The Last W

David Helton

Table of Contents

PART ONE

THE LONG WALK OUT

CHAPTER ONE

When your life is over, it's the same as when anything is over – it just turns into another story. It went this way for a while, and then that way, and then this other way, and then here we are. In no more than a few days, they'd all be sitting around the Ledge saying, "Did I ever tell you about the time old Gibbous Moon and I did this or did that?" "Yeah, but was that before or after the time we went to wherever and did something else?" And then they'd all agree "before", and there would be the story of the life of Gibbous Moon coming into shape. It would be wrong, half of it, but it would stick and, for a while, be a minor myth. Maybe there was some episode that was so good or funny or revealing of truth that it would hang on past the present generation and become a medium-sized myth, growing completely out of shape in everything but its essence – the thing that made it good or funny or revealing of truth. But Gibbous couldn't begin to imagine what that episode might be.

And Gibbous knew his episodes – he was the chief storyteller around here. Or had been. As his seventieth birthday approached and he'd finally decided to resurrect the custom of the Long Walk Out – the ancient option that used to spare the relatives and everyone else a lot of protracted dying – he called the whole settlement together and told them. And then told them that, to his mind, young (or maybe not that young) Two Tornadoes seemed to have the knack and ought to take over the ceremonies. It was after that, when left to listen instead of talk or to sit alone and think about the way things used to be, that Gibbous started to see his own life pulling itself into just another story, with maybe only a punchline lying ahead.

"At least take the new poncho," said Paintbrush, his grandson's wife.

"What for?"

"It's new. And you've got a long way to go."

"But not a long time, Paintbrush. Not in poncho time. That could last somebody maybe five years. The old one's fine." He laid the old one out on the floor with his other things – the goatskin trousers, the water skin, the salt, the meat, the two shirts, the satchel, the blankets, the rope, the twine, the knife, the flints, the blowpipe, darts, poison sachet, birdlime sachet and the best red-oak walking stick in the Seven Settlements, the one that – with its knob, its width and its perfect, gentle curve – might have been grown to order. He'd found it three years ago, just when his knee was first starting to hurt. It had been lying, like a gift from the ancestors, in the middle of the Trail.

"Don't tell me you're still not going to wear shoes."

"I've never worn shoes in my life. It's a little late to start."

"But you don't know where you're going to go. It might be cold." Paintbrush had a problem. She imagined she could see the future, and it made her permanently anxious. "You'll have to go over the mountains. Sometimes they're white on top. That could be snow, you know.

"I don't wear shoes when it snows down here. But look, if my feet ever start getting too cold, then I'll stop and make some shoes. Okay? Don't worry."

"Yeah, why should I worry?" she said. She picked the baby up out of his hammock, even though he wasn't even crying – he was asleep, in fact, a highly desirable condition – and held him close. "According to you, when you walk out of here tomorrow you're officially dead. I guess it's stupid to worry about somebody who's dead."

He'd been kneeling over his things, and now he stood up, his left knee popping painfully. "Paintbrush, I know what you're saying, but you don't have to tell me you'll miss me. Not again. I know that. I know a lot of people will miss me, and I like the feeling. And I know what else you're saying – that nobody goes on the Long Walk Out any more. Well, people ought to. When I was a boy, all the old folks did – at least the ones did that didn't die before they got it organised. But look what happens now. Look at old Pecan Shell and old Pigtrotter, turning into corpses while the whole settlement watches. I couldn't stand that. Going is the considerate thing to do – and I'm going."

As Paintbrush glowered at him, a shout from outside the housecave proclaimed, "Oh, he's going all right." This was Breeze, his daughter-in-law. She'd been out in front all day tanning leather and holding loud

6

conversations with other women doing various other things in front of other housecaves. "He's plenty strong enough," she yelled in reply to something, then pausing to listen to an indistinct voice, "Sure, he stopped big hunting years ago. But he still climbs the wall. Killed this goat, in fact." That, apparently, shut everybody up, and for about the first time today, there was silence.

But it was getting late already, and maybe they were just tired of shouting. Outside, the sun had been behind the Gorge wall for a while, and now its light, as it did most evenings, filtered down from the sky in general in a bluish haze – a haze that even came inside the housecave. Paintbrush stood in this light, the blueness diluting the blue in her eyes and in the patterns on her dress. Holding the baby, who miraculously was still asleep, she seemed to want to cry but was too generally annoyed to let herself. He'd miss her, too – a lot. Hell, he'd miss everybody and everything. But as it was, he already missed three quarters of the people he'd ever known – including two brothers, two sons, a sister, a daughter and his wife Spiderweb – because they'd died on him. One thing he wouldn't miss, though, was being alive, because for a while, at least, he would actually be alive, if unofficially. All considered, the Long Walk Out was probably the least bad way to go, and that was the real reason he wanted to do it – a long solitary journey while he still had most of his faculties. Seeing other things he only knew from the stories or had guessed might be out there – vast forests and deserts and mountains and plains – and finally seeing the fabled endless water and, to pay for all he had seen, just keeping on walking. Old-fashioned? Just because something was out of fashion didn't mean it had never been a good idea.

Another advantage of the Long Walk Out was that you got to go to your own funeral. "I need to finish getting this stuff together," Gibbous said. "They're starting right after dark."

"I'm not going," said Paintbrush. She turned her back to him – suddenly, in a swirl of red hair. Now she was probably crying a little. And the baby was starting to. Gibbous had never seen a baby quite like this particular great-grandson of his. He'd take several minutes to wind up for a cry, whimpering, pausing, whimpering louder, pausing, yelling a little and so on until he had a face to match the evening air and a sound like an elephant. With those lungs he'd grow up to be the champion Gorge-wall racer. His legs would fall off before he'd run out of breath.

Anyway, wasn't Two Tornadoes supposed to name the baby tonight? This was one of the storyteller's many responsibilities. It always happened at the end of whatever ceremony or storytelling session the settlement was having. Any mother with an infant who needed a name would come into the circle with the child and put it in the storyteller's lap. The storyteller would drink a cup of naming brew, go into a trance, eventually have a vision and, when he did, shout out what he saw, which became the new name. (The reason this event was always scheduled last was that after drinking the naming brew, the storyteller was no good for anything else for several hours. It was the part of the job Gibbous missed the least.) "You've got to come, Paintbrush. The baby gets his name tonight. I don't want to go not knowing what he's called."

She said something, but she still had her back to him, and the baby was already halfway to the top of his howl.

"What'd you say?"

"I said …" She whipped around. She did have tears on her face. "Dead men don't know anything."

"I'm not dead yet," he said. "Take it easy."

"And you won't be for a long time. I don't care whether it's official or unofficial – you're going to be out there by yourself, and things are going to be hard for you. I know it. I dreamt it." Paintbrush was, in fact, a good dreamer. She'd predicted at least two deaths (of pretty frail people, admittedly), a lot of minor accidents and the sighting, last year, of a skyman. Nobody had seen a skyman around here for a generation, and then Paintbrush dreamt about one and told everybody about it the next morning, and that afternoon Breeze looked up and saw a skyman way over on the south Gorge rim. For a long time he looked down at the settlement through that big eye he had, and then – when he realised, maybe, that he'd been spotted – he disappeared. Flew away probably. Skymen could fly, of course.

The baby was fully wound up now, but Paintbrush hardly seemed to notice. Gibbous shouted, just as the baby took a breathless pause, "What kind of hard …?" Then, in a normal voice, "Couldn't you feed him or something?"

Paintbrush sighed, opened her dress and collapsed into a hammock. The baby was instantly quiet, kneading furiously.

Gibbous found a stool, put it next to the hammock and sat. He leaned forward and shooed some flies away from Paintbrush and the baby. "How are things going to be hard for me?"

"You're going to have to fight. In the dream I saw you fighting."

"Fighting? Me? I'm seventy years old and on my way to die. Why would I fight? Who was I fighting for God's sake?"

"I couldn't see them. I don't think you could, either."

"Were they spirits or something?"

"No, I don't think that's what they were."

"What then? Invisible people? Air animals?" Air animals were the inverse images of all the animals that were alive at any one time. When you killed an animal, its air image slipped into the carcass and gave it its nutrition. It was a very intricate piece of theology and, in Gibbous's opinion, totally unnecessary. Why couldn't an animal just have its own nutrition already? But this was a question that, even with his age and authority, he would never dare ask. Besides, there wouldn't be anybody to ask. The storyteller was the chief theologian too.

"They were people, real people, but I think they were just far away."

"I don't believe this is a valid dream, Paintbrush. Not your fault – sometimes dreams are just dreams, even for you. I mean, how could I fight somebody who's far away? For that matter, how could I fight somebody at all? Don't worry about the dream. I'll have a fine, slow journey and a painless end. I plan to sing all the songs, one after another, and think about them."

"The fighting wasn't all that was in the dream, Granddad. There were worse things. Please stay. I'll make it my special job to take care of you – not that you need much taking care of. Did you hear what Breeze was saying out there? Look at you. You've got most of your teeth. Your beard's grey, but you keep it trim. Your hair's still got black in it, and it's all mostly there. You're pretty strong. Your eyes are ... You've always done your eye exercises, and they're as sharp as ever. You're healthy. You'll be healthy at eighty. If you have to go, go when you're eighty. Go when you're ninety."

Outside suddenly, dogs were whimpering and panting. The hunters were coming through the settlement, shouting about having killed a cow. The women were shouting, too, teasing them about taking all day to bring down one skinny heifer. No matter what the hunters brought back, the women always teased them. When he was young, Gibbous had never failed to find

9

this maddening. He thought then and still thought that if only the hunters would refrain from carrying on about their kill, however splendid it might be, the women wouldn't taunt them. But the hunters always did, and the women always did. It was one of those things, apparently, that could never change.

Breeze was saying, "Have all the cows up there sprouted wings or something?" The dog family that shared the housecave came in, doing the sniffy things that dogs do, mainly looking for food and not finding any.

"There was a problem, Mother."

"Paintbrush," said Gibbous, ignoring the clamour. "I couldn't change my mind now, even if I wanted to." Comet Tail, Flickering Star and Partial Eclipse, respectively Gibbous's son and two grandsons, all shed their knives and bows and other stuff at the housecave entrance and then stumbled inside. The young male dog that had, for some reason, recently taken a liking to Gibbous came over, jumped up, tried to lick his face and, as usual, got pushed away and had to settle for his hand.

Comet and Flicker – sighing, sweating and blood-splashed – went straight to their hammocks. It was the pink phase of the evening now and soon would be gloomy and purple, and Eclipse immediately started building a fire. Breeze carried her leather in and hung it on the wall rack.

"This boy is some hunter," Comet yelled over to Gibbous.

"It was an accident, Dad," Flicker said.

"We did get a nice cow for your funeral, Granddad," said Eclipse, fanning the new flames. "A pretty nice one."

"He missed a cow by about a cow's height," said Comet, stretching his arms apart.

"Everybody misses," Gibbous said, pushing the dog away again. "I always missed more than I hit."

"Well, he did more than just miss."

"It was an accident," said Flicker.

"Of course it was an accident," Comet said. "I didn't think you meant to do it, even if it looked like you did. If you could shoot straight, if you'd practise …" Flicker, the younger of Comet's sons, did tend to have a hard time pleasing his father. Eclipse, on the other hand, was responsibility itself. Now that he'd got the fire going, he was lighting wall torches. Then he came over to his wife Paintbrush, kissed her on the forehead and stroked the baby's hair. "It was an unlucky accident," he said solemnly to both Paintbrush and Gibbous, "a pretty nasty one."

"It wouldn't be the world's first hunting accident," said Gibbous. "What happened?"

From his hammock, Comet said, "Well, Dad …"

"I don't think I want to hear this," said Paintbrush, getting up to lay the now sleeping baby in his own hammock, fastening her dress.

"… you know how we've been hunting with the Little Rimmers lately?" Little Rim was the nearest settlement, right at the top of the Gorge and almost directly above the Ledge, although actually getting to the place meant going two miles up the Trail and then two miles back.

"I've heard mention of it." Gibbous said. "Alliances are good things, I guess. But why the Little Rimmers?"

"It doesn't matter, Granddad," said Eclipse. "I think the alliance is over anyway."

Comet said, "It's over all right."

"I'm sorry," said Flicker. "I'm really, really sorry about what happened. But you have to admit, Dad, the Little Rimmers have been pretty horrible allies. They're so grim. They never smile and never speak up so you can hear them. They're all sort of skinny and unhappy and take all the fun out of hunting."

"Hunting's not supposed to be fun," said Comet. "Anyway that's just how Little Rimmers are, and you have to be extra careful around them. You've got to pay attention. Not like you …"

"It's their religion, Flicker," Gibbous said. "They take it very seriously. It's against their religion, for instance, to eat fat. That's why they're all so skinny. They don't believe in singing, either, which may be why they seem unhappy. At least that's what I've always thought. "

"What happened?" Breeze said, standing in front of the fire with her arms folded. "Just say. Why does everybody in this family always have to spin things out?"

"'It's probably my fault," said Gibbous. "Not every family has a storyteller for a grandfather."

"We won't have one much longer," Paintbrush said. She had wandered over to Gibbous's belongings and was gazing down at them. "I can't believe this is all you're taking, Granddad. Look, he's not even taking shoes."

"Granddad's never worn shoes in his life," said Flicker. "Have you, Granddad?"

"Not since I was old enough to make up my own mind about it."

"He's grown shoes," said Flicker. "Look at his feet. There must be a thumb-length of callous there."

"That's what callous is for," Gibbous said. "You'd all have good callous, too, if shoes hadn't come back into fashion."

"I give up," Breeze said. "I don't care what happened. I'm going to help with the cow." She started towards the doorway.

"Wait," said Comet. "You need to hear this. You need to hear what a great hunter your son is." He sat up sideways in his hammock. Gibbous could tell it had been pretty hard day. Comet had sweated through his hunting paint, and it was smeared down one side of his face and neck. All that sweat really didn't tally with one cow. And Comet had a whole night ahead of him, because that was how long funerals had to last. Gibbous did hope that his only remaining son would stay awake until dawn and be able to see him off. "Anyway," said Comet, "we were hunting with the Little Rimmers, like I said, and Flickerhead here missed this cow by about a cow's height. He doesn't practise, Dad. He doesn't practise, and he doesn't pay attention to what's on the other side of the animal he's shooting at—"

"I didn't see him," said Flicker. "The cows were in the way."

"You knew how we'd agreed to do it. They and their dogs were coming from that side, and we and our dogs were coming from this side, and we were supposed to move the cows into a tighter herd, so that maybe we could get more than just one or two for a day's work. Sometimes the women are right to jeer at us, you know. Anyway, you weren't even supposed to be shooting yet. You were supposed to be herding. You're not coming on another hunt until you learn to pay attention to the tactics. And until you've done some target practice."

Eclipse said to Paintbrush, "Isn't it a little early for the baby to be sleeping?"

"Oh God," said Gibbous, "don't wake him up."

"If I don't, he'll be up all night."

"So will we, remember?"

"Oh. Oh yeah," Eclipse said to Gibbous. "But wouldn't it be better if he was sleeping then instead of screaming? That he does his screaming now, I mean? Otherwise Paintbrush will have to take him outside and will miss everything."

"We've already been through a screaming session," Gibbous said. "At least wait a few more minutes."

"And so," said Comet, "he lets loose this arrow. It goes way past the cow he's shooting at, right over the top of another cow and straight into this Little Rimmer's neck. The man died standing up. His name was Jones, I think – you know how Little Rimmers' names don't mean anything? Jones, I think. Anyway, they were pretty upset. We'd already shot four cows, and we let them take three of them, but they were still upset. I don't blame them either. But they walked away carrying the cows and Jones and talking about war."

"Oh no," said Paintbrush. "Not again."

Thank God, thought Gibbous – thank God I'm getting out of here. He'd long ago begun to think of wars as a silly waste of time and energy, not to mention life. One group would get fiercely painted up and slink towards the enemy settlement, and the settlement's warriors (otherwise known as the hunters and otherwise as the young men) would paint fiercely up and go out and meet them. Arrows and darts would fly, a lot of people would get hurt and maybe one or two would be killed, and when the attackers judged that they'd caused enough damage to cover whatever the defenders' crime had been, they'd turn around and run home. When he was young, Gibbous had found the occasional war to be, if not exactly exciting, at least a break in routine. Now it just seemed sad and pointless. After all, his other two sons would be still be alive if it hadn't been for wars. One had been killed by the Waterfallers in a war caused by an argument over the ownership of a dead horse; and the other had died during a raid on Deep Gorge. That was a raid to steal wives, though – which, to Gibbous's mind, was the only possible excuse for a war: settlements that didn't do enough outside marrying often ended up with weak blood, not to mention too many bleeding babies (back, that is, when there still were bleeding babies). But there were plenty of other ways of recruiting wives – simple courtship, for a start. No, in wars, you went out and got scared and got shot at and maybe even got wounded, and then came back to the settlement and talked about it for a long time. Told stories.

That was it, wasn't it?. Why hadn't it occurred to him before? War was just another way of generating stories.

CHAPTER TWO

"How long has it been," asked Two Tornadoes, raising his arms for silence, "since anybody's heard The First Story of All?"

The truth, for almost everybody here, was not very long, and Gibbous imagined he could hear a few moans among the Ledgers. Two Tornadoes was good enough at telling stories – was excellent, in fact – but he did have this weakness for The First Story of All, and he would tell it about every tenth time he told anything. It wasn't that people always wanted brand new stories, but certain cycles would go in and out of fashion, and the storyteller had to be sensitive to that. Lately, Gibbous could feel a general hankering after the Ledge string, about the very complicated events that led the ancestors to put a settlement on this fine wide ledge – not at the bottom of the Gorge and not up on the rim, but halfway between. About how they first settled here in the Cavern and then over the years – even over the generations – gradually, rock by rock, dug out the housecaves. Made an enduring settlement for a group that would always be distinct from the other six, from the Riversiders, the Waterfallers, the Big Rimmers, the Little Rimmers, the Deep Gorgers and the Salters – in other words, all the other people in the world. It was a fine story, if well told, but Gibbous doubted if Two Tornadoes had used it more than twice since he'd taken over. How many times, though, had he done The First Story of All? That one was more spectacular, of course, and more suited to Two Tornadoes' particular talents, but what a storyteller needed was to adapt himself to the story, not the other way around. It was a shame, Gibbous thought, that he'd never taken Two Tornadoes aside and reminded him of that. Now, of course, it was too late. Damn. How much else would he be leaving undone?

The funeral, like every other settlement gathering, was being held in the Cavern, and all fifty-three of the Ledgers were there. Usually, no matter how important the event, at least a few people would opt to stay home. They'd be sick or generally decrepit or just not in the mood – nobody had to come to anything. So it was a nice compliment, Gibbous thought: every single one of them, from the babies through to the likes of Pecan Shell and even Pigtrotter, who had had to be led in by his family and didn't seem to have any idea where he was. The Weather Clan, the Sky Clan, the Animal Clan, the Sacred Object Clan – they were all here. The cow had been roasted and reduced to bones, a lot of cactus had been drunk and now everybody was gathered in the Cavern's main chamber, sitting on the rocks, ledges and floor, around the circle of elders, the storyteller and the effigy of Gibbous Moon, wrapped in a shroud and waiting to be taken to the Cave of Bones. (Since this was the Ledge's first Long Walk Out in maybe fifty years, an elder had given a little talk while the cow was being carved, explaining about the effigy and how it was Gibbous's body as surely as if it were a real dead man, as surely as this cow was a real dead cow.)

Wall torches fluttered, sending waves of light and shadow across the paintings on the walls and making the hunters and animals seem to move. The Cavern's paintings were among Gibbous's favorite things in life and certainly among the things he'd miss the most. He liked the idea of all those Ledgers all through the ages standing at the Cavern walls with their paintbrushes thinking about all the Ledgers before them standing at the Cavern walls. It gave him a sense of eternity – and of how, in eternity, nothing ever really changes. The figures on the walls were the same kinds of people with the same kinds of weapons hunting the same kinds of animals that people still hunted and painted – the cows, the deer, the horses, sheep, pigs and goats, lions, dogs, and even rabbits, squirrels, small cats, rats, guinea pigs, gerbils and other animals whose killing, you'd think, wouldn't really be glorious enough to rate a picture. (At the other extreme, way back in the chamber was a picture of an elephant with a lot of arrows sticking out of it, something Gibbous had always taken to be a kind of ancestral whopper, and a sacrilegious one at that.) But even squirrels and cats looked alive and a little magnificent in the torchlight.

Except for a couple of whimpering babies, the Cavern was mostly silent, everyone watching Two Tornadoes – who, Gibbous thought, had great presence. He was big, even fat – a good quality in a storyteller (Gibbous had always regarded himself as a little too ropy to be ideal for the job) – and he had a way of looking around the chamber, from one face to another, as though he were talking to everyone individually. His eyes would widen so far that sometimes they seemed all white, and then as he spoke they would narrow down to slits before widening again. And his arms and hands did as much talking as his mouth. His laugh was loud and contagious, and he even danced a little dance sometimes. Of course, Gibbous had taught him those tricks and some others, but once taught he was very good at them. (If he hadn't picked up a point or two of the philosophy of storytelling, it probably didn't much matter.) Now Two Tornadoes made a low, slow sweeping motion with both arms. "In the beginning," he began, "the world was nothing but a river of blood." He pretended to wade, as if the blood was up to his chest.

There were different ways of telling this story – it was really up to the storyteller to inject the variations he wanted – and Two Tornadoes' way tended towards the dramatic and heavily illustrated. There was nothing wrong with that – the kids, especially, liked it – but Gibbous's touch had always been a little, well, subtler. He'd never pretended to wade, for instance. And when he'd got to the part about how the first people rose out of the blood, he'd never stood on his tiptoes and raised his arms towards the Cavern's ceiling, as Two Tornadoes was doing now.

Gibbous was also finding that his new seat gave him an interesting perspective. Ever since he'd been made storyteller thirty or so years ago, he'd always been down in the circle, either telling the stories himself or, lately, sitting right next to Two Tornadoes as he told them. But tonight, being represented in the circle of elders by his effigy, he himself could sit back with the people – with his immediate family and the rest of the Sky Clan. He was half-lying on a largish flat rock with, on one side, Paintbrush, Eclipse and the awake but puzzlingly silent baby and, on the other, Comet and Breeze. (Flicker, as usual, was over with the people his age – the clan of the unmated young being always more tightly bound to each other than to any stratum of family.) At a distance, Two Tornadoes' gestures and effects worked a lot better than they had when was doing them more or less in Gibbous's face.

A half an hour on, they'd reached the point in the story when the hero, Hero, knee-deep in blood and mud, appeals to the great white birds to show his newly created but much beleaguered people a way out of their mess and misery. Two Tornadoes was holding his hands under his chin and, as he'd been doing for much of the story, was shouting at the ceiling. "'Listen,' Hero yelled at the birds, who were soaring higher and higher in spiralling circles, 'you can fly. You can see the whole big world just by looking down. Lead us out of here. Show us somewhere clean to go.' But the birds kept flying higher until they were out of sight – until there wasn't a bird left in the air, and the air was just as bleak and bloody and stinking as the land."

There was a lot of story left to go. Two Tornadoes hadn't even got to the Mother Elephant yet, much less the Winged Penis – and even that wasn't a third of the way through. And when The First Story of All finally did finish, there'd be a singing-and-dancing break and a session of different people telling anecdotes about Gibbous. Then a funeral oration. Then there'd be the baby's naming ceremony, and then with luck the sun would start to rise. In all the funerals before Long Walks Out that Gibbous could recall from his youth, it had never quite occurred to him as a problem that the poor walker-out would be starting his journey after a night without sleep. But the funeral was, of course, supposed to be authentic, and Gibbous and everybody else (he'd never even heard anyone remark on this sleepless-night paradox) would end up more or less regarding the person as really dead. Come to think of it, there had never been any big send-off for a walker-out, no waves goodbye – only a few immediate relatives quietly watching him, or sometimes her, disappear up the Trail. After the procession that carried the effigy to the Cave of Bones, everyone else always went to their housecaves and their hammocks just as if they'd been to a normal all-night funeral.

The way he was half-sitting, half-lying eventually began to make his knee ache. He sat up straighter and in the process glanced at Paintbrush. She was staring at him with what seemed to be injured anger. He pretended not to notice, to be interested in the story, which had almost reached Mother Elephant. Then Paintbrush's mouth was next to his ear. "You're not dead," she whispered, "and you won't be for a long, long time."

"... and so Gibbous and I went ahead and followed the goat farther up the path," Spotted Pig was saying, "even though the path was hardly wide enough for the goat to walk on, much less us. I swear – only half my foot fit on it. The other half was standing on the Gorge air. Up ahead, Gibbous was trying to draw his bow, but every time he started to pull back on it he'd wobble a little and would have to stop and put his hand on the wall. I'd been in a lot of precarious places around this Gorge – and so had Gibbous – but I don't know how we'd let that goat lure us up a path like that. Way up ahead there was a pretty good ledge – we thought that was probably where the goat was heading – and we talked about it and decided we had to go there, too. We had to. It was a no-turning-around path, and it was either make to the ledge or try to walk back backwards. The goat … well, never mind the goat …"

Yeah, thought Gibbous, never mind the facts either. That ledge wasn't that far ahead. It was about five steps away, and the goat was already on it. What he'd been waiting for was the goat to get there, so that it would be cornered and so that, when he shot it, it wouldn't fall into the Gorge. (Hunters usually spent more effort trying to retrieve smashed-up goats than they did stalking them.) As for the path, yes, it was pretty skimpy right where they were, but he hadn't been so stupid as to try to draw a bow while he was on it. He'd been aiming with his blowpipe. It made you wonder about the truly old stories, all the way back to The First Story of All, if something that only happened about twenty-five years ago, and with both the people in it still alive, could get distorted so much. He knew, of course, that there were exaggeration and manipulation in all stories – there had to be or they would be boring – but how much? Was there one single thing in the ancient stories that actually happened? And if so, what? You could never know. You just had to believe them, or you'd miss their point. (Hero could talk to animals because that was back in the days before animals lost their speech. Sure.)

The proceedings were at the testimonial stage and near the end of it at that. A couple of more tales about Gibbous Moon and then Two Tornadoes would say his piece. Then the baby would be named and the sun would come up. The singing and dancing had taken a lot out of people, and as usual at this point of a funeral, a good proportion of them were asleep, a few snoring. Eclipse, who had had hard day at the cowhunt, was sprawled out on his back, sleeping through tributes to his grandfather. But because the baby was also asleep, nestling on Eclipse's chest, Gibbous forgave him. He had to hand it to Comet, though – he'd been through the same hard hunt, but there he was awake and paying attention (to a lot of lies, but nevertheless …). So was Breeze, and so was Paintbrush.

Paintbrush puzzled him. She always had. She was the first Sacred Object woman to marry into Gibbous's immediate family since … well, since his older brother Winter Sun had married Cooking Stone. Cooking Stone died giving birth the next year (to one of the last bleeding babies he could recall, taking its first breath and then turning into a cascade of blood). Gibbous had only been about Flicker's age when Cooking Stone was in the family, but he did remember that she had a pretty bad temper and that she'd spend hours, it seemed, just sitting in her hammock and staring at nothing, and you didn't dare speak to her then or she'd shout. Or cry. Poor woman. Nobody ever tried to find out what was bothering her. Everybody just stayed out of her way, Winter Sun included. Yeah, she had been strange, and Paintbrush was sometimes strange, too, but they were very different kinds of strangeness.

Paintbrush was a worrier. It had to do with her vivid dreams – she seemed to be able, or to say she was able, to see the future about as clearly as she could see the other side of the Gorge, but in no more detail than that. That much was all right, and a handy enough talent to have in the family, but then she'd want to make sure everybody around her did everything that was absolutely necessary to avoid that future if it was a bad one or achieve it if it was good. It meant she nagged a lot. Whenever she relaxed – and she wasn't always worrying – she was good-natured, pleasant, sweet even. She had that sandstone-coloured hair, a fine, intelligent face, searching eyes and a way of moving that was never awkward or sudden. She flowed. The general theory was that the name you were given by the storyteller (in Paintbrush's case, by Gibbous himself), under the influence of the magic naming brew, would somehow predict what you would be like when you grew up (though Gibbous never had figured out what a three-quarters-full moon said about him), and Paintbrush could be a little like a paintbrush, making smooth strokes and leaving interesting colours. But show any resistance to her, and those colours got dark or livid and occasionally scary.

And she was certainly in a livid mood at the moment. He wasn't sure whether it was because she was genuinely concerned for him or because he was so off-handedly ignoring her precious dream and its warnings. And what perverse warnings: the predicted doom was that he wasn't going to die, not that he was. His general intention, of course, was to walk and walk until the land ran out and then to walk off into the endless water, if such a thing really existed. That was the intention of everybody who'd ever set off on the exercise, but no one knew what actually happened to any of them. There were no memories, no stories, of anyone coming back from a Long Walk Out, saying he'd changed his mind and reporting his adventures. As far as Gibbous was concerned, the unknown about it was one of the main attractions. And the point of it wasn't suicide – it was a long walk, a final excursion. That was all, and if Paintbrush wanted to, she could glower and mutter at him for the rest of his life on the Ledge – all two hours of it.

Then he'd be gone – out of the Gorge, across the plains and to the mountains, the western edge of the known world. He had no idea how far the mountains stretched. Or if they actually had another side. Or whether they went down again or just kept going up. He didn't know how far was it from the mountains to the endless water. There could be anything along the way. There could be other people, for example. It was always assumed that the inhabitants of the Seven Settlements were all the people there were, but who could say? Some argued that if there were other people, they'd have found their way to the Gorge by now. But why? Had anyone from the Gorge ever tried to find anyone else? Well, yes, come to think about it. Every now and then, maybe once every couple of generations, some explorer or small group of explorers would set out from the Seven Settlements to see what was over there, but like people on Long Walks Out, none of them had ever come back and reported. No one knew whether that meant there was danger and death out there or if it was all so wonderful that the explorers didn't want to come back. Most people, though, were of the danger persuasion, and that tended to discourage exploration – and was one reason why the Long Walk Out went out of fashion – but Gibbous somehow wasn't sure. Not that he'd mind if there was danger – he was going to die anyway – but it stood to reason that once you started going you would want to keep going. And once you came to a barrier – the endless water, say – you would want to veer in another direction or just stay put. Once you'd gone so far, it would be against all instinct to turn back. Anyway, it was about ten days to the mountains, and then he'd start to find out. He was itching to get going …

… and he suddenly realised he hadn't been paying attention. Imagine being able to attend your own funeral and then letting your mind wander. Old Spotted Pig had finished, and now the old widow Warm Water had the floor. And the story she was telling – if it was what Gibbous was afraid it was – was one he'd rather she'd forgotten. No mistake: she was confessing to that afternoon when they were both about fifteen and she was getting ready to get married soon and he was out collecting lizards (which was something he did when he was fifteen) and came across her gathering honey and … Even though the people of the Ledge thrived on stories – always told each other almost everything that happened and a lot that hadn't happened – sometimes there were some things … It had been the first time for both of them, it had been clumsy and, as he remembered it, they'd agreed afterwards never to tell anyone. He never had, and on the evidence of the absence of gossip about it, neither had she. But now she was standing in front of the whole settlement – every single Ledger – and going into detail, even the details about the swarm of bees, the cactus thorns and the loose lizards. And possibly because the story had never been told before and had had no chance to evolve, it was absolutely as he remembered it. Flicker's group was in hysterics, and there were plenty of hoots and guffaws from other parts of the cavern. Everybody who'd been asleep, including Eclipse, seemed to have woken up. But why was she doing it? Why now?

Then he noticed something. As she revealed these bumblings and toe-curling intimacies, she never once glanced in his direction. Neither did anyone else. When they glanced, they glanced at the effigy. Some even craned to see it. And then he remembered the exact terms of his and Warm Water's pledge: they would never tell another person as long as both of them were still alive. "It had its funny moments," she was saying, "and its painful ones. But it was the nicest, most exciting, most tender afternoon of my life." Her conclusion, however flattering and pleasant, couldn't compete with unexpected discomfort of realising that the illusion of the effigy and the funeral had worked just as they were meant to, that in the minds of Warm Water and everyone else in the Cavern, Gibbous Moon was genuinely, irrevocably dead.

But someone squeezed his hand. Paintbrush. She at least was looking at him, and not, for once, with fury. Just Paintbrush wasn't enough, though. He felt embarrassed and an imposter. He got up. "I'm going now," he whispered to Paintbrush. "Goodbye."

"Wait, Granddad," she said. "I'll walk you to the Trail."

As the two of them began to move around and behind the crowd and towards the Cavern entrance, only Comet, of the rest of the family, seemed to notice, and all he did was give a little wave. Breeze and Eclipse, who still held the baby, were watching the next speaker come down to the circle and didn't even turn their heads. That speaker, incidentally, was Hand Axe, his old pebbles partner, who was probably going to bore them all with a description of a very intricate, close, improbable and long-gone pebbles game. This really is, Gibbous thought, the right time to go.

"I think I know why, Granddad," Paintbrush said when they got outside. "That must have been embarrassing."

"It was a little, but that wasn't the reason."

21

"And it must be a little strange having all those people think of you as dead. Listen, I know I've been angry with you. Well, I still am and I still know you're alive. And I still think it's a stupid, selfish decision—"

"Come on, Paintbrush—"

"... but you've got a long, hard journey ahead of you—"

"Long, yes, but—"

"... and I don't want you remembering me only as angry."

They came into the housecave, two entrances down from the Cavern. Except for the glowing fireplace, it was dark. Gibbous felt along the wall for a torch and then brought it over, shoved it into the coals and blew it into life. He said, "I don't just think of you as angry, even when that's all you seem to be. You're just a very smart young woman. Too smart, probably. You've got the burden of knowing things other people don't. That would make anybody mad. Here, hold the torch for me."

"I know. I can never figure whether people don't believe me or just don't care."

He had a quick look through his satchel, making sure he hadn't forgotten anything. Then he went over and untied his hammock, folded it and packed it on top of everything else. He shouldered the satchel and his water skin and put on his dart belt, and just as he was kneeling down to pick up his walking stick, he felt a familiar wetness on his arm. "Hello, dog," he said, standing up and pushing the animal away. "Give me your opinion on this one, smart young woman. Why does that dog like me so much?"

"It might be because your soul and his air animal like each other. Or it might be because you gave him some salt pork that time."

"Did I? Oh yeah. Once."

"If you give food to a dog, that's what can happen. Why don't you take him with you?" She went to put the torch on the wall.

"Take a dog? The Long Walk Out is supposed to be done alone."

"You'd still be alone as a human. I'll tell you what. You want to take some of the selfishness out of what you're doing? You want to show me that it's possible for you to have a little respect for what I can see and you can't? Just once do what I ask. Take the dog. He'll be a help."

"How do you know the dog wants to come?"

"He does. I know."

Gibbous could never get over the feeling that talking to Paintbrush was like talking to someone twice his age rather than less than a third. How could a thoroughly dull boy like Eclipse ever have courted her? What did they say to each other? He'd be talking about the five steps to laying a perfect fire, and she'd be predicting death and calamity. There she was in the torchlight, a wispy silhouette of a long-haired girl telling him with absolute certainty what his moral obligations were and what a dog thinks and wants and will do.

"Okay, okay," Gibbous said. "Come on, dog." And, sure enough, the dog followed the two of them out of the housecave and along the Ledge towards the Trail. It was a warm night with a little breeze and enough moonlight to see clearly the Man with the Nose, a rock formation that rose up from the Gorge floor. He had climbed it once. No one else could say that.

"I suppose I should admit it," Paintbrush said. "I'm the one being selfish when I say I don't want you to go. Or did say. Don't worry – I'm giving up now."

"You're selfish?"

"Yeah. Without you around, it's just going to be me and Breeze and the baby in the housecave all day. Breeze is all right, but – I don't know. You're a storyteller. You talk, and I really like listening to you. It's been great having the settlement storyteller all to myself. When I was little, I used to love coming to the Cavern and hearing you. You were much better than Two Tornadoes is. He overcooks it – acts it out too much. You're better just with words."

"So is that it, Paintbrush? That dream about me fighting far-away people and living a long time? Did you make that up?"

"Oh no. That was real enough. But I don't even want to think about it now. Since you don't want to listen to it, I don't know why I should have to think about it."

They reached the Trail, and they stopped. The dog trotted up it a short distance and then looked back to see if anyone was coming. "I suppose he thinks he's going hunting," Gibbous said. "It seems a kind of cruel trick – taking him on what he thinks is a hunt and then walking him to the edge of the world."

"He knows he's not going hunting. There aren't any other dogs or any other hunters."

"You're right. You're always right. And I'm sorry I'm not going to be around to entertain you."

"You know it's not just that, Granddad." She kissed him on the cheek. Then she hugged him, holding her face in his neck for what seemed a very long time. Finally she pulled away and said, "I guess they'll be starting the naming ceremony pretty soon."

"Goodbye, Paintbrush," he said. "Try to enjoy your life." He watched her all the way to the Cavern, and then he turned towards the Trail. "All right, dog. Let's walk."

CHAPTER THREE

The only thing Gibbous regretted about his early departure from the funeral was that now he'd never know what the baby had been named. Otherwise, he wondered why he'd gone to the thing in the first place. But of course he did know why: it was customary, and it was, to say the least, a once-in-a-lifetime experience. Now that lifetime was over, and even though he and the dog had only been walking for the length of the morning, it already seemed like something that had happened to another person in another world. Or maybe that was the way he just wanted it to seem.

And he did already feel lonely, exquisitely so. This hurt a little, even physically, in his chest and stomach. On the other hand, he couldn't remember when he'd last had the sensation of so much future lying ahead. Ageing is standing still while your life runs through you like a rope, and it comes to the point where you've got great heavy coils of it behind and the flapping end coming at you at a rate of speed. Now, with the long part amputated, the short part was the long part. The future had expanded. There was a whole lot of life to go – months of it, maybe.

Then why was he pushing himself so hard? The lack of sleep was getting to him, his knee was hurting, and there wasn't any reason why he couldn't stop here for the rest of the day and the night. It was a pleasant enough place – a wooded strip that ran along the bank of the fast, rocky, broad river that eventually turned into the waterfall. The trees were mainly cottonwood, birch and low-slung oak, and they gave shade and plenty of purchases for a hammock. He knew the woods well. He'd hunted here. It was good for rabbits, squirrels and various birds and their eggs, there were fish and terrapins in the river, and it was generally the easiest spot for small game before another expanse of plain began, about an hour ahead, once he'd walked to the nearest crossing. Stopping now made sense, but he just couldn't get his legs to quit. He wanted to go on, to get into territory far enough away from the Seven Settlements so that he couldn't accidentally run into a hunting party or something. But he badly needed a breather, and even the dog was starting to dawdle, stopping at every animal hole he came across, sniffing it, inexpertly digging at it and generally falling behind. Finally, giving himself the excuse that he needed to let the dog catch up, he was able to unshoulder his satchel, lay down his walking stick and sit under a tree.

And when he sat he realised how very, very tired he really was. He'd been going like a horse. As soon as he'd come to the top of the Trail – it was just about sun-up then – he'd headed on a huge detour around the settlement of Big Rim, going about three miles to cover one. He knew most of the Big Rimmers and even had a few relatives, including a sister, among them, and the last thing he wanted was to run into anybody there or near there. They wouldn't have known he was on his Long Walk Out and would have treated him like plain old living Gibbous Moon – maybe even invited him to eat or drink something. Then he would have had to explain, and then they'd have been uncomfortable and wouldn't have known what to do. Some people might even have nightmares after talking to a man who was officially dead.

So he and the dog had gone straight up over the low ridge parallel to the Gorge and down through the patch of cedar trees on the other side – at that point, the dog had been running ahead – then about four miles across the plain, with its far-flung scatterings of cattle, deer and horses. (This must have been where the hunters were hunting when Flicker made his unlucky shot: a pass to the south led to the Gorge rim, and that's probably where they would have wanted to corner the cows.)

It had been hot, if still very green from last month's rain, and the sky was big again. Since he'd stopped going out with the hunters, Gibbous had been pretty much confined to the Ledge, with the skinny sky you get from inside a gorge. For a Ledger it was always a little intimidating to be out in the open under the full blue emptiness, and if it had been a long time since you'd been under it, the feeling was practically phobic, as if nothing were holding you to the ground. (And what did hold you to the ground? It was something he'd wondered again and again, without any help at all from the old stories.) So he was glad, after a few hours under the sky and sun, to make it to the woods, where it was cooler and where there were trees for his mind to fasten to.

And now as he sat under one of those trees, feeling a separate ache in almost every inch of his body, he thought a little about his itinerary, which, put simply, was to go where the sun goes. West was where the endless water was. Admittedly, his only authority for that was the old stories, but they were the only authority anybody had, and they consistently described the endless water as being the place where the sun went down. It went down into the water, which put it out. Then Mother Elephant had to retrieve it and spend all night carrying it through Hell so that she could light it and launch it again from the dry side of the world – the east. Whenever Gibbous had mentioned this during the course of some story or other, there was a chance that someone, a child usually, would ask what would happen if Mother Elephant got tired of making the Hell trip and decided one day just to launch the sun from the west. It would make its arc in the sky, Gibbous would say, and come down on dry land. What would happen then – would the world burn up? Maybe. So it had to go from east to west, even if that did mean a lot of never-ending drudgery for poor old Mother Elephant.

But telling and retelling these things – and, after all, he'd spent his whole life at it – had done nothing for Gibbous himself but fill him with doubt. Could that really be the only explanation for night and day? Sometimes it sounded to him like something some ancestor had made up on the spot. And if it wasn't the explanation, if there was another reason, it might mean that there was no endless water out to the west at all – that he could walk and walk and finally expire on dry land. But what was it about the story, he asked himself, that didn't ring true? Was it the endless water, the sun going out or even – perish the thought – Mother Elephant herself. Now, the sun went out at night for some reason. That much was obvious. And water extinguished fire – that was certain, too. The sun had to be made of fire – what else? It disappeared in the west and reappeared in the east, and something had to get it to the other side of the world somehow. But was it necessarily Mother Elephant who did it? And if not her, who or what?

And this was about as far as he ever got analysing these stories. He knew that in all of them something was wrong, and in some of them, something was probably right. But what? A person could go crazy trying to figure it all out. And so the only thing he could do, in the end, was accept that the endless water was out to the west. And if it wasn't and he just walked until he collapsed, so what? It wouldn't make any difference to anyone or anything.

Except maybe this dog. The animal had caught up now, had had a drink from the river and was now lying under a tree about five paces away, with his head on his paws and his eyes on Gibbous. It still seemed wrong somehow to take a dog on a Long Walk Out, for a couple of reasons. One,

Gibbous wasn't truly alone and free – he always had to be conscious of the dog, which wasn't much more than a pup, after all, and might do something stupid and get hurt. There wasn't much evidence, either, that the dog could feed himself. You could tell by the way he dug at animal holes that the older members of his family hadn't got around to telling him about patience and stealth. In fact, he looked to be a kind of canine Flicker. Did this mean Gibbous was going to have to hunt for two, or teach the dog to hunt – or, worse, try to keep the dog out of the way so he didn't spoil the hunt? For that matter, how do you teach a dog to hunt? Only other dogs would know that. There was also a mild taboo against separating a dog from its family and making it think it belonged to a human family, or even to a single human. Everybody was aware that it could be done, and sometimes had been done, but it was considered a little perverse and highly unfair to the dog, which would never get a chance to fight for leadership – would, no matter how talented it was in dog terms, always be an underling.

Nevertheless, Paintbrush had said the dog would be a help, and if she thought he would, he probably would. Anyway, it was Gibbous's own fault for having given the animal salt pork that time. You weren't supposed to feed dogs. They earned their share of any animal they helped kill and generally ate it on the spot. Otherwise they hunted on their own. He'd known feeding them was wrong, but it had been raining for days, and the dogs hadn't had much luck in hunting. This dog in particular seemed very hungry. He, Paintbrush and Breeze were sitting there eating salt pork, river greens and cactus apples, and over in their corner, the dogs were sitting there with their big eyes watching them. Then this dog, with his big sad eyes and his tongue hanging out, came over and sat right next to Gibbous. It was putting him off his own meal, and so finally, right in the middle of a little story he was telling, he said, "I can't stand it," went over to the haunch of pork, chopped off a big piece and tossed it to the dog. Paintbrush was right – that was exactly when this dog took a liking to him.

And now the dog, who was still prone under the tree opposite, had his gaze trained on Gibbous's face, his eyes flickering with every small movement the man made. The animal was obviously hungry and expected Gibbous to feed him. But then Gibbous was suddenly feeling a little hungry himself, and maybe this dog was just reminding him that in his determination to get out of the range of the Seven Settlements he might be forgetting an important fundamental.

All right, they would eat. There was plenty of salt pork – along with salt goat and salt beef – in Gibbous's satchel, but there were also a couple of squirrels on the branch of an oak tree over there, and they were entirely absorbed with each other. Gibbous had always liked to watch what animals do – it was what had made him one of the Ledge's best hunters – and the difference between what they actually do and what, in the animal stories, they were supposed to do had produced the first doubts he'd ever had about all the old stories. These two squirrels, for instance: when they behaved this way in the stories they were playing some kind of game and were making their noises for the fun of it. But look at them – they were obviously fighting. They were two males, and one was intent on getting on a big branch that apparently belonged to the other one. They'd both chatter and wave their tails back and forth. Then the owner would lunge, and the intruder would make a sudden, noisy swoop through the tree, trying to flank the owner, to get behind him and get to whatever the owner owned – maybe a female, maybe a stash of acorns or maybe just a branch with potential. Anyway, wherever the invader went, he found that the owner was there first, facing him, chattering, tail-shaking and lunging. The invader, in fact, didn't have a chance, because the other squirrel was bigger and smarter and, most important, had more to lose. So what Gibbous took out of his satchel wasn't salted meat – which, anyway, was for emergencies – but his blowpipe, a dart and a second dart, just in case. He took the protective leaves off the points of both darts, and without getting up or moving any more than was necessary, he put a dart in the pipe and the pipe to his lips, aimed, blew and solved the branch-owner's problem.

The invader squirrel fell to the ground under the oak, but unless the fall killed it, it wasn't dead – the poison on the dart only stunned the animals it was used for – and the interesting thing to Gibbous right now was seeing what the dog would do. An educated dog would run over to the squirrel and, with a tooth to the throat, finish it off. Then it would bring the carcass to the hunter to be skinned and shared. But just as Gibbous had half expected, this dog wasn't up to that. He responded to the whip of the dart and the thud of the body all right, but ran over to the squirrel, picked it up, took it to a juniper bush by the river and, tail wagging, started to eat it. Great, Gibbous thought – thanks, Paintbrush. He got up, achingly, and went to the dog, which of course picked up the squirrel again and retreated just out of reach, putting the bush between himself and Gibbous. Gibbous, though, could still see his eyes through the foliage. The dog growled now.

"Look, dog," Gibbous said, sitting on his haunches and staring him in the eye, "I'm not on this trip as your special squirrel-shooter."

Another growl.

"Bring me the squirrel."

A growl.

What were his choices? He could let the dog get away with it, in which case every time he shot a bit of small game from now on – and small game was going to be his main subsistence – he was going to have to shoot one for the dog and one for himself. That wouldn't be much trouble on the face of it, except that once you shoot one small animal, all the other small animals tend to disappear. He glanced at the oak tree, and the vanished owner-squirrel was a case in point. Or he could chase the dog or throw rocks at him, which would be useless and ridiculous and maybe a good way of giving an impressionable young dog a nervous or surly personality. So he went for a third option. He still had the pipe and the spare dart in his hand, and he loaded up now, aimed at an unobstructed front paw and blew. The dog yelped, left the squirrel, took a couple of steps away from the bush, reeled a little and fell on his side. His eyes were still open – but he would be feeling terrible. Gibbous had been accidentally shot by a dart a few times, and several times he'd pricked his finger while applying poison. It was a sort of joke accident. Your head seemed to shrink until it was about the size of your fist, your eyes felt like melon seeds, your ears roared, and the world came at you as though it were trying to fit in beside the brain in your already tiny head. People, if there were any people around, would waver back and forth above you saying such things as, "He must have pricked his finger, the idiot."

Of course, Gibbous couldn't know how that translated to the experience of a dog, but he could be sure it wasn't nice and that it would last at least an eternal ten minutes. He was sorry – the dog would be horribly bewildered – but if he intended to keep the animal with him at all, it would have to be on equal terms. He pulled the dart out of the dog's paw – it had been a good shot, leaving only a pimple of blood. Then he stepped over the dog, picked up the squirrel – noting that the dog had at least known how to kill it correctly – and carried it back to the tree where his satchel was lying. He put both darts back in their case, found his goathorn knife and in about five strokes skinned the squirrel. Then he took his hand-axe, his salt box and the slippery pink carcass to the bank of the river, to a place where the ground sloped down to a small shaded eddy. He was just going to tenderise it because he didn't feel like building a whole fire for one little lunch and, anyway, didn't want to make telltale smoke so close to the settlements. He cut the squirrel in a couple of strategic places to bleed it, washed it, put it on a flat rock by the water and rubbed it with salt and a bit of sage that happened to be growing within reach. Using a couple of stones, he pounded the meat for a while and then picked up everything and went back to his tree.

It was as he was cutting the squirrel down the middle that the dog stirred and feebly got up. "Now look at this," said Gibbous. "This is how we do things from now on." He tossed the dog's half of the squirrel a pace or two forward, and the dog staggered over to it, his tail dragging and his eyes alternately on the meat, Gibbous and Gibbous's blowpipe, which was lying on top of the satchel. If he can eat while he's still feeling like that, Gibbous thought, he is a very hungry animal. The dog did eat his half. And Gibbous ate his. And a point seemed to have been made and understood.

****

It took them about an hour to reach the crossing, which was a fortuitous series of flat boulders that made it just possible, by way of a little stretching and balancing, to get across the river without getting too wet. Actually, the river was shallow enough – about neck-deep at the deepest – to cross almost anywhere, but the current was strong, Gibbous wasn't young, and the dog … well, there was no knowing about the dog. He might be able to swim like a water rat – most educated hunting dogs could – or he might panic and never be seen again this side of the bottom of the waterfall. This was really, really not how a Long Walk Out was supposed to be – he shouldn't be worrying about a damned dog. He should be completely self-absorbed, meditative even. On the other hand – and maybe this was what Paintbrush had been thinking – Gibbous had spent a large proportion of his life meditating, or at least quietly wondering, and maybe the real point of the Long Walk Out was to do things that you've never done before, or even imagined doing – such as sharing your life with an animal. It already seemed more natural than by rights it should have been. The dog already appeared to have almost as much personality as a lot of people he'd known. Next, Gibbous thought, I'll be giving him a name.

That idea came to him as he was resting before making the crossing. He was sitting on the first big stepping-stone, dangling his tired feet in the cold water. With so many boulders in its way, the river here was at its most thunderous, and the mist made a rainbow on the far bank, right in front of the trees and beside a group of drinking horses. Here on this bank was the dog, in what had become his customary starting position – head on paws, eyes on Gibbous, tail alert and signalling that he would spring into motion the moment Gibbous did. Give him a name? A strange, almost creepy idea.

Names, after all, were sacred things. And it was the sanctity of their names that gave the Ledgers their essential dignity and distinguished them from the inhabitants of the other six settlements. (Well, Waterfall and Big Rim had descriptive names and naming ceremonies of sorts, but the names there were almost like jokes, like nicknames, and were attached to people retrospectively, after their personalities had become obvious. As for Little Rim, Riverside, Deep Gorge and Salt, they just used names that either had no meaning or had meanings that no one remembered.) A name was unique to every individual Ledger and was what made that individual human and distinct. Gibbous had never heard anyone suggest that a name could be given to an animal – even to a dog. Anyway, dogs were thought to have their own names, bestowed by the other dogs, completely understandable in dog terms, unknowable to humans and expressed in whines or yips or just special looks in the eye or turns of the head. A human name for a dog would be as silly as a dog name for a human.

On the other hand – and Gibbous now took his feet out of the river and began to rub them dry with his goatskin – maybe dogs did have names for humans. How could you know? Anyway, he wasn't a Ledger any more. He wasn't even officially alive. In the world he now inhabited there were, for all practical purposes, only two sentient beings – him and the dog – and if he gave the dog a name, nobody would ever know, and certainly nobody could give him funny looks for it. He stared at the dog, and the dog kept staring at him. He would do it, but he would do it completely without ceremony and without thinking much about it. What was that dog's main characteristic? Quick. His colour: yellow. Of course, all dogs were yellow, but – again – for all practical purposes, he was the all the dogs there were. So his name was Yellow. Gibbous could have just called him Dog, maybe, but somehow Yellow was a little friendlier. Levering on his walking stick, Gibbous got up, adjusted his satchel, cocked his head at the dog and said, "Come on, Yellow." And Yellow came on. He would have anyway, of course, and anyway couldn't have heard Gibbous over the roar of the river. But the fact that Yellow followed – as Yellow – gave Gibbous a type of satisfaction that he'd never quite known before. Creepy? It wasn't creepy at all.

Paintbrush, he thought as he secured his footing on the second stepping stone, how in hell did you know? How do you always know?

CHAPTER FOUR

They crossed. It took longer than it used to take in the days when Gibbous was a hunter, but he didn't know whether to blame that on his memory, his age or the fact that he slipped a couple of times, nearly lost his walking stick once and had to drag himself back onto large, smooth stones with no handholds. This, while Yellow stood above him with patient curiosity, as though the old man had suddenly decided to take a bath. Everything in his satchel was soaked, and when he was finally on the other side, he had to stop, pour water out and make an inventory to see if anything had washed away. Nothing had. But he would need to stop for the rest of the day soon, to let his clothes and blankets dry out.

Now, though, stopping didn't seem such a bad idea. He had crossed the river. He was really on his way. All of the settlements were on the other side, and at this time of year all of the hunters from them did all their hunting on what was known as the Near Plain, the one Gibbous had crossed this morning. The Far Plain was for more desperate projects – for expeditions that could last, sometimes, several days. While he found it lucky, if not a little odd, that he hadn't encountered any hunters from any of the settlements while crossing the Near Plain, he was sure he wouldn't run into any here. It was too soon after the rains. Game was wonderfully abundant on the Near Plain, and there was no point in coming this far. There were also more risks this side of the river. While the hunters kept the Near Plain pretty clear of big predators – lions or wild dogs, once sighted, were usually mobbed and killed or chased away – there was a full complement of them over here. When Gibbous was a boy, he and his friends used to like to come to the river to set fish traps as much for the fish they caught as for the chance to wade out and throw rocks at the occasional lion drinking on the other side. Now, as Gibbous made his way up the slope and through the woods towards the beginnings of the Far Plain, he reminded himself to be a little careful, and especially to watch out for Yellow, because somewhere right around here – and this had been true for generations – was the base camp of a lion pride.

Where was the dog anyway? He'd been behaving differently ever since the episode with the dart. Instead of dawdling at animal holes and making Gibbous wait for him, he was now trotting ahead and then stopping to wait for Gibbous, who could only guess why the poison should have had that particular effect on him. Had he had a vision while he was lying there? Had some ancestral dog appeared to him and said that a dog's duty in a one-to-one long-distance walking relationship with a human was to scout ahead? Was it? It was true that, in hunting, the dogs as a group often selected the target and went for it first, tiring the animal out and steering it towards the bows and arrows. And … no, that was preposterous. But something, obviously, had happened, and now Yellow was up ahead and out of sight. But he'd probably be waiting just beyond the lip of the slope, and when Gibbous reached level ground, there, sure enough, Yellow was. But also, sure enough, about thirty paces farther on and mostly obscured by trees and bushes, was a lion. Two lions. Several of them. He couldn't see any very clearly, but the scattered tawny patches that showed through the foliage were unmistakable. It was the whole pride, probably asleep, since that's what lions usually were, especially in the afternoon.

People had been eaten by lions before – there were plenty of stories to that effect – but Gibbous had never personally known anyone who had. A few years ago, a Big Rimmer by the name of Fat Laughing Man was supposed to have been killed by lions during an attempt, while on a Far Plain expedition, to steal a carcass the lions were eating, but Gibbous reckoned that Fat Laughing Man got exactly what he deserved. No, in Gibbous's opinion, humans weren't worth a lion's effort. They weren't meaty enough and, with their knives, spears and arrows, were unpredictably prickly. But what lions definitely did like to kill, and went for with no provocation at all, were dogs, and the breeze was blowing off the river, which meant they would smell Yellow before he smelled them.

The dog, who'd been sitting as he waited for Gibbous, was now up on four feet again and about to set off in the lions' direction. Gibbous reached down quickly and grabbed him by the scruff of the neck. Then he tried to turn right with him, to pull him north, parallel to the river. But Yellow just planted his feet. Gibbous dragged him along the ground a little way, but that was slow and tiresome and a bit too rustly and crackly. He was also afraid that the dog might be tempted to growl or yelp, and so there was nothing for it but to pick him up and carry him.

Yellow struggled, as apparently surprised to be carried as Gibbous was to be carrying him (in his whole life, he'd never seen anybody carry a dog that wasn't either wounded or dead), and combined with the satchel and the walking stick, he was heavy. Gibbous was an old man with a bad knee, he'd been up all night and he'd just walked fifteen miles without eating anything but a bit of raw squirrel. He'd fallen in the river twice and was still soaking wet, he was trying to get out of the way of some lions, and it was all he could do to hold the wriggling animal and stagger about ten paces – until he had an idea. Still holding Yellow's scruff, he put him down. Then with his other hand he felt in his satchel, took out his blowpipe and let Yellow see him put it to his lips. The dog instantly assumed a cringe – down on his legs with his tail tucked under and his eyes wide.

"Good," whispered Gibbous. "Now we walk this way." He pointed his stick north. "And stay with me." He patted his thigh. "And stop cringing." They walked north briskly, the dog trotting right at Gibbous's heel. When they'd got at least two hundred paces from the lions, Gibbous turned west again, and the dog followed. It was mid-afternoon now and definitely time to look for a place to camp.

He found that place at a point where the woods were just beginning to peter out. It was about fifty paces from where the Far Plain could be said to begin, but there were still enough trees to offer shelter, shade and support for the hammock (there would probably be many nights ahead when he'd have to sleep on the ground – might as well enjoy a little luxury now). As soon as Yellow saw Gibbous put down and start to unpack his satchel, he seemed to know that the day's walking was finally over and found a soft and shady bit of ground to collapse on. Almost immediately he was asleep. Gibbous stopped unpacking for a moment to look at Yellow and wonder if he'd been too hard on him today, and then, feeling the array of aches in his own body, decided that the day had been hard all around. He was tempted just to forget everything else and to curl up like Yellow … but no, if he went to sleep now, he'd wake up in the middle of the night, and everything would be out of kilter – no food, no fire, no dry clothes. So, aches or no aches, he kept unpacking, took off his wet clothes, hung them and his blankets on a cottonwood tree, slung his hammock between a couple of other cottonwoods and found some stones for a fireplace and some leaves and kindling for a fire. Then he gathered some bigger wood until he had a nice pile of it. He built the fireplace, arranged the leaves and kindling ready to light and found his flints at the bottom of his satchel.

But he stopped there. It would probably be better to have something ready to cook before he actually got the fire going – the smell of smoke tended to scare things away. So he left his flints on the fireplace and, carrying his blowpipe and a couple of darts, began to stalk the immediate area for a likely meal. He was almost at the edge of the woods and was about to raise his pipe to aim at a crow in a small group pecking the dirt when something disturbed the birds, causing some to fly and some to hop out of the way. It was a man walking past. Gibbous dropped down and crouched behind a bush. A man, hell – it was a skyman.

He'd never been close to one before. The skyman – and Gibbous was now looking at him from behind – was very tall and was wearing a suit the colour, naturally, of the sky, with a white something on his back that might have been a satchel. And he wore the kind of hat you use when you want to keep the sun off your neck. In fact, the hat and the rest of his clothes seemed to be all one thing, as if he were wearing the sun-hat over his whole body, even his hands and feet. Then again, that might have been his body, and maybe skymen were blue the way some birds were blue. The skyman walked a few more paces and then stopped and put down a load of spears he was carrying. They were very thin, were impossibly straight and at the blunt end had largish black knobs. If you threw one of those, Gibbous reckoned, it would flip around and travel blunt-end first, or just keep flipping end over end. But when the skyman, who still had his back to Gibbous, picked one out of the pile, he didn't try to throw it. Instead he jammed the sharp end into the ground, put his head right against the black knob and seemed to twist the spear a little this way and little the other. Then he came around to the other side of the spear, and Gibbous, shrinking as deep into the shadow of the bush as he could, got a front view, only slightly obstructed by leaves and branches.

Skymen, on the rare occasions when they were ever seen, were always seen from great distances, and they were said to have a face composed entirely of one huge eye. And that's what this one had – or would seem to have if viewed from far away. Up close, though, you could tell that it wasn't an eye at all. It was shaped like a big eyeball all right, but it was more of a mask, a very strange kind of mask. Masks were what you wore when you wanted to disguise yourself, or when you wanted to pretend to be something else – as when in a dance you put on a horse's head or a cow's head. But the skyman's mask was no disguise at all, because you could see right through it, the way you could see through water or thin ice, with the same sort of flickering glints on the surface. And what Gibbous saw on the other side of the glinting surface was a man's face. There was no beard, but otherwise it was just an ordinary man's face – a young man, about thirty maybe, with ordinary blonde hair and an expression of concentration. God. Skymen were just men with see-through masks on. Skymen were men. Were they?

Gibbous had an urge to stand up and reveal himself, to say hello to the skyman and ask him why he was wearing all that on such a hot day and why he was sticking spears in the ground, and he might have done it except that he'd have been revealing more of himself than he'd really have liked: his clothes were hanging from a tree back there. Somehow, when you're meeting someone for the first time, you really shouldn't be naked. Anyway, the skyman seemed to be finished with that spear and was picking up the bundle of others. He had one last look at the one he'd planted and then walked on, south. If Gibbous had indeed stood up and met the man, he could now be warning him that there was a pride of lions in that direction. On the other hand, lions were probably as disinclined to attack a skyman as any other kind of man. Skymen were just men. They were men. Amazing.

Ridiculous. What about all those stories that had skymen flying? If that one could fly, why would he walk, carrying those spears? And he didn't have any wings or feathers, either. Gibbous went over to a tree, stood behind it and watched the skyman stride away. He kept right at the border of the plain and the trees and, after about a hundred paces, stopped again, picked out another spear and repeated the routine. Then he walked on. How many times had Gibbous told stories with skymen in them? Thousands. Tens of thousands. The skymen helped Hero find the Gorge and went to all the other people wandering alone in desolation, taking them to the Gorge, too, and telling Hero to look after them. And they did it by flying. They would swoop through the air using their huge cycloptic eyes to look for the lonely and would swoop down and pick them up and carry them to safety and hope … It really was crap, wasn't it? This was far from the first time Gibbous had made an observation that contradicted the stories he told, and whenever he did he wondered if he ought to be ashamed. His life's work, after all, had been a process of systematic lie-telling. But whenever he wondered that, he told himself that the facts didn't matter if the essence was true – that the truth grew out of the lies like a seedling out of cowshit. That didn't keep him, though, from wondering – desperately sometimes – what the actual, factual truth was. Why had he let a little thing like nakedness keep him from speaking to the skyman, who might have known plenty of facts? Gibbous could have learned some real truth for once and died with some answers in his head. Damn. He'd probably never have as good a chance again.

The skyman was well off into the distance now, planting another spear. Gibbous waited a moment to make sure the lions didn't get him, and then, still holding his blowpipe and darts, he glanced around again for a target. The crows had settled and were working the same patch of dirt as before, and so Gibbous aimed, shot twice in quick succession and returned to the campsite with two big birds, some tree fungus and a couple of onions that he'd spotted and pulled up. Yellow was still asleep – half on his side, half on his back, with a rear leg in the air and a powwow of flies around his mouth and nostrils. This made him snort about every third breath and ineffectively wave the hind leg in a scratching motion. Oh well, Gibbous thought, as the first shoots of flame twined around the kindling sticks, I've always known stories are only stories. The only sane policy is just to hear what you hear, see what you see and keep your mind open. And, anyway, it had been a thrill to discover at least one big truth about skymen.

The roasting crows woke Yellow up, and Gibbous tossed over the raw half-bird he'd saved for him. (The whole crow that was cooking was destined to be salted, dried and stashed in the satchel.) The fact that the dog looked a little groggy didn't keep him from practically swallowing the thing whole – or at least cleaning the bigger bones in what seemed about five swipes of his teeth and then starting to break and lick the bones themselves. Gibbous had rehung his clothes on a branch over the fire, and before the meal was ready they were dry enough to put back on. But instead of doing that, he left the birds on the spit and took his dry clothes and his drying skin on a ten-minute walk to the river. Yellow followed. "I wonder if there are such things as skydogs," Gibbous commented as they walked down the slope through the thickening woods. "I wonder if they wear masks, too." Then he reflected on two absurdities: putting a mask on a dog and trying to have a conversation with one. What he wondered next was whether loneliness would eventually skew his thinking.

At the river, as Yellow drank, Gibbous stood about one pace into the water and washed off the dirt he'd accumulated walking around naked. Then he, too, had a drink, and then he had a pee. It was late afternoon, a couple of ospreys were soaring and swooping and catching fish, and not three paces away, a little green kingfisher disappeared into the water and came out and up with a minnow. The mist on the river was just getting some colour now – light blue and the tiniest hint of orange. And by the time the sky in the west was thoroughly red, not to say violet, he had come back up from the river and past the campsite and was sitting against a tree finishing his meal and looking out over the plain. Yellow was beside him, looking, too. Just off to the left was the skyman's spear, and he planned to give it a good examination – maybe tomorrow, before he set out. Now, though, he was tired beyond tiredness, and it was all he could do to gnaw on his food and stare out at the world he was about to cross.

The plain rolled and rolled and looked as if it went on forever. But one thing Gibbous knew for sure was that it didn't. He'd been on a hunting expedition once that lasted twelve nights and went so far that the hunters came almost right up to the mountains. The old stories mentioned the mountains a lot, too, as a sort of border of the known world, and there was a claim by a group of Little Rimmers – though Little Rimmers were notorious liars, even by Seven Settlements standards – to have actually walked a way up one of the mountains. Was it a lie? Was it important? Whatever, in a matter of days, Gibbous Moon would be doing a whole lot better.

A matter of days, though, was a long time into Gibbous's future. At the moment he was only at the beginning of the Far Plain, and for all his tiredness and loneliness (or maybe because of those things), it was a very pleasant place to be. At this time of year, the grass was green and long, and it bent in the breezes. And on the expanse, with its undulations and hillocks, these breezes weren't always uniform, so that the grass in one place was bending one way and in another another and in another yet another. This combined with the light of the sunset to give different places slightly different shades, as though someone were shaking out the landscape the way you shake out a blanket. Then out among those shades, from Gibbous all the way to the horizon, were the animals – the silhouettes of animals. Closest to him, maybe a hundred paces off to the left, was a herd of thirty or forty grunting cows – grazing, looking up and around, moving a little forward whenever the lead cow did, grazing, looking up, grunting. Farther away and more or less straight ahead were horses. Two stallions were rearing up and trying to hit each other with their front hooves, while the other horses grazed or watched or got out of the way. Every now and then, through the noise of the cows, he could hear high-pitched whinnies. Beyond the horses were deer, more cows and a trotting pack of dogs, and at the horizon to the right – about two miles away, almost too far to distinguish – was a herd of elephants. Or he thought that was what he saw. It was getting dark, they were far away, and they might have been boulders or a patch of trees or nothing at all. Overhead, bats were streaming out of the woods, behind him an owl woke up with a shriek, and way off to the left, the first two lionesses from the local pride ventured out for a night's hunt. Others followed – six or seven of them, with several large cubs. The last to emerge were two males, which walked a certain distance from the woods and then sat and watched as the lionesses continued on, shoulder-deep in the grass. Gibbous wondered if the lionesses would go for the cattle nearest him, but they walked right past them and, as cows' heads all turned to follow them, kept walking. Maybe, he supposed, they weren't in the mood for beef. It was just as well, too, because while harassing those cows, the lions might have spotted Yellow.

A bigger danger, now, was the skunk. Gibbous hadn't seen where it had come from, only that it was crossing in front of them, about five paces away. Then it stopped and stood completely still, staring at the man and the dog. Yellow was suddenly on his feet, and Gibbous just managed to grab him by the hind leg and then the scruff of the neck. "Shh," Gibbous said in his ear. "Come on." Was he going to have to teach him everything? But they needed to get back to the campsite anyway – it was all but dark now. So he pulled Yellow a short way in that direction and then found no resistance. He let go and walked, and Yellow walked with him. The dog, he supposed, was doing his best. Imagine being a young predator and resisting the impulse to turn around and chase a not-very-big animal with a challenging stare, even if you didn't know that a skunk could afford to be challenging. "You're pretty good," Gibbous said, "pretty smart." The woods were dark, and Gibbous lost his bearings a little, but then all he had to do was push Yellow ahead and follow him. This was a dog being useful for something other than hunting. In fact, this was a dog agreeing not to hunt. This was a dog, he thought, being a companion. He also thought that that might have been putting it a little too strongly, but he felt that today, at least, he'd discovered something about dogs and regretted that he'd never be able to tell it to anybody. And that brought another pang of loneliness.

The fire was down to coals. It was important that it burn big and bright all night, because Gibbous and Yellow were, after all, camped in woods between an animal-abundant plain and a drinking-water river. And as

Gibbous laid about half his woodpile on the coals, he could hear large-scale rustlings and snortings not very far away. Horses, it sounded like. Yellow's ears turned forward, and he was on his feet, but that was all – he didn't chase any noises, which was good. When the flames were finally high, Gibbous put some more wood on, raising them almost to the lower branches of the tree. Even so, he was going to have to wake up at some point and build the fire up again. But if he was so tired that he didn't wake up, it wouldn't really matter – he'd be oblivious of anything bad that happened.

Lying in the hammock, with Yellow stretched out by the fire, Gibbous thought briefly about the world. He liked it and knew a lot about it, and he knew nothing at all. He thought about the skyman for a moment and what the skyman must know, and then he vanished into sleep. He didn't dream. He didn't wake up to rebuild the fire. In fact, he didn't wake up at all until he heard the baby screaming.

CHAPTER FIVE

Paintbrush was incoherent. She kept saying that, while she was tracking him here, she'd rehearsed again and again but that she just didn't know how to say it – how to start. The baby was screaming, Yellow was howling in response, and Paintbrush was crying and saying it was her fault, all her fault. "I dreamt about the enemies that couldn't be seen and thought it meant you couldn't see them, Granddad. I didn't think it meant … If I'd warned them instead of you—"

"Who? Warned who? Feed the baby or something, Paintbrush. I can hardly hear you. Shut up, Yellow." Yellow didn't shut up, Paintbrush didn't try to feed the baby, and the baby kept screaming. What was going on? Was this a dream? He was dead and on his Long Walk Out. What was Paintbrush doing here? Gibbous was still in his hammock, sitting up now. Whatever else was happening, he was desperate for a pee.

"Look," he shouted, "I need a pee. While I'm doing that, get the baby settled. When the baby stops, the dog will stop. When they both stop, I'll be back." He got up and walked to a part of the woods a little farther from the campsite than was strictly necessary. When he'd finished and retied his trousers, he waited where he was until the baby and then Yellow ended their respective howling. Now he could think. Now he could be a little indignant about being tracked down when he was on his Long Walk Out. If it had been anybody but Paintbrush … But Paintbrush – she was obviously in a bad way. He shouldn't have shouted at her. (Well, he had to shout to be heard, but he shouldn't have shouted quite the way he did shout.)

When he got back to the campsite, Paintbrush was in the hammock weeping and feeding the baby. Her face was dirty, the sleeve of her wet dress was torn and had blood on it, and she was missing a shoe – a serious matter for a person without Gibbous's kind of callous. She managed, somehow, to look both very tough and very frail. It dawned on him, too, that she must have tracked him at night, with nothing to see by but moonlight, which was almost nothing at all when she was in woods. She'd made that river crossing at night. With the baby on her back. And that had been the next night after the funeral, which meant she hadn't slept for two nights running. Had she slept during the day yesterday? Was she hungry? Was she thirsty? He stood beside the hammock. "Paintbrush," he said, "I'm sorry. But you can imagine. You surprised me."

"Granddad, I—"

"Tell me when you can tell me. Do you want a drink of water?"

"I've got a lot of the river in me at the moment. No thanks." She almost smiled, but then she looked more desperate even than before.

"There's some crowmeat drying over there. There are onions around. Do you want—"

"No, no, I can't … Yes, I can. Some onions. Some crowmeat, yes. Thank you, Granddad."

He went to the fireplace, found the crowmeat and tore off a piece of breast and brought it to her, putting it in the hand she wasn't using to hold the baby. "The onions are just over there a way," he said. "I'll be right back." But when he'd pulled the onions and come back, Paintbrush was asleep, and the crowmeat was on the ground under the hammock. The baby was asleep, too, having thrown up on his mother. Gibbous used his drying skin to clean up as much as he could without waking either of them, and he worried about Paintbrush's wet dress and the cut on her arm. Scouting around, he found a birch with some moss on it, scraped a bit off, brought it back, spat on it and laid it on the cut, which didn't seem too deep. And since the day was promising to be a hot one, the wet dress probably didn't matter. She needed to sleep, and he let her.

But what in hell happened to bring her here? It was the first time since waking up that he'd had a moment to fully wonder that. Where was Eclipse? Had they had a fight, or had he had an accident? No, a fight was out. Eclipse always did as Paintbrush told. And if it was an accident, Comet or Breeze could have seen to it – no need to track down an officially dead man fifteen miles away and on the other side of the river. She'd been carrying on about that dream of unseen enemies, but how … No, forget it, he told himself. Whatever had happened, it wouldn't unhappen just because he heard about it later rather than sooner. It was more important for Paintbrush to sleep, and since it was clear he wouldn't be travelling today, the most useful thing he could do now was get some more food in.

He took Yellow with him. In a way, he felt sorry for Yellow. He realised that, in just a day and some, he'd struck up a partnership with the dog. Now that there were suddenly another two humans around, Yellow would be the odd animal out. It wasn't fair. For that matter, it wasn't fair to him –

to Gibbous – either. What kind of solitary, meditative Long Walk Out was this turning into? He'd started with a dog that he had to protect and teach, and now he had a young woman and a tumultuous baby as well. Were they going to go all the way to the endless water with him?

He had his darts and pipe, and he and the dog were on the edge of the plain. Yellow had forgotten some of his discipline suddenly – a result, possibly, of the new humans – and was sniffing around the opening of a prairie dog burrow, which pretty much guaranteed that, whatever Gibbous shot, it wouldn't be any prairie dogs. But never mind. He walked out to where the grass was taller, stopped and tried to think. Then he sat down and tried to think. He wasn't a rigid person. When things didn't go to plan, he could usually manage. He could adjust. But this time … It wasn't fair, and he couldn't think. He wanted to think about something else, and then he remembered the skyman's spear, which was just over there. He wasn't tired now, and he had time, so he got up and went to it.

He'd thought of it as a spear, but that obviously wasn't what it was. It was some kind of … something. The shaft of the thing was absolutely straight, as black as coal, about as tall as he was and made out of a material that he didn't recognise. It certainly wasn't wood. It was more like … coal, or stone or some kind of mineral. Obsidian, maybe. (There was a lot of obsidian down around Deep Gorge. The Deep Gorgers carved little statues out of it.) Gibbous ran his hand up and down the shaft, marvelling at its perfect smoothness and wondering how the skyman had managed to get it into that shape. The knob at the top, though it was also black, glistened. Or at least it did on one side – so much so that he could see his reflection in it, just as clearly as if he were looking into a black bowl of water, except that his face was distorted – too big at the nose and too little at the ears. He peered at it, feeling his beard and noting that he needed to cut it at bit at the bottom and around the mouth. Then he stood back and saw that even at a short distance he could get a reflection, and that if he stood back even farther and if Yellow came and stood beside him – which Yellow, having driven all the prairie dogs to the deepest depths, happened to do – he could see the two of them in the glistening knob, bigger in the middle than at the sides. "Huh," he said aloud, but he didn't know where to begin imagining what the thing might be. It was more than an aid to beard-cutting – he was sure of that. He was tempted to pull it out of the ground and take it back to the campsite, to examine it some more or maybe even use it for some barbering, but he thought about the skyman and the expression of concentration on his face when he'd stuck it in and wiggled it, and supposed it must be there for a serious purpose – maybe as some kind of cutting that was going to grow there, or maybe as some religious thing, like a totem pole – and so instead he waved his arms a bit, reflecting on his own reflection. But that was it. Unless he ever got close to a skyman again and could ask him, he'd never know what it was.

There would have been better small-game hunting in the woods, but he'd been visualising striking out across this plain for so long that he couldn't resist just taking a walk on it now. It wasn't very hot yet, and a light breeze carried brisk smells of grass and dung. There were no big animals very near, and so no danger of Yellow either getting hurt or starting a panic. In fact, the world was perfect, except for the fact that he wasn't actually continuing his walk to the endless water today and that Paintbrush was here and had been in such distress. Something truly bad had happened, and now Gibbous admitted to himself that he really didn't want to know what it was. That was why he hadn't encouraged her to keep talking, diverted her with food, let her sleep. It was why he was walking here now. He felt almost as if he'd entered some kind of afterlife and shouldn't be bothered with the problems of mortals, no matter how awful they were. He found a little high point on the plain and sat down again in the tall grass. Yellow wandered around and sniffed things, using Gibbous as a sort of base.

Something else that bothered Gibbous was the unnecessary revival of his fondness for Paintbrush. He loved her in a way. It wasn't because she was related to him – granddaughter-in-law was, at best, a pretty tenuous connection – and there certainly wasn't anything sexual about it. The very thought made him laugh aloud at himself. He hadn't had sex or any hankerings after it since Spiderweb had died and for a few years before that. He just liked who Paintbrush was – her intelligence and prescience, the way she treated him both as a respected old man and an almost girlish confidante, the way she could get genuinely, intimately angry with him. He felt tender towards her. He guessed that he and Paintbrush were just two like-minded humans whose years in the world had happened to overlap a little, and under normal circumstances he'd been grateful for that. But now? Here?

Nevertheless, here was where she was, and he ought to be concentrating on getting some food and then getting back to the campsite with her. Enough of this playing at walking across the Far Plain – he had to accept that his afterlife had been interrupted, but could be resumed, presumably, when Paintbrush's problem was solved, if it could be. At least he wasn't lonely now. He got up, caught Yellow with his eyes, flicked his head and then started back towards the trees. The prairie dogs had come up again and two or three were standing half out of their holes and looking around. They were a long shot for a dart, but Yellow had almost caught up with him, prairie dogs were delicious, and it was worth a quick try. The dart made a long arch, missed the target by about half a pace and stuck in a bit of the prairie dog pilings. But the animal, instead of ducking back down, went over to see what it was, and Gibbous got it with the second shot. Yellow was off almost as fast as the dart, reaching the prairie dog and biting its throat. Gibbous arrived holding up the pipe, and Yellow brought the animal over. The man had to hand it to himself – he was almost as good as a dog as a teacher of dogs.

****

By the time Paintbrush woke up, in the early evening, Gibbous had managed to make the campsite a little more livable. He had granted that Paintbrush and the baby needed the hammock now and so had built himself a sort of platform out of tree branches and had covered it with leaves and moss. He'd also made a couple of stools. The fire was going well, the prairie dog was roasted, and he'd used its salted skin, with some stretched gut, to make Paintbrush a shoe. He'd brought in onions, greens, mushrooms, sage and mint. For tomorrow, just in case, there was a fish trap in the river. Yellow had actually killed himself something – a duck, while Gibbous was laying the fish trap – and even though he'd brought it over and dropped it on the bank nearest Gibbous, Gibbous had let him keep it and eat it, which meant that the dog was now full, satisfied and not particularly interested in anybody else's food. He was just lying, half dozing, by the fire. Not far away some cows were trudging towards the river, and Gibbous, almost without being conscious of it, was quietly singing the Rattlesnake Song as he sat on his stool and from his poison sachet carefully retipped the darts he'd used in the past two days. That done, he retied the sachet and laid it beside the blowpipe on one of the fireplace stones. The darts were lined up there, too, ready to be leaf-sheathed. Then he put some more wood on the fire and poked at it with a stick. And that was when he realised that Paintbrush was standing beside him, holding and jostling the baby.

"There's another stool there," Gibbous said.

She found it, brought it to a spot beside Gibbous and, thank God, started to feed the baby before the baby had a chance to start crying. "I could use some water," she said. Gibbous reached for the water-skin and handed it to her. She drank and handed it back, and he folded and tied it. Then he gave her a little prairie dog chop, which she tore at. He hoped she'd hurry and get it all down, because, until she did, she didn't seem to be willing to breathe. She'd fallen asleep this morning before she could eat anything, and how long was it before that since she'd had any food? And she was nursing, too. Women could lose their milk by not eating. "When did you eat last?" Gibbous said.

"I don't know, Granddad. I don't know. It doesn't matter. You shouldn't have let me sleep."

He handed her some roasted mushrooms, which she ate a little more slowly and self-consciously. But he could tell she wanted to gulp them down. "Well, you obviously needed to sleep. And now you need to eat."

She didn't speak again until after she'd had a pile of boiled greens, some more meat and another drink of water. Now she was eating roasted onions. "I wonder if I should have come here." She took an apple-sized bite.

"That particular wonderment has crossed my mind, too."

"I had to go somewhere. I couldn't think of anything else to do. Granddad, it's too terrible to talk about. I don't know where to start."

Gibbous poked the fire again. A raucous flock of budgerigars was descending from the sky, apparently intent on roosting, smoke or no smoke, right around the campsite. It was getting dark fast. "Well," said Gibbous, "as a storyteller I've always gone by the rule that says, when in doubt, start at the beginning. But if you still have doubts, start in the middle and fill in. You can even start at the end sometimes. There are some more onions here."

"No thanks, Granddad." That desperately sad look on her face had returned in force. Her eyes were reddening.

"Looks like we've got budgerigars for company tonight. Hear them?"

"How could I not hear … Granddad, you don't want to know, do you? You think it must be bad, and you don't want to know about it. You think you're dead and have a right not to know. Let me tell you …" Tears were flowing now. "… you're not dead. I'm not dead. He's not dead." She squeezed the baby. Her voice shook. "Two Tornadoes isn't dead. Flicker and a few of his friends aren't dead. Poor old Pigtrotter isn't dead. The wounded aren't dead – yet. And that's about it. Now do you want to listen?"

CHAPTER SIX

"Everybody's dead? Is that what you're telling me?"

"Oh, Granddad, what am I doing here? I should have let you walk on. What's the point in you knowing this? What was I thinking about? All I thought, almost from the beginning, was that I had to find you. But I don't know why. There's nothing you can do about it – nothing anybody can do. I'm so sorry, Granddad. Look at your face. I'm so—"

"Paintbrush. Please."

"I think I just wanted to be with you, Granddad. It was selfish. And I felt ashamed about the dream. I hate myself. I've got this gift of dreaming, but I don't have a enough sense to get the picture right."

"Paintbrush, don't talk about the damned dream."

"Sorry, Granddad. But now I have to tell you everything, don't I?"

"Of course you do. That's what you came here for, isn't it?"

"No. Like I said, I needed you. I just wanted to be with you."

"Well, you can't be with me and not tell me. So tell me. Just tell me what's happened."

Gibbous turned from staring at her face to staring into the fire. He wasn't grasping this. How could everybody be dead?

"All right. I'll do what you said and start at the beginning. I need to get it straight in my own head, too. But I have to think about what the beginning actually was. I guess it was after the naming ceremony and before the funeral procession, when I went back to the housecave. I didn't want to go on the procession. It wasn't disrespect, Granddad – you know that – it's just that I didn't think of you as dead. I mean, I'd just seen you off and kissed you goodbye. Anyway, Skyman was getting grizzly, and I thought—"

"What?"

"The baby was getting grizzly, and I didn't feel like … Oh yeah. His name is Skyman."

Skyman? Gibbous had a good look at his great-grandson. The boy had finished feeding now, Paintbrush had retied her dress, and the baby was just propped on her knee, sucking his thumb and looking at the fire. He seemed to be moving his head slightly in rhythm with the flames. To Gibbous, somehow, it was like seeing him for the first time. When he wasn't crying, his face was pleasant, if very dirty. His eyes were big and blue, and he had full black hair. Two Tornadoes had named him Skyman.

"Two Tornadoes named him Skyman?"

"Yeah. I'm not very happy with it, but … but it doesn't matter, Granddad. Not now."

"Of course not. Go on. It's just that I saw … No, go on."

"All right, I was back at the housecave putting the baby down. I fed him and put him down, and I was just about to get in my hammock. Then it hit. Outside, this enormous splash and whoosh. It was so quick, Granddad. I heard screams – lots of screams – but by the time I got from the hammock to the doorway, a lot of the screaming had stopped. I couldn't go out on the Ledge, though, because it was on fire. I couldn't see where everyone was – there were flames right at the entrance, and this burning liquid was sort of splashing and popping in. All I could think of was to keep the fire out of the housecave, and I got a blanket and was beating it back. In a while, though, it pretty much died down by itself, and I was finally able to get out."

"What was it?"

"What was what?"

"That was burning?"

"Fat, Granddad. I'll get to that. When I got outside, I couldn't see right away where the screams were coming from – they were mainly groans and whines now, anyway – because there was so much smoke. The ground was all slippery and there were little fires like little campfires burning all around. The bushes were burning, and the cactus. I was afraid to walk because I was afraid I might slip and fall into a fire. I was thinking about Skyman and what might happen to him if something happened to me …"

Skyman, as if already knowing his name, made a little chuckle. Gibbous was able to detach himself from the horror for a split second in order to wonder again at Two Tornadoes naming the boy that.

"… so I just stood there in the smoke – it really hurt my eyes, and I must have been crying, but I was crying anyway. And shouting and asking them where they were, but there were really only about two or three people groaning now. Then I heard some other shouts coming from somewhere else. That was Flicker and his friends. They hadn't been in the procession.

They'd sneaked away to some housecave – four boys and four girls doing what kids that age do …"

"Wait a minute. Are you saying that something happened to the procession? To my funeral procession?"

"Oh, Granddad. Don't look at it that way."

"Oh, God."

"Granddad, listen. Don't think of it that way. Just listen."

"Oh my God. It's my fault. I didn't have to have a funeral. I didn't have to—"

"It's not your fault. It's my fault. And the Little Rimmers' fault.

"The Little Rimmers?"

"Yes, I'll get to that, too.

"The Little Rimmers?"

Ignoring that, Paintbrush went on. She told him how, when the smoke began to clear, she made her way along the hot, greasy ground to the remains of the funeral procession. Flicker and his friends were already there, either standing around stunned or crying and wailing or, in the case of a couple of the boys, trying to sort through the blackened, hot, smoking, barely recognisable bodies for anyone who was still alive enough to moan. "I tried to help them," Paintbrush said. "We found three, in the end – all Sacred Object people, who were at the back of the procession and didn't get the full splash."

"Splash?"

"The splash of burning fat. They were Hunting Horn, Five Knives and my cousin Turning Spit. Spittie could even talk a little, but she was just babbling really. We took them into a Weather Clan housecave – that's where they were when it happened, about Weather Clan level – and poured water over them. But their burns are just terrible. Five Knives – you couldn't bear to look at him. I'm sure he's dead by now. Spittie might be all right. Her face didn't even get burned. But her legs and back, oh. And Hunting Horn's not much better than Five Knives. I left them there – a couple of the girls stayed with them, pouring water on them and trying to get them to drink – and I found Flicker, who …"

Who was, she said, laying out the bodies of Breeze, Eclipse and Comet. Gibbous had been staring into the fire so intently that his eyes hurt. He'd been seeing burning people in there. Now he stood up, turned his back to the fire and looked into the darkness; there was still fire, though, dancing on the backs of his eyes. Paintbrush and Flicker didn't know what had happened and didn't know what to do. They just stood there by the bodies. Flicker was sobbing, and all Paintbrush could think was that she had to reach him, Gibbous. Then she found herself looking up the side of the Gorge as it rose above the Ledge – shading her eyes and looking all the way up the side to where the rim met the blue sky – and all the way up, in a broad swathe, there were black, burning, burnt and smoking bushes, cactus and grass. She thought she could even see smoke curling into the sky from an overhang at the Gorge's very lip, which was right by the settlement of Little Rim.

"The Little Rimmers," she said to Flicker, and pointed. "It was the Little Rimmers. This is their war."

"That sort of snapped us out of it for a minute, Granddad, and Flicker and I and a couple of the other kids decided to go down to the Cavern and see if we could wake up Two Tornadoes, who would have been lying there sleeping off the naming brew. Flicker was having a hard time. He was walking along saying, 'I did it' and 'It's my fault'. I put my arm around him and tried to tell him that shooting that Little Rimmer was just an accident, but he was getting hysterical by the time we reached the Cavern and was going on about not ever practising or paying attention or appreciating his father. Then I remembered about the dream and realised it was much more my fault than his."

"It's mine," Gibbous said, almost to himself. "It's mine." The Long Walk Out was supposed to be a proud, transcendent, unselfish thing. Now it just seemed frivolous and a little stupid. And yet it had already had an irredeemable effect on him: he'd just lost a son – his last surviving one – a grandson and a daughter-in-law, not to mention almost everyone else he knew, but the future imbedded in his mind still had him walking on towards the endless water. And that made him feel even guiltier. He should have been thinking about taking Paintbrush and going back to the Ledge, helping Flicker and the rest of the kids do whatever needed to be done to keep the Ledge as a settlement alive. But then if he went back to the Ledge now, everyone in the funeral procession really would have died for nothing. Was that right or not?

"No it's my fault," Paintbrush said. "I dreamt of enemies that couldn't be seen and didn't warn anybody but you – who turned out to be the only person who was safe from them."

There was silence for a little while, not because Gibbous accepted for a moment that Paintbrush deserved any blame, but because he didn't know if he was ready to hear any more of her story. He paced. Then, when he sat on his stool again, he saw that Paintbrush had been quietly weeping. The baby was still gazing into the fire, and Yellow, who had woken up, was resting his head on Paintbrush's knee, looking up at her as though he understood. Maybe he did. Dogs were very close to each other, and maybe he'd lost relatives, too. But no. That he'd even think such a thing at such a time just showed how much a couple of days dead, alone and in partnership with a dog had altered his thinking. "Go on," he said. "What happened when you got to the Cavern?"

"Well, we couldn't wake up Two Tornadoes."

"I'm not surprised. It's not just sleep you get with the naming brew. It takes you to other worlds. It's a good thing that only the storyteller ever has to drink it."

"And the really sad thing was that old Pigtrotter was there – just sitting on a rock and waiting for his family to come pick him up. One of the boys – you know, Stalking Fox – was Pigtrotter's great-nephew, and he took him home. God knows what he told him. Or how he told him. Or what he did with him – they would have had to go past the bodies. Anyway, what I decided then was that we needed help from another settlement. So I got Skyman and strapped him on my back and told the kids – three or four them were still trying to identify people and lay them out – that Flicker and I were going to Big Rim, and we did. But you know, Granddad, as soon as we were on the Trail, I knew I'd never go back to the Ledge. I knew I'd be tracking you."

"So you don't think you and I ought to go back?"

"God, Granddad, what for?"

"To help the kids."

"Oh, they've got help now. Two Tornadoes is there, and …Well, let me tell you what happened in Big Rim. About an hour from Big Rim, we ran into a Big Rim hunting party and told them what the Little Rimmers had done – though we still didn't know exactly what they'd done, just that they'd done it. There were about a dozen of them. Some stayed with us, a couple of them ran ahead to Big Rim, four of them ran to the Ledge to see what they could do, and a couple decided to run to Little Rim, to find out what the story was."

"That was brave," said Gibbous.

"I know. Little Rimmers hate Big Rimmers even more than they hate us. But they're not at war with each other or anything. Or weren't then."

"You mean they are now?"

"Well, yes, because … Well, when we finally got to Big Rim, the runners had got there about half an hour earlier, and the whole settlement was already in that meeting house they have and were discussing whether to go to war with Little Rim. When Flicker and Skyman and I came in, they got Flicker to stand in front of them and tell them all about what happened. Then they got me to do it. Neither of us did it very well. We kept crying and mixing things up, but they got a sort of story out of us. They didn't disbelieve us or anything, but they were really puzzled by the burning stuff. It was the worst thing they'd ever heard of anybody doing in a war."

"It's the worst I've ever heard of, even from the old stories."

"The Big Rimmers have a chief, um … "

"His name is Always Standing Up. He's my brother-in-law."

"So Always Standing Up said they should wait for the runners to get back from Little Rim. In the meantime, they'd send runners to all of the other settlements – even Salt, even though Salt never fights wars – to ask for representatives to come to Big Rim. Has that kind of thing ever happened before, Granddad?"

"Not that I know of."

"I mean, the idea seemed to be to get all the settlements to gang up. Anyway, while we were waiting they offered us some food, and Flicker and I tried to eat it, but neither of us could. Both of us retched. It was cooked meat, Granddad, and all I could think of were those burnt bodies. I guess I'd got over it a bit when you gave me your meat. And I was really hungry by the time I got here."

"How do you feel now?"

"Awful. But better than I felt then. And I can think now. I couldn't think then. Telling you this makes me realise things I didn't realise then, and should have. I mean, it was fat. Of course it was fat. It smelled like fat. It burned like fat. It was slippery. But I didn't think of fat because there was so much of it. They dumped about an elephant's weight of burning fat onto the Ledge."

"Did the runners say the Little Rimmers said it was fat?"

"Yes. They got back late in the afternoon. They were clever, you know. They'd just strolled into Little Rim saying greetings from Big Rim and we hear you really gave a good one to the Ledge, and the arrogant bastards couldn't help bragging about it. They even said some of them were laughing, and nobody could ever remember hearing Little Rimmers laugh.

They said that man Jones, the one Flicker killed, was a holy man, and only the worst punishment they could think of could make up for losing him. But what the Big Rimmers hadn't realised, and I didn't either – I don't know if you ever knew this, Granddad – was that when they drain the fat out of the animals they cook, they don't just throw it away. They save it. In big vats – hollowed-out stones. They've been doing it for generations."

"I knew they did that."

"Did you? Why then?"

"Well, they don't eat fat in the first place, or try not to – you can't absolutely avoid it – for lots of reasons. I'm not sure what the reasons all are, because their religion's got a lot of secrets, and if a Little Rimmer ever tells any of them to an outsider, that Little Rimmer, then and there, dies and goes to Hell. But don't forget that there have been a few Little Rim women marrying into the Ledge. They get their names changed to Ledge names, and you tend to think of them as Ledgers, but they're so scared of their old religion they still keep its secrets. One did once tell me this much, though. That saving pure fat – and if it's pure enough it does keep, sort of – meant that no matter what happened they'd never go hungry."

"Yes they would."

"Why?"

"They don't eat fat."

"Well, yeah. But the theory is that they would eat it if they were hungry enough."

"Well, judging by the amount of fat that hit the Ledge they haven't been hungry enough in about two hundred years. Imagine saving all that stinking, rancid—"

"You know, Paintbrush, I think you've just made a good point. They don't eat it, and they wouldn't ever eat it, no matter how hungry they got. I think old Blue Butterfly – that was the ex-Little Rim woman who told me why they saved fat, she died before you were born – she might have been just saying that so that I wouldn't think Little Rimmers were entirely crazy. But of course they don't eat fat because it's against their religion, and that's all there is to say about it."

"What do you mean, Granddad?"

"Maybe there was a famine or something God knows how long ago, and their ancestors got in the habit of hedging against another one by saving fat, and as generations passed, fat became sacred, and the habit of saving it became a tenet of religion – nothing to do with famines any more. That might be how most religions get their tenets. It could be how ours did."

"Granddad, how can you say that? You taught us our religion. It's a beautiful religion, not nasty like Little Rim's."

"Theirs may be a bit grim. Everybody agrees with that. But that doesn't make it any more or less true."

"What's happened to you, Granddad? Of course their religion isn't true. Fat isn't sacred. What's sacred are things like the air animals and the labours of Mother Elephant. Dreams. The heroism of Hero. Spiritual things. How can you say …"

"All seven religions have Hero in them. It's the only thing that makes me believe in Hero. But take the air animals. Do the Big Rimmers have air animals? Do the Waterfallers? No. No other religion has air animals. What is it about the Ledgers that has made us uniquely able to recognise air animals? Anyway, are air animals important, other than as a nice, warm basis for stories?" Never, ever, in his previous life would Gibbous have said this. He had been the Ledge's storyteller, for all practical purposes its priest. He was almost as shocked at himself as Paintbrush seemed to be.

"Are you saying there's no such thing as air animals?"

"No, Paintbrush. No. I'm just—"

"Granddad, I've just seen the dead, burnt bodies of my husband, my mother-in-law and my father-in-law. I've seen my cousin suffering. I've seen my whole settlement – my whole world – destroyed. And now you're trying to destroy my belief in my religion. You, of all people."

"No, Paintbrush, I'm trying to give you a better religion – one that really is true, one I've been looking for all my life. But never mind. It's no time to be talking about such things."

"You're right about that, and I forgive you. That's because my religion – the religion you taught me – taught me to forgive. I forgive you because I love you – you taught me about love, too. But I think this Long Walk Out, from the funeral on, has affected your mind."

"No, it's not that, but I think my mind has been overwhelmed all right. I think it's struggling to find another subject to think about. So forget all the religion talk. What else did the runners say?"

Yellow suddenly growled. He'd wandered to the edge of the firelight and was looking into the darkness and growling and snarling. Gibbous got up slowly, walked over to the dog and quickly grabbed his scruff. Then he dragged him back to the fireside and, still holding him, sat down. "There hasn't been a chance to tell you, Paintbrush, but there's a pride of lions based not far from here. If I hadn't been so tired at the time I'd probably have pitched camp a little farther away."

Her eyes widened a little, and she instinctively held the baby closer. "Would lions bother us?"

"No, lions don't bother people much. But they hate dogs. That might have been a lion passing just then."

"The dog's still growling. Do you think it's still there?"

"Maybe. But as long as it sees us and sees the fire, the dog will be all right." Still holding Yellow with one hand, Gibbous got up and threw some more firewood on. Then he sat again. "Go on," he said to Paintbrush. But he was puzzled by Yellow's behavior. A dog wouldn't growl at a lion. It would cringe or run like hell. That is, if it had a normal sense of survival, which might disqualify Yellow.

"Yes. Sure. The runners said ... well, you know that big flat stone overhang outside Little Rim? My father had to visit Little Rim once, and he took me with him ... Oh God, Granddad. I didn't even look for my family's bodies. It was too much. It's still too much. Oh. It hurts, Granddad." She went quiet. There was indeed something rustling very near. Yellow's growl intensified. "Anyway," Paintbrush said, "my father showed me this stone overhang, and I lay down on my stomach with just my head over the edge, and when I shaded my eyes, I could see right down to the Ledge and see people walking around like ants. Well, that's where they did it. They somehow got their big, heavy vats of fat, all that fat the mean skinny bastards don't eat because it's against their religion, their nasty, nasty religion – I don't care what you say. They got that fat, got it to the overhang, got it burning and dumped it onto the Ledge." She went quiet again, weeping again.

The horrible thought that was rising in Gibbous's mind was, why hadn't they ever done anything like this before? Despite the long history of warfare between Little Rim and the Ledge, the Little Rimmers had never so much as dropped a pebble on the settlement below. They'd always behaved like everybody else – got painted up and came down the Trail and attacked. Fought. Wars were fights, contests. Who had Jones the holy man been that they, even they, would do something so atrocious? Could they have seen that the whole settlement was out in the open? No, it would have taken them a long time to move the vats, and if they did see a funeral procession when they were getting ready to pour, that would only have been a bonus. Anger at the death of Jones just happened to coincide with some Little Rimmer's bright idea, and that coincided with Gibbous's funeral. And what it meant was that the Ledge would never be safe to live on again. All thoughts of Two Tornadoes and the eight kids somehow regenerating …

And all thoughts stopped suddenly because Yellow jerked free of Gibbous's grasp and ran snarling into the darkness. Gibbous tried to find his knife but instead found, on a stone on the fireplace, his blowpipe and fresh darts. As he loaded he said to Paintbrush, "I don't know what it is, but I don't think even that dog would try to attack a lion."

"What then, Granddad?" She was standing now and holding the baby so tight he was starting to cry again.

Gibbous raised his pipe and aimed at a spot in the darkness a little above Yellow's growls. He shot and had time to take one more step towards the darkness when the object of Yellow's attack – Yellow's teeth clenched on a leg whose thigh had a dart sticking out of it – toppled into the firelight. It was the skyman.

PART TWO

MOTHER GRAVITY

CHAPTER SEVEN

"Mars is furious," Templeton said. "I tried to explain. I told them what you told me, but the best I ever got was a bitter laugh. God, Allaby, do you know what it's like trying to argue and make lame excuses about something you didn't even do – I mean I didn't do, you did – when they're so unreasonable anyway, and with that damned two-minute delay. And I still haven't heard from Titan yet. What will it be like when they get on the comms? Those people make the Martians seem cheerful, and the delay's eight minutes. I could kill you for this, Allaby."

"I'm sor—"

"I mean, what were you thinking about? You could have put them anywhere in your territory. You've got two million square kilometres, for Christ's sake."

"I know. It's just that it's a really nice place. It's got a perfect mix of big animals, a great vista and … Oh, I know. It was stupid. I'm sorry."

"You're sorry all right. I don't think you have any idea what this means. And a thought just hit me. If you like that place so much, that means you must have done it before from there. Have you?"

"A few times. It's very popular."

"You have done it before."

"They don't go there in this season. They never have."

"Well, one has, hasn't he? Are there any others?"

"I don't know. I haven't had a chance—"

"Not that it matters now. You've turned the sensors off, I hope."

"Of course. I did that right away, as soon as I knew."

"You mean as soon as I told you. Even on the Moon it caused a stir, and Moon people are sophisticated. We've always pretty much known about the goddamned Immyos, at least on a mythic level. On Mars, there may or may not be myths about them – the controller said that at one park there was a huge crowd standing around the guy and following him – but on Titan nobody knows anything about anything on any level. They live their lives in the dark – still in the Dark Age, too. Have you ever been ... Oh. Oh yeah. Ha. You were born there, of course."

"Yeah. In Jerusalem."

Templeton got up from his desk and, turning his back to Allaby, stared through his holowindow at the skyline of Armstrong, his home town. Templeton could have chosen among any number of views for that window, including plenty of Earth ones, but he'd picked ugly Armstrong, with the cablecars flying past its stony terraced buildings and the girdered sky that was the underside of the dome. Allaby sometimes felt a little sorry for the man. He was just a Mooner civil servant who'd found himself promoted to a job in an office in Earth Headquarters Satellite, and all he really lived for were his quarterly visits home. Most people on EHQS thought they were in heaven – artificial gravity everywhere except at the centre of the centrifuge, where there was a huge freefall gym and recreation lounge. Otherwise, there were hotels, theatres, auditoriums, a convention centre, parks, small farms and all the rest of it, including a bar district and even a discreet red-light area. A lot of EHQS workers didn't even bother with their quarterly leave, but Templeton never missed a minute of it. Of course, a life on EHQS wouldn't have appealed to Allaby either, but Allaby was only interested in the Earth itself. He certainly would have preferred the satellite to a dull place like Armstrong. He was sure of that – he'd gone to university in Armstrong.

Templeton turned around again. He was framed by Armstrong's everlasting glare, and it made it hard to see his face. "You know, I actually forget you're from Titan. When I look at you, I just see you, and you seem so normal most of the time. Good at your job, or used to be. Best Ranger. Best imager. I'll tell you a secret – some people on the board didn't want to promote you last time. But I stood up for you. They said your kind couldn't be trusted to take such a prime sector, and such a big one. I knew what they meant – that you were a Titanian – but I just said that you were better than anyone else on Earth, and that was all there was to it. I pointed out your PhD from the University of Armstrong—"

"Two PhDs."

"... but they were afraid that 'your kind', just by being 'your kind', would fuck up, and you know what? They were right. And I might be going down with you now, you bastard."

"Going down?"

"Yes."

"What do you mean?"

"What do you think? You still don't understand what you've done, do you?"

"I do. I know it's serious. I'm sorry, and I'm ready to take my punishment. But it's the first thing I've ever done wrong, and I won't do it again. I can't be fired."

"Oh yes you can. The procedures are already—"

Allaby then did something he'd never before imagined doing. He switched Templeton off. Well, just switching him off wouldn't have done any good – he'd have barged back on in ten seconds. So Allaby switched him off and instantly switched on the test gram – a half-room-sized spheroid of swirling colors that left the comms occupied and impenetrable. This was very, very bad of Allaby, but hell, he'd just been fired. The best job in the Solar System and the only thing he'd ever wanted to do in his whole life, and they'd fired him. How did it happen? How did he let it happen?

And what was going to happen now? Well, nothing very quickly, he supposed. There'd have to be a formal hearing, and they'd have to find a replacement, and the union would have to have a say, although he didn't imagine he'd be getting much sympathy there either. What Allaby had done, he supposed, was the single worst thing he could have done. He'd broken a kind of taboo. After twelve years on Earth and being promoted – thanks to his reputation for initiative and responsibility – to one of the few sectors where there was even a danger of this happening, he'd calculated the odds against and decided they were too large to consider. And then it had happened, just like that. And it could never be made all right. The Moon had had its transmission, Mars had had its, and even though the signal hadn't reached Titan yet, there was no way of intercepting it or even of warning the Titanian authorities so that they could turn the holoparks off. Laser signals went at an absolute speed – the speed of light – whether they were carrying pictures or voices, and you couldn't just send one out to overtake another. The only glimmer of luck was that Jupiter and its moons were on the other side of the Sun right now, and Ganymede wasn't receiving.

"Maybe I can start a new life on Ganymede," Allaby said aloud as he went into the kitchen. He shuddered at the thought of that and poured a larger-than-usual scotch. Outside, the sky was just starting to darken, and as he did every evening when he wasn't out in the field, he took his scotch to the glassed-in balcony. Now that his future on Earth had suddenly been cut short, the planet was looking more stunningly beautiful than ever. Allaby's station was on a lower slope of Pike's Peak, and his balcony had a view of about two hundred kilometres of descending mountain, hills, plains, forests and two rivers. After the recent rains, everything was green and glistening – from the most distant plains, which were so green they almost looked purple, to the trees blanketing the lower part of the mountain, to the little scrubby cedars that hugged the rocks just next to the balcony. From here he could look down on eagles. He could see four without turning his head – one soaring far below, two perched near the tops of huge pines and one motionless on the wind, pinions fluttering. It made you feel like God, standing here. What could ever come after this? What if it was Ganymede? Or for that matter the Moon, or back to Titan? Mars might just be bearable, he supposed, but no. Ugh. Mars was just a parody of Earth.

There was nothing, anywhere, remotely like this wonderful place. He sat back in the chaise longue and watched a herd of high, slow-moving cirrus clouds barely start to pinken. Evening after evening, when he was young, he'd done this on Titan. It wasn't long after holoparks had first been built, and his father had got a franchise on one in Jerusalem. It meant that his family lived actually inside the park. Of course, it got turned off out of hours, but before it went off there was usually a sunset. Allaby would go into the back yard, lie down and gaze up at the clouds. What a place – so light and so many colours. Then maybe he would stand up and lean on the back-yard fence and watch the darkening plain – with its herds and hawks and vultures and predators – trying to ignore the crowds of Titanians walking among and through them. Or maybe today it was a rainforest, and when he looked up he would be seeing shafts of light through the dark green canopy, hearing the birds and monkeys call and occasionally seeing one flash through the light.

Whatever he was experiencing, though – forest, desert, mountains, seashore – he came to be certain that one day he would live on Earth. He

63

would work there. He would be one of the ones who sent these scenes out. And he wouldn't just be seeing and hearing Earth – he would be standing on it, touching it, feeling the weight of the wind, standing under a sun that was only a hundred and fifty million kilometres away. For that matter, by God, he'd be under a sun at all. There was no sun on Titan, just thick, dark, green-tinged clouds, usually raining methane. To Allaby the boy, nothing was more depressing than when, after church usually, the family put on their suits and took their excursion outside the dome. It was always dull and nasty. There was a methane lake nearby – the Sea of Galilee, it was called – and you could go sailing on it, and lots of people liked to climb the ice mountains or just stay outside for several days, camping or something. There was a movement in Jerusalem – and not just Jerusalem – known as the Titanists, who spurned the holoparks and spent a lot of time outside the domes, treating Titan as though it were a place where humans were actually meant to live. The movement was strongest in Jericho, where they even had a couple of external villages, with houses made out of ice bricks and people spending their whole lives in suits, just going through the nearest dome door from time to time in order to replenish their oxygen, eat real food and have the unencumbered use of a toilet. But to Allaby, growing up in a Terra-Holopark, Titan was Purgatory. Once he got to the Heaven of Earth, he'd sworn, he'd never leave it.

"Goddamn it," Allaby said, getting up to refill his glass. As he poured the scotch and sipped, through the kitchen window he saw movement up the mountainside. It was that flock of sheep. He watched them against the red sky picking their way over the rocks, and he realised that – in how long? a month, two months? – he'd never see such a thing in the flesh again. He felt like crying. He felt like harming himself, hanging himself. He felt like running outside without his suit and dying painfully of the Abunga, bleeding through all his pores. Instead, he filled the glass with whisky and drank it like water. Then he filled it again. And then he got a grip. He'd better, he decided, turn the comms back on. Templeton would be even more furious now, but it was certain that leaving him disconnected wasn't going to improve anything. When he went into the comms room, though, and turned off the test gram, it wasn't Templeton who was waiting. It was Jenny.

"I was about to give up," she said. She was sitting on a sofa wearing a short blue nightshirt and, unusually for her, looking a little sombre. "Who were you with for so long?"

"Nobody." Allaby said. "Just Templeton. You're up late." Jenny was Ranger for Africa East, and it was the middle of the night there.

"Don't let it go to your head, but I was dreaming about you. Then I woke up and couldn't go back to sleep. Then I thought Ranger Regular over there will just be knocking off now and might like some company."

"Thoughtful."

"If you don't want to see me, I'll switch—"

"Don't go, Jenny. No." If she disappeared, Templeton would instantly take her place, and Allaby's grip was suddenly slackening again. Anyway, he was supposed to be in love with Jenny.

She smiled and made a little snort. "That sounded desperate. Is something wrong?"

"You might say that."

"In my dream you were on a giant tongue, and it was curling up around you. I wanted to help you, but I was in this giant hand and couldn't get loose. I think I was next for the tongue. Don't dreams sound stupid when you try to describe them? But I woke up in a sweat."

"You? In a sweat?"

"Oh, I get into conditions you couldn't imagine."

"Sometimes I try."

"I'll bet you do. But take it easy. It's only two months till the Confab."

Oh God. The Confab. It was the semi-annual get-together on EHQS, when Rangers were supposed to discuss techniques, problems and general ecology but were mainly coming up from their lonely stations and seeing – and more than seeing – each other in the flesh. But he wouldn't be there this year. The firing procedure would be well over in two months. He wouldn't even be a Ranger. The thought, when it hit, almost took his wind away. "Shit, Jenny."

"What do you mean, 'Shit, Jenny'? Are you trying to tell me something? Not looking forward to the Confab? Not looking forward to me? Well, don't worry. Ben Haymark's been calling a lot lately, and I'm—"

"No, Jenny. It's not—"

"… and I'm pulling your leg, moron. Where's your sense of humour tonight? What is wrong? What's happened?"

"Never mind," Allaby said. "You'll find out soon enough. It's so embarrassing I don't even want to talk about it."

"Embarrassing? What embarrassing could happen to you?"

"Never mind, I said. But if you want to know why you had trouble getting to me, it was because the test gram was on. And the test gram was on because I didn't want to talk to Templeton any more."

"But you're Gus Templeton's best boy. What did you do? Cut him off? You'll get hell for that."

"I've got hell. I'm fired. Hold on. I'll be back. I just want to get some more scotch."

When he returned from the kitchen – his glass full again – Jenny was standing up, arms crossed, and staring at him as though she was waiting to yank thoughts out of his brain. One thing Allaby loved about Jenny was that Mars look she had – long-legged, tall and supremely confident, with black hair, brown skin and glistening black eyes. But she was one more thing he'd just lost, unless she joined him in exile on Ganymede or wherever. "Peter, you can't be fired," she said.

"Why don't you get a drink, too?" said Allaby. "It'll help you sleep. It'll soften the blow, too. It's softening it for me."

"Peter, I don't know what you're supposed to have done, but they can't fire you. They just can't. You're too good. God knows, it's hard enough to fire bad people. Do you remember Callaghan in Australia Northwest – the one who claimed the forests needed fire and kept burning everything down?"

"Of course I remem—"

"It took them years to get rid of him."

"But, Jenny, that's because he was right – those Australian forests do need fires. And he had union backing. Anyway, I wish all I'd done is burn down some trees."

"What did you do, then?" She was sounding angry now. He stepped forward and put his hand out to calm her down, and of course it went right through her face. He stepped back, surprised that he'd do such a thing. He was wavering a little and realising how much scotch he'd drunk and in how short a time. "Why are they firing you?" Jenny said.

"Will you come with me to Ganymede?"

"Ganymede?

"It's sun-blocked right now. So it's okay. It won't get …" He finished off the whisky in his glass. "… the transmission. Not that that really makes any difference."

"Peter, what are you talking about?"

"Never mind. I'm talking about what I feel like talking about, not what I don't feel like talking about. Just tell me you'll come with me to wherever."

"Peter, I think you need to sober up. You know it's not safe to get too drunk. What if you did something and let some air in? Take some Antialks. Don't make me worry about you."

"No, I won't let any goddamned air in. I'm okay."

"And I think you're probably drunk and imagining you've been fired. You're not a big drinker, and you've never been in much trouble before, have you? I think you're probably in a little trouble with Templeton, and you're overreacting."

"I'm in big trouble with Templeton. Templeton's in big trouble, too, poor guy. I've got no excuse, you know. I should never have put the sensors there, even though it's a great place. It's got everything, and it stretches forever. I'm sure when I was a kid we used to get that particular place, and it was my favorite one of all. But there was a risk. He's right. It was stupid."

"Are you or aren't you going to tell me what happened?"

"I haven't run it back on the flat-screen log – I can't bear to – so I can't tell you exactly. But, Jenny, I caught a human."

"A human? Who?"

"Some old Immyo. And his dog."

"You put sensors in an Immyo reservation?"

"Not anywhere near where Immyos ought to have been, but yeah. The sensors were inside the reservation."

"When did it happen?"

"This morning. The guy's already been to the Moon and Mars. And Titan too, by now."

"Jesus. How could you?'

"My words exactly. Templeton's too."

"Jesus. Jesus. Jesus." She fell back onto the sofa, her hands over her face. "Jesus."

"Maybe you ought to get yourself that drink now. I know I'm having another one."

When he came back this time, she had tears on her face. "Oh, Peter," she said. "You really are fired, aren't you? I'll never see you again."

"Not unless you come with me to—"

"No, I'm not going to Ganymede or anywhere else. Goddamn you, Peter. Anyway, you might not get a choice about where you go. While you were whiskying up, it occurred to me that you could end up in Collins Central."

"In prison? Really? Why?

"You've broken part of the National Park Act." Jenny said.

"The National Park Act? How? Templeton didn't say anything about the goddamned National Park Act."

"Maybe he doesn't realise it himself, but the law is there. Don't forget I studied law, and I'm telling you that those people are a state secret. Anybody who does anything to reveal their existence to anyone beyond the Moon and its dominions—"

"The Moon has dominions?"

"Yeah, of course. Us, Venus and Mercury." .

"Nobody lives on Venus and Mercury. God, they'd be worse than Titan. You can't even land on Venus or Mercury."

"Mercury and Venus are still dominions. They're claimed by the Moon."

"You know, Jenny, I never knew that before. Why would the Moon bother to claim a couple of hellholes like that?"

"Minerals, moron. Before the Apocalypse people landed on both those planets. It's in the records."

"Yeah, I guess you're right. I don't think we'll ever catch up with the Ancients."

"Peter. Why in hell are we talking about this? You know perfectly well the Moon claims Venus and Mercury. Why are you playing stupid? Why are you trying to get me off the subject?"

"I don't know. It was just nice to talk about something else. I need another drink."

"No you don't. Now listen to me." Her sadness at his coming departure – if, indeed, that's what the tears had been about – had been entirely replaced by what seemed to be fury. No head in hands now. In fact, her hands had become fists, occasionally pounding her thighs. Beautiful thighs. Shit. "You could be," she went on, "in real legal trouble."

"Jenny, I knew I was supposed to do everything I could to keep Immyos out of the scenery. I know they're not supposed to see us or any of our machinery. But I didn't know there was a law, for Christ's sake. And I'm not playing stupid when I say that. I'm sure Templeton doesn't know either, or he'd have beaten me over the head with it. Does anybody but you know about this law?"

"It's a footnote to clause fourteen. I guess it isn't well known because it's never been broken. Well, it's broken all the time, but nobody's ever been arrested for it. You can't keep every traveller from the Moon who's heard stories about the Immyos from mentioning them. You can't monitor every radio conversation. I remember being vaguely aware of them before I left Mars, but if I thought about them at all, I thought of them as something like fairies, something only stupid people believed in. And that's the point—"

"I still need a drink."

"No you don't."

"Yes I do. Just a minute." In the kitchen, he had to open a fresh bottle – next month's bottle out of a Ranger's twelve-bottle yearly ration, and he had to hammer open a time-lock to get it. As a result, a little red light would now be flashing in Templeton's office. But all he could think – as he poured, drank and poured again – was that he was suddenly a criminal. Not just fired, but a criminal. But wait. No. No. Back in the comms room, he said, "So if nobody's ever been arrested, that's okay then."

"Try to listen to me, Peter. And for God's sake put that glass down. People can talk about the Immyos all they want, but if there are no published studies of them, no reputable references to them anywhere and especially no images of them, then everyone who might have heard of them will suppose they're not really real. And it's easy to keep it that way, because the only people allowed on Earth, besides them, are us. And all we have to do – or have had to do since the holoparks were invented – is keep them from wandering into our transmissions. And you do that by not doing any transmissions in the Immyo reservations. So why did you do a transmission in your Immyo reservation?"

"I know where my Immyos go and don't go, and they don't go that far from the settlements in this season. They've got all the game they need right nearby. They're not going to walk past all those animals just to hunt the same kind of animals farther away and across a river and then carry the carcasses all that way back. I know what they do. I know a lot about them. I've even picked up their speech, their speaking, and have tried to work out their language. You know they've still got a lot of words that aren't too different from our words? And they got a kind of same constructing. Construction. Same kind of construction. Oh, Jesus," Allaby sighed and clumped down on his desk chair.

"How do you pick up their language?"

"With a, you know, an old old-fashioned whatchamacallit … a phonoscope. It works like a dream in those open spaces."

"God, you've been disobeying rules all over the place, haven't you?"

"Yeah, I guess you're not supposed to do that, either. But fuck it. Why shouldn't I try to pick up their language? Just because Daddy Templeton says no? Or is eavesdropping on Immyos against the law, too?"

"Against regulations, yes, but not against the law. At least I don't think so. I'll say this for you, though – you're a real dark horse. I thought I knew you."

"Nobody knows everything much about anybody."

"Peter, you're too drunk right now to be profound. Just listen. If you're not prosecuted under the National Park Act and are only fired and have to go away, I think that's the best thing that could happen to you."

"Do you?"

"Yes."

"But why? Do you want me gone?'

"Of course not. But, in a way, yes. For your own sake. I mean, I've always stayed good and clear of my Immyos, and not just because of the law and the regulations. I'm a little scared of them. Well, not of the poor old people, but somebody else, I think."

"Who?"

"I don't know. But somebody – whoever it is that doesn't want us to learn anything about them and doesn't want the rest of the Solar System to even know they exist. Do the Immyos know something that we're not supposed to? I know that the usual story is that people wouldn't understand about them being naturally immune and would want to know why some people can live on Earth and everybody else can't. But that shouldn't be too hard to explain. It's never sounded good enough to me."

"Me neither, I guess."

"So what do you think, then?'

"I don't know. I do think something, but I can't remember what it is. And what thinking I'm trying to do right now is giving me a headache. Can I get another drink?'

"Oh hell, get one. You seem to be having the original bad day. And don't ask my permission. I'm really not that kind of woman."

"You're a goddamned good woman," Allaby said as he lurched out of the chair and towards the kitchen. At the doorway he turned, steadying himself on the jamb. "You're goddamned beautiful, too. When I get back, let's masturbate."

"Peter, tonight's not the night, I think. Just get your whisky."

He got it, and when he came back this time, Jenny wasn't on her sofa. She was gone, in fact, and so was the sofa. What he saw – and his first thought was that maybe he should try going out and coming in again – was Templeton standing there in front of that big holowindow view of Armstrong.

"What the—"

"It is possible to override," Templeton said. "I've never had to do it before, and believe me it's an administrative and technical bastard. I had to sign some papers and call in an engineer. But it can be done, goddamn it. Don't you ever think you can … "

And so on. He shouted, muttered, whispered, paced a little and made emphatic hand gestures. Allaby just sat in his desk chair with his drink and wished and wished it was still Jenny on the comms. He wanted to ask her what she meant about the Immyos knowing something that other people weren't supposed to. What could that possibly be? Why had he got himself drunk, of all idiocies? He couldn't think. He needed to think, but his concentration just bounced off the surface of things. He found himself pondering the view of Armstrong, remembering his university days and thinking, what a hole.

"… didn't realise it was as serious as that," Templeton was saying. Yeah, Allaby thought, I've got to find the Antialks. There must be some in the medikit.

"… hearing's on the fourteenth," Templeton was saying. "Then on the eighteenth you'll be told what the sentence will be. It's up to me, they say, to get you a damned lawyer, too, because you're on Earth and it's not so easy, they say … "

I'm on Earth, Allaby thought. I'm not on EHQS. I'm not in Armstrong or anywhere else on the Moon. I'm not on Mars, Ganymede or especially Titan. I'm on Earth. I'm on Earth. Just a little to his right, within easy reach, was the comms control console. On it were two finger-screws that if un-finger-screwed made it possible to lift the top up. He put his drink down on his desk. The first screw he loosened too far, and it plinked onto the floor somewhere. The second one he loosened too far but caught, and he tossed it towards Templeton and through his left eye. "What are you doing?" Templeton said. "What are you fiddling with? Are you even listening? Do you know what's at stake? Your whole life is in …"

Allaby lifted the top of the control console up and half stood to peer inside. There sure was a lot of stuff in there – transpheres and flanges and array after array of tiny diomes that he knew would be whirling, though the whirl was so fast they seemed to be still. An interesting optical illusion. And little coloured receptors here and there.

"Allaby. What are you doing?"

"Just looking."

"What at? Is there a problem?"

"Yes. No." He picked up his whisky. "No problem. But I just thought of something."

"What? If you don't—"

"It just occurred to me …" Allaby said, pausing as he wavered over the console.

"What, damn it?"

"… that I'm on Earth," he said, and he slowly poured the whisky over the transpheres and flanges and invisibly whirling diomes. Then he looked up and said, "Override that, you son of a bitch."

CHAPTER EIGHT

The dog was running around, apparently chasing little animals, and the old man was just sitting in a clearing in the grass, holding a stick across his lap and gazing at the scenery. He looked like he was enjoying it, enjoying being on Earth as much as Allaby did when he was outside doing his rangering and his imaging – enjoying it even more, of course, because he was breathing air, smelling the grass and feeling breezes and sunshine on his skin. Never in his life had Allaby breathed anything but a manufactured and mechanically mixed concoction of nitrogen, oxygen and carbon dioxide, and the only breezes he knew came out of vents. If he went outside now without his suit, he wondered idly, how long would it be before the virus hit him? How many breaths of fresh air could he savour before the bleeding started? People had always said that it was instantaneous, but who really knew? Maybe you could get in two, three or four powerful inhalations – big, chest-filling pulls of the air that humans were born to breathe. What would it be like? More to the point, would it be worth it? The way Allaby was feeling right now, he almost thought so.

He was watching the old man and the dog on what was known as the flat-screen log. No one had ever come up with a way of recording ultraholography. It was about the only modern invention that wasn't just a recent rediscovery of something ancient. Of course, the Ancients had had holography, too, but for some reason they'd never really taken to it. Then about seventy years ago, a 'Martian named Manny Underwood Lopez not only resurrected the old technology but, by adapting the laws of exponential signals to it, gave it a sharpness, naturalness, scope and scale that had never existed before. The trouble was, nothing in ancient recording technology could handle it, and neither Lopez nor anybody who followed him had ever been able to develop a new one. So all ultraholograms had to go out live. That was too fucking bad, Allaby thought, taking a moment to be pissed off at Manny Underwood Lopez for not finishing the job. Just think. With a ultrahologram recorder, transmissions could be vetted first, and there would never have been any of this trouble at all.

The only recording, then, that was done during an ultrahologram transmission was on an ordinary video chip installed in each sensor, with the images radioed to terminals in the Ranger station and park headquarters on EHQS, stored in those places for the record and played back, if they ever needed to be, on ordinary video screens. It was this morning's recording from sensor 27G that Allaby, with yet another glass of whisky in his hand, was watching now. He'd found the Antialks in the medikit all right, but he'd never taken any before and hadn't realised that, while the pills did sober you up in a spacey sort of way, they also gave you a powerful, instant, eye-aching, hand-shaking hangover. It was as though much of Allaby's brain had been lying quietly in a darkened room, and someone had suddenly turned on a spotlight and a fire alarm. The whisky now was to get over that a bit. It seemed to be working, too, without getting him drunk again. It was also still working on the comms control console: as Allaby sat on one side of the room in front of the flickering video screen, the other side was filled with a tableau of Templeton's office – the big desk, the view of Armstrong and, in front of both of them, a holographic statue of Templeton himself, mouth open, foot poised in a step forward and finger pointing straight out at Allaby. Strange. Allaby hadn't thought much about what might happen before he soaked the controls. Actually, he hadn't thought at all, but if he had, he'd have expected that the scene would just go away, in a puff of smoke maybe. Instead it froze. Of course, he could turn it off, but what for? There was something about the stopped-in-his-tracks Templeton that seemed just fine.

The old man finally got up, leaning slightly on the stick. It was interesting what he was wearing: a brown, woven shirt-sweater thing and trousers made out of some kind of skin. There was nothing crude about his outfit – in fact, he looked almost dapper. No shoes, though. Imagine that, Allaby thought. Not only was he feeling the air and the sunshine, but the grass and the dirt, the Earth. And he seemed to be walking right towards the sensor. Yes he was – it was the sensor itself he was interested in. It was the sensor that had inspired him to get up. In the ultrahologram he would have been part of the landscape, no matter how near to or far from a sensor he happened to be, and the visitors to a holopark might just take him as another, if eccentrically dressed, member of the public – that is, until he walked through somebody, which he would be bound to do. But on this flat recording, he just kept getting bigger and bigger. Finally, his face filled the screen. Then his big grey beard did, with a big hand feeling it. Allaby could see right up his hairy nostrils, could see the wet on his lower lip as his tongue stroked it. And at either side of the top of the screen, his eyes stared right down at Allaby. By God, he was looking at his reflection, as if he wanted to shave or something (Allaby couldn't remember if any of these people ever did shave – but he thought not, somehow). He kept doing that for about another minute and then backed off a short way and cocked his head from side to side – still, apparently, marvelling at his reflection. He backed off still farther, and you could see that the dog was now beside him, looking up at him. The old man did a quick little dance, stopped, leaned on the stick again and said, "Huh." He lost interest then and went back to his clearing in the grass and sat down.

Allaby found himself saying "Huh," too. What in the world would that have looked like in a holopark? On Mars, Templeton had said, crowds had gathered around the man. They'd have been poking at him, probably, throwing things through him – anything to demonstrate to themselves that he wasn't just another person in the holopark. He was a human living on Earth – walking around without a suit on, breathing the air they'd all always been told was instantly lethal.

As a boy, Allaby would ask why people couldn't go back to Earth anyway and live in domes and suits, the way they did on Titan. What difference would it make? And at least they'd be on Earth. And the answer was, you just don't realise how insidious the Abunga virus is. Look at this dome. Bits of Titanian methane leak in all the time and turn to gas, but it doesn't much matter, as long as we keep the ban on open flames. All it would take on Earth would be for about a thimbleful of air to get in and get in the ventilation, and everybody – everybody – would die. The people who do live on Earth, he was told – the Rangers, the ones who manage the place and send out the holograms – have to go through years of training, just in how to stay absolutely sterile. Their Ranger stations have quadruple, sometimes quintuple, walls and glazing. When they come in through the airlocks, they have to dispose of their suits and tanks and wear brand-new equipment every time they go out. They have to live alone, so that they always know, all the time, exactly what's going on in their stations – so that nobody's ever at the mercy of anybody else's mistakes. The Rangers are strictly selected and highly paid. They're the most responsible people who can be found anywhere in the Solar System. And even then, sometimes, one or another of them keels over with Abunga. You can't have populations there, not even small groups, not even pairs … And there were those Martian crowds today, looking, poking, at an old man with the breeze riffling through his beard, sitting with his dog in the tall grass, barefooted.

At some point along here, most of the holopark managements would probably have realised or been told what was going on and would have turned their systems off. But for the people in the parks – now suddenly big, empty, brightly lit rooms – that would only have been final confirmation that they'd seen what they thought they'd seen. Were there riots? Templeton hadn't mentioned such a thing, and since he was at pains to mention every horrible consequence he could, it was probably safe to assume that there weren't. Anyway, Martians as a nation were too phlegmatic to riot, and the planet itself, having been terraformed by the Ancients – who had warmed it up with orbiting mirrors, melted its water and planted crops and grassland and forests – was a little like Earth anyway. In some places, people lived in houses on streets and walked around outside in ordinary clothes, with just oxygen-supplement breathers. But there still would have been some pretty loud mutterings, and the media now would be full of it. If there were going to be any riots, though, they would be on Titan. The Back-to-Earth nutters, if no one else, would see to that.

But what Allaby suddenly realised was that he didn't give a damn. Let them riot. Let the authorities try to calm them down by explaining about the Immyos, and then let them explain why they'd been kept a secret – for centuries, even all through the Dark Age. Kept a secret from all other humans and all other humans kept a secret from them. Allaby was suddenly amazed at himself for never having wondered about this before. Jenny had wondered. How many other Rangers had? Here was young Peter Allaby, the best and brightest of the best and brightest, and he'd always just swallowed everything he'd been told and did everything he'd been told. And now he was in such a fix that he probably never have a chance of finding out the truth. On the other hand – on the other hand – he was on Earth, wasn't he? But, oh God, what had he done? Feeling a pang of terror, he took a gulp of the scotch and directed his attention back to the old man, who was finally getting up again.

This time he seemed to walking with more purpose, heading towards what, if Allaby had his bearings right, would be the Flaco River – or that strip of mainly cottonwood trees that bordered the Flaco. Another few steps, and he'd be out of shot from 27G, and so Allaby noted the time code and switched to the same one on 27F. F was farther away, and the man was suddenly very small. But he was plain enough, and Allaby could watch as he stopped, brought his blowpipe up and shot a couple of darts. Whatever he was shooting at was out of frame (and would have been out of the hologram), but he must have hit it, because the dog instantly took off in the direction the darts had gone. Then the man followed at a limping lope, finally disappearing.

Allaby switched off the flat-screen log. He wondered two things: why was the man hunting – alone and with a single dog instead in a group with a pack of dogs, as the Immyos always did – on that side of the river in this season; and would any holopark anywhere – the Moon and Mars today and Titan tomorrow – be kept running long enough for the people to see that wonderful blowpipe scene, for people to see someone living where people were supposed to live and making a living the way people were meant to? One of those questions he might be able to find the answer to; the other was something he'd probably never know.

Back in the kitchen he poured what would be his last whisky and went to the glass balcony. Up on EHQS, they might have been willing to go through the slow process of law on the Clause Fourteen charge, but now that he'd sabotaged the comms – not to mention smashed the emergency radio and thrown the portable handset into the chemical toilet – they'd be on their way. It would take a little while maybe to find some people who were Earth-adapted and knew all the sterility drills, but they'd find them all right, suit them up and see them off in a ship of some kind. Or if they couldn't find them, they'd have to send somebody all the way from the Moon or even, it occurred to him, from the Europe training school, if there were any people there almost through their adaptations. Or – who knew? – maybe they'd send another Ranger, saying that Allaby had gone crazy and needed to be stopped from harming himself. He doubted that, but – whatever – somebody from somewhere was on the way, and what Allaby needed to do now wasn't to stand around sipping whisky and looking out at the night. He needed to hurry a little. Nevertheless, he stood there. He stood gazing at the Moon, of all places. It was all but full now and looked both mysterious and perfectly harmless. And yet people up on that shiny thing were planning terrible things for Ranger Allaby – Ranger First Class Doctor Peter James Allaby, pride of the profession. At the very least, they'd take him to Collins Central and leave him there to rot. Try him in his absence – they did that on the Moon in state security cases, which this probably was by now – and then come along at some point and tell him how many years he was going to serve (all the years he had, no doubt). On the other hand, if he went ahead and did what he now planned to do, when they found him they'd probably feel free to kill him. God, he wished he could talk to Jenny.

Quit it, he told himself. Things will never be normal again. Just get going. He tossed down the rest of the whisky in his glass and then stood for a moment with his eyes shut tight, clasping the glass against his chest. "Now," he said aloud. "Now." As he passed through the kitchen, he threw the glass into the sink, shattering it. He went through the comms room past the Templeton tableau, crossed the living room with its low-slung, minimalist Olympus Mons-style furniture (he'd ordered it specially, to replace the clunky Moon stuff that stations were usually furnished with), and half-ran down the corridor to the supply room. The first thing he did was take a sterile suit out of the suit-locker, unwrap it and take the mike and the radio-tracker out of the helmet. He took off his indoor clothes and put it all on. Then he quickly slung a clean tank on his back, connected the hose, and breathed. He found his holster – gun still in it – and strapped it around his thigh. Next he took the whole crate of feeding cans – nearly a year's supply – off its shelf and dragged it across the floor and down the corridor to the rear airlocks. He did the same with the crate of air-tanks and the same with the bag of suit-latrines. Exhausted and breathing hard, he stood with his hand on the handle of airlock E.

Whatever he'd done so far, this was the moment. This was when he'd burn the bridge – the link between anything he'd be from now on and anything he'd ever been. He turned the handle and slid E-port back. But instead of shutting it again, he stepped over to D-port. The automatic locking system wouldn't let him open that until E-port was shut, but he overrode the system fairly easily by drawing his gun and turning the D-port lock into a lock-sized hole. He opened D-port. (In Templeton's office now, alarms would be shrieking.) Then, blasting away, he opened C, B, A and the heavy outside door. Air wafted out, air wafted in, seeping into everywhere, including the ventilation. Ranger Station North America Mid South West was now uninhabitable, and it would take about a year of sterilisation and two of quarantine to restore it. He holstered the gun. This wasn't vandalism, he'd already told himself. This was making sure that he'd never be tempted to come back, that he'd never exchange his freedom, his new life on Earth, for a shower, a change of clothes and a little time without the suit on. Not that any such temptation would ever have to be endured for long. He had, in theory, almost a year's supply of food, air and suit-latrines, but if you were in your suit constantly, day and night, it only added up to enough for about two months. After that? Well, he wasn't thinking about after that. He was just substituting a couple of months free on Earth for a long lifetime in Collins Central.

And there was another good reason for letting the air in. It meant they couldn't station a new Ranger here for ages. Of course, someone could sit around the place in a suit, but no one could live here, and by and large, there wouldn't be anybody permanently monitoring the territory – making Allaby just that much harder to find. They'd have to operate straight out of EHQS or add this sector to Jack Jackson's station, way up on Vancouver Island. And since Allaby had taken the radio-tracker out of his helmet, they wouldn't be able to find him that way. (It had been easy to remove because it was essentially a benign device, in case of an accident or something, and no Ranger in his right mind would ever want to be without it. What no one had anticipated was a Ranger not precisely in his right mind.) They'd have to look for him, with their scanners and their sensors and their telescopes and their goddamned naked eyes, and the North America Mid South West territory was vast.

It took him about twenty minutes to drag the two crates and the big bag through the open airlocks, and puffing, he figured that at this rate it would take another hour to get them down the winding path to the hangar, and an hour, really – now that he'd spent so much time in front of the flat-screen log and otherwise generally building himself up to this – was too long. He'd have to bring the pickup to the door. That wouldn't be easy because the wind, as usual up here, was blowing pretty hard, this part of the mountain was just a steep slope, and there wasn't any place nearby that was flat enough and big enough to put the pickup down on. In fact, the nearest level ledge was where the hangar already was. (It was also the reason why this station, alone, lacked a directly connecting hangar.) If he brought the pickup here, he'd have to set it on hover, get out of it without breaking any bones and then load the stuff into the hold. It was all beginning to seem impossible. Whoever was on the way to get him could be here at any moment, and again he was overcome by indecision, standing in the moonlight on the scraggy side of a mountain and trying to keep from being blown over. It didn't help either that the Antialks somehow seemed not to have penetrated his whole brain. The frontal lobe was more or less ticking over, but some of the motor parts still seemed to need attention, and when he finally did decide to start down the steep, gravelly path, he wobbled, slipped, slid and fell down.

And then, as this time he was lying on the scraggy mountainside in the moonlight, he thought of something else he absolutely had to do before he left. God, how could he have overlooked it? If it meant he didn't get away, it wouldn't matter. There'd be no point in everything he'd just put himself through and anything he now planned if he didn't go back into the station and … He got up, struggled up the slope and in through the destroyed airlocks. The panel he was looking for was halfway along the corridor, disguised as part of the wall, because he wasn't officially supposed to know it was there. By moving his gun and holding the control down, he peeled the panel away, and underneath was an ancient array of wires and dusty little buttons that had long since ceased to light up. After centuries, though, they still worked. He pressed them all, about twenty of them, and one blue button that hadn't been needed in all those centuries did light up. Then he took out his gun, held down the firing lever and swished the barrel back and forth, creating a sort of button stew and correcting what in his opinion was one of history's nastiest injustices. What he had just done was set a people free. He stared at the stew for a proud moment before the shakes, the panic and the need to hurry returned in force. He started again to the hangar.

By the time he got there, he'd fallen twice more and had slid the last twenty or so metres to the hangar door. His suit was rugged, though, and he wasn't particularly hurt. After three tries, he turned on the light, brushed bits of gravel off his suit and then pulled the handle that opened the roof. The panels groaned and lurched and slowly began to draw apart (he'd been asking for a new assembly for more than a year), and at about halfway open they started screeching. They always did this, but this time he jumped as if something were coming at him from the sky. "Eeeeee," he screeched back. Half his nerves were dead, and the rest were pure electricity. His hands were shaking so much that when he tried to open the pickup door he missed the button and actually bent his knuckle back against the innocuous spot he did punch. Finally he got the button with his thumb and, trying the shake the pain out of his finger, flopped into the seat. He sighed, closed the door and closed his eyes, held the hurting finger and slowly tried to clear his mind, to calm down a little. He took a deep breath, and Templeton shouted, "What the hell do you think you're doing?"

What?

"What are you doing there? What did you do to the airlocks?"

Oh God, the pickup radio. How could he have forgotten about the pickup radio? And it couldn't be turned off, unless Templeton did it from his end. And Templeton – with all his lights and buzzers and alarms and whatever the fuck else (no videochips, though: a hard-won point by the union, against voyeuristic controllers) – knew exactly where Allaby was and what he was doing. "Deputies in a cruiser will be there in about five minutes, Allaby. Go back up to the station. You hear me? Answer me. Now. Answer me. Answer me and then go back to the station."

Well, he couldn't answer because there was no longer a mike in his helmet – not that he would have answered anyway. Five minutes. With a little more time, he could dismantle this radio, too, but he only had five minutes – not enough even to pick up the crates. If he hadn't gone back to destroy those buttons ...

"Everything you're doing is making it worse; worse, for you. What's the matter with you, Allaby?"

Or maybe he had more than five minutes. Maybe Templeton was bluffing, trying to scare him. But no – Allaby couldn't take the chance. He started the pickup, put it on climb, rose through the open roof and then shot forward, down the slope over the tops of the spruce and pine trees. "Allaby, you're moving. Where are you going? I can't find your tracker chip. Oh there it is. It's still in the station. Did you take it out? Go back to the station, Allaby. Allaby. You're obviously off your rocker. You need help. When you get up here I promise I'll get you help. I can deal with the police. Allaby, listen, listen ..."

Listen, eh? If I can't turn him off on the controls, Allaby told himself, at least I can do it in my head. I can stop listening, can pretend that his voice is just static or something. And he really did need to ignore Templeton. He needed total concentration now, because he was flying without lights and trying to stay low so that the cruiser wouldn't be able to spot him against the moonlit sky.

"... are there now, and they say the airlocks are wide open ..."

The mountain slope was getting much gentler, and now that he was lower down, the forest seemed endless. It was a carpet of treetops, black and prickly under the moon, and Allaby was trying to hold his altitude at about twenty metres above the tallest pine trees. The trouble was, he couldn't know how tall the tallest of the tall trees might be and he'd already had to bank around a couple of them.

"… committing suicide. I mean, how long will that tank last? A day? A day and a half? Come back, now, Allaby. You don't want to die. Nobody wants you to die, for Christ's sake …"

Now the trees were starting to peter out, and there were more clearings, some of them very large. He pushed the pickup faster, faster than he'd ever gone in the thing, but it was still only a tiny fraction of the speed the cruiser could go. There'd be prairies soon, though, and he'd feel better then – and the deputies, anyway, wouldn't know where to look for him. For all he knew, they might be going another way – north or west towards the Pacific. Ah yes, the trees were pretty much gone now, and the landscape was almost as flat as water. Even though the sky was clear, way off to the left, practically below the horizon, lightning was flashing – little distant momentary domes of whiteness. He didn't have long to live, and that was exactly the sort of thing he wanted to see now – Earth just being Earth.

"… Jenny Romero. I know you two are …"

He could make out faraway, shadowy animals, a massive herd of cows ahead, grazing. Not native to this continent – he remembered that from Ancient Ecology. Hell, most of the wildlife came from some other continent, domesticated and brought over by humans, who then wiped out most of the native animals. What humans, though? The Clovis people? No, they just did for the mammoths and the sabre-tooths. Where did the elephants come from then? No, people – later people, Europeans, Asians and Africans – brought the cows and horses and elephants and even the lions and tigers, which they displayed in parks or used to keep as pets. Incredible? Who'd want a pet lion? The Ancients were insane sometimes. How many people who went to holoparks knew that most of the animals didn't come … He suddenly realised that flying over the cows so low might stampede them, and he silently veered off before he reached them, straightening up just as he crossed the ruins of Alamosa and the Arkansas River. That was close … Jenny? Did he say Jenny?

"… so here she is. Hear her out. Let her know if you're still all right."

"Are you there, Peter?" She paused for a few seconds and then said, "Are you sure he can hear me?"

"I'm sure he's in his pickup," Templeton said. "But he hasn't answered. He might have disabled the radio or something. He disabled the one in his station. Try anyway. There's a chance."

"Peter, I'm calling from my station. It's been a hell of a night. I couldn't sleep after we got cut off – I was so worried about the mood you were in. And now Gus tells me you've gone berserk or something. Oh Peter, come on. Answer."

"I can't, Jenny. Sorry."

"I don't think he's hearing us. Where is he?"

Templeton said, "If I knew that—"

"Can't you trace him?"

"No. I told you—"

"Oh yeah, yeah. Peter, listen. It's a very bad idea, what you're doing – whatever it is. In fact, it's no idea. It's stupid. You'll die. If it means anything at all, I don't want you to die. I love you. Do you remember the last Confab? Do you remember when we went down to the … Oh, I feel like an idiot, Gus. He's not hearing. I'm just saying embarrassing things into nothing."

"But, Jenny, do you have any idea where he might be going?"

They were obviously convinced by now that Allaby couldn't hear them. He was over desert, and there were great boulders and saguaros everywhere. He had to pay attention. He crossed the Rio Grande and instantly had to climb, to reach a pass he knew in the San Juan Mountains, which loomed across the southern sky.

"How would I know? That's an enormous territory, and I've never even been there." A few moments of silence. "But … well—"

"But what?"

"Yeah," said Allaby. "But what?"

"You know, it's funny – I was thinking just then that I didn't want to get him into trouble."

"That is funny," Templeton said.

"It's probably nothing, Gus. It's only a thought, but he's fascinated by his Immyos. He's been recording their language with a phonoscope. He's got a doctorate in Ancient Languages, you know, besides the one in Terrestrial Ecology. Now if he only had one day to live, I think he'd—"

"Oh my God," said Templeton.

"Jenny," said Allaby. The radio went dead.

He was right up against the San Juans. He'd found the pass, but it was too black in there, and so he shifted into lift. He'd go over. No point in being excessively cryptic now – the cruiser would be heading straight here, to stop him from reaching the Immyo settlements. And once the cruiser got close to the pickup, the pickup would be detected no matter how low or how dark it was flying. When he got past the mountains and over the foothills, he'd have to make a dash for the Flaco Plain and the Immyo reservation, because the cruiser couldn't follow him there: it was forbidden – with absolutely no exceptions – to fly a ship where Immyos might see it. But wait a minute. If it were in pursuit of a ship that was breaking that very law … He didn't know. There'd probably never been a precedent. He just didn't know. And something else occurred to him: up to now they'd been chasing him to catch him, to bring him back, essentially to save his life. Now that they knew where he was headed, they'd be chasing him to stop him, to kill him if necessary. Once they had a fix on the pickup, they'd just shoot him down. Thanks a lot, Jenny.

His original plan – the one that expired ten minutes ago when he had to abandon the crates – was to hide the pickup near one of the settlements, walk in, introduce himself, stay with the people and put a final polish on the language and then, on one hand, learn from them what it meant to be a real human and, on the other, tell them everything that, as real humans, they deserved to know. As a plan, it was impulsively conceived and full of holes, but at least it was a plan. Now he didn't have any idea what he was he was going to do, other than die tomorrow. But before he did that, he guessed he just wanted to meet some Immyos and to let them meet him – to show them that they weren't alone in the universe. Exactly why they'd never been shown this before was something, now, he'd never discover.

He rounded a rock formation that was immensely tall and topheavy. The San Juans seemed endless. They were a mixture of mesas and peaks and expanses of bare earth fringed by thick stands of, if he remembered, aspen and juniper. There were also rivers and several lakes down there, and occasionally a lake would shine through a black blanket of trees, the moon floating in its middle. Mainly, though, the mountains were just a dark, high, craggy greyness whose primary importance at this point was that it was Allaby's final hurdle. As Allaby flew, he kept checking his monitors for any sign of the cruiser and considered it a miracle that it hadn't shown up yet. But after a day like today, a miracle was the least he deserved.

But if it was a miracle, it didn't last long. He'd come part of the way off the San Juans and was approaching the plain – intending to fly higher now, mainly to keep from disturbing any of the Flaco's superabundance of animals (how could anyone blame him for wanting to do imaging there?) – when he caught the cruiser's glint, magnified by the overhead monitor. The cruiser must have been looking for him from space, and now it was diving out of the stratosphere and levelling off and hovering high above the mountains. Allaby was about thirty seconds away from the border of the Immyo reservation, and so he swooped in, gave the pickup its last ounce of speed, and dashed for it. The cruiser still didn't move. Only its missiles did. The ship wasn't using lasers, of course, which would have left wreckage, but its particle missiles. Allaby could see them in the monitor, two of them arching down and coming at him, ready to transform him and the pickup into so many quintillion new constituents of the air and the soil.

Not knowing what else to do, he performed a manouevre that Jenny had once told him about (Martian joyriders, apparently, used to use it), but of course he'd never attempted it before because it was guaranteed to destroy the pickup's drive box. Travelling just four metres off the ground, he put the controls on hover and full forward at the same time. Because both controls were trying to switch off, it took all his strength to hold them in place. But he did hold them, and the pickup scooted ahead on a magnetic cushion, three times as fast as the old clanker had ever gone in its life. Allaby knew that right now he'd be terrorising animals, sucking up grass by the roots and trailing a sonic boom, and he was sorry but … The drive box lasted about twenty seconds, and yet he'd covered maybe fifteen kilometres in that time. Then, when he heard the box shatter, he fired the emergency retro and felt the speed slam down. He could take his hands off the controls now, which was a good thing because he needed both arms to brace himself. But then when the retro burnt out the pickup, instead of settling down into a gentle landing, still seemed to be going, at fifty-five kilometres an hour according to the speed display. He scanned the panel and saw why: the hover function was still on. It must have stopped resisting when the drive box went – which meant that the pickup was, in effect, skidding on magnetism. There was no way of stopping it without turning the hover off and crashing, and so he just opened the door and tumbled out, hitting the ground with a roll. And when he stopped rolling, he was lying in the soft grass with nothing worse, as far as he could tell, than a threatening pain in his wrist. Then, about ten seconds later and a hundred metres ahead, the missiles caught up. With a whoosh and a flash, one particled the pickup. The other particled something else – he had no idea what.

He didn't move. The hurt wrist was on the same side, the right, as the swollen forefinger, and now the finger, which he'd almost forgotten about,

85

seemed to have taken a new infusion of pain from higher up. As for the wrist, it might have been broken, or at least sprained. Holding his right arm against his chest, he levered with his left and sat up in the grass. Then he did an inventory of the rest of himself, and nothing else seemed to be hurting. The suit was intact. And since he was breathing, so, obviously, was the breathing gear. The gun wasn't in the holster, though. He looked around. The grass was tall and thick, and he was sure he'd never find it. It served him right for forgetting to click the flap down, and anyway, what did he need a gun for? With his left hand he unstrapped the holster and tossed it away, too. He stood up. Somewhere, horses whinnied. Somewhere else, a screech owl screeched. Bats streamed across the moon. He was alive. Not for long, but he was alive now, and he was at home on Earth. Nobody would be looking for him any more, because they'd assume he'd been in the pickup when the missile hit.

Well, he thought, you wonder idly all your life where you're going to be when you die, but he could never – not even as a boy dreaming in his father's holopark – have imagined this. He was going to die outdoors on Earth. What was more, tomorrow when he felt his air-tank going, he wouldn't just wait to suffocate – he'd unscrew the helmet and take that deep breath of real air. He was almost looking forward to it. But no, no, of course he wasn't, and don't dwell on it either, he told himself. Right now there was the last day of his life to live and lots of things to do. The first was to attend to this arm. He felt the wrist with his left hand. It was hard to know, through a glove and the sleeve of a suit, if it was broken, but he had to assume it was (it felt broken from the inside anyway) in case a bone pierced the skin and he started bleeding into the suit. The suit had tool pockets at chest level, and he tried to see if he could raise his arm and rest his hand … ow, no. And all his tools were still in the pickup – rather, were integral parts of the planet Earth – otherwise he could cut the side of the left pocket with a knife or shears. And, of course, he could have made a sling out of the holster. Where had he thrown it? He couldn't remember. Should he look for …? Oh, to hell with it, he thought, just hold the wrist against your stomach.

And so, grasping his wrist tightly, he started walking towards the settlements. An hour or so later – having moved in a daze through his very own living, moonlit, mooing, whinnying, hooting, grunting, rustling, roaring, real holopark – he even imagined he could smell it – he reached the strip of cottonwoods that bordered the Flaco River and could see, down among the trees, a fire burning.

CHAPTER NINE

"Poor man," Gibbous said. The baby was crying, Yellow was whining and cowering (Gibbous had had to be pretty rough with him just then), Paintbrush wasn't screaming exactly but was making a succession of sharp, frightened-animal noises, and the skyman was lying on his back in the firelight with that just-been-darted glaze on his eyes. Or at least Gibbous – on his knees, bending over him – assumed that was what he'd be looking like. It was hard to see much at all of his face, with the flames reflecting off that mask he wore. "He is a man, you know," he said half to Paintbrush, half to himself. Then he looked back at Paintbrush. She had stopped whimpering and was just staring. Instead of holding Skyman too tight, she now looked as if she might drop him, and Skyman's yells suggested that he sensed the same thing. Gibbous straightened up quickly and stepped over to her, putting his arms around both her and the baby, who instantly stopped crying and just started grabbing for breath. "Don't worry," Gibbous said to Paintbrush. "He's only a man. He doesn't have wings. He can't fly. He's not magic. He's a man."

"It's a, a ..."

"I know. He's a skyman. But under that thing, that mask thing, he's got a man's face. I saw him yesterday, up close. Let me show you. Come on."

"No."

She pulled away, and Gibbous was suddenly holding the baby. And the baby was holding him, both arms tight around Gibbous's neck, breathing hard in his ear. "Listen, Paintbrush. Really. He's nothing to be afraid of. I saw him. He just wanders around sticking sticks in the ground. And in the stories skymen are always friendly, and they help Hero, remember? In some versions, Hero's a skyman himself."

Paintbrush shut her eyes tight and opened them, as if the skyman might not be there the second time she looked. But he was, of course, and she said, "God, Granddad. This can't be happening."

"Here, take Skyman."

He prized the baby's arms loose and handed him to Paintbrush, who held him all right now. She looked at Skyman and then at the skyman. "Two Tornadoes knew."

"I guess he did. That naming brew really does have powers. Or it might be a coincidence. Who knows? Let's see if we can help him."

When Gibbous kneeled down and bent over the man this time, Paintbrush knelt beside him. "It's not a coincidence," she said. "Have you ever heard of anybody else getting named Skyman?"

"Have you heard of anybody else named Gibbous Moon or Paintbrush? Storytellers try for originality in this – to go with the original nature of the person. Maybe we're running out of sky names." He took the dart out of the skyman's thigh. "You know, I know it's a horrible experience this man's having, but it can't be helping that he's got that thing on his head. I don't know how he breathes in there."

"Not any more. We're not running out of them any more," Paintbrush said.

"Out of what? Maybe I ought to try to get it off."

"Sky names. Any kind of names."

He looked around at Paintbrush. Her eyes were welling up again. If Gibbous had any reason for being grateful to the skyman, it was that for a few moments he hadn't been able to think about the atrocity at the Ledge. "I'm sorry, Paintbrush. I, uh … I don't know."

"Never mind, Granddad. It's happened. And now this is happening. Things that can't happen are happening. I think the world's coming to an end."

Gibbous could only look at her – her face orange and black in the firelight, the fatherless baby going to sleep with his head on her shoulder. What could he say? It was true: the world was certainly ending for him, for Gibbous. After all, he was on his Long Walk Out if there was anything left of it. In reality, even his new world, his afterlife, had come to an end. Her world, the Ledge, was finished, and the wider world (whatever and wherever that was) was delivering a skyman straight out of The First Story of All and into their campsite. He wouldn't have been surprised if Mother Elephant herself turned up next, hunkering down at the fire and saying she'd got tired of launching the sun every day and that people would have to live in the dark from now on. All he could think to do was to put his hand on Paintbrush's arm and say again, "I don't know."

But Paintbrush said, "Granddad, maybe he's been sent?"

"Sent?"

"Think about it. Two Tornadoes drinks the naming brew. He goes to another world – you said that's what happens – and in that other world he's shown the rain of fire that's just about to come down, but because he's drunk the naming brew, he can't wake up and warn us. The only way he can communicate is through the baby's name."

"Phew, Paintbrush. Hold on."

"What's he going to do then? Because maybe there's more to the story that we don't know because it hasn't happened yet. Maybe the skyman is being sent to save us, to save the settlement somehow. Remember that story about how Hero stopped the sun? If he can stop it maybe he can make it go backwards – make it go backwards two days' worth ..."

"Paintbrush."

"... and then he does something to stop the Little Rimmers doing what they're planning to do. So instead of trying to warn us by naming the baby something like, well, Fire Is Coming From The Sky – which nobody would take as a warning, would just take as a stupid name – Two Tornadoes tells us that there's hope, that a skyman will come and everything will be all right."

"Is that all?"

"It's only just occurred to me."

"Paintbrush, I think ..." But what did he think? Her idea was not only impossible and preposterous but unreality to the point of madness.

"Now if he has a face," she said, "a man's face – I can't see it – but if he has one and is a man, maybe you're right. You ought to get that thing off him before he smothers. He'll never be able to help us if we don't help him now."

"I don't think ... " Gibbous said. "All right. All right. I'll try."

"What's the hat made of?"

Gibbous got up, put the dart by the other darts on the fireplace and then squatted behind the top of the skyman's head. "Well, it's like rock right here at the top. Over the face it's hard, too, but you can see through it, except for the reflection. It's like ice but not cold. Then, hm, down here in front of his mouth it's kind of soft and pushy. Pushy over the ears, too. But the rest of it's hard." He tapped on the mask. "Very hard." Then he regretted tapping. The man was awake. He could see and hear. He was just very miserable and very sensitive and couldn't move.

Paintbrush said, "Look, Granddad. There's some kind of seam connecting the hat thing to the body thing, right there at the bottom of the neck. Oh, I just saw his face. He does have a face."

Gibbous pulled on the hard hat and mask but only managed to drag the whole skyman a short way across the ground. All this suddenly became interesting to Yellow, who abandoned his mope and, wagging his tail, began sniffing around the skyman's feet. Then he quickly progressed up a leg to the crotch. "Yellow," Gibbous said, "be careful." The dog glanced at Gibbous and then went on sniffing.

"Granddad," said Paintbrush, who was standing behind him now, "I've been meaning to ask. Have you given the dog a name?"

Pulling obviously wasn't doing any good, and it certainly wouldn't be making the man feel any better. So he stopped. "Yeah. I have. Look, the man's chest is moving. He is breathing. He'll be coming out of this before too long, and then maybe … I don't think we should—"

"A dog having a name. It's just one more strange thing. Maybe that's a sign, too." She pondered for a few moments, and said, "Does it come apart at that seam?"

Gibbous examined the seam, looking for a thread or something, so that he could unpick it. But it was as stony as the hat. "It's not a sign. It was just that he didn't have any dogs to give him a dog name, and if that dog family in the housecave had already given him one, I didn't know what it was and probably couldn't say it anyway. And at the time it was just me and him in whole world. So, yeah. I named him Yellow."

When he spoke the word, Yellow looked up from his sniffing. "Come over here, Yellow. Leave the poor man alone." Yellow came over and stood beside Gibbous, lowering his head and sticking out his nose as though he, too, were examining the seam. "See? The name works, and he's only had it for about a day. Uh, Paintbrush, this isn't a seam as you and I know seams. The body covering, though, is cloth – not any kind I've ever seen before – but … can you hand me the knife? It's on the fireplace."

She brought it to him, and he tried to see if he could pick at the cloth just beneath the seam, but there was no picking place that he could find. The cloth, somehow, didn't seem to be woven and was almost as impervious as the headpiece. And come to think about it, Yellow's teeth hadn't been enough to tear it. The dart had gone through it, though. So if he could just stab at it, maybe, without also stabbing the man … But no. He was already doing more harm than good. He wished he'd never wondered aloud about whether the man could breathe.

Then, just in time, the skyman moaned. It wasn't muffled a bit by the mask. It was there. It was clear. It was definitely a moan, a human moan. Gibbous said, "He's coming around," and stood up. Paintbrush stood tight next to him, and he put his arm around her.

"I'm sure of it, Granddad," she said. "I'm sure of it. He's been sent."

"Whatever you say. But don't get your hopes—"

This time it was a full-fledged groan, and abruptly, the skyman sat up, scattering Yellow to a safe distance. Then the man did something odd. The universal reaction of people coming out of a dart spell was exactly that moan, but it was also palms held over temples. The skyman, though, was grasping his right wrist. In fact, still moaning, he was starting to double up over it. "Granddad," said Paintbrush, "he's hurt. Here, hold the baby." She passed a sound-asleep baby to Gibbous and then knelt in front of the skyman. That was when Gibbous, trying to keep the baby's head from lolling, saw how the man managed to breathe. Low down on the back of the headpiece, just above the seam, there was a big hole. Simple. "What's wrong with your arm?" Paintbrush said. "Can I see it?" She started to pry his fingers loose but didn't have to. He simply opened his hand and, with the wrist resting on it, let her feel. "I think it's broken," she said. "Did you break it? Did you fall down? His arm's broken, Granddad."

"Ease naking," the skyman said in a deep human voice. "Ooh. Fut heatem."

Trying to peer into the mask, Paintbrush said, "What?"

"Oh. Uh. Aaaahhh. What? What? Heaead? Hit?" His speaking was bit like coughing.

Paintbrush looked up at Gibbous. "He can't talk," she said. "I never knew darts did that to you."

"Me neither," said Gibbous. "But you don't feel much like talking. In fact, once you can move again you feel like crawling away and dying. Don't worry, friend," he said to the skyman. "It was just a dart. You'll feel better in a little while. Paintbrush, I think I'll put the baby in the hammock. Then I can make the man a splint."

"But it's a bit dark over there, and you said there were lions."

"All right then. I'll move the hammock closer to the fire. Take the baby." Paintbrush by now was sitting, legs crossed, in front of the skyman –

squinting as she tried to peer into the mask – and Gibbous put the baby in her lap.

"Were you sent to us?" Paintbrush was asking.

"Uh. Hi. Hi. Neame ease Perterr."

"What?"

Gibbous spotted a couple of nearby cottonwoods that would do, and as he was untying the hammock, he was still hearing the totally unrewarding conversation – her asking the skyman a question, him jabbering and her saying, "What?" As far as Gibbous knew, there was nothing about dart poison that made people jabber. It was almost as though the man really couldn't talk. If that turned out to be true, what a disappointment. How could a skyman, of all people, not be able to talk? Could it be that he was the only skyman, even the last skyman, and had never had any other skymen to talk to?

"By the way, Paintbrush," Gibbous said as he was putting the hammock up again. "All that trying to pull his headpiece off was waste of time. There's an airhole at the back."

"Oh yeah? Where?"

"Just at the back of his neck. Here, I'll take Skyman. He's really worn out, poor kid." He put him in the hammock and put the blanket around him.

"Why do you wear that thing on your head?" Paintbrush persisted. "We thought you couldn't breathe. That's why we tried to pull it off."

"Heaead. Heaed. Head. Head."

"Granddad, he said 'head'".

"But did he mean 'head'?"

"Yes, head," Paintbrush said, reaching over and patting the top of his headpiece. "We're sorry. We thought you couldn't breathe. That's why we tried to pull it off. We didn't know you had an airhole." She tapped the back of her own neck. "We didn't know about this," she said, leaning forward and reaching around the headpiece.

"Down some," said Gibbous.

"We didn't know about this." Then she quickly pulled her hand away. "Oh, Granddad, I touched his neck. He really is human."

"Yeah, and he's got a broken wrist. Maybe one of those firesticks—"

"Granddad, look at him." The skyman had let drop his right wrist, leaving the hand lying in a very painful-looking position on the ground, and with his left hand he was feeling his own neck through the airhole. For a while, he just stayed that way. Then suddenly he jumped up and began moving his left arm up and down his back – going up as far as he could reach, as though he were putting himself in a wrestling hold.

"I remember," said Gibbous. "Yesterday he had a satchel on his back. He's lost his satchel."

"Uh oh," said Paintbrush. "I hope—"

"Yaaaaaaahooooo," the skyman screamed. He bent over and, broken wrist or not, grabbed Paintbrush by the shoulders and shook her. "Yaaahaaa, yaaaahaaa. Ibn cun birth. Ibn cun birth."

"Birth?" said Paintbrush. "Granddad, he's scaring me."

"Calm down, skyman," Gibbous said, pulling at his shoulder, pulling him away. Then the skyman turned and grabbed Gibbous's shoulders. "Ibn cun birth. Ankee. Ankee."

Then – again, with both hands – he grasped the sides of his headpiece and began to turn it around, so that very quickly Gibbous was looking at the back of it. Then it turned all the way around, and the skyman lifted it off (so that's how you do it, Gibbous couldn't help thinking) and tossed it into the darkness. It was, in fact, the same tall, beardless, blond young man Gibbous had seen yesterday, but the earnest expression was very definitely gone. He was beaming and laughing and circling around in the campsite taking in huge gasps of air. Every now and then he'd say, "Ibn cun birth" or "Ibnm viab" or "Ibnm in art."

All the shouting had woken the baby up, but he wasn't crying, just lying in the hammock sleepily sucking his thumb, apparently fascinated by the skyman. Yellow, too, was fascinated, stretched out by the fire with his head on the ground, his eyes following everything the skyman did. Paintbrush was holding her wrist up and pointing at it, saying, "Be careful. Be careful." As for Gibbous, he was glad, in a way, that something had happened to make the skyman so happy, but he was also annoyed that, not only could the man not talk, he might even be crazy. Look at him, he thought, he's just emerged from one of the nastiest experiences known, he's got a broken wrist that he's bound to have made much worse in the past couple of minutes, and he's pacing around laughing and whooping as if he were having the time of his life. And jabbering. Only yesterday Gibbous had wondered if maybe the skyman could answer some of the questions that had nagged at him all his life, and when he finally appears, right here, he turns out to be an inarticulate, nerveless idiot. As for Paintbrush thinking he was some kind of saviour … Gibbous looked at her,

94

saw the concern on her face and realised that that was still exactly what she thought, or at least desperately hoped.

She went up to the skyman now and put her hands on his arms just above the elbows, stopping him. "Please calm down," she said. "Granddad, help me." But before Gibbous could move, the skyman started hugging her and bending to kiss her on the head and face. Then Gibbous did move. He reached the skyman, grabbed him from behind, pulled him backwards and turned him around, appreciating in the process just how tall he really was – at close quarters, Gibbous's head only came up to his chest. Nevertheless, he jabbed that chest with a finger and, looking up, said, "I don't know where skymen come from, but where I come from you don't kiss women without asking. Or being asked."

The skyman raised his hands in appeasement – or would have if one of them wasn't just flopping uselessly at the end of its wrist. "Ibnm opolo," he said. "Ibnm jut osoo ippa. Uh, uh, surrie."

"Sorry," said Paintbrush. "He's saying 'sorry'."

"Sor-ry," said the skyman.

Paintbrush said, "It was all right. I didn't mind. There was no harm." She was standing beside Gibbous now, and very gently she took the skyman's wrist in both her hands. "Doesn't it hurt?"

"Hurrt," he nodded, smiling. "Hurrt."

"Granddad, could you make a splint now?"

Gibbous picked up his knife and went to the woodpile, muttering, "Sorry, sor-ry." He threw a few sticks on the fire and picked out another one of about the right thickness. Then, stabbing it with the knife and twisting slightly, he split it. With several strokes of the blade, he smoothed the splinters off. The spool of twine was in his satchel, and on his way to get that, he saw that Paintbrush was trying to persuade the man to take off his shirt or whatever the thing was that he wore. In the dark, Gibbous rummaged in the satchel, felt the twine and returned to the firelight to find the skyman naked except for a pair of very short trousers. The body-thing was lying in a heap, the man was still grinning, and Paintbrush was again holding his wrist. "I've never seen anything like it," she said. "He did something with that seam, that collar, and all his clothes just came apart and fell off. And he's lucky, Granddad. Look. The bone hasn't stuck through. I don't know why."

"He's lucky all right. He's lucky he didn't get another dart in him, kissing you like that.

95

"Oh, Granddad, it doesn't matter. He's just happy about something. He's kind of beautiful, too, isn't he? Maybe he's happy because he can help us, can help the Ledge."

"Paintbrush, you're not still thinking that this person – this jabberer – is going to—"

"No. I think I kind of understood him a couple of times. And sometimes he does seem to try to talk right."

"I don't know. I find Yellow easier." He brought a stool over and put it down behind the skyman. "Get him to sit down. I don't care how happy he is – this is going to hurt like hell."

Still cradling his wrist with one hand, with the other she reached up and pressed on his shoulder. "You have to sit down," she said. "Sit down."

"Siate dow. Siat dow."

"Downnn," said Paintbrush.

"Aaaah," he said. "Sit downna." And he sat down on the stool, with Paintbrush going down in concert, kneeling and still holding the wrist.

"All right," Gibbous said, kneeling next to her and putting down the splint and twine. "Give it to me." Paintbrush passed the man's wrist to Gibbous, who started feeling for the break. Feeling for and setting broken bones was something most Ledgers were pretty good at, living as they did in a hard, vertical landscape (part of every child's education was practising with skeletons), and he found the fracture right away. "He is lucky," he said. "It's a clean break, and it's sharp, but it hasn't cut through anything outside or inside as far as I can tell. He doesn't even have much of a bruise. Yeah, here's the other side. It's got a little way to go. All right, skyman, ready? Get him to shut his mouth, Paintbrush, make him clench his teeth. Otherwise he'll bite his tongue off." (Not that that would make much difference, he refrained from adding.) Paintbrush showed clenched teeth to the skyman, but he seemed to take that as a smile and smiled broadly back. "Oh God," said Gibbous. "Give him the knife. Make him bite the knife." Paintbrush picked up the knife and put it between her own teeth, showing him what to do. Then she gave it to him, and a little to Gibbous's surprise, he actually put the knife between his teeth and bit down, raising his eyebrows in an "Is that right?" expression.

"See, Granddad?" said Paintbrush. "He even put it in the right way around – sharp side out."

"I should hope so. All right then." Gibbous already had a grip on each end of the broken bone, and now, pushing hard, he moved the two ends until they met. Then he held them that way with one hand while he picked up the splint with the other and wedged the two sides of it under his own clenched fingers and thumb. He unspooled some twine, and holding the end in his mouth, ran the spool around and around the splint, laying the twine on it as tightly and neatly as he could, with no gaps, for the splint's full length. Now all he needed to do was to get Paintbrush to cut the twine and ... damn. With one hand he was supporting the wrist and holding the twine in place, with the other keeping the twine taut at the spool end and holding the place where it needed to be cut, and with his mouth keeping the other end taut. He nudged Paintbrush and said through his teeth, "Get the knife."

"What?"

"The knife. The knife." He signalled as well as he could with his head. "Get the knife."

"Oh, he looks all right. A little pale."

Gibbous didn't move and just closed his eyes. A thought occurred: this must be what the skyman has been feeling like – saying things that can't be understood. Maybe he wasn't jabbering. Maybe he was ... but the thought stopped when Paintbrush said, "Do I need to cut that for you, Granddad? Can I take the knife out of his mouth now?"

"Umm," Gibbous said.

Then he heard her say, "Let go. You can let go now. Granddad, he won't open his teeth. His eyes look funny."

"Slap him," Gibbous said.

"What?"

Oh hell. Gibbous half-turned and was able to use his knee to support the splint. Then, taking the twine out of his mouth and keeping it taut with his hand, he said, "Slap him."

"Really?"

"Yes. Hard."

So she slapped him hard. The skyman shook his head, refocussed his eyes and relaxed his jaw. Paintbrush took the knife.

"Cut it here."

She did, and Gibbous quickly tied the knot. He held the splint and looked at it. It was as good a one as he'd ever made. It would probably last the full month and a half.

****

That seemed to have done it for the skyman. Just a few minutes after having his wrist set, he was curled up on the ground by the fire, as close to being dead as sleep ever takes a person. Yellow was curled up with him. And Paintbrush, even though she'd slept all day, still hadn't really had enough. She went to the hammock, she said, to fix Skyman's blanket, and when Gibbous looked again, she was in with him, also asleep. Gibbous was exhausted, too – it had been a day the likes of which he'd never known and would be impossible ever to know again. In fact, too much had happened for it to end with something as innocent and ordinary as sleeping.

There was only one blanket besides the one Paintbrush was using, and that was rolled up on the bed that Gibbous had made for himself an age ago today. The skyman, though, didn't even seem to have any clothes (it was indeed, as Paintbrush had observed, like nothing ever seen: the body thing was now just a pile of rags), and so Gibbous got the blanket and laid it over the skyman and the dog. The coolness would come more from the ground than the air, but maybe if the man shivered himself awake, he'd have the instinct or the presence of mind to wrap the blanket all the way around – not that there was any telling. Anyway, Yellow would warm him, and dawn wasn't that far off.

Gibbous decided he'd try to see the dawn in. He put on his poncho, built up the fire a little and put the stool close to it. As he settled down and poked the coals with a stick, he had a brief pang of a feeling that surprised him. He wanted Yellow to rest his head on his knee, and Yellow, the traitor, was sleeping with the skyman. It was jealousy – over a dog. It wasn't much, and he scoffed it away, but it was a feeling that he could never, a day or two ago, have even imagined – have even imagined existing. God, what in the world had happened in two days? Paintbrush's wild hope about the skyman running the sun backwards was as understandable as it was crazy. It sounded simple enough, and if it worked, it would certainly make the world all right again – about the only thing that would. But no. In the story, Hero had only stopped the sun, so that he and the skymen and the ancestors didn't fall behind schedule. He never made it go backwards. For one thing, it would have hit on the land side of the world and burnt everything up. And anyway, where would Mother Elephant have fit into all that? Then again, if events are all going backwards instead of forward, then Mother Elephant would be unlighting the sun, running backwards through Hell and … and Paintbrush and the baby would be crossing the river backwards, and later Gibbous would be walking backwards across the near plain, having unkilled that squirrel by sucking the dart back into his pipe … Of course it was preposterous. But he couldn't blame Paintbrush for hoping. He almost wanted to hope it himself – the carnage at the Ledge was too awful to think about. But at least Gibbous hadn't seen it happen. Unlike Paintbrush, he didn't have the real, permanent picture in his mind of the groans and the stinking smoke and the burnt bodies. He also had the detachment of a dead man – an outlook that wouldn't go away. When he'd left the Ledge, something had snapped that couldn't be rejoined, and the worst misfortune in the world – he couldn't imagine how anything could be worse – wasn't enough bring him back to worldly life. He felt dead. He felt gone. And he felt terrible for feeling that way.

And he didn't want to feel terrible. His feeling terrible was one more dire result of his deciding to have a funeral and to go away in the first place – and of the Little Rimmers' wild overreaction to the death of Jones. For that matter, of Flicker not being able to shoot straight. If the sun ever could be run backwards, Gibbous supposed he would have it go to the point where Flicker was drawing his bow and then somehow have him lower his aim by about an inch, so that the arrow hit the cow instead of the man behind it. An inch. That one inch and then everything could proceed normally – the wake, the funeral, the Long Walk Out – and tonight he, with Yellow, would be camping somewhere out on the far plain, never even doubting that everything on the Ledge was as fine as when he'd left it. In fact, he'd hardly be thinking about the Ledge at all – he'd be thinking about the next day's walking. In fact, he wouldn't be thinking at all – he'd be asleep.

Oh, Paintbrush. The truth is – I'm sorry, but it is – the skyman can't make the sun go backwards. It's not possible, not conceivable, and anyway, that particular skyman can't even talk or, on the evidence, understand talking. Gibbous then remembered the thought he'd had when he was holding the twine in his teeth, and then what came to mind were the Salters. Salt had always been a strange settlement. The people there didn't hunt and didn't fight wars. They didn't have to hunt, because what they did do was dig salt. Their settlement was built on the only known salt deposit, and people from the other settlements brought the Salters all the food, clothes and everything else they needed, in exchange for the vital salt. Nobody ever fought wars with them because nobody could afford to have them as enemies. And they couldn't afford to have enemies, either. Salters weren't very likable, though – were hard-faced, hard bargainers – and when they weren't digging salt or meeting trading parties, they were generally inside those big, windowless mud houses they had. They didn't see outsiders if they didn't need to, never went to powwows and didn't often bring outside women in or let their own women marry out. And though they could talk all right pretty much all of the time, when they thought no one was listening – and this was the point – they'd speak gibberish to each other. Gibbous had overheard them a couple of times and so had other people. It had always been dismissed as grunting, the way pigs grunt, but once Gibbous had watched a couple of Salters at this for two or three minutes, and what they were doing seemed to him to be – except that it wasn't – real talking. They were doing all the other things people do when they talk – changing expressions, moving their hands – but they weren't actually saying anything. He'd never much thought about this afterwards (Salters were weird, that was all), but what if they had been talking?

It was something else to add to his accumulation of sacrilegious ponderings. Just as names were sacred, so were all words. They were, in fact, the most fundamental sanctity. This was true in all the religions (except maybe Salt's, as it now began to seem). People couldn't exist without words – words were what connected them together – and it was the obligation of everyone not to distort them, to use them as they were meant to be used. True, there were differences of opinion among the settlements about what was exactly right – you could even tell which settlement a person came from by the way he spoke – but nobody misused words to such an extent that there could be no understanding at all. Anyway, what would be the point? Gibbous glanced at the skyman. What indeed? What if everybody you knew misused words in the same way? This thought immediately led to another, almost frightening one. That man lying there was a skyman, after all, just short of a god if the stories were to be believed (though the skyman's behaviour tonight hadn't done a lot to add to Gibbous's confidence in them), and the words he used were more likely to be the real, the correct, the sacred ones than the words of plain humans.

Anyway, how long had it been since skymen and humans had had any direct contact? Not since about the time of the Beginning, probably, whenever that actually was – but a long, long time ago. Down in Deep Gorge, every new storyteller, before he could be confirmed in the job, had to memorise a list of the chief's generations, and the last Gibbous had heard, there'd been roughly forty of them (though how far you could trust the long-term memory of the Deep Gorgers, he wouldn't have liked to say). Skymen were certainly seen from time to time, and had been seen all through the ages, but they were always at a distance – even in the Cavern paintings, they were often tiny and indistinct. There were some big ones, too, but they were obviously made up – their heads consisted entirely of a big friendly-looking eyeball, and they had enormous feathery wings on their backs. They were always far away in most of the stories as well, when they figured at all. The Ledge cycle, about the founding of the settlement, was the last time skymen appeared as characters. So, through all those generations, skymen and humans hadn't talked to each other. And it wouldn't be surprising if, through all those generations, humans had developed some bad habits with their words.

Or maybe not. There was no way to know. But it had taken some sitting and some thinking for Gibbous to realise – and now he'd have to operate on this assumption – that the skyman, when he seemed to be jabbering, was actually making talk, unknown talk. He looked again at the skyman – the first one to get in contact with people since the Beginning, picking out for the honour none other than young Paintbrush, her son and her old grandfather-in-law Gibbous Moon. "Sor-ry," he said under his breath, and he had to admit that it certainly did seem more than a coincidence. For the first time in memory and legend, one settlement has all but wiped out another one, and right afterwards three of the survivors – four, if you counted Yellow – experience the first visit by a skyman since the Beginning.

Suddenly there was immense crashing nearby, and Gibbous quickly stood up and tried to look in its general direction. It went on, spread out, came nearer and got louder, with creaks and snaps and groans and rumbles. He thought he knew what it was. He stepped out of the firelight and shut his eyes for a few moments to let them adjust and then peered into the woods. Yes, there were great shadowy forms there, spotted with moonlight – a herd of elephants, the nearest one about fifty paces away. They'd be on their way to the river, apparently lingering to break some trees. They did that sometimes – they liked the bark and the leaves, and they'd knock down the trees, especially the spindly younger trees, to get at the foliage. Elephants. It was all right – they probably wouldn't come near the fire. But elephants. Out on the plain, the only elephants he'd seen, or thought he'd seen, had been a couple of miles away. The river wound from places that would have been much closer to them than this, but they'd made their way here. And the trees in this bit of woods had shown no sign of elephant damage. There'd been no signs of elephants at all. They obviously didn't ever come here. Except tonight.

He felt like going over to them, to look at them, to touch one maybe. But he knew better. He'd probably only startle them and get trampled or slammed to death. So he went back and sat at his place by the fire and, as the thrashing and crashing carried on, speculated about this onslaught of signs and visitations. Earlier he'd pictured Mother Elephant coming in and sitting down, and now he wondered more realistically if somehow Mother Elephant had sent that herd here. (He also wondered if he even believed in Mother Elephant, but that, right now, was way beside the point.) He certainly couldn't escape the feeling that somebody somewhere was trying to tell him something – something no doubt about the events at the Ledge. But what? As things stood, asking the skyman wasn't going to help. Paintbrush wouldn't know, or would, in her present state of mind, fly into absurd fantasies. He might as well ask the baby or Yellow. No, the answer was inside him, Gibbous. It was in his own head, and he and only he could winkle it out.

He reflected again on Paintbrush's story, on the rain of fire, the burnt bodies, the wretched kids sorting through them. Then what? Two Tornadoes sleeping, poor old Pigtrotter being led away, Paintbrush and Flicker heading for Big Rim. And then they'd left the Ledge behind. He went back over the story and tried to remember every word she'd said – he was supposed to be good at that. He was a purveyor of stories. The fire, the bodies, the kids – and, oh yes, the discovery that it had all come from Little Rim – Two Tornadoes, Pigtrotter … and then they leave.

Was it Gibbous's imagination or were the elephants getting closer? They were louder. They were working their way towards the campsite, pulling down trees now not thirty paces away. He looked around. Despite the noise, everybody here was still sleeping – even Yellow, who should at least have had the instinct to wake up and get out of the way of a herd of elephants. (Maybe it was just because he was under the blanket.) Would the fire really keep them away? He didn't know. Fires kept most animals away, but elephants were rarities, and he'd never had this particular problem before. Besides, why would elephants ever be afraid of anything? He decided he'd better not wait and see, that he should wake up everybody now and clear the campsite. But as he stood up to do that, it seemed that maybe the elephants weren't coming any closer after all, that they might have turned and were working their way more towards the river. He changed his mind, put the last of the sticks on the fire, picked up the water skin, sat again and had a long drink. As he retied the skin, it occurred to him that if the elephants had been sent, they might have been sent not as a sign so much as an intimidation: think, or be trampled.

Think from another angle maybe. I'm dead, I'm detached, I've had my funeral, as disastrous as it turned out to be. But being dead and detached can be an advantage maybe. And I'm really still a living human – that's a great advantage. The skyman's a living human, too, and he's detached. What would he think? What's he even here for? To help? To help do what? To save humans? To save culture? But the Ledge's culture, for one, is all but wiped out – left in the minds of Two Tornadoes and the six kids and at the mercy of vengeful Little Rimmers. But wait – after the Ledge. What happens then? Paintbrush and Flicker leave. They go to Big Rim and tell their story. What does Big Rim do? It sends out runners. Chief Always Standing Up is calling a council, a war council – all the settlements, maybe even including Salt this time, against Little Rim. It has never happened before. It's not a contest. There are no rules this time, no traditions. The Little Rimmers are caught in a surprise attack and outnumbered four or five to one. The aim is not to punish Little Rim but to wipe it out – no more Little Rim with its mean, sanctimonious, skinny, scowling grumps, spoilsports and, now, multiple murderers. And then instead of seven settlements there'll be five – or five and a mutilated stump at the Ledge. But then what happens? Precedents have been set. The next time someone in one settlement slights someone in another, will a simple flurry of arrow-shooting be enough? The concept of wiping out people wholesale has been established, and though it may not be possible every time there's a war, it will still be the ideal. War will involve more and more ingenuity, more fear, constant fear. Anything will go. How long will it all last? There are, or were, only seven settlements, and there's a limit. Paintbrush was right. It's the end of the world, or at least the beginning of the end. It has to be stopped now, while it still can be stopped. The atrocity at the Ledge has to be known as having happened once, until it fades in the collective memory and becomes once upon a time. Meanwhile, the Little Rimmers have to be made aware of the enormity of what they've done. They're the ones who have to feel the guilt, and they can't do that if they're wiped out. The only way to save the world now is to save Little Rim.

103

It had gone quiet. The elephants must have got tired of eating trees and were probably almost at the river now.

CHAPTER TEN

It was the morning after to end all mornings after. There'd been a morning at a Confab once when he'd woken up in an alleyway in EHQS's red-light district without any money or identification, without even his shoes, and had spent several foolish hours at a registration and supply centre trying to replace those things before an afternoon meeting on herbivore ecology where he was scheduled to deliver a paper. And back in university days there'd been a few typically painful and disoriented mornings, occasionally featuring strange rooms and strange women with Lunar accents. But all that, now, was frivolous and, essentially, nothing. That was another universe. That was the world as he'd never again know it. Now he had both the ordinary hangover and the heightened effects of the Antialk devastation, not to mention the skull-splitting residue of whatever had been on that dart (the cutaneous secretions, he suspected, of rana anesthiesis, an ancient genetically engineered frog that managed to hop away), but he also had an aching, throbbing wrist, spots of itches salted over his body and a shaft of real, unfiltered and unrefined sunlight directly on his closed eyelids, suffusing his wretched brain with a haze of hot scarlet. And there were the sounds – various birds, mainly, and rustling leaves; he'd heard those sounds before, though – what he'd never experienced until now were the smells.

The strongest was what he presumed was the dog. Allaby knew dogs. He knew their history. He knew that the dog, with the possible exception of the cat, was the first species to be domesticated by humans. That had happened at least fifteen thousand years ago, when packs of dogs and packs of men would hunt together, but there were some anthropologists who even had dogs and humans, more than a hundred thousand years ago, evolving together – a partnership of the brain and the nose. He knew how dogs socialised, and why. He knew dog anatomy, dog taxonomy, dog hunting techniques. Why, for an exam once he had to draw part of the dog – the grey wolf – genome. But this dog curled up against him now was the first dog he'd ever touched and certainly the first he'd ever smelled. Smelling an animal for the first time was, of course, thrilling, but that

105

didn't mean it was particularly pleasant. The closest thing he could imagine to it was a dirty towel that had been lying on a wet bathroom floor for a month, or certain corners of the compost wing of the Jerusalem hydroponics plant. But no, the dog's smell was more definite than that: singular, strong – mammalian, carnivorous, metabolising, respirating, farting, sleeping, dreaming, slightly snoring, hind-leg-jerking, down-to-earth, real, dogged dog.

There were other smells, too – dirt, dust, a dying fire, some kind of droppings – but the dog overpowered all of them. The only thing it didn't overpower was the air itself, a flux of genuine, natural Earth air. Air that he was breathing. That wasn't killing him – that wasn't killing him. Smelling the dog may not have been exactly pleasant, but on the other hand it was a magnificent privilege. He finally, slowly opened his eyes, converting the scarlet into a mixture of bright yellow, blue and dark green. He was alive. It was the Abunga that was dead.

The thought came upon him in a *whoosh* and was forceful enough to yank him into a sitting position. His lurch jolted the dog awake, and it yipped and half got up, too – the half being its front legs. The hind ones stayed folded on the ground for the moment, under a rough brown blanket and alongside Allaby's own legs. He was touched: last night, somebody – the pretty Immyo girl probably – had covered him up. He looked around for her now and spotted her long auburn hair hanging over the side of the hammock. Then he looked in the other direction, towards what was left of the fire, and there in dapples of sunlight was the old man, slumped forward on his stool with his chin on his chest. The dog finally got up all the way, stretched, shook dust off itself, went over to the old man and, whining a little, rested its head on his knee.

It was the Abunga that was dead. The Abunga was dead – dead and gone. There was a lot in the way of pain going on in Allaby's head right now, but at least he was thoroughly, even starkly, sober – sober and able to realise that it wasn't just his own survival that was the miracle here (and last night that was all he'd been able to think about) but that, unless he'd somehow been born with an Immyo's immunity (about, he reckoned, a ten-million-to-one shot), there was no more Abunga virus in the Earth's air – the Abunga, the nano-particle of RNA that, when it escaped from or was let out of an ancient laboratory (that, at least, was the assumption, based on a general prejudice against the ancients and their chronic carelessness: nobody, in fact, knew where the virus had come from) did more to change the course of humanity than any other force, factor or form of life in the whole of history. For all practical purposes, it ended human history. In fact, it ended humanity – or at least, except for Immyos, humanity on Earth. And now the Abunga was gone. What he, Allaby, had just discovered was nothing less than the most momentous discovery of all time. As such, it was clearly something he had to do something about. He had to get word to people. The millennial wait for the all-clear was over, and the Solar System's human diaspora needed to know – now. Wasn't that right?

Of course it was. Of course. But how? He scratched and scratched again. These damned red spots were probably the result of some kind of dog parasites. Fleas, they were called. He was sitting in a campsite with a flea-ridden dog, a baby and a couple of primitives whose language he hadn't even tried out yet. His only clothes were his underpants, he'd been given up for dead (for killed), his pickup had been particled, the nearest communications centre was at his Ranger station about six hundred kilometres north of here, and anyway, he'd destroyed those communications, even down to the emergency radios. The nearest working comms centre, then, was either at Vancouver Island or Yucatan, and how far away were … But of course there were still mikes and headphones in the helmet supply … but no, the helmets, the suits, everything would all be disposed of, having been contaminated by Abunga, or so people would think. But what people? Obviously, the people restoring the Pike's Peak station. They were probably working on it already. There were people there, and if he could just get there, he could … Jesus, his head was hurting worse than ever. The pain was actually sawing at it … He could what? All they needed to do was see him – see him walking around in the open, breathing. Then they would know, wouldn't they? Would they? The same sort of people had already tried to kill him once, and anyway how would they know who he was? How would they know he wasn't just some stray Immyo – made possible, they would know, by the sheared-off panel and immolated buttons. Stray Immyos, by definition, should be dead, and they would make sure … But no, he could talk to them, and once they heard him … Jenny … Jenny had said something last night. What was it? Jesus, Jenny, the Abunga's not killing me, but my head is. What was it you said?

For the last minute or so he'd been sitting with his hand over his eyes, trying both to cradle his headache and to give his thinking a free run. And when he moved his hand now, he saw that the dog had woken the old man up. He was sitting straight on the stool, had his eyes open and unfocused and was holding the back of his neck in the universal gesture of someone who's just been sleeping without lying down. It then struck Allaby that since the old man was the only one without a blanket, it must have been him, not the girl, who'd covered him up – a tender thing to do for someone who'd, earlier, seemed so grumpy. On the other hand, he had put the splint on Allaby's wrist – not tenderly, for sure, but expertly and carefully – and so maybe grumpiness was just part of his charm. Anyway, grumpy was something he deserved to be. Here he'd been on a hunting and camping trip with his daughter or granddaughter or whoever (for all Allaby knew, his youngest wife), and this goddamned alien drops in, acting outlandishly and needing medical attention. On yet another hand, it was actually he, Allaby, who might have deserved to be out of sorts: if it hadn't been for this old man's unseasonal expedition (and looking at them now, there was no doubt that those two over there were the very man and dog in the errant ultraholograph), he'd now be waking up in his own bed in his own Ranger station with a solid reputation, a secure job and a decent, if intermittent, love life. But with no knowledge, Allaby pointed out to himself, of the truth about the Abunga virus. He – not to mention the rest of humanity – owed a lot to that old man, or would owe a lot if Allaby and the rest of humanity could ever manage to regain contact.

The old man suddenly got up off the stool, walked past Allaby as if Allaby didn't exist, went to the hammock and started shaking it, gently at first and then a little harder. Allaby watched as the faces of both the girl and the baby emerged from under their blanket. The old man said something in an urgent tone, and the baby whimpered and began to cry. The girl seemed mystified and drowsily asked something, but the baby's rising screams cancelled all immediate chances of Allaby understanding anything. He stood up now, the blanket around his shoulders, and smiled in their direction, but only the girl acknowledged him. She smiled shyly back and then equally shyly began to feed the baby. This brought sudden silence, which the old man used to quietly explain something at some length. Allaby recognised the words for "river", "save", "meal" and "five" – which meant he could understand almost every word he could hear.

That was encouraging, but the point of the moment was that he wasn't, after all, going to die today – or any day for a long while. Before he started on the trek to Pike's Peak, he'd need clothes and provisions, which he could only get from Immyos. And to get them – and to inform the Immyos about himself, about other people and about their place in the universe,

108

which was just as important in its way as telling the Solar System about the extinction of the Abunga – he'd have to test his knowledge, or lack of it, of this language. He would either start speaking it right away or need a little time. But now, happily, a little time, even a long time, was something he had. In fact, as much as he appreciated the importance of getting to the Ranger station, he was still running on last night's momentum away from there and was having trouble making himself, rather than just appreciate, actually feel the importance of going back. What he really wanted to do, he realised – stroking the ground with a bare foot, savouring a breath, scratching his thigh and becoming aware of both a raging thirst and a bladder with a reservoir of poisons to expel – was just to live for a while as a human on the human planet.

He wanted to say "back in a minute" but wasn't certain he'd say it right, and so he waved to catch their attention (the girl was the one looking grumpy now; the old man looked, if anything, a bit crazy) and said a word he was sure of – "river" – pointed that way, pointed at himself and then circled his finger around to indicate that he was coming back. Though both of them gave short nods, neither of them seemed to care very much, and on the way to the river, Allaby felt slightly foolish for having said anything at all. But how could he feel foolish about that, considering the display he'd put on last night? He wondered when he'd ever be able to explain to them what it was like to be ready for certain death, to think, after the dart hit, that death had come even earlier than expected, and then to find that it was all a big mistake followed by an even bigger one, a colossal one, an historical one.

That thought came in the rush of relief as he unloosed a whopping urination. There'd been many times in the field when he would be using his suit-latrine and wondering what it would be like just to pee into a pile of leaves or against the side of a tree. And now he was doing it: tree first, then leaves, then a patch of dirt, little glistening rivulets branching out from a lakelet, finding their level and sinking into the ground. That's me going down there, he thought. That's me directly wired to the planet Earth. Oh, what a big thought, he thought as he eventually finished and shook off, and oh what a day. Much of the headache seemed to have diffused since he left the campsite, and what remained was no worse than, say, a very heavy hat. He could focus better. As he picked his way down the slope to the river, trying to avoid skinning or impaling his membrane-tender feet on a stick or a ragged pebble, he was able to see in a way he never could from inside a helmet. The sunlight, when it fell through the branches, was so sharp – the greens so olive or emerald and the browns so cinnamon or faecal. He'd made images in woods on the Flaco River before – not right here because it really was too close to the settlements and people sometimes appeared on the opposite bank, but upstream where the elephants usually drank (come to think about it, there were signs of elephants down here, too) – but it still felt as if, until now, he'd never been anywhere that was anything remotely like this.

Down at the river, the blanket still hanging across his shoulders, he stood on a cool, flat stone and stared across the almost blindingly brilliant, rushing, splashing, white-on-white water – listened to the clamour of it, smelled it. The smell was like the olfactory equivalent of white noise, blotting out all other smells without actually replacing them with anything, or anything other than a general tinge of the wet essence of life (liquid water, the magic potion that made all the difference between the inert and the animate). Were there fish? Was he smelling fish? Well, of course there were fish, but if that was their smell, it wasn't anything like the stink that accompanied the Jerusalem market fish, fresh from the tanks, or the generated fish cakes that came out of the Ranger-station freezer. But don't be stupid, Allaby told himself, you can't smell fish that are still alive and under water. This was vegetation he smelled – moss, ferns, algae, grass, whatever – carried on the little breeze that was whipped up by the current itself. The current also created a fine, low haze, especially towards the far bank, where it skirted the lower trunks of, mainly, sprawling cottonwood trees, every other of which seemed to support a big, black ospreys' nest, a few with single ospreys sitting in them or perched beside them. Other ospreys – maybe five or six altogether, along with a couple of zone-tailed hawks – hung in the sky over the river, and now one osprey bunched itself up and hurtled down, rising again with a flapping fish in its talons. It pumped hard to carry its catch upriver, to its nest obviously, where there would be a chick or two waiting – or so Allaby reasoned, knowing that young ospreys had hatched last month and would take all summer to fledge.

Knowing. There was so much he knew and so much he didn't – or rather so much he could only be beginning, like an infant, to experience. He dropped the blanket off his shoulders, and as he bent to pick it up, his back to the river, he felt for the first time ever the sensation of the sun shining directly on his whole body. Of course, in the Ranger station he'd felt it through glass – on most mornings on the glass porch, he'd spend a little time sunbathing, but he'd never had it straight, as it were, or mixed with a bit of wind and river spray. He tossed the blanket onto a grassy patch up the bank and then took off his underpants and tossed them on top of it. Turning around and spreading his arms (like an osprey, he imagined, even though one wing was broken), he felt the sun's full blast: it was as if he were being held in gigantic hands, all hot and wet. He turned again and again – sun on his side, sun on his back, sun on his front. Finally, facing the river and standing at the edge of the rock, he let himself fall forward.

The idea was just to have a bath. This was the idea, if vague, when he first left the campsite – a pee, a bath, a long drink of water. Then back to the campsite to see what was next, food maybe. So he wasn't doing anything he hadn't meant to do – he even fell more or less to his left, with his right hand raised so that the splint wouldn't get wet. He also knew the river was generally pretty shallow, especially near the bank. He was aware that the current was strong, too, but, hell, he'd once taken a graduate course in fluid dynamics, and he knew that standing up here would be no harder than, say, standing up in a strong wind. But what he hadn't taken into account was that the riverbed was pebbly, rocky, slatey and slick. And rather than just easing himself in, he'd made a bit of a dive. He'd also gone in off the end of a long, flat rock, and his point of entry was a little deeper than he'd bargained for. But, mainly, it was cold. Allaby had spent his whole life in controlled temperatures, and though he knew what a cold shower was like, or a sauna, or a swimming pool (not that he could swim), he'd never quite had the sensation of sun-heated skin getting suddenly immersed in water that felt as though it had no right to be in a liquid state. It was a shock, and with his head under, it was only conscious self-control that kept him from gasping. And he couldn't get his head up because he couldn't find his feet. He knew they were somewhere – they were feeling the shock, too – but wherever he thrust them they only met water or, he imagined at one split-second, air. The wrist with the splint was in the river with the rest of his body, but that, right now, was the least of his problems. The biggest was the current. It was damned fast, and until he could get a foothold he was at its mercy. It rolled him over and tumbled him over. His eyes were open, and he could see the sun flash past and suddenly turn into riverbottom, which he couldn't reach with hands or feet before the sun flashed past again. At one point he did get his feet down, and his head up (the water reached his chin) for as long as it took to catch one breath and glimpse what seemed to be an unreasonably distant bank, but then his feet simply slid away, and he was tumbling again.

Towards the Flaco Falls. It was near, but he didn't know how near. Near enough, though – and a good deal nearer than it had been half a minute ago, when he'd last stood on dry land. What he did know for sure was that the Flaco was something like four hundred and fifty metres high, the second highest waterfall in the whole sector, after Yosemite. This fact actually rolled through his head as he rolled through the water, offering itself, almost, as some kind of solution. But its only effect, of course, was to accelerate the panic. He thrashed, got a foothold, breathed, slipped again, tumbled, thrashed, got a foothold, slipped ... and then hit something. And held on.

It was a tree, or a big branch of a tree. Why it should be floating on its side and stationary out in a raging river wasn't something he dwelt on for the moment. It was enough that it was there and had come to his rescue. It had rough bark and little twigs that stabbed him under his arm and in his ribs, but that didn't matter either – once again he'd been on his way to die, and once again something had stopped him. There were branches, still with leaves, between him and the immediate bank, and so he couldn't see it, but he could see the bank farther upriver, and it wasn't as distant as it had seemed last time he been able to look. Everything was okay. All he had to do was make his way along the trunk and hope that it reached the shore or extended close enough for him to wade the rest of the way. He tried to climb out of the water and onto the trunk, but with his bad wrist he couldn't get the leverage. So he decided, as the river battered him, just to tunnel through the foliage. His legs and feet, which were hanging under the tree, were able to find submerged branches to push against, and at one point they found a rock, which answered the question of why the tree wasn't moving. This wasn't altogether easy. It involved a lot of thrashing around and getting scratched and being careful of his eyes, but he did finally find the end (it was broken off and jagged with, in the place of the tree's pith, a black fungus; the fungus had weakened it, Allaby figured without even realising he was figuring such a thing at such a moment, and a push by an elephant probably finished it off). The shore was about two metres away, and the water where he was standing now – a swirling eddy, shaded by an overhanging willow – was only knee-deep. After the brightness of the river and the sun and with water still in his eyes, he found it hard to see much, especially in the shadows right under the tree. But he did see one thing, and it saw him. Raising its head, its tongue still hanging out and dripping, was a big male lion, interrupted while having a drink.

The feeling Allaby had then was both entirely natural and, to him, entirely new. It wasn't the panic he'd felt in the river or the confused resignation of last night. It certainly wasn't any of the I'll-have-to-deal-with-this-quick reactions that accompanied the various scrapes and emergencies he'd ever encountered in the past. And it wasn't as though he hadn't been around lions before. He'd often imaged among them (they were very popular in the holoparks), but safely in his suit and with his gun on his thigh. Now, though, he was as transfixed as any small cornered animal. No gun now. No suit. No clothes at all. He was standing naked and bleeding and with no possibility of retreat, and he was staring a lion in the eyes. He even thought he knew this lion personally: it was probably one of the old males that younger males had recently ejected from the local pride – alone now and living out its life without any difficult hunting. It couldn't stand up to strong young lions and probably couldn't bring down a cow, but that didn't mean it couldn't, with a short leap, finish off a puny human, delivered like a gift from out of the river. And even though that leap was the last thing Allaby wanted to have happen, it almost seemed right that it should. Life on Earth survived by consuming other life on Earth, and Allaby, imported somehow from a satellite of Saturn, was now just another poor creature on Earth having its turn. There was a chill to the transfixion. It stemmed from the back of his neck and spread in one direction across his scalp and, in the other, deep into his bowels, which he was only just able to keep closed. Breathing was impossible. So was moving.

The lion blinked. To Allaby, now conditioned as an imminent prey item, that seemed odd. The lion, by now, ought to have been hunching its shoulders and tensing its hindquarters. Its head should have been lower down, and above all, its stare should have been constant, unremitting: that was how transfixion worked. Instead, the lion blinked again. Its hindquarters, far from being tense, seemed to have collapsed. And the next blink wasn't a blink at all – the eyes simply closed. Then the big head and the black shaggy mane lay gently on one paw. With a thump, the rest of the lion fell and sprawled out, as if asleep. Air surged into Allaby's lungs, and he took a very shaky step forward. Had it died or something? Had a heart attack? Another step brought him right up to the animal, and then he could see, imbedded in the haunch, two darts, next to each other.

Christ almighty, how embarrassing. It was worse, somehow, than if the lion had actually pounced. Where was the old man then? But Allaby didn't have to look far. He was standing in the shadows by the trunk of the tree, his pipe in his hand and something like disgust on his face. It was possible that Allaby misread that – he couldn't see his face that clearly – but if the man did have disgust on it he wouldn't have blamed him. Or maybe it was just puzzlement, wonder at how this stranger could get himself into such a ridiculous spot. Whatever, Allaby felt like a throwback. Had he actually thought of these people as primitive? The old man lived on this planet and lived well. He was wearing woven clothes and had a weapon in his hand – a chemical weapon powerful enough to stun a lion. Above all, he knew what he was doing. He could take care of himself and could take care of other people if he had to – including Allaby. But look at me, Allaby thought, glancing down at his scratched, dripping, naked body. I can't even go to the river for a bath without being nearly eaten by a lion as an alternative to taking a four-hundred-and-fifty-metre dive. I can't even speak the language. It's not that I'm an innocent infant with a lot of simple skills to learn. Well, it is, but it's more that I'm just a pitiful, helpless baby.

As if cued by Allaby's own assessment of himself, the old man laughed. It was a bit wheezy, the laugh, and Allaby realised that he must have had to run to get here. He must have seen Allaby get whipped away by the current, and then, gimpy leg and all, he must have run along the bank – or above the bank or wherever, watching Allaby being swept towards a snagged tree – and would have come upon one end of the lion just as Allaby was facing the other. Allaby also became aware of the dog, higher up the slope, sitting with his tongue hanging out. So the old man and the dog would have been running after him … In that case, where were the girl and the baby? Why weren't they here too, to pile on the humiliation? But they weren't, and the old man didn't laugh again. Instead, he stuck his pipe in a sort of pipe-holder at the top of his trousers, said something, came over to Allaby and, shaking his head and stepping past the recumbent lion, took his wrist – the broken one. Allaby's hand was blue. The water had swollen the sticks and the string wrapping, and now the splint was cutting off circulation. The old man took a knife out of a knife-holder and quickly and deftly severed the strings, letting the splint fall to the ground. Everything's starting over again, Allaby thought. Still shaking his head, the old man took Allaby by the other wrist and started to lead him up the slope. Allaby, his right hand dangling, trudged along, realising without caring very much that he was lacerating his feet. Never mind, he told himself. I'm just new here. Things are bound to hurt.

And he was, he supposed, at least still alive – still breathing, still the only non-immune human breathing Earth air and the only human from the Solar System stations who knew that the Abunga was gone. That was still, despite everything, some kind of distinction, some kind of responsibility. He'd survive because he had to, or maybe – considering the miraculous escapes he'd been having – was meant to.

Boy, the Titanian Lazarines would have liked that last thought. They believed absolutely in destiny, and destiny included the fact that humanity was going to return to Earth. As Allaby, the dog and the old man finally reached the spot where Allaby had tossed the blanket and his underpants, Allaby was still contemplating the Lazarines. The return to Earth wouldn't happen until the day of the Rapture, they said, when Jesus would appear to all the humans in all the stations and take them there all at once. In the meantime, Earth was where the souls of the dead went. Once there (or here, he reminded himself, almost with a smile) the souls remained invisible also until the Rapture, when they would suddenly materialise and be joined by the not-dead-yet people from the stations, and in time the Earth would again have as burgeoning a population as it had had before the Apocalypse – even worse than that, because all the people would also be immortal. Allaby, who had been raised a Lazarine, had once innocently asked in Sunday School if immortal people could have babies and was sent home that day for, however obliquely, alluding to sex. As he trudged on, wearing his underpants and shouldering the blanket and with his feet freely bleeding now, Allaby reflected on yet another silver lining to this whole holopark mess: the goddamned Titanian Lazarines, who had made his early and especially adolescent years an uninterrupted misery, would now have the central plank of their doctrine nullified. There was a mortal man on Earth, and everybody at the holoparks could see him.

Even back at the campsite, with plenty to distract him, he couldn't get the Lazarines out of his head. He was sitting on a stool while the girl tended his cuts, scratches and bites with what seemed to be a mixture of spit and spider web (never mind: he had no doubt now that these two were experts at whatever they tried to do), and the old man was getting another splint ready. As the girl administered to him (and the firelight last night hadn't created an illusion – she really was that pretty), her hair would fall across his shoulders or a leg, and some of his cuts and bites were in fairly intimate places. He was also having his stomach tortured by the smell of a roasting spitload of very small plucked birds – budgerigars probably. He was ravenous, but even the prospect of food wasn't enough to stop him thinking about the Lazarines.

That was strange, because he hadn't given them much thought in years, not since he'd left Titan, and he hadn't really thought about them while he was there – just believed everything they said when he was younger and believed anything else when he was older. Most of their dogma was the usual stuff: God, Jesus, Satan, Heaven, Hell (ie, Venus) and take one wrong step and you're damned. To prevent the domed and finite Titanian cities from having an unsupportable population boom (Allaby worked this motive out only later, and anyway, the draconian legal system, with its wide range of death penalties, did a lot more than the Lazarines to prevent that), the most wrong step was any step that might conceivably lead to unmarried sex. This was birth control of sorts and the main reason why the ruling Scientific Committee and the established church, the Keepers of Jerusalem, tolerated the Lazarines. The main split between the churches, though, wasn't about sex – on that they generally agreed. It was more finely theological. It was over specific words in the Lord's Prayer: "… on Earth as it is in Heaven." To the Keepers, those words proved that Heaven and Earth were different places, but to the Lazarines they proved that the two were definitely the same.

Then, of course, there were the Back-to-Earthers. They had a theology, too, but Allaby had no idea what it was, because they weren't so much a sect as a cult, a secret cult – secret because they were illegal and illegal because they believed that the virus was a lie propagated by the Solar System's various governments for their own nefarious purposes. That was all Allaby and most other people knew about them. The Back-to-Earthers were always trying to steal ships to fly to Earth and were always caught and, to prevent them going away and dying of Abunga, usually killed.

So the apparition of the old man in the holopark would probably discredit the Lazarines and, by default, strengthen the Keepers. As for the Back-to-Earthers, who must have believed that there had always been people here anyway, they would just stay as crazy as ever.

Part of the reason Allaby had been pondering these things was to keep his mind off the constant pricks and stings the girl was inflicting with her disinfectant or whatever it was. He'd been resting his gaze on her hair, her hands and her legs and feet, but now he glanced up at the trees and the sun, wondering what time it was. It was mid-morning, maybe ten-thirty or eleven here, on the day after that transmission had hit EHQS, the Moon, Mars and Titan. All those people in the Titanian cities had seen a man a with a beard walking around on Earth and breathing the air as if there were no such thing as the Abunga virus – which, in preposterous fact, there wasn't. Then Allaby had another thought, but one that needed to wait a while …

… mainly because of a shock that seemed to affect every bone in his body – everything with calcium in it, including fingernails, toenails and teeth. Last time the girl had given him a knife to bite, but this time she'd forgotten or something, and he could feel warmth in his mouth and a scorching pain in his tongue. The girl's face, green eyes wide, was suddenly very close to his own face, and she shouted at the old man. The old man, who was now the one kneeling in front of Allaby, spoke but didn't look up – he was too busy tying the splint. The girl disappeared for an instant and then was back with a cloth, dabbing it over Allaby's mouth and chin. She pulled his teeth apart, looked inside, touched his tongue and, wiping off her finger, said in a normal tone of voice words Allaby could actually understand: "It's not too bad." The pain from his wrist disappeared as quickly as it had come, but the tongue burned on.

It was still sore about half an hour later as he was trying to steer hot budgerigar-meat past it, but at least the bleeding had stopped, the whole tongue was intact, and the pain wasn't so bad that he couldn't watch and be puzzled by some other things that were going on. The girl and the old man were arguing again. He kept insisting he had to do something, and she was saying "no" a lot. And then, instead of eating his share of the meat, he was putting it into a small bag, which he tied to his waist, beside a water bag. As they argued, he would point at Allaby – "Look at him," he said a few times – or he would point beyond, in the direction of the river. Then, sometimes, he'd point at her. Her gestures were predominately arms spread out from the elbows, open palms and a slight crouch. Sometimes, she seemed furious, almost dangerously so. At one point, the old man sat on the stool and put his head in his hands, and then looked up and spoke in a low voice, as if trying to be reasonable, saying again, "I have to do it."

Eventually, she just shrugged. What was obvious was that the old man was going somewhere, that the girl had desperately tried to dissuade him, that she'd failed and that now she was resigned to it. When they spoke now the tones were amicable, even affectionate. He was ready to go and seemed

117

to be in a hurry, but before he went he came over to Allaby and gave him something of a physical. He looked at his lacerated feet and scratched legs, arms and torso, had a last glance at the splint and pulled Allaby's mouth open to examine his tongue. Then, with a sigh and a short shake of his head, he put his hand on Allaby's shoulder, looked into his eyes and gave him a few solemn admonitions. Allaby, of course, couldn't grasp the gist of them – the word 'trust' kept popping up – but they were delivered in the same tone of voice his father had used just before young Peter had boarded the ship to the Moon: "Study hard, stay away from drink and women and don't spend all the money in the first term." Now, having delivered his 'trust' speech, the old man turned to the girl and, for good measure, gave her a speech, too, his eyes flicking towards Allaby and then towards the knife, which was lying by the fireplace. Finally, he picked up his walking stick and shoulder bag – which was bulging, even though almost everything he might be expected to carry in it was somewhere around the campsite – and after hugging the girl one last time, he was off. The dog, which had been lying under a tree watching all this, sprang up and started to follow, but the old man looked back and shouted something, and the girl grabbed the dog by the scruff. The old man, walking in the direction of the river, didn't look back again.

Let's work this out, Allaby told himself. The old man's gone but not for long – he didn't take much with him, not even his knife. Wherever he's going and whatever he's going to do or get, it's important to him or he wouldn't have gone through such a row with the girl in order to do or get it. It's even important enough to leave her alone with me, a stranger from nowhere, and after he'd been so protective of her last night. So he'll be back soon but not that soon. My responsibility now, Allaby decided as he gazed again at the girl, who seemed to get prettier by the minute, has a hell of a lot to do with trust.

CHAPTER ELEVEN

"I can't tell you how strange it feels," said Always Standing Up, "to be talking to a dead man."

"I'm not dead," said Gibbous, "not really."

"Well, I know that, Gibbous. I can see that. But when I heard you'd had a funeral, I said to myself, 'Old Gibbous is dead. Too bad.' And in my heart you were dead. Now here I am talking to you. You did a Long Walk Out – is that it?"

"Yeah."

"It doesn't look like it was very long Long Walk Out. I don't think I was born the last time somebody from here did a Long Walk Out, but I never heard of a person coming back from one. My father used to say that walkers actually did die as soon as they got close to the mountains. Did you get to the mountains?"

"I barely made it to the Far Plain."

"What happened?"

"You know what happened."

Chief Always Standing Up, who'd long outlived his name, was sitting on a cushion on the other side of his little "thinking" room from Gibbous, who was also sitting on a cushion, his walking stick and satchel at his side. As the Chief looked down at his hands and watched himself clasp and unclasp his fingers, Gibbous realised that the Chief hadn't known whether he, Gibbous, knew about the atrocity at the Ledge and probably hoped he didn't. Still looking down, the Chief said, "It was terrible. How did you find out?"

"My granddaughter – rather, my grandson's wife … widow – found me."

"She should have let you walk on." He looked at Gibbous. His dark blue eyes said nothing. Gibbous remembered that this was the best pebbles player he'd ever met, a man whose face never gave anything away. He also remembered when Always Standing Up had come to take his older sister Raincloud to Big Rim, to marry her. She was laughing and crying with excitement. Everybody in the family was laughing and talking and celebrating her having landed such an up-and-coming warrior, and Always

119

Standing Up, who'd been courting her for about two years, was positioned at the doorway wearing his wedding costume but otherwise looking as stiff and still as a birch tree. "Is she the smart one with the baby?" he now said. "She should have been smart enough to let you walk on."

"She didn't know what to do. What would you have done in her place?"

"I'd have let you walk on. But why are you back here now? Why didn't you walk on anyway?"

"Chief, you're doing what you've always done as long as I've known you."

"What?"

"You always ask two questions at the same time, and it's hard to know which one to answer."

"The two questions are two ways of asking the same thing. Why are you here?"

Gibbous had to admit that, however it was phrased, it was a good question. On his way to Big Rim today, he'd had to keep reminding himself why he was doing this, and it was certainly the question Paintbrush had been asking this morning, though not as nearly as matter-of-factly as the Chief. But she'd also asked it in lots of different ways. One was, "Why in the world would anyone, especially you, want to do anything to save those nasty, evil, mean-spirited murderers?" Another was, "If I thought you were going to go help kill them, I'd say go ahead. But to try to save them ..." Still, he'd more or less convinced her in the end. At least he thought so – she might have just got tired. The Chief, though, was a different proposition. The reasoning would have to be right. He'd need to know everything that led to the decision. And there wasn't much time – Gibbous had noticed when he was sneaking past the settlement to the Chief's house that there were no young men around, and he'd just crossed the Near Plain without seeing any hunting parties. He wondered how many settlements had finally been persuaded to participate and what the assembled warriors were doing right now. Getting organised? Rehearsing tactics? Working themselves up? He hoped that was all.

"I'm here," Gibbous said, "because something occurred to me last night. Believe me, I would have walked on, and taken Paintbrush and Skyman with me, except ..."

"Skyman?"

"That's the baby's name."

"Funny name. Is he called that because he's got a big eyeball on his shoulders? Ah, but all you Ledgers have funny names. I used to tease Raincloud about that, but you know she's never changed to a Big Rim name, even though years ago the name committee invented a perfectly good one for her."

"What was that?"

"Always Busy. The committee thought it went well with Always Standing Up."

"Always Busy is better than Raincloud?"

"Well, the way we look at it, Gibbous, is that Raincloud doesn't mean anything, doesn't say anything about her. It's almost as bad as the Little Rimmers, with their Wilsons and Baldwins ..."

"... and Joneses," Gibbous said.

"Yes," said the Chief. "Their names don't mean anything at all, not even something you can see in the sky."

"That's what I've come to talk to you about, Chief – Jones the former holy man, and the rest of them. I've come to talk about the Little Rimmers."

"Well, you'd better talk fast, Gibbous, because pretty soon there won't be any point, because there won't be any Little Rimmers. "

"Why, Chief?"

"Why? Because we're going to wipe them out. The boys are. All the boys from everywhere. Except Salt. We didn't even ask Salt. We knew they'd be against it because they wouldn't want to lose another settlement of customers, and they might have tipped Little Rim off. Those Salt boys don't know how to fight anyway."

"I mean," said Gibbous, "why wipe them out?" There, he'd said it. But damn it, he'd said it too soon. He'd rehearsed all the way here and had intended to work up to it, to show the reasoning behind sparing Little Rim before actually saying what he thought should be done or, in this case, not done. You told stories that way, saving the main point for last. Now he might have blown it.

Always Standing Up cocked his head a little to one side and came very close to letting an expression creep onto his face. There was, indeed, a flash of puzzlement – a couple of the many little lines in the space between his eyes briefly deepening. Seconds passed before he spoke again. When he did, he said, "Gibbous, did that granddaughter or whatever of yours tell you exactly what happened?"

"I'm sure she did. She couldn't have made it sound any worse."

"They wiped out your settlement, the whole settlement. There's no more Ledge. Even the seven or eight survivors have come to us, because they're afraid the Little Rimmers will do it again. The Deep Gorgers have been talking about evacuating their settlement – they're below Little Rim, too – not straight below, but below – and they were thinking it could happen to them. So why are you saying why?"

"The Little Rimmers won't do anything to Deep Gorge. They won't do anything like that ever again to anybody. That is, they won't if you—"

"Well, you're right about that, Gibbous. They won't because they won't exist. You know, I think we should have some tea. I'll make some tea. I've become very good at that since Raincloud got sick. Be sure and look in on her while you're here. Or are you still playing dead?" He got up.

Raincloud had been sick off and on for years – sometimes she shook all the time and couldn't get off her pallet – and it would have been thoughtful and brotherly to drop in on her. But Gibbous said, "No, I don't want to be seen by anyone. By anyone but you. Which means you're going to have to be the one to do it. You're going to have to call off the attack, and then you're going to have to be in charge of making the Little Rimmers realise the awfulness of what they've done." That sounded lame even to Gibbous.

The Chief plopped down again. "What have I just heard you say? Maybe you really did die, Gibbous Moon, and have come back as somebody stupid. We're talking about the Little Rimmers. Remember them? Have you ever heard of anybody ever convincing a Little Rimmer of one thing? They're too damned smug to think anything but what they already think. It's one of the reasons everybody else in world hates them. Or everybody but the Salters, I guess."

"Not everybody."

"Well, I guess not you, either – though God knows why."

"I don't mean me. They killed my family, all my people. That was my funeral procession they burned. What I mean is not everybody else in the world."

"I'm losing you, Gibbous."

"What would you say if I told you I've met someone who's probably never even heard of Little Rim?"

"Well, in this very settlement there's a man named Dripping Spittle who's probably never heard of Little Rim. He's probably never even heard of Big Rim. He can't even talk – he just wanders around howling – but I don't take that to mean I should call off the attack."

That made a better point, Gibbous thought, than the Chief could have realised. This was getting nowhere. Not only that, he couldn't back up and start again, short of Paintbrush's version of the skyman reversing the sun a little. There was now really only one thing left to try. "Let me show you something." He reached over to his satchel, untied it and took out the skyman's big ball of a mask. Then he rolled it across the platform to the Chief. It came to a stop at the edge of the cushion, and without moving, the Chief stared at it. Gibbous had found the mask this morning, glistening in the bush where the skyman had thrown it last night. He hadn't looked for it – he'd forgotten about it, in fact – and he didn't know why he'd brought it with him or what good it would do his cause. But since all his rehearsed arguments had unravelled before he'd had a chance to use them, he thought he might as well see what the mask could make happen.

"What's this, Gibbous?"

"Guess."

"Don't make me guess." He picked it up and tapped it with his knuckles. "I've never seen anything like it."

"Are you sure? Think. Think where you might have seen one before."

"I've never seen anything like it. What is it?"

"It's a mask," Gibbous said.

"A mask of what? It doesn't look like an animal or a devil or anything."

"No, you're right, it doesn't. It's a mask that's not a mask. It's a mask of nothing. Put it on. You'll see."

"How?"

"Just put it over your head, with the blue part at the back."

"You're making me feel silly."

"Go ahead, Chief. Do it."

The Chief shrugged, lifted the mask and put it over his head. Widening his eyes a little, he stared out at Gibbous. "I can see you as clear as if there's nothing there." He tapped on the mask at eye level. "Even though there is something there."

"I think it's a kind of warm ice," said Gibbous.

"I can hear you all right, too. It's not like putting my head in a bucket or something."

"And I can hear you. If you feel, you'll find soft places by your mouth and ears."

Always Standing Up felt. "Oh yeah. But what's it for? What is it?"

"It's a skyman's mask," Gibbous said.

"Say that again."

"A skyman's mask. A mask that belongs to a skyman."

The Chief's hands suddenly shoved upwards, and the mask flew in an arc, hit the floor, bounced and rolled into a corner. There was a definite expression on the Chief's face now: it was horror. He glared at the mask, and then he stood up and glared at Gibbous. "What have you done to me?"

"Nothing. I just—"

"You made me—"

"I didn't make—"

"I recognise it now. It's not a skyman's mask. Skymen don't have masks. It's a head. It's a skyman's head. You must have cut his head off and scooped out the inside, scooped out the big eyeball. Then you made me—"

"No, no," Gibbous said, standing up too. "Calm down, Chief." He put his hand on the Chief's shoulder. "It's only a mask."

"It's a head."

"It's a mask. I swear. I wouldn't ask you to put on an empty head. Skymen are only people. It's just that they wear these masks. When they take the masks off, they're just people, the same as us."

"How do you know?"

"I know because that mask came off a skyman. And he's just a man. In fact, if you ask me, he's not that much of a man."

"I don't believe you. Where did you meet a skyman? Where could you … Oh. Oh no."

"Oh no what?" said Gibbous.

Always Standing Up was peering into his eyes. "You really are dead, aren't you?"

"What? No."

"You made it to the mountains, just as my father said."

"No, I only got to the—"

"You made it to the mountains. You died. You've been to the other world. You've mingled with skymen. And now you've come back to talk to me."

"Chief, no."

"Why are you lying about it?"

Gibbous sighed and sat back down on the cushion. He closed his eyes. He'd come here to impress the Chief with the reason – the reason – for not slaughtering the Little Rimmers. He was supposed to be making him think about the future of mankind in a world where it was permissible, maybe even normal, to eradicate whole groups of people, whole cultures, just because there was a good excuse – and really, in this case, because nobody liked the particular people or their culture very much. Instead, he'd brought the damned skyman into it. Why? What did he think would happen? He supposed he had meant to show the Chief that there were other people in the world, people who might not even have heard of the Little Rimmers. But how did that advance the argument? At one point, he'd even been tempted to bring the skyman himself, and he might have done it if he hadn't needed to hurry and if the idiot hadn't ripped his feet to shreds. At least, then, the Chief could have seen that the skyman was human, that humanity was bigger than the Seven Settlements, even if only by one man. But that would have pushed the argument the wrong way, because the Chief could have said that in that case it mattered even less what happened to Little Rim: in a world with more people, the Little Rimmers became more expendable. Gibbous couldn't think this through – he didn't have time, and the Chief was hovering, looming, over him. Mother Elephant had given him, Gibbous Moon, a mission, and he'd blown … Wait a minute, Gibbous thought. I don't even know if I believe in Mother Elephant, but what if she or something else – something inside me, inspiration even – made me pick up that mask?

The voice of the Chief, coming as if out of the sky, said, "I don't mean to interrupt a soul's meditations, Gibbous, but I think it's all right now to tell me the truth."

Of course, thought Gibbous, reason would be wasted on him. He's a living person, part of a group of people. Part of it, hell – he's head of it. He believes what his people believe, what he's been taught to believe and what he tells others to believe. Do I want to win an argument or get the job done? When did all this dedication to reason and the doubts about the stories come along anyway? Well, that's been growing in me all my life, Gibbous supposed, but it ripened when I got detached. When I died. I'm dead, and I've returned briefly to deliver a message to the living. The Chief is absolutely right.

CHAPTER TWELVE

At first, the atmosphere at the campsite was a little awkward. Well, right at first it was okay because they were both busy. Allaby's immediate priority, after he'd finished eating, was to see to his feet, and in casting around for something to wrap them in, he spotted the remains of his Earth suit. The suits were made to disintegrate chemically, boots and all, as soon as the collar was loosened, so that even if a Ranger was stupid or absentminded enough to try to walk into his station still wearing one, he wouldn't be able to. At any rate, the suits and helmets were always stripped away in the second airlock – after decontamination in the first – and put down a chute to a photovoltaic incinerator, and Allaby had never even looked closely at a suit in its pile-of-rags stage. But now, walking on tiptoe on one foot and on the heel of the other, he went over to the rags, sat down and, under the nose of a fascinated dog, started to sort through them, mainly reducing them to dust as he handled them.

The girl, meanwhile, was wandering around the edges of the campsite picking up firesticks. Every now and then she'd cock her head sideways, like a foraging bird checking for danger. Allaby wondered if this was a natural reflex, something to do with being a certain distance from her baby – who was watching her, in turn, from the hammock – or whether she was just nervous to be away from her settlement, away from the old man, with a stranger and out in the woods (and he did know this: somewhere in the neighbourhood right now there would be at least one very miserable, possibly very angry, old lion). When she had a good armload, she brought the sticks over and laid them down by the fire, taking a few off the top of the pile and dropping them into the flames. Allaby was absently holding a couple of shreds of the suit in his hand as he watched her do all this, admiring the graceful ways she had of moving, and not realising he was staring until she stared back.

That was when the awkwardness set in. He felt himself blush. And to catch himself doing such a coy, silly thing as blushing made him blush even more. (Even the dog seemed to sense the blush and made a low whine.) Was there no end to the embarrassments he was going to have to

126

suffer in front of these people? He looked down at the rags again and, still feeling the heat in his ears and cheeks, very busily sorted through them. She was only a young Immyo woman, for God's sake. But, God, her creamy skin and her shining green eyes and that hair, and her legs and hips when she was picking up the … Don't think about that, he told himself just as he came across a miracle – the sole of a boot. It was whole – intact – and here was the other one. Soles, it seemed, were the only part of the suit that didn't disintegrate. It was the next best thing to finding an abandoned pickup – these thick plastic slabs were going to be his transport to Pike's Peak.

"Look," he announced to the girl, holding them up. "I'll walk again." She seemed puzzled and little wary, but she came over, and Allaby, raising a foot, held a sole against it. She made a smile of comprehension, kneeled down, moved his hand and, pushing the sole away, examined the foot and then said something and held a finger up in a wait-a-minute gesture.

And while he was waiting, he had a chance to examine his feet himself. They didn't look as bad as they felt: about three small punctures, a few scratches and a little gash – none of them bleeding now, thanks, no doubt, to the spit-and-spiderweb treatment. (Her spit, he had to stop himself from thinking; it was getting ridiculous – he'd just been having his Earthly experiences as a helpless baby, and now he was a slavering teenager.) It also occurred to him that, as miraculous as the soles were – and if he could find a way of attaching them to his feet and if his feet didn't get infected before they healed – he'd still need something more than a blanket to wear if he was going to march off to Pike's Peak. Ah, but he'd manage, maybe with the help of the old man. They could kill a cow, maybe, and make a suit out of the hide. Allaby was an Earthman now, and he'd have to learn to live like one. This morning's scrapes were obviously an initiation, just something to toughen him up. The biggest obstacle at the moment – narrowly topping a list so long he couldn't see the bottom of it – was the language, but that was ridiculous, because he knew he was able to understand and speak it. After all, he'd done nearly two years of groundwork with the phonoscope. He had taught himself plenty of vocabulary, not to mention pronunciation, syntax and grammar. He could even distinguish what passed for slang. But he'd, of course, never actually conversed in it, and that fact was creating some kind of block – not unlike the shyness that had just made him blush. Right now what he needed was an intensive talking session with somebody, and right now the only somebody around was the girl (oh, the girl).

When she came back, it was with some more of what he presumed were medicaments, the giveaway being the little ball of spider web. But there was also what he recognised as the water bag, something that might have been moss, some leaves, some string, a cloth, the knife, some other things and a kind of fungus that, for all his studies in terrestrial ecology and his duties on Earth, he was sure he'd never seen or heard of. She hadn't been gone that long, which meant that all this stuff must have come from right around here, more or less at arm's reach. Fair enough, a lot of it had been carried here in the old man's shoulder bag, but a lot obviously hadn't. This was human resourcefulness at its purest: this woman (he was really going to have to quit thinking of her as the girl) – this descendant of a people once so intensively mechanised, chemicalised, energised and civilised that they practically eradicated the real Earth – now treated the real Earth as though it were her own kitchen, with cupboards and drawers and spice racks. She was perfectly at home and was on the way to making him at home, too.

What she finally, exactly did with everything was a little hard for Allaby to tell, partly because of her tendency to lean forward over his feet and obscure them with her hair – he was still sitting on the ground, legs outstretched now and his good arm braced behind him – and partly because the dog wanted to investigate every procedure and was getting in the way, but she'd lean aside and pat something, pull something, pour water on something or cut something, and then he'd feel a tickle or stroke on the soles of his feet, added to the tickle or the stroke of her hair on his ankles and shins. For God's sake, he thought – feeling a the beginning of a swell where he had no business feeling one and remembering that all he was wearing was a blanket and a pair of underpants – think about something else. Let's see: the Immyo verb endings. Very much the same as ours, apparently, except in the almost universal irregularity of the past participles … It took her a little while, but when she finally sat up on her haunches, pushed her hair back and smiled at him, Allaby was shod.

The girl (that is, the woman) gestured to him to stand up. After a glance to see if the review of verb endings had prevented what would have been the worst embarrassment yet – and it had, oh thank God – he started to stand but found that he couldn't. The right arm, obviously, was no help, and the left had been propping up his torso for so long that it seemed to have turned to wood. As he was squirming to his knees, the blanket having fallen off, he felt a lift under his armpits and was finally able, with a squat march forward, to gain his feet. As he stood, he was less impressed at first by his new cloth, ankle-high shoes than by the fact that she had lifted him up and was now standing beside him holding him around his waist. She looked down at his shoes and then looked up at him expectantly.

He could feel his feet all right – or hardly feel them. What had she done? He was standing perfectly flat-footed, and there wasn't any pain. He pushed down on one foot and then the other, and again, and it was as though nothing had ever happened to them. She'd obviously used his boot soles as a base, but what had she put on them? He took a step, and she stepped with him, her arm still around him. These were better than any cushioned shoes he'd ever had – spongier. As a kid, Allaby and the other kids used to play around the outfall of the Jerusalem hydroponics plant, where water mixed with accumulated dirt and debris and made what on Earth might be thought of as mud. They'd take their shoes off and walk through it, and the feeling now was a little like that, but without the ooze – just very soft. It must be the moss, he thought. More puzzling, though, was the fact that his feet had stopped hurting. How had she done that?

Then he thought, never mind – she did it. Somehow she did it. She lives on Earth, and she knows some kind of magic. He lifted a foot sideways and looked at the shoe. It was bound up with twine, almost in the style of the splint, which meant it would be hell to get off and worse to put on again. But right now he didn't care. He took a couple of more steps, and she stepped with him, holding his arm now. Then he stopped and pointed at a shoe. "Good, good," he said. "Name?"

"Name?"

"What name?"

And she told him the Immyo name for "shoe". He was on his way.
****

The sun had just set as Gibbous left the Chief's house, and he hadn't gone far when the moon rose – properly full tonight. He'd got away earlier than he'd expected – things happen fast when you don't have to argue – and though another all-nighter lay ahead, there was no reason for him not to stretch it a little more and take a last chance to stock up on dart poison. So he stuck close to the rim this time and headed for the frog pools by the waterfall. He'd always liked walking along the rim, especially at night. Aside from the occasional prickly pear or small, gnarled creosote tree –

usually looking like a crouching animal in the moonlight – it was mostly rocky, barc and flat with more bluish grey flatness off to the left (crazy with crickets tonight) and a black emptiness to the right. Well, mostly black – the Gorge's ragged far rim was moonlit and so were the three overbalanced rock formations that grew up from the depths. At one point, too, he spotted dots of firelight all the way at the bottom. That was Deep Gorge, where, presumably, the women, children and older men were sitting around worrying about an imminent fat attack from Little Rim.

The next time he saw firelight was a good deal later, as he was approaching the settlement of Waterfall. He could also see, against the sky, the distant outlines of those pointy rock buildings the Waterfallers lived in. He didn't get much closer, though, because this was also the beginning of the Poison Path, which led down into the Gorge for a short way and then along a ledge to the pools.

They were small rock basins sitting at various levels all the way down the side of the waterfall. The best and biggest were at either of the two places where the torrent hit a ledge and flattened out for a short distance before plunging on, and one of those was just below Waterfall the settlement and was in fact an extension of the Poison Path ledge. The pools, which at most were about fifteen paces from the thundering water, were weedy and still and constantly renewed by the settling mist. In the light of a full moon, the mist – which, this close to the waterfall, was everywhere in the air, was the air – turned into a uniform moon glow that was all but impossible to see through. In fact, the combination of the glow and the roar of the waterfall took away both eyes and ears as guides to anything. To Gibbous, the approach to the pools on a night like this always felt like stepping through the sky, like entering a world where there were no ups or downs or sideways. The trouble was, all those dimensions were, in fact, still there – most importantly the down one – and as he walked he had to keep one hand on the rocky side of the gorge and use the walking stick in the other hand to feel for the bushes and vines waiting to trip him over, for the ledge's edge in places where it narrowed and for the one point where it simply disappeared and a gap had to be stepped across. Altogether, it was chilly, wet, slick and very slow going.

But that step across the gap was one of the last few steps before the edge of the first frog pool, and pretty soon Gibbous's stick told him he'd reached that. Then he crouched down, laid the stick on the ground and unshouldered his satchel. The easiest time to catch frogs was during the mating season, when they were all in the pools and preoccupied and could just be scooped up, but the mating season was over now by a couple of months, and most of the big frogs would be roaming around elsewhere looking for food. There would be lots of little frogs in the pool, though, and weight for weight they had the strongest poison. But little frogs were quick and slippery, stayed close to the bottom and were pretty much immune to simple scooping. There was a way, though.

First Gibbous scraped his fingers around on the rocks that lined the pool until he scratched up a decent-sized handful of moss. He squeezed as much moisture out of that as he could and put it inside his shirt, against his chest. He took his pipe out of his belt, put his open and empty food pouch beside him and lay prone with his face just above the surface of the pool. This close up, he could see the water clearly enough – black with sparkles of yellow from the luminescent mist. He could also see the dark mass of plants – the kind, mainly, that didn't have roots and just floated around and generally clogged the water. Putting his pipe in his mouth and his face so close the pool that his beard floated with the vegetation and his lips actually touched the surface, he very softly blew – so softly that it couldn't really be called blowing, softer even than an ordinary exhalation. He made one little bubble and then another and another. At about the sixth or seventh bubble, he could feel that the pipe was blocked. So he sucked hard, put his finger over his end of the pipe, pulled the pipe out, grabbed the thumb-sized froglet dangling at the other end, dropped it in the food pouch and folded the pouch shut. Then he lay forward again and made more bubbles.

He decided he'd done enough when the bag held about twenty-five froglets. So he sat up cross-legged and reached inside his shirt for the lump of moss. His shirt, of course, was soaked but was moderately drier on the inside than the outside, and the moss was pretty dry, too – probably the driest lump of anything for about fifty paces from the falls. It was also pretty warm (a little warmth, somehow, made the frogs respond quicker). He now reached for the food bag and, one by one, took the frogs out, squeezed their backs hard against the moss and plopped them back them in the pool. He then put the moss in the food bag, tied it doubly tight and hung it on its string at the top of his trousers.

It was when he was well out of the mist and almost at the top of the Poison Path that he began to wonder, for the first time he could remember, why it was possible to catch froglets with bubbles. All his life, it had just been a trick he knew. That was the way you caught froglets, and that was all there was to it. But he didn't think you could catch big frogs that way – not that you'd ever need to – and it certainly didn't work with fish, even little ones. Why just froglets? What did they think the bubbles were – food? Little drops of air wouldn't have been like any other food they had down there. Maybe, waterfall or no waterfall, the bottom of the pool was silent – it was always quieter under water than above it – and maybe the bubbles made an interesting sound. Maybe the froglets were trying to breathe, or learning to breathe. Or maybe there was no reason at all – just something in froglets that made them go for bubbles.

It bothered him, and he cogitated on it all the way past Waterfall and much of the way along the river as he headed for the crossing. He was still thinking about it when he sat at a little eddy to drink, rest and soak his feet. And then he started thinking about something else: about the Chief and how much easier everything had been after the Chief had begun to believe that his old brother-in-law was back from the dead. Gibbous had simply told him that, over in the other world, the gods and the skymen and all the rest (he couldn't remember every Big Rim deity, but he knew that Mother Elephant was only a minor one and that skymen were more important to Big Rimmers than they were to Ledgers) were alarmed at the prospect of Little Rim being wiped out, that they didn't like the whole idea of wiping people out and that they had their own ways of punishing Little Rim. What they needed the Chief and his alliance to do (and Gibbous had had to think fast here, because he'd expected to discuss philosophy, policy and strategy with the Chief and so had arrived without a specific plan) was to surround the settlement, effectively capturing the Little Rimmers, and to take them in small groups to the Ledge to see the carnage and eventually to bury the bodies. This, Gibbous hoped, would make the Little Rimmers, not to mention the escorting warriors, good and sick.

What the Chief did further to that, Gibbous had said, was up to him. Over in the other world they didn't like getting too detailed in their dealings with mortals, and so he could try anything he thought might work, provided there was no unnecessary killing. A little killing probably couldn't be avoided – but no wiping out. Exactly how the Chief was going to sell this general idea to a convocation of warriors interrupted while working up their bloodlust might be a problem for the Chief, but he was the Chief, and everybody, even from the other settlements, usually did what he told them to do. And he had the skyman's mask now, which would be bound to help.

Gibbous had done more or less everything he'd set out to do – even getting the Chief to donate some clothes for the skyman (a sacred offering, Gibbous had told him) – but he still, somehow, felt defeated. He'd got what he wanted by nothing more than trickery, by lies. Of course, to be tricked and lied to was exactly what Always Standing Up deserved, since he wouldn't listen to Gibbous's reasoning, but what was it – not just about the Chief, but about everybody he'd spent his life telling stories to – that made people love lies so much? "Ha," Gibbous said aloud, pulling his feet out of the water, "I'll understand that when I understand why froglets like bubbles."

As he walked on, he soon gave up thinking about either question. What arose instead was something he'd deliberately blanked out of his mind when he'd first left the campsite: would Paintbrush and the baby be all right with the skyman? He'd convinced himself they would or, peacemaking mission or not, he wouldn't have gone. And while he was gone there'd been no point in worrying about it. But what if he'd been wrong? What if he got back to find … what? What did he actually know about the skyman or skymen in general? On the other hand, no – Paintbrush was, if anything, tough. Add maternal instinct to that. Forget it, Gibbous told himself. He'd be back at the campsite soon, and he'd find out. Anyway, he was slightly shocked to realise that, of everybody there, the one he'd be happiest to see right now was Yellow.

CHAPTER THIRTEEN

Now, when she most needed to know, no one could tell her anything. The last person to speak to her was Gus Templeton's secretary, who said Gus had been arrested by the EHQS police. That was in the early hours of the morning. First Gus had been saying, yes, that the National Park Service cruiser had spotted Peter and was gaining on him and would catch him all right. Then she asked what they were going to do with him, and Gus had got out the words, "They'll bring him …" when he looked in direction of his office door, which was out of range of the comms image, and the image went off. Jenny was left staring at the swirling test gram for several minutes, and then the comms came on again, only with the secretary – her name was Mrs Parker, if Jenny remembered – standing behind Gus's desk. She was leaning forward with one hand on the comms controls, and the other she held in the distress position on top of her head. She'd been looking down, and now she looked up, eyes wide.

"What happened?" Jenny asked. "Where's Gus?"

"Oh it's you, Ranger Romero," Mrs Parker said. "It's … I don't know. The police. The police came. The police took him."

"Took him where?"

"I don't know. Wherever police take people."

"But Mrs Parker, why?"

"I don't know. They didn't say."

"They have to say. It's the law."

"They just said clause something and a number."

"Listen," Jenny said. "Try to remember. Did Gus say whether the Park Service cruiser had caught up with Peter … with Ranger Allaby?"

"He didn't say. He didn't have time to say anything. They just came in and … What am I supposed to do?"

Then before Jenny could answer (not that she had any idea what the woman actually was supposed to do), Mrs Parker herself vanished.

Jenny stared at the test gram for a while before it occurred to her to try raising Ben Haymark in Africa South and then her nearest neighbour Silvia Francisco in Arabia, but the gram wouldn't let her through. And neither the

134

emergency radios nor the helmet sets were producing anything but an ear-splitting static. Her concern for Peter and Gus had finally been joined by concern for herself and even a little concern for poor Mrs Parker, which altogether was too much concern. She spent until daybreak and beyond in a kind of aimless desperation that had her picking things up and putting them down somewhere else and wandering from room to room for no reason. She had a feeling that she needed to get dressed (all the time she'd been talking to Gus and then Mrs Parker she'd still been wearing the short blue nightgown she'd put on for Peter), but for all her wandering she couldn't seem to steer herself towards her bedroom and her closet – possibly because the sight of her bed might have been too tempting. It had been an exhausting night and morning. She could have just fallen on the bed and slept, woken up later and seen if anything had improved. On the other hand, she'd known she couldn't – shouldn't – sleep. Something was going to happen. It had to.

Then, at about noon, it did. She was wandering around and thinking very little beyond where's Peter, where's Gus, why am I cut off and what can I do, when the voice came: "Ranger Romero," the wall speakers said, "please report to your comms unit." Waiting in the comms room were two men she'd never seen before, sitting behind a shuttle control console and telling her to comb her hair and put on her uniform. Trying not to show how very relieved she was to see them, she asked them if they knew anything about Peter or Gus, but they only said they'd be docking at her airlocks in fifteen minutes, that she was needed at a meeting at EHQS. She wasn't to worry – all her questions would be answered then.

And at a meeting at EHQS was where she was an hour later – with four more people she'd never seen before. Jenny had been attending semi-annual Confabs at EHQS for nearly six years now, and between that and her regular work contacts, she thought she knew, at least by sight, just about everyone who worked there. So it surprised her that in an hour she could meet a total of six strangers. In fact, more than that: even granted that it was still fairly early in the morning – EHQS operated on Greenwich Mean Time – and that any people she passed in the corridors would have been night-shifters, she'd still have expected to see one or two recognisable faces. But out of a dozen people she'd passed there wasn't a single one. And she was in a part of the satellite she didn't remember having been to before – hadn't really realised existed. While still adjusting her pace to EHQS's Lunar gravity, she'd been taken to the left out of the shuttle dock and through a door that she'd always assumed had something to do with maintenance. And it looked like a maintenance block. There were a lot of corridors – all uncharacteristically stark for the satellite. No holowindows anywhere. No signs or names on doors. And the room she was in now was just foursquare with bare, greenish walls, an assortment of spare parts and a conference table with exactly enough chairs for her and the four people she'd been brought to meet.

Four people who still weren't telling her anything. In fact, for a few minutes, they didn't talk to her at all. She'd been the first in the room, had sat where the shuttle men had sat her and, after they'd gone, had been alone and left to look around at absolutely nothing that was interesting. In fact, the room was so dull and Jenny was so tired that she'd shut her eyes and almost nodded off before the people came in. And when they did file in, murmuring to each other in their ugly Lunar twang, they looked pretty dull, too. One or another would glance at Jenny from time to time as they all arranged their meeting paraphernalia in front of themselves. There were no introductions, no real acknowledgement, other than the glances, that Jenny was even there.

Finally, when all the meeting things seemed to have found their places, Jenny realised that the people had stopped just glancing at her and were staring. They were three men and a woman, something she only now seemed to notice, maybe because they were all so … so what? So alike, so strange and, at the same time, so unremarkable – all neat and pressed and in their forties, but with these deep, earnest, almost unblinking eyes, as though they'd all been taking the same narcotic, and not a very fun one. Another quirk was that, even though they were all in ordinary office clothes, every one of them was wearing something – a tie, a handkerchief, a pin – that was the same odd reddish orange.

After a short silence, the man directly across from Jenny (distinguishable from the others mainly because his hair was longer than theirs and had a little grey in it) tapped his chin and said, "Ranger First Class Jennifer Romero?" His voice, Mooner twang or no Mooner twang, was gentle. On the other hand, no: it was bland.

"I only want to know," said Jenny, "what's happened to Peter Allaby. And to Gus Temp—"

"You are Ranger First Class Jennifer Romero?"

"Yes I am, of course. Would you please tell me—"

"I have to ask, for the record."

"What record?"

"All interviews are on the record," the woman offered, nodding.

"Is that what this is? An interview?" Jenny said to the woman. "I thought it was a meeting. I assumed you were going to tell me …" She looked back at the greying man. "Who are you anyway? You haven't told me. Are you police?" If they were, they'd failed to identify themselves, something else that was illegal. But they didn't really seem like police. They seemed, at the same time, both less and more threatening.

The greying man didn't answer that. Instead he asked, "Is your sector Africa East?"

"Yes. Yes, it is. Really, do you mind if I ask who you are and why you brought me here?"

"How long," asked another man, the one on the left, "have you been the Ranger there?"

"Oh, for God's sake."

Throats cleared around the table.

"Please," said the man on the left.

"Please?" said Jenny. "Please what?"

"Please cooperate. We're trying to help."

"Well then help. Tell me—"

"You have to understand," said the man on the left, "that we can only help if you cooperate."

"What do you mean 'cooperate'? Tell you things you already know, or could find out by pressing a button?"

"It's just for the record," the woman said.

"I've been there five and a half years. Okay?"

"Thank you," said the man on the left. "And where were you before that?"

"Oh come on. Don't you know there's an emergency—"

"Where?" His voice was losing some of its blandness.

"I was studying at the University of Armstrong. Law first and then terrestrial ecology. Five years. PhD. Where is Peter Allaby?"

"You're Martian, aren't you?" said the man on the left.

"Yes. I come from Tharsis City, which you may have heard of. It's a pretty place, well known for its floral displays. Now who are you people, why am I here and where is Peter Allaby?"

Jenny's first reflex, whenever she felt she was being mistreated, was to go on the offensive. But somehow, with this group, it wasn't working.

They seemed more perplexed than offended – they behaved as though they'd never had anyone speak to them with anything less than – what? Respect? Deference? Reverence even? They seemed to expect that Jenny should know who they were without having to ask. But she didn't know, and so to hell with them. Whoever they were, she was Jenny Romero. She was also an Earth Ranger, which by itself made her one in a thousand – the number of people who'd applied to train for her job. She walked the Earth and sent images of Africa into outer space. What did these people do? If anybody here deserved respect, it was her, damn it.

The man on the left said to the woman, "Is the record satisfied on Ranger Romero's identification?"

"Yes. Thank you, Arthur … Oh."

The woman blushed, Arthur made a quick little frown, and Jenny realised that, for some reason, they weren't supposed to use each other's names. But would that be just not in front of Jenny, or did they never do it? She wouldn't have been surprised if they called each other by numbers.

To Jenny, Arthur said, "That's done then. Now we have some questions for you."

"What do you want to know now? My DNA reading?" Stop it, Jenny told herself.

"You and Ranger Allaby were good friends. Is that correct?"

"Were?"

"Is that correct?"

"What do you mean 'were'?"

"All right, are."

"No, you said 'were'."

"Please answer the question."

"Yes, Peter and I are good friends. If it turns out he's dead, we were."

"Does he regularly confide in you."

"Yes he does, or did. Couldn't anybody catch him? Don't write him off. You know, he's still got enough air to last most of today. It's still possi—. But you said 'were' now, didn't you? That means he's already dead. Did somebody kill him? Did you? Any of you?"

"We don't kill people," said the greying man.

"I'll bet," said Jenny. "Anyway, if I don't know who you are, how do I know you don't kill people?"

The greying man said, "Because I'm telling you we don't."

"I should take it on faith, then?"

"Some things can be taken on faith."

"Like what?"

"Like whatever I say, for a start."

Jenny suppressed a gasp.

Arthur said, "Can we return to the interview?" It had suddenly become clear that Arthur wasn't the one in charge here. He was only the main question-asker, and the man on the right seemed to be mainly a note-taker, maybe a backup for the woman. No, the chief bastard was the greying man.

The woman said, leaning forward and looking even more earnest than before, "Why does Ranger Allaby confide in you?"

"Why shouldn't he?" Jenny said.

"Is it because you're lovers?"

"That helps." Typical, Jenny thought – leave it to the woman to ask the sex questions.

"It must be very hard," the woman said, "to be lovers when you have to spend almost all your time in isolation."

"Well, we meet at the Confab twice a year, and we visit on the comms most nights. It's not a bad way to have a relationship, in fact."

"And is that when he confides in you? When you visit on the comms?"

"Yes. How else? Except at the Confabs."

Arthur said, "You never, for instance, meet?"

"Meet? How? Our only transport is our pickups. I don't know if you've noticed, but between Pike's Peak and the Ngorongoro Crater there's the best part of a planet."

"Pickups aren't that slow," Arthur said. "You could meet halfway and then get back to your stations in time for bed. Nobody would ever be the wiser."

It was hard to know where to begin with these people. "That's the most absurd thing I've ever heard," Jenny said. "Aside from the fact that we'd be breaking half the clauses in our contracts, not to mention neglecting our day's work, and aside from the other fact that we'd be rendezvousing in the middle of the Atlantic while wearing a couple of clunky Earth suits, why in hell would we want to meet? To pass confidences? As for nobody being the wiser, we've got tracker chips in our helmets."

"I didn't know that," said the greying man.

"You didn't?"

"No, we haven't really had time to study the details of the working conditions of Rangers. I have the general impression, though, that the rules are too lenient. For instance, I was surprised to discover that you can't be watched while you're in your stations. And that there aren't any transcripts of your comms conversations."

"The union fought hard for … Wait a minute. What do you mean you don't know about Rangers? Who are you? I thought you were going to have some information about Peter, but you don't seem to know anything about anything. Where's my controller, by the way? Where's Gus Templeton? Was it you who arrested him? I'm not answering another question until you either tell me who you are or you bring Gus here."

"At the moment," said the greying man, "it wouldn't be possible to contact your controller. So forget that. And who we are is none of your business. But I will say this – our job is to decide how to respond to your lover's little indiscretion, the man that he's broadcasting all over the Solar System. He looks like some horrible aboriginal to me, but other people have other ideas. Now, what I want to know – what we want to know – is what you know about Ranger Allaby and that man."

"I don't know anything, and I wouldn't tell you if I did."

"Is that man the only one, or are there others? One of your people has said there are. Are there?"

"Who are my people?"

"You know who your people are."

"I don't know if I do. Anyway, I'm not answering."

To the woman, the greying man said, "You've got a fixer on that thing, haven't you?"

The woman nodded.

"Okay. Every time she refuses to answer, have her say 'yes'."

"What?" Jenny said.

"Now," said the greying man, "this man …" He indicated Arthur. "… is going to ask you some questions. Your answers will be truly recorded. But any question you don't answer will be answered for you. I probably don't need to emphasise that this record will be very important – vital – when it comes to be used." He looked hard at Jenny and then glanced at Arthur. "Okay?"

Arthur looked down at his notebook and pressed a couple of buttons. What was important about these people, Jenny realised, wasn't so much who they were as what they were. What was their status, their power? They were either entirely outside the law or, somehow, were the law. But what law and whose law – whose authority? And as for the default "yes", why through the ages had people been tortured by people like this, if getting the "right" answers could be so simple? She didn't see any choice – she had to respond to their questions, and she wasn't even sure if she could use "I don't know" as an honest answer. She was ashamed to notice that her hands were trembling. So were her jaw and her lips.

Arthur said, "Has Ranger Allaby ever confided in you about this man or anybody like him?"

"Only once. Last night."

"What did he say about him or them?"

"Nothing really. He was drunk."

"What did he say?" said the man on the right.

"He said he'd been trying to learn their language."

"So he was mixing with him or them," Arthur said.

"No," said Jenny. "It's them, by the way, plenty of them. I don't know how you don't know that. But no, he didn't need to mix. He said he used a phonoscope. I'm sure they've never seen him. You might not realise, but Peter is one of the best, most responsible Rangers on—"

"Drunk was he?" said the greying man.

"He'd just found out what he'd done and what the penalties for it were."

"Do other rangers drink?" said Arthur. "Do you?"

"At our stations we're rationed to one bottle of spirits a month. And five bottles of wine."

"And you drink all that?" said Arthur.

"It's not so much. It comes to a drink before dinner, a glass of wine with it and maybe a nightcap. It's civilised. Rangering is a great job, but it's lonely and a long way from anywhere. Little touches of civilisation help."

"It never occurred to me," said the greying man, "that drinking alcohol had anything to do with civilisation."

If she hadn't been bone tired, frightened and completely bewildered by these people, Jenny might have developed the argument that, on the contrary, drinking and civilisation were intimately connected. All the most malign dictators and repressive religions were usually teetotal. A friend of hers at university had once written a dissertation on the subject. But now, no. It was bad enough that she had to answer all their questions, without starting an academic lecture. What she did say, glancing down at her quivering hands, was, "I've been up all night, and I'm very tired and, as you can see, getting pretty nervous. I appreciate that you have some questions you want to ask, but I don't see how those questions are getting us any closer to helping Peter. If he hasn't been caught, he's out there somewhere. He's out there somewhere with less than a day's—"

"To tell the truth," said the greying man, "we couldn't care less about that."

And Arthur said, "Do you have any aborigines in your sector?"

"What do you mean you couldn't care less?" Jenny said. "I thought … The shuttle men said—"

"Register that as a 'yes'," the greying man said to the woman.

"The answer is 'yes'." Jenny said. "Yes. There are some in my sector. Their reservation is in the Serengeti. Why don't you care about—"

"Have you ever sent images from their, uh, reservation?"

"No."

The greying man said, "I visited the Serengeti in a holopark once. Wasn't that from you?"

"The Serengeti is a very big place, and the reservation is a very small part of it. It was wrong – illegal, even – of Peter to do what he did, but he doesn't deserve to die for it."

"If you knew what he actually did do," said the greying man, "you might think he did deserve to die."

"What?"

"Have you ever gone into your reservation at all," Arthur said.

"What did he actually do?" said Jenny.

"That's a 'yes'," said the greying man.

"No, that's a 'no'," said Jenny. "I've never gone onto the reservation. I've never even seen those people."

"Aren't you curious about them?"

"Of course. But we're ordered not to go near them. Not to risk being seen by them."

"Why?"

"I don't know. Tell me what you think Peter actually did."

"I'll tell you what I feel like telling you," the greying man said. "Now you tell me – do you care about those people?"

"To a certain extent, yes. They are people, after all."

"Well, I guess if you want to stretch a point—"

"Of course they're people. What's more, they're people living where people are supposed to live, not out on a bunch of grim rocks in the sky. We're the freaks, you know. How anybody who lives in some dump of a Moon city could judge—"

142

"Do you care about them enough to care if they disappeared?"

Before Jenny could answer, the woman said, "How do you know we live on the Moon?" The three men in unison gave her sharp, quick looks.

"With accents like yours? Where else? Either that or here on the satellite. If you ever moved to Mars, they'd make you take elocution lessons."

The woman flushed. "No need to be rude," she said.

"I'm only being rude back," Jenny said. "It's rude to ask someone a bunch of personal questions without at least introducing yourselves. It's rude to tell a woman that what happens to her lover doesn't matter. It's rude to say that people who obviously are people aren't people and could be made to disappear. It's rude in a way only Moon people can be rude."

Arthur said, "Can we get back to the ques—"

"Oh, you snooty Martians," the woman said. "You think just because you don't live under domes and can walk around in the open air – not that you can breathe it – that you're the great cultured race. You make fun of our accents and our heritage, our architecture, everything we do. But let me tell you something, young woman, you Martians aren't the only ones, not any more. How about walking around outside and breathing? How about—"

"Get out." It was the greying man. He was standing up and leaning across the table on stiff arms and closed fists.

The woman, her eyes wide with fury, put her hand over her mouth. Then her eyes, still wide, welled with tears.

"Get the hell out."

"I'm sorry, Simon. She just—"

"Don't say another word. Get out of here. Wait outside. Wait in the corridor. You," he said to the man on the right, "you keep keeping the record."

The woman tried to gather up some of her stuff, but a few pieces of it fell on the floor. So she abandoned it all and half-ran to the door, slamming it as she disappeared.

Sitting down again, Simon (too bad, Jenny thought, that the woman left before naming the third man) said to Arthur, "I told you."

"Sorry," Arthur said. "There just wasn't time to get another—"

"I know," Simon said, sighing. "Never mind. As for you," he said to Jenny, "you had no right to talk to her that way."

"I was talking to all of you," Jenny said. What had just happened hadn't quite sunk in. What had the woman said to get her thrown out? Or was it just because she'd broken the blandness by losing her temper? No, the

143

blandness had already been broken by Simon. But she'd said something about walking around outside and breathing. Where could you do that? Had the Moon got an atmosphere suddenly? Jenny said, "What did she mean about—"

"Never mind what she meant," Simon said. "We've got to get these questions answered." He nodded at Arthur. "Go on."

Arthur looked a little irritated. His eyes darted from Simon to the third man to Jenny before he pressed a button on his notebook and said, "Last night you knew, didn't you, that Ranger Allaby would be heading for those people?"

"No," said Jenny, "I didn't know."

"Oh yes you did," said Simon. "That's how they found him. We've got the transcripts. But in the transcripts you called those aborigines a funny name."

"You mean Immyos?"

"Yes. Why did you …" Then to the third man, he said, "Do you know how to work the fixer on that thing?"

"So they did find him?" Jenny said. "Did they catch him?"

"I'm not sure," the third man was saying. "Is it the blue button? What does it do exactly – retrack the record and pick out—"

"Hell, give it to me," said Simon. The third man pushed the record-taker across the table, and Simon picked it up and punched a couple of buttons.

"Did they catch him?" Jenny said.

"No, it's not that one either," Simon said. "Damn. Now the goddamned thing's stopped altogether."

Arthur said, "Do you want me to bring Martha back in?"

"No."

"Did they or didn't they catch him? Tell me."

"Oh no," said Simon. "Did you press the blue button?"

"Yeah," said the other man, "Didn't you tell me to?"

"I certainly didn't. You know what you goddamned did? You erased the whole goddamned record."

"Please tell me," Jenny screamed.

There was silence for moment. Simon, his forehead in his hand, stared at the little machine, while the third man sat with his arms crossed and an it's-not-my-fault expression on his face. Finally, Arthur said, "What happens now? Do we start over?"

144

"Not with me you don't," Jenny said. "You got me here under false pretences, but you've blown those now. You're obviously not going to tell me anything about Peter, and so I'm going." She stood up. She didn't know quite where she'd go. You couldn't just book a shuttle – you needed authorisation. But there were hotels on EHQS. Maybe she could get a room and then work things out from there.

"You sit down," Simon said.

"Screw you," Jenny said and started for the door.

"Remember those men who brought you here? They're right outside, and they're armed."

Jenny opened the door, and sure enough, there was one of them turning his head to give her a surprised look. The other one, she presumed, was on the other side of the door. So she shut the door again and leaned against it. "Okay, Simon, but what are you going to do? None of you can work that stupid thing, and even if you swallowed your pride and called Martha back, you'd be afraid she'd blab some more. Come on, Simon – where do you walk around outside and breathe?"

"That remark didn't miss you, did it?"

All of them were staring at her, even Arthur, who'd been sitting with his back to the door and was now twisted around in his chair. "It sure didn't," Jenny said.

"You know," said Simon, "I think there's only one way of handling this."

"How? Kill me?"

"Nah. We didn't bring you all this way to kill you. You'll join us. We've got a project, you see, and you can help."

"Are you kidding? I don't want to help you."

"It doesn't matter what you want. You'll help. Anyway, there's no point in going back to your station. As of this morning, thanks to your lover – who's dead, by the way – all Rangers are redundant. And yes, he's dead. He's been particled. The National Park Service did it. So you can be glad there's no such thing as the National Park Service any more. He's as dead and gone as a person can be. So you might as well come with us."

"No National ... He's been particled? Come with you where?"

"I might as well say it myself – where you can walk around outside and breathe."

CHAPTER FOURTEEN

After visiting the Chief, after going to the poison pool, after the hike back to the campsite, after darting an early-rising turkey just at the crack of dawn, Gibbous arrived to find Paintbrush and the skyman deep in conversation. The sun was just up, the fire was high – as though they'd been sitting up all night stoking it – the baby was asleep in the hammock, Yellow was asleep under it, and Paintbrush and the skyman, the blanket still around his shoulders, were sitting by the fire on the two stools, both leaning forward so far that their heads almost touched. They were murmuring to each other. They looked tired, and neither of them seemed to notice that Gibbous was there. So, noisily dropping his satchel, turkey and stick, he said, "I'm back."

They both straightened up slowly and looked at him from the other side of the fire. Paintbrush said, "Granddad, the most wonderful thing …" and the skyman said in a strangely orotund voice, "Welcome, Gibbous Moon. Was your mission a success?" Then the two of them turned and giggled at each other.

There was an old Ledge expression: "I could have choked on the smell of flowers." Gibbous had never liked the expression very much – mainly because he'd never quite seen the logic of it and also because people used it over and over, to cover almost anything that wasn't precisely expected – but he understood it all right now. The jabberer had spoken. Gibbous had been gone for a day, or almost a day, and in that time …

"Paintbrush," the skyman said, standing up, "has been teaching me your way to speak."

"Of speaking," Paintbrush said.

"Your way of speaking," the skyman said. "Of course – of speaking. The prepositional gerund, not the infinitive."

Well, Gibbous thought, he hasn't entirely stopped jabbering. But never mind. In a day. In a day, Paintbrush has …

"My name is Peter. Peter Allaby. And I thank you for rescuing me from the lion."

146

Several thoughts hit Gibbous. One was that skymen had names like the Little Rimmers' names, totally meaningless and hard to say or remember. Another was that Paintbrush had him talking like Two Tornadoes working up to the climax of an epic. And another was still the marvel that he was talking at all. Gibbous also realised that he himself hadn't said anything since announcing he was back – that, in fact, he couldn't think of anything to say that would cover his astonishment. He was exhausted, too. He wanted to take the discovery of the suddenly articulate skyman and go to sleep with it, getting it ready to deal with when he woke up. There were too many questions that needed to be asked, and he needed to work out where to start.

"Granddad," Paintbrush said, "you know what? Skymen really do come from the sky. Allaby – he likes to be called Allaby ..."

Allaby, Allaby, Gibbous tried to register.

"... was born way up in the sky – way far away."

"Really?" Gibbous finally said.

"I told him that we already knew that, that you'd told us that."

"Yeah, but ..."

"Yes," said the skyman. "I am very interested in knowing how you knew."

God, Gibbous thought, he's asking me a question. "It just ... I don't know. It's in the stories. I just ... Paintbrush ... What's his name again?"

"Allaby," they both said at the same time.

"Allaby and Paintbrush, I'm very, very tired. And I guess you are, too. Have you been at this all night? All day and all night?"

They both nodded. Whatever experience they'd had appeared to have turned them into twins.

"I think we should all try to get some sleep – or at least a little before Skyman wakes up. Skyman, Allaby, is the baby's name."

"I know. Your Two Tornadoes must be prescient."

Prescient? Did Paintbrush teach him the word 'prescient'? And did he really think Two Tornadoes was prescient? And did their conversation really get as far as Two Tornadoes and the baby's name? Well, obviously it had, but had they had time to do anything but learn how to talk and then talk? Had they gathered wood, fetched water, cooked and eaten, seen to the baby, found some food for Yellow? They must have, but ... It was too much to think about. "Look," Gibbous said, "I killed us a turkey, and I picked up some stuff in Big Rim." He kneeled down, moved the turkey aside and opened the satchel. "Two more blankets and another hammock." He took them out and tossed them on the ground. "I wanted two hammocks, but the Chief only had one – he must be sleeping on his cushions these days – and the Chief's house was the only place I went …"

"Were you able to prevent the war?" the skyman – Allaby, Allaby – said.

Gibbous looked up. "What war?"

"The war on Small Rim."

"Little Rim," Paintbrush said.

"You know about that?" said Gibbous.

"Paintbrush and I have talked and talked. Was your plan effective?"

"It was the plan I had, but I think it worked," Gibbous said. "Here, the Chief gave me some clothes for you, uh, Allaby."

"Granddad? You went all the way there and you only think you stopped the attack?"

"I always thought the Chief was pretty tall, but he's still a lot shorter than you." Gibbous stood up with a pigskin shirt in one hand and a pair of goathair trousers in the other. He came around the fire to Allaby. "Big Rimmers," he said, "wear a lot of goathair. I find it itchy myself, but I guess …"

"Granddad," said Paintbrush, who was now standing beside Allaby and, by God, was clutching his arm, "how can you not be sure what happened?"

Gibbous draped the clothes across Allaby's free arm, which, fortunately, was also the unbroken one. "Are you two, uh … Did you … You haven't …"

Paintbrush quickly let go of Allaby. "Oh no, Granddad. No. We've just been learning to talk."

And then Allaby, having taken a couple of moments to catch Gibbous's meaning, said even more emphatically, "No, no, no."

Gibbous wasn't sure. Paintbrush had held Allaby's arm as naturally and casually as if they were married or something. She'd even, he thought, touched her cheek to it. What was going on? Whatever, it was his, Gibbous's, fault. He'd left them alone. But he'd thought that if Paintbrush had the knife … That wasn't the problem, though, was it? It had never occurred to him that Paintbrush herself would want … would want what? What? Oh God, it was just something else he was too tired to contemplate. Later, later, he decided, wondering once again what a skyman was doing here in the first place. "Never mind," Gibbous said. "Let's get some sleep." He went back towards the satchel. "I'll put this hammock up. You can use

148

it, Allaby ." He was going to make damned sure it was a distance from Paintbrush's hammock. "And you can keep the blanket, too. I'll use the Chief's and sleep on that bed-thing I made ..."

"Granddad, I swear ..."

"I swear also," said Allaby.

"Never mind, I said." He reached into the satchel again. "I got you some shoes, too. They're probably too small, but if they are ... Oh. What the hell are those?"

"I made them, Granddad."

Carrying the shoes he'd brought, Gibbous came closer and looked down at the ones Allaby already had on. He recognised the cloth – it was his drying cloth, cut up and tied around the man's feet and ankles like bandages. "Are those comfortable?"

Allaby seemed to think this over. Then he said, "Comfortable?"

"Do they feel okay?"

"Oh, comfortable. Yes, very comfortable. Paintbrush is magic. She made the hurt just vanish."

"Paintbrush," said Gibbous, "what did you do?"

She was smiling down at her handiwork and damned if she wasn't – unconsciously, no doubt – holding the man's arm again, with both hands. "I used some moss and—"

"And what?"

"Some other things."

"What other things? What made his, uh, hurt vanish?"

"Oh, well, I dug up some numbing fungus."

"He's had numbing fungus on open cuts all day – all day and all night? You're not supposed ..."

"I know you're not supposed to," Paintbrush said, "but I've never understood—"

"You're just supposed to dab the cut with it. Otherwise you can forget you have a wound and forget to be careful with it. It can get into the rest of your body, too. It even gets into your head sometimes. How do you feel, Allaby? I mean, feel all over? Good? Bad?"

"I feel good," Allaby said, grinning.

Oh, what the hell, Gibbous thought, he feels good. Let him. As for what he and Paintbrush might or might not have done or been doing, let them do it or not do it, as they wish. She's already a widow, for God's sake, and old enough to know her own mind. And if any woman ever deserved a

149

skyman, it would probably be her. But this skyman? Gibbous couldn't help feeling a very unpleasant pang. There was no choice, though, but to go ahead and feel it, or to think about something else – hanging the turkey, for instance, or putting up the hammock and persuading these two to try to get some sleep (separately, though, separately – his tolerance would never extend to seeing Allaby climbing in with Paintbrush and the baby). "Well, keep feeling good," he said to Allaby, "but be sure and take your new shoes off before you go to sleep."

****

Sleeping wasn't easy. Back in the housecave, he'd been able to snooze during the daytime because it was always pretty dark and pretty cool even when it was blazing outside, but there was no way of escaping the heat and light here. As the sun got higher, the trees seemed to get flimsier, and lying with his shirt off and an arm slung across his eyes just made him feel hotter. The fact that Yellow kept nudging and sometimes licking him didn't help either. And as tired as he was, he couldn't get his mind to shut up about Allaby and Paintbrush or just about Allaby by himself. Skymen, he presumed, knew everything about everything. He'd know about God and Hell and Mother Elephant, about whether the endless water really existed, where the sun really went at night and what the stories of the Beginning were really about. It had been strange going back, seeing the Chief and leaving again. In a way, it had been like dying a second time – or at least cutting a link with the world that hadn't quite been cut after the first departure. Then he'd left the company of people – or thought he had – but this time, after seeing how fundamentally stupid the Chief had been when misinterpreting the skyman's mask, Gibbous had come away not wondering so much about the truth of the stories as being certain that they were lies, or largely lies. Now he had to fill up on the truth, and only Allaby knew what the truth was.

On the other hand, if Allaby knew everything, why was he so damned inept? Why would he leap into the rapids? Why would he let his feet get torn up? Why did he have to be taught to speak? And why would he say, when he finally could speak, that Two Tornadoes must be prescient? Gibbous had drunk the naming brew hundreds of times, and one of the things it damn sure didn't do was make you prescient. What it did was to put all your concentration on one single thing and enable you to utter one or two words before going to sleep – dreamless sleep. Oh, sleep. He could have used some naming brew now.

And what about Allaby and Paintbrush? Gibbous let his arm slip and turned onto his side to look at them in their respective hammocks, about twenty paces apart. Neither was sleeping. Over in her hammock, Paintbrush had Skyman sitting on her stomach and, although the sound barely carried to Gibbous, seemed to be baby-talking to him. She was bouncing him a little, and he would smile, laugh and then earnestly try to make his lips make the sounds she made (the same as she'd been doing with Allaby, he presumed). As for Allaby, he was just lying there in his shorts and, yes, his shoes (he still hadn't tried on his clothes, either; they were now draped over a branch just above him), his head cradled on his broken arm, drowsily gazing in Paintbrush's direction. Gibbous felt the pang again (it was nothing but jealousy – he knew that) and then suddenly felt something else too: a twinge of a kind of fear that he didn't think he'd ever felt before and couldn't quite isolate. Maybe it wasn't really fear, only apprehension maybe, but not apprehension just for himself – for all of them together. The first time he'd walked away from the Seven Settlements, he'd been feeling a deathly detachment, and that had been fine, necessary even, and not scary at all. It had been something of a handicap when he unexpectedly had to deal with Paintbrush again and her terrible story, but on the whole it had been a blessing.

This time, though, he'd left the settlements to go to something, to this group of people. Before, he hadn't had any people, and now he suddenly did. Before, he had been detached. Now everyone was. No one had a base. The Ledge was gone, and Paintbrush and Skyman had nowhere to go back to. Well, they could conceivably go back and settle in Big Rim, but he couldn't see Paintbrush ever wanting to do that – she'd left Big Rim to join him, and there was nothing about that particular foreign settlement that would have any kind of appeal for her. Even Yellow, who had now given up trying to rouse Gibbous and had gone to sit and stare at the high tree branch where the turkey was hanging … Even Yellow couldn't go back to being a regular dog: his dog education had been interrupted and lost, and he was a member of a family of humans now, getting a human education. Allaby, too – judging by his disorientation and general craziness – seemed to have cut whatever connections he might have had, as if this campsite, randomly chosen by Gibbous as an overnight stop just three days ago, had been his actual destination (as if he's been sent, Gibbous thought in spite of himself). But whatever brought him here, he is here, and he's one of us now. That's it, Gibbous told himself – we're now 'us'. We're it. We're the world, and we only have each other. By God, that really was frightening.

What were they going to do? Where go? They were starting all over. They might find some place they liked, with some natural shelter maybe, and just stop there and start a whole new settlement – which could mean, he imagined, that some day we'll be, or at least Paintbrush and Allaby will be, somebody's original ancestors. People will tell stories about us, as if we sprang from nothing, or from the hand of God or the trunk of Mother Elephant. We're probably right at the beginning of another Beginning. Is that the way Beginnings always are, he wondered, just something that happens after the ending of something else – one before the other before the other before the other …

(About then Gibbous finally slept.)

CHAPTER FIFTEEN

It was morning, the sun was behind them, and at last, Gibbous and Yellow were striking out across the Far Plain. Except that they weren't exactly striking out. Yellow, having lost his some of the discipline he'd briefly acquired when the company consisted of just him and Gibbous, was back to his old habit of running ahead and waiting, with sometimes only his head and tail showing above the grass. But Gibbous could sympathise – because it wasn't just the two of them any more, and the going was a whole lot slower. He'd finally persuaded – well, almost forced – Allaby to take the numbing fungus out of his shoes, and now the man was limping again. It wasn't nearly as bad as before – and Paintbrush was letting him put his arm around her shoulder, or as much shoulder as he could reach past the baby on her back – but the occasional little hop he was doing off his right foot (oh, but he was doing it bravely, Gibbous had to admit, and was looking even braver, somehow, for his trousers and shirt being much too short in the legs and sleeves) meant that both Gibbous and Yellow seemed to spend a lot of time standing still and surveying the landscape – the endless rolling, waving, blue-tinged plains, with enough cows, horses and deer right there now to feed all of humanity for the rest of time – or so Gibbous figured, simultaneously wondering if there wasn't something wrong about figuring cows, horses and deer that way.

But that was the way everyone had always figured them: food on legs. Right now he and Yellow, who'd come back to see what was wrong, were more or less in the middle of a group of grazing horses – six or seven mares and some foals – all of which were apparently unconcerned by the humans', not to mention the canine's, attitude towards them. Maybe they could tell, in their horse way, that neither the man nor the dog was in a hunting frame of mind. Or maybe they knew that, whatever the two were thinking, there wasn't much these two little predators could do to harm a group of powerful, hard-kicking, fast-running horses. Of course, they made sure that Gibbous and Yellow were aware that they were aware they were there – there was a lot of looking up and snorting and staring into Gibbous's eyes, and the lead mare – an old grey horse with large black patches, one around one of her eyes – didn't graze at all, just regarded and contemplated and sized up and, as far as Gibbous could tell, wondered whether she should move the other mares off a distance. But she didn't, and Gibbous just regarded her back. This was food on legs?

Of course, it was a tenet of religion – a command of Mother Elephant – that animals be respected for their unique individuality, and words were said over every carcass before it was butchered and cooked. But those words were often said very fast, and early on in his tenure as storyteller, Gibbous had given up trying to get people to slow down and think, to reflect on the end of a life. Anyway, his own reflections had led him to realise that somehow Mother Elephant's command only seemed to stretch to big animals. The likes of squirrels, rabbits, birds and prairie dogs were cut up and eaten with no ceremony at all, as though they were pieces of fruit or something. Why wasn't a squirrel as much a unique individual as a horse? Had Mother Elephant really left squirrels out, or had people, over time, quit bothering about the squirrel end of killed animals? If the storyteller couldn't answer that, no one could, and Gibbous had had to stop pressing the matter. It was the imperfection of things, the inconsistency of things and the way people didn't even seem to notice that, that would have driven him crazy if he hadn't retreated to the company of his own, often heretical, thoughts. And a final reliance on the company of his own thoughts, he realised now – feeling, in a way, that he was sharing this particular thought with the lead mare – could have been why he'd opted, for the first time in a couple of generations, for a Long Walk Out.

But now the Long Walk Out had been transformed into some kind of migration. He and Paintbrush had had a conversation of sorts with Allaby, before sunrise and while they were striking camp, and though it wasn't really possible to comprehend most of what the man was getting at (being able to hear him talk was far from a solution to understanding him), he at least seemed to have an objective. He needed to go to a place that was important to him. Gibbous couldn't remember what Allaby had called it exactly, but as far as he could tell it was a house of some kind, maybe even Allaby's own house while he dwelt on the ground. He lived there alone, it seemed. He had a family, he'd said, but he'd left them back in their settlement in the sky. Anyway, there were things Allaby needed to do when he got to his house or whatever – skyman things – but Gibbous suspected he only wanted to go home. Which was fine. Home seemed to be in the general direction Gibbous had been heading anyway, and Allaby seemed helpfully anxious to reach it, so much so that Gibbous's offer of another day or two at the campsite, while the feet finished healing, was turned down out of hand. So Allaby's home was generally where they'd go, if very slowly and, for Allaby, painfully. And – who could know?– maybe they'd start their new Beginning from there. At some point he'd really have to ask Allaby about new Beginnings.

The lead mare made a whinny so low it was almost a sigh. She jerked her head, scratched at the ground and then walked away by several horse-paces. The other mares, one by one, followed. And then the reasons for that – Paintbrush and Allaby – caught up. Both of them were puffing a little, Allaby through the effort of limping and Paintbrush because she was carrying two people on her back. She was even sweating, something he couldn't remember her having done very much before. In the hot sun, it made her look a little rough, red and desperate, but within the bounds of her usual composure, something Gibbous had only ever seen broken when she'd told him about the atrocity at the Ledge. And even then, she'd kept that quality about her that made you want to push her hair back and kiss her on the forehead, to hold her hands and look her in the eyes and say, "Damn, you're good." It bothered him to see Allaby using his limp to take advantage.

Paintbrush said, "I'm afraid we're not going very fast, Granddad," and gazed across the endless plain.

"We've made a start," Gibbous said. "You don't get anywhere if you don't make a start."

"Yeah, but look, Granddad." She glanced over her shoulder. "The sun's getting hot, and the woods back there still don't seem that far away."

Gibbous had to agree, but he said, "Well, we're going faster than if we weren't going at all. How's the foot, Allaby?"

"Not too bad," Allaby said. "I think I can … I'm very sorry about this." He was still leaning on Paintbrush and, like her, seemed to be contemplating the apparent infinity of the Far Plain. Then he looked over at the group of mares, "I don't suppose you know how to break horses. No, of course you don't."

Gibbous had to think for a moment and then, reckoning Allaby was still having talking problems, said, "Of course I do. But I don't have a bow and don't have any arrows. I only brought this pipe. I guess you could use a pipe, but it would take two or three darts, and by the time you blew the second, the horse would be halfway to the mountains, which we can't even see yet."

"That's not what I meant," Allaby said. "Forget it."

"Anyway," said Gibbous, "what would we want a horse for? We couldn't eat it all here and we couldn't drag it with us. There's enough dragging going on as it is." Here was the supposedly all-knowing skyman coming up with another a stupid idea. And it wasn't as though there wasn't enough food. What was already in the satchel would last a couple of days.

The baby, covered all over in a piece of Paintbrush's dress that had been specially cut off for the purpose (Gibbous, as he cut it, had hoped that her legs wouldn't burn), began to whimper.

"I'll bet he could eat a horse if he could," Paintbrush said. "I'd just fed him before we started. Now he wants to be fed again."

"Feed him then," Gibbous said. "We can't have him crying. Sit here in the grass. We'll burn the ticks off later."

As Paintbrush sat and fed Skyman – just her bowed head and back visible above the grass – Gibbous took a few slow steps towards the mares. Under normal circumstances, he figured, they would have bolted by now, but this was the lushest of the lush seasons, and the plain was so crowded with grazing animals that they'd have had to go some way to find another spot where they could spread out a bit. Oh, well, there was room just over there, but why should they move – they'd already established that the humans and the dog had no intentions towards them. Not counting Allaby, of course, but who, human or horse, could ever know what Allaby was intending? Then he realised that Allaby was standing beside him, also looking at the mares.

"I wish I could remember how you do it," Allaby said.

"How I do what?"

"No. How it's done. That was the impersonal 'you'."

"The what me?" God, the more Allaby talked, the more irritating he could be. The what me?

"No, what I mean is how does a person break a horse. You still use the word 'break', don't you?" He picked a long blade of grass, put one end between his teeth and, using his good hand, jerked it in two. He spat out the short end. "Break," he said.

"Um. Yeah," Gibbous said. "More 'tear', but yeah. Are you saying you want to break a horse?" He imitated Allaby 'breaking' the blade of grass. "Like that?"

"No, you wouldn't be breaking the actual horse so much as breaking its – how would you put it? – its spirit. Its freedom."

"What the hell for?"

"So you can ride it."

"So I can what it?"

"Look, Gibbous," Allaby said, "for thousands of years, your ancestors, my ancestors – they're the same ancestors, you know – rode horses. They broke the horses' spirit so they could get on a horse's back and let the horse do the walking – even do the running. It was easier than, well, doing their own walking or running. And not just easier – a horse could go faster and farther, and in any direction the human wanted it to go. By breaking the horse, the human took over the horse's mind – became the horse's mind. Now if we could break two or three horses ..."

"Wait," Gibbous said.

"Wait for what?"

"Just wait. Wait while I think about that."

Allaby shrugged and, still staring at the mares, crossed his arms. And Gibbous stared at Allaby, who was standing there poking out of his too-small clothes, the breeze ruffling his blonde hair and, yes, the seedlings of a beard showing on his cheeks. He was a skyman all right, but he was definitely a man too. He'd said it: they had the same ancestors. That had to be true, or Allaby would have been something else: a horse even – or a dog or a pig or something like the skymen on the Cavern walls, with big eyeballs for heads and eagles' wings on their backs. No, humans could only be produced by humans, and so Allaby had to have the same ancestors as Gibbous, Paintbrush, the Chief and everybody else in world. It was something he'd known from the first time he'd ever seen Allaby, inside his mask and with that earnest expression on his face. It's one of those things you can know, Gibbous told himself, but still take a while to realise: he and Allaby had the same ancestors.

And over the ancestors' generations, the same kind of stories had drifted down – some true, some not, and no way of telling the difference. Except maybe by thinking about them, reasoning about them, actually trying to picture Mother Elephant lugging the sun through Hell, the air animals bestowing nutrition on corpses, Hero swimming in blood or, now, a human taking over a horse's mind, sitting on its back and commanding it to go places. As a man, of course, Allaby had all a man's weaknesses, chief among them the ability to swallow lies and then burp them up again. The fact was that Allaby no more knew the truth than Gibbous did, and that, somehow, was even more disappointing than when he'd been nothing but a jabberer.

"The prospect of breaking a horse," Allaby said, "doesn't seem to have filled you with enthusiasm."

"Well," said Gibbous, "It's an interesting idea. I'll give it that."

"Yes," Allaby sighed. "It can be done, but I don't know how and neither do you. Look, Paintbrush is getting up."

Indeed she was, and soon they were all moving in the direction that they knew would, sooner or later, reveal mountains. This time Gibbous tried to keep pace with the other two, purposely carrying his stick instead of using it, so that he would slowly limp as well, and finally just giving the stick to Allaby and some relief to Paintbrush. Even Yellow got tired of running ahead and crept along with them. When they set up camp that evening, there was still no sign of mountains, and the woods they'd left this morning were still on the other horizon. It had been one of the slowest travelling days Gibbous had ever experienced.

But who cared anyway? Gibbous gathered a few armloads of cow dung, got a fire started and showed Allaby how to dig beds in the plain's hard soil and how to gather grass to soften them, and Paintbrush found enough rocks to build a stove around the fire and to get a meal started. It was budgerigar and mushrooms again, but Gibbous didn't mind – there were some kinds of food you could eat night after night, and as long as you ate it in a different place each time, it seemed, in a way, like different food.

In fact, Gibbous was so glad to be out on the Far Plain at last, dug in and camping, that he was almost able to forget the weak side of Allaby's humanness. He was feeling comfortable again with the idea of the new Beginning. Allaby and Paintbrush were playing with the baby, jostling him and making him laugh, and Yellow was wandering from point to point around the campsite, as though he were standing guard (and he was – it had always been one of the dog pack's jobs out in the open like this). The moon was a little fainter than last night but was still pretty bright and still nicely silhouetting wispy clouds and whizzing bats. Burrowing owls squeaked and dark figures of cows shuffled and lowed, slowly mowing through the grass. The general smell was good, too. Gibbous liked dung fires. Ever since he was boy, the pungency and the heavy, hanging smoke had always meant a quiet moment in the middle of an adventure of some kind, a next morning to look forward to. And there was hardly any breeze tonight, which made the smoke that much heavier and tastier. It had gone well with the budgerigars and mushrooms.

In time, the baby got tired and fussy, and by rocking him in her arms and quietly singing the cactus apple song, Paintbrush was able to get him to sleep. Allaby – a few paces away, wrapped in his blanket and lying on his back in his bed-pit – seemed to be drifting off, too. Gibbous put some more cowpats on the fire and was getting ready to lie down when Allaby, as if coming out of a dream, said, "I've just remembered."

"What did you remember?" Paintbrush said. "Tell us a story about it."

"It's about breaking horses. I've remembered the principle."

"Oh God," said Gibbous, lying down and pulling his blanket around him. "Haven't you been thinking about anything else?"

"I remember. I read about it once."

"You what?" Gibbous said, wondering if all conversations with Allaby from now on were going to be peppered with 'whats' and whether he ought to just to stop asking, let Allaby talk and try to work it out afterwards.

"I read about it," Allaby said. "It's a way, I guess, of, uh, hearing stories. You look at little marks … I can't explain it right now."

"That's all right," Paintbrush said sleepily. "Just tell us the story."

Gibbous grunted.

"Well, it's got to do with strength," Allaby said. "The main thing horses are is strong. Not intelligent, but strong. And strength is what they respect in other animals."

Gibbous grunted again.

"So a human, to get a horse's respect, needs to make it think that a human is stronger than a horse. I think I've even remembered what they used to call the thing you do that with. It's a snubbing post. And you need a rope. And I think you need other things, too, but I can't remember what they all are. But I don't think you need them right at first. Just a rope and a snubbing post. You tie a rope around the snubbing post and the other end around the horse's neck and then stand between the horse and the snubbing post holding the rope. That makes the horse think it's your strength that's keeping it from running away."

"And that works?" Paintbrush said.

"I don't really know, but I guess so," said Allaby. "I just remembered reading about it, that's all. But I really don't know."

"Is that what 'snubbing' is, then? Pretending to hold the rope?"

159

"I don't know that either. Maybe snubbing is some other part of the process. I can't remember."

He can't remember, Gibbous thought. Few things annoyed him more than someone trying to tell a story, true or not, and being vague with the details – it showed lack of imagination. He wished Allaby would just shut up and go to sleep and would have told him to if Paintbrush hadn't seemed so, well, happy with the man. But she sounded as though she herself might fall asleep at any moment, and when she did, then he'd tell Allaby to shut up. On the other hand, maybe he could gradually change the subject. There were a lot of things he wanted to talk to Allaby about, but none of them concerned obvious lies about horses, ropes and snubbing posts, whatever 'snubbing' actually did mean. "These ancestors of ours," Gibbous said, "did all of them snub horses?"

"You mean did they ride them? I think most of them did. Or used them to pull things, heavy things."

"How come, then, that in the old stories there's nothing – nothing at all – about horses? Well, they're hard animals to hunt, and there are stories about that, but … ut you know the stories. I don't have to—"

"No I don't," Allaby said.

"Don't what?"

"Know any of your stories. I'll want you to tell me some time. Paintbrush says you're a brilliant storyteller."

God, Allaby was hard going. Every time he said something, you had to stop and think and reassess. The man didn't know any of the stories. Of course a lot of them covered the time between the last contact with a skyman and more or less now. But there were also plenty that came before skymen or had skymen in them. Didn't he know those? Surely skypeople had stories about how they saved ordinary humans from the floods of blood, gathered all the lonely souls together and carried them through the air to the blessed Gorge. So what did they have stories about, besides taking over the minds of horses? There would never be a point, it seemed, where he could start with Allaby. As for "Paintbrush says you're a brilliant storyteller," it looked like talking to him was going to involve being patronised as well, something Gibbous wasn't used to and definitely didn't like. Always Standing Up might patronise Gibbous sometimes (though he never would again), and sometimes even Two Tornadoes – although Two Tornadoes had never realised that he was being humoured in return – but an inept like Allaby, no.

Forget that for now, Gibbous told himself. There was an opportunity here, an entry point. "We have stories about the Beginning," Gibbous said. "Do you?"

"The beginning of what?"

"The Beginning."

"The very beginning, of everything? Yes, we have stories about that. Actually, 'theories' would be a better word."

"Theories?" said Paintbrush, who Gibbous thought might have fallen asleep.

"I think he means 'ideas'," Gibbous said.

"Ideas, okay," said Allaby.

Gibbous said, "And what are the skymen's ideas about the Beginning."

"Granddad," said Paintbrush, "this is a big thing to ask. When you used to talk about the Beginning it would take almost a whole night's session." She seemed to be wide awake now. "And to tell you the truth, it always left me with the same questions."

"What are they?"

"Where did the floods of blood come from? And where did the people come from who were drowning in the blood?"

"Floods of blood?" said Allaby.

"Those are pretty good questions, Paintbrush," Gibbous said.

"They are? I was always afraid to ask. So was everybody, I think."

"I think I was too," Gibbous said. "I think the very thought was a little heretical. But I'm not afraid any more, and neither obviously are you. You know why I think that is? I think it's because ..." He stopped. He was going to say, "I think it's because we're having a new Beginning now," but he hadn't developed that thought – that theory – to the point where he could talk about it. Talking about it now would jinx it somehow.

"Because what?" Paintbrush said.

"Floods of blood." said Allaby. "That's really interesting."

Gibbous said, "Not as interesting, I'll bet, as your answer, the real answer – if you think you skypeople have the real answer."

"So you really mean," said Paintbrush, "that the floods of blood aren't the real answer? Granddad, why did you always tell us—"

"We're pretty sure we have it," Allaby said. "There are some who don't think so, but most do. There's an argument about whether, when we look at the stars, we're seeing the Doppler effect or the Compton effect. And then, of course, there are the religious people, but they have their own ideas and don't care much about either of the effects."

"What do you mean religious people?" Paintbrush said.

"Well, you know, people who, uh, believe things that aren't, uh, proven. Can't be proven."

"Is that all?" Paintbrush said. "Is that all religion means? I've never thought of it that way. In fact, I've never heard of anybody who thought of it that way, or of anybody who didn't even have a religion to believe in, but … Allaby, do you? Do you have a religion?

"Uh, no, Paintbrush, not really. I used to, when I was younger, but I guess I grew out of it."

"But," said Paintbrush, "Skymen are a part of religion. All the religions."

Gibbous said, "I'll bet skymen aren't part of the skyman religion. Are they?"

"Well, yes and no. We don't think of ourselves as skymen. You think of us as that. We just think we're people, the same as you. And in all the religions – and we have different kinds, too – there are people. So yes and no."

The three of them fell quiet. They were all lying on their backs in the dark, each wrapped in a blanket and looking up at the stars and the moon and the wisps of smoke and the bats. All around cattle grazed and grunted, and Yellow was making a noise that sounded like digging – maybe he was digging for an animal or digging a bed for himself, although whenever he wanted, Gibbous reflected, he could crawl in with him or Allaby. Last night, though, Allaby had pushed Yellow away, and the dog had slept with Gibbous. Why had Allaby done that? He'd seemed to like him fine the night before.

Finally Paintbrush spoke. "I can't imagine what it must be like not to have a religion. I can even imagine having a bad religion, the kind the Little Rimmers have, but not no religion. Do you believe anything at all?"

"Well," said Allaby, "I, uh …"

"He believes what he sees," Gibbous said. "Is that right, Allaby?"

"Granddad, I don't know about you any more. You're getting … I don't know. Is that right, Allaby? Do you only believe what you see."

"Well, yes, more or less. And what I've been taught."

"But isn't that kind of what religion is? What you've been taught?" By the sound of Paintbrush's voice, she wasn't lying down any more. She

162

must have been leaning up or sitting up. And her voice had a note of pleading.

"Not necessarily," said Allaby.

But that was all he said, and the conversation paused again until Gibbous spoke. "Come on. What about the Beginning?"

"It's a little hard to explain," Allaby said. "And you've got to understand that our science, our seeing and believing, if you want to put it that way, was badly interrupted by … well, actually by what you call the floods of blood, I imagine. After that, the people out in the … the sky were too busy just surviving to—"

Gibbous said, "So there were floods of blood?"

"Uh, yeah," Allaby said, and Gibbous had the distinct feeling that he was skimping on the truth in some way, just to make life easier for himself.

"See, Granddad?" Paintbrush said. "Every time you start to question the stories, Allaby comes up and says they're right. That's what religion is, Allaby. You've got a religion, all right. You've got our religion."

"But I'll bet you something, Paintbrush," Gibbous said. "I'll bet Allaby doesn't think the floods of blood were the Beginning. They weren't, were they, Allaby? I'll bet you know where the blood came from and the people, too."

"What exactly is your version of the Beginning?" Allaby said.

"Don't ask him," said Paintbrush. "He takes all night to tell it."

"Don't worry," said Gibbous. "I'm not going to be the one answering questions tonight. I want to ask them. Now tell me the real Beginning. Start by telling me how long ago it happened. How many generations?"

"I wouldn't put it in generations," Allaby said. "Generations are too vague. Years. You have to put it in years."

"A year's kind of short," Gibbous said.

"Not that short," said Paintbrush.

"Anyway, how many?"

"Well," said Allaby, sighing, "if you accept that it's the Doppler effect we're seeing – that is, the astronomers are seeing, and I accept that's what it is … you know, you're right, Paintbrush, you've got to make up your mind to accept something … nd if you accept that the stars are moving away from each other at a certain speed …"

"The stars?" said Gibbous. "They don't move away from each other."

"Yes they do," said Allaby, and Gibbous thought he heard a touch of impatience in the man's tone. It reminded him somehow of old White

163

Water, who'd been the storyteller when Gibbous was a boy. If you ever made an obvious but unacknowledged observation, he'd sigh in that same way and come just short of calling you stupid. "And the farther away they are from the centre, the faster they're moving."

"Even if stars did move away from each other," Gibbous said, "what's that got to do—"

"By working out the speeds, astronomers have been able to figure out when it all started. It was about fourteen billion years ago."

Silence again. Crickets. Cows. The burrowing owl, twice. Then Paintbrush said, "Allaby, what's an astronomer?"

"That's somebody who spends his life looking at the stars."

"Oh," she said, thought a few moments and then said, "Half his life. The other half, it would be daytime."

"Okay," Allaby said. "Half his life."

"Less than that," Paintbrush said, "because there are a lot of cloudy nights."

"Yes," Allaby said. "Of course."

"I'm thirsty," Gibbous said. "Who's got the water bag?" He didn't see who'd tossed it, but the water bag thumped onto his stomach. He sat up, untied it, drank and tied it. Still sitting, looking out away from the fire at the dark shapes of animals, he said, "Fourteen how many years?"

"Billion. Fourteen billion."

"I never heard of a number like that. Is it a real number or just something you make up, to mean a lot?"

"It means a lot all right," Allaby said, "but it's real enough. Let me see. Do you know how long a thousand years is?"

There was something Gibbous both liked and didn't like about this conversation now. He liked the fact that they were having it, that at last he was hearing and about to hear something that wasn't in the old stories, something new for a change. But he wasn't ecstatic about the content so far. He didn't believe any of it, for one thing. Stars didn't move away from each other. They moved through the night, and they moved with the seasons, but they all moved together (except for the Red Star, the Silver Star and the Flickering Star, which seemed to have minds of their own and were known as the Bad Children). Why would Allaby say such a thing? Was he teasing? He didn't seem to be. He seemed patronising, but he also seemed serious. And right now Allaby's survival entirely depended on Gibbous and Paintbrush; it would have been stupid of him to taunt them.

Anyway, he wasn't the type – Gibbous was sure of that much. "Well," Gibbous said, "I know a hundred. When I was born, my father was thirty. So a hundred years is how long ago my father was born. And if that happened ten times, that would be a thousand. And there are a thousand paces in a mile, and if you think of a pace as a year … So, yeah, I know a thousand years. But I still think doing it by generations makes more sense."

"Okay," Allaby said. "A thousand years – a lot more but … I'll tell you – it's been about a thousand years since your floods of blood. You think of that as the Beginning, but for us—"

"Has it really been that long?" Paintbrush said. "Imagine, Granddad. All those storytellers in all that time, and none of them changed the story. I think that's—"

"Storytellers don't change the stories," Gibbous said sternly. "They might overdo them, the way Two Tornadoes does, but they don't change them. People would know if a storyteller changed them, and he wouldn't be a storyteller any more." But, damn it, Gibbous knew that storytellers did change the stories – in little ways, he'd done it himself – and it was the cumulative effect of that that was the whole problem.

"I didn't mean—" Paintbrush said.

"Okay, Allaby," Gibbous said, standing up, dropping the water bag on Allaby's stomach and, for something to do, walking over to the fire. "We know now that the floods of blood weren't the real Beginning. So what was?" He put two cowpats on and squatted, warming his hands. "And never mind how many years ago. Or how people who watch stars all their lives – half their lives – know. I just want to know what they think they know."

"All right," Allaby said. He sat up crosslegged in his bedpit and pulled the blanket around his shoulders. Paintbrush was sitting up, too, the sleeping baby in her lap. Allaby said, "There was a thing called a singularity."

"Tell me what a singularity is or was and then go on."

"Well, it's kind of hard to say what it is, was. Nobody really knows. It was just everything packed into … into a … a point. It wasn't anything you could see, not that anybody would have been there to see it. It was just … nothing. Everything, but nothing. Everything and nothing. And then it exploded."

"Everything and nothing," Gibbous said, concentrating on his fingers held up against the light of the fire, "and it exploded. Like when something explodes in a fire?"

"Yes," Allaby said. "It's called the Big Bang."

Paintbrush said, "Bang? As in bang? Just bang?"

"Yeah," Allaby said. "The Big Bang. It's a complicated idea, and scientists – astronomers are scientists – always try to put complicated ideas into simple terms. That's where they're different from religious people, Paintbrush. Religious people always try to put simple ideas into complicated terms."

To Gibbous, it sounded very much as if Allaby had said that before, maybe many times. He was storytelling now. Why? Trying to impress Paintbrush?

"Anyway, everything that now exists – us, those cows over there, the moon, the stars, everything – is a result of the Big Bang. Everything just blasted out from the singularity."

"Cows?" said Gibbous, still concentrating on his fingers. "Cows blasted out from the singularity?"

"Well, it took a long time for cows to exist, as cows. But all the little particles in a ... all the little things that, put together, make a cow a cow were there then. Light and heat started then. Even time started then. And time, lots of it, brought us the world we know now."

Paintbrush said, "Time? Did it? Really? Did it really begin in the bang?"

Oh God, thought Gibbous, time. Don't get her started on time. Before you know it she'll have the sun going backwards again.

"So was there a time before time?" Paintbrush said.

Allaby sighed. "This gets difficult, Paintbrush." He started to get up but sat down again. Gibbous sensed that he wanted to stop talking about all this now and just go curl up with Paintbrush, and the only reason he didn't was that he, Gibbous, was watching. The way Allaby looked at her and strained in her direction was painful to see. "If there's no time," Allaby said, "there can't be a 'before'."

"So it was just bang," Paintbrush said, "and everything started."

"Uh, yeah," Allaby said.

"Well, that's simple enough," she said. "There's something I like about that – I think I even dreamt it once – but, Granddad, compared to the floods of blood, it's not nearly as good a story. Allaby, does that mean time's a thing?"

Here we go, Gibbous thought.

"What do you mean?" Allaby said.

She picked up what looked like a lump of dirt – it was hard to tell in the moonlight. "That's a thing, isn't it?"

"Yeah."

"I can pick it up and turn it over, hold it up, put it down, crumble it up. Can't I?"

"Yes, sure."

"And it came out of the bang?"

"Well, yes. Okay. Yes."

"And time came out of the bang, too. Right?"

"Uh, right."

"So can I do all that to time?"

"Well, time is dif—"

"That would be real magic," Paintbrush said. "Except that it wouldn't be magic. It would be real. If there was a bit of time that was really bad – rotten – if I could just reach out and take out that bit of rotten time and just throw it away, or stick it in somebody else's time …"

"Paintbrush," said Allaby, "I don't know what you mean."

"Oh I do," said Gibbous. "Paintbrush, stop right now."

"You've got to know how to do this, Allaby – you're a skyman. You know what the real Beginning was. I believe what you say. It sounds right. It sounds wonderful. Nothing at all and then bang – the light and the dark and time, and then time, all by itself, turns everything into stars and water and sunshine and cactus and grass and all the things that make life good. After Skyman was born what I used to like best was carrying him outside in the morning when things were still a bit wet from the night and sitting on a rock and giving him his feed and watching the sunshine crawl through the Gorge, turning it into colour, like a big paintbrush. It was so wonderful I want to cry to think about it, and now I want to cry because it won't ever happen again – I'll never see the Gorge again. And I don't want to now. Now I'm crying because the Ledge is burnt and stinking of dead bodies, and time did that, too. If you could just take that bit of time out, the way you take out a rotten tooth—"

"Stop it, Paintbrush," Gibbous said. He stepped over to her sleeping-pit and put his arm around her. She was shuddering with sobs and holding the baby so tight he was afraid she might suffocate him. The baby had woken up and was whimpering and gasping a little, and Gibbous tugged at her arm to loosen her hold. Allaby had come over, too, and was now squatting in front of her with his hand on her cheek. Gibbous said in her ear, "It's really not time's fault."

And Allaby added, "It doesn't work that way, Paintbrush. Time is just … I don't know how to put it … what happens happens. You can't change—"

"Are you saying you can't?" Paintbrush said.

"No, I can't. Nobody can."

"Time's a thing. You said so."

"I didn't say that. Or I didn't mean that. Not exactly. Time is what's called a dimension, like, uh, like distance. A certain distance is a certain distance. You can't change that."

Gibbous could feel Paintbrush relax a little. She sniffed, raised her head and loosened her hold on the baby. "Oh yes you can," she said.

"No," said Allaby. "I'm sorry Paintbrush, but—"

"Yes you can. Otherwise, why are you talking about snubbing horses? You want us to get on top of horses and go faster. How far is it to the mountains? Two days? On top of a horse it might be one day. That makes the distance shorter. It cuts something out of it. You said – you told me this when you were learning to speak – you said when you came here you came in a way that was very fast, that it was only moments from the mountains to the river. That made the distance almost go away completely. If time and distance are the same thing why can't you …" She stopped, staring at Allaby.

"Allaby, I think she's got you there," Gibbous said, mainly to make Paintbrush feel better but also to lighten things a little while he absorbed this new information about Allaby travelling from the mountains to the river in moments. His first thought was, if so, why aren't we travelling back that way? And the thought that followed was that Allaby must be lying again. But why? What good does it do him to say things that are so obviously untrue – that stars move away from each other and that he went from the mountains to the river just like that? And why is Paintbrush so quick to believe him, or to believe him until he says something that obviously is true – that you can't change the past – and then to argue with him? Well, of course he knew the answer to the last bit: the atrocity had affected her in her heart. He knew Paintbrush all right – it was Allaby he couldn't fathom. Over the course of his life and especially in the past few days, Gibbous had been developing a new way of looking at the world – of taking it as it seemed to be and not using some old corrupted story to

168

explain every little thing that happened – and he'd expected Allaby to back him up and to give him some information he could work with. Instead, he got a story of the Beginning that wasn't even as good as the Little Rimmers' version, which had God pointing his finger out of the sky and creating light and land and animals and a man and a woman, or the Big Rim and Deep Gorge Beginning, where God as a baby finds some thunderbolts lying around and accidentally drops one into a pond, which magically makes plants, animals and people. All of these stories neglected the same fundamental question: what happened before that? And Allaby's was just the same. Saying there was no time so there could be no 'before' was just shrugging the question off, and believing that there was a time of no time was no different from Paintbrush believing you could extract bad times like bad teeth. Another Damned Disappointment: that was the name he'd give Allaby if he ever had the chance.

Allaby and Paintbrush had kept on talking for a while, but Gibbous hadn't listened. He'd gone to the fire again and then back to his bedpit. Then Allaby went back to his, and though no one was talking any more, no one was sleeping either. Gibbous could hear Allaby crunching around as he tried to get comfortable, and Paintbrush was singing softly, getting the baby back to sleep. Even Yellow had woken up and was scratching the ground again. Why was he doing that, Gibbous wondered and then decided it was one too many things to wonder about. Then, just as he was dropping off, Paintbrush spoke. Her voice was soft, clear, slow and sleepy. "Allaby, Granddad, I think time is a thing, and if neither of you can change it, I'll have to, because I can do something neither of you can. I can dream better than anybody in the world. I'll get my hands on that rotten piece of time and kill it in my dreams."

CHAPTER SIXTEEN

"No, Caleb, it wasn't a soul," the Chief Deacon said, "not unless souls are very short and have beards and bare feet and walking sticks and have wolves with them. Well, you know what a soul ought to look like. It would be—"

"Do you know what a soul looks like? Have you ever seen one?"

" … it would be, I've always thought, tall and translucent, and light on its feet, maybe even with wings. That wasn't at all like a soul. That was a man for sure, an old man."

"Would you please pass the potatoes?" Caleb Hook, the Grand Marshal of the Keepers of Jerusalem, received the dish, took the last two potatoes, put the bowl down, cut both potatoes in half and poured butter-oil on them. Chewing, he said, "Is anybody saying it was a soul?"

"It's hard to know. It was only a couple of hours ago. The news is getting around, though."

"I don't know what would be worse," Caleb said.

"What do you mean?" said the Deacon. He had very small eyes, close set, and during a conversation he never seemed to blink. And in a crisis – and this was the first crisis he could ever remember the Deacon being involved in – he didn't seem to be able to talk and eat at the same time. His lunch was getting cold. It made Caleb feel greedy.

"Eat," Caleb said.

The Chief Deacon took a small bite of bread and swallowed it quickly. "What do you mean you don't know what would be worse?"

Caleb was suddenly aware that other people in the Garden of Gethsemane were staring in their direction. There was nothing unusual about that – he was head of the established Church, after all, and was used to being stared at in public. Most of the time he even liked it, believed, in a way, that he deserved it. But today … today he felt that they weren't looking at him so much as to him. What was he going to say in his sermon tomorrow? This was a theological policy decision, and it had to be sorted out with the Chief Deacon, now – there was only a day before they had to present the Keepers' official opinion to the Head of Station, and maybe even him and some of the Cabinet – the summons had come through while he was on his way here. And before that, there was tomorrow morning's sermon. "Look," Caleb said, leaning forward and speaking just above a whisper, "Forget the soul nonsense. It's a man, and people are going to be wondering what he's doing there. How can a living, breathing man be in a place where no living, breathing man can possibly be? They'll be thinking – well, God knows what they'll be thinking, what they're already thinking. That we've been lying, probably – both us and the Government. Remember the Back-to-Earthers?"

"Yes, but they were crackpots."

"Well, they won't look like crackpots now. And there's no 'were' to it. I happen to know that the police broke up a cell in Canaan just last year. They were going to steal a ship again."

"So what? It would have been suicide."

"Would it? There was a man there. You saw him, didn't you?"

"No not me." The Chief Deacon said. "I didn't see him. It was my son and his family. They always go on Saturday morning. My son says it makes their whole week."

"Okay, your son then. And his family. And how many other people?"

"A couple of hundred maybe. I don't know. Saturday morning's a pretty big—"

"That's just great. Two hundred. You can't argue with two hundred witnesses, not to mention the ones—"

"That did occur to me, Caleb, and I wondered if we could call it mass hysteria or something. Remember those schoolgirls, the ones who thought they saw the Virgin Mary?"

"I remember."

"They saw her right here in the Garden of Gethsemane. In the leaves of that lime tree over there."

"Deacon, this isn't helpful."

"And you called it mass hysteria."

"I wish you'd eat your lunch. I hate watching gravy congeal."

The Deacon swirled his fork around in his gravy as Caleb finished the last of his potatoes and took the last bite of his drumstick. Then the Deacon said with a tone of finality, "I honestly don't see why we can't call it mass hysteria."

"Because," said Caleb, his mouth still full, "it honestly wasn't." He swallowed. "And what about Jericho? Jerusalem isn't the only city with an

Earth holopark. Was it mass hysteria there, too? And in Canaan? And Bethle—"

"Oh," said the Deacon. "Oh yeah. Of course, I haven't heard any reports from—"

"Try to concentrate, will you? I need your help."

"We could just ignore it."

"No we couldn't. Think."

"Would you like anything else, Reverend Hook?"

This was the waiter, whom Caleb hadn't noticed. How long had he been standing there – standing there listening to two Church leaders trying to cook up a story to feed to the Government and then the people? "Oh, yes, thanks," Caleb said. "I'll have – what was your special? – the cherry pie. Yes. And ice cream. And take the Deacon's plate away. He's not hungry."

"But I'm—"

"Take it away and put the food in a box or something. He can eat it later."

"Certainly, Reverend." The waiter and both plates – one finished, one full – disappeared.

"Now," said Caleb, "let's think about what it means if people think it was a soul."

"They'd be wrong. It couldn't have been."

"Because it – he – wasn't tall, translucent and light on his feet?"

"Well, yes. But no. There's more to it than that."

"What?" said Caleb. "What more is there to it?"

"Souls just don't—"

"Don't what?"

"Caleb, are you saying that it might really have been a soul? That would be heresy, you know."

"Why?"

"You know why, Caleb. Please, what are you—"

"I know why, yes. I was just checking to see if you do."

"Heresy's heresy. What do you mean why?"

"I'll tell you why it's heresy. And why it's worth knowing a little Church history sometimes. Everybody thinks it's something to do with transubstantiation, but seeing souls is the very point, in 2821, that caused the schism with the Lazarines: they said you could see them; we said you couldn't. They said souls went to Earth, we said they went to Heaven, the ones that didn't go to Hell. They said Earth was Heaven, and Venus was

Hell. And Titan was Purgatory, where we were all waiting, as it were, for our orders. It was all too … this universe for us. We let the question hang. We let people believe what they wanted in that department. It was the easy way, and we took it because no one ever imagined there would ever be any proof one way or the other. Then a couple of centuries later the holoparks came along and there was proof, in our favour. There were no souls to be seen. The Lazarines withered."

"There's still that church over on Luke Street," the Deacon said.

"Yes, one church. One little church. And two, I believe, in Jericho. But they used to be bigger than us. People liked the idea of their souls walking around on Earth and … and … feeling the rain and basking in the sunshine, whatever – basking in the goddamned sunshine. And now a human figure's been seen doing just that."

"Sorry, Reverend, there was only strawberry," the waiter said. "I know it doesn't go very well with cherry pie, but I took the liberty." He set the dish in front of Caleb.

"Thanks," said Caleb, looking around at the other tables. Had the waiter heard that? Had anybody else? "Thank you. Strawberry is fine." Had he raised his voice? He couldn't remember. People were still slyly staring his way, but not, it seemed, in shock. So maybe everything was fine. The Garden of Gethsemane, which was the 'outdoor' restaurant attached to the central market, was probably not a good place to be making theological policy. But he and the Deacon always met here on the Saturday before the Sunday comms sermon, and today there hadn't been time to change plans. So now they were here, and they had to make a decision, one that might alter centuries of church teaching, and in less than two hours. And then get the Head of Station and the rest of the Government on side and then after that write a new sermon, possibly the most important sermon he'd ever had to write. Caleb felt a hot pang of panic in his chest, and he sent some strawberry ice cream down to cool it off. The waiter said, "You're welcome, Reverend," and left. The Deacon called after him, "Could I have some coffee, please?" Caleb could tell that the waiter hadn't heard the Deacon.

"Well," Caleb said, "any ideas?"

"I don't know, Caleb. If it can't be a man and can't be a soul and can't be mass hysteria, what can it be?"

"I don't know either. And neither does anybody else, and that's the problem. The Head of Station needs to be told something, or he'll—"

173

"He'll what, Caleb?"

"Well, I don't know. Without us – without us, clear and firm – he might do something stupid. He's certain to, in fact. He's probably already talking to the Scientific Committee."

"What do you think they'll say?"

"God only knows. They're probably as baffled as we are, but … Oh, I know what they'll say. That it has to be investigated – in other words, that they don't know either and it's going to take them a long time to find out. But that's not good enough. It's dangerous. People will start inventing their own stories, and that'll make them unhappy and restless, maybe even rebellious, maybe even ready to believe in a soul and the Lazarines or a man and, God help us, the Back-to-Earthers. What the Keepers of Jerusalem, the established Church of Titan, can offer, and what no one else can, is certainty. We're needed now."

"Okay," said the Deacon, "what was he then?"

CHAPTER SEVENTEEN

Probably the hardest thing to get used to, other than being imprisoned in her hotel room, was looking out of her window and down at the Strip and seeing it deserted. Normally, it was the centre of a district that could only exist on EHQS, a place without any real residents or residences other than a few dormitories for technicians and civil servants and walk-up flats for caterers and entertainers. At any given time, most of the people on EHQS were tourists. They came from all four of the stations (though overwhelmingly, by reasons of proximity and sovereignty, the Moon) for a week or two or three of relaxing, drinking, gambling and general carousing, and the place where most of that happened was up and down the several hundred metres of the Strip. The whole satellite was a 900-metre diameter, 400-metre thick wheel that created centrifugal gravity as it turned around its hollow hub – which had no gravity itself and had been fitted out as an enormous and enormously entertaining free-fall gym. There were two circular 'levels', an inner one for offices and labs and an outer one, nearly three kilometres around, for accommodation, gardens, factories and the main money-maker, fun.

Most fun was the Strip. It was where the hotels were, and the theatres and the bars, and at any time brash light and music would be blasting out of open doors, and the street and its connecting alleyways would be thronged. To Jenny – to most people, even people who'd never actually been to EHQS – it was the most exciting district in the Solar System. Images of it were beamed out to the city equivalents of holoparks so that people at the distant stations could have the illusion, at least, of being there too. Nearly everyone everywhere knew the names of all the Strip's establishments, and most of the music that most people listened to had first been played and heard somewhere along this place.

So to look at it now was like witnessing doomsday. It was all quiet, empty and closed. The only lights came from the sky-ceiling and the windows of the hotel across the way, and the only people in sight were the orange-uniformed soldiers. There seemed to be one stationed in every doorway she could see – standing, slouching, often gazing up at Jenny's

175

hotel and sometimes even at Jenny gazing back at them. Who these soldiers were and who they represented – and, for that matter, what they'd done with everybody – was something Jenny still hadn't been told. In fact, she still hadn't been told what had been done with Gus Templeton, never mind the throngs in the street. She'd been told about Peter, though. They – and 'they' were mainly that bastard Simon – said he'd been killed, particled, by the National Park Service; it was that agency's fault, and she should be grateful that it had now been forced to disband.

But she wasn't grateful. She herself was an officer in the National Park Service and had always been proud to be. And she was probably the only member of the Earth staff who knew, if not exactly what was happening at EHQS, at least that something was. So it was probably more her responsibility than anyone else's to try to save the Service, if it could be saved. But for the millionth time in the past two days she asked herself what and who she'd be saving it from. Obviously, the Park Service was just one of many victims, up to and including, apparently, the Government. Whether that meant the administration of EHQS or the whole Government of the Moon was something else she didn't know. In fact, beyond what she could see from the window, she had to admit that she didn't really know anything. She couldn't even be sure that Peter was dead, if believing that meant believing a shit like Simon.

Oh, but Peter was dead of course – it didn't take Simon to say it. At best, he'd only had a day's worth of air. In a way, she hoped that he actually had been particled, if the alternative was suffocating or dying in agony of the Abunga, something she couldn't bear to imagine. She'd loved the man and, by God, she missed him. She missed all the Rangers, for that matter, but losing Peter was like losing a lobe of her brain. When she'd first started as a Ranger, it had always been Peter, a veteran of a good two years by then, that she'd relied on for guidance. He was so straight up and, well, ranger-like – the pride of the force and the fount of all biological knowledge, earthcraft and imaging techniques. But it wasn't until she discovered his deep naïve streak (the Titanian in him, she figured) that she began to pity him a little, then like him a little, then like him a lot, then … well, it first happened at a Confab three years ago. Now, every night, or most nights, she'd go to bed, sleep a few hours and then get up, go to the comms and catch Peter just as he was knocking off for the day. She'd tell him what she'd been doing and thinking and even dreaming, and Peter being there to hear it and respond to it seemed to make it actual. She often thought that their relationship was the nearest thing Rangers could know to marriage.

And then when they touched … They were together twice a year, every year, at EHQS. The fact that, on Earth, she almost always visited Peter during the wee hours and went back to bed afterwards – along with the fact that she only saw him by way of a holograph – sometimes made him indistinguishable from figures in her ordinary dreams. So when, at the Confabs, they actually touched again, it was literally dreams coming true. She'd mentioned that to Peter once, in a hotel room exactly like this one, and he'd teased her about it as post-coital sentimentality, as something that, in her right mind, she'd never think or say – not at all Jenny. But that was what it did seem like, she'd told him, and anyway, he had plenty of soft spots of his own. What about the way, after a few days at EHQS, he always itched to get back to Earth – to what he'd once called 'the real holopark'?

"What's sentimental about that?" he'd asked.

"Because you were born or whatever in a holopark," she said. "It's homesickness. It's homesickness for a goddamned holographic image."

"But it's not an image. That's the whole point."

"It might as well be," Jenny had said, "for all the actual contact any of us ever have with the place. At least in a holopark you don't have to wear a goddamned Earth suit."

He was slow to answer that and finally muttered, as he turned over to a spoon position, nudging her in the back of the neck, "It's just knowing I'm there."

"I know what you think," Jenny said. "You think Earth is Heaven. You think you're living in Heaven. How sentimental is that?"

Much too loudly and just behind her ear, he said, "I don't think Earth is Heaven. I don't think anything of the kind."

She'd certainly pressed a button then. He'd always claimed to scorn the religion he'd been brought up in, but his overreaction now was enough to convince her that Heaven was exactly what he thought Earth was. It was obvious why he eventually ended up getting drunk and going berserk: the devils were going to kick him out of Heaven.

Jenny suddenly realised that one of the soldiers across the street had been staring at her for a while, and so she turned away from the window and did practically the only other thing there was to do in this room – lie on the bed. The little comms unit could be turned on, but that was all: there was never an answer when she tried to call out and nothing at all coming in (even the holowindow was blank) and otherwise only this hundred-year-old story on the flatscreen about titanium miners in the Sea of Serenity. Nothing else: as soon as it ended it started over again, and at one point she'd been so bored she'd watched it twice in succession, having already watched it once the night before. The hero, an exaggerated, swaggering, musclebound Mooner, discovered the fabled motherlode against all the connivances of the villains (Martian corporatists, of course), blew up their dome, rescued the girl and her prospector father and saved the Lunar expedition to Venus (the thing was so old it was still thought landing on Venus was possible – ah, the surgent optimism of the late Renaissance).

She was almost tempted to watch it again, maybe this time for its wealth of continuity blunders, when she felt a sudden surge of anger and shame and sat up on the edge of the bed. Important things – evil things – were happening out there, and she was being held prisoner. But instead of trying to do something about that – to think of a way out – she was just alternately gazing out the window, lying on the bed and watching a crappy old propaganda story. She was actually cooperating with her captors. Exactly what they'd want would be for her to sit here and dull her mind until she was so docile she'd do anything just to be doing it.

In fact, if she thought Simon and his people were really smart enough to plan such a thing, she'd have suspected that this imprisonment was custom-made to break her down. If she'd been in a real prison or a torture chamber, she'd have had something to do, or if not exactly to do, at least to resist. But two days of sitting here in ignorance and silence just made the same thoughts wheel around and around in her head – one after another, repeating until she was weary of thinking them: how had Peter really died? Where were Gus and the rest of the bureaucrats? What was happening back at her station, back in her sector, in all the sectors? Why were Simon and the others so concerned about the Immyos? Why had they taken over EHQS, as they apparently had? Who the hell were they? And, above all, where was the place where you could walk around outside and breathe?

Because once Simon and his group had abandoned their interview with her, they hadn't spoken to her again. Simon's last remarks were that Peter was dead and Jenny could be useful, and from then and there she'd been escorted by the two shuttle guys all the way across the satellite and to this room. Door locked. Unbreakable window also locked. Food sent in on the room-service chute: plain stuff – generated stuff made to look like bread and noodles, green cakes that didn't look or taste like anything, orange-coloured juice, water, no salt, no meat, no wine, no …

"Goddamn it," she said aloud, standing up off the bed so forcefully that, in the Lunar-gauge gravity, she bounced on the balls of her feet. And that reminded her that she still had Earth strength in Moon gravity and still would for a couple of months. Why hadn't she thought of that when those guys were escorting her here? They'd looked pretty big, but they were Mooners. They'd had guns or at least implied they had guns, but there weren't any guns in sight, and she could probably have pushed them aside and, before they could reach their under-jacket holsters or pockets, at least have run – hell, bounded – away. She knew EHQS pretty well and knew places where she could hide.

But of course, the EHQS she knew wasn't the EHQS now. There were these orange soldiers all over the streets, and hardly anyone else. They'd have caught her wherever she went. Even the hotel staff seemed to have been replaced by soldiers – her escorts had pulled her past them on the way to the elevator. Still – despite all that – if she was going to stay sane, she was going to have to think of a way out of here. Just the planning by itself would at least keep her brain working.

Jenny went back to the window, looked down at the empty Strip and began her escape plan by thinking about what she'd been thinking about. Had she been thinking at all, or was she just in the grip of a kind of paralysing but low-key panic? After all, she'd been concentrating on problems, not solutions. She'd been thinking about everything she didn't know and nothing about what she did. She must know something for certain … She closed her eyes for a moment to focus on this, and when she opened them again she noticed that the soldier who'd been staring at her had left his doorway and was talking to the soldier in the next doorway down. Then, at the same time, they both looked directly up at Jenny, grinned and laughed in an unpleasant way. Or so it seemed: she couldn't hear them, of course, and they were four storeys down, but the laughs didn't look very nice – slimy, in fact. Then one of the soldiers gave her a fluttery wave. "Damn," Jenny said, and she pulled the blinds shut and went back to sit on the bed.

So much for concentrating. She was furious: she couldn't even look out the window now. Damn those soldiers, damn that … And then, effortlessly, a plan floated into her head. Those soldiers, offensive as they were, were at least a form of human contact. She could see them and they could see her – never mind what they thought they saw when they saw her. In fact, what they thought they saw could be an advantage. She could go to the window, strike some kind of sexy pose and signal to them to come up. They were soldiers, and the hotel lobby was full of soldiers just like them. They could walk right through to the lift, come up and … But she wouldn't be able to let them in. They'd need to get a key. They'd need to go to the desk and ask for … But how could she tell them they'd need to do that? And if they knew they'd need to do that, they'd realise she was a prisoner. And would the soldier at the desk give them the key just for the asking?

No … The plan was disintegrating as fast as it had materialised. So she skipped past the locked-door problem to the part where they came barging in and she used her Earth strength to shove them aside or even knock them out and then to bound down the corridor – when the actual door in this actual room actually opened and two actual soldiers came in.

Followed by Simon. With a jerk of his head, he ordered the soldiers out again and shut the door after them. So much for shoving aside and bounding. In fact, Jenny hadn't had time to move from the edge of the bed. Simon, with a nod hello (these people were not strong on opening greetings), pulled out the dressing-table chair and, without turning it around, straddled it, his arms across the back. It was the way the Martian-fighting Mooner on the flatscreen sat.

He smiled, the first time Jenny had seen him do that. "It took almost a day longer than I thought it would," he said, "but everything's ready. Are you ready?"

"Ready?"

"Yes. Ready to go. Packed and everything?"

"I came up here for a meeting, remember? I didn't bring anything. I've been combing my hair with my fingers and washing my underwear in the—"

"That's fine then. You're ready."

"Ready for what? And what's the idea of keeping me prisoner?"

"Prisoner? Is that what you think you are?" Still smiling, Simon cocked his head a little.

"What else?"

"No. We just locked you in because we didn't want you to go away. We wanted to know where you were when we needed you."

"But isn't that what a prisoner is? Somebody who's locked—"

"You're not," said Simon, "the easiest person to get along with." His smile had gone. "You're not exactly cooperative. You're in on the project of the millennium, and all you can think to do is be awkward. We thought we could count on a little more gratitude from you."

"Gratitude? You've been keeping me a fucking prisoner."

"Well, being a fucking prisoner in a fucking luxury hotel room—"

"Luxury—"

"… is a lot fucking better … See? I can use the word, too … than what's happening to everyone else on this satellite, this Gomorrah. And it serves every one of them fucking right – the dancers and singers, the music-players, the gamblers, the liars and sons of liars, the bureaucrats, the sybarites, the scientists – but you don't care about any of them, do you? You only care about your fucking lover."

He was leaning far forward against the back, now the front, of the chair, and his long grey hair had somehow uncombed itself. His face was the colour of Martian dirt. "You only care about Peter fucking Allaby. I can't stand to imagine what kind of nasty things a man and a woman can do by hologram, but then I don't have to imagine it because he's smithereens, zillions of invisible smithereens, and it was your own fucking National Park Ser—"

"Shut your dirty mouth."

She was off the bed and conscious again of her Earth strength, which this time she used. Simon's pink and grey head projected from her fist to the side of the dressing table, and when he hit it the mirror hit him, crashing onto his face, splintering. Then he was on his back on the floor. She had just enough time to see the blood start running from his forehead and down into his ear when the two soldiers were suddenly there, almost ladylike in their expressions of astonishment. Their guns were out and their hands were shaking. One said to the other, "Did she kill him?" And to Jenny he said, "Turn around, you."

"No, he's not dead," the other soldier said. "God willing, he'll be okay." She couldn't see him now, but the soldier must have been kneeling. "Put your hands behind you. You got the handcuffs, Amos?"

"Yeah."

"Put them on her."

As she felt the metal close around her wrists, the soldier who was doing it said, "Why would you want to hurt him?"

"Why the fuck not?"

"But him, of all people."

"All what people?"

"Don't you know who he is?"

"He's Simon, and he's a shit."

"No. He's our inspiration. God, she doesn't know who he is, Marcus." He paused for a moment and then said in a quieter voice, "He's the prophet. He's Moses. He's the President."

CHAPTER EIGHTEEN

It was Allaby's third day of rising into consciousness in the open air of the planet Earth. This time it wasn't the smell of the dog or the soreness of his feet that had occupied his first thoughts but, as his grass mattress had compacted, the innumerable stones and clods that were bruising his body and the various mites and ticks that were dining on it. There was also the sensation that something very large and not necessarily very friendly was very near. He opened his eyes. The fire had burned out, but it wasn't dawn yet (he made a mental note to volunteer to take turns with Gibbous in keeping it stoked) – just the slightest tinge of purple over the woods in the east, and, yes … in the air above him was something dark, massive and warm. With legs. With one leg, one foot – when he turned over to face west – just a short kicking distance from his face. He instinctively turned his face away, looking up and either seeing or sensing or just reasoning somehow that right above him was an udder. The cow grunted.

"Uh, help," he said quietly, because the last thing he wanted was to startle the animal. On the other hand, Gibbous and Paintbrush wouldn't be able to hear him, and anyway what could they do to help? He was on his own again, and he heard the hoof scrape. So he rolled over, and in the midst of a frantic movement that was something between a crawl and a wriggle got a hard hoof in his ribcage. By the time Paintbrush sleepily said, "Did something just happen?", the cow had loped back to her group of grey eminences about twenty metres away.

"A cow stepped on me," Allaby groaned. He tried to sit up, but it hurt too much.

"The fire's out," Paintbrush said. "Granddad, you let the fire go out, and now a cow's stepped on Allaby."

"What?" said Gibbous.

"You let the fire go—"

"What happened?"

"Where are you, Allaby?" said Paintbrush.

"What happened?"

"A cow," Allaby and Paintbrush said together. Allaby kept trying and failing to sit up. This was very worrying. He already had a broken wrist and shredded feet. Add a couple of cracked ribs, and he might as well be put out to die. And his side was certainly hurting enough for ribs to be cracked.

"Oh there you are," Paintbrush said. "Over here, Granddad. Why are you just lying there, Allaby?" She squatted down and put her hand on top of the hand Allaby was using to hold his side. In a quiet voice, she said, "Is it there?" She pressed lightly.

"Uh. Ow. Yeah."

"Oh, Granddad, come here. I think he's—"

"… cracked some ribs?" Gibbous said as came up and also squatted. "Move your hand, Allaby. Let me feel." Gibbous pushed a lot less lightly than Paintbrush had, and Allaby felt a flash of heart-stopping pain that seemed to go from the top of his head to somewhere in his stomach. "I don't know," Gibbous said. "It could just be a bruise. It's hard to tell with ribs."

Allaby choked and coughed, which was excruciating. He said, "It feels like more than a bruise."

"Really?" Gibbous said. "Damn."

"Granddad, why did you let the fire go out?"

"It's hard to say," Gibbous said, almost philosophically, as he continued to prod Allaby's ribs. "I woke up all right. But I don't know. The fire was dying, and all I had to do was get up and put some more cowpats on it. But I don't know …"

"What do you mean you don't know?" Paintbrush said. "What if the cow had stepped on Skyman? God, he's over there by himself now." Allaby could hear her suddenly scuttling back to her bedpit and then her voice from a short distance: "He's okay. He's asleep. Granddad, if you woke up, why—"

"Like I say, I don't know. I meant to. But then I think I started thinking about the Beginning again. About Allaby's 'bang' thing and all the rest of the Beginnings and sort of comparing them—"

"Ow," Allaby said. "Yi."

"There's one there," said Gibbous. "There's another one. And … three of them. All cracked all right, but not broken in two or anything."

"Ah. Stop. Please."

"Well, we've got them located anyway."

"But couldn't you have thought about all that," Paintbrush said, "while you were stoking the fire?"

"Sure," said Gibbous. "And I'm sorry, Allaby and Paintbrush. But I was really trying to get to the bottom of what makes all the Beginnings alike somehow and how there's something wrong with all of them, including your 'bang' Beginning. These ribs of yours could be a real problem. Let's see if I can get you sitting up." Gibbous grabbed Allaby by the upper arms and pulled.

To Allaby it felt as if Gibbous had reached inside him and was pulling him up by the cracked ribs. But once he was sitting it wasn't quite as bad – in the way a bed of nails wouldn't be quite as bad as a bed of burning coals. He hugged himself, and that lowered the pain a little more, to about the level of the bed he'd just been sleeping in.

"Better?" Gibbous said.

"Yeah, a little. Oh goddamn."

"Granddad," said Paintbrush, "I still don't understand—"

"… why I didn't stoke the fire? I don't either, to tell the truth. Allaby, just sit that way for a minute while I figure out what to do. Ribs are hard. You can't put a splint on them, but you've got to be careful—"

"Granddad."

"Okay, okay. All I can do is tell you what I was thinking about. I was thinking that – like you, Allaby – you've got accept something or you'll stop thinking altogether. It's like, well, the paintings on the Cavern wall. If you don't have a wall you can't have the paintings. See? The Beginning's like that. There's no argument there. Everything came out of it – all the versions agree. So I thought I'd pick a version – yours, Allaby. To be honest, it sounded preposterous to me, but so do the others, so why not?"

I don't care, Allaby thought, still hugging himself. Doesn't he realise I might not be able to travel with these ribs?

Gibbous was standing up now. The sky was brightening behind his head, but his face was still a dark blank. "And then the more I thought about it, the more it began to sound right. You see, Allaby, the main difference between your 'bang' thing and the others is that you have time starting at the same time as everything else, and that's how you get around what happened before that. The others just have God always having been there. Even the Big Rimmers' baby God wasn't exactly born, didn't have parents as far as I know. The other versions all have forever in them – yours doesn't. But then I started thinking that maybe, just maybe – and I have to admit that I was just lying there watching the coals die down – something did come before. Something had to, because how did that – what did you call it, the single thing—"

"Singularity," Allaby coughed.

"Singularity. How did that get there?"

"I really don't know," Allaby said. All he could think was that, if he couldn't walk, they were going to have to devise some way of carrying him. But there were the San Juan mountains to cross. Well, they could make it to the pass, but even that … Oh Jesus, it hurt.

"There had to be a world before the singularity or there wouldn't have been a singularity. Maybe the singularity was the end of the other world, or maybe the other world just produced the singularity, the way a plant produces a seed. But then I thought, a plant produces lots of seeds. So maybe this is just one of many worlds the other world produced. There could be whole forest of worlds – a whole world of them. And that world would have had to start somewhere, too. The thought was getting too big and, well, too annoying. I couldn't get out of it – Beginning after Beginning after Beginning, as well as bunches of Beginnings all at once. The idea gets you everywhere and nowhere, and you might as well have God or Mother Elephant. It was making me hate the whole idea of Beginnings. It even made me hate the world for a moment. It certainly didn't put me in a mood to get up and rebuild the fire, and I was glad when I felt myself going back to sleep. Now I'm really sorry, though, because that cow wouldn't have come anywhere near a properly burning fire."

In other words, Allaby thought, if I hadn't talked about the Big Bang, my ribs would be intact. It was strange to be in such agony and have cosmology to blame for it. He stopped hugging himself to see if that helped at all. It didn't. It just changed the focus of the pain. So he hugged himself again.

Paintbrush said, "Do you know what you did, Granddad?"

"Of course I do. I—"

"You had a tantrum. You had a tantrum about the beginning of the world, for God's sake, and now Allaby's suffering for it."

"I wouldn't call it—"

"Well, I would. Seventy–year-old men don't fall down and kick and scream, no. But they do things like you did. They sulk, and that's the same as a tantrum and a lot more dangerous. In all the time I've known you, I've never seen you sulk before. Sulking's for people who aren't in control of things, and in control of things is something … well, something you've always been."

"Well," Gibbous said, "I wasn't in control of those thoughts I was having and probably never will be, damn it. I can't help it, Allaby. I can't help being disappointed in you. You're a goddamn skyman. You should be able to tell me things, definite things – not raise questions that are too big for a man to think about." There was enough light now for Allaby to see Gibbous's face and the expression on it, and he wondered if the old man was going to kick him or something, in the ribs maybe.

"Granddad," Paintbrush said, "don't talk to Allaby that way. He's got cracked ribs. You should be helping him. If I could get over to him right now, I'd do it." Allaby was able to turn his head enough to see that Paintbrush was feeding the baby. Then suddenly all he could see was the dog, which gave him a lick up the middle of his face. "See, Granddad? Even your Yellow is worried about him."

The smell was almost as overpowering as the pain, and for some seconds he couldn't move his hand either to push the dog away or wipe his face. And when he finally did manage, it was with the wrong hand, and he conked his nose with the splint. "Damn," he said to Gibbous. "You think *you* wish I hadn't told you about the Big Bang." The dog now decided to sit beside Allaby and lean on him.

Gibbous sighed. "I know, Paintbrush. You're right. Sorry, Allaby. Get out of the way, Yellow." He knelt, pushed the dog a little and looked Allaby in the eye. "I am sorry," he said.

Through his pain, Allaby suddenly thought he understood something, because he – it wasn't as though he were thinking this but almost as if he could hear himself think it – because he felt that some of the Earth's charm, especially after that cow, was wearing thin. The Earth of the holoparks and even the Earth from inside the station and inside the suit was a willowy, pretty, glorious, soft place and, yes, a sort of Heaven. But the Earth out here was hard as knuckles. Disappointment – of course. He and Gibbous were both disappointed. Disappointed in the world. "I'm sorry myself," he said. "There are plenty of things I ought to be telling you about. I didn't need to start with the Big Bang."

"Oh why not, if you thought it was the Beginning? And I did ask. Look, I've got to get you to stand up now."

"I don't think I can. Not yet."

"You've got to."

"Yes," said Paintbrush. "If you can't stand up or can't walk, we're stuck here until your ribs heal. This is nowhere, here. If we can get to the mountains, there'll be at least be trees. Water too, probably."

"That's true," said Gibbous. "Or maybe we could make it back to the river."

"No, no." Allaby said. "We've got to keep going. Oh, damn that cow. Damn these ribs."

"Can you explain again," Gibbous said, "where we're going and why. I wasn't paying much attention the first time you said it, and just going anywhere seemed fine with me."

Allaby inadvertently took a deep breath, which hurt a lot. He followed that with a shallower one and a firmer hug on himself. He looked towards the woods, where the sky was staging a full-blown sunrise, and then in the direction of the mountains, which were still below the horizon. And even after they crossed the boundary and went up into the mountains and got through them somehow, it was still a long, long way to Pike's Peak. He said to Gibbous, "I've got to get in touch with some people – people like me, people, uh, in the sky. And to do that I've got to go to my house, my house on Earth."

"I won't say I understand why you have to go to your house to do that, but don't tell me. More important, why do you want to do it? Do you want them to come get you?"

"No. I have to tell them something. I have to tell them that you can breathe on Earth. And not die."

"You mean they don't know that?"

The pain was unremitting. Was Allaby now expected to sit here as he suffered and explain twelve hundred years of history? And he was suddenly aware that he had to pee. How in hell was he going to manage that? Gibbous and Paintbrush were right – he had to get on his feet. "Maybe you could help me stand up now."

Paintbrush said, "Why do they think you can't breathe here? That's ridiculous."

"Until very recently," Allaby said, "you couldn't. Well, you could. They couldn't. I couldn't."

"Why not?" Gibbous said.

"Please help me up. I've got to pee."

"Oh, okay," Gibbous said, squatting and putting his hands under Allaby's armpits. "Take it slow. Bend one leg now. Just concentrate on your legs. Forget your ribs."

"Ow," Allaby said as he bent his leg and planted his foot.

"Just concentrate on your legs, I said."

"I am. I forgot how much my feet hurt."

"Okay, now push up ... I'm holding you ... and get the other foot on the ground. Good. Now." Gibbous lifted Allaby as though he were doing a press with a barbell. Allaby was up, and the main threat to his staying up was fainting from the pain – pain everywhere, his side, his feet. Even his wrist had started to throb. "Pee over there," Gibbous said. "We'll be leaving this campsite soon. And turn your back to Paintbrush, please."

"Oh, Granddad, I won't look. Anyway, do you think I haven't seen ..." Even in the agony of taking a step, Allaby was aware of how Paintbrush was leaving her sentence in the air. Please don't say it, he thought – not yet.

"Haven't seen what?" Gibbous said.

"A man's thing before," she said quickly. "Look, this is a baby. How do you think it got here?"

"From your husband. But I don't think what you said was what you were getting ready to say."

"Then what was I getting ready to say?"

"Never mind, Paintbrush. I was just telling him as a matter of courtesy. Men should always turn their back to women when they pee, even women they've ... you know."

"No, I don't know. What are you trying to say?"

Throughout this and with the dog beside him, Allaby had taken four steps, each one of them memorable. Now his ribs, his feet and his bladder all told him that four steps were enough. He managed to negotiate the unnecessarily complicated string system on Immyo flies and finally did, copiously, what he'd got up to do. Some of it splashed on Yellow, and some soaked into his cloth shoes, but he didn't care – it was strange how relief could sometimes be stronger than the worst pain. He retied the trousers, and while scratching at some of his bites and gazing for a time at the scarlet sunrise, the brown-green, still shadowy plain and its herds of animals – including, not that far away, some elephants – he asked the Earth to forgive him and to be a little easier on him. Then he painfully turned around. Gibbous and Paintbrush had brought their exchange to what seemed to be a stalemate, with nothing really revealed. "What now?" Allaby said to Gibbous.

"Let's have breakfast," Gibbous said, "and we can work out what to do with you."

CHAPTER NINETEEN

Gibbous, skinning and quartering a couple of prairie dogs, was feeling ashamed of himself. It had been bad enough letting the fire go out and causing Allaby's cracked ribs, but he hadn't been as kind as he could have afterwards. And then, even though he'd resolved not to, he'd tried to tease the truth out of Paintbrush about what she and Allaby had done while he'd been visiting the Chief. Anyway, it was obvious what they'd done, and – also anyway – it didn't matter. He was feeling a little jealous, of course, and that was an irritant – a truly stupid one if it had anything to do with sexual jealousy (how could that persist so long after sex itself had stopped?) – while on the whole, any mating of Paintbrush and Allaby had to be good: that is, if this was going to be the nub of a new Beginning. But Allaby – and Gibbous knew, knew, knew the man hadn't meant to – had soured his search not only for the true Beginning, but for every subsequent one, because the later ones couldn't exist without the true one, the first one, and that had turned into a morass. And without doubt Allaby would have more disillusionment to come. Paintbrush was right – in a way, Gibbous had been sulking – but, damn it, he had a right to sulk. He then missed with a whack of the knife and chopped off a prairie dog's leg without taking in the thigh.

He sighed and looked up. Allaby, once standing, had stayed standing, as though he didn't want to go through the ordeal of getting up again. But he was standing next to Paintbrush's bedpit, and she – the baby on her back – was standing in front of him with her arms around him and her chin on his chest. They were talking, but with all the morning animal noises around – especially a particular bellowing bull trying to keep another bull away from the nearest herd of cows – he couldn't make out what they were saying to each other, not that they would have wanted him to. Of course they had mated. That was a fact, and Gibbous, watching them, now accepted it in its fullness. It was a relief, in a way. He still didn't like the idea of Allaby sleeping with Paintbrush, especially with the baby there, too, but hell, Allaby had broken ribs now. Would that keep him from … Well, if he lay on his back and was very still and if Paintbrush was very caref—

It then occurred to Gibbous that, in the interest of his own peace of mind, he shouldn't think about the details. Instead, and in the interest of everybody's peace of mind, he ought to let them know that he knew and more or less didn't mind that much. He ought to make a gesture.

A gesture, yes – something that would not only seal their mating, but would establish the whole group – Gibbous, Skyman and Yellow included. It would make them a family. Hell, it would make them a tribe. Yes, he'd do it for certain, but not just now. Just now there was the matter of Allaby's ribs and whether – for how many times in his life? – Gibbous and the group he was with would fail to make it to the mountains.

And every time it had been the fault of someone else. Every time, Gibbous had wanted to press on, and so usually had a couple of others, but there would always be somebody who was hurt or homesick or, the most usual problem, scared. Except for a few Little Rimmers once – and they had probably been lying – no one had ever reached the mountains, gone any way up them and come back to tell about it. People had set off with the expressed purpose – not simply as something extra to do during a Far Plain hunting trip – and that would be the last time they'd be seen. So most people were like the Chief's father, believing that there was something in the mountains that killed you. But that wasn't Gibbous's persuasion. He thought that, for some reason, the travellers didn't want to come back – that there was something up there or on the other side that was … what? Better, but how could he know?

He would have known, about now, if he'd still been on his Long Walk Out. But that came to an end four days ago. Four days? It seemed like a year. It was another life. It was the end of a life after the end of a life and before the new Beginning. Before Paintbrush turned up. Before Allaby did. He looked up from basting the prairie dogs and studied the pair of them. Allaby was so much taller than Paintbrush it was almost comical – especially with the added effect of the man's arms and legs sticking so far out of the Chief's old clothes. And probably because of his ribs, he couldn't even bend a little to compensate. When he spoke to her, only his neck craned downwards, while hers was bent all the way back, occasionally bumping the top of the baby's head. The sun was well up now, and it was starting to get hot out here, but Allaby and Paintbrush held on to each other as if they were doing it for the body warmth. It occurred to Gibbous then that if, as Paintbrush had at first insisted, Allaby had been sent by some power or other, he might have been sent just for her – maybe to keep her on this side of sanity. Yes, their mating was definitely a good thing, and he was truly sorry about Allaby's ribs.

In a while the prairie dogs were ready, and Gibbous called Allaby and Paintbrush over. Yellow hadn't needed to be called. Something dogs always knew was when a piece of meat was done. Spiderweb – Gibbous remembered – had always used the housecave dogs as a gauge – as soon as they started to move towards the fire, she knew the meal was ready. They very seldom got any of it, of course, but they did once in a while, and that was enough to make getting up every time worth the effort. And as far as Yellow was concerned now, he did get something every time, and the only problem was that he might start coming to the fire too soon. Anyway, he was the first there and the first to take his portion away and start gnawing it. Allaby and Paintbrush, meanwhile, were taking an age – step, rest, step, rest ... It occurred to Gibbous that he could have brought the meat to them, but this was an interesting experiment, and a depressing one. Cracked ribs shouldn't keep Allaby from being able to walk, but he was probably suffering now from the initial soreness, the bruising. How long would they be stuck here waiting for him to get over that? Three or four days? Longer? It was great being out on the Far Plain, but only if you were in the process of crossing it. It wasn't a place where you wanted to live.

"Granddad," Paintbrush said as she handed a piece of meat to Allaby and took another one for herself, "Allaby and I've been talking—"

"I noticed."

"... and he's worried that he won't be able to go any farther. He thinks that we should—"

"Wait a minute," Gibbous said. "He's only got cracked—"

"... and he thinks we're going to have to figure out a way of carrying him. He's got an idea, too."

"What's that?" Gibbous said, moving from his squatting position to sit crosslegged on the ground. The other two were eating standing up, and with their backs to the sun it was uncomfortable to look at them. So he looked at his piece of meat, and when he spoke, that's what he spoke to.

Paintbrush said, "He thinks we could make a ... What did you call it, Allaby?"

"A trolley," Allaby said.

Paintbrush said, "It's like a bed that you pull."

"Who pulls? Me?"

"Well, the two of you," said Allaby. "And there's a way even the dog could help."

"Hey, Yellow," Gibbous shouted, and Yellow, the meat between his teeth, actually flicked his eyes in Gibbous's direction. "You want to drag Allaby to the mountains?"

To Allaby, he said, "Is that something skymen do? Get dragged around in beds by dogs? I hate to say it, Allaby, but it's not the best idea I ever heard. All of us together – even if we waited for the baby to grow up into a strong man – wouldn't be able to drag you and a bed very far. Anyway, your ribs would pop out. Tell you what. Why don't we just snub a horse?"

"The trouble is," said Allaby, obviously taking Gibbous seriously, "we don't really know how to do that. Sure, I remembered the principle, but there must be important things I don't know, and you or Paintbrush could get hurt. But I could show you how to make a trolley. Or how I think you could make one"

"It's a sort of magical thing," Paintbrush said. "You don't drag it, Granddad. Just pull it, and it comes right along. Isn't that right, Allaby?"

"That's right," Allaby said. "All we need is some branches and a couple of logs. They don't have to be very big logs. Just about that big around, maybe. That long. And straight."

Gibbous shaded his eyes and looked up at Allaby's hands describing the dimensions of a log. It was big enough. And they were on a treeless plain. "I'm sorry, Allaby, but look around. How many logs do you see? And why do you think we're burning cowshit?" He lowered his eyes again and took a bite.

"We realise that, Granddad. We talked about that, too. It means one of us going back to the woods."

"Okay, Paintbrush. We'll wait here. See you later."

"I can't, Granddad. You know that. Not with Skyman. I couldn't do all that and carry Skyman, too."

"So I guess it's no trouble at all for a seventy-year-old man with a bad knee."

"Allaby, tell him."

"Here's the idea, Gibbous. I can tell you now how to make a trolley. Then you go back to the woods, find what you need and make it. Then you can pull it back here. It'll be easier than carrying everything. Otherwise, what are we going to do?"

What indeed? Gibbous had to remind himself again that Allaby's condition was his fault. The least he could do was listen to the man's idea. "Sit down, Allaby. I know it's hard getting up again, but you can't stay standing forever. Come on. Sit there so we can talk. Here, I'll help." Holding his breakfast in one hand, Gibbous stood up and with his other hand held Allaby's upper arm. "You take that arm, Paintbrush. Okay, easy. Bend your knees but keep your back straight." God, he thought as Allaby was lowered, this really is going to take some kind of magic. Of course, they could always make a stretcher, but the thought of stretchering him the rest of the way felt almost as exhausting as dragging him. Anyway, they'd need poles for a stretcher and would probably have to go back to the woods for those. "Okay, Allaby, what's a trolley?"

Allaby explained. What he described was like a bed all right, although he kept emphasising that it had to be as strong as possible while being as light as possible, which made sense in theory but was going to be damned hard to do. It meant branches of cottonwood, Gibbous supposed, or willow. Yes, willow. There were some willows by the river. Allaby was very vague on lashing and general stringwork – and in fact Gibbous had to correct him a few times and do some explaining himself – but what the man was really good at was making pictures with his finger in the dirt. He angled it in a way that made it seem to stand out, to come real. He would have been a revelation, given some colours and a brush and a place on the cavern wall. This was pleasing to Gibbous because not only did it help him understand how to build this trolley thing, it showed that Allaby – now, after all, an integral part of Gibbous's new Beginning – was proficient at something, wasn't totally inept. And when the picture was finished, Gibbous was pretty clear about what he had to do. Well, except for the circles. Pointing at them, he said, "I still don't know what those mean."

"Granddad," Paintbrush said, "those are what make it come right along."

"Yeah, that's what you've both been saying. But I don't see—"

"Paintbrush," Allaby said, "could you find something, uh … what have we got here? Uh."

"What do you want, Allaby?" Paintbrush said.

"Something round. What's round around here?"

"What for?" Gibbous said.

"I want to show you—"

Paintbrush said, "Those cowpats are round. Kind of."

"Yeah," said Allaby, "get one of the … get two of the roundest ones in the pile. They're all dry, aren't they?"

"Sure," said Gibbous. "They don't burn wet. Wet ones aren't very nice to pick up, either." As he watched Paintbrush sorting through the cowpats, he noticed that in the grass beyond her a little, a lioness – body almost flat to the ground and front elbows and shoulder blades raised – was stalking some cows, or cows with calves. The very cows, as it happened – the group that included the cow that had stepped on Allaby. There would be other lionesses around, but he couldn't see them for the grass. They must have had an unlucky night and were still hunting as they were heading back to the woods.

He couldn't have that. If the lionesses charged, cows would be running all over the place. "Just a moment, Allaby," he said, and stood up. "Hey," he shouted at the lioness. "Hey, lion." Both Paintbrush and the lioness looked his way, one startled, one telling him to shut up – or so Gibbous imagined. As Paintbrush hurried back towards him, clutching a couple of cowpats and glancing over her shoulder and the baby's head, the lioness resumed peering in the direction of the cows and began to stretch into another of her very, very slow stalking steps. Passing Paintbrush – who he realised was going to Allaby, not him – he reached the fire and grabbed a burning cowpat by an edge that hadn't caught yet, shouted "Hey, lion" again and sailed the cowpat towards the animal. When it hit her on the flank, she sprang sideways, shot a look at Gibbous and bounded away – with Yellow, out of nowhere, suddenly at her heels. "Stupid dog," Gibbous yelled. "Get back here, Yellow! Yellow!"

A little to Gibbous's surprise, Yellow did stop, and though he didn't come back, he didn't go on either, watching the lioness run a distance further. Then she herself stopped, closed her eyes, jutted her chin and made a loud, sad, moaning call in the direction of the cows. Two other lionesses, on the other side of the cows, became visible above the grassline and made their way towards her. And Yellow slowly – as though it had just dawned on him what he'd had the temerity to try – started back to the campsite. The lionesses, exposed now, walked towards and past the cows as if nothing was there, and the eyes of every cow followed every step they took.

As did the eyes of Paintbrush and Allaby. When Gibbous finally sat down again, Allaby turned to him and said, "How did you learn to throw that way?"

"What way?"

"You didn't throw overhand, like … uh." He'd started to demonstrate an overhand throw and got a reminder from his ribs. "You threw that cowpat backhanded and sideways," he said in a pinched voice. He didn't try the sideways gesture.

"That's just the way you throw cowpats, I guess. Why?"

"If you were throwing a spear at the lion, how would you throw it?"

"It was very brave of you, Granddad," Paintbrush said, still watching the lionesses.

"I had to do something or there'd been a stampede."

"You'd throw it overhand, wouldn't you?"

What was Allaby going on about? "Look, finish telling me about the trolley. If I'm going to do this, I've got to get moving. Yes, I'd throw it overhand."

"What I'm trying to say is that different shapes do different things. You throw a spear overhand because it's straight and long, and you throw a cowpat sideways because it's round and flat."

"Yeah. So?"

"Well, there's one use for round and flat, and another use for straight and long. Give me the cowpats, Paintbrush, and Gibbous, you give me your pipe."

"Why?"

"I'm going to show you something." Paintbrush put the cowpats in front of Allaby, and Allaby held his hand out for the pipe.

"Will you be careful with it? If anything happens to it, we'll get very hungry out here."

"It's the only thing I can think of that's the right shape."

Gibbous shrugged, unsheathed the pipe and gave it to Allaby, who immediately stuck one end of it into the middle of a cowpat. "Damn, Allaby. I've got to put that in my mouth." Gibbous tried to reach for the pipe.

"Wait," Allaby said, and he turned the cowpat over and stuck the other end of the pipe in the other cowpat. Then he put both cowpats, held up by the pipe, on their edges. "Now, look," he said, and turned the cowpats and pipe towards a smooth bit of ground and gave them a push. They rolled about four paces and, when they left the bare ground and hit the high grass, came to a stop. So what, Gibbous was tempted to say. Everybody knew round cowpats – or, better yet, round rocks or balls of sap – would roll if thrown or pushed. After all, there were lots of games played with balls. In fact, there was even a kid's game – flopover – that used dry, circular cowpats. What did Allaby think he was proving? Gibbous stared at Allaby's construction – what was new? Then he realised something: the loser of flopover was the kid whose cowpat was the first to slow down enough to fall flat. These were stock still but hadn't fallen. Because of the pipe.

Gibbous got up, went to the pipe-and-cowpats and, with his foot, pushed it back towards Allaby. He hadn't pushed it hard at all, and though wasn't going fast and wobbled a lot, it didn't stop until it came to rest against Paintbrush's leg. She said, "It's pretty good, isn't it, Granddad?"

"It's interesting," Gibbous said, grabbing the thing and sitting down again. He pushed it back and forth on the ground between him and Allaby. "What do you call it?"

"The cowpats are now what are known as wheels. Those are the circles in the picture."

"Not the cowpats," Gibbous said. "Everybody knows round things roll. But what do you call that – the pipe?"

"Oh, that's an axle."

"Axle, eh? That's interesting. Interesting." Suddenly he had a couple of ideas the likes of which he'd never had before, but they whizzed in and out of this thoughts so fast he couldn't identify them. All he gleaned in their passing was that this axle thing could indeed be useful. You'd have to think of a way of attaching things to it without stopping it turning, but … He leaned forward again to look at Allaby's drawing, but it had been pretty much obliterated by having cowpats rolled over it. "Allaby," he said, "show me again how you … how you, you know … how you keep the bed bit from rolling off the axle."

"I think just a loop of something there. Some rope or something. Not too tight, so that the axle can still go around."

"Yeah," said Paintbrush. "That's all you'd need."

Then as suddenly as the axle had seemed a good idea, it seemed full of holes. "That wouldn't work," Gibbous said.

"Sure it would," said Allaby.

"Why not?" said Paintbrush.

"Because the whole point is that you'd be in the bed thing."

"Of course," Allaby said.

"And you're a big man."

"Yes I am, but this—"

"There'd be so much weight on the axle that, uh, the bottom of the bed would stop it turning. It might even break. And the wheel things, if I made them light enough – with water-bent willow or something – would break, too. And your log idea, that's … It would be heavy. Have you ever tried to roll a log? I mean, is the axle something skypeople use a lot?"

"Well, yes, quite a lot. Not as much as people used to, because we've got other ways of getting around. But yeah, there are a lot of things that still roll. All in all, the wheel – the axle – is one of the foundations of civilisation."

"Oh is it then? How is that we've managed to have a civilisation without it?"

"It depends on what you mean by civilisation."

"Well, what do you mean by it?" It was getting very hot out here, they weren't going anywhere, the baby was starting to moan, and Allaby's latest great suggestion was seeming less great by the moment."

"Well …" said Allaby.

And then Paintbrush said. "You know, it seems hotter when you're just sitting still than it does when you're walking. I think I'm going to put a blanket up or something. I take it, Granddad, that you're not even going to try to make a trolley." She went to her bedpit and started shaking the dust out of her blanket. The baby was further winding up for a cry. Everybody, Gibbous noticed, was getting very dirty. It would be worth reaching the mountains just so they could find some water and bathe.

"No, I'm not," Gibbous said loudly. "For a moment there I thought it might work. I was tempted to go back and give it a try just to see what would happen – just to build something interesting. But now I can see that it won't work, and Allaby doesn't need it anyway."

"Don't I?"

"Nah. You could be ready to walk tomorrow. You're only bruised now. Cracked ribs won't stop you, if you're careful."

"Are you sure about that?"

"Well, pretty sure. Or maybe the next day. Don't people ever get cracked ribs in the sky?"

"I guess sometimes they do. Maybe not as much as here because life's not so rough and the gravity isn't as strong, but then our bones are weaker than yours, also from the lower gravity, from growing up in it. It makes us taller than you, too."

Paintbrush, who was sitting in her bedpit with the blanket over her and the baby's heads, said, "What was it you grew up in, Allaby?"

"Lower gravity," Allaby said to the blanket. "In the, uh, sky, people are lighter."

"But you're not light," Gibbous said. "I know. I've just lifted you. And I've worked out that you're too heavy for a trolley."

"I'm not light here," Allaby said. "In fact, when we get stationed on Earth, we have to spend half a year just learning how to … how can I put it? … how to be heavy. Strengthening our muscles and our bones."

"Wait a minute," Gibbous said, "Just wait." He closed his eyes and tried to imagine what Allaby was getting at. But his concentration wasn't helped by the fact that the baby was now in full cry. Paintbrush would be going deaf under that blanket. "Feed him," Gibbous shouted.

"He's not hungry," came the shout back.

"Then why's he crying?"

"He's hot. I'm hot."

"Then come out from under the blanket."

"No, the sun's even worse. Damn it, Granddad, we'd be walking now if you hadn't let that cow step on Allaby. Allaby, don't tell him anything else that's new to him. He wants to know too much, and when he hears it, it confuses him and makes him grumpy. People in the sky being lighter makes perfect sense to me."

At that, everyone stopped shouting and just let the baby cry. Gibbous got up and stepped to the edge of the clearing. He threw his prairie dog bones into the grass and then wiped his hands on his shirt and stared at the horizon where the sun would eventually set and where – some day, at some point and with luck – hazy mountaintops would appear. About halfway between Gibbous and that damned blue-blank horizon a couple of white-headed eagles were doing the sky dance they do, flying way up, locking talons and then plunging towards the ground – unhooking before they actually hurt themselves, and flying up again. Was that really dancing – everybody always called it that – or was it the way eagles argue? Right now, that made more sense.

Paintbrush, as usual, was right. He'd been getting grumpy. On the other hand, Allaby was saying such damnable, maddening things. Gibbous had always been better than anybody he knew at working out problems and mysteries, but some of the things Allaby said only left his mind as helpless as the crying baby. How was it possible to be heavy in one place and light in some place else? A certain weight was a certain weight, just as – and Allaby had agreed with this last night – a certain time is a certain time and a distance a distance. The mountains get near only if you walk towards them. You have to cover a certain distance. You can't just sit here and expect, one morning, to wake up and see the mountaintops. That is, unless you get up high. You see farther the higher you get, but that doesn't get you any closer. Anyway, out here there was nothing to climb, and also anyway, his thoughts had wandered way off the point. Allaby's outrageous, impossible, offhand remarks had a way of making his thoughts do that.

The eagles had flown up high again. But this time they didn't dance or argue or do anything that involved locking talons. They'd finished with that and were simply soaring, almost wing to wing and, as if to taunt him, off in the direction of the mountains. Some small birds – hard to tell from here what kind they were, hardly more than dots – fluttered around them, the way small birds often do. The eagle on the right gave a pump of its wings and rose higher still, scattering the small birds as it veered away from the other eagle. It seemed to swim in the air, Gibbous thought, just as an odd second thought also swam into his head.

You're lighter in water than out of it.

Yes. Maybe it had something to do with that. Maybe the sky was water. The sky was about the same colour as water, and water came out of it sometimes, if not out of the blue part. But it was still something to think about. And it would answer why Allaby and the skypeople thought you couldn't breathe down here. Fish can't breathe out of water, and skypeople could be like fish, or think they're like fish. They look out of their watery sky and see dry land and think we can't breathe down there, and so whenever they do come here they wear a mask full of water. Of water.

Of course. And so when Allaby had his accident, when he fell out of the sky somehow, all the water leaked out of his mask, and Allaby didn't realise it until Paintbrush pointed out the hole – that hole at the back of his neck – where it had leaked out, and Allaby realised that he could breathe out of water. That was why he'd been so happy and also why he had to get to his house – why there in particular God only knew, but never mind – so that he could tell the other skypeople that they could breathe down here, could come live down here, among ordinary humans.

And that would be good, wouldn't it? Good for the people down here? Allaby, as maddening as he was, seemed a decent and peaceable man, and the others would probably be the same. Knowledge, Gibbous was pretty sure, made you that way. If you know the real truth about things – even if it was as confounding as Allaby's 'bang' (and as much as it irritated him, he suspected there was truth in it) – you don't do stupid things for bad reasons. You don't kill each other because of petty disputes. You don't go around believing in holy men and wiping out whole settlements because some boy missed with his arrow. They'd teach us things. We'd be travelling around on the backs of horses, pulling trolleys on axles and God knew what else.

So it really was necessary to get to Allaby's house or whatever and tell the skypeople that they could breathe here and were welcome. And if he, Gibbous Moon, could help Allaby get home, it would be the most important thing he'd done in his life – and all this after he'd had his funeral and was on his way to die.

But would skypeople really want to come here? Why?

Maybe because it's not so nice in the sky.

Now, that was a thought. It was something that had never occurred to him before – to him or anybody he knew. There was supposed to be a paradise up there. Why would anyone want to leave that to come here? But if they're all always swimming around in water, maybe they'd want to … Nah. Look at Allaby (which he turned around and did). He was sitting exactly where he'd been sitting a minute ago, his head bowed as he rummaged through his hair, picking things out of it. Look at him. He's been on the ground all of three days, and he's a wreck. Bones broken everywhere, scabs on his hands and lower legs, feet torn up, face pink as raw meat from the sun, his body host to every flea, tick, mite, biting fly, mosquito and grub on the Far Plain. Never in his life had Gibbous seen anyone attract itchers and biters the way Allaby did. Not even babies. Not even dogs. Gibbous himself hadn't had fleas since he was boy, and nowadays ticks, when they turned up, only turned up one or two at a time. But Allaby was infested with the damned things. If this was what the ground did to skypeople, the sky would have to be pretty damned bad for them to want to leave it.

The baby was only sobbing now (maybe it really was cooler under the blanket), and so Gibbous was able to say, in an almost normal voice, "Allaby, can I ask you something?"

Allaby, head still down, grunted, "Uh-huh."

"Do you like it here?"

"Where?" he said. "Right here?"

"No, I mean here on the ground. This world."

"On Earth?

"Earth, ground, yeah," Gibbous said.

"Put it this way," he said, raising his head and wincing. "It's the only place I ever wanted to be."

"Hmph." Gibbous looked beyond Allaby at the expanse of grass between him and the woods, at the sky and the birds and the grazing animals, the heat shimmers and the little finger of a whirlwind way off to the right, flicking up dust, and he thought he could almost see Allaby's point. Unlike Allaby, he didn't have a life in the sky to compare it with. He didn't even know what this world was like beyond the Far Plain, but most of his life and especially in the short but, he now realised, intense time when he thought he was walking to his death, he'd felt it was worthwhile being here. If Allaby, in his condition and with his experience of other places, could feel the same way, maybe this was as good as worlds got. It wasn't perfect, the way paradise was imagined to be, but you could be who you were and live here. Maybe the 'bang' thing did make a morass of worlds, but there were a lot of ways any or all of them could be worse than this. No, it wasn't perfect, but you could make yourself comfortable in it. So could the skypeople. And so could Allaby now. So, for that matter, could this whole group. "I've got an idea," Gibbous said. "Paintbrush, are you asleep under there?"

"Shh. No, Granddad." He could see that she was sitting and leaning forward, with her arms spread, turning herself and the blanket into a kind of root for the now sleeping baby. He went over and folded the blanket back, so that he could see her face at least. "Look, Paintbrush. Allaby. We're going to be stuck here for a while, and we're going to need shelter. I think I will go back to the woods, for some poles to hold blankets up with. I could get some extra water while I'm at it."

"How long do you think it'll take, Granddad?"

"If I start now, by the time I get there, do everything and get back, it might be pretty late, maybe even morning. But at least I don't have to build a trolley thing. At one point there, I thought that might have been something to do, but it wasn't very realistic. I'd have been a couple of days getting back, and you'd be roasted, and the axle wouldn't have worked anyway – though, I've got to say, Allaby, it was a pretty interesting idea. Interesting, yeah."

"You'd better go now, then, Granddad."

"Yeah. A couple of other things, though."

He paused, and Paintbrush and Allaby said together, "What?"

"Uh, there's plenty of food here and enough water in the skin," he said, as he picked up the axle, extracted it from the cowpats, knocked it clean and turned it back into a pipe. "I'll take this and Yellow and hunt for us two as we go. You be sure and keep the fire burning, Paintbrush, and …" He paused again.

"And what, Granddad?"

"Well, it'll be cold again tonight, and I think it'll be warmer and safer if you two sleep together."

"What?" Allaby said.

"Granddad, what do you mean?"

"I mean you should sleep together."

"But Granddad, I thought you didn't—"

"You would have anyway, wouldn't you?"

"Not if you didn't approve," Allaby said.

"You don't need to lie any more," Gibbous said.

"But we—"

"So just one thing before I go."

"Well, you'd better hurry, Granddad."

"I am – or was – a storyteller, right? And this used to be one of the storyteller's duties. And we're a new group now, a new tribe, and I'm appointing myself this tribe's storyteller."

"Fine, Granddad, but you'd better—"

"So, Paintbrush, come out from that blanket and stand beside Allaby. And Allaby, you've got to stand up again."

"Oh God," Allaby said. "Why?"

"Because I'm going to marry the two of you."

CHAPTER TWENTY

As it turned out, Simon had hardly been hurt at all. He hadn't lain on the hotel bed for more than about fifteen minutes – and the doctor hadn't been there for more than five – before his eyes fluttered open. And it had only taken about ten seconds more for the evillest scowl Jenny had ever seen on a face to install itself on Simon's.

"Where is that woman?" he said in a low voice as he sat up. He'd had to ask because by this time the room was packed with soldiers, and Jenny, even though she was handcuffed, was being pressed against a wall by six or seven of them – full Earth strength was obviously something they didn't know much about, and it obviously worried them.

"Over there," a soldier said.

"Bring her here."

Jenny resisted, not because she thought there would be any point in it but, as much as anything, to see how many of the soldiers it really would take to get her to Simon's bedside. The answer was five, two on each arm and one pushing. What she'd noticed most as they ground and dragged her towards the bed wasn't so much Simon's scowl or what he was saying to her ("… opportunity of a lifetime – of a hundred lifetimes – and you threw it in my face, with your fist. Well, we don't need you. Not any more. You can go rot with the rest …") as the consternation on the face of the doctor, not for Simon, who was about to be injected with something (the pansy – it had only been a punch in face and a little cut), but for her and for the whole bustling room – soldiers going in and out, examining this, opening that, signalling out the window, talking to each other, talking on their comms kits, looking Jenny over, nudging each other, swinging their guns and generally getting out of the way of Jenny and her team of escorts. The doctor was a nice-looking, open-faced man with a wide forehead and fringe of beard in the Ganymedian fashion. Then she couldn't see him – a soldier suddenly had her in a headlock – but she'd seen enough. The doctor was Ganymedian, and that, somehow, in a room full of Mooners, was a straw of hope.

She didn't really have the time to think any more deeply about the doctor or his home moon – just to go from his round face and brown eyes looking deeply into hers as he stepped towards her to a picture of Ganymede sliding in its orbit around Jupiter, innocent of Peter's old Immyo and of the disturbances here and God knew where else in the Solar System. That was it: just a moon among several moons and a giant planet safely on the other side of the sun.

And the image was still there when she started coming to. But she was seeing it from a different perspective now. She saw it the way she could see the whole Solar System in the Tharsis City planetarium, with dominant Jupiter and its sixteen moons in a riot of orbits but with sturdy Ganymede the largest of the lot – even larger than, way over there, Mercury, and way over in the other direction, Pluto (not counting Charon). And then there was Mars, such a tidy little planet with two neat little moons. And on the other side of Jupiter, Saturn, not quite as big but with much more decoration – the coloured rings and the shepherds and even more moons than Jupiter. And the largest of those is impenetrably grey Titan, origin of Peter Allaby. Where is Peter? Peter's dead, particled. Vanished. Whooph. But where am I? Where am … That goddamned bastard Ganymedian doctor gave me a shot of something and knocked me out.

"Is that what happened, honey?" a voice said. It seemed to be right at her ear, if not inside her head, but was still barely audible against a huge din of other human voices.

"Did I say that out loud?" Jenny opened her eyes.

"Loud enough, honey." Right in front of Jenny's face was the face of a young woman – pale and lipsticked with long ringlets of blonde hair fanning out around her head. The woman's face was so close to hers that Jenny couldn't see where the hair ended. Was this a new style, she wondered vaguely. And who was making all that noise? The woman said, half shouting, "They shouldn't have done that. They shouldn't just throw you in here unconscious and handcuffed. You could really hurt yourself. I've been watching out for you, though."

"What? Where …" Jenny turned her head, effectively turning her whole body. People – men and women – were everywhere, all floating and almost all talking or shouting, a noise compounded by incessant echoes. Then it dawned on her: they were in the free-fall gym, right at the centre of EHQS. It was the hub of the wheel that, in turning, gave centrifugal force and thus gravity to the rest of the satellite. But the hub, of course, couldn't have gravity. So it was used as a recreation facility, with parallel bars and rings, free-fall trampolines and free-fall game courts, all inside six vast polished wooden walls or floors or whatever you wanted to call them. Most of the EHQS residents used the gym from time to time (there weren't many other ways of getting exercise on the satellite), and lot of tourists visited EHQS for no other reason. There was no other place like it in the Solar System.

"Yeah, it's the gym," the woman said, hovering back in front of Jenny's face. "We're all locked in here, about a thousand of us it looks like. Certainly all us working girls are here, and a lot more besides."

"Working girls?"

"Yeah, they rounded us up, every single one of us. Nobody knows what they're going to do to us. They're fruitcakes, those people. My name's Louise."

"Jenny," Jenny said.

The top of a man's head bumped the top of Louise's head, and the two of them bounced away from each other. Louise was holding Jenny's arms, though, and so Jenny drifted with her, until in a few seconds their feet found someone's back, and they stabilised a little.

"It's awful," Louise said. "They threw food in a couple of times, and people batted it around trying to catch it. And it was all breaking open and crumbling and going everywhere. Look." She reached out. "Here's a raisin. You want a raisin?"

Jenny shook her head.

Louise swallowed the raisin. "It's the only way to eat now. But you've got to look before you grab because of the horrible toilet situation. Those doors are locked, too. So not everything floating around is food. You can tell by the smell."

Jenny had been aware of a smell, but it was a bit down the list of suddenly awakened and assaulted senses. She sniffed. "Ew," she said. "Jesus. How long have people been in here?"

"Well, I've been here about three days. It wasn't so crowded at first, but more and more people keep getting thrown in. You're the first I've seen in handcuffs, though. And the first unconscious one. People sleep, of course, but they go to sleep knowing where they are. I thought, that poor woman. She'll wake up in here not knowing she's here. So I sort of … Well, I just happened to be floating by Portal C a couple of hours ago when they threw you in. I know your uniform – it's Earth Ranger, isn't it? I see some of them when you people have your convention. I see some of them hanging

207

on the back of my chair, too – and I thought you deserved respect and help. I've always liked Earth Rangers. They're gentlemen and pay in advance. Anyway, you'd vomited – that's all floating around, too, somewhere, along with all the other vomit – and it looked like there was still some in your mouth. I thought you were going to choke and die. I had to clear your mouth and throat with my fingers."

"Oh God, sorry," said Jenny. "Sorry. But thanks."

A woman sailed past screaming, followed by another one who was apparently trying to catch her. "Don't worry," Louise shouted over the screaming. "I have to do worse than that all the time. Sometimes I think hooking's a lot like being a doctor. You know, dealing with bodily stuff … Oh, Isobel, hi." Louise grabbed the ankle of a woman who was passing above their heads and pulled her down to them, or them up to her. Whichever, the gesture set the three of them into motion, and they were slowly cruising now, head-first. "I was telling Jenny here how hookers are like doctors."

Hookers are more honest than doctors, Jenny thought. That Ganymedian had looked so nice, and so concerned.

"Oh that chestnut," Isobel said. She was quite a bit older than Louise, had short dyed black hair and the sharp, hard face that long-time whores are supposed to have. "I like a girl in a uniform," she said to Jenny. "Ooh, and handcuffs, too."

Jenny looked at her handcuffs and shrugged. Then something very obvious occurred to her for the first time. In the hotel room, her hands had been cuffed behind her. Now they were in front. Those guys hadn't just forgotten to take them off. They must have gone to the trouble of unlocking them, taking them off, moving her arms and putting them on again. It was more comfortable with them in front, but why do it at all? Was it some sinister way of being nice? They'd knocked her out. They didn't need to put … But no. They wouldn't bother to do that. "My hands are in front," she said absently

"Oh, I fixed that first thing," Louise said. "You know – put your legs through your arms? It's easy in here."

In that case, she thought, thank God for Louise, who now had one arm hooked in Jenny's and was carrying her along as she talked to Isobel, mostly about the toilet situation, the food situation and the what-are-they-going-to-do-to-us situation.

They finally floated to a stop in a relatively unpopulated space at about the centre of the gym. The nearest hovering bodies were six or seven metres away, and Jenny had a chance to take in almost the whole scene. Louise was right – you'd have to say there were about a thousand people in here. Jenny had once taken a course that touched on fluid dynamics and Brownian motion, and this seemed to illustrate some principle or other that she couldn't exactly name any more. But it was like solids in a solution, gently stirred. People – arms and legs moving as though they were slowly drowning, others in conglomerations of bodies – seemed to be rotating, overall, clockwise. That was from one perspective, beyond her feet. When she bent her head back and looked from that perspective, they were moving anti-clockwise – along, of course, with all the inert things: pieces of food, containers, clothes, shoes, socks, a belt over there, a dental plate, turds – lots of turds – blobs and hazes of liquid (could be anything but was probably mainly vomit, blood and pee), and just bits and bits of things: things that come out of people's pockets and off their straps, from pens to handkerchiefs to cards to money to combs to comms kits. It really was like being part of a liquid solution of humans, their artifacts and their excretions. And it was obvious by the stench that the vents weren't coping. People might even start suffocating at some point. Whose perverse idea had it been to throw this many people into what amounted to a free-fall dungeon? And, for Christ's sake, why? Never mind what they're planning to do with us all – we'll know that soon enough – but why in hell are they doing it?

"Are you talking to us or yourself?" Imogen said.

"Did I say ... Not again. Sorry."

Louise said, "She was slagging some doctor the last time she did that. She was really giving it to him. What doctor was it, Jenny?"

"Sorry. Nothing. Nobody. Just some Ganymedian. He gave me a knock-out shot. I guess that's how I got here."

"A Ganymedian doctor?" Imogen said. "Was it Dr Ferrer? Omar Ferrer? There can't be two Ganymedian doctors on this satellite. There can't be much more than two Ganymedians period, except for some tourists. Where were you?"

"In a hotel room. The Collins."

"Yeah, it was Omar," Imogen said. "He's the Collins Hotel doctor. He does us girls when we want to work the Collins – you know, the inspections. I like being inspected by him. He's one of the good ones. He talks to you. They're all some funny religion, Ganymedians, but they treat ladies with respect. "

"I've never worked the Collins," Louise said. "I usually work the Bean when I work a hotel. But I don't really like working hotels that much. I like—"

Jenny said, "He's one of the good ones?" She surprised herself with her obsession about the doctor. Hell, she'd only even seen him for a few seconds. If she was obsessing about anyone, it ought to have been Simon. Him or herself, for God's sake. But she'd briefly seen the doctor, this Omar, as a spark of hope, and then he was the one who'd …

"Yeah," said Imogen. "I offered him a freebie once, and he turned me down, and in a really nice way. Men don't come much better than that."

"Then why is he helping those bastards?"

"Search me. Maybe …" Imogen said, and it was the last thing she said. Something had started them drifting again, and suddenly they were in a whole tangle of people. Jenny thought she saw Imogen's foot (the same foot Louise had first grabbed to pull Imogen, as it were, into existence) sticking out from under a man's armpit, and then other arms, legs, heads and torsos intervened in front of that, and Imogen was gone. Louise was still there because she was holding on to Jenny's arms but, even so, a leg had come down between them – a woman's bare leg and foot – and after that had been extracted, Louise had had to hold Jenny in a hug. This was just as well because it brought their mouths to each other's ears, the only way they would ever be able to hear each other over the clamour of voices in the tangle. A lot of voices were in a rage, a lot in a fright, and almost all were cursing. Jenny, over Louise's shoulder and through curls of hair, stared right into the close-up and upside-down face of a deranged-looking, sweating man who was shouting, "Get away! Get the hell away. Get away from me …"

"Can we get away," Jenny said to Louise's ear.

"I'll try," squealed Louise. "But I was caught in one of these for an hour yesterday."

Jenny could feel Louise pushing with her legs, and so Jenny pushed, too, but they didn't seem to be budging – that, or the whole ball of people, the whole wriggling moonlet of them, was moving all at once in the same direction. "What's stopping us?" Jenny said.

"My shirt's caught on something. Can you see?"

Jenny looked down Louise's back and, sure enough, a hand was holding her shirt tail. "Let go," she shouted at the hand. "Let that shirt go." Through hair that, maddeningly, she couldn't bat away, she tried to follow the hand along the arm to a head and face, but in a tangle of arms there were four faces down there – three men's and a woman's – a crying woman's. She tried to concentrate, to cool her thinking, and she followed the arm again, got to the shoulder and this time thought she got to the right face. It was the same sweaty man who had been and was still shouting, "Get away!" This time, though, the face was right side up, and she recognised it.

Just then Louise gave another push – a leap – with her legs, and Jenny, startled and shocked by what she was seeing, instinctively gave a mighty push, too. They tore loose from both Louise's shirt and the human ball. They'd sprung free and, with Louise still hugging tight, were speeding towards another side of the gym. But Louise's shirt, presumably, was still in the human ball, still being clutched by that demented man. That wouldn't matter much to Louise, who turned out to be wearing some kind of chemise, but Jenny was going to have to convince her that they had to go back anyway – not for the shirt, of course, but for the man who was holding it. The face Jenny had recognised was Gus Templeton's.

CHAPTER TWENTY-ONE

"Get away!" Gus shouted again. "Get away from me."

"Gus, Gus, look at me. It's Jenny Romero. Come on. Come with us."

His pupils disappeared under the tops of his eyelids, leaving just the whites. In trying to jerk away he nearly pulled them back into the mass of bodies, something it had just taken an hour to extract him from.

"Try to hold on to him," Louise said, "and I'll hold on to you."

Holding his arm wasn't easy. It was bad enough that her wrists were cuffed, but he tried to thrash every time he was touched. So as Louise continued to grasp the ankles of both Jenny and Gus, Jenny put her hands around Gus's neck. The eyeballs stayed blank. "Okay," Jenny shouted, "now work your way up me!"

"Wait," said Louise. "My feet are touching something. Stiffen your body. Can you do that?"

"Okay."

"Okay. You ready? I'm going to push."

Gus was trying to say something – "Get away!" no doubt – but the way Jenny was holding his neck meant that the handcuff chain was pressing against his adam's apple, and so he just gasped and moved his lips. In the process of general stiffening, she realised she had stiffened her grip – it was hard not to. Anyway, being strangled seemed to subdue him a little. He stopped thrashing, and his pupils returned as his eyes popped. Then Louise pushed, and as they were moving again, Jenny could feel Louise slowly – trying not to reduce their momentum too much – climbing up the backs of her legs and then her back.

"Don't kill him," Louise said, putting her arms under Jenny's and clasping her wrists in front. "Not after all the trouble we had getting him. I hope he turns out to be worth it."

"That'll depend," Jenny said, relaxing her grip a little, "on whether he's still got a mind in there. Gus, do you recognise me? It's Jenny. And this is my friend Louise. Don't think you should recognise her, but it's her shirt you tore off." Gus's pupils were still there, but they didn't seem to be receiving anything. And it was pretty certain that his ears weren't operating either. She wondered if indeed he did have a mind left. It would be bad enough seeing anybody in such a state, but Gus Templeton, every Ranger's rock? A free-fall dungeon was, of course, not the sanest place to find yourself in, and the enormous gym was echoing with angry shouting and demented screaming. But Gus Templeton? He'd seen her through her training, her apprenticeship, her first posting … "Gus, please. Focus your eyes. It's Jenny."

"Look up," Louise said. "We're not that far from a wall."

Jenny craned her head back and looked. Not only was a wall coming obliquely towards them, but the part of the wall with the exercise bars and hand-swings. In the days when this was nothing but a gym, people would use these to launch themselves across the room to a similar set on the other side. It was hard to imagine now, but that used to be fun. Now the bars and swings were dense with people hanging on. She bent her neck a little farther and could see that there was a least one struggle in progress, between a thin man who was hanging on a hand-swing and a fat man who wanted to. But a lot of people in this place were losing all judgment, because not far from the two men was about a three-metre stretch of bar that was unoccupied.

"See that?" Jenny said to Louise.

"See what?"

"That bare piece of bar. Look where I'm looking."

"Uh, oh yeah."

"Can we get there?"

"We'll have to push against some of those people, but I think so."

In fact, there wasn't going to be any choice. They were heading right for another body-ball, differing from Gus's former one only by not circulating through the gym – it was anchored to a hand-swing and was doing a slow pendulum. Whatever the cause of Gus's state of mind, Jenny was pretty sure that being caught in one of those things – and God knew how long he'd been there – hadn't helped, and what was important now was that, if he could see at all, he didn't see another one coming. She held his neck so that he was facing firmly away from it and towards her face. He'd at least given up thrashing and was now just limp and staring – though what at was indecipherable and probably not in this universe. The body-ball was getting closer.

213

"Get ready," Louise said. "Don't give anybody a chance to grab us. There's a nice broad back right ahead. I'm going to have to change my grip here."

The hands that Louise had clasped in front of Jenny were now manoeuvred into one arm crooked around Jenny's neck, the other arm presumably free to push. The groaning, shouting and cursing from the ball – which a moment ago had only been part of the general din – had now become more specific. People just wouldn't stop holding on to each other. Each person wanted everybody to let go of that particular person, but nobody wanted to let go of whoever he or she was holding. It was a contained and permanent panic – a fear-fuelled implosion, the inverse of a stampede to the exits.

They were right at the broad back now, and Louise let their momentum carry them a little bit farther, so that she could bend her elbow and aim, and then she gave a gentle push that sent the pendulum swinging away and herself, Jenny and Gus on a straight trajectory feet first towards the vacant stretch of bar. "You're getting pretty good at this," Jenny said.

"Yeah," said Louise. "I always knew I must have a talent for something besides what I do. I never imagined flying, though."

They passed a wall of people hanging off the bar at all angles, passed under (from their perspective) the two men still fighting over the hand-swing – which was veering wildly as each held on with one hand while trying to punch the other with the other – and reached their target. Jenny let her feet touch the wall about half a metre beyond the bar and then crossed her ankles as she bounced back. Louise, as far as she could tell, had done the same thing, and they both swung into a sort of sitting position, crossing their legs at the knees. Gus, who was as limp as somebody who'd just died (he hadn't, Jenny assured herself, he hadn't), had swung in another direction and was now perpendicular to her, legs straight out and feet in the face of the next man along the bar. When the man pushed the feet away – and he pushed hard – it almost caused Jenny to lose her grip on Gus's neck, but even though it made her cuffed wrists hurt to do it, she was able to pull Gus into a kind of crumpled position between the bar and the wall. She held him there.

"I won't be able keep this up," Jenny said. "We've got to anchor him somehow."

"He's wearing a belt, isn't he?" Louise said.

"Uh, yeah."

"Can you take it … No, you can't do it with those things on. Just hold him. I guess this is something else I'm pretty good at."

Louise came around to face Jenny and then, hanging on to the bar with one hand, reached Gus's belt, undid it and pulled it off so fast that it reminded Jenny of the old trick with the tablecloth – where you yank it away without disturbing the crockery. Then, holding on to the bar with her legs, she turned it over, passed it back through Gus's rear belt loop and buckled it around the bar. With some relief, Jenny let go of Gus's neck, and he hovered between the two women, secured by the seat of his trousers. Louise then pulled his face towards hers, upside-down, and peered at it.

"You didn't kill him, did you?" She put her ear to his mouth and then looked up and said, "No, I can hear breathing. Whew. I had a guy die in my bed once. I couldn't believe it. He lay there all night, and I kept listening like that, hoping he was just kidding or that I'd made a mistake." She squinted at Gus again. "But if you just had his eyes to go by, you might think he was … You know what I bet he needs? We don't know how long he was caught in that thing. He probably needs some water."

"God, how are we going to manage that?" Jenny said, realising suddenly how thirsty she was herself.

"When we first got here, they threw in water bottles with the food, but I haven't seen any bottles for a while, not any full ones, and I finished my last one hours ago. There are water fountains in here, though. Somewhere."

Jenny looked along the part of the wall they were on for a sign of one of the water fountains spotted here and there around the gym. No pipes jutted out – she knew that – in case people got hurt by bumping against them. They were just holes in the wall – valves – each marked by a blue circle and accompanied by a strap. You approached it like a bee to a flower – holding on to the strap, putting your mouth to the valve, pressing it with your tongue and sucking. But now a strap would be another of the room's precious purchase points, with the bonus of a water source beside it. If you wanted to spot a fountain now, you'd have to look for somebody smack against the wall in a place where there weren't any bars, hand-swings or other gym equipment. So she looked, and sure enough, about fifty metres away, near the junction with another wall, was a crowd of a dozen or so people holding on to each other, but in an organised way – not so much a body ball as an undulating body pancake. Pointing with both hands, she said, "I think that could be a fountain there, by that bunch of people. The oncs at the corner." And as she spoke, she noticed that a woman in the group did appear to havc her face to the wall. "Yeah, someone's drinking. Look."

Louise, who had swung around to face in the same direction Jenny was facing, said, "Oh yeah. Okay. I'll go get some."

"What'll you carry it in?"

"I don't know. I'll find something. There are a lot of empty bottles floating around. Stay here and don't let anybody take my bit of bar." She looked back at Jenny and laughed. "You know, we've got a saying – whatever you do, don't lose your place at the bar. I never thought it would ever mean this kind."

Holding on, she drew her feet up under her, looked, let go and launched. There was no gravity in here, but there was air, which meant slight air resistance and a tendency for people's clothes to billow as they floated or sailed. Louise's chemise was very loose-fitting, and as she progressed towards the water fountain she looked as if she were being carried there by balloon. As Jenny watched, she had a chance to realise how grateful she was to the woman, and then when some bodies intervened and blocked her view of Louise, she had a chance to wonder – for the first time, practically, since she'd woken up in here – what this was all for.

Okay, there'd been a coup d'état. That was clear. A coup d'état involving Simon and his strange, unpleasant people. And in coups d'état citizens often get rounded up and imprisoned in some way or another. In the history of Mars there'd been a few coups, and on the Moon, too. Such things happen. There must have been a coup on the Moon this time and on EHQS, too, as the Moon's only inhabited outlying dominion, a place where elements of the overthrown establishment might otherwise retreat to and regroup. That much made sense. From there on, though, as far as Jenny could see, nothing did.

"I'll bet you know," she said to Gus. "I wish you'd get your damned mind back." He'd swivelled on his belt so that he was now facing flat against the wall. Probably the best thing for him, Jenny thought, holding herself to the bar by her crossed legs and cuffed hands and more or less sitting at Gus's feet. The less he can see of this place – if he can see anything at all – the more likely he is to come around, maybe. Just the same, she nudged him by the ankle and got him away from the wall and on the same general plane that she was. I'll call this 'up', she told herself. Then she leaned forward, pulled him into something resembling a sitting position, gave him a tap on the cheek and looked him in the vacant eye. "Gus, for God's sake, wake up." On the other hand, what if he woke up and didn't turn into Gus but into that maniac he'd been earlier?

Getting him out of that body-ball had been one of the most complicated and, yes, dangerous things she'd ever had to do. And she'd been charged by buffalo twice, had stepped on a Nile crocodile once and once had fought off an attack by hyenas. But nothing like that ever compared to the dangers humans could manufacture. It was only Louise – a real fighter – who had made rescuing Gus possible. In fact, to everybody's gratitude, she and Jenny had broken up the whole body-ball mélange. One elderly weeping woman, before drifting away, had kissed Jenny on the forehead and said she'd been caught in the ball for a whole day and that Gus – who Jenny, at this point, had been holding by the ankle – had been there at least as long as she had. "He's gone crazy," she'd said helpfully.

Peter had gone crazy, too, she now reminded herself, and she'd been right there on the comms while he was doing it (at the time, she thought he was only getting drunk). Somehow, he managed to destroy everything he lived for and then, for all practical purposes, to kill himself. She couldn't let that happen to Gus as well. She had needed to save him.

"Gus," she said, pulling his head towards her so that she didn't have to shout. "I don't care if you're not hearing me. I'm going to talk to you anyway. I remember being embarrassed when you made me talk to Peter when I didn't think he was listening, and because of it I probably didn't say what I probably should have said. I don't know what that would have been, but what I did say wasn't enough to talk him out of killing himself, if he actually was listening. So I'm just going to say what I think now – or tell you what it is I don't understand about this mess – and if you want to come to at any point and set me straight, feel free."

She looked up to see if Louise was on her way back yet, but there'd been a surge of bodies between Jenny and the fountain, and so there was no way of telling. She looked back at Gus looking at nothing. "The only thing that's clear to me is that there's been a coup, a coup on the Moon, not just on this satellite, or the Lunar Army would have been here by now sorting those bastards out. I also realise that after a coup, certain people get rounded up and thrown in prisons – makeshift ones usually and this is about as makeshift as they come.

"And the people they round up are usually people who might conceivably threaten the new, what will we call it, regime, or likely at least

217

to be hostile to it. So I can understand why I'm here. God, Gus, I've met the guy who goes around calling himself the prophet. He brought me up from my station to do something for him – I've never had any idea what – but in the end I just hit him, knocked him out. So if nobody else was floating around in here, I would be. And I imagine you must have put up some resistance, too, and so it can't be much of surprise that you're here. I can even understand Louise being here. People like Simon – that's the name of the new prophet, in case you don't know – don't like people like Louise, or the idea of them anyway, and so those are the first people they go for. They see themselves as cleaning up morals. I mean, historically, people who overthrow democracies are always very moral, in a perverse sort of way.

"But, Gus, tell me this. Why are all these other people here? Why so many? Louise and I reckoned there were about a thousand, but when I look around now I think it's closer to two. Gus, that's about the whole population of the satellite, maybe with a few tourists thrown in. I floated past a guy I recognised who's an oxygen synthesiser. What threat is he to them, and why isn't he at work synthesising oxygen? There are probably hydroponic farmers here. How are Simon and those stupid bastards going to eat? What's the point of taking over and ruling a place if all your subjects are in the dungeon? And why, if Simon's the prophet, isn't he prophesying on the Moon? And the biggest question of all is who the hell is he? Who the hell are they?"

Jenny had worked herself up so much (while Gus had been worked up not at all) that she had failed to notice the arrival of Louise, at least not until the back of Louise's head interposed itself in front of Gus's face. Then she was doing something to his face. Jenny twisted around to see: she was kissing him. And still kissing him. Jenny had time to say, "Louise ..." before Gus suddenly pulled his head back and choked violently, spraying water into Louise's face and throwing himself into reverse so hard that he almost tore off his belt loop.

"Damn," said Louise. "He wasted it." She looked at Jenny with sparkling water droplets floating off her nose and cheeks. "I couldn't catch a bottle without going way off course. So all I could do is bring the water here in my mouth. Now it's wasted."

Gus choked and coughed until one final spurt of liquid shot out. Then he groaned.

"He's made a sound, Jenny. That's something."

218

It was then Jenny noticed that Gus was looking at her, actually looking at her. And he opened his mouth, cleared his throat and, in a sleepy, croaky voice, actually spoke: "Jenny, don't you know? They're Back-to-Earthers."

"Hah," Louise said. "All we needed was to make him choke."

CHAPTER TWENTY-TWO

The little blue light on the panel went on. In the sensor studio, the Eminently Reverend Caleb Hook, standing behind the pulpit and wearing his highest-occasion regalia, concentrated on the focus point, aware that he would be watched by absolutely everyone today, even the Lazarines. The Government hadn't made any kind of statement yet. The Head of Station had overruled the Scientific Committee and – on faith, as it were – left that to the Church, to him. The little yellow light went on. And that was just as well, because Caleb at the moment (but for not much longer) was probably the only person on Titan who knew the truth, and he was, in a way, still awed by it. The little green light went on.

"Good morning," he said. "Thy Kingdom come, Thy will be done, on Earth as it is in Heaven. My theme today is what is Earth and what is Heaven." He did his start-of-sermon pause, looking hard at the focus point.

"Let's begin with Heaven," he said. "It's a place none of us knows anything about – except that God, Jesus and the angels reside there, along with the souls of the faithful. It's not of this Universe or defined by any of the eleven known dimensions. It's not any place we could ever go physically, and it's certainly not anywhere in this Solar System. It is definitely not, as some people preach and seem to believe, the Earth. The Earth is only a planet – the most blessed of all our planets, but a planet just the same. So if anyone believes he saw a human in a holopark transmission yesterday morning, that's exactly what he saw, a human, not a soul, because souls can't be seen by the living. In my researches last night, I discovered how a human came to be there, and I'll get to that presently. But bear with me for a few minutes, because first I want to talk about the Earth, how it began and what it is now.

"The Earth was the third thing God created, after the sun, when He said, 'Let there be light,' and after the firmament – the sky and the stars, which are taken to include our splendid planet Saturn. That in itself is a wonderful stroke of creation. Saturn is something every Titanian has a duty to see at least once in his or her life – not in a picture, not in an ultrahologram, but at the very least from the window of the Keepers of Jerusalem's holy

220

excursion ship as it lifts above our orange atmosphere. At the same time – many of you know this, but some may not – you'll be able to see the Sun. It isn't as it is from Earth, as seen in the holoparks, but small and distant. Nevertheless, it's so strong that it ties our magnificent Saturn – and us – into an eternal orbit, so that we'll always have a set place in the Universe and always be safely in the same Solar System as our holy mother planet, the Earth. Praise God."

Caleb bowed his head, a cue for everybody attending the holoservice to do the same. It was a silent prayer, during which it was understood that everyone would thank God for the existence of, well, everything. But what Caleb himself was being grateful for – to God, of course, but also his own resourcefulness – was the Church vaults and the sacred safe there that hadn't been opened in more than a thousand years, was never supposed to be opened, under pain of damnation, and was opened last night by a safecracker he'd borrowed from the Jerusalem Penitentiary. Caleb was sure that, under the circumstances – mainly a threat of civil unrest – God would forgive him and suspend the hellfire. He was very tired, though. He'd been up all night both planning this sermon and trying to decipher Ancient English.

After about thirty seconds, Caleb opened his eyes, raised his head, stared at the focus point again and said, "God is glorious. On the third day, after He'd created the Sun, the Solar System and the rest of the Universe – after, so to speak, He'd set the stage – He said, 'Let the waters under the heavens be gathered together into one place, and let the land appear.' Note 'the waters'. The orbit He'd chosen for his pinnacle of creation was exactly the right distance from the Sun for water to exist mainly as liquid. Life as we know it, as we are it, could never have come to exist without liquid water and a combination of liquid water and land. Land, earth – the Earth.

"Between the third day and the fifth day, life evolved. Now let's pause here to think of the meaning of a day to an immortal entity. In the long history of Church and the even longer history of the Bible, there have been disputes between those who insist that God's day was an actual Earth day – the time it takes for that planet to revolve once – and those who say that a day to God is simply the time it takes for Him to perform a particular task. All of you, including the Lazarines who may be attending this morning, know the stance of the Keepers of Jerusalem on this question. We say that an Earth day is meaningless to God, except as part of the maintenance of life on his chosen planet."

With so many Lazarines listening, Caleb hadn't been able to resist the opportunity to taunt them a little on basic doctrine. Much of what he'd said already – that Earth isn't Heaven, in particular – would have them frothing, but they wouldn't dare switch off before hearing about the man in the holoparks. Caleb had realised during the course of the night that he was in the best position he'd ever been to talk to and influence Lazarines from the pulpit of Titan's established church. In fact, if all this weren't so essentially serious, he'd almost be tempted to smile.

"We on Titan should have a special sympathy with that view – because, if we're to be honest, an Earth day, Earth time, should perhaps be meaningless to us as well. It has nothing to do with how long it takes Titan to revolve, and an Earth year doesn't reflect the time it takes this moon to go around Saturn, or for Saturn to orbit the Sun. The only reason Earth time means anything to us is that ever since our ancestors established a station here, we've always used it. I know that some of the more extreme Titanists want to impose a system of Titan time, but it would make our days too long, our years too short or much too long – longer than three or four generations, if we chose to measure time by Saturn's orbit. The surviving colonies on the Moon and Ganymede take similar views to ours. Only on Mars, where conditions and scales are very like the Earth's, do people commonly use that planet's own time, and they still refer to Earth time when they're being technical or formal or dealing with the other worlds.

"But does God use Earth time? The God of the whole Universe? The Bible says it took two days to create all the life on Earth before the appearance of man, but we know for a fact that that actually took four and half billion years. For God, though, who has all the time there is and will ever be, would there really be any difference among two days, two weeks, two years and four and a half billion years?"

This was getting well off the track, of course, but that wasn't necessarily a bad thing at the beginning of a sermon. It lulled people, encouraged their minds to wander, even bored them a little and calmed them down. Besides, it was another point of contention with the Lazarines, whose line on God and time was that, God being God, He could do anything he wanted in whatever time he decided. If He wanted to run through all evolution in one second, He could do that. So if the Bible said a day, a day it was. The Keepers had long rejected this view as unscientific, and in Caleb's personal opinion, the Lazarines made the deity seem like some hocus-pocus magician.

"Besides," Caleb said, "it's pleasing – the idea of God taking four and a half billion years. It shows how much He cared, how He laboured over every single detail – every leaf, every insect, every monster that he tried, found wanting and allowed to go extinct – how thorough he was in his preparation for the advent of humanity. And when humans did arrive, they found themselves in a world that was absolutely perfect for them, in Eden, in Paradise. But as we know, however perfect God's Earth was, the humans He created – He allowed to evolve – were less than perfect. Now, that wasn't His fault. His ambition was to populate the Earth with creatures that lived by the same laws that governed the rest of life on the planet but were also like little gods themselves, capable of independence, capable of predicting the future, of knowing about and preparing for their own mortality.

"They had the power, they had the ability and the talent and the intellect, but they lacked something – basic morality, I say, something wrong at the interface between the animal and the god – and they behaved in ways that were against their own best interests and the interests of the planet God had so carefully crafted. So He decided to gather, as it were, a seed bank of humans and to wipe the rest out and start again. That was the Great Flood, and Noah and his family were the seed bank. That remedy worked for a little while, until humans proliferated again and went back to their old ways. The stick hadn't worked, and so this time he tried the carrot. He had a Son and gave Him the power to forgive all the people for their endless transgressions, cruelties and sheer stupidities and to have him take upon himself the punishment for all of that."

Caleb took out his handkerchief, dabbed at the corners of his mouth and put it back in his pocket. "But that didn't work either, not well enough. A great religion was founded on Jesus and purveyed his story and his teachings and his sufferings far into the future, but people – and even Christians themselves, often – generally reverted to what was beginning to seem simply innate human ways. And this time it was much worse than ever. This time humans proliferated to the point that they became, in their combined weight, the most massive single form of life on the planet. They couldn't control their reproduction. There were six billion of them – then quickly ten billion, twelve billion. They ransacked the planet of its resources. Species of life that God had so painstakingly created and committed to their care died out in millions simply for the lack of places to live.

"We think of the Earth today as paradise – some of you even regard it as Heaven – but the people then just took it as the world that they happened to find themselves in and abused it at their pleasure. So God went back to the stick, and He struck again. This time it was a new, fast-travelling, thoroughly lethal virus. It was also very specific. It only affected humans and a few other primates, even though it could replicate itself in almost any animal – as though the animals themselves were taking revenge. As we all know, the virus – the disease, the Abunga – wiped out Earthly humanity in a matter of days.

"But as we also know and are thankful for, God kept His seed banks again. Humans, by this time, had colonised other bodies in the Solar System, and all but three of them are still going. We've all heard the old story of the horrible demise of the stations on Io, Callisto and Europa – extremely hostile moons of Jupiter where humans couldn't last without constant support from the Earth and the other colonies. To this day, a stain remains on the name of the people of Ganymede, the only other colonised moon of Jupiter, for never going to their rescue. It's unfair, undoubtedly, for present-day Ganymedians to continue to bear that ancient blame, but they still do, and they feel the guilt themselves, which may be why they're so inward and isolated.

"But you know that, most of you. Most of you already know most of what I've been telling you. But I felt a reprise would be a good idea before I tell you something you definitely don't know, something that goes all the way back to the Great Apocalypse and will explain what many of you saw and all of you have heard about. It will explain the human in the holoparks."

Caleb, who had been delivering sermons since he was thirteen years old, felt a pang of something he hadn't felt since he was, well, thirteen years old – stage fright. He paused now and wondered why. Even while planning the sermon, he'd felt that pang when he'd reached this point. Maybe it was because theology and a little history are a standardised mix – codified and ritualised. Almost never, in delivering a sermon, did he ever say anything that hadn't already been said innumerable times. And now he was getting ready to tell a story that, as far as every Titanian was concerned, was brand new. He coughed into his fist, took a long breath, stared hard and went on.

"All along, God has had another seed bank. This is the truth, and before I tell you any more, I'll tell you my source. It's the log of one of our ancient forebears – Colonel Albert A. Schwinn, Head of Station from 2172 to 2190." Caleb extracted the stack of paper from the tray in the pulpit. He held it up for a moment and then put it in front of himself, beside his notes, and turned to the page that he'd marked. "This, the relevant section of the log, was written in 2176, twenty-three years after the Apocalypse. I found it last night in a safe in the Church crypt." This was tricky. The existence of the Forbidden Safe, as well as the fact that it was forbidden, was only ever known to Church elders. At the risk of outraging the Chief Deacon and few others, he couldn't very well stop and explain that the safe was forbidden and then explain that he'd had it opened anyway on the grounds that sometimes there's a point when forbiddenness runs out. He'd been forced, for the common good and to quell the nascent uprising already being provoked by the Back-to-Earthers, to discover what that man in the holoparks was. He took another deep breath – God, he was nervous – and went on.

"This is a print-out, on plastic paper, which is just as well, since the only other things in the safe were quantum computer drives, for a type of machine that hasn't been built in centuries. There's undoubtedly much more on those drives than in the paper log, but until someone can replicate the old computer – which, like so many things ancient, is more sophisticated than the ones we use now – we won't know what that is. But this paper log, for the moment, is plenty to be going on with, and its story more than answers the question about how that man got to be on Earth. It's written in Ancient English, of course, but, like every other graduate of the Jericho Seminary, I was taught the old language and have used it several times in addressing ancient texts. I'm even able, I think, to translate as I go along.

"But first let me give you some background. The date of the second Lunar expedition to Earth was 2176. The first expedition, in 2174, had established that it was possible for humans wearing sterility suits to visit the planet for short periods and to decontaminate and return safely. But that, really, was all that it established. People were so worried at the time that the suits might not work, that outside air might leak in somehow or that the virus might accidentally be brought back to the Moon, that the only purpose of that expedition was to establish the viability of the suits. I think that we have never given enough credit to the brave men and women who went to the Earth way back then. For all they knew, they were going to die, either of the virus itself or of eventual suffocation if they couldn't be allowed back. It turned out, though, that God was with them. He didn't want all humans to die. He only wanted their contact with Earth to be as severely limited as possible. It was still a punishment and remains so. Whatever some misguided people may say – and I'll be quite specific here: I'm talking about yesterday's pronouncement by the insane, irresponsible and illegal Back-to-Earth Movement – we cannot go to Earth and live there the way humans did before the Apocalypse. Air samples are constantly analysed by Earth Rangers, and they always show that the virus is as alive and deadly as ever. Don't take the sightings of the man in the holoparks as evidence to the contrary. I'll now tell you why – or let Colonel Schwinn help me tell you.

"The second expedition – the 2176 one, led by the same man who led the earlier expedition, one Robert Heron – was the first to actually explore parts of the planet, to see first-hand what had happened to the Earth after twenty-three years without humans. They stayed about six weeks, decontaminating every night as they returned to their ship and putting on new suits every morning. But that's a detail. Here's what Colonel Schwinn wrote about part of their final report." Caleb paused, cleared his throat, adjusted his glasses and read. "'Very interesting dispatch from the Lunar Colony today. The Heron expedition has made its final report. Heartening to know that the mother planet has regenerated so well in such a short time. Not too surprising, but heartening. What is surprising, however, is a discovery made in the ruins of Philadelphia. The Lunar authorities order me to tell no one of this ...' You have to remember," Caleb said, looking up, "that in those days, the Moon was in command of all the other stations. '... to tell no one of this. They have good reasons, but I still feel compelled to write it here. Heron has found a man – alive, alone, wildly bearded and quite mad from years of solitude. He was – is – apparently immune to the virus. They wonder if elsewhere on the planet there are others who ...' Now this is where ... What?"

As Caleb had looked up, his eye caught a little bit of colour on the pulpit panel – a colour that shouldn't have been there. Red. Now he stared at it. The little red light was on.

He'd been cut off. "Hey," he shouted, turning to his right and looking at the technicians' window. No one was there, but he shouted at the empty window anyway. "Who cut me off? How long have I been cut off?" He stepped away from the pulpit and ran (as much as he was capable of running) to the door. It was locked. "Hey," he shouted.

CHAPTER TWENTY-THREE

Gus's mind had returned all right. He could focus his eyes and speak a little and even manage a weak grimace as Jenny brought him up to date on what she was doing here (again, but there was no way of knowing how much, if anything, he'd taken in before, and anyway, this was a version re-edited in light of her new knowledge that Simon and his bastards were actually Back-to-Earthers). In the midst of this, Louise, declaring once more that her job was a lot like a doctor's, had prescribed another attempt at water and some food if she could grab any and launched herself back towards the drinking fountain.

Gus, still anchored to the bar by his trousers, floated a looped belt's length from it and parallel to both it and the wall, while Jenny, legs crossed around the bar so that she was perpendicular to Gus, looked 'down' on his upside-down face. It wasn't a very comfortable way to talk to someone, but it was the best she could do for the moment. The prospect that frightened her most, especially with Louise off foraging, was accidentally springing away and finding herself sailing, rudderless and handcuffed, to some remote quarter of the gym. She needed to stay with Gus and felt a measure of security on their two-metre length of bar. It was funny, she thought, that even in such a hellish circumstance, the instinct for home territory could be so strong. Damn those bastards for reducing people to this.

"Gus," Jenny said. "I always thought Back-to-Earthers were just a few religious nutters. How did they get strong enough to … I mean, where did they come from?"

"From the Moon," Gus said, his voice so weak it was nearly lost in the general din.

"Yeah, obviously, but—"

"They say the Government has been lying about the Earth, that there's no more virus."

"But they've always said that, haven't they? The Martian ones certainly have."

"Jenny, how can I turn around? Talking upside-down is making me feel sicker than I already am."

"Yeah, I keep looking at the wrinkles in your forehead instead of your mouth. Let me see."

"I can't move. Why can't I move?

"It's your belt. It's holding you to the bar. We shouldn't undo it, though. Could lose you. Reach down behind your bottom and grab the bar. Here." She guided his hands to the bar, and when he grasped it, he floated as far upright as the belt would allow – which was a little more than forty-five degrees and, of course, with his back to Jenny.

"Shit," she said. In a room where movement spanned all three dimensions, she and Gus, in negotiating the bar, seemed to be confined to one, as though they lived in a comic strip. "Of all people," she muttered as she grabbed the bar, unlocked her ankles and then swung out and inched her cuffed hands under Gus's left leg. "I thought they were pretty much defunct."

As she finally got to Gus's other side, he said, "So did most people."

"So where did they all come from?" She gave the bar another ankle lock and swung over to Gus's level. It was the nearest anyone could ever manage in here to facing each other in a pair of chairs.

"They've always been illegal, Jenny. So who knew how many there ever were?"

"But what made them crawl out now?"

"What do you think?"

"I don't know."

"I do. Allaby's old Immyo. Proof that humans live on Earth."

"No, Gus, no. They already knew about Immyos. They asked me about them. That can't be—"

"But did they know that Immyos were immune?"

"Of course. I mean, I assume … They'd have to, wouldn't they?"

"Tell me, did they call them Immyos?"

"Sure. What else?

"Think."

"Oh."

"What?"

"Oh yeah."

"What?"

"Aborigines."

"Jenny, I'm sorry, but if your boyfriend wasn't already dead, I'd kill him. Look around. Look at what he's done."

"I don't see how you can blame Peter for … Gus, you actually did kill him, you know. You're the Controller of the National Park Service, and the National Park Service particled him. At least that's what the Back-to-Earthers told me."

"It's the drill, Jenny. Standing orders. We've never activated them before, but we never had a Ranger go so far off his rocker before. I mean, imaging on an Immyo reservation? What's the first, last and most important thing they tell you at the Academy? Huh? Huh?"

If Gus had been capable, he'd have been yelling, and from a man whose voice was so initially weak, the effect was the same. His face, which had been pale, was now almost purple. "I'll tell you what they tell you, in case you've forgotten. They tell you that the Immyos exist, and then they tell you to stay away from them. Don't fly over them, don't set foot on their reservations. And for God's sake, they don't even bother to say don't image them." He made a pistol-to-temple sign with his forefinger and then, with his open palm, he indicated the whole gym. "And this is why." He was hoarse now.

"I didn't have to go all the way to the drinking fountain," Louise said, making a soft landing on the bar behind Gus and bouncing a little as she crossed her ankles, "because this big bag of soup came by. It's really lucky, you know. There's not a whole lot of food around any more. They stopped throwing it in two days ago. The air's getting really stale, too, and I don't mean just stinky. And before we drink this stuff – the label says it's gazpacho, wow – have you got anything we can wipe the bag with? It's been in a collision with a turd."

Jenny raised her cuffed hands, undid her uniform neckband and, with a little push, set it gliding past Gus to Louise and the bag of gazpacho.

Gus said, "Jenny, who is this woman?"

"Lie that way again," Jenny said, giving Gus's shoulders a shove, "and meet Louise. She's saved your life at least twice, and mine so many times I've quit counting. She's our friend. Be nice to her."

"Aw," Louise said, smiling to herself as she wiped the bag, adding "yech" as she sent the neckband off to join the general circulation of detritus. She uncapped the soup bag, sucked at the spout for a few moments, replaced the cap without taking the spout out of her mouth and then took it out and passed the bag to Gus, who slowly turned it around, as if checking to see how well she'd cleaned it. Then he took the cap off and started to wipe the open spout on his sleeve. A spurt of lumpy red and green gazpacho mushroomed out, splattering his forehead and hair before tumbling off into the greater gymnasium. "Watch it," Louise said as she reached down and shoved the spout into Gus's mouth.

"For God's sake, Gus," Jenny said, "what a time and place to be fastidious."

Louise said, "Oh, he's probably still groggy. Have you got something else to wipe with? I had a couple of hankies, but they were in my shirt."

"Not unless I give you my shirt. Leave it, Louise. It won't hurt him to have a little soup on his head." Jenny was peeved at Gus's attitude since waking up. After all the trouble she and especially Louise had been to, after the fighting to extract him from the body ball – after everything – his return to consciousness had been marked by a diatribe against poor Peter and a sneer at Louise.

"We can't just leave him like that," Louise said. "It's undignified. You said he was an important man."

"Yeah. He is, or was."

"Well, we can't have him like that, then."

Gus was still drinking, or seemed to be. His adam's apple was working double time, but his cheeks were also swelling, and spots of gazpacho were coming from the corners of his mouth.

"Gus," Jenny said, "you're not sucking. You can't just gulp it down – there's no down. Suck."

Gus's eyes popped a little as he looked at Jenny. Then, with his thumb over the spout, he took it out of his mouth, apparently sucked down what was in his cheeks, inhaled deeply, exhaled, mouthed the spout again and did it right, nodding thanks at Jenny.

"You act like you've never been in zero-G. You go to the Moon and back twice a year – to see your mother, isn't it? How do you eat on the ship?"

Gus made a dismissive gesture with his hand, and Louise said, "Jenny, really, he's just groggy and probably confused, and very hungry and thirsty, I'll bet. And I can't stand seeing him messy. Look, Mister, uh, uh …"

"Just call him Gus."

"I couldn't. Not an important man like him."

"Templeton, then. Mister Templeton."

"Mister Templeton, I'm going to clean that soup off you. You just keep on drinking, and don't be startled. It's nothing personal." With one hand holding on to Gus's shoulder, Louise lifted him off the bar and into a sort

231

of 'standing' position next to it. Then she curled around him from behind and brought her face and free hand to his soup-splattered and now deeply furrowed brow. She scraped soup off his face and hair with her fingers and licked them. After doing this half a dozen times, she began licking directly, reminding Jenny of nothing so much as a big cat with her kitten. Gus was blushing mightily, but he tolerated it and, as Louise had ordered, kept drinking. When, in about five minutes, Gus's face and hair were sparkling clean, Louise unwrapped herself and returned him to his place along the bar. "That's better," she said, admiring his face as she pulled a hair from her teeth. "Thanks for letting me do that."

Gus finished drinking and properly capped the spout. With his eyes on Louise, he passed the soup to Jenny. "Don't thank me," he said. "And I'm, uh, I'm sorry."

"What for, Mister Templeton?"

"Just sorry. Very sorry. Nobody's ever ... well ..."

His voice trailed off before he could say what nobody had ever done, but Jenny supposed it was a fair bet that nobody had ever licked him clean before. And she herself had never met anybody who would do the sort of things Louise seemed happy to do. As Jenny sucked what was left of the soup – God, she was thirsty, and it was almost gone – she reflected that Louise was more than just a whore with a heart of gold. She was probably a whore because of her heart of gold. She probably earned her living the way she did because she considered it kind to give people satisfaction – unencumbered by any sort of intimacy barrier. In a way, she really was like a doctor – better than a doctor, because doctors, no matter how hard they might try not to, always seemed to hint at a residual unease when performing some of their dirtier duties. Louise, though, seemed to revel in such stuff. Jenny looked at Gus looking at Louise and wondered if she'd just witnessed the instant when a man fell in love. Or maybe he'd just been taken to some previously undiscovered place beyond his threshold of disgust.

But in the present circumstances either love or disgust was pointless. The soup was finished. She tossed the bag away and watched as it drifted into what was beginning to look like a gargantuan slow-flushing toilet. Even people were looking discarded somehow. As a mass, they seemed suddenly listless – there wasn't so much screaming and shouting any more and not so many body balls, as though fear itself was becoming superfluous. Also, Louise was right – the air had a new staleness to it, and Jenny realised she'd probably been breathing harder than usual. Then, as if to underline these thoughts, several metres away a dead man floated by. She didn't know how she immediately knew he was dead – something about the odd angles of his arms and legs and the way his head flopped back and forth – but she had no doubt. "Look," she said to Gus and Louise.

Gus took his eyes off Louise and looked where Jenny's two hands were pointing. "Oh," he said.

"Poor man," Louise said. "I wonder what happened."

"A heart attack, maybe," Gus said. "It could be anything, though."

"In here," said Jenny, "it could be suicide."

They were all quiet for a moment as they watched the body pass by, and then Gus said, almost to himself, "It's really time we got out of here."

"Oh, Gus," Jenny said, "what a great idea. I knew there'd be a solution to all this. Let's just go. Yeah, I've had enough fun in the free-fall gym for a while."

"Actually," Gus said, "I've got a way out."

"Really?" said Louise. "Do you really?"

"If you've got a way out," Jenny said, "why aren't you out?"

"That's where I was going when I got caught in that … that mob, and people kept holding me back. I was so near, too. Finally it got so frustrating, I just went blank. I don't even remember how long I was there. How long was I there? Do either of you know?"

"What day did you get thrown in?" Louise said. "I got thrown in on Thursday myself. "

"Friday night," Gus said.

"It's Sunday evening," said Louise.

"Damn it," Gus said

"Never mind what day it is," Jenny said. "How do you suppose you're going to get us out?"

"Oh, I can get us out all right." he said, patting his shirt pocket. "I've got a key. Getting out isn't the problem now. The problem is that it's Sunday evening. Too late to stop them. They'll all be gone."

"Who'll be gone?" Jenny said.

"The Back-to-Earthers."

"They've gone?" said Louise. "Where've they gone?"

"Back to Earth, of course."

Jenny and Louise looked at each other. Then Louise looked at Gus. She seemed to want to say something but just opened her mouth and closed it again. Then Jenny remembered that meeting or interview or whatever it was and the talk about the place where you could walk around outside and breathe. "Gus, tell me something. Would they have taken sterility suits?"

"No, of course not. They don't believe in the virus. And now that they've seen a man in a holopark walking around unprotected they know they're right, or think they do. I suppose, until then, in their heart of hearts they were a little unsure. Now they're not."

"No, Gus, I told you – they know about the Immyos."

"No. Remember? They know about the aborigines. What they don't know about is the immunity."

Louise said, "You two are going a little too fast for me. I know you're an important person, Mister Templeton, and you're an Earth Ranger, Jenny, and I'm only a ... I mean, I don't really understand, but I've heard of Back-to-Earthers all right and how crazy they are. And now you say – or I think you said – that they're the ones who did all this to us. So this is good news, isn't it? What do they call that – what you get when you breathe Earth air? Bungle, or ..."

"Abunga," Jenny said gently.

"Abunga," said Louise. "They'll just open the ship's portal and die of Abunga, and that'll be that. And you've got a key, Mister Templeton, that'll get us out of here, along with everybody else, except the poor dead people, and we can all go home or go to work and—"

"She's right," said Jenny. "What's the problem?"

"It's the children," Gus said.

"What children?"

"For a start, the children from this satellite. How many kids have you seen in here? Look around. How many do you see now?"

Jenny didn't have to look around. She realised he was right. There were no kids. A few mothers and babies, yes, and an occasional crying baby was part of the general commotion, but no child bigger than a toddler. It wasn't that there were ever very many kids on EHQS – the kind of work you could do here appealed mainly to singles – but there were a few families, and the tourists often came as families. "What have they done with them?"

"They've taken them along."

"For God's sake why?"

"They're the basis of the new humanity," Gus said. "I think that's the way I heard it put. They've got some of their own children with them, too. And some they stole out of a school when they left the Moon."

'The basis of the new humanity': when Simon had said that, he'd been talking about kidnapped kids – the evil bastard moron.

The light flickered. It was a sudden dimness as quick as a blink that started at the end by Louise's water fountain and moved across the enormous gym like the negative of lightning. And the general mood of listlessness instantly disappeared. Screams and shouts and a rumble of voices followed like thunder. Once the dimness passed, the light was as good as ever, but as anyone knew who lived with shadowless free-photon illumination – and it was pretty much universal these days – the flash of dimness meant an impending power failure. Normally, a little attention to a generator or, in this case the solar transmission system, would put things right, but everybody knew that all the technicians capable of giving that attention were floating around in here. That was upsetting enough to cause the overall reverberation, but there would also have been the assumption, of anyone who was thinking clearly, that the flicker would have gone through the whole satellite and that somebody on the other side of the gym's portals would get the system fixed. But what only Jenny, Gus and Louise knew was that there wasn't anybody on the other side of the portals. All the people who were presumed to be there were probably now lying dead on the surface of the Earth.

On the other hand, what exactly had Gus meant? Jenny shouted, "Did they all plan to go, Gus? Weren't they going to leave anybody behind to run the satellite?"

Gus shook his head. "They were going to abandon the satellite. They weren't interested in it. Everybody wanted to go to Earth. But they didn't want to blow it up or sabotage it or anything, because it might be useful later – as a defence if, say, the Martians attacked. But the Martians couldn't get here for weeks."

Louise shouted (everybody was shouting now because everybody else was), "You mean they've left all the people here to float around in the dark until they die? What does your key open? Which portal is it?"

"It's more a door," Gus said. "I think it's about right straight over there." He pointed at the opposite wall.

Because of all the people, it was hard to see the opposite wall at all, much less whether there was a door in it, but Jenny couldn't remember there being any doors in any of the walls, except the locked toilet door – which, on thought, was on that wall, too. "You've got the key to the toilet, then?"

235

"Yes and no," Gus said. "Not the toilet you're thinking about. The executive toilet. We call it the washroom, though, the executive washroom."

"What?" Jenny said. "I never heard of that? And I never saw a door to it."

"You wouldn't," Gus said. "It's discreet – you can't tell it from the rest of the wall. We don't want people knowing we don't use the same toilets they do. It seems so, uh, undemocratic. So the door looks like part of the wall. We only use it during executive exercise hours. And we go out through a plain door on the executive corridor. Or did."

"Oh, Gus, Gus, Gus." Louise was right. They were going to float around in the dark until they died. And when the lights went the heat and ventilation would go. It was a question of whether they'd freeze first or suffocate.

"What's the matter, Jenny?" Louise said. "Let's go."

"There's no point," Jenny said.

"Why?"

"It'll be locked from the other side. Or the keys will be deactivated or something."

"No they won't," Gus said. "There's no way the Back-to-Earthers could have known about the executive washroom. Hell, almost nobody but us knew about the place. It was embarrassing."

"But why hasn't some other executive opened it by now?"

"Jenny, all the other executives are dead. Killed. Lined up and shot. I swear, this is the only remaining key to—"

"Shot?"

"Yeah."

"How come you weren't— "

"I'll tell you when there's more time. Now let's go."

"Yeah, let's do," said Louise, who already had a hand on Gus's belt. "Now, you cross your legs around the bar. This is no time to lose you." Gus did as he was told, and Louise unbuckled the belt, whipped it out of his rear belt-loop and then strung it back through all the loops and buckled it again, patting the buckle when she'd finished. Gus stared at the buckle for a second or two, gazed wondrously at Louise for another couple of seconds and then looked over at Jenny and said, "You two got me out of that mob and got me here and revived me. So I'm going to let you two decide how we get to the other wall without, uh, without—"

"Getting thrown off course?" Louise said. "Getting caught in another body ball? Don't worry. I can take care of that."

Even though Jenny trusted Louise to get them there – that, after all, was Louise's newly discovered specialty – she still couldn't help feeling a deep pang of fear and, despite the urgency, a reluctance to move. This was partly because she was having trouble believing in the existence of Gus's invisible door and of Gus's key actually opening it, and partly because – she was ashamed to admit to herself – she didn't want to desert their two metres of exercise bar. She'd been keeping Gus talking instead of moving because staying here somehow seemed more important even than staying alive, and she knew that if she gave in to this fear she'd be literally scaring herself to death. But there was still another dimension of fear, a contradictory one and one that defied reason and had developed since the floating corpse and then the flickering light: she wanted gravity – here, now, where she was. She was comprehensively sick of free-fall, which after all was the same sensation as actually falling – in fact, it was falling. All those people out in the vastness Jenny was about to fly across were falling. They were in a bottomless pit, falling and falling through a haze of blood, vomit and piss and a perpetually echoing lamentation of human voices. She maintained her scissorhold on the bar as though the bar were a lucky tree-root that she'd happened to catch at the edge of the pit, to break her own eternal fall. She did realise, of course, that what was scaring her was as stupid as it was morbid. On the other side of Gus's little door, there would be gravity, if there really was a door and if it really could be opened. Even though she wanted to scream, she only shouted, in a forcibly cheery if breathless, voice, "Okay, Louise?"

Louise said, "Okay. Now, Mister Templeton, Jenny can't use her arms, so she goes in the middle. You and I travel on the outside, and when I say to push against something or somebody, you push, okay? And when you push, pull your hand or foot right back so nobody grabs it. Ready, Jenny?"

"Yes."

"Okay," Louise said. "Here we go."

CHAPTER TWENTY-FOUR

There had been better wedding nights, he supposed – ones that didn't involve broken ribs, a broken wrist, sore feet, a bed of rocks, a painful sunburn, a crying baby, a thousand itching and biting things, scratchy blankets, large animals walking by, the need for the bride to get up in the dark and gather cowpats, and this all-pervading night-time chill. But as Allaby lay on his back now, gazing up at the, yes, gibbous moon and the strands of smoke drifting across it – what would it be now, about two in the morning? – there might conceivably have been worse wedding nights as well. Paintbrush, asleep now, lay against him with her head on his right shoulder and the sleeping baby between them, and the dog was curled up on his left arm and against his left side, so that a little warmth was seeping in from two directions. As long as he didn't move, nothing hurt very much, not even the sunburn on his neck. The fire was going well – no need to worry about that now – and he wasn't hungry or thirsty and didn't need to pee. It was a moment of peace, and he savoured it. He did love Paintbrush and was happy to think of her as his wife, however dubious the half-minute-long marriage ceremony might have been. For this moment, things were okay – good even. And then, almost for the first time since tumbling out of the pickup, he thought of Jenny.

"You what?" she'd say. "You married an Immyo?" Of course, Jenny would probably have been thinking he was dead, and so she might precede that with "Peter, you're alive ..." but there wouldn't be very many more words before she got to "You married an Immyo? Immyos aren't even supposed to know you exist. Don't you think that marrying one, having sex with one, is getting a bit close? Don't you think that ..."

What would she be doing now, he wondered, feeling a little unfaithful to Paintbrush as he wondered it. It was hard to believe she was still on the same planet as him, just a continent, an ocean and another continent away (God, distances had been different last week – he wondered now if he'd ever even see the San Juans again). Well, what would she be doing? Two in the morning here – if that's what it was – would be noon there. She'd have had a morning with, maybe, migrating wildebeest and would be back in her station for lunch. Oh, but today was Sunday, if he wasn't mistaken – air-sample day. Before lunch she'd have had to stop to do the air samples – was probably doing them right now, checking to see if the Abunga was still alive and well and ubiquitous (and boy was there something fundamentally flawed in that procedure). Then she'd be back for lunch. It was her main meal, and she usually had put a casserole in the oven before she left in the morning and at lunch would get it out and eat it at a properly set table while she watched the news from Mars. In fact, she had her comms set up so that the newsreader sat across from her.

A casserole. Chicken was her favourite, if he remembered. Anyway, it was a chicken casserole that she'd cooked for him once on EHQS, at one of the Confabs, and it was the best … Stop it, he told himself – you'll be drooling in a minute. Paintbrush had done a fine job last night with roasted prairie dog. It wasn't quite chicken casserole, of course, but she'd found a couple of peppery spices, and … Oh, come off it – roasted prairie dog was not anywhere near chicken casserole. Jenny had always accused him of romanticising the Earth, and he'd really be doing that if he pretended that prairie dog, with or without spices, was anything but vile. The only thing that had made it seem okay last night was that Paintbrush – lovely, flowing, fluid Paintbrush, his wife, now asleep at his shoulder – had cooked it. She only needed to touch a thing to make it all right. But, God, was he … Would Jenny say that his feelings for Paintbrush were also part of his romanticising the Earth? Of course she would. She'd say, "Look at her, Peter. She's way too short for you, for a start. And too young probably. No education whatsoever – doesn't know anything at all. At all – can't even read or write. Doesn't even know what reading or writing is. And a baby, for Christ's sake. Okay, she's got a lovely body in a miniature way, pretty face, striking jade-coloured eyes, beautiful hair …" Even Jenny would have to concede that. "… but the body, face and hair are so smudged and dirty and matted at the moment you can hardly tell. And you're a match, Peter. You love the Earth? Well, you've got it all over you, and the little beard's crap, too …"

God. He was lying in a scrape on the Flaco Plain at two o'clock in the morning having a row with an imaginary jealous Jenny, a person he'd probably never see again. Of course, if he did somehow make it to Pike's Peak, he'd be back in her world, but at the rate he was travelling, it was going to take a hundred years. And he didn't really want to have that argument with Jenny – didn't really want to reach Pike's Peak, for that matter. He was only headed that way because he had a duty, a responsibility to humanity. What he'd really like to do was find a nice spot – on the lower slopes of the San Juans, maybe – and settle down with Paintbrush and the baby, help form that tribe Gibbous was talking about, get Gibbous to teach him to hunt and fish, and just live on Earth. But that would probably be the most selfish thing anybody in all of history had ever done. All those people surviving on those unfit-for-humans heavenly bodies would have to go on surviving there for generations more – until someone else had an accident like his and discovered that the air tests were faulty and the Earth was fine. He wouldn't be able to live with himself if he didn't at least try to get there, and he could never have been content in the San Juans or anywhere else, even with Paintbrush, if he was always obsessed by his terrible, overriding sin of omission.

At this point, the moon disappeared. For a second he imagined he might have sleepily closed his eyes, but he blinked, and, no, they were open, and what he was seeing instead of the moon were a lot of little lights – three red lights forming a T with a long row of blue lights, all inside an oblong fringe of white ones. The overall sense was of something huge and heavy, not unlike his first impression, yesterday morning, of the cow. Then a spotlight came on, illuminating the ground somewhere way off to his left, to the west. He couldn't see exactly where because – with Paintbrush pinning one arm and the dog the other, and his ribs not allowing the necessary exertion – he couldn't move to sit up. He could only turn his head and follow all the lights as they travelled very gradually westwards and downwards until he couldn't see them any more. He looked straight up again: the moon was back, with the wisps of smoke trailing over it and, briefly, an owl flying across.

It had been a ship, of course – a very big one, much bigger than a cruiser – and it had been coming in for a landing. In fact, it was big enough to be the kind of ship he himself had once travelled on, during the ten-month journey from Titan to the Moon when he was on his way to university. It looked like – it was – a liner. It had to be. Definitely, a liner. But liners were designed to carry people in their hundreds and were only used for long hauls. There weren't even any based at EHQS, because there weren't docking facilities for them. The ship had to have come direct from the Moon at the very least, if not from farther. A liner. A liner from somewhere in the Solar System had just landed somewhere on the Flaco Plain.

But, he reminded himself, this was still an Immyo reservation, and flying over it, not to mention landing on it, was illegal. So where was the National Park Service? It had been quick enough to particle his little pickup – how could it ever have let a goddamned liner through? So maybe he hadn't really seen it. He couldn't have, because it was impossible, and if he still had any grasp on rationality, that had to be that. Hallucinations could happen, after all. It was late at night, and he was lying here broken, bitten and battered in what was, to be honest, an alien environment, and at the same time he was feeling highly emotional because he was so in love. Hell, he'd just had an argument with Jenny, and she wasn't on the Flaco Plain either. Maybe there was an subconscious part of his mind that didn't like being on Earth and out in the air, and maybe that part of his mind wanted him to see a liner. Maybe it was like the chariot in that church hymn, and he had an unrecognised desire for a big ship to swing low and carry him home. There was no sign of it now – no lights in the distance that, by craning his neck, he could see. Whew. It had certainly been realistic, though. It was good thing he knew something about psychology. Otherwise …

But wait a minute. How much did he know about psychology? He'd never taken a course in it, never gone deeply into the subject at all. He didn't know what hallucinations were really like – whether a person who was having one usually knew he was having one while he was having it, or whether, as he himself had just done, decided it was an hallucination after he'd had it. Wouldn't it be a sort of hallucination to deny what you'd just seen, your subconscious mind intervening because that was the easiest way to cope? But no, no – it all came down to the National Park Service. There could not be a massive liner over and then on an Immyo reservation. There simply could not. It and everybody in it would now be part of the landscape and the atmosphere. Or maybe it had been particled after it had left his vision. He hadn't seen a cruiser or any particle missiles, but maybe they'd come from the other direction, from the north-west, over the San Juans. That was where they'd come from when he'd been – or rather his pickup had been – destroyed.

But wait another minute. The National Park Service had only known where he was because Jenny had told them where to look, because when he'd destroyed his station he'd destroyed all this sector's tracking and warning systems. So a ship, even a big one, could conceivably come here and land here without being noticed – that is, if there hadn't been time to get the systems repaired yet. But they'd only needed to reconnect a few terminals. That couldn't take … he groaned. All this was giving him a headache, and he said aloud but in an undertone, "Just an hallucination."

"What, Allaby?" Paintbrush whispered.

"Shh. Nothing. Don't wake up the baby."

"He won't wake up," she said softly, pulling the baby's lambskin tighter around him. Then she rose to her knees and, with both arms under him, carefully moved him to the edge of the bedpit. She rummaged under the blankets until she found the baby's fleece hat, which she gingerly pulled onto his head and, after giving him a pat, lay down again, her back to him as she snuggled up to Allaby. "Now tell me what you were saying." She kissed Allaby's ear.

"I don't know. I guess I was talking in my sleep."

"You weren't asleep."

"Why do you say that?"

She laid her head on his chest. "You didn't feel asleep."

"But weren't you asleep?"

"Yes, but I could still feel that you weren't. It came into my dream."

"How can that happen?"

"I don't know how, but it can. I'm a good dreamer. You know that. I've told you that."

"What was your dream then?" The dog was still lying across his left arm, but his right was finally moveable again. It was the arm with the splint, but he still had bare fingers, and now he used them to comb through Paintbrush's hair. Imaginary Jenny had been right. It was getting matted. He hoped Gibbous could manage to bring enough water back so that they could all have a wash, even if a little one. The dog was scratching himself in his sleep, and Allaby imagined he could feel the fleas hopping on to him. (That liner had definitely been an hallucination. Nothing had happened.)

"I can't tell you. My dreams are too powerful. I have to think about them before I can talk about them."

"Wouldn't it be better to talk about them while they're fresh?" (Forget about the liner.)

She raised up on an elbow and looked down at him. He couldn't make out her face, but in the moonlight she'd have been able to see his. "They're always fresh," she said. "I can usually remember dreams better than things that happen when I'm awake."

"Come on. Tell me now. I'm your husband. You can tell me." There was nothing more boring than hearing dreams described, even if you were in love with the describer, who also happened to be, as it were, a professional dreamer. But Allaby was ready to hear anything that would keep his mind off his own hallucination. (If there really was a liner out there, he was going to have to do something. What?)

"No, Allaby, you don't want me to. It's a responsibility." She smoothed his hair and kissed him on the forehead, which made Allaby feel about ten years younger than her. "I have to make sure what it means before I talk about it, because my dreams have a way of coming true, and if I give it the wrong meaning, the wrong people can suffer. I had a dream that I thought was a warning to Granddad and told him about it, and it turned out to be a warning to everybody but him. That was a bad, bad mistake."

"Where do the dreams come from, Paintbrush?" (Yes, it had definitely been his subconscious, yearning for a chariot. Well, to hell with his subconscious. His conscious was in charge now.)

"I don't know," she said. "Sometimes I think God or Mother Elephant puts them there, but my father used to say that spiders whispered them into my ear. I was a little girl then, though, and people will tell children anything. I asked Granddad once what he thought, and he said dreams probably came from the air animals. That was back when he still believed in air animals. I don't think he believes in anything now, not even God or Mother Elephant, not since he started his Long Walk Out. Something's happened to him – I don't know what. Maybe the atrocity did it. Anyway, Allaby, it doesn't matter how the dreams get there. If I haven't planned a dream, and it—"

"Planned a dream?"

"Uh huh." Two kisses, one on each side of his nose. "That's the best part of being a dreamer. The dreams I don't plan are, like I said, a responsibility. But mostly I decide what I'm going to dream before I go to sleep, and then I sleep and dream it. I can do anything then. Fly, anything. I did it last night, too – before I had the dream I'm not telling you about."

"Can you tell me about that one then?" This was getting serious. How could anyone have that much control over her subconscious? And was there a subconscious to her subconscious?

"I can, but I don't know if I want to."

"Now why not?"

"Well, okay. It's a little intimate is all. But okay. You know last night when we made love, and you had to lie on your back because of your broken ribs and I had to be careful not to jar you too much and … everything?"

"I know, yeah. It was—"

"It was wonderful, Allaby, but—"

"I know, Paintbrush. I know. But my ribs won't be cracked all my life, and—"

"Shh, Allaby, no. I love you, and I loved that, but, um, before I went to sleep, I decided to dream that your ribs weren't cracked."

"Oh?"

"And we made beautiful, beautiful love, Allaby. It was even better than that first time, when Granddad went to see the Chief and before the cow ever stepped on you."

Well, that made him forget about the liner. According to Paintbrush, he'd just cuckolded himself. But he hadn't done it, not him – some dream him, who not only had sturdy ribs but was Paintbrush's idea of a perfect lover. If she could conjure up that Allaby every night, what was the point, from her perspective, of this Allaby even existing, especially considering that he wasn't any good for anything else at the moment, not even walking? "Paintbrush, don't you think you take this dreaming business too far? I don't like you dreaming that kind of dream."

"In the dream you loved it. And keep your voice down. Skyman is—"

"Okay, I'll whisper." She was right. There had been a cough and a whimper, and the last thing he wanted at the moment was another bout of crying. "But listen," he said. "That wasn't me in the dream. I didn't dream that my ribs were okay and I was making beautiful, beautiful love with you. I wasn't there. It was just you, in your head. I don't want you dreaming that dream any more. It makes me jealous of myself, which is crazy – almost as crazy as having to tell you what not to dream."

"It is crazy," Paintbrush said, giggling. She snuggled down and, still giggling, nudged her head under his chin. "I think I'll go to sleep now," she said with a mock yawn.

"Don't you dare."

"Aha, Allaby. You are jealous of yourself." She leaned up on her elbow again and kissed him, this time on the mouth, but before he could decide whether he ought to respond (he was doing his best, after all, to be stern with her), she pulled away and said, "Let me tell you something about

244

dreams. They don't really happen. They seem real, and you can remember them as clearly as real things, but it's like when a storyteller tells stories – especially a good storyteller like Granddad. He'd start telling a story – Hero and the first Ledgers, let's say – and the way he used his hands and his eyes and his words, pretty soon you'd be seeing the story, not just hearing it. You'd be right there with Hero, right beside him, right inside him sometimes as he swooped into the floods of blood and plucked people out. He'd fly with maybe a man under one arm and a woman under the other, and you'd be up there in the sky with them, looking down over the whole world through the eyes of the man or the woman or Hero himself or even through your own eyes just flying along with them. But you'd also know you were in the Cavern sitting still with your legs crossed and maybe biting your fingertips. You weren't really up there with Hero, and you knew you weren't. Well, dreams are stories, too – you just don't always know who's telling them. When the dream Allaby was making love to me, I knew it wasn't really happening. It wasn't even happening to me. It was happening to the dream Paintbrush. The real Paintbrush was lying here curled up with the real Allaby. And the dream loving was no more real loving than flying with Hero in the story was real flying. People who dream without thinking about what they're doing don't often realise that, but if you're a good dreamer like me, you always do. That's how I can plan dreams. I know I'm making things seem to happen, not really happen. And I'll tell you this, Allaby. I'd much rather make love with the real you, even if every bone in your body was broken, than to sleep for the rest of my life while I watched or even felt something pretending to be me making love with something pretending to be a perfect you. So don't worry."

After that, Allaby completely forgot not only about the liner hallucination, but about Jenny, about chicken casserole and roast prairie dog, about Pike's Peak, about the bites and the stones and the night's chill, about everything in the Universe except cracked ribs (only because he had to keep reminding himself to stay on his back) and Paintbrush. The baby stayed asleep, and the dog soon moved to a less hectic spot. After a while – he had no idea how long – and with her on top of him ("It's warmer this way," he said, and she said, "It's softer"), they slept. But not for long. The sky was only just starting to lighten when Allaby realised that what had woken him up was a prod on the foot from Gibbous's walking stick, followed by the observation that "You'd think you of all people would remember to keep the fire going."

After the several seconds it took Allaby to appreciate where he was, what he'd been doing and the wonderment of it all, he mumbled, "Go out?"

"Yeah, but I suppose you don't really need to worry about it." Gibbous's voice was now coming from the region of the firepit, along with some scraping and clinking that must have been him trying to get the flames up again. "Nobody's hurt, and after all, I let it go out the night before. I'm sure your excuse is better than mine was."

"You're back, Granddad." It was a very small voice, with the words spoken directly into the side of Allaby's neck.

"Yep," Gibbous said. "Walked all morning, gathered stuff all afternoon. Had a meal and a bath and spent all night lugging everything back. I'd have slept, but I couldn't let you and the baby and your poor injured husband there spend another day in the sun."

"Thanks, Granddad."

"Thanks," Allaby said, closing his eyes again.

"God, am I tired. Hello, Yellow. Glad to see you, too. As soon as I get this going and we get some shelter up, it'll be my turn to sleep a while."

"That's good, Granddad." She still hadn't moved or raised her voice at all.

"But in a way, I'm glad I walked all night. I mean, I'm glad I was up."

"That's good," Paintbrush said.

"Yeah. Because something very, very interesting happened."

He seemed to be waiting for one of them to say, "What was that?" but neither Paintbrush nor Allaby obliged.

"Yeah, as I was walking along, it suddenly got very dark. And I looked up, and the moon was gone. And you won't believe what was there instead. I'm not sure I believe it myself – lots of stars, bright stars – red ones and blue ones and white ones ..."

CHAPTER TWENTY-FIVE

The free-fall gym was essentially a box inside a cylinder. It would have been possible, when the satellite was built, to dispense with the box and to have an even larger, cylindrical gym, but the satellite's architects, way back in the twenty-third century, were concerned that weightlessness in such a huge space would be disorienting enough without at least the comfort and security of six flat walls to look at and vault off. There were also several zero-gravity sports that needed flat surfaces. Once, in the twenty-eighth century, the walls were removed during one of the satellite's regular renovations, and a cylindrical gym was installed, but it was soon discovered that the original architects had been right: people found the shape nauseating and a little scary, and the free-fall polo, football and hockey leagues were forced either to rewrite their rules or cancel their schedules. The former proved impossible, mainly because parallelepipedous ball-bouncing was integral to all three sports (the bright spark from Armstrong who'd designed the new gym had even put rounded ends on it), and the abandonment of the season's matches, which became the only choice, was so resented that there was a popular uprising, leading to a brief (two days in all) secession of the satellite from the Moon. So the box-shaped gym was rebuilt as quickly as it could be, and the Polo Putsch, as it was later called, became a quirk of history.

Jenny had recalled and dwelt on this little fact in all its classroom clarity (she could even picture Lunar History 2.02 and herself and couple of fellow Martians laughing out loud at yet another example of the idiocy of Mooners) as a way of not dwelling on what was happening at the moment. And it did have relevance: even though the executive-showers door was now safely closed behind them, they were still weightless because they were in a passage between the straight wall of the gym and the curved wall of the cylinder. It was just the three of them because Gus had thought it was too dangerous to leave such a small door open for people to try to crush through. If their panic, he'd argued, made them form body balls or fight over bits of exercise bar, what would they do if they saw an escape hole? Louise had thought the three of them could hang by the door and

247

usher people through in an orderly manner, but Gus had said that would be murder, not to mention suicide – that they should get through the door quickly, shut it, take the lift and then go to the control deck – next to the Head of Station's office and right down the corridor from the executive washroom – and open the four large portals. Because Gus was an important man, Louise had agreed instantly. Jenny, for her part, had no opinion and barely heard the discussion. She had a brand new fear to control, and she could concentrate on that, since she was in the middle, her hands were useless, and she was, in effect, just along for the ride.

As they'd floated on towards the place where the door was supposed to be, she'd become less sceptical about it, partly because, having abandoned their base, there was no point any more, and partly because the trip across was turning out to be so unexpectedly easy. Though there was still a certain amount of shouting and grabbing here and there, a lot of people seemed to be beyond either panic or aggression – seemed, for the most part, to be waiting to die (two or three, in fact, weren't having to wait any more). If the course they were on needed correcting, Gus or Louise would simply push somebody and regain bearings while the person pushed would passively veer away in the opposite direction, bumping into other people and sending them veering as well. In fact the main hazards turned out not to be people but the various manifestations of gunge that kept getting in their eyes, adding to the unremitting low-key sting of urine.

But quicker than Jenny had at first dared hope, they arrived at an unremarkable bit of wall, and when Gus had passed his key over a little red spot, a door slid open and a brightly lit and splendidly ungungy passageway materialised. They'd gone in, the door had shut, and at the corridor's other end, Gus and Louise used the handles provided to swing themselves feet first, flipping Jenny over in the process. Then that door slid open, revealing a ladder and the sparkling tiled floor of the lift. "I've always loved this bit," Louise said, "and I'm really going to love it now."

"You first then," Gus said.

Holding the railings that started in the corridor, Louise clamped her feet on the top rung of the ladder. "Ouwee," she said. "My feet forgot they existed." At about three rungs down, she added, "Wow. Something else forgot, too. Talk about the shivers. Ahahahaha." And once on the floor, she looked up and said, "Come on, Jenny. You two look funny standing on air."

The handcuffs, again, were a problem. Jenny couldn't re-enter gravity evenly, with a hand on each railing, and she couldn't ask Gus to lower her or he'd be jerked through the hatch, and they'd both end up in a pile. In Lunar-gauge gravity, that wouldn't be a problem for her, but Gus had never known anything else, and his bones were correspondingly breakable. So to hell with it: she gave a push on a handle and, in effect, jumped. She'd aimed to land a metre or so away from Louise but of course forgot about the Coriolis effect (the most noticeable way centrifugal gravity differs from real gravity: things fall at angles) and landed on top of her, knocking her over. The fall had been just slow enough for Jenny to avoid hitting Louise feet first and to raise her arms over her head so that she didn't knock her with the handcuffs, but she did hit her with a full-body crash. To Jenny, it was a soft landing, with even a bit of bounce, but it seemed to have taken the wind out of Louise, who made a *'hhhhh'* sound, gasped mightily and finally gathered enough breath to cough and say, "Damn, Jenny."

"God, I'm sorry," Jenny said, lying on top of her and looking at her surprised face. For the first time since she'd met Louise, her hair wasn't billowing out around her head. Well, it was, but it was spread out on the floor. And her face was specked and smeared with black and brown gunge. "Are you okay?" Jenny asked.

"Yeah, I think so. Boy, that was gravity with a bang."

"What the hell did you do?" Gus yelled from the hatch.

Jenny turned her head sideways. "I forgot about the ... Oh, come on, Gus. Come down." She looked back at Louise's face, and then – without realising she was going to – gave her a kiss. Because of the taste of gunge on both their mouths, it wasn't a very pleasant thing to have done, but at the moment it had seemed the best way to express her relief and gratitude. Pulling back, she said, "Thanks, Louise. Thanks for everything. I mean it. Thanks for saving us." Then she started trying to get up, but without having experienced her own weight for a while and without the use of her hands, she wasn't getting very far.

Louise stopped Jenny's struggle to rise by grasping the back of her neck. She said, "Thanks for thanking me, Jenny. Wow."

"Ladies, please," Gus said. "We've got a lot to do." He was tugging at Jenny's arm, and she let him pull her up. The lift quickly arrived at the Inner Ring, the door opened, and Jenny and Gus stepped out into a big empty, silvery room.

"Sorry, Mister Templeton," Louise said as she, too, got up and stepped out. "But I've been holding back in there, and since there are toilets somewhere here, I'd really like to—"

"People are dying in that gym," Gus said, pointing at the lift.

"Then go let them out," Jenny said. "You said the control deck was just down the corridor. You don't need us. I want to use the toilets, too. And God knows, we could all do with a shower."

"I just don't want ... I mean, I think it would be better if ..."

Louise was quick to assess what the real problem was. She took Gus's hand, pressed it to her breast, looked him in the eyes and said, "We're only going to be using the toilets, Mister Templeton. You go do what you have to do and come right back, and we'll be right here waiting for you. You don't have to worry now. We've got gravity, and there are no bad people out there. No people at all, you said. And don't worry about Jenny and me having a little kiss. We were just thanking each other. And I'd like to thank you, too." She then gave him about twenty times the kiss Jenny had given her. When she'd finished, she stroked his hair and said, "Thank you very much for having the key that got us out of that awful place."

"Now which way to the toilets?" Jenny said.

The silvery room they were in contained nothing but the lift and its door and two other doors, one of which Gus now waved a finger towards. Then without saying a word, he turned and dazedly, even robotically, walked to the other one, opened it and closed it behind him.

Jenny and Louise half-ran to the door Gus had indicated. Louise opened it and, as badly as Jenny needed to get to a toilet, she couldn't help stopping at the threshold. Louise had taken a step inside and had stopped, too. "My God," she said.

"The executive fucking washroom," Jenny said.

It was gold. The whole room – from the tiles in the ceiling to the tiles on the walls to the tiles on the floor – was gold. And not just painted gold either. At the very least it was gold plate, and each tile was carved or moulded or whatever in a motif that was vaguely, Jenny thought, Ganymedian – lots of intricate abstract patterns. The only parts of the room that weren't gold were what were presumably the toilet doors, and they looked like they might be obsidian. Jenny couldn't decide whether she was more dazzled or disgusted by the spectacle, but right now she didn't have time to be much of either. "I'll take this one," she said, going to the nearest door.

Louise headed for the one next to that, and as soon they were both inside, Louise said – her voice coming over the partition – "This is bigger than the place I live in."

Jenny only saw the golden toilet, and it wasn't until her trousers were down and she was sitting on it that she could do any surveying. This might have been King Midas's convenience. Next to her on her right was a gold sink with the circumference of a bathtub and a row of spigots shaped like lions' heads (a departure from the Ganymedian theme, she observed, since Ganymedians didn't believe in graven images). On her left was a gold urinal, then a gold bidet and, jutting out from the wall, what appeared to be a wooden, perhaps mahogany, massage table. (How were they getting hardwood? Mars, supplier of timber to the Solar System, didn't have hardwoods. So either it was being supplied from Earth – one of the most difficult, dangerous and illegal practices Jenny could imagine – or it was pre-Apocalypse mahogany, in which case it was worth all the gold put together.) There was a large, wardrobe-like cabinet – a locker, she guessed – and a rack of soaps, unguents and other assorted toiletries. The wall opposite, including the inside of the door, was entirely mirrored, so that the occupying executive, presumably, could keep an eye on himself in his various glories of undress and bodily functioning. (She paused to look at her own reflection and moved quickly on – the grime and dishevelment were revolting.) Over by the partition was a shower tray the size of a large carpet and in the ceiling above, another gold lion-head with its mouth open. Between that and the sink was a rack of rails with about twenty different sizes of gold-coloured washrags, towels and bathmats. "It's not hard to understand why Gus is embarrassed about this place," she said to the top of the partition.

"You know, Jenny," said Louise's voice, "I make pretty good money, but I figure I'd have to turn ten tricks a night for about ten years just to pay for what I'm pooping in. Imagine – me, Louise Leblanc, on a solid-gold karzy."

Leblanc? Jenny had never wondered about Louise's last name. She seemed too, somehow, familiar to have such a thing. And was it a real name or a professional one? It would have been impolite to ask – so she said something else: "They had all this, and now they're all just as dead as people who never used anything but porcelain."

"All except Mister Templeton."

251

Jenny tried to picture Gus doing his toilet in these surroundings, and she couldn't, not without laughing.

"What's funny?"

"I was just thinking about Gus sitting on … You know, Louise, he never did tell us how he got away."

"I think he thought it was too long a story. And he didn't really get away, did he? He got thrown in the gym like everybody else. Boy, I can't wait to get off this thing and get under the shower. I couldn't bring myself to do what all those other people were doing – just kind of letting loose into the air. It didn't seem right. I've always had good control around that area of my body, but now I've got about three days' worth in me … Maybe he wasn't important enough to shoot. How important is he really?"

"Earth Controller? Pretty important. I don't think they were supposed to have a pecking order, though. They were a council of democrats – so-called, hah. I mean, look at this place. No, only the Head of Station was higher ranking … Uh, you know what, Louise?"

"What?"

"It's kind of hard to believe, but it would have to be … With the others dead, Gus – Gus Templeton – is now Head of Station. I'll bet he doesn't even realise that himself."

"Wow," said Louise. "And I kissed him."

"You also licked gazpacho off his face ."

"I did that, too. And now I'm sitting on a golden commode. What a day!"

They went quiet for a while. Never mind, Jenny thought, what else had happened to Louise recently, to her it was all worth it, because of the licked-up gazpacho, a kiss with the Head of Station and a gold toilet. There were probably a dozen other events that she'd also recall fondly – from the exciting body-ball fight and the discovery of her talent for flying to the nice chat with her colleague Imogen. Jenny couldn't help being fond of the woman. She had spent so much of her recent life entirely on her own that she'd wholly forgotten such a feeling – the whole concept of friendship, of comradeship. Before he'd been killed, she'd had Peter, of course, but that was different. That was a love affair, based in a large part on sex, even if sex conducted mainly by ultrahologram. With Louise, though, it was … it was … Ah., she didn't know and she didn't want to analyse it any more.

And another line of analysis revealed that she didn't need to be sitting here any more. She pressed the airwipe and then stood up and activated the decompositor, which made its whistling noise. Louise said, "I'm finished, too," and her decompositor whistled. "Now for that shower."

"Me, too." She pulled her shoes off with her feet, stepped out of her trousers and started to unbutton her shirt. Then she looked at her hands. "Oh, damn."

"What's the matter, Jenny?"

"The damned handcuffs. I won't be able to get my shirt off."

"Jenny, just tear it off. It's covered in crap anyway."

She started to object that it was her best uniform shirt, and then felt silly for even thinking it. So she went to the next objection: "Then what would I wear after the shower?"

"Well, you don't want to wear that filthy shirt, or any of your filthy clothes. Wait a minute." Her voice was a little more distant. "Do you have a big cabinet in your room?"

"Yeah."

"There are bound to be some kind of clothes in ... Damn, it's locked. Is yours locked, Jenny?"

"Just a second." She went over to the cabinet and opened it. "It's not locked," she yelled. "And there are clothes. Gym stuff, it looks like."

"I'm coming over," Louise shouted.

There were about eight big shelves in the cabinet, the top three of which held all kinds of sports equipment – various balls and racquets and gloves and clubs and mallets and bats, as well as a big first-aid box. The rest of the shelves had shirts, socks, shorts, jock straps, zero-G springshoes and a lot of other things to wear, all in the colours and cuts appropriate to different games and activities. It was hard to see it all, but Jenny had the feeling of peering into some sort of sportsman's Sesame. The striking thing about the collection, though, was that none of it looked used. Everything seemed brand new.

"I've got a brother," Louise said from behind Jenny's shoulder, startling her slightly, "who'd give everything he has for this stuff. Not that he has anything. Sorry. Did I make you jump?"

"I just didn't hear you come in."

"It's because I'm barefoot, I guess." She stepped forward and started flipping through the gym clothes. She was barefoot all right, to the top of her head. "Here's a nice colour." She pulled out a lime-green jersey and held it up in front of Jenny. "It's a polo shirt, isn't it? You'd look good in that. You've got such beautiful black hair, and this would really make it stand out. Or it will when you've washed and combed it. Right now it looks like crap, because that's mainly what it is. Mine is, too. Phew. Let's shower first. We can pick the clothes out later." She tossed the polo shirt over the cabinet door.

"I've still got to get this shirt off."

Louise looked at the handcuffs and the uniform shirt and for a few seconds generally studied the problem. Then she said, "What do we have to do? Get it into two halves?"

"I don't know," Jenny said. "What if I unbutton it and just flip it over my head …"

"Oh yeah. And then I'll tear the sleeves … What we really need are some scissors."

"There's a first-aid kit," Jenny said, nodding towards the cabinet. "See if there are any in there."

Louise took down the box and found scissors in it while Jenny finished unbuttoning her shirt. She'd almost forgotten she was wearing a camisole, but as long as there were scissors and Louise to use them, it was no problem. What did seem to be a problem was that Louise was naked and Jenny was as good as. But that was absurd. How many times in her life had she been in toilets and changing rooms and any number of other places where she was naked in the company of other naked women – friends, acquaintances, strangers even? When she was off Ranger duty, it was an almost everyday occurrence. So why should she feel uneasy now? But of course it had something to do with the fondness she felt for Louise. Of course. She didn't want to have sex with her or anything. She had had sex with a woman once in her university days, just to see what it was like, and it wasn't all that bad. So she wasn't against the notion in principle. She just didn't want it with Louise in particular, and she didn't like the fact that she was having to tell herself that. No, her feelings towards Louise were comradely, yes. Friendly. Grateful. Anyway, what was sex to Louise? Her job, for Christ's sake.

When the last of Jenny's camisole was cut away, Louise dropped the scissors into the first-aid box (Jenny noticed how second-nature the Coriolis effect was to her: she'd held them about ten centimetres to the left of the box when she let them go) and said, "I'll get the soap and shampoo. You get the shower going." She went to the shelves and got the two bottles, and when she turned around and saw that Jenny hadn't moved, she said, "Oh, Jenny, I'm sorry. I just thought it would be easier, with your handcuffs and everything, if we … I'll go to the other shower, of course. I just don't think about people's feelings sometimes – modesty and all, you know. Here's your stuff." She handed the soap and shampoo to Jenny, averting her eyes a little. "I'm really sorry, Jenny."

If there was such a thing as a full-body blush, Jenny was having one now. Of course, Louise's only idea was to take a shower and to help her wash her hair. What did she think Louise had wanted? Undressed, dressed, man, woman, sex act, shower – it was all the same to Louise. And now Jenny was betraying her own sense of comradeship and so on. And to make matters worse, she had embarrassed Louise. Why? She really didn't want her to go to the other shower, but she still felt she couldn't …

"Which compartments are you ladies in?" Gus shouted.

Oh no, not now, Jenny thought … On the other hand, "We're both in this one," she shouted back.

"Both of you?"

"Yeah, we're just about to get in the shower. Louise is going to help me wash my hair. The handcuffs, you know."

Louise looked at Jenny and grinned.

"Oh, okay. I'll just use the next one here, so I can talk to you. I opened the portals all right and turned on the emergency power and air, and I watched the people on the monitors for a bit, and they were starting to come out. It wasn't a rush, though. They all looked so exhausted. Sorry about the opulence, by the way. It dates from the Ganymedian Caliphate. The story goes that they discovered a little asteroid that was almost solid gold, and this is one thing they did with it. Are these your clothes, Louise?"

"Yes, Mister Templeton."

"Do you want them?"

"God, no, Mister Templeton."

Jenny turned on the shower, and they both got under it without waiting for it to warm up. The cold water felt good, and Jenny threw her head back a bit and let it hit her in the face. (The Coriolis effect worked with water, too. It showered at about a seventy-five-degree angle.)

"Just decomp them," Louise went on. "We've got some clean clothes over here. Oh, but not my shoes, and take my cards and things out of my pockets. Thanks. Sorry about that, sir."

The water was suddenly warm, and Jenny lowered her face. "Sir?" she whispered.

Whispering back, Louise said, "He's Head of Station now. Remember?"

"My uniform's too filthy to clean, too." Jenny said, trying to soap herself while wearing handcuffs. "The shirt's already in shreds because I couldn't get it off with handcuffs on."

"Here, let me," said Louise. She turned Jenny around and began soaping her back.

"Jenny, that's not going to be a problem any more," Gus said. "There was a tool box in the Control Deck. So I've brought a metal-cutter with me. Just tell me when you're ready."

"Oh Gus, thank God. Louise, I'm going to have arms again. Hallelujah. There are a lot of reasons for hating those idiot bastards," she shouted to Gus, "but at the top of my list are these goddamned handcuffs."

"The handcuffs haven't been all bad," Louise whispered.

Jenny lowered her voice. "Louise, I know you're in the habit of seeing good where other people can't. But if you can tell me one good thing about these damned ..."

"Mr Templeton," Louise said loudly, "have you got time now to tell us how it is you didn't get shot?"

"I guess so. It's pretty simple, really. I was in jail when it all happened."

"You, in jail?" Louise said. "What for, Mr Templeton?" Then in Jenny's ear she whispered, "Because without them, I'd never have noticed you and felt sorry for you. We'd never have met. And I'm so glad we did."

Jenny turned around to face Louise, and leaned forward to whisper, "Oh, Louise. I'm sorry. Of course. I didn't mean ... "

"I think Jenny knows what for," Gus was saying. "For allowing the transmission of a forbidden image, thanks to that goddamned boyfriend of hers. I was in a police cell waiting to be taken to the Moon, to Collins Central. There was going to be a secret trial and everything."

"And you'd never have needed me." Louise whispered. "I'd never have had the chance to fly you around in there. I loved that, you know. Actually, Jenny, don't be shocked or anything, but I want to tell you something." She put her arms around Jenny and kissed her on the ear she'd been whispering into. And as she pressed a little closer, Jenny couldn't help it: her cuffed hands were touching Louise where she definitely didn't want them to.

"Then suddenly there was this battle going on right inside the police station. You can say what you like, Jenny, about the Back-to-Earthers being stupid – and in their basic premise that's of course what they are – but when it comes to strategy and tactics, they are, or were, brilliant.

They'd been planning this for years and managed to put it all into effect in about two days – after Allaby's old Immyo had turned up in the holoparks. They took over the Moon and the satellite at the same time. More people were mobilised than you'd ever have imagined. And God could they fight."

Louise pressed even closer.

"They killed every single policeman in the station, about a half a dozen of them, with the loss of no Back-to-Earthers. At the same time others of them were shooting the executives and kidnapping children and rounding up people to throw in the gym. I knew what they were doing because I could hear them organising it. There's only one cell in that station, and it's small and kind of off another room, and for a long time they didn't even know it was there – didn't know I was there. And they'd made the station a kind of headquarters for, I guess, the more middle-ranking ones, the ones who were doing most of the fighting and kidnapping and ..."

Jenny couldn't help it. Her hands were where they were, and Louise was where she was. She said, "Listen, Louise. You're one of the best, most generous people I've ever met. In my life. And you saved my life. But I don't want—"

"Jenny, what I want is to give you a present."

"... talking about taking all the ships in the docks and heading for all what they thought were the most fertile parts of the planet, six of which are in and around the Immyo reservations, I'm sorry to say, but of course that's why the ancients put the Immyos in those areas in the first place. And now all over the Earth, Immyos are going to be finding these puzzling ships full of dead people. And so many of them children ... Ships, big ships, were coming direct from the Moon, too. And Jenny, you know where their main colony was going to be? Their headquarters? Their capital? Their nursery, as they called it. Your sector. That's probably why they took you away from there, so that you, in their deluded view, couldn't cause them any trouble. Or maybe when they talked to you they wanted you as a guide or something. Anyway, they said that Africa East was where humans evolved and that was where humans would start again. It makes you sick to think ..."

She felt Louise moving her fingers as if she were somehow arranging them. She whispered, "Jenny, are you ready?"

"Ready? For what?"

Louise's fingers kept probing. Then they were still. "Okay," Louise said. "And because of Mister Templeton over there, I'm going to have to do this, too." She put her other hand over Jenny's mouth. Then the fingers moved again, and for some reason Jenny became almost rigidly tense.

What happened right after that, she couldn't have said exactly. She couldn't even have said how long it lasted. All she knew, both while it was happening and afterwards, was that it was sudden, entirely unexpected and explosive, and seemed to involve every muscle fibre, every nerve, every cell in her body. The tension that Louise, with a touch, had apparently induced was, with another touch, immediately dissipated, and the result was pure, unrefined essence of pleasure. It came in pump after pump after wave after wave. Jenny was vaguely aware of other things happening, of her moans and shrieks into Louise's hand, of her shortness of breath, of the collapse of her knees and Louise lowering her to the shower floor, but all that was incidental to a total onslaught of ecstasy.

It hadn't made her pass out or anything (in fact, it had been the opposite of passing out – the most awake she'd ever known herself to be), but when it was over, she was left with the sensation of coming to. Had that been an orgasm? If so, every orgasm she'd ever had before was no more than a belly laugh. She was sitting there, feet far apart, still shuddering, still breathing hard, and feeling unnaturally happy. Warm water was running over her, and a beautiful, dripping Louise was kneeling in front of her stroking her hair.

"Are you two all right?" Gus said.

"We're fine, Mister Templeton. Are you all right?"

"Yeah, yeah. But I thought I heard, not loud, but a kind of yelling."

"Oh that was just me, Mister Templeton. I got soap in my eye. But I'm all right now. And please go on filling us in on everything that's happened."

"Okay," he said. His decompositor whistled. "I'm going to have my shower now." His shower started. "Where was I? Oh yeah, they finally came across my cell about three hours after they'd taken the station. I don't think it worried them that I'd been eavesdropping on them all that time. They thought it was kind of funny that I could be there. They didn't know who I was, of course – just assumed I was a burglar or a drunk or something … You know, they could be so clever in some ways and so stupid in others. All they had to do was check the records. And of course going to Earth without sanitation suits is the ultimate stupidity. Anyway,

258

they turned me over to one of the gangs that were rounding up people for the gym …

Jenny looped her handcuffs over Louise's head and, with her hands on the back of her neck pulled her to her. Jenny whispered, "What did you just do?"

"It's a kind of trick, I suppose. An old woman taught it to me. With the fingers of one hand you can make – right away and all at once, Jenny – all three kinds of orgasm. It's hard to learn, though. It takes a lot of practice. I had a friend once who said it was harder than the violin. She tried but couldn't quite learn. To do that, I mean. She was a good violinist."

"Jesus, Louise, I've never … God, who are you?"

Louise kept whispering: "But the trouble is, nobody else nowadays seems to want to learn, especially not any men, and you know what men are like – they've got something they'd rather use than their fingers, bless their hearts. Nobody wants to do all that practising, and it doesn't quite work when you do it to yourself. I haven't felt what you've just felt since the old woman died. I've felt parts of it from other people and from myself, too, but it always takes a while, and it's not the whole caboodle. Now that we know each other better, would you do me a lovely favour and let me teach you?"

"Sure, Louise, of course, of course. But for right now, would you, would you—"

"What?"

"… would you do it again?"

"Okay, but in a minute. Let me shampoo you first."

"… and the rest," Gus was saying, "is history – you two turned up, thank God."

CHAPTER TWENTY-SIX

It was hard enough to understand what Allaby was talking about, but it was even harder to understand his attitude to it. Sometimes he seemed excited, sometimes unhappy, sometimes puzzled – which was doubly puzzling to Gibbous: how could Allaby fail to comprehend anything skypeople did? As far as Gibbous could make out, which was not very far, the moon had disappeared last night because a big something – Allaby had been calling it either a 'ship' or a 'liner', neither of which words were much help – came between the moon and the ground. And it now it could be on the ground, somewhere over that way, towards the mountains but a bit south of the direction they were heading in (or, as was the case, not heading in), and there could be a whole lot of skypeople with it. If there were, this meant that it wasn't necessary any longer to go to Allaby's house, wherever that was anyway, so that he could tell the other skypeople that they could live on the ground and breathe, because they obviously already knew that – an idea that Allaby seemed to like and then not like. But then Allaby would say that maybe they weren't there, that they'd been somehow made to disappear or had decided not to be there or somesuch, in which case it might or might not still be necessary to get to Allaby's house, to tell other skypeople that these skypeople were there or might be somewhere else or weren't anywhere at all … and that was where Gibbous would lose track. What was hard to tell was whether Allaby hoped they were there or hoped they weren't. One way or the other, Gibbous himself was having a hard time caring. He, Allaby and Paintbrush were working on a new Beginning here, and if they didn't have to go to Allaby's house any more because there were skypeople over yonder, fine – then they could really concentrate on their own project. But if there weren't any … and Gibbous found himself going around the tree again.

"But, Gibbous, we've got to find out. There's no way of avoiding that."

"We could just go over there and have a look, but you can't walk. Or I could go over by myself and look, if it really matters that much to you. Or best of all, we could wait until you can walk, which will probably be another couple of days, and then walk past the place on our way to the mountains."

It was the middle of the afternoon. Gibbous had slept well under the shelter he'd built and had had a delicious late breakfast, served by Paintbrush, of prairie dog and cactus apple (he hoped Allaby appreciated what a magnificent cook he'd married) and was in a mood too good to be spoiled by Allaby's convoluted problem. Or non-problem. Allaby sat propped against one of the shelter's poles, and Paintbrush sat between his knees using some of the extra water Gibbous had brought to wash the baby down, having already cleaned herself and Allaby around the face, hands and hair. Yellow was off somewhere – last seen chasing a hare. There was a little breeze blowing across the plain and through the shelter, and with that, their new shade and the soft grass Paintbrush had gathered this morning, it was as comfortable out here as could ever be expected. Waiting a couple of more days didn't seem so bad now, and he hoped Allaby would see it that way, too. Having to walk what Allaby had estimated was about ten miles just to see what was there or wasn't there and then to turn around and walk back seemed a pointless exertion. But if they were on their way to the mountains anyway, why not go a little south?

"While you were asleep," Paintbrush said, rubbing dirt off the squirming baby's neck, "Allaby did do a bit of walking."

"It was more riding on your back than walking," Allaby said, "but we did go some distance, about over to where those horses are now. Who knows? I might be all right tomorrow."

Those horses were almost close enough to look in the eye. Gibbous could see the flies they were swishing with their tails. "One of the many things I'm failing to understand, Allaby, is why there's such a hurry. I'd have thought you'd want to feel as good as you could before we started off again."

"Well, I do, but it's really hard to explain, Gibbous."

"I've noticed."

"Okay, let's start over."

"Oh, what's the point, Allaby? If you couldn't explain it the first time …"

"Granddad and Allaby," Paintbrush said, drying the baby with a cloth, "I think I know what's wrong."

"What's that?" Gibbous said.

"When I didn't know how to tell you about the atrocity, you told me about telling stories – about starting at the beginning, the middle or even the end sometimes, but all in all it was best to start at the beginning. Remember?"

"Sort of." He didn't remember saying that last bit, but never mind.

"Well, I don't think Allaby's starting – and I don't mean this as a criticism, love – I don't think you're starting at the beginning. I mean, you've told us about the bang beginning, but that seems a bit far back. There's a lot in between that you haven't got around to yet, and I think that if we're going to understand why it matters that a bunch of skypeople might be walking around ten miles over there, there's something else you've got to tell us. Isn't that right?" She took Allaby's hand and kissed it.

"Let's see," Allaby said. "How far back would I ..."

"I'll tell you where you could start. Tell us how skypeople came to be."

"I've told you. Skypeople are just people, just like you and Gibbous, and people evolved – that is, people first appeared on Earth in East Africa about a hundred thousand—"

"No, no, Love. How did they get to be skypeople?"

"Where is that?" Gibbous said.

"Where is what?"

"Where you said people first appeared."

"Oh, East Africa." Allaby pointed in the direction, roughly, of the woods. "That's about—"

"No," said Paintbrush. "Stop it, both of you. That's what happens, Granddad. You get Allaby off the subject."

"Do I?"

"You know you do, Granddad."

Well, yes, he supposed he did, but all the most interesting things Allaby had to say he seemed to say as asides. That was fascinating, that people began in the east, where the sun rose, and he wondered if there was a connection. No, maybe not. But maybe. He'd have to ask Allaby some time when Paintbrush wasn't around – although separating the two of them now, even for a minute, would be about as easy as uprooting a cactus.

"Now, Allaby, Love," Paintbrush said, "I'm just going ask some questions, and all you have to do is answer them. And Granddad, you just listen. First question. How long have people been living in the sky? Longer than on the ground or not as long?"

"Not as long. Not nearly as long. Only about twelve hundred years. As I said, people first appeared on Earth – on the ground – more than a hundred thousand years ago."

"In the east," Gibbous said.

"East Africa, yes. That is east of here. That is to say you'd get there a little quicker going east than going west … but no, I won't get into that."

"Good," said Paintbrush. "Now remember we're trying to find out about skypeople and why it's important that there might be a bunch of them over there."

Did he say that that place was both east and west of here? Why did he say that? It seemed a deliberate attempt to confuse and confound, to ruin a perfectly pleasant afternoon. The baby was awake but not crying – just happily sitting in his mother's lap, sucking on the cloth and looking from Gibbous to Allaby as though he were listening to the conversation. And with Paintbrush herself sitting with her back to Allaby, the three of them together, all freshly washed, looked like the perfect loving family. The breeze was nice. There were no worries about food or water or anything else. There was nothing to do, really, but sit and talk – a nice opportunity. And then Allaby has to say something that slices through the middle of your mind. "Sorry, Paintbrush. I won't be quiet about this. I can't let him get away with saying that one place is both to the east and to the west."

"Granddad, please …"

"No, I'm sorry, Paintbrush," Allaby said. "I didn't mean to say that. It just slipped …"

"You might not have meant to say it," Gibbous said, hearing a touch of anger in his own voice, "but did you mean it?"

"Yes."

"Oh, Allaby, we'll never …"

"This isn't working, is it – dribbling information to you little by little, so that I don't disturb your world view too much or shock you or anything. To hell with it, Gibbous. The world is round. We're sitting on the outside of an enormous ball, stuck to it by something called gravity. If you travel west long enough and far enough, you can not only manage to get to East Africa, you can keep on going and end up right back here, and the same goes for east. So this spot where we're sitting is not only here, it's west and east of here, not to mention north and south. Understand? That's the way it works when you live on a ball.

"Is that really true?" Paintbrush said, bending her head back to look up at Allaby.

"It's true."

"It can't be true," Gibbous said. He didn't know why he'd said it, though – except that it was an explanation that, in a lifetime of pondering such things, had never occurred to him.

Allaby went on. Gibbous and Paintbrush were being asked to imagine a fly walking on that big round rock formation over by Deep Gorge, then to think of a much-smaller-than-usual fly and of a big round rock much bigger than the one they'd already been asked to think about. "To the fly it would look flat," Allaby said, "and the direction 'down' would be towards the rock, wherever on the rock the fly was." But while the fly stuck to the rock because it had sticky feet, people stuck to the ground because of this gravity thing that Allaby had mentioned before – which was like invisible strings always pulling at you and everything else. Then somehow he got to the sun and the moon, which were also big balls, and the stars, which were mostly even bigger than the sun but a lot farther away. Then came something about gravity making things go in circles around other things and the world not being just a ball that was sitting there or hanging there but was going in a circle around the sun and was spinning while it did it, which made night and day, and so on and so on. Gibbous didn't know if he was taking in half of what Allaby was saying, but he was beginning to feel more and more like the fly on the rock – very small and stupid. Of course, he didn't know how much of what Allaby was saying was actually true and how much was based on the skypeople's equivalent of the Old Stories, but Allaby did come from the sky, where most of this stuff was happening, and he might have seen it all in action. Finally, though, Gibbous quit trying to keep up and let Allaby talk on while he pondered the part about the round world. Thinking about some of the implications made him a little dizzy (about the surface of a ball, for instance, not having a beginning or an end), but it did seem to answer at least one thing he'd always wondered about. He interrupted to say, "If the world is round, Allaby, would that be why we can't see the mountains?"

"Gibbous, you've just grasped something that took the rest of humanity the best part of its existence to grasp. Yes. We can't see them from here because a small bit of the curve of the ball is between us and them. If we went out from under this shelter and looked, we could see the sun, which is a hell of a lot farther away than the mountains, because we'd be looking at it in a straight line. But if we wanted to look at the mountains in a straight line, and could see through the ground, we'd be looking in about that direction." With his good hand, he pointed straight ahead and then lowered his arm a little. "And that would just be the mountaintops."

"Or," Gibbous said, "if we could get up high ..."

"Right. Then you'd see over the curve."

Paintbrush took the hand Allaby had been pointing with and held it against her cheek. "It's a beautiful idea, living on a ball. I like it a lot better than some big flat slab. Do you believe it now, Granddad?"

"I guess I do," Gibbous said. "I just don't know why I never figured it out myself." That was the reason Allaby's explanations annoyed him sometimes – they were so blindingly obvious they made him feel simple-minded. It was like the axle. How could he go all his life without thinking to put a stick between two cowpats?

"Gibbous, you can't be expected to have figured it out. As I said, it took all the people in the world thousands and thousands of years – generations after generations – to realise the shape of the rock they were sitting on. And it's a scandal that such a basic fact hasn't been passed on to you. It's cruel. The whole predicament of your people is cruel. Well, now that I'm one of your people and married to one of your people, the finest, the brightest, the internally and externally most beautiful woman I've ever met or ever thought I'd meet, I'll tell you that your people have been imprisoned and kept in ignorance by my former people since the first of your ancestors were discovered more than a thousand years ago. All because of jealousy ."

"Allaby, love," Paintbrush said, "you're wearing out my head. Who is it that's jealous?"

"The skypeople."

"What of?"

"You. Your people. Because you can live here. That's the way it must have started, anyway. Most skypeople now don't even know you exist – they're kept in ignorance, too, at least on the subject of you. The only ones who are supposed to know about you are people like me, working on Earth, and the people supervising us."

"Why can't they know about us?"

"I think maybe it's a case of a secret that's been kept so long it has to keep being kept. If people found out about you now, they might think it was okay to return to Earth. Of course it is okay, but that's beside the point. Back when it wasn't – and as far as all skypeople but me are concerned, it still isn't … I think … But then we don't know what those people from that liner know … Ah, I'm getting tied up again, aren't I?

"Yeah," Gibbous said. "You might have talked yourself out. But you've just given us the round world, and we're grateful. Go on, though, if you think you can." It was satisfying in a way to see Allaby struggling with something he didn't know everything about.

"I'll tell you what the problem is," Allaby said. "Because we're not supposed to know you exist, we don't get any history of you. All we were told in Earth training was that you are descendants of people who were immune to the, uh, the disease that killed everybody else on Earth. Your ancestors were sought out and rounded up – they were all very isolated cases – and put on the richest land around so that they and their descendants could make a living far into the future by hunting and gathering. There was no problem with migration – that is, moving somewhere else – because, for one thing, your land was so permanently rich you wouldn't particularly want to leave it, and for another, there were detection systems around your reservations so that any human with an immunity gene walking across the boundary got … Oh, I don't know. I made sure it doesn't happen any more anyway. At least not here."

"I don't understand," Paintbrush said. "What did you call it, that system?"

"Detection system," Allaby said. "It just means that if anybody like you steps across a certain line, that person is particled. That person dies. Vanishes. There's a line like that at the foothills of the San Juans – the mountains. Except that there isn't one now, because I destroyed it. Really destroyed it. They can rebuild almost everything else about my station – except that they don't need to now, only they probably don't know that, or might know it, who knows? – but I hated that system so much that … Nobody ever explained to us why our ancients didn't want you to leave your reservation or why the damned system stayed in place all this time. I mean, it wasn't as though there were any other humans around …"

Allaby, who was very agitated now, seemed to have reverted to jabbering. When he'd been talking about round worlds and gravity, he'd been pretty clear, if exhausting. Now, though, Gibbous (and to judge by the mystified look on her face, Paintbrush, too) was comprehending very little. But he did think he'd caught the gist of the 'system' or whatever it was. The skypeople had made a kind of trip-rope, like the trip-ropes you'd put around a campsite on a war expedition. It meant the Chief's father and a lot of other people had been right: anybody who tried to go to the mountains or, if they were so moved, to any of the deserts in the north, east and south would trip the rope and be killed by the skypeople. That's why no explorers ever came back, and why no one ever had ever returned in embarrassment from a Long Walk Out. It banished Gibbous's vague notion of a place over there so wonderful that no one who reached it would ever want to leave again. But it also meant that when the Little Rimmers had said they'd gone up a mountain, they had indeed been lying, just as Gibbous had always thought. Then there was his own Long Walk Out. If it had turned out the way he'd planned it – with no Paintbrush and Skyman and no Allaby, a normal Long Walk Out to the endless water – it would be over now. Something horrible would have happened to him.

But Allaby said he'd destroyed the trip-rope (he had said that, hadn't he?). That would mean that, if they ever got going again, Gibbous, Paintbrush and Skyman would be the first people from any of the Seven Settlements ever to venture beyond the Far Plain, ever to go into the mountains. No matter how you looked at it, that was exciting. But there was a bleak side to it, too: skypeople were not, as the stories depicted them, entirely benign. Allaby himself seemed to hate his own people because they murdered, or did something worse to, innocent people who only wanted to see the world or just quietly go off and die. That there might be a big group of skypeople just ten miles away became a little unsettling – now that they knew they could breathe on the ground, the skypeople might want the ground all to themselves. Allaby was right – it was important to find out if they were really there. This small party could easily skirt around them and go on travelling, but what about the Seven, rather the Six, Settlements? What would the skypeople do to them?

"… immunity is carried by a dominant gene, which means that one out of four of your babies bleed to death as soon as it takes its first breath, and so your population never grows …"

"Wait, Allaby," Gibbous said. "Hold on. If you're still able to talk so that I can understand you, can you answer a question for me?"

"You haven't been understanding? Oh, sorry. I guess I was getting carried away. Of course. I can go over it again, this time using words that—"

"No, no. You don't need to go over it again. I just want to ask a question."

"Okay."

"I've got a question, too," Paintbrush said.

"Sure, ask, one of you."

"If there are skypeople over there," Gibbous said, pointing, "are they dangerous?"

"I don't know," Allaby said. "All I do know is, if they are there, they're not supposed to be. If the people I used to work for caught them, they would kill them. They might even already have."

"Would they do anything to our people – our people back at the Gorge?"

"I don't know," Allaby said. "I just don't know. They might be entirely peaceable. But I don't know."

"Sounds like I'd better have a look then, just to see if they're there. If they are, maybe I could go back and warn the Chief. I could go look for them tonight."

"Oh, Granddad, no." Paintbrush said. She was feeding the baby now, the final touch to the perfect family picture (except that Allaby was looking a little red-faced and wild-eyed). "Not another all-night walk. And if they are there and are dangerous, something might happen to you, especially if you're alone."

"Nah. If they're anything like your husband here, they should be pretty easy to size up without getting caught. Sorry, Allaby, but you know what I mean."

"I do know. And right now they'd be a lot worse than me. They wouldn't be used to the Earth – the ground – at all. For one thing, they'd hardly be able to move, because they're so much heavier than they've ever been ..."

Not that one again, Gibbous thought.

"... but they might have guns, something you've never seen. If you decide to go, you'd better let me tell you everything to watch out for."

"I wish you wouldn't, Granddad."

"Thanks for worrying about me, Paintbrush – for all the worrying about me you've ever done. I don't think anyone, even Spiderweb, ever worried about me as well as you do. But I think this might be important, and there's nobody else who can do it. Anyway, I'm just going to look and see if they're there and maybe see how many of them there are. I'm not going to go up and say hello or try to start a fight or anything." Then he remembered all the times he'd almost made it to the mountains. It was pure luck that he hadn't. "Although I wouldn't mind telling them what I think of them, the bastards."

Allaby said, "I think you need to get one thing straight, Gibbous, because I don't want you losing your temper and doing anything stupid."

"I've never lost my temper in my life."

"That's true," Paintbrush said, "and he's never done anything stupid. Until now."

"Just the same," Allaby said, "those people, if they are there, will never have heard of your people. The ones you call 'the bastards', the ones who decided on the detection system and set it up, are all long dead, and the ones who operate it now would never let a ship come near here. I have no idea who they are, but I'm certain who they aren't. That's not to say that those people can't be dangerous, or bastards, too, in some other way. We just don't know. At the very least, if they saw you, you might scare them, and no telling what they would do then."

"Granddad, I have a terrible feeling about this. It reminds me of a dream. Allaby, love, tell him not to do it."

"Gibbous, think about it. Are you sure you want to?"

"I don't want to walk twenty miles tonight, no. But I have to. So I'm going, Paintbrush. I'll have a little more to eat now, and then Allaby's going to tell me what to look out for and point me in the direction he thinks they are – because of the curved world, we can't see them from here. I'll start out while it's still light. After sunset, I'll rest until the moon rises and then go on."

Paintbrush shrugged. As she looked down at the baby and stroked his head, Gibbous thought he'd seen tears. "Whatever you say, Granddad." Then, still looking down, she shifted the baby to the other breast, and there was silence for a while as the baby sucked and pumped. Gibbous finally got up, went a couple of paces out into the sun and stoked the fire. He added a cowpat, dug up a skinned prairie dog, knocked and shook the dirt and worms off and put it on the spit he'd brought back last night from the old campsite. Then he looked out across rippling grass at the horizon a little west of south. Damned if there wasn't – way beyond the cows, horses and deer – a herd of elephants out there. He'd be walking right past them.

From the shelter, Paintbrush was saying, "Oh yes, Allaby – the question I meant to ask. Did you say something about a lot of our babies bleeding to death?"

"Yes I did. Do you want me to explain why?"

"No, you don't need to, love, because it doesn't happen. It used to, I think, but I've never seen it happen. Granddad, there used to be bleeding babies, didn't there."

"Oh yeah, all the time," Gibbous said. "People used to consider themselves really lucky if they didn't have a bleeder." He lowered the spit a notch. "Then one year it just stopped happening, and it's never happened since. I remember that year, mainly because it was so smoky, with all the burnt offerings to Mother Elephant. It stopped in all the settlements, too, not just the Ledge. Funny thing was, everybody thought it was their own gods that had done it."

"Gibbous," Allaby said, "how old were you then?"

"Oh, let's see. It was the year before Spiderweb and I got married. And I'll tell you, we were really happy to think we weren't going to have to go through that. It was awful – gruesome, really sad. So I guess I was twenty, about twenty, yeah."

"And now you're … "

"He's seventy, Allaby."

"I'll be damned."

"What's the matter, Love?"

"I can't believe this. All that time. All that sterilisation rigmarole and everything. Are you sure you were twenty, Gibbous?"

"Sure I'm sure."

"You know what that means?"

"What, Love?"

"The goddamned virus has been gone for fifty years."

CHAPTER TWENTY-SEVEN

Gibbous had gone about three hundred paces when Yellow joined him. He hadn't seen where the dog had come from – at the time he'd been concentrating on the elephants up ahead, wondering if he'd be able to get past them before sunset – and then had looked down to see Yellow in the grass walking beside him as though he had been there all along. This was a very dirty dog. He'd obviously been down a hole somewhere and was now covered in lumps of soil and strands of root. Gibbous stopped, put down his stick, held Yellow by the scruff and brushed as much as he could off him. Then he stood up again and waved his stick at Paintbrush and Allaby, who were still watching him from the campsite. They waved back. "No, no," he mouthed. "Yellow's here. Yellow." He pointed at the dog, even though he'd be hidden from them by grass. They waved again. So he said to Yellow, "You go back. Go back, Yellow." Yellow trotted about ten paces in the other direction and sat down, waiting. Gibbous trudged after him, saying, "I don't want you on this trip. It's too dangerous. Go back there." He pointed at the campsite behind. Yellow got up and went another ten paces west, and that was when Gibbous realised something: both times he'd left Yellow before, he'd been going east, back to where they'd already been. Yellow wasn't interested in that. He wanted to go west – or southwest at least – but to go on, which he must have thought Gibbous was now doing. As far as Yellow was concerned, there'd been some interruptions, but now they were back on the Long Walk Out. This gave Gibbous two choices – he could either pick the dog up and carry him back to campsite and maybe tie him to something, or he could let him come along. This time, when he was about two paces from Yellow, the dog got up, trotted another ten, and sat. The choice, it appeared, was not really there. So Gibbous, following Yellow, walked on.

Because if that was the way Yellow wanted to look at this little expedition, why argue? For a while, Gibbous could pretend things were as he thought they were back on the first and only day of his long-planned Long Walk Out – with the Ledge intact behind him and no inkling of the skypeople's trip-rope lying ahead (it was the most disturbing piece of information Allaby had so far given him, mainly because it invalidated a whole lifetime of imagining). But what a day: cut his ties to his past, got to know a dog better than he ever thought he would, had squirrel for lunch, wondered about Mother Elephant, speculated about the endless water, watched the sunset over the Far Plain – just as he would be doing again now. In fact, as far as the endless water went, he hadn't got around to asking Allaby about that, and so he could still speculate … But, no. No, he couldn't. Endless water was impossible, of course. He lived on the surface of a ball now, and the only way you could have endless water is if you didn't have any land whatsoever. The world according to Allaby was all wrapped around itself. Damn.

He didn't doubt Allaby. It was just that, after years of trying to reason out the truth, finally getting it – not through reasoning at all, but on the say-so of someone who was bound to know – was an anticlimax. So that was it: a whole bunch of balls going around in circles out in the sky, all the result of a bang in some other part of the sky. He'd been a long time not quite trusting the Old Stories, partly because he knew how much he'd embellished them himself, but now he felt a little sad at their passing. Paintbrush had said they were beautiful, and they were, most of them, even if they were all utterly wrong. But what he was left with seemed so impersonal and precarious. He had a lot of questions for Allaby, even though he wasn't sure he wanted to ask them. For instance, how come some things are alive and some things aren't? In the Old Stories, everything was alive – rocks, trees, everything – they were just alive in different ways. He was pretty sure that wasn't true, but he was afraid now of Allaby's possible answer. He had no idea what that would be – and there was no point in even guessing – but he now knew it would manage to be disappointing somehow.

Maybe what was really true was that every time you learned something you lost something. Maybe all the questions you have are automatically answered to your own satisfaction, whether the answers are right or not, and when the genuine right answer comes along, you have to make way for it by throwing one away that you've always been perfectly happy with. Of course, in my case, Gibbous thought, I haven't been perfectly happy with the automatic answers, and so I'm getting exactly what I've asked for. It serves me right. Once upon a time, Mother Elephant used to spend all night carrying the sun through Hell so that she could come out at the eastern edge of the world and launch another day. It made you feel warm inside that Mother Elephant should care so much. But now it's goodbye, Mother Elephant. Now the world is a big ball that – for no reason Allaby has so far explained – spins around, so that night is when the part you're on isn't facing the sun, and day is when it is. (But why does it keep spinning? Why doesn't it just flop over like a top? Probably something to do with gravity – Allaby's own Mother Elephant, in that it seems to be involved in the last-resort answer to everything.) It was better to know the truth – Gibbous was resolute in that opinion – but at least until he could explore it some more, the truth felt uncaring and accidental, almost bleak.

Even worse was the disgrace of the skypeople. Once, they were part gods, with big eyeballs for heads and wings on their backs. They were allies of Hero, who may or may not have been a skyman himself. They helped him found the Seven Settlements after saving the ancestors from the rivers of blood. It had been comforting to know that they were up there, and it was a rare cause for gratitude when one was spotted on the ground. But now what were they? Ordinary people, and not very nice ones either. They killed innocent travellers, and others – so far from caring about the inhabitants of the ground – didn't even know the ground people existed. The world, thanks to the truth, had lost a whole layer of goodness – and not to nothingness this time, but to a new layer of what could very well be evil. (Except for Allaby, but then Allaby had deserted the sky and was a ground person now.) That truth about the skypeople was even worse than bleak – it was ominous. And here he was on his way to a whole nest of the bastards.

The sun had dropped to a point almost straight ahead of him, and the breeze that had been so pleasant earlier in the afternoon was now on the verge of becoming a proper wind. It was blowing from behind him and was making his shirt and trousers flap a little as it ruffled the hair on Yellow's back and bent the grass towards the white glare of the sun. He hoped that, before the wind got any stronger, Paintbrush and Allaby would think to take the shelter down. Otherwise they could lose a blanket and have a pretty miserable night. He took a look back, but he had walked nearly a mile by now, and there was a landscape full of animals between him and the campsite. He couldn't see the shelter, but just in case, he sent a mental message to Paintbrush (she sometimes claimed to be able to receive these) and then figured that was the most he could be expected to do about the problem, if it actually was a problem.

And whether it was or not, it was a strange problem for him to be worrying about, considering the size of the one that might be lying ahead.

Allaby had told him about several skyman things he might see and would have to watch out for. Gibbous wasn't sure he could remember all the names and which did which, but he was pretty firm on the 'ship' itself, a kind of massive house that, if it wanted to, could fly, as well as smaller flying things called 'pickups' and 'outriggers' and a bigger something else – the name had gone. Allaby had been detailed in his descriptions and had drawn pictures in the dirt, but even though Gibbous had tried hard, he hadn't been able to lodge all of them of them in his head and had finally decided that he'd know them if and when he saw them. Then there was a 'rover', which couldn't fly but was actually a little exciting, because if he saw one of those he'd be seeing axles in action. The worst thing was the 'gun'. It was like a bow and arrow, in that it could kill from a distance, but there was no bow, and it was small enough to be held in one hand. What was more, you couldn't even see the arrow it shot, not that it was an arrow. Gibbous had had real trouble following this part, but Allaby had described it as a little ball of light so fast and hot that it burned a hole in whatever it was shot at. And the little balls could be shot in quick succession, so that if the first one missed, any one of the others wouldn't. Guns were a genuinely frightening prospect, mainly because they were so small. Allaby had said that by the time you noticed that a person was holding one and if he could see you and had a mind to kill you, you'd already be dead. So there was only one solution to that: stay out of sight. Allaby had mentioned other things, too, but when he'd talked about them, he'd been talking so fast – to the point, sometimes, of jabbering again – that Gibbous had just said never mind, that if he came across any of those, he'd have to guess what they were for and use his wits. Altogether, it had been the most intensive short intake of new information he'd ever experienced, and it had given him a throbbing pain just above the eyebrows.

It hadn't helped, either, that every time Paintbrush had heard of another horrible possibility, she'd pleaded with him again not to go and then pleaded with Allaby to plead with him, and Allaby would ask a half-hearted question about whether he really wanted to, and Gibbous would have to say all over again why he thought it was important and how he wasn't going to go all the way back to Big Rim or even to the nearest settlement, Waterfall (no, it had to be the Chief – Gibbous didn't even know who Waterfall's Headman was these days), if there wasn't a danger, and if there was, he'd have to see what it was for himself – how many people there were, exactly where they were, what they looked like and what they were doing. If you were going to start a scare, he'd told them, you shouldn't be half-cocked. Anyway, Paintbrush's pleas had been counter-productive: the more he had to defend his intention to go, the more firmly he was able to convince himself.

By the time the sun had turned from bright and white to large and orange, there were elephants silhouetted in it. And since the wind had picked up even more, Gibbous knew that the elephants were already aware that a man and a dog were coming their way. All of them – it was a herd of about a dozen, not counting three or four babies – had turned to face in Gibbous's and Yellow's direction, even though they were still a good two hundred paces away. Why elephants should have as much as a flicker of worry about relatively puny and harmless creatures was usually taken as one of life's puzzles (by contrast, cows, which were regularly hunted by men and dogs, always seemed surprised when bad things happened to them), but in Gibbous's opinion, it was because elephants had such lofty principles. They chased lions, for instance. Gibbous had never seen lions with any designs on elephants, not even baby elephants, but elephants nevertheless tormented lions at every opportunity. What they liked to do best, it seemed, was to find a pride in repose – asleep or just lying around after filling up on something – and charge in and make the poor belly-heavy things scatter. To Gibbous it looked like righteous retribution on the part of animals that didn't approve of killing other animals – a way of scolding lions for being lions and being nasty to peaceable grass-eaters. And of course they could as easily have the same low regard of men and dogs, which weren't any nicer to grass-eaters than lions were. That was probably why the ancestors had chosen to worship elephants – they represented a fierce and unattainable morality. Given that meat was most of what humans ate (and all that dogs did), if you actually behaved in the beatific way elephants would have you behave, you'd starve to death, though afterwards you'd probably go to some kind of elephant heaven.

Elephants were the only animals Gibbous was really nervous of. He'd been worried since he'd started this hike that he'd reach the herd right at sundown and would have to stop near them while he waited for the moon to rise. He'd half expected that the elephants would have moved on by the time he got here, but they hadn't, and with the wind blowing the way it was, even stopping this far away didn't feel comfortable. It wasn't unheard-of for elephants to attack people who approached too close to a herd, but most of the time what looked like an attack – the matriarch's raised trunk, the flapping ears, the glaring eyes, the angry trumpeting, the feinted charges – was nothing but an admonition, and if the object of the elephants' efforts looked suitably scolded and slinked away, that would be that. The trouble was, if you added pitch darkness to the mix, not to mention a confusing wind, there could be an accident.

So he decided, while there was still some light, to go due south for a while. He'd make a big arc around the elephants, adding maybe a mile to the trip, which wasn't too much (especially considering that Allaby's guess about the location of the skypeople was, at best, very, very rough), and he could spend his short time in the dark well out of the elephants' range. "Come on, Yellow," he said. "Let's go this way," and he started walking south. But after a few paces, it became clear that Yellow didn't want to go this way. The damned dog was fixated on southwest and kept trotting towards the elephants. "Yellow!" Gibbous shouted, his voice carrying on the wind all the way to the silhouette of the matriarch, who raised her trunk. She might have trumpeted then, but if so, the sound was blown away. "Yellow!" Yellow, now about thirty paces from Gibbous, stopped and sat, facing towards the elephants and showing no sign of wanting to join Gibbous on any journey in what he considered an inferior direction.

Never mind, Gibbous told himself, just start walking and he'll have to come. Trying to look resolute, Gibbous strode south, his stick hitting the ground firmly with each step. He wouldn't look back. The wind was buffeting him from the side now, whipping through his hair and beard and beginning to feel a good deal cooler. Before too long he was going to have to stop and take the poncho out of his satchel. Well, he'd take it out now. He stopped, squatted and opened the satchel, and as he was pulling out the poncho, he stole a look at where he'd last seen Yellow. Because the wind had nearly flattened the grass, he could see clearly that the dog wasn't there. He stood up, put on the poncho and had another look. Yellow was, in fact, farther on his way towards the elephants.

Okay, then, that was it – the parting of the ways. A man and a dog could get along pretty well – better than he'd ever imagined – but there comes a point when they're each on their own again. Otherwise what could Gibbous do? Run after him? Snatch him from under an indignant elephant? Well, for a start, Gibbous wasn't able to run, and that eliminated anything else. Go be a dog, Yellow, and maybe you'll find some dog way of getting out and staying out of trouble. I just hope I've taught you to take care of yourself as well as another dog could have. The sun was almost gone, and the sky was purple and darkening fast. He had a last look at Yellow – the wind blowing his fur upright as he still trotted towards the elephants. Then Gibbous turned away and resumed walking south.

He wasn't bent double with guilt, but it felt like it. Even the guilt he'd experienced for having an unnecessary funeral and getting his whole settlement wiped out wasn't this intense. That guilt had been more thoughtful, more justified – deep sorrow and a true self-recrimination for a disaster that he'd inadvertently caused. This was just irrational and stomach-wringing. When he looked back yet again, it was too dark to see much more than the now safely distant (for Gibbous, anyway) outlines of the elephants, all still facing in the same direction, which could only mean that they were still watching the dog approach. Any other dog trotting across the plain wouldn't have been worth a glance from the herd, but this one had been with a man and was tainted by that fact. It was as if Gibbous had left his spirit with Yellow, and the matriarch was at least going to punish that. He had to keep telling himself that if Yellow was determined to keep going, there was nothing he could have done about it … except …

… he could have darted him.

Damn it. In any emergency, his pipe was usually the first thing he thought of. Why hadn't he thought of it this time? He'd even had the wind behind him … What was wrong with him?

When the darkness was total, he stopped walking. With his stick he thrashed the grass in a circle around himself, making sure there were no snakes, and then he sank to a squat. The wind had reached battering force, whistling and moaning over the grass, whipping his clothes and tearing at his beard. He hated wind in the dark because it made him as deaf as he was blind, and he had no way of knowing if anything was coming. It even eliminated smell as a guide. The only things available to any sense now were the stars, which despite their uncountable number never gave off any usable light. They just hung there – giant, faraway suns and fireballs, Allaby had said, not supports for the sky and aids to storytelling, as Gibbous had been brought up to believe …

Why hadn't he darted the dog? He could have darted him, gone over and picked him up and carried him to somewhere around where he was now. Had something happened to his ability to think? He couldn't explain this. It was as if all the new information had not only crowded out his old theories but had taken his practical instincts with them. He was in another world now, a round one, and nothing he ever thought he might know seemed to apply any longer. All of a sudden, he was a newcomer here, and the more he learned about this place, the less he seemed to understand. But was that an excuse for not darting the dog?

If so, it was pretty lame. He had taken responsibility for the animal, and he'd let him trot to his probable death – innocently. Gibbous remembered that when he'd called Yellow the second time, the dog had stopped. That was the way they walked together, with Yellow always several paces ahead. When he got too far, Gibbous would call him, and he'd wait. The dog wouldn't look back. He'd just wait until he reckoned Gibbous had caught up a little and then go on some more. That was all he'd been doing. Actually, there wouldn't have been any need for anything as drastic as a dart. It would have been enough just to throw a clod at him or something, to get his attention. Yellow wasn't aware of the elephants. He either didn't see them or didn't know what they were, and with the wind blowing the way it was, he couldn't have smelled them. The fact is, Gibbous told himself, I panicked. And Yellow's probably dead.

Maybe in the end the matriarch hadn't charged, or maybe she had, and Yellow had evaded her somehow. But at the very least, he'd be lost and confused in the dark, in the wind and among animals hundreds of times bigger than him – and frantically looking for Gibbous. This would be happening about now, Gibbous realised – right now. He'd never been so ashamed.

The moon rose on a very abject old man. He didn't want to go any farther, but he certainly didn't want to go back, especially without having gone any farther. What he really wanted to do was stay where he was and bury himself alive. But of course he did go on. As he continued south, the wind seemed to have got, if anything, stronger, and he had to lean against it as he walked, his poncho billowing out to his right as if it were trying to pull him west. The low moon – noticeably less bright than last night's – gave him a long, faint shadow off to his right, and when he turned west it stretched out in front of him across the flattened but fluttering grass. The shadow seemed to be taunting him, reaching out to the place Yellow should have been. It was a nuisance, too, because it obscured the ground in front, and after every few steps he'd have to poke with his stick for possible snakes. He passed a huge herd of horses – there must have been seventy or eighty of them – all standing stock still with their hindquarters to the wind, their tails between their legs or over their backs and their manes over their eyes. In a while, as the moon got higher, he could make out the elephants off to the north. They were formed into what seemed to be a tight group now, probably sheltering the babies, having done their worst to the terrible little dog with the spirit of a man. Gibbous hated those elephants, for the obvious reason but also because they'd left him hating himself. He was lonely, too – something that, in the past, he'd either relished or was indifferent to. Now, though, the feeling was something else he hated.

He was about a mile past the elephants when he first saw the light. It was a soft glow right on the west-north-western horizon, as though the missing piece of the moon were lying there. He actually pointed at it with his stick, instantly feeling foolish for showing something to himself, but he also sent a mental message to Paintbrush (feeling foolish for doing that, too), telling her to compliment Allaby on getting the location of the skypeople almost right – if the glow did in fact mean skypeople (and what else could it mean?). The wind was blowing as hard as ever, and Gibbous realised that so far he'd been resisting it, making it push him. But now he began to walk ahead of it, with it. He went faster. He'd had enough of this whole expedition and wanted to get it over with as soon as possible.

He kept walking, and the glow grew. It was a colour of light that he couldn't remember having seen before, not coming from the ground, anyway. It was nothing like firelight and really was as yellow as the moon – though as he got closer, it seemed to get whiter, as if it were gradually changing from the moon to the sun. He thought Allaby had said something about the ship making light, but by that point Gibbous had been having trouble paying attention, had still been absorbing earlier information – the bit about the guns in particular. Trying to picture the guns had kept him from catching a lot of the last part of Allaby's briefing.

In time, he began to see something inside the glow. All he could tell, really, was that it was a shape. There was still a long way to go, and so it must have been pretty big. For that matter, the glow itself was enormous. The shape, oblong and black without much else to distinguish it, was probably two miles away now, but the glow was illuminating grass not a mile in front of him. Because of the wind, he couldn't hear anything from that direction – in fact, all he'd been able to hear for what seemed a very long time was whistling, whishing and howling. He was impatient with the wind. Whatever he was going to have to do in a short while, one thing was certain: it was going to require some stealth, and stealth is hard to manage when there's a big wind blowing. It also made the night colder than it should have been. Gibbous's ears were sore, and his poncho was flapping so much it was practically useless. What he really wanted now wasn't a great oblong thing inside a mysterious glow but some shelter and a fire and maybe something warm to drink, not to mention a solution to these pangs of guilt about Yellow. And as he got closer, he noticed that there were fewer animals around, as though the glow was a great campfire that they wanted to stay clear of. In fact, except for a small group of cows off to his left – all down on all four haunches, all with their heads bowed against the wind – there seemed to be nothing left but flattened grass, which made him feel even more remorseful, and lonelier.

It wasn't easy to tell where the pure moonlight stopped and the glow began. At first he'd thought it was receding, mirage-like, ahead of him, but then he realised that the grass at his feet was dark green instead of grey and that he must have entered the glow's dimmer fringes. The oblong thing, which he now presumed was the ship, was taking on some detail. It seemed to be a little thicker on the left than on the right and, instead of sitting squarely on the ground, was raised up a bit on stilts, like the houses in Deep Gorge (a precaution against the occasions when the river below the waterfall flooded). There were also some decorations of some kind on it. He couldn't quite tell from this distance, but they didn't seem to be either pictures or anything very symmetrical – though he couldn't be sure. But the main thing about it was its hugeness. Allaby had described it a kind of house that could fly, but as a house – a flying one or not – it was bigger than a whole settlement, than two settlements. The nearest thing to it he'd ever seen was that windowless long-house that all the Salters lived in, but that would have fitted inside this thing, along with most of the salt flat.

It was as light as day. He stopped and, shielding his eyes from the wind, looked around. There wasn't an animal in sight – not a bird, not a bat, not an insect. It was too windy for flying things anyway, but he had a feeling they would have avoided this place even in stillness. The piece of plain inside the glow was like a world of its own, or like the end of a world. He couldn't see anything beyond the glow's great dome. There were no stars, no sun, no moon – just whiteness – and when he looked back in the direction he'd come from, he saw whiteness dimming to nothingness. It was eeriest, though, when he looked down. For one thing, he wasn't casting any kind of shadow, and for another, the wind-whipped grass was a light, bright green, not the rich, darker green it would have been in the sun. This was the colour of the first sprouts after the first rains, the grass the deer and the hares liked to eat. But it was too long to be that colour now – as though the glow had sucked all the ripeness out. This was light without warmth. He was colder than ever, and as he walked on he tried to hold his poncho tight around him, to stop it flapping and billowing so much and letting so much wind in.

Allaby had said there would be light around the ship, but Gibbous wasn't aware of his saying anything about what kind or how much. He had imagined small circles of torchlight or firelight that he could hide beyond as he spied on the skypeople. But he didn't know what he was going to do in this weird daytime. When he got closer, he'd have to get down and crawl, he guessed – a thought he didn't exactly savour. He wondered if it was going to be impossible to hide and if he should go back now. After all, there was no doubt that the skypeople were here, and here in numbers. What was the point in going on and risking showing himself to them and maybe, as Allaby had suggested, scaring them and getting himself shot with their guns? No warning would get back to the Chief that way. None of those doubts, though, was enough to make him even break his stride. He had come all this way for a look at the skypeople, and it just wasn't possible for him to turn around when he was right on the verge of doing that. If he had to crawl, he'd crawl.

Allaby had made some other predictions, too, and Gibbous strained to remember them (why hadn't Allaby mentioned the guns last instead of first, so that Gibbous could have concentrated better on everything else?). Oh yes, the smaller flying things – the pickup and the other thing … no evidence of them anywhere. Likewise the thing with the axles, the rover. And, oh, there was one thing he really had forgotten. He couldn't remember what Allaby had called it, but it was some way of seeing things from a distance. Would the skypeople be using that now, and would it mean they were already looking at him? It was hard to imagine how something like that would work, but he supposed that if they could turn night into day and get that monstrosity up ahead to fly, they could do anything. Anyway, how it worked wasn't the question. The question was, were they looking at him? If they were, approaching the ship by crawling would be pointless. But then they might not be looking at him. How the hell could he know? Damn it, he couldn't think in this wind.

By the time he was close enough to the ship to imagine he could see figures, yes, under it, he still hadn't answered the crawling question. He stopped. There was probably half a mile to go – a short enough walk but a damned long crawl, especially down with the snakes and the ants and the beetles. It was something he really didn't want to do, and he began to search for reasons why he shouldn't. Okay, he asked himself, what's the danger? That I'll scare them, and they'll shoot me with their guns. Why would I scare them? Because they don't know there are people down here. They don't know I exis—

Of course. That settled it. He'd walk on for a while and not start crawling until he was a lot closer. Holding his flapping poncho with one hand and his stick with the other, he continued towards the ship. It was simple. If they didn't think there were people here, they wouldn't be looking for any. And there were no dangerous big animals around – they'd seen to that with their enormous, ugly light. As far as they were concerned, there was nothing to look for. Why, he could probably walk right up to them and they wouldn't see him.

Still, as he went on, he couldn't help suspecting that he was being a little foolhardy. For a start, there was a severe limit to what he actually knew about skypeople. Even if Allaby had wanted to tell him absolutely everything, he wouldn't have had time, and Gibbous either hadn't understood or hadn't paid attention to a lot of what Allaby did say. He also wondered if his remorse about Yellow hadn't affected his judgment. He'd made a bad, panicky decision then, and maybe he was reacting with a bad, reckless one now. But whatever, the decision had been made, and it was too late – if they were inclined to see him, they already would have, because now he could see them, or some of them.

The stilts of the ship seemed to raise it to about twice a man's height, the grass had been cleared under it, and there looked to be some sort of gathering of people there, not in the ship's shadow or anything because there wasn't a shadow. The area under the ship was illuminated by the same glow that was everywhere else. And after another hundred or so paces, it became clear that all of the people (and there were a lot of them, more than a settlement's worth, more than he'd ever seen before all at the same time) were sitting on the ground and facing the same way – away from him. This was the kind of luck that was impossible to ignore: they hadn't seen him coming only because every single one of them – however many of them there were – happened to be looking the other way. And any one of them could turn around at any moment. It was time to repent foolhardiness and procrastination and to start crawling.

But before he did, he thought he'd better have his pipe handy. He unshouldered his satchel and reached for the pipe and a dart. Then he slung the satchel over his back and, holding the pipe and dart in one hand and the stick in the other, got down and began to move forward on his elbows, his beard dragging across the grass and the dirt. He supposed there was at least one consolation down here: for the first time in hours, the wind wasn't pummelling him. On the other hand, the grass was. It whipped and flicked at the back of his neck and his already sore ears. He also felt more vulnerable down with the ants, the beetles and the snakes, not because he was particularly bothered by any of those things – it was just the feeling that in this creepy world, he was now one of them and that some great foot might come along and crush him.

What made crawling particularly creepy now was that in this glow you could see everything. Forgetting the fact that, by rights, it was the middle of the night, the things that lived down here were even bereft of shades and shadows. Keeping as low as possible meant that he couldn't see very far ahead, and so as he pulled himself along there wasn't much else to look at but the grass he was crawling over and occasional spots of bare ground. And every one seemed to have some kind of creature on it probably wishing it could hide. A few he was just as glad to have seen and avoided – one centipede, one small scorpion and the tail of a coral snake – but mostly they were various kinds of beetles (including a couple of impressive stag beetles), wood lice and spiders, lots of spiders. Watching crawling creatures seemed a strange thing to do while he was in the process of stalking a crowd of skypeople, but travelling this way was slow and tiring, and the bugs kept his mind off his exertions. In truth, he was too old for this. All his joints were aching, especially the knee of his good leg – which was having do the work of two, because the other one was useless at this angle and just bumped along like some kind of heavy tail.

After what seemed a very long time, he stopped, looked up and then crouched in the grass. He was closer than he thought he'd be, though not really close enough for a lot of detail. Still, the ship seemed to loom across the whole western sky, and it was clear from this distance that there was something odd, even accounting for the fact that these were skypeople, about the big group seated under it. He couldn't say what it was, though, other than the fact they were all wearing the same colour clothes – a green like the phony green that the glow gave the grass. They also seemed to bend a little as the wind gusted, also like the grass. The wind kept him from telling if they were making any noise, but he had a feeling they weren't, that they were just sitting there silently, arranged in rows, as if they were waiting for something.

He decided to crawl a little closer, and when he did and crouched again, he noticed something else: they all had their hands behind their backs. No, their hands were tied behind their backs. Just as he was realising that, an especially heavy gust blew through, and several of them toppled over. And stayed toppled, lying on their sides in the dirt or across their neighbours' laps, not even trying to get up. He couldn't really see, but that probably meant their feet were tied, too. As Gibbous was wondering why, it dawned on him what the oddest thing about them was: they were a lot of different sizes, and it didn't look as though any of them were very tall, not like Allaby – who had said once that all people in the sky were taller than people on the ground (that had been Mother Gravity again, hadn't it?). Of course, it was hard to tell when all of them were sitting or, now, lying on their sides, but ... by God, they were kids!

Children!

As if to validate this observation, six or seven adults appeared from somewhere – they'd probably been inside the ship, though he hadn't seen how they'd come out – and started putting the toppled kids back upright. But they did it very slowly, as if they were trying to walk under water. Every move they made seemed a huge effort, and when they tried to move against the wind they were almost stopped in their tracks. As for lifting the kids, they might have been doing strong-man stunts with boulders. Allaby had been right – they were very tall, probably taller even than Allaby, and they wore the same kind of whole-body clothes the kids wore, except that theirs were reddish orange instead of early-grass green, though there was no telling what the colour would really be in sunlight. Gibbous counted four men – all beardless, the way Allaby had been when he first appeared – and three women, and they all seemed to be shouting things at each other and at the kids. He couldn't hear them, just bits of voice that occasionally penetrated the wind and sounded like faraway birds chirping.

He had no idea what was going on, but he did know this: he didn't much like these people. Whatever their reason, they were obviously mistreating children – tying them up and making them sit out in a cold night wind and then shouting at them when the wind blew them over. And why were the kids so still and stiff-looking? Were they even alive? He had yet to see a child's face, to see if its eyes were open. He also looked for evidence of guns. Allaby had said they carried them on their belts, the way Gibbous often carried his pipe, and they did have belts on, all of them with something hanging where their right hands could reach. He supposed he could only assume that guns were what those things were. And then what? Just keep an eye on them, he guessed. What else?

And he wondered what he'd tell the Chief, and whether he even needed to bother. Call out the warriors, Chief – there's a huge bunch of dead-looking kids way over there, along with a few tall adults who look weak and move slowly. But oh yeah, hadn't Allaby said they'd be heavier than they'd ever been before? Gibbous had discounted that because he didn't believe it, couldn't rationalise it – but there they were, moving as if they were made out of rocks. About twenty-five or thirty of the kids had been blown over, but the seven adults between them had still only uprighted about ten, and each time one of them did, there would be a long pause for catching breath and looking balefully into the wind. It struck Gibbous that there might not be a problem here at all (other than the mistreated kids, but then how did he know this wasn't a normal part of a skychild's upbringing?), because they were so obviously unsuited to life on the ground. It had been bad enough for Allaby, with all his bites and wounds and broken bones, but at least Allaby didn't feel as heavy as a horse. He sent a mental apology to the man – gravity really was something to be reckoned with – and if Gibbous were one of these skypeople, he was sure he'd have wanted to get the kids back inside the ship and fly the ship away.

On the other hand, it was as long ago as last night that the ship had arrived, and the skypeople hadn't left yet. And Allaby had said that eventually they could build up enough strength to start feeling normal on the ground. Also, Gibbous had no idea how many more adults might still be inside the ship – there'd have to be a lot to have this many children. So he supposed he ought to warn the Chief after all. Maybe if the people of the ground were going to deal with the skypeople, it would be better to do it soon, while the skypeople were still having gravity trouble.

That was that, then. He'd wait for the adults to go back inside, and then he'd start his return trip to Paintbrush and Allaby and go on from there to Big Rim. For the moment, though, all he needed to do was wait and watch.

There were only four or five kids left to attend to, and while some adults were creakily doing that, a man and a woman came to the edge of their clearing, and with their arms around each other (more like mutual support than affection, Gibbous thought, crouching lower and bending forward) they gazed over Gibbous's head and across the plain. Gibbous had to admit that as they stood smiling a little, with their black (his) and blonde (hers) hair streaming in the wind, they looked like people who were basically content to be on the ground and weren't about to turn around and leave … until both their smiles dissolved into looks of horror. They were staring down at something. Bent over in the grass, Gibbous could only see the couple from waist up, and so he didn't know what was bothering them, and if he straightened up to see, they might see him. But because the man was slowly moving his hand towards the thing on his belt and because they weren't looking his way now anyway, Gibbous thought he'd better take the chance. So he straightened up. There at their feet – sitting on haunches, head tilted back and tail sweeping the ground – was a dog.

Gibbous stood up. The man's hand had reached his belt, but before it could move much more, Gibbous had loaded his pipe and shot the dart, hitting him in the arm he'd been about to use. As the man crumpled towards the ground and the woman, with even more horror on her face, watched him fall, Gibbous shouted as loud as he knew how, "Yelllllooooooooww!"

Yellow turned his head, looked hard and then hared towards Gibbous, who instantly wondered what kind of stupid thing he'd just done. He was standing in full view, one hand on his stick and one holding the pipe, his beard, hair and poncho whipping in the wind. But never mind, he thought – Yellow didn't die, Yellow wasn't killed, I didn't get him killed. When Yellow reached a couple of paces from Gibbous, he leapt, and Gibbous caught him in the crook of the arm that was holding the pipe. As the dog frantically licked the side of Gibbous's face, Gibbous looked back towards the ship. There was the man crumpled on the ground, and beside him, the woman had fallen to her knees. She was looking right at Gibbous, her eyes wide. And under her chin, she was holding her hands flat together, fingers closed and pointing upwards. Then he looked at the scene behind her, under the ship. All the rest of the adults were on their knees in exactly the same pose.

CHAPTER TWENTY-EIGHT

For the first time in his life, Caleb Hook was glad to see Jedidiah Bates, Primary Preacher of the Lazarines, but right now he'd have been glad to see absolutely anyone. For the past three days his only human contact – if it could be called that and not just evidence that humanity still existed – was the hand that put the food through the slit in the door. This time the hand had opened the door and had displayed an attached arm and shoulder and even the side of a face. And then a whole Jedidiah had strolled in, resplendent in his full ceremonial attire – a brown pinstripe, twenty-second-century suit' with brown, tasseled 'loafers' and a red 'necktie'. And since Caleb himself was still in his scarlet robes, the two of them, in their splendour, were probably making the windowless, free-photon-lit cell look even dingier than it was. The door clanged shut, Titan's two most important church leaders shook hands and said how good it was to see each other, and Jedidiah immediately sat down on Caleb's bed, smiling that smile of his and crossing a red-socked ankle over his knee. He pushed at the mattress and said, "Yours is a lot springier than mine."

"You're in here, too?" There weren't any chairs in the cell, and the only other place to sit was the toilet. So Caleb stayed standing.

"Was, Caleb. Was. I've been out since yesterday. I came to terms, I guess. How are you holding up?"

"Came to terms? With what, Jed? I don't even know who's doing—"

"Ah, but I do, Caleb. And that's why I've come to see you. Don't worry. You'll be out, too."

"I should hope so. Do I have you to thank somehow?"

"Are the doctrinaire Keepers of Jerusalem going to be in debt to the misguided Lazarines? I'm afraid not, Caleb. They already had the idea. They just thought you'd be more likely to listen to me than if they sent one of their own."

"No offence, Jed, but who would I be less likely to listen to than you?"

"The Devil himself, maybe." The smile again. Caleb could have sworn he had more teeth than other people.

"I guess you've got a point – either the Devil himself or the people who put me in here. Who are they, Jed?"

"A group. A group that's a lot larger and stronger than anybody ever gave them credit for being. And I might add, a lot more reasonable and daring."

"Not the Titanists?"

Jed uncrossed his legs, barked a laugh and hit both knees with his palms. "The Titanists? They've rounded them up. The entire Titanist board's in this jail too. Think again, Caleb. Come on."

"Oh no, not the … Nah."

"Yep, Caleb. You got it in two. It took them a little while to convince me and for me to convince the elders, but we Lazarines, we're firmly on side now. And you could be, too. It's a great mission, Caleb – probably the greatest in history. And you and the Keepers are welcome to be part of it."

For the moment, Caleb couldn't keep watching Jed and his damned teeth. He turned around and closed his eyes. As much as he disapproved of the Lazarines and their conviction that Earth was Heaven, he didn't still want to imagine them committing mass suicide. Jed must have been brainwashed somehow – that could happen in a prison. He told himself to be calm. He made himself smile, and then he turned back around. "Has this got to do with the holopark man?"

"He was the trigger, I think – the signal that their time had come. Accept it. In fact, be joyous."

"Did you hear any of my sermon?

"It was cut off about two minutes in, but I heard enough to get the drift."

"What drift was that?"

"You were going to call it contagious mass hysteria or something. I know you. I've been alert to you all my life. You're have a weakness for psychology."

"I wasn't going to call it contagious mass hysteria."

"What then? Hallucinogenics in the drinking water? You've always got some way of explaining away miracles."

"I was going to tell the truth, Jed."

"Caleb, of course you were."

"Well, Jed, of course I was.

Jed's smile was showing strain – always a prelude to an expression that was much more sinister. Caleb had watched him deliver a sermon once. He'd started off with his piano-keys smile, but not five minutes had gone before he was snarling and spitting and condemning his terrified congregation to Hell (which according to the Lazarines was the planet Venus). Caleb didn't approve of the religion, but he did pity the people. Now Jed said, "So what was the truth I didn't hear?"

"It's as simple as this, Jed. There are people living on Earth who are immune to the virus. And there always have been, ever since the Apocalypse."

Jed leaned forward, a hand under his chin. "You believe that, do you?"

"Yes I do, Jed. And I'll tell you something. It's much easier to believe than you selling out your church to those lunatics."

"They're not lunatics – they're very smart people. And nobody's sold anybody anything. Sometimes it happens that interests converge. You see, we don't even agree about the meaning of the holopark man. But we know and they know what needs to be done now that he's appeared."

"What would that be?"

"What do you think, Caleb?"

"Well, if you've thrown in with the Back-to-Earthers, I suppose you must be planning to go back to Earth. I'm not a perfect man, Jed, and there's a little bit of me, deep inside, that wishes you'd do it. But just you and not your poor followers. If you did that, there are a lot of problems, my problems, that would be solved. But for you, it would be difficult, uh, theologically. For instance, when you go to Earth believing Earth is Heaven and you step out of the ship and die of the virus, where do you go? If you die in Heaven, do you go somewhere else or just stay there, except dead?"

"We won't die of the virus, Caleb, because the virus is gone."

"Do you believe that baloney because of the holopark man? I told you, Jed – there are people who are immune—"

"No." The smile finally disappeared. But the teeth were still visible, only now as part of a sneer. "Don't talk garbage, and don't talk theology – not to me. You're a theological illiterate. You say Heaven is in some kind of unreal place, in no dimension even. But it's got to be somewhere. Everything is somewhere. What you say you believe is the same as saying there's no such place as Heaven, that you don't really believe in it. And if you don't believe in Heaven, as far as I'm concerned, you don't believe in God."

"God is beyond the—"

"... beyond the physical. Yes, I know. God's universe is nothing to do with this universe – that's your line. Your God is some figure of speech, some kind of fairy-tale character, something out of fiction. That's why the Science Committee and the Head of Station always liked you so much, and why yours was the established church. They liked a fictional God in a fictional universe that never got in the way of what they saw as the only real universe – one that didn't have an awkward God or Heaven in it."

"There's a suspicious amount of past tense in what you're saying."

Jed folded his arms and, smiling again, leaned back against the wall. "Those Back-to-Earthers ..." He shook his head and then pinned Caleb with a stare that didn't go, somehow, with the smile. "Lunatics, hah. They liked to let people think they were lunatics, but all the time they were planning. They've been planning for years, all over the Solar System. Years and years. You know, Caleb, the uprising happened right when you thought you were delivering your sermon. Just like that." He clapped his hands once and held them together. "No more Head of Station." He clapped again. "No more Science Committee." Again. "No more you. Except that the Head of Station and the Science Committee are a lot no more than you are. They'll never be again. You, you've got a chance. That's why I'm here – to offer you a chance, not to discuss theology."

"You mean you killed Thurman? And the whole Science Comm—"

"Not me. Not any Lazarines, unless some of the Back-to-Earthers happen to be Lazarines too. But of course they're a religious movement in their own right. You'll be glad to know that they believe in a kind of nowhere Heaven like yours, but they think the Earth has been promised to them exclusively. That's why I was really grateful when they let us in on it. But they do need friends – we're all so far away here. I mean, Caleb, the Mooner Back-to Earthers are already there. It's going to take us months. More maybe."

"Already where?"

"On Earth, of course. We've been picking up comms signals this morning. They're saying they're on Earth and outside, feeling the wind and the sun. It's a done deed, Caleb. They've taken over the whole Moon and have even knocked out Earth Headquarters Satellite, turned off the power or something – I don't know exactly."

"But what happened to the people on it?"

"I don't know. I guess they're dead. There haven't been any comms coming from there, that's for sure. Mars still seems to be in the hands of

Xanthe City, but we're getting Back-to-Earther comms from somewhere around Syrtis Major. They've got about a battalion and a bunch of ships, and they say they're getting ready to attack Xanthe. Comms from Mars are taking about twenty hours – so I guess by now they've done it. Ganymede, though, is sun-blocked."

Caleb had to sit down, and if he didn't feel like sitting next to Jed on the bed – and he didn't – the toilet lid was the only place. He sat and sighed and instantly decided that, except for Ganymede being sun-blocked, he didn't believe a word of the horrific things he'd just heard. Somebody somewhere along the line was lying. But wait, he told himself, I have the evidence of my own predicament that at least what he's saying about Titan is pretty likely. And Mars and the Moon and poor EHQS – that could be true, too. He put his face in his hands. But something isn't true. He looked up. "They can't be feeling the wind and the sun, Jed. They can't be."

"Oh yeah? Why not"

"The virus of course."

"I told you, Caleb – the virus is gone. It's been gone for years. I didn't know this either. But the Back-to-Earthers swear it's true."

"That doesn't make any sense, Jed. If the virus has been gone for years and they knew it, why wait till now?"

"Caleb, how should I know? Something to do with the holopark man, I'm sure. But I haven't grilled them. They tell me what they want to tell me. I'm grateful just to be asked to be on their side. What they sent me in here to explain to you is that you could be on their side, too. It's enough to them that you're head of a religion. They've got nothing against the Keepers – they just don't want secularists, atheists, science-supremacists, people like that. But they also want a big force from Titan. To be frank, Caleb, I think they're scared that the Mooner and Martian Back-to-Earthers will have claimed all the best places – especially the original Jerusalem – and our ones want to be ready to fight if they have to. That's just my guess, though."

"For Christ's sake, Jed—"

"Don't you take the Lord's—"

"… how do you feel about going to your goddamned Heaven to fight a goddamned war?"

In an instant it was Jed who was standing up. He planted himself in front of Caleb, leaning forward and pushing at his shoulders, his teeth looking like fangs now. "You're a disgrace," he said. "How can the leader of a

Christian church speak in blasphemies? But I guess I know. It's because you're not really a Christian at all. You're just a fat man with red robes and a plum job got by kissing atheistic backsides. Let me tell you something about Christians." He'd reached the spitting stage now. "Christians are fighters and always have been. We'd never have got anywhere, on Earth or off it, without our glorious wars. And now, now—"

"Damn, Jed, you're soaking me."

"Don't you understand, you fat pig – this is it. This is the Rapture. Don't you think the Rapture is worth fighting for? Everything predicted in Revelation is happening right now, and all you can do is utter sarcasms and blasphemies."

When Caleb stood up, their faces were so close that their noses nearly touched. Caleb attempted a threatening glare into Jed's eyes, but Caleb was a little long-sighted, and Jed's eyes were too near. So with his hands and his belly, he gave Jed a shove that sent him bicycling backwards until he hit the cell door, bumping his head with a clang on the metal. Jed put a hand to the back of his head and looked a little dazed. Caleb said, "You're a moron, and your allies are still lunatics. They've been saying the virus is gone ever since I can remember, and before that. Back-to-Earthers date from a couple of centuries ago, and their main line has always been that the virus is gone and governments are keeping people off the Earth for some kind of secret reason. Of course they're going to tell you the virus has been gone for years because they've been saying it for years. You're nothing but a sucker, Jed. The Rapture, my arse."

"More blasphemy," he said almost absent-mindedly. He was still holding his head. His back was still against the cell door, his eyes weren't quite focusing, and for once his teeth weren't on display.

He looked as if he might have been seriously hurt, but Caleb didn't think he could have hit the door that hard. It had clanged, but in a jail things were always clanging. He was probably, having lost the argument, playing for sympathy. "Tell me something," Caleb said. "Who do the Back-to-Earthers say the holopark man is?"

Slowly and dreamily, he said, "They don't."

"Don't what?"

"Say. They say they know. But they don't say. Not to me."

"If you're not going to believe me about the immune people, then who do you think he is?"

"Oh I know who he is. I know that." His words were even slower and more slurred, and his hand was still on his head.

"Who then?"

Jed's pupils rolled back into his skull, and with his eyes wide and white, he slid down the cell door. "Him," he said. "Him."

CHAPTER TWENTY-NINE

"The only way we can know, Jenny," Gus said, "is for you to go back to Earth and see."

"Alone?"

"Of course. You're the only one here who's Earth-adapted."

"What about the couriers, the station-maintenance guys, the cargo pilots, the—"

"No, Jenny. They wouldn't … I couldn't … What's come over you? Why would I want to send somebody like that? I trust you, Jenny. It can only be you. As for being alone, you're an Earth Ranger, damn it. Alone is what you do."

Jenny had two reservations: she didn't feel like spending one more moment in free-fall; and indeed, she didn't want to be alone any more, to be away from Louise. Louise right now was installed in the apartment Gus had found yesterday for her and Jenny in the Bachelor Technicians' Quarters and was waiting there for Jenny to come home. And now Gus was saying that Jenny was going to have to go to Earth and … "When would you want me to go?"

"The sooner the better," Gus said. "We can't stay invisible here forever."

By that Gus meant comms invisible. The junta running the Moon was assuming, according to intercepted comms, that everybody on EHQS was dead, and as long as that assumption lasted, the satellite would be safe from a second invasion. So the first thing Gus had done when he realised he was Head of Station was to have all the transmitters disconnected. Then he turned off all the outside lights (he'd done it very realistically, a little at a time with lots of flickering, as though the power was slowly fizzling away). After that he'd made an announcement on the internal comms telling everyone what was happening, to stay calm and, unless they were in the hospital (which was crammed), too worried about their children or otherwise indisposed, to go to their jobs and help make the satellite as secure and viable as possible.

And now, as she sat in the Head of Station's office, Jenny was being reminded that her job was in the Africa East sector and that was where he wanted her to go.

"I can't understand," Gus said, "how they're on Earth and not dead. We're only getting voices, though. Either they don't have any imagers with them or are too stupid to use them, or they're lying to the junta, saying they've been outside and are fine, when they're actually sitting in the ships with the portals shut wondering what to do next."

"They probably did take suits. Otherwise, why would they suddenly—"

"You don't understand. I don't understand. We can't radio them and ask. That's why you've got to go and see."

"Could I do it in the morning? I'm really tired."

"What's the matter with you, Jenny? You've had all night and most of the day to ... You have slept, haven't you?"

"Uh, not that well, to tell the truth."

"Well, you look fine. In fact, I'd almost say there's a glow about you. Listen, I know the gym was a horrible experience and that you feel you need some more recuperation – and of course I'll always be grateful to you and Louise for saving me – but we're having an emergency here, Jenny, and you're the only one who can do this. And I want you to start within the next, say, two hours, when the sun's setting on your sector."

Jenny shrugged. Gus would want her to report back as quickly as she could, and so she'd probably only miss one night with Louise. "Okay, Gus. Brief me." Still, it wasn't right – people in the first flush of a relationship ought to be excused all duties, even in emergencies.

He briefed her. Five ships had reported back to the junta: two cruisers that had left from the satellite and a cruiser and – would you believe it? – two liners direct from the Moon. There was a cruiser, the command ship, in Jenny's sector and a cruiser each in Asia North and Australia. The liners were in Europe North and North America Southwest, Peter's former sector. These were only the ships that had reported back – how many had actually gone to Earth was, Gus said, anybody's guess. Because of comms invisibility, Gus couldn't try to contact any Earth Rangers, but oddly no Rangers had tried to contact him. Even if they didn't know anything was amiss (and it would be hard for them not to know at this point), normal routine would have had them trying to get in touch at least once every day or two. But from the Rangers, nothing.

Many private citizens on the Moon had told the authorities on Mars about the coup, but repeated attempts by Mars to contact the junta hadn't been answered. In the most recent communiqué, the Martian Prime Minister had made a veiled threat to send a fleet. Messages from the Moon had also been sent to Titan, but it was much too soon to know Titan's response. And Ganymede, of course, was still sun-blocked. What Jenny had to do was find the command ship – it had been pinpointed to an area near the Ngorongoro Crater – and see whether the Back-to-Earthers and the kidnapped children really were walking around outside without suits or were just sitting in the ship and lying to the junta. She would have a flat-screen recorder but no comms equipment at all, which because of piracy clause in the Interstation Convention on Control of Illegal Interception meant she wouldn't have a tracker either. This would mean no one could know her exact coordinates and, more important, neither could she. Moreover, she couldn't use lights, and, as soon as she checked out the command ship, she was to fly on to Africa South and see if there was anything wrong at the Ranger station there. Then she was to fly straight back here and dock with no comms and so no help from a controller. "By the way," Gus said, "can you fly a shuttle?"

"A shuttle? God no, Gus. I didn't know one person could fly a shuttle."

"If runarounds could operate in atmosphere or pickups could operate in space, you could have one of those. But all we've got left that operate in both are a few shuttles. Only shuttles. That's all that's still here. So have you ever flown one?"

"I did once, when I was about five years old and sitting in the pilot's lap. Don't you have to go to school to learn to fly those things? And I'd have to land it. And dock it. And without a controller. Jesus."

"Well, you know, Jenny, these ships nowadays pretty much fly and land themselves. Dock themselves, too. You'll be all right. Just glide straight into the clampers."

"Oh, thanks for the tip, Gus." She wondered if he himself had ever flown a ship, any kind of ship, but right now it wasn't a point worth pressing. What was, was: "Why don't you just give me a pilot?"

"No, Jenny. If you see what, unthinkable as it is, you might see, I don't want anybody but you to see it. What kind of effect do you think it would have on the people here if word got out that … well, you know."

"No I don't, quite."

"Well, believe me, it would."

"What would?"

"Just take my word for it. Look, you've got about an hour and a half. Why don't you go back to your apartment, clean up, get something to eat – whatever you want to do. The clothes I had put in your closet include a flight suit—"

"I noticed that. I'd hoped it was a mistake."

"Take it out, bring it back and put it on here, and I'll get someone to check you out on a shuttle. I'll make sure there are sterility suits on it, too, just in case."

"Just in case of what?"

"Uh, in case you have to get out of the shuttle."

"Of course I'm going to have to get out of the shuttle. But that's not what you meant, was it?"

"Well, yes but ... no ... I, uh ..."

"You don't believe the Back-to-Earthers are lying, do you?"

"Well, when you think about five ships all telling the same story, and to their own commanders—"

"Gus, all they'd need in common is a last-minute reluctance to bleed to death."

"Well, you'll see, won't you?. That's why I'm sending you. Oh, and by the way ..."

"Yeah?"

"When you're at the apartment, give Louise my regards, will you?"

"Sure, Gus."

"She is remarkable, isn't she? She was a real hero in the gym."

"She was, yeah."

"You know, I don't even know what she does."

"What do you mean?"

"For a living."

"Oh, oh yeah."

"What does she do?"

"Oh, she's a ... uh ... a sort of a ... charity worker, I think."

"She would be, you know. Is she, uh ... Has she got a man, a husband, anything like that?"

"Yes, Gus. She's getting married next week. To a really nice guy."

Gus's face dropped. "Oh. Well, I'm sure he would be nice. So, like I say, give her my regards. And my congratulations, too, of course."

"Of course. I'll see you in an hour and a half," Jenny said, adding under her breath, "if I haven't killed myself."

"What?"

"Nothing, Gus. See you later."

"See you later, Jenny."

Jenny was ashamed. As she waited for the lift down to the outer ring, she reflected that she'd just had her first touch of a new relationship's nastiest side-effect – jealousy. It was a strange kind, though. The thought of Louise carrying on as a whore didn't bother her at all, and in the couple of seconds when she'd speculated about any kind of future with Louise, she'd assumed Louise would continue doing what she did. It was her living, she was undoubtedly good at it, and she talked as though she enjoyed it. But the idea of Gus courting Louise – or whatever he had in mind – made Jenny feel a little nauseous. She wondered if she shouldn't have been honest with him about Louise's trade – but no, that had been right: she hadn't wanted him to think less of the woman. What was wrong was telling him Louise was getting married. It was unkind – both to shy, lonely old Gus and to Louise, who would have revelled in the attentions of the Head of Station.

The lift came, and at the bottom, Jenny and the other passengers stepped out into the satellite's big park. Unlike any of the hotels, which for the most part faced only each other, the Bachelor Technicians' Quarters overlooked this ancient piece of artificial landscape. Jenny, as both a Martian and an Earth Ranger, had always been dismissive of such a poor replica of a piece of the home planet – made to seem even poorer by contrast with the holopark that sat on one of its perimeters. But right at the moment, with the holopark closed – maybe permanently – and Earth looming as something scary, this safe bit of make-believe was as close to the planet as she felt like getting. Anyway, the grass, the trees and the flowers were real enough – it was just the robotic songbirds and the herd of robotic horses that made it seem hopelessly hokey.

She sat on a bench. Straight across from her, rising above a line of silver birch, was the Bachelor Technicians' Quarters, and the other side of the seventh-storey window on the far left was where Louise was. Jenny wanted to be up there with her – and there wasn't much time before she had to report back to Gus – but she needed to sit and think for a few minutes about what she'd done and what she was going to have to do. Down the path, the lift opened again, and half a dozen people came out – as dazed-looking and foot-heavy as everybody else on the satellite seemed to be. She watched them pass, and by their appearance, she wasn't the only one who'd needed a longer break before going back to work. In fact, working or not, it was going to be quite a while before the population here got over the free-fall dungeon – except Louise. For her it had been a moment of glory. As Gus had said, she was a remarkable person. For that matter, Gus himself had been pretty remarkable, to act so fast and so decisively. He had just saved and then hidden the entire population of the satellite and was counting on her, Jenny, to help him know what to do next. He expected her to go, to look and to come back and report. This was like some pre-Ancient conflict, a Peloponnesian War or something, with a scout riding ahead to see where and how big the other army was. Gus was being resourceful and level-headed while she was nursing reluctance and fear. Maybe it was her turn, after all, to be remarkable. She still wasn't sure, but she did get up from the bench and head for the BTQ.

Then she was in another lift – on her way to the seventh floor. Also in it were two what she presumed were bachelor technicians. Deep in self-criticism, she'd hardly noticed them, but now that she was focusing again, she saw that while one was staring straight ahead with that universal dazed expression, the other was actively looking her over – she could follow his eyes following her contours. He was a handsome man with Martian bearing and the dark Martian skin and hair, not to mention a grin and a dimple. Just as the lift reached the seventh floor, Jenny looked him in the eye, smiled broadly and winked, and as she started down the corridor, she heard a chuckle. She'd genuinely meant that smile and wink, and if she'd had time and if he'd asked, she might have gone straight to bed with him – that was how achingly sexual she was feeling at the moment. What had Louise done to her? It wasn't so much that Jenny was a lesbian now, but more anything and everything to do with sex. It felt both frustrating and fantastic, and it definitely had to stop. Maybe being away and alone for a day and night was exactly what she needed.

The apartment was just as she'd left it when she'd got Gus's summons. Throughout the night and day, Jenny and Louise had been taking food breaks – nothing that involved anything as orderly as cooking or even warming up, but just opening boxes and packets from the food chest, consuming whatever was inside and letting the packaging drop – and now Jenny kicked bits of the mess aside as she crossed to the bedroom. This was very un-Jenny-like, too, as anybody who'd ever seen her faultlessly tidy Ranger station could have sworn (she'd have at least to get this stuff to the rubbish decomper before she went back to Gus). In the bedroom, Louise was still asleep, in the same position she'd been in while Jenny had been dressing to go – on her left side, face half under the sheet and her long, thick curls fanned out across the pillow and on to Jenny's pillow. (Funny about Louise's hair: Jenny had assumed in the gym that it was lack of gravity that caused it to explode from her head that way, but even with gravity it seemed to behave the same at every opportunity.) At the bottom of the bed, the sheet had ridden up, and from the knees down, Louise's legs were sticking out. Jenny sat on the edge of the bed now and absently stroked a leg as she looked at Louise's hair and at her form under the sheet.

She wondered if she loved her, and she wondered if any love could be separable from her dependence on her in the gym and from her astonishing touch. It occurred to Jenny that it might not be. And now that she wasn't dependent on Louise any more, that would only leave the sex. Not that there was anything wrong with that – altogether, the experience had been among the most exciting and self-revealing she'd ever had, and she hoped it would continue. But she didn't have to kid herself either: whether it was real love or not, it couldn't be all-important, and she had to sober up.

She checked the time – there was a little less than an hour left. She pulled the sheet over Louise's legs, got up and undressed, and instead of throwing her clothes on the floor – as she'd done when they first stepped into this bedroom – she hung them over the rail provided. Then she crawled into the other side of the bed and, from behind Louise, put one arm over her and squeezed the other one under. She lay that way –snuggling against her back and nosing into her hair – for many minutes, until Louise sleepily turned over and laid her head on Jenny's arm. "Where were you?" she whispered.

"I did say goodbye," Jenny said, "but I don't think you woke up. I had to report to Gus."

"How is Mister Templeton?"

"Fine. In charge. Trying to save our lives."

"Is he doing it?"

"Doing what?"

"Saving our lives."

"He's trying, but he needs help."

"Help from you?"

"Yeah."

Louise leaned up on an elbow, kissed Jenny on the tip of the nose and pushed her hair back. "You're beautiful, you know. I love black hair and dark skin. I wish I looked like you. What kind of help?"

"I don't think I can tell you. It's sort of a secret mission."

"A secret mission? Wow."

"It won't take long, though. I have to go pretty soon, but I'll be back tomorrow."

"How long is pretty soon?"

"Twenty minutes maybe."

Louise snuggled down, her lips at Jenny's ear. "My beautiful, brave hero – going on a secret mission in twenty minutes." Jenny could feel Louise's fingers working themselves into position. "Here, let me do you before you go."

Jenny wasn't sure she wanted that. Well, she wanted nothing more, but it left her feeling distracted, and she was going to need all her strength and concentration to fly that shuttle. On the other hand, if she still had this yearning, that would be distracting, too. She said, "It's three kinds of orgasm instantly and all at once. Isn't that right?"

"That's right." Louise wasn't waiting. Her fingers were moving.

Jenny put her hand over Louise's and stopped the motion. "Louise …"

"What's the matter?"

"Louise, would you do it slowly, and give me just one kind?"

CHAPTER THIRTY

Louise had done as she was asked, but it hadn't made any difference. The man who was checking Jenny out on the shuttle controls – Brewster, he was called – had to demonstrate the glide-conversion procedure three times before she could finally focus and absorb. She'd been focusing and absorbing the first two times, but it had nothing to do with the glide-conversion procedure. She had been focusing on Brewster's rather fetching Roman profile, the muscle in his right forearm, his hand – a very nice hand, with long, slightly concave fingers. And after the third time, when he looked over and asked her, unnecessarily slowly, if she understood now, she said, "Yeah, yeah. I was just missing the engage step. I see. Sure." He had nice eyes, too. He looked like an altogether nice man. She was embarrassed.

"Don't worry," he said. "It's a lot to take in. What I don't understand is why Templeton's sending you out in this. Why doesn't he send a qualified pilot?"

"I asked him the same thing," Jenny said.

"What did he say?"

"I can't tell you."

"You mean it's a secret?"

Jenny nodded.

Brewster cleared his throat and looked straight ahead. "How can there be any secrets here? We're secrets ourselves. We're all invisible here together. First we were all weightless together, and if we had any secrets before we went into the gym, we sure didn't have any when we came out. Now we're all invisible. So what else don't you know about this thing?"

"Landing. Docking."

"Landing?" He turned towards her again. "Where are you going to land?"

"Haven't you noticed the sterility suits?"

"No but, yeah, I see." He faced the controls. "You're going to Earth for some reason. But you're an Earth Ranger, and so I suppose that makes some kind of sense. Okay. You're in glide mode. You've done the glide-conversion procedure – you remember it now ..."

"Yes."

"... and you slow right back to about twenty, turn on the ... I get it. You're going to Earth to confirm they're all dead. It's obvious. Why make a secret of that? Anyway, a pilot could do it as easy as you."

"Gus has his reasons, I guess." She was beginning to wish she hadn't insisted on this little pre-flight lesson. Brewster was right – it would be stupid to send an inexperienced pilot down, alone and in a shuttle, just to confirm that the Back-to-Earthers and their hostages were outside and dead. And it wouldn't take a huge leap of logic now for Brewster to hit on the possibility that, in Gus's surmise anyway, they might be outside and alive. Of course, Jenny, who herself did an air test every week, had no doubt at all: anyone who had left the ship was dead, and anyone who'd had an attack of sanity and stayed in it was alive and lying to the unreconstructed nutters on the Moon. Even though Gus had more or less ordered her to go on this mission, she was sure she could have got out of it somehow, and she'd only really agreed to go to put Gus's mind at rest. He was Head of Station now, EHQS was having an unprecedented crisis, and Gus didn't need to worry about any more than was absolutely necessary.

As for what Jenny didn't need, the main thing right now was any more of Brewster. He was doing a perfectly good job of explaining the shuttle, but he was too close to her at the moment, too alone with her and too obvious an answer to her craving. Whether Louise had meant to or not, she and her little violinist's trick had afflicted Jenny with an appetite she would have encouraged almost anyone to satisfy. This didn't matter a lot when she and Louise were together, but Jenny in this condition wasn't really fit to be out in the wider world. What used to be a just another functioning part of her body – albeit a function that was occasionally capable of giving and receiving pleasure – had become the focus of her every conscious moment and probably most of her unconscious ones. She still didn't know if her feelings for Louise had anything to do with love, though she certainly liked her and was grateful to her for saving her life, but the woman had also put some kind of hex on Jenny. She'd manipulated her into what seemed to be an animal oestrus, and Jenny had to find a way of getting it to stop. How did animals do that? They could wait for it to go away when the season was over, but that was only if they were very unlucky. What they usually did was mate and conceive.

"… slow to two. Then you just lower the support scaffolding with this and very slowly – this slow: ease … off … the … hover. Give it about five seconds. Got it? God, I don't know. To get a pilot's licence, you've got to do this again and again, with the examiner sitting right where you are. Now you're just going to go away and try to do it on my say-so. If something happens to you, I'm going to feel really … really, you know … Now repeat what I've just told you. Come on."

"What are you going to feel?"

"What?"

"If something happens to me?"

He looked at her with one eye squinting a little. "Uh, bad, of course. I'd feel responsible. I'd feel I hadn't done my job."

"That's really nice of you." Quit it, Jenny told herself. She felt a flush of warmth all the way to her feet, and she forced herself to stare straight ahead.

"Nice? I wouldn't say nice, Ranger Romero. It's … It's responsible. That's all. And if you ask me, it looks irresponsible of Templeton to send you down alone in this. I can't figure out why he's doing it."

"Don't try, Brewster. Please. And you can call me Jenny." She looked over at him and then very quickly straight ahead again. She didn't trust what her eyes might be saying. She wanted him to get up and get out of here before it was too late. "So just show me docking, and then it'll be almost time for me to go."

"No. First I want you to repeat to me how you land."

"Jenny?" It was Gus's voice.

"Hi, Gus."

"How's it going, Jenny?"

"Fine, Gus. Brewster's just going to show me how to dock, and then I'll be—"

"He hasn't shown you yet? What have you been doing, Brewster?"

"There was a lot she didn't know, sir. I really don't think she ought to be—"

"Well, show her quick, and get out of the shuttle. I'm launching her in five minutes. And Jenny, when I do launch you, let me remind you that there won't be any more comms. The internal will cut off automatically, and all other comms capability has been taken out of there. So I'll say good luck now, and I'll see you when you get back. And you hurry, Brewster. Five minutes. Bye."

"Jesus," Brewster said. "Five minutes to explain docking. Okay, then, Ranger Ro … Jenny, watch the simulation here. When you get to this position, and the satellite looks like this, you rotate …"

Five minutes? Suddenly, the last thing Jenny wanted was for Brewster to go. Five minutes, followed by hours and hours all alone with this huge ship with this goddamned itch.

"… you've done that, the ship is what we call synchronised. That means you can start your glide …"

And when Brewster went, Gus would launch her into weightlessness. The satellite was over the mid-Pacific now. How many hours of orbiting would there be before Africa East? Four? Five??

"… when you approach, watch this figure here. I know this manoeuvre can be done automatically, but you're not going to have any comms guidance – or even any lights, as I understand it, and without comms, no positioning either – and so it's best to know exactly …"

He was right. She'd have to know where she was by sight, and those maps Gus gave her. How much could she tell from orbit, for Christ's sake. What did Gus think she was? She was going to have to leave this ship now.

"… the point now when you ought to see the clampers. I've never had to do it without lights – I don't think anyone has – but if I were you, I'd … Ranger Ro … Jenny?" He was looking at her empty seat. "Jenny?"

She had taken one step, changed her mind, changed it again and changed it back. "I'm right here, Brewster." Right here turned out to be directly behind his seat, where she stood frozen in indecision.

"Oh. Good idea. Good thinking. From behind me you get the pilot's perspective on the simulator. Now, if it turns out you can't see the clampers and if there's anything wrong with the autofinder – and that does depend on light to some extent – you should be able to see the triangle at the top of the dock. That one there. See?" As he pointed at it, he turned in his seat and looked Jenny in the face. "See it?"

All she could think to do was nod. If she walked quietly down the aisle past the seats, she could nip out the hatch and be back in the satellite.

He faced forward again. "So you only have to align it with this triangle here. This one. It's a safety device, and for once I think …"

But once in the satellite, she'd have to hide from Gus, for a very long time, probably. Maybe she could get Louise to take her to the district where all the whores live. Then she could start a new life in a place where Gus would never think of looking. Would it be so bad to work as a whore?

After the way Louise had supersensitised her, the thought was almost exciting. But no. Oh no it wasn't. It was sordid. It was an insane notion. Would she rather work as a whore for the rest of her life than take a day trip to Africa? Wasn't she supposed to be a hero? Isn't that what Louise called her – on her secret mission, wow?

She was still standing behind Brewster's seat, still motionless, when Gus's voice came on: "Okay, Brewster, have you got her in the dock?"

He was at least two minutes early. There wasn't time to decide anything, to do anything even if she could decide. While Brewster was saying that he still hadn't explained the speed into the clampers, Jenny swallowed her fear and bore her itch and sat in her seat again.

Gus said, "Is she completely briefed?"

"Yeah, I guess so – if she can remember it all. I thought we still had a couple of minutes more. If I could test her—"

"Can you remember it all, Jenny?"

"Yes, Gus," she said, crossing her arms and sinking into the cushion. "Except I didn't hear what Brewster said about the speed into the clampers."

"Four point four," Brewster said.

"Four point four," said Jenny. "I guess I've got it."

"Okay, Brewster," Gus said. "Time to go."

Brewster swung out of his seat. "I sure do wish you luck," he said, and he leaned forward and kissed her lightly on the forehead, making her actually tremble. "I'm really glad to have met you, and please make it back so I don't feel … you know, like I said."

Jenny said, "Brewster, I—"

"Brewster, are you out yet?"

"I'm going. I'm going. Goodbye, Jenny." He brushed past her – reigniting the tremble – and went towards the hatch at the rear. He paused there and shouted, "I hope Templeton knows what he's doing – what you're doing. Please be careful.

"Brewster, are you gone?"

"He's gone," Jenny said, hearing in her own voice a distinct plaintiveness.

"Jenny, switch over to the pilot's seat. You there?"

"Yes, Gus," she said, getting up and sitting down.

"Strapped in?"

"Yes, Gus." She strapped herself in.

"Okay, Jenny. Good luck. You're off."

Two things hit her at once: weightlessness and the best idea she'd had all day. She was off the satellite and looking at the Earth, and right below her was the mid-Pacific Ocean at both the equator and noon. Up here she was suffused with that terrible insubstantiality that she'd thought she'd take to her death in the gym, but she hadn't panicked yet, not quite. According to Gus's orders, there were hours of orbit to go before she could descend to Africa East. But she was alone in a ship with no comms and thus no tracker, and no one, not even Gus, knew where she was or what she was doing. So she would do what she felt like doing, and right now she was going to head for the mid-Pacific. She would air-fly to Africa East. Air-flying was slower and Gus's timing would be thrown off, but if Gus didn't know, who was there to care?

Hawaii was up ahead and to her left, and a quick look at a map showed her that a line almost due east from the main island would eventually get her across Mesoamerica, the Atlantic and Africa to the Serengeti, and that was the only bearing she needed. To use it, though, she was going to have to de-orbit quick, and she couldn't quite remember how to do that. Had Brewster even told her? Maybe he had, but she guessed she hadn't always been listening. Her hand twice shot to the control she suspected was the right one, and twice she stopped herself. But just as Hawaii was about to pass her by, she went ahead and hit it.

And it worked. The shuttle slowed, dipped and soared down into the mesosphere. Assuming she was still going a little too fast to enter the stratosphere, she throttled back, hit the same control and steered sharp left. Sure enough, the shuttle pointed north, cruised across the stratopause, dipped again and finally levelled out in the lovely troposphere. She was air-flying, and she had weight – beautiful, firm Earth weight.

She was low over the ocean, heading towards a part of the planet always described in histories as a kind of paradise. Of course, there were fewer islands now than in the histories – the lower ones had all sunk – but the high ones were also the big ones, and they were coming up fast. And Gus had been right about one thing: these machines more or less did fly themselves. In fact, after years of using something as basic as a pickup, she thought she could learn to like, really like, this ship. It had an automatic pilot, too, and when she was right over the main island – she had glimpses of high waterfalls, dark green mountainsides and a scarlet, oozing volcano – she turned right, set a course just a few degrees south of east, and turned on the automatic. She was flying very low, but the ship could read topography, and when it was over land, it would rise and fall as the land did. So that was it. She didn't have to do any hands-on flying again until she reached Africa East – probably about ten hours from now.

Now she could relax. And after a few minutes of watching the empty seascape, she realised that she really was relaxing. Somehow, during the excitement of manouevring the shuttle, the little itch had vanished. Or could it be the heavy gravity? Or maybe it was just the total relief from having de-orbited so easily, so adroitly, if she did think so herself. Either shuttle-flying was as simple as Gus had said or more of Brewster's briefing had sunk in than she imagined. Whichever, she felt more at ease – the genuine ease of being competent and in control, rather than the Louise-induced kind of ecstatic ease – than at any time since waking up in the gym. She pushed back in the pilot's seat with her knees against the control console and watched blue sky and dark but white-capped sea go by, thinking, here I am alone and in charge of my very own passenger shuttle without comms or tracker. At peace.

She dozed for a little while and woke up to the same sea and sky, but with her peacefulness slightly disturbed by a pang of hunger. She hadn't eaten, she realised, since some time last night, when she and Louise were raiding the apartment's food chest. All shuttles had galleys, though, and the only question was whether the one in this shuttle was stocked. She went down the aisle to the door behind the last passenger seat and opened it. It was the galley all right – a small kitchen – and it certainly was stocked. There was enough food here to feed a full ship on a trip to the Moon and back. What was more, it was already prepared and on plates with freefall-proof covers, slotted into the freezer waiting to be warmed up. And in a holder on the wall was a sheaf of menus. She opened one. For the main course there was a choice among steak Ganymede (kebab style), generated protein paddies and chicken casserole. "I'll be damned," Jenny said aloud and began unscrewing the plates' covers until she found a chicken casserole. She also found baby asparagus and potatoes au gratin. She put the vegetables on the plate and the plate in the oven. While it was heating, she went through the cupboards until she discovered the wine rack and picked out and opened an eighty-year-old Lower Olympus Mons cabernet sauvignon. Because these meals were meant to be eaten in zero gravity, there weren't any ordinary wine glasses anywhere, just beakers, but she finally came across some plain tumblers that staff must have used before and after landing or docking. In the same locker there were ordinary utensils and a tray, and she put the warmed plate, a knife, a fork, a napkin, salt, pepper, wine bottle and tumbler on the tray, which she carried back to the pilot's seat. Because of the zero-G eating arrangements, there weren't any tables anywhere, but the console was largely horizontal, and she was able to unload the tray onto the various flat spaces among the buttons and levers, with the plate right in front of the seat and the wine bottle and glass in easy reach. She chucked the tray over to the co-pilot's seat, sat, put the napkin in her lap, took a bite of casserole (nothing like her own – it was generated food, to start with, and half the spices seemed to have been left out) and poured wine into the tumbler. After a long drink, she held the cool glass against her cheek, looked out on a rolling sea (no sign of land yet, not even any birds) and reflected on how very, very good that had tasted. She took another sip. Then she ate.

She couldn't have finished the meal any faster if she'd inhaled it. She'd probably gone all day not realising how hungry she was because her attention had been so focused on that other appetite. Now with both of them gone, she could concentrate on other things – her mission, for example. She put the dish and other stuff on the tray – leaving only the wine bottle and glass on the console – took the tray to the galley and left it beside the sink. Back in the pilot's seat, she poured some more cabernet sauvignon, gazed at the black and white ocean and the now-greying sky and, as she sipped the wine, tried to plan what she'd do when she got to the Serengeti. According to Gus, it was all very simple. He had given her an exact reading on where the cruiser was – right at the eastern edge of the Ngorongoro Crater – and all she had to do was land a safe distance away, put on a sterility suit (shuttles, which were often used for ferrying Earth Rangers to EHQS and back, all had sterile airlocks) and simply walk or creep over to the cruiser and see if the Back-to-Earthers were milling around outside or holed up in the ship. That was all. Then back to the shuttle and fly to Ben Haymark's station in Africa South and see what was going on there, why he wasn't routinely reporting in. Then straight back to EHQS. What she wasn't to do was try to go to her own station – too dangerous: they'd be watching it – or go to any other stations besides Ben's, however urgent she thought such a trip might be. She could come back later, after discussing everything with Gus, but on this trip she was to take no initiatives, none at all. None.

Well, Gus was very busy and under terrible pressure, and he wasn't always thinking clearly. For one thing, he was allowing for the chance – by his lights, slim but real – that those maniacs were going around outside without sterility suits, and all the precautions he'd told her to take were based on that possibility. But they wouldn't be watching Jenny's station because they couldn't be – they were stuck inside their ship. But why would they want to watch it anyway? That was Simon and his gang parked at the Ngorongoro, and they had thrown her into the gym personally. She was, as far as they were concerned, dead. So why would they watch her station even if they could? She poured another glass of wine and was glad to see that the heavy clouds she'd been flying under were starting to thin out, and a few shafts of sunlight were hitting the water. She thought she could see birds in the distance, too. Her first landfall would be the west coast of Mesoamerica – part of the ancient republic of Mexico – and by her reckoning she'd be seeing that in about fifteen minutes. She sipped her wine. She was glad now that she was doing this alone. She still felt peaceful and comfortable, and the Pacific lit by sun shafts was beautiful.

The main thing was that she was alone. Alone and without communications. She could take any initiative she felt like, and Gus wouldn't have to know about it. In fact, she was taking one now, by air-flying instead of orbiting and by getting to her sector a few hours later than Gus had wanted her to. And if she decided to stop at her station and, say, trade the shuttle for her pickup, that's what she'd do, because then she'd only have to land the shuttle once and take off once, and could do her running around in a machine that was second nature to her and easier to handle over short distances. That didn't mean she didn't appreciate the qualities of this ship. It was luxurious, and she was loving it, and then she remembered that on commercial shuttle trips there was usually something happening on the in-ship comms – music or a light show or a story in the space by the ceiling. She wasn't in the mood for a story now – she'd rather watch the Earth go by – but she thought music might be nice, and she wondered where the comms kit was. She looked over the console and found one thing that looked like a comms control, but that turned out to be the now-dead external connection. There was nothing on the co-pilot's side either. Then she remembered that it was the attendants who seemed to supervise that sort of thing, and so she poured herself the last of the wine and, with the glass in her hand, went back to the galley. There were plenty of controls along the walls and by the door, but they all seemed to be

310

concerned with cooking, refrigeration or housekeeping. She left the galley wondering if she really needed music but decided to try the door across from the galley, and sure enough, it opened to a little room with soft chairs and a low table – an off-duty staff lounge, she supposed. And on the wall opposite the door was an entertainment control panel exactly like the one in her station.

She made her selection and then sat in one of the chairs, her feet on the table, as she sipped the wine and bathed herself in the music – melodic ancient classical music, the kind she sometimes played at home. This particular piece – and there would be more like it to come – was one she hadn't heard before. It was sung by what sounded like a quartet in, of course, Ancient English, with beautiful harmonies and accompanied by ancient instruments making sounds that no one in the whole history of the post-Apocalypse era had ever quite duplicated. It made her think of Peter, who'd been able to translate this kind of singing – who, in fact, had introduced her to it – and the words almost always turned out to be about sexual love. So she was glad she couldn't understand them. Of all the things that made this trip so peaceful and pleasant so far, the most notable was the absence of that damned itch. She didn't need that, and she didn't need anybody to satisfy her or perform anything of any description for her. It was something else Gus had been right about: alone was what she did. She was a natural-born Earth Ranger.

She emptied the glass and felt like going over to the galley for another bottle (she'd seen cognac there, too, hadn't she?), but she reminded herself that she was flying a kind of ship she'd never flown before, and because she was in a good enough mood already, more wine would be lily-gilding, not to say risky. She'd had her casserole. She'd had a little to drink. And the music was on. The least she could do was go sit in the pilot's seat while she listened to it. But when she got up and was about to leave the lounge, she noticed another door. It was in the opposite corner of the room – a narrow door, painted the same general maroon as the walls – and had been easy to miss. There was no question of her not going over and opening it, and when she did she discovered a little bathroom, complete with a little shower. Ever since she escaped from the gunge of the gym, showers were high of the list of experiences she couldn't get enough of – she and Louise had showered four or five times last night – and so she had another shower now, once again washing off the piss, shit, vomit and blood that she would never in her life forget. Before the shower she'd felt better than ever, and now she felt better even than that. With her hair wet and her teeth brushed and a light touch of perfume behind each ear (there'd been a fully stocked cabinet above the little sink) and while ancient classical music filled the shuttle, Jenny made her way back to the pilot's seat. She was carrying her clothes – her underwear and the flight suit – and before she sat down, she folded them and put them on the co-pilot's seat. Right now she felt too clean for clothes. There were no comms and no tracker, and nobody anywhere for thousands of kilometres. Lone nakedness was the ultimate in comfort. She'd get dressed later.

While she'd been lounging and showering, land had come into view. What she could see now made her remember why she'd ever wanted to work for the National Park Service, whose greatest accomplishment, over the centuries since the Apocalypse, was to have restored the seas. They'd been all but dead at one point, poisoned and fished out. Long-term reseeding and, most important, the absence of humans, had resurrected them. If she'd been straining to see birds over the open ocean, now she had them in what looked to be their millions. She hadn't realised that this particular part of the North American coast was such a rich feeding ground – something to do with the Humboldt Current, she supposed – but so many birds were hitting the water and coming out of it that from up here it looked as if the offshore sea was boiling. Even though the sun was full out now, she was a bit too high up to tell what all the different species were, but she did manage to pick out both brown and white pelicans and frigatebirds, cormorants and tropicbirds. The smaller ones were undoubtedly different kinds of gulls and terns, and there were so many of them they seemed like snowflakes in a blizzard. She thought she could see sealions in the water, too – yes, here they would probably be sealions – and what might have been a pod of orcas. On the fast-approaching beach ahead was a vast colony of elephant seals, and right on the horizon, shimmering in and out of a haze, the Sierra Madre del Sur was taking shape.

As much as it thrilled her to view the planet this way, it helped her remember how much she hated the Back-to-Earthers – and not just for what they did, or thought they finally did, to her and the rest of the people on the satellite, or for what they must be doing to those children. She'd never known very much about their philosophy (and never wanted to), but she did know that it was based on something in the Bible and that they thought they and only they had a divine right to live on Earth, which God had made for them. Exclusively them – because they believed something or other. They didn't like wild animals either. She remembered that much from a pamphlet of theirs she'd read once, but she couldn't remember why. Was it because animals weren't capable of believing in God and so had no right to life? She didn't know, but whatever the reason, they would have hated a scene like this and wouldn't mind stopping it happening. And she couldn't even hope they were all dead by now, because that would have meant the children were, too.

Or would they be? What about this – she wondered as the ship passed over the elephant seals and the Earth's surface turned into a scrubland – what if they believe that the children can't breathe the air until they've been converted or something? The adults would go outside and collapse, leaving only the children and some babysitters inside the ship. Then the babysitters, seeing that the others had died, would lie to the Moon while they tried to figure out what to do – unable to admit, even (or especially) to their own leaders, that the most fundamental tenet of their faith was bullshit.

There was real hope in that, she thought – as she happened to notice, to her left and exactly on the northern horizon, what seemed to be a vast ruins, stretching maybe a hundred kilometres in from the coast. And directly below her were other ruins, overgrown and mostly buried but recognisable, of what must have been buildings and wide roads. And off to the right, damned if there wasn't another big city's remains. What would these have been? She couldn't remember if there were any cities that size on this part of the Mesoamerican coast. Inland, there were a couple of big ones – Guadalajara and Mexico City – but not on the coast. There was no point in looking at a map, since the ones Gus had given her didn't show ruins. She just couldn't remember where all the old cities used to be, and anyway North America had never been a specialty of hers – only Africa was.

She refused to worry. The ship was on auto and knew where it was going, and the Sierra Madre was right where it was supposed to be – ragged, rocky, snowy in spots and straight ahead. Those ruins had been a puzzle, though, and she wondered if maybe a small cognac would help take her mind off them. For a little while she argued with herself about that. But finally, as the mountains were fast approaching, she decided it would be appropriate to drink a toast to them, and when she walked back from the galley this time, it was with the music a little louder and half-full tumbler in her hand. She'd told herself that she'd drink it very slowly and that this was absolutely the only … But what was that up ahead? Trees? Trees. Green trees. Spruce, they were. Rocks. It was a mountain. But why so close? The topography reader … She dropped the tumbler and plunged towards the console, grabbing the manual control with both hands and pulling the ship straight up, climbing almost right at the sun. She didn't know how high the mountain was or where she was in relation to it. It was just her and the sun, loud music and sticky cognac running down her stomach and left leg. In about five seconds, when she checked the rear monitor and saw she was past the top of the mountain, she levelled off. But where was she? Well, flying over mountaintops, snowfields, valleys and shining green forests – over the Sierra Madre, obviously. But what the hell had happened to the topography reader? She wondered if Gus had sent her out in a faulty ship. But Gus couldn't have known, and there hadn't been time for a full mechanical check. Anyway, at this instant she was too relieved not to have crashed into the mountain to blame anybody for anything. But obviously the topography reader didn't work, which meant that if she was going to keep flying low, she couldn't use the autopilot, and that meant, damn it, she was going to have to stay at the controls for the rest of the way.

She could fly higher, of course, and maybe she would, but what else couldn't she trust about the autopilot? She couldn't know and she couldn't think. Her hands on the controls were shaking. What she really needed right now was that cognac, but the tumbler was lying empty somewhere behind her, and she didn't dare leave the controls to go to the galley again. The music didn't help, either – it was too fast and too loud, and she couldn't go back and turn it down or off. She was just going to steady herself through her own sheer will. She could do that. She'd be all right. She was above any dangerous mountains now, and so it was safe enough to close her eyes just for a minute. She closed them and, breathing deeply, lay back in the seat with her feet propped against the console. One hand, she realised, was resting on the sticky patch on her stomach, and she ran a finger over it and raised it to touch her tongue. It was good, and she did it again and then retrieved some spillage from her thigh. The music hadn't got any quieter, but at least it had slowed down a little, and she immersed herself in that and the taste of the cognac. Everything was going to be okay, she told herself – she'd just had a scare. As she was licking her finger for maybe the fourth or fifth time, she thought she sensed something. She opened her eyes, took in some fluffy clouds and snowy mountaintops and then, for no particular reason, turned her head to the left. Not ten metres away a man was looking at her.

A boy, really. He was probably in his late teens. He had orange hair and an orange collar, and on his acned face was the angriest look she'd seen since … well, that time when Simon had been so angry with her. The boy was at the controls of a ship, and he was signalling at her by repeatedly pointing to his ear. Jenny was transfixed. This was not possible. She might as well be seeing an angel or, in this case maybe, a devil. Where had he come from? How could he be there? The ship was a kind you didn't see very often – an outrigger. Much bigger ships kept them in their holds and used them when someone on board needed something small and speedy. But what was this one doing over the Sierra Madre? The boy kept pointing at his ear and was now mouthing something. "Comms," yes – that's what it was.

As she wondered how to signal back, she realised she hadn't moved since she'd first seen him. Even her finger was still in her mouth. She dropped her legs quickly, folded her arms across her chest and, feeling a furnace of a blush, shook her head at him. He furiously repeated the comms gesture, looking as if he might poke out his eardrum. The only way she could think to reply was to make a broad shrug, palms up (even though she was still blushing, it was way too late for modesty). Then she shook her head again, waved a hand over her own ear and mouthed, "No comms."

He reached for something on his control console, did something to it and then held up to his window a writing tablet. It said: "TURN ON YOUR COMMS."

Again she shrugged and shook her head. She looked around quickly but couldn't see a writing tablet anywhere around her own controls.

He banged the erasure button and wrote again (God, he was angry). This time the message read: "I AM FULLY ARMED AND FASTER THAN YOU. I WILL EXCORT YOU TO A LANDING PLAICE."

What could she do but nod? Looking straight ahead, she put her hands on the controls. She thought without much confidence that there might be a chance at some point to slip away from him. Then she looked back at him and saw that he'd written another message: "GOD PUNISHES MASTERBAITERS."

CHAPTER THIRTY-ONE

It was the middle of the afternoon, and there was still no sign of Gibbous. They'd expected him back early in the morning, but they all, the baby included, had slept through the morning. This was because no one had slept through the night, which they'd mostly spent trying to keep from being blown away. And they might have been – or at least everything they needed for survival out here might have been – if Paintbrush hadn't suddenly decided, not long after Gibbous had set off, that the breeze was picking up a bit too much for her liking. She'd taken down the shelter and had Allaby sitting on the blankets and holding the baby while she dug their (now double) bedpit deeper and wider, using the rocks she was prying up to weigh various things down. She'd even managed to pull one pretty big rock out of one end of the bedpit (she was a hell of a lot stronger than she looked), leaving a hole large enough for Allaby (and he could actually do this now) to build a little fire in. So while they couldn't sleep and, because there was no way of keeping a bed of grass down, couldn't even rest very well (the baby cried a lot but not constantly, and anyway the shrieking wind took the edge off his screams), they'd at least been able to keep warm and to eat. Allaby had even begun to understand what might conceivably be good about prairie dog (Paintbrush had been teaching him how to suck and finally eat the bits he'd been spitting out).

The wind had dropped at about the same time as the sun rose. So the shelter had gone back up, and with neither Paintbrush nor Allaby daring to observe aloud that Gibbous wasn't back, they'd arranged themselves and the baby on a pile of newly cut grass and had slept. Then they'd woken up in the early afternoon and had finished another meal before Paintbrush, now feeding the baby, sighed and finally said, "He's not back, Allaby."

Allaby was stretched out on his side, his head propped on his good arm, as he stared in the direction Gibbous had gone yesterday. "Maybe," he said, "he's still looking for them. Or maybe he decided to sit out the wind last night and is going to look for them tonight. Whatever happened to the dog, Paintbrush? He didn't take the dog, did he? I don't remember."

"I don't know what happened to the dog," Paintbrush said, "but Granddad didn't take him. I guess the dog's just deserted us. Or he's dead."

Neither Allaby nor Paintbrush uttered the obvious next sentence – or even the next word: "too." To Allaby, the prospect of Gibbous being dead was awful, not only for the sake of poor Gibbous himself – who had become, he realised, possibly the best friend he'd ever had – but for what it would mean for this little family stuck in the middle of nowhere, and for a hell of a lot beyond that. It would mean that those people in that liner were hostile. At the very least, they would be ignorant, because nobody officially sent here would ever harm an Immyo still on an Immyo reservation. Allaby silently cursed himself. He was the one who should have been checking out that liner, and he would have been if he hadn't been so inept and let himself get crippled. On the other hand, if he hadn't been crippled they'd all be well into the San Juans by now and probably wouldn't even have seen the liner. Anyway, he could be reading too much into Gibbous's failure to show. Any number of things could have held him up. There wasn't that much reason to worry, not yet. He looked back at Paintbrush to say as much and saw that she was weeping.

The baby was pumping and sucking, and Paintbrush was sitting there wide-eyed and with tears running down in dirty streaks. Allaby got up – noticing vaguely how much less of an effort getting up was today – went over to her, sat and put his arm around her. He said, "There could be a lot of reasons why he isn't back. It doesn't have to be a bad one."

"Why did you make him go, Allaby?"

"I didn't make him—"

"Yes you did. I was begging him not to, and then you would say something like 'Are you sure you want to?' and he would say 'Yes I am,' and then you both would ignore me while you told him about the skypeople and all the horrible things they could kill him with. You wanted him to go."

He tried to pull her a little closer, but she resisted. So he took his hand off her shoulder and self-consciously put it in his lap, looking at it as though it had done something wrong. "I didn't want him to go if he didn't want to. I told him about the guns and things so he'd know how dangerous it was."

"The more dangerous you made it sound, the more he wanted to go. Granddad's always done that. He loves proving that things aren't as dangerous as people say."

"He is brave, Paintbrush. He's smart, too. He wouldn't—"

"It's not bravery, damn it, Allaby. It's mockery. He climbed the Old Man with the Nose once – not because he was being brave but because he'd been sitting and studying it. It's a huge rock formation, you know, and he could see a way up. Then he announced to everybody that he was going to climb it. He was a young man then. It was way before I was born, but the old people still tell the story, or did before they got killed by those nasty bastards." She started crying harder, actually sobbing.

"Paintbrush, please." He tried putting his arm around her again, this time not pulling her closer to him, and that seemed to be tolerable to her, if she even noticed.

She sniffed and inhaled. "He said he was going to climb it, and everybody said don't try, it's not possible, you'll die, and he just sat there and let them talk at him, and one old man told me once that what had started out as a little grin or smirk just gradually grew as the people kept telling him not to do it – and that included his wife Spiderweb, they had little kids by then – and by the time he got up and was starting towards the trail down the Gorge to the bottom of the thing, he looked like he had two faces he was smiling so much. He loved that. He loved knowing he could do it and loved all those people pleading with him not to. And do you remember when he threw that burning cowpat at that lion? Nobody else would do that. They'd be scared to unless there were a whole lot of people around with rocks and spears and things. But Granddad knew exactly what that lion would do, that it wasn't dangerous to throw a burning cowpat at it. But yesterday he didn't know. He thought he did, maybe, but he didn't. This time it was too much for him. Damn him. Damn him. Damn you." She wiped her eyes with the back of her hand and gave Allaby a searing sideways glance that felt like, well, like a burning cowpat. Then she looked down as she carefully shifted the baby to her other breast.

Then she wasn't crying any more. There was some residual catching of breath, but she was mainly angry now – angry at him, Allaby. It was something he hadn't experienced from Paintbrush so far, and he didn't have any idea what to expect or what to do about it. Anyway, he was also worried about Gibbous and was capable of blaming himself without any encouragement from her. He felt terrible. He felt alone – without Gibbous and with a furious Paintbrush. Not even the dog to give him a consoling lick. There was a whole liner full of his own people over there, but they apparently were hostile and dangerous. Why? Who were they? He had to think this out: what group of people, enough of them to need a liner, would come to Earth with hostile intent? Did they know the virus was gone? Yes, they'd have to – otherwise why bother? And why come now, when the damned thing's been gone for fifty years? In fact, right at the moment, Allaby almost wished the virus would come back. It would be the end of him personally, but an end was something he felt he'd just about reached anyway. And it would wipe out all those people and leave Paintbrush and the baby to go back to their settlements. That is, if they were immune. They'd both been born after the disappearance of the virus, and there was a one in four chance that …

"Allaby."

"Yes?"

"What are you thinking about?"

"Where do I start? You and the baby, among other things."

She pushed Allaby's hand off her shoulder. "Don't waste time thinking about us. We're all right. You should be thinking about yourself and what you made Granddad do."

"I was thinking about that, too. It would be terrible if something's happened to him – terrible in ways you probably haven't realised yet. But don't give up so quickly. He could still be—"

"No, he'd be back, Allaby. If he couldn't find them or something, he'd come back anyway. He wouldn't do this to me."

Allaby stood up, stood over her and halfway raised his hands in a shrug. "Do what? Make you worry? You just said yourself that he likes to make people worry. That's why, according to you, he tried to climb that rock formation. And I've heard him say to you that you worried about him better than anybody. Better, he said. By the way, did he finally climb the thing?"

"Of course he did. And they say he did a little dance on the top. Spiderweb fainted."

He crossed his arms. "There. You see? He's probably just lying up somewhere to make you worry. Us worry. He ought to be ashamed."

"Don't say that about Granddad. Don't … Oh, Allaby." Tears returned.

"What?"

"Allaby, I know you tried a little bit to argue with him, but he's … Oh, sit down and put your arm around me."

Was that it? He sat, put his arm around her and pulled her to him. Among all the reasons to love Paintbrush, this could be top of the list: she didn't stay mad. He'd had a girlfriend in university once who could string out a sulk for weeks, and even Jenny could do a day or two. And neither of them could ever have been angry about anything as serious as this. Allaby had no illusions – Paintbrush loved Gibbous more than she loved anybody, including him – and here he'd been instrumental in sending the old man off on a mission that was beyond anything he could ever have imagined. Here had been someone who'd only just been introduced to the wheel – how could he comprehend photon guns, zoom monitors and different models of ships? But, yes, he had badly wanted Gibbous to go. Of course, Gibbous himself had wanted to go, and if Paintbrush couldn't talk him out of it, what chance would Allaby have had? Then again – and Allaby was having to concentrate hard to reconstruct exactly what had been said – he had started out by convincing Gibbous that going and having a look was important, and once Gibbous was convinced, there was no unconvincing him. But it really had been important to find out … except that they now knew nothing more than they'd known yesterday, and now there was no Gibbous. "Shit," Allaby said.

Paintbrush, her mouth next to Allaby's ear, said, "I take that to mean that you've just thought through what you've done and are finally wishing you hadn't done it."

"Uh …"

"Good," she said. "Now I want you to show me something." She pulled away from him again. "You've hardly moved today. I want to see you move."

"What do you mean?"

"Get up and try to walk around. Let's see how you are." With her elbow, she gave him a little poke in the sore ribs. "Go on."

That hurt. Maybe, in fact, she was still mad but just had a peculiarly Paintbrush way of expressing it. But he did get up, and stepped out from under the shelter. Once again, he gazed over the plain, willing a distant Gibbous to reappear where he'd seen him disappear yesterday evening. But there was still only the sea of grass, the herds of grazing animals and a broad heat shimmer where a returning Gibbous should have been. Of course Paintbrush was still angry with him – in a way that would permanently diminish him: he would always be the man who sent her beloved Granddad to his death.

"How was that?" Paintbrush said.

"How was what?"

"Getting up and taking two steps."

"It's kind of hard to tell after being hit in the ribs." In fact, he realised, he had got up and stepped over here as though it was the most natural thing in the world.

"Walk some more, Allaby. Walk to the edge of the clearing and back."

Allaby walked to the edge of the clearing and stopped, still trying to conjure Gibbous out of the heat shimmer. Then off to his left an all-white stallion, with much wild-eyed whinnying, mounted a chestnut mare, while twenty or so other mares and foals alternately grazed and looked on. It was an impressive thing to see, but instead of relishing the sight, he felt sad and wished he was a horse himself. Horses belonged here, were as much a part of the Earth as the ground they were standing on. He was an alien. He came from a city under a dome on a faraway moon – an artificial world without insects to bite you, sun to burn you, wind to batter you, wild animals to crack your ribs. His great discovery that it was possible to live and breathe on Earth had led in the end to nothing but failure. Allaby lacked the stamina for this hard-edged planet, and as a result Gibbous was probably gone for good.

"Now walk back to me," Paintbrush called.

He shrugged and did.

And when he reached the shelter and sat down against a pole, she said, "Allaby, you're okay. You can walk again."

"I guess I can. The bruising must have gone down."

"Granddad said it would. He even said when it would."

"And you know," Allaby said, looking at his feet spread in front of him and encased in the shoes Paintbrush had made, "I think not walking for a while has helped my feet heal up a little." Paintbrush's wonderful, preposterous bandages of shoes – what a day that had been. All that promise. Starting his new life as an Immyo. Tuning in to the language. Falling in love with the beautiful Immyo girl. Making love to her. Who had instigated that? As far as he could remember, neither and both. It had just happened as if it had been the next thing on the schedule. Then waiting for Gibbous to get back, in perfect confidence that he would. In fact, worrying about him getting back too soon and catching them. Allaby sighed.

"They ought to be healing. I put enough gumplant in those shoes. Yes, I think walking what's you need now, Allaby."

"What do you mean?"

"We can't just sit here any longer."

"Gibbous could still turn up. And if we're not here—"

"Allaby, I hate to say it, but you're not thinking straight." The baby, it appeared, had fallen asleep on the nipple. Paintbrush laid him on her lap, shooed some flies away, wiped his mouth and started retying her shirt. "We're both telling ourselves Granddad must be dead because if we think the worst, and the worst is true, that somehow doesn't make it quite as bad as it could be. But we've got to think that it might not be true, too."

"But that's what I was saying."

"Yeah, Allaby, but you were saying it because you didn't want to think the worst. But I think now you've thought the worst, and so we can start thinking other things. Hand me Skyman's blanket."

He got up, found the blanket and gave it to her. "Believe me, I was thinking the worst," he said, sitting again and trying to dissect her logic.

She began swaddling the baby. "No you weren't. You were trying to be cheerful and to cheer me up, which only leaves me to think the worst by myself. I needed you to be with me, Allaby, and you weren't. That's why I was angry, or mainly why. I had to get you thinking it was your fault." She got up and laid the baby in a little grass-lined pit that Allaby had begun to regard as the cradle, and then she came over to Allaby and sat between his outstretched legs with her back to him. She pulled his arms around her. "He had to go, didn't he?"

"Well, he thought he did."

"You thought he did, too."

"Well, I—"

"Don't deny it, Allaby, or we'll start going around the tree again."

"I thought it was important, yes."

"Well, maybe it was," Paintbrush said. "Maybe those people over there are just Little Rimmers from higher in the sky. Do you think that's possible?"

"I don't know. I didn't know yesterday, and I still don't know. But with Gibbous not being back—"

"So it's up to us to find out."

"What?"

"You can walk now. And that's what I mean about Granddad and his mockery. He knew you'd be able to walk today. You might not have believed him, but he knew. And he couldn't put off going for a single day so that—"

"I could go?"

"Yeah."

"Um. Yeah. It should have been me."

"Well, it will be now."

"But would you be all right if—"

"And me. And Skyman."

"Oh no, Paintbrush. You can't. Not … you and the baby. No."

"What do you want us to do? Squat out here until you vanish too?" She'd been sitting with her back to him, and now she turned around, put her legs over his and wriggled herself as close as she could get. She pressed his crotch with hers and put her open hands on the sides of his face. Peering into his eyes, she said, "Allaby, in case you've forgotten, I'm your wife. I know wives often sit at home while their husbands go out and do things, but damn it, Allaby, this isn't home. This is nowhere. I'm not going to be stranded in nowhere while you go disappear. What are you thinking about?"

"I just thought you might want to go wait by the river or maybe back to your settlements. That's all. This is obviously going to be dangerous."

"Dangerous for Granddad alone, sure. Dangerous for you, maybe – even though they are your people. Dangerous for you, me and Skyman – maybe that, too. But Allaby … Oh, Allaby, I'm not letting you go without me. I'd never see you again." She began kissing him around the face. "We had such a horrible night last night, and today we've argued. The baby's asleep now. Just lie back, Allaby. We need something to give us energy."

Allaby had never quite looked at lovemaking as a way of gaining energy, but he was happy to go along with the notion. And his happiness increased exponentially as the seconds and minutes passed, until at last, as they were lying still, eyes closed and basking in each other's substantial smells, a voice came from above, saying, "When I'm away, is this all you two ever do?"

CHAPTER THIRTY-TWO

Allaby's eyes popped open only to see the dog's mouth, teeth and tongue just before a long, wet lick was administered. Paintbrush had been instantly on her feet, and by the time Allaby managed to push the dog away and pull his trousers to a decent level, he could see that she had her arms around Gibbous and was crying over him, oblivious of the fact that her skirt was up around her shoulders. Holding his trousers with his good hand, Allaby got up and used the hand with the splint to pull the skirt down. He said, "Gibbous, I've never been so glad to see anybody in my ... What the ... "

There, parked at the edge of the clearing, was a fluorescent orange pickup. He took a few seconds to register what he was seeing, but while he was registering, he heard a man's voice say in modern English and a Lunar accent, "... quite a reception ..." The voice kept on, but it had dropped too low for Allaby to understand. Then a woman said something about a little girl. At the same time that he confirmed to himself that he really was looking at a pickup, he also realised that its door was open and the voices were coming from inside.

Gibbous said, "Allaby, do you know how to jabber back at those people? The only way I can get them to do anything is to talk with my hands or draw pictures. They've got this flat thing that turns your finger into a paintbrush."

"What people?" Paintbrush said, drying her eyes and looking up for the first time. "What's that?" She stepped back from Gibbous.

Gibbous gestured towards it. "It's one of the things Allaby described to me. Good description, too, Allaby. It's very small inside, Paintbrush, but it flies through the air faster than a hawk in a dive. We got here just like that." He clapped his hands. "But, Allaby, I can't remember what you called it."

Keeping his voice low, Allaby said, "A pickup."

"That's it. A pickup. Anyway, Allaby, can you go jabber to them? They want something from me, but I don't know what it is. And they're kind of stupid, to tell you the truth. They've been jabbering at me for most of the night and day. They don't seem to understand anything about anything. I had to do some pretty good drawing and hand-talking to get them to bring me here. And be careful. They have those guns you told me about. One of them almost used one on Yellow. I had to dart the man."

"You darted one of them?"

"Not one of those. There are hundreds of people back at the liner, but there are only two in the pickup. That's all there was room for, what with me and Yellow and my satchel and stick. And they're afraid of Yellow, which made it seem even more crowded because I had to keep him away from them. Now I don't think they want to get out. They don't walk very well, and they spend a lot of time on their knees for some reason."

It struck Allaby that Gibbous was being as knowing and enthusiastic as a child, to whom everything is new and thus possible ("then the witch got on the broomstick, and when the cat got on too, they took off over the ..."). Paintbrush, on the other hand, was rivetted. When she'd first seen the pickup, her jaw had dropped – it was still dropped – and she was still staring at the machine. Now she said, "Allaby, what makes it fly? It doesn't have wings."

He knew she meant something like eagle's wings, but it was still a pretty good observation. "Uh, air-particle quantum displacement," he said. "I'll tell you about it some time."

Gibbous said, "Allaby, let's go over there. Come on."

Allaby realised that his hesitation was caused by, as much as anything, embarrassment. He was a filthy mess – matted hair and beard, bites all over him, bandages for shoes, a makeshift splint, clothes cut for someone almost a metre shorter, so much dirt on his face he could feel it through his skin and a smell that only God and Paintbrush knew the full extent of. And with the shelter open at the sides, those people had just seen him and Paintbrush in coitus, for Christ's sake. Then that made him aware that he was still holding up his trousers with his hand. So he started trying to retie the damnably complex string system, something that normally took him a couple of minutes. And now his fingers were shaking.

"Oh God, Allaby," Paintbrush said, "let me do that."

As she knelt in front of him, he thought he heard a little shriek from the pickup, and that replaced some of his embarrassment with resentment. What business was it of theirs if his wife had to do up his flies – or, if that's what they thought was happening, to administer oral sex. He'd got used to a world with just four people in it. What were those extras doing here? What were hundreds of them doing in a liner on an Immyo reservation? On the other hand, he thought, they hadn't harmed Gibbous, and he was immensely grateful for that. It meant they weren't entirely sinister. Maybe they were no worse than, as Gibbous had suggested, stupid. "Thanks Love," he said to Paintbrush as she tied the last knot and stood up. "Okay, Gibbous. You coming, Paintbrush?"

"No thanks," she said. "I'm staying with Skyman. Look, the dog's licking him again. He'll wake him up."

Paintbrush headed for the cradle, and Gibbous and Allaby walked over to the pickup. It was only about twenty steps away, but to Allaby it felt like a hike. They were, after all, travelling between worlds, between universes, through an epoch of time. And as he got closer to it, he found the colour of the thing increasingly offensive. There was no orange like that anywhere around, anywhere on Earth probably. Even at his station, there was never any screaming orange – things were painted white or dark green. This was the kind of colour you'd find all over Armstrong. What business … Oh hell, stop it, he told himself as they reached the pickup. Try to be friendly.

Because the sun had been glinting off the glass, Allaby hadn't been able to see quite what the two Mooners looked like, but now, peering past Gibbous through the open door, he saw them as if they were figures in an illumination. The first thing that struck him was how pasty-faced they were. This was accentuated by the sunlight, but still … It was just that after days with the tanned Paintbrush and the weathered Gibbous (even the baby looked more robust than these two) it was a shock to see the colouring, or lack of it, that Allaby had always regarded as normal. Both looked to be in their forties and were wearing red-orange uniforms with green collars and green epaulettes with crosses on them. The man had a shaved head and pencil-thin eyebrows, as though he'd plucked them, and the woman was a white-blonde with her hair pulled back and no apparent eyebrows at all. And her pupils were so pale that in the glare they seemed to have vanished as well. As for the man, his eyes were shiny and black. Gibbous said, "Oh, shit," and did a little jump backwards, bumping against Allaby, who was now able to see that the woman had her gun out.

When Gibbous jumped, the man, who was sitting nearest the door, looked over at the woman and said, "Oh put that away."

"No. Look at him," she said. "That's the dirtiest, scariest man I've ever seen. He's a monster. And I swear he was raping that little girl."

"I'm telling you he wasn't," he said. "He couldn't have been. She was on top. Anyway, look. She's not a little girl. She's got a baby."

"That doesn't mean …"

Allaby said, "She's my wife. And she was on top because I've got cracked ribs. Hello, I'm Peter Allaby."

The gun dropped out of the woman's hand. The man swung around, and they both stared at Allaby. Gibbous, stepping aside, said, "Hey, they understand your jabber all right. What did you say?"

"Nothing much yet," he said to Gibbous. And to the Mooners he said, "I want to thank you for taking care of my friend and returning him safely. He's my wife's grandfather." That wasn't strictly true, but it saved explaining how Gibbous could be his wife's former grandfather-in-law.

Finally, the man said, "You … you speak English."

"Yes, and so does he," Allaby said, putting a hand on Gibbous's shoulder. "It's just a different, uh, evolution of English."

The man glanced at the woman and said, "I told you it wasn't Aramaic."

"Aramaic?" Allaby said. "Nobody's spoken that in more than three thousand years."

"What are you jabbering about?" Gibbous said. "Are you really talking?"

"Yeah, we're talking about Aramaic, the language – the jabbering – of Jesus."

"Who's Jesus?"

"An ancient holy man. Some people – and I suspect these are a couple of them – still think of him as a kind of god."

The woman said, "Did I hear you call the old man Jesus?"

"No." said Allaby. "His name's Gibbous. Gibbous Moon. My wife over there is called Paintbrush, and the dog's called Yellow. The baby, ironically enough, is Skyman, not that you'd understand that particular irony, although Gibbous Moon is kind of ironic, too, come to think about it. And your names are …"

"I'm Jacob," the man said, "and she's Rachel. We come from Conrad. That's in Crater Korola. Far Side."

"They're called Jacob and Rachel," he said to Gibbous, "and they come from the other side of the Moon." To them he said, "Very glad to meet you, and thanks again for taking care of Gibbous. Can I ask you something, though? I've been a little out of touch lately, but how come a liner full of people is allowed to land on an Immyo reservation?"

"A what?" Jacob said.

"A liner, full of people."

"No, I mean what we've landed on."

"An Immyo reservation."

"Well, I don't know what that is, but we're Planet Pilgrims, you see, and we were assigned to this place."

Rachel leaned partly across Jacob and, with a nod, said, "We're regenerating the Earth."

Planet Pilgrims? Allaby had heard of Planet Pilgrims, he thought, but while he was trying to remember where and how, the pickup's comms went on. A voice said, "Are you there yet?"

"Yes, sir," Jacob said.

"What's it like?"

"Kind of out in the open. Not really where you'd expect ..."

Of course – Planet Pilgrims was what Back-to-Earthers called themselves. Nutters. Religious nutters. Dangerous, illegal religious nutters.

"... no source of water or anything. And there are only four of them, counting the old man and a baby. And you won't believe this. One of them speaks English." But the last sentence wasn't transmitted, because Allaby had quickly reached in and switched off the comms. "Get your hand off that," Jacob said.

"Okay," Allaby said, and he grabbed Jacob's gun.

"What are you doing?" Gibbous said.

"For one thing, getting us a pickup."

"But they've been pretty nice to me," Gibbous said.

Allaby took a couple of steps back. "Okay, get out of there, both of you. Rachel, if you reach any closer to the gun on the floor, I'll blow your goddamned God-bothering head off."

"I told you he was a monster," Rachel said. Her lower lip began to tremble, and tears appeared in her blank eyes. In fact, they brought her pupils into view – a very light hazel. "I didn't want to do this, you know. I didn't want to leave Conrad. I hate this place."

"Get out."

"We can't move fast," Jacob said. "The gravity." But he did move his legs towards the door and very gingerly began to lower himself, while Rachel managed to progress from her seat to Jacob's.

"Hold him," Allaby said to Gibbous. "Don't worry. He's tall, but he's a whole lot weaker than you."

"Okay," Gibbous said, grabbing Jacob's arms from behind. "They may have been nice to me, but now that I think about it, they weren't very nice to those children."

"What children?"

"About a hundred. And they make them sit outside all night in the cold. And last night in that wind."

Paintbrush called, "What's going on over there?"

And Jacob said, "You realise you're not going to get away with this. Command's got a reading on our position."

"So what? Hurry up, Rachel."

It took about as long for Paintbrush, carrying the baby, to arrive at Allaby's side as it did for Rachel to lower herself out of the pickup. And when her feet touched the ground, her knees buckled, and she fell into a kind of squat that she didn't seem able to struggle out of. At the same time she was having a sobbing fit.

"Allaby, what's happening to these people?" Paintbrush said. "That woman is scared to death. Here, hold Skyman." She plopped the baby onto Allaby's good arm – the one the gun was at the end of – and to keep the baby from falling, he very quickly had to bring his arm around so that the gun was pointing entirely the wrong way. And while he was able to use the fingers of his broken arm for a lot of things, the splint would have kept him from holding a gun – which, of course, Paintbrush didn't know he was doing. Anyway, the baby was squirming so much that Allaby needed both arms for him, and by the time he adjusted to that and turned sideways so that the gun was pointing in roughly the right direction, Paintbrush was kneeling in front of Rachel, saying, "Please don't cry. Let me help you up."

Then Allaby decided that Paintbrush, whether she knew it or not, was right: there was no longer any point in holding a gun on these two. "Bring them over to the shelter," he said. "I've got a hell of a lot of questions to ask."

And Gibbous said, "Don't forget to ask about the kids."

As the three pairs – Gibbous marching Jacob, Paintbrush supporting Rachel, and Allaby carrying the baby and patting him with the gun – slowly walked back, Allaby said to Gibbous, "Tell me again about the children."

"It was the damnedest thing I ever saw," Gibbous said, as though everything else he'd seen last night and today wasn't also the damnedest thing. "It was cold, and that nasty wind was blowing, and they had these kids outside and sort of tied up and sitting in rows. Sometimes they'd blow over, and the grown-ups would go around and sit them up again. A lot of them were little kids, too. And when they were taking me into the liner …"

Gibbous has been inside a liner, Allaby reflected. Gibbous Moon in a liner.

"… I could see the kids' faces. They were just staring straight ahead, with a funny look in their eyes. I had a feeling they were frozen. Almost dead, they were. Ask them about it, Allaby."

"I will," Allaby said. "Let's get them settled."

At the shelter, Gibbous let go of Jacob's arms, turned him around and pointed to the ground in front of one of the poles.

"He wants you to sit there," Allaby said.

Jacob slowly sat, saying, "I'll just have to get up again in a minute."

"Why?"

"That's about how long it'll take the outrigger to get here."

"The outrigger?"

"That pickup isn't the only ship attached to the liner. There's an outrigger, too, and it could be here in less than a minute."

"What makes you so sure they'll send it?" Allaby said.

"Our comms have gone dead. What do you think they're going to do?"

Paintbrush, meanwhile, had eased Rachel down so that she could sit against one of the other poles. She was still terrified and was breathing in long, wheezing gasps, while Paintbrush, holding the water skin, was dabbing at the tear stains with a wet cloth – forgetting, apparently, that she still hadn't wiped earlier tear stains off her own face. "Don't worry," Paintbrush was saying. "We won't hurt you. Allaby, tell her we won't hurt her."

"Ask him," Gibbous said.

"Gibbous says you have about a hundred children at the liner and that you make them—"

"Allaby."

"What, Love?"

"Tell her. She's about to have a fit."

"Rachel, it's all right. Nobody's going to hurt you." He said to Paintbrush, "She'll calm down, Love. Just keep being nice to her." He turned back to Jacob. "You make these children sit outside in the cold—"

"I loved Conrad!" a crimson-faced Rachel shouted through her sobs and wheezes. "It was my home, my beautiful home. You made me leave to come to this filthy place. And those are our children, too, he's talking about. Pumped full of dope and sat out …"

"Shut up, Rachel," Jacob said. "I knew you wouldn't have the stamina—"

"Stamina? Look at you. You can hardly walk yourself. We're both crippled and stuck God knows where with these creatures," she said, batting at some flies, "and these … savages."

"Shut up, I said."

Rachel returned to loud sobbing, and the baby, who was wriggling hard enough to make Allaby worry about his ribs, was himself beginning to whimper. Full-blown screaming was about a minute away. (As was, according to Jacob, the outrigger. What was he going to do about that? He needed to think.) "Paintbrush, can you take him? He's going to start—"

"Allaby, what are they shouting at each other?"

Gibbous said, "Yeah, she's really mad about something.

"And I want to know what you did to this woman to scare her so much."

"Pointed a gun at her, I guess. Can you please take him, or I'll just put him in the cradle, even if he is awake."

Paintbrush stood up. "Pointed a gun? What gun?"

"The one in my hand."

"That's a gun? My God, Allaby, you're holding Skyman with a gun in your hand. Give him here."

"Thank you," Allaby said when Paintbrush took the baby. "And please try to stop him from crying. We really don't need that now." He needed to think. He needed … Of course, he had Jacob and Rachel as hostages, and the outrigger wouldn't do anything to anybody if … Or would it? These were Back-to-Earthers, lunatics. They might just think Jacob and Rachel were being sent to Heaven. Back-to Earthers were notoriously and maddeningly beyond logic.

Rachel's sobbing had reached a higher pitch, and her face was streaked with tears and snot, attracting new detachments of flies. "My home. My home. My children," she kept saying to no one in particular.

"Allaby," Gibbous said, "are you going to ask him about those kids or not?"

"That might have to wait, Gibbous. I really have to figure out what to do about the outrigger."

"The what?"

"How do you suggest I stop him crying? And be careful with that gun. You're pointing it everywhere."

"Try feeding him."

"How can I feed him with all this going on?"

Then Jacob said, "Rachel, if you don't quit blubbering, I'm going to ask that man to shoot you."

This, of course, made Rachel howl, which tipped the baby into full cry. And from somewhere – Allaby couldn't see where and didn't feel he had the leisure to look – the dog started howling, too. A group of cows, uncomfortably close to the shelter, raised their heads from grazing, cast their eyes around wildly and started to move away at a trot. Rachel screamed, "Where is that outrigger, then, you stupid man! You said it would be here by now. You haven't made one right prediction yet. Paradise, you said. It's shit!"

"Just be quiet," Allaby said, "or I will shoot you."

"Don't talk to her that way," Paintbrush shouted over the baby's noise.

Oh God, Allaby thought – now I'm getting my damned languages mixed up. Checking first that he was about to use the right one, he stepped over to Gibbous and said, "We need to get Jacob back to the pickup. It's the only way we can stop the outrigger."

"The what?"

"Another ship, Gibbous. Come on, let's get him up."

Jacob said, "Did you say you could see the outrigger?"

"Nope. Get up, Jacob."

Allaby and Gibbous pulled Jacob up by the arms. "You help him, Gibbous, and I'll hold the gun."

Jacob said, "I hope you're taking me a long way from that woman. I'm just sorry I can't move faster."

"Where are you going?" Paintbrush and Rachel yelled in their respective tongues.

"Just to the pickup," Allaby told Paintbrush. "Stay with Rachel. Maybe she'll calm down once I'm not near her. Or once Jacob isn't." As they trudged along, he said to Jacob, "When we get there, I'm going to get in first and sit in the off-seat. Then you're going to get in and turn on the comms. You'll tell them it was just a technical hitch and that you're all right. All right?" Allaby knew he was going to have trust Jacob to certain extent to respond without being prompted and to sound convincing. He was also going to rely on him not wanting to die and go to Heaven.

Another risk was that even dying and not going to Heaven might have been preferable to any more of a life with Rachel.

"I don't mind," Jacob said. "It's too late for that anyway. The outrigger's been dispatched."

"How do you know, and where is it?"

Gibbous said, "Are you talking about those kids yet?"

"Not yet, Gibbous. I promise, as soon as we get this out of the way."

At the pickup, Allaby got in, and then he pulled Jacob while Gibbous pushed him. Gibbous said, "You're not going somewhere in this, are you?"

"No. Don't worry. We're just getting in here to talk to … uh, Gibbous, you're going to hear a voice now without seeing whose voice it is …"

"Oh, I've heard that voice. It comes from there," he said, pointing.

God, Allaby thought, he's already blasé. "Anyway, don't say anything while Jacob's talking."

"Why not? The voice knows about me. It's you it doesn't know about."

"You're right, Gibbous, of course. But still don't say anything."

"I wasn't planning to. There's a lot going on here, Allaby, and I think what you need is to stop and take a deep breath."

He was right. Allaby took the breath, paused, looked around at the plain and the animals and shelter, checked the western sky for an oncoming outrigger and saw only half a dozen red-tailed hawks and slow spiral of turkey vultures. Then he said, "Okay, Jacob, turn it on."

Jacob did. "… in, P-U. Come in, P-U. Come …"

"Here I am," Jacob said.

"Oh, whew. He's back, he's back. What happened? We thought we'd lost you."

"No, it was Rachel. She was fooling around and broke the switch."

"Broke the switch? How can you break the switch?"

Allaby nudged the gun against Jacob's temple. Was the man being stupid or purposely implausible?

"It's not easy," Jacob said, his eyes darting towards Allaby. "But you know Rachel. If she puts her mind to it, she can break anything."

"But in what way does a switch break? It's only a … Oh, never mind. It's obviously okay now. I didn't like the idea of sending a couple with the old man, especially not a couple that fights as much as you two. But you know – it's less threatening with a woman along, and it's better to have a man there, too, and marrieds are better than unmarried. All that. Anyway, we almost sent the outrigger for you. I guess we would have, if we hadn't …"

"You didn't send it?"

"No. No, the outrigger's not here now."

"Where is it?"

Allaby gave the gun a push.

"Well, you're okay. So it doesn't matter."

"Where?"

"Jacob, what does it ma … I don't know – some unidentified ship west of here. Young Hiram's checking it out – we wanted someone with a bit of a ruthless streak. Anyway, he was an apprentice nuclear-waste inspector and, in case anything happens, is Earth-adapted. Paul's on the comms to him, if you want to … No, you can find out when you get back."

Jacob said, "How long will it be?"

"Will what be?"

"The outrigger."

"I don't know. Hiram's got to find out where the ship's from. Then he's got to shoot it down or force it down or something. Why do you want to … Look, you are all right, aren't …"

Allaby switched off the comms. "That takes care of the outrigger," he said.

"Blast the luck," Jacob said glumly. "How am I going to tell Rachel?"

It struck Allaby that this man was awfully human for a Back-to-Earther. The sect, which was illegal throughout the Solar System, was made up of people who were always having to be stopped from killing themselves, each other or someone else and were generally regarded as unpleasant, unhinged, austere and – because of their illegality, of course – highly secretive. But Jacob was just a harried husband from an ordinary small town on the Far Side. On the other hand, he'd done something strange with his and Rachel's children – not to mention other people's. "Gibbous, the outrigger – that other ship – is away doing something else. So I've got time now to ask him about those kids."

"Finally," Gibbous said.

To Jacob, Allaby said, "Gibbous wants to know about those children he saw. Why did your people have them out in the cold and the wind, and what was wrong with them? I thought I heard Rachel say they'd been drugged."

Jacob turned his head sharply and gave Allaby a hard, dark look. "Those children are none of your business."

"Oh yes they are," Allaby said.

"It's Planet Pilgrim policy, and I don't have to explain it to you, unless you're a Planet Pilgrim yourself, which I seriously doubt."

"But you do have to explain it because I'm pointing a gun at you and will shoot you if you don't. That's the rule, with guns." Shit, Allaby thought, maybe he's decided it's go-to-Heaven time. "And if I do have to shoot you, I can still get the answer from Rachel. She seems anxious enough to talk about the subject."

"You're right about that. But she'd get it wrong. She never has liked the policy, or understood it. You know ... What did you say your name was?"

"Allaby."

"You know, Allaby, I think I've finally located that boondocks accent of yours. It's Titanian, isn't it? I thought at first it might be Ganymedian, but the little beard was throwing me. What's a Titanian doing here, and in the state you're in?"

"Never mind me. You people have broken every law ever made about the planet Earth, and I want some questions answered. Start with the one I asked."

"We made the Earth habitable again. You wouldn't be sitting here breathing air if it weren't for us. You'd be dead."

"You made the Earth habitable again? You did?"

"Us. The Pilgrims. It was our scientists, using our money. And now it's our planet. Shoot me if you like, but you won't change that fact."

"How?"

"How what?"

"How did you do it? Your scientists, I mean. How did they do it?"

"Allaby, I honestly don't know. Until a couple of weeks ago, I didn't even know we had scientists. None of the ordinary members knew. We were just told that when the time was right, God would send a sign, the Government would fall, and the Pilgrimage would start. And that's pretty much what's happened. Most of the Pilgrims still believe it's been as simple as that, but being with the Liner Command now, I've been let in on a few things, and it hasn't been quite so simple. But exactly how it happened is something only the top leadership knows. You'll have to ask them, not that there's a chance in Hades you'd ever be able to."

"Are the top leaders in your liner?"

"Lord no. But they are on Earth."

"Where?" Allaby said, as he began to grasp that the Government of the Moon had fallen. He'd never had any particular love of the Government of the Moon, but at least it had been nominally democratic and was bound to have been better than whatever had replaced it, especially if these imbeciles had anything to do with it.

"It's no secret. They're setting up the new capital of the planet, in the very cradle of humanity. The Garden of Eden, some people say."

"Where's that?"

"In Africa. In a crater. It was news to me, to tell the truth, that Earth even had craters. And I can never remember the name. Gong Gong or something."

"Ngorongoro?"

"That's it."

Jesus, Allaby thought – these people have spent their whole lives yearning, straining, to go the Earth, and they don't know a goddamned thing about the place. And the Ngorongoro was in Jenny's sector. He wondered what might have happened to her with this new 'capital' plonked down at her feet and no Moon Government to appeal to for help, and that made him feel uncomfortable – not because he was particularly worried about Jenny (right at the moment, he didn't have the mental or emotional room for that) but because Jenny was central to his old life. As inadequate as he'd been feeling about his poor adaptation to the raw Earth and the new life – Gibbous's new beginning and new tribe – that was still exactly what he wanted. And now these ignorant, superstitious bastards had made that all but impossible.

Gibbous stuck his head in the pickup and said, "Finding out about those kids is sure taking a lot of jabbering. What does he say about them?"

"Sorry, Gibbous, but he doesn't want to answer that. So we're going to have to talk a little longer. But listen – that outrigger isn't going to be otherwise occupied forever. It might be an idea for you to get Paintbrush and the baby ready to go."

"Go? Go where?"

"I don't know yet. Anywhere. But wherever we decide, we're going in this."

"Yeah, I guess we can go anywhere in this. The Endless Water – if there is Endless Water – anywhere we want. It doesn't seem right, though."

"What do you mean?"

"Well, you can go from one place to another. You can do that. I mean, we were at the liner, and then suddenly we were here. And I suppose wherever you go, it's the same thing. You go, but you don't do any travelling."

"We haven't done a lot of travelling without it, either."

"We would have, though. It's sad, in a way."

"I know," Allaby said. "But we don't have any choice now. You'd better go get them ready."

"I think I'll eat something while I'm at it. They tried to give me some food at the liner, but it was horrible. It didn't look like it came from anything that ever lived."

"It didn't. It's called generated food. But there's some prairie dog already cooked."

"Good," Gibbous said, and he started towards the shelter.

His eyes following Gibbous, Jacob said, "We'd never have hurt him, you know."

"No, I don't know. I didn't, and I still don't. What are you people planning to do about the Immyos, anyway?"

"What are Immyos?"

"Him. My wife. And the rest, including me now, I guess."

"There are others?"

Oh shit, Allaby thought, I'm the one who's talking too much. I might as well give him the gun and let him grill me. "Never mind," Allaby said.

"I mean, we have had a preliminary directive from the top leadership that we haven't been able to make much sense of. About aborigines. We'd never heard of aborigines, but there are some in this area, the directive says, and we're supposed to find them. Do you know about any aborigines?"

"No I don't. What else does the directive say?"

"Nothing. It doesn't even describe them. It just says find them and that we'll get another directive after we do. So when your friend there turned up at the ship, we thought – well, some of us, the ones who knew about the directive thought ... I mean, the ones who don't know about it – we call them the Congregation – have a pretty clear idea about who they think he is. Anyway, we in Command thought that he might be an aborigine, or at least know where some aborigines were and we thought we'd get him to let us take him home. So he brought us here. But I don't think we've quite hit the jackpot. All we've got is the Solar System's filthiest Titanian and his tiny wife."

"Correction," Allaby said. "The filthy Titanian has you."

"A technicality," Jacob said. "As desperate as you look, I don't think you've got it in you to kill a person. Now, your friend – he's different. He's already shot one of the men in the Congregation."

"With his pipe, yes."

"His what?"

"His blowpipe, and dart. It doesn't kill."

"It doesn't? Are you sure?"

"Well, the man he shot – is he dead?"

"No he isn't. Not now."

"What do you mean not now?"

"Well, I wasn't there, but the ones who were said that – they were all pretty excited, so it was hard to get a clear story – said that it had something to do with that wolf over there. Our man was going to shoot it, but before he could, your friend shot him, and he fell down dead. Then a little later when your friend was being led to the liner, he stopped by the man's body and bent down and touched him on his wound, and he started breathing again …"

"Wait a minute," Allaby said. "Did anybody check if he was breathing before he was touched?"

"I don't know. Maybe not."

"Did anyone see what Gibbous shot him with?"

"A gun, they said. But he didn't seem to have one later."

"Did they see a gun?"

"I don't know. I guess not. They didn't see him until after he'd shot the man."

"So all your people who saw it assumed Gibbous had a gun and assumed your man was dead – because people who are shot with guns usually are. Then when Gibbous reached down and, as you say, touched him on his wound – when he was only retrieving his goddamned dart, for Christ's sake – somebody noticed the man was breathing. What a bunch of morons."

"I don't know. I'm not convinced either way. You see, when the man finally came around, he said he'd been in Hell and that your friend – Gibbous, yes – not only saved his life but rescued him from eternal perdition. He's very grateful and very ashamed that he'd gone to Hell. He reckons his thoughts haven't been pure enough, and right now what he's doing is scourging himself."

"Let me get something straight, Jacob. Who do your people think Gibbous is? Is he supposed to be Jesus or something, raising the dead?"

"I don't know what I believe, but it's not too farfetched. This is Earth, after all. It's where Jesus lived."

"As well as everybody else who ever lived, until people started colonising other planets. If it weren't so pitiful, it would be hilarious. I can't wait to tell Jesus – uh, Gibbous – what idiots you all are."

"Don't you dare laugh at us. This is our planet now. And anyway, there's no doubt about this – he was the sign from God."

"Now what do you mean?"

"He was the man in the holoparks. I'm sure of it. Everybody at the liner is sure of it, Congregation and Command both."

"The man in the holoparks was the sign from God? The thing that got all this lunacy started? Is that what you're telling me?"

"He's him. I'm sure."

"Oh my God," Allaby said. "Oh goddamn! Oh Jesus fucking hell!"

"Allaby, we in the Command are often a little more tolerant of blasphemies than the members of the Congrega—"

"Please shut up, Jacob." The image that sprang instantly to the front of his mind – so clearly that he felt he was seeing it with his eyes – was the one of Templeton after Allaby had poured the whiskey in the comms controls. He was standing there frozen with his finger pointing. You. You. But that was all. Allaby couldn't gauge the enormity of it. The fall of the Government of the Moon. The invasion of the Earth. What did it mean, other than blood draining down from his head, rising up from his legs and congealing in a solid lump in his midsection? It was hard to breathe. You. You. But Templeton, it was the best area for wildlife in the whole … Immyos never go there in this … Oh, God, what he needed to do now was just turn the gun on himself and …

"Okay, Allaby," Gibbous said, leaning into the pickup. "I ate fast, and we're all ready. Even Yellow's ready. How much of this stuff do you think we have to take? Will we need blankets? Rope? I've left the shelter up so that poor woman and this man here will have a place to sit. I've left some prairie dog, too, but the woman doesn't seem interested. In fact, she yelped when I handed it to her. Do you think … Allaby? Allaby."

From behind Gibbous, Paintbrush said, "Are you all right, Love? You look funny."

Jacob said, "Are you people planning to go somewhere?"

339

"Yes," Allaby said absently. "You'd better get out now."

"Whatever you say, but I don't think you'll go very far."

"Why not?'

"Because, look – here comes the outrigger."

CHAPTER THIRTY-THREE

No, there was no way she could give him the slip. It would have been suicide to try. Her orders, delivered by writing tablet held against glass, were to fall back and follow him. His rear monitor would be trained on her, as would the guns in the turret. Without comms, he couldn't give her a warning, and so there couldn't be a second chance. Her hands were to be kept on the control panel, where he could see them in the rear monitor, and she wasn't to move out of her seat. Anything Jenny did that he didn't particularly like or understand would result in annihilation. He hadn't said so, but in his series of scrawled, unpunctuated orders, he gave the impression that it would be a lot less trouble for him than having to guide her down. Or trying to spell 'annihilation', for that matter.

And she supposed that if she were a really good soldier on a secret mission, she'd be actually hoping he would annihilate her. That way these people would never know where the ship had come from, and the secret of the satellite would be safe. On the other hand, they might still be able to make an educated guess, and Jenny wasn't feeling much like a soldier anyway. She felt like a naked former Earth Ranger who'd just been perceived to be masturbating and wasn't allowed to move now even to get dressed. Quickly glancing at her flight suit, which was folded and lying on the co-pilot's seat, she wondered if it would be safe to grab it, and then she decided it definitely wouldn't. Besides, that red-faced punk had already seen everything of her there was to see and was still seeing a lot of it now. But let him, she decided – her nakedness at the moment was not the biggest of her problems, and anyway, she was proud of her Earth-fit body. It was probably a better one than a puritanical boy like him had ever witnessed or ever would again. Much more pressing questions were where he had come from, where he was taking her and how she had let this happen.

It was that last consideration, she thought, that should have been causing shame. She'd been weak. She'd developed a phobia about zero-G, which had caused her to flout Gus's orders by dropping out of orbit too soon, and had been indulging in the luxury of her very own passenger shuttle. Even now, the too-loud music was torturing her for that. On the other hand, she'd been careful to stay well out of range of the nearest Back-to-Earthers, parked far north of here in Peter's former sector, and though she was being led somewhere now, she was still on course. She was over the eastern slopes of the Sierra Madre del Sur, with more mountains – the Sierra Madre Oriental, presumably – in the far distance. Coming up below was desert – yellow, red and brown desert. It was true that most of the Earth's tropics was desert, but only had been for a millennium or two. She wasn't an expert on the Americas, but this wasn't a relatively new wasteland. It looked ancient and settled, somehow. She should have been too far south for this. And the Oriental – did it extend this far south?

It struck her that this was more like the wide part of the continent, where the Sierra Nevada cut off the western rains and the Atlantic was too far to the east … Then she remembered the two enormous ruins that she couldn't place. What if … She had trouble letting herself think this, and the music was battering her brain … What if those had been the ancient mega-city Los Nuevos Angeles and … what was the other one's name? A saint's name … yes, Nuevo San Diego, both called 'new' because they'd been rebuilt after an earthquake. She couldn't check the locator because it was part of the comms system, and Gus's maps, even if she could reach them, didn't show ruins. Of course she could call up the ship's atlas – all ships had them – and almost did, when she remembered that it would appear in front of her and obscure the forward view and, more significantly, herself from the outrigger's rear monitor – an action that boy would have tolerated for about half a second. God, she'd nearly killed herself for something that didn't really matter. Wherever she was, she was where she was – following the outrigger – to its mother ship no doubt.

There was no question, though: that was ancient desert down there, and she was a long way off course. But why? Maybe it wasn't only the topography reader that was faulty – it must have been the whole autopilot. It had aimed her a little northeast when she should have been heading a little southeast, something that makes a bit of difference after a few thousand kilometres. Or maybe she'd set it wrong. But could she really be so stupid? What she needed was to check the autolog – just what she'd been hoping Gus would neglect to do when she got back. But how? That, too, might obscure her from the rear monitor and get her annihilated. Or would it? She really needed to know what had happened. To hell with it, it was only text, and he could see past it. "Go ahead," she said aloud. "Annihilate away," and she called up the autolog.

The outrigger did a little wobble – probably the only way the boy had of emphasising how close to annihilation Jenny was getting. But nothing else happened, and so she concentrated on the log, scrolling back to where she first set the autopilot. That would have been just after she'd turned east at Hawaii, and sure enough, there it was – "auto on, 47° ESE". That was at "00:12:43" after the "00:00:00" that represented entry into the troposphere and the beginning of atmospheric flight. Then she scrolled ahead a few lines and saw "00:13:13: auto off." Why, half an hour after heading east, did she turn the thing off? That was why the topography reader hadn't been working – the goddamned autopilot hadn't even been on. The main way you turn the pilot off is just to take over the manual controls, but she hadn't done that. She might have knocked something, though – accidentally. What had she been doing half an hour after setting the pilot? Eating, that's what. Sipping wine. Plates, utensils, a glass, a bottle, all over the console … Oh, God, Jenny told herself … do you realise what you've done? You've indulged yourself into getting captured … maybe even, once we've reached the mother ship, getting killed. Or tortured and then killed.

She turned off the log by slamming the control with her fist, and this appeared to be the cause of another angry wobble from the outrigger. But again, that was all. Was the boy being told on his comms not to consign the shuttle to smithereens before finding out what it was? She could imagine his side of the conversation. "She's got no comms and no clothes, and do you know what she was doing?" Maybe, being cultists themselves, they could imagine Jenny as belonging to some kind of thrills cult whose members, for years, have been secretly flying unmarked ships through the Earth's atmosphere to enhance their auto-orgasms. Maybe, when they began to grill her, that was what she should say. What she'd been caught at was preposterous enough and the Back-to-Earthers were credulous enough for the story to work. Maybe. Or maybe not. She'd have to tell them something, though.

They were fast approaching the mountains she'd seen in the distance earlier, as they were coming down from what she now was sure had been the Sierra Nevada. She couldn't remember what these were called, but all of the mountains on this part of the continent were branches of the Rockies. And she did remember that on the eastern edge of this particular branch there ought to be a particularly lush plain. When and if she saw that, she'd have no doubt about where she was – poor Peter's favourite part of his sector or, as it had been put in Earth Geography 304, the grassy plains watered seasonally by clouds that came from the recently enlarged Gulf of Mexico and were gathered in by the mountains. It was the hunting grounds of Peter's beloved Immyos – the damned Immyos that had got him killed – and, according to the little lights on the map in Gus's office, it was also the place where the Back-to-Earthers had chosen to land a liner. And there was a cruiser – Simon's cruiser – parked right by her own Immyos. And at least one other ship on another reservation. Had they picked the reservations on purpose, or was it because those also happened to be some of the most fertile spots on the planet?

You well might wonder, she told herself – that was one of the bits of intelligence you could have come back with. Talk about fucking up. On the other hand, if she could allow herself a little optimistic consolation, she was going to learn most of what she needed to know once she was at the mother ship – including the most important of all, whether they really were outside and breathing the air. Then she would only need to get the information to Gus … but there was an extremely fat chance of that.

Mountains again. High lakes, juniper forests and, a glimpse between the mountains of a green plain. The liner, surely, would only be minutes away now. Would they fly into its hold? A shuttle was slower than an outrigger, but it was whole lot bigger. Would it fit inside a liner? Was there a way for a shuttle to dock with a liner on the outside? Either way, she'd had no instruction on how to dock in or on another ship. Otherwise she was going to have to land the thing, and she was so shaken now and the music was driving her to such distraction she wasn't sure if she could even remember how to do that. She just hadn't paid enough attention to Brewster – at least not to what he was saying. She thought she knew a couple of the principles, but the rest she'd have to do by logic and instinct, neither of which, under the circumstances, was at its operational best. Her stomach tightened, and she pleaded with herself not to panic, not now. It was too late, though. She was panicking.

She needed to forget about the fact that she was going to have to land or to manouevre into the liner until the second she had to start doing it. What was important now was to concentrate only on following the outrigger. But she couldn't help it. All that was in her head was a cauldron of incomplete thoughts about the hover function and glide-conversion procedure and the scaffolding and how to slow to a stop without toppling and crashing, along with an undertone of the irony in the fact that what was scaring her most wasn't the angry boy or the outrigger's annihilation capacity or even the prospect of torture and death at the hands of the people in the liner, but having to do something that anyone flying a shuttle ought to know how to do by second nature.

And she'd have to do it any minute now. It was an effort to keep from just peeling away from the outrigger or even ramming it from behind, something she might be able to manage before the boy had a chance to fire, even though, of course, it would mean both ships crashing. Still, it was simple and, right now, was what she really wanted to do, and she had to force her shaking hand away from the throttle. They were leaving the mountains, and the plain was there. The outrigger slowed and dipped, and she was able to slow and dip with it, getting her first look at the liner, about twenty kilometres away, before the outrigger obstructed it again. Still shaking, she laid a hand on the hover control.

But then the outrigger speeded up again. It had levelled off and actually speeded up. He didn't seem to be taking her to the liner after all. It made no sense, but she didn't care. What was important was that docking with the liner would be out of the question now, and landing, at the very least, would be delayed. The panic dissolved almost instantly. Her heart was still thumping and the music was still blaring, but her mind had pulled out of its cauldron and was coming into the clear. As the liner passed below, she remembered something Brewster had said about the speed into the hover and also remembered about the scaffolding control and how you slow to five, hit the hover, count to five (Was it five? Slow to five, count to five? Both fives? Was that right?) and then release the scaffolding and turn off the hover. But at what altitude? Oh yes, the altimeter actually spoke to you and told you when. Yes. Okay. And just as she thought she had it, the outrigger dipped and slowed again, so suddenly that she almost did ram it from behind.

This time, for sure, it was going to land. An outrigger was small enough not to need scaffolding. It would just hover and lower itself onto legs. She wondered if, while it was doing that, she could quickly rise and shoot away. But no – he'd be after her and would catch her in half a minute, if he didn't just destroy her from where he stood. She kept following and slowing. And then the time came to upend, so that she was facing empty blue sky and guiding by the rear monitor, which showed nothing now but grassy ground, and it was hard to tell exactly where they were putting down. At her last good look, there didn't seem to be anything here but herds and herds of cows and horses. Lower and slower. She was down to eight, seven, six and five. The altimeter wasn't saying anything yet, which meant that even though her speed was five, she's was still a little too high. Never mind – the worst that would happen would be an uncomfortable jolt. She held the speed, counted to five and hit the hover. Then she released the scaffolding and turned the hover off.

The next step, after the shuttle finally settled down, would be to swing it level. Then, she told herself, she'd skip the flight suit and go straight for the sterility suit and the airlock. The Back-to-Earthers didn't have sterility suits, or so Gus had said, but Jenny didn't believe that any more than she believed the virus was magically gone – they'd be sure to have at least some suits, especially one for an outrigger pilot. On the other hand, what if they truly didn't have any at all? A gamble was called for now, and she might as well bet on the possibility that the boy would be stuck in his ship. She might have a chance. It was a preposterous thing to think, but she still might be able to get away – by keeping the shuttle between herself and the outrigger, dodging among the herds and then simply walking on. But that wouldn't work, of course. He'd just fly up and find her. Anyway, even if it did work, where would she go?

****

When she came to, she was still wondering that. In her mind, she had a picture of herself trudging across this vast plain with her air running out and her … and slowly she realised she was picturing this while lying on her back – with a whopping pain on the top of her head. She felt where it hurt and then looked at her hand: blood. Sensations followed: stinging in her eyes and nose and the realisation that smoke was coming from somewhere; the shuttle's seats, her seat and the controls hanging from the ceiling. No, she was the one on the ceiling. The shuttle was upside-down. Where was the smoke coming from? It was hard to tell from here. Wait. There were the controls, and there was the smoke. Flames, too. The other end – the galley. The ceiling, now the floor, appeared to have been crumpled upwards right at about the galley and the little music lounge across from it (oh, at last, the music had stopped), and there was now a jumbled wall of metal there. The airlock was right at the rear, beyond the wall and the flames, and she'd never be able to reach it. But of course, she didn't need to now. The airlock was only a way of protecting the air inside the ship, and at this point the air inside the ship was becoming as deadly as the air outside. What she really needed was her sterility suit.

And there it was – where it had always been, lashed to one of the seats and now well out of reach. The smoke there was getting heavy, too. Her flight suit and underwear were in a heap beside her, but what good was any of that? As she sat up and then stood up, she suddenly realised that, ever since she'd been conscious, she'd been hearing a steady banging. It was coming from the direction of the door – not the airlock but the ordinary hatch, which was on this side of the galley and locked from the inside. Somebody was out there – probably the boy – banging the door with something hard. That meant he had a sterility suit. If she could just reach hers, she could put it on and go out through the hatch, if she could get to the hatch – the flames were heading that way, and the hatch was now pretty high up the wall. It was right next to the crumpled metal, though. If she could get a foothold on that … but what was the point until she could work out how to reach the suit?

And she couldn't possibly reach it – not before the flames obliterated the hatch. That left one possibility, one hope: that the Back-to-Earthers weren't lying, and the virus really was gone. Not very likely, but a ninety-nine per cent chance of dying of the Abunga was better than a hundred per cent chance of asphyxiating in here. She had to get to the hatch now, just the way she was. But no – not just the way she was, damn it. That boy had seen enough of sights he'd never seen before. No more peep show, even if she died in front of him. Her eyes were being sandpapered, her throat might as well have been the inside of a chimney, and blood was leaking out of her head and onto her face and neck – but she took a few moments to assume some belated dignity and got into her flight suit.

And there was a reward before she even reached the hatch. The crumpled metal next to it was hot, and the flight suit had built-in boots. It was bad enough having to grab, briefly, a jutting piece of iron before she got her insulated foothold, but at least there was no burnt skin after that – the manual latch was made of cool graphite. She held, turned and pulled hard, and the hatch slid halfway open and jammed. Smoke poured past her. From outside the ship, what seemed to be a metal pole – no doubt the pole that had been doing the banging – was pushing at the door. But the door wasn't budging, and the pole was keeping her from trying to squeeze through. So she grabbed it, jerked it away from whoever was holding it – almost certainly the boy – and let it drop. She got a leg, hip, arm, shoulder, head and neck out, and by exhaling totally and turning, she extracted the rest of her body. Now facing into the ship and the smoke, she balanced in the doorway on one leg and jumped backwards.

As she turned in the air she could watch the grassy ground as she fell and at a couple of metres from the side of the shuttle made a pretty good landing, squatting and with her hands down. It had jarred her knees and elbows, but the grass was long and soft and it was still only the top of her head, her throat and her eyes that really hurt. She stood up and took a few steps backwards, and her thoughts, when untangled, went like this: "I'm not breathing smoke, I am breathing Earth air, and what's more, I'm alive. I'll dwell on this later, though, because what I'm seeing in front of me – besides some Immyo standing just over there – is the rear section of the outrigger sticking out from under the upside-down shuttle. The shuttle has fallen across the outrigger, and the outrigger's flattened. I was obviously way too high when I lowered the scaffolding, and … there's no way the boy can be alive under there – at least I hope he can't … and I toppled the thing. I truly fucked up the fucking landing, thank the Lord. Now for this Immyo …"

That he was an Immyo wasn't a big surprise – this, after all, was an Immyo reservation – but as Immyos went, he was a very tall and very dirty specimen. But he must have been the person who'd been banging the door with the pole, which not only showed courage (he might never have seen ships before, much less one crashing on top of another) but also perception and initiative: how did he know a hatch was a hatch, especially on a shuttle, where it blended so well with the rest of the outside of the ship? Then she noticed that stuck under his belt, which was a rope, was a gun – no, two guns – which had to mean that he'd already been corrupted by those damned maniacs. Had they shown him how to use a gun? Why? And why, for that matter, had the boy pilot skipped over his mother ship to bring Jenny here, to an Immyo? Or several Immyos – because she could hear voices now, a woman's and a man's shouting in an Immyo language, another woman screaming and, yes, a baby crying.

But she couldn't take her eyes off the Immyo in front of her, and he apparently couldn't take his eyes off her. He squinted a little as he looked her over, and then he stepped towards her, peering harder. Because he had guns, she didn't want to make a sudden move or alarm him in any other way. So she simply stood still and kept her eyes on his eyes. When he was right in front of her, he raised a hand to her face – which, she realised, would be covered in blood and probably blackened by smoke. He rubbed his fingers across her cheek. Then he licked his fingers and rubbed again – forehead, cheeks, chin. He stepped back, mouth open.

"Jenny?" he said.

PART THREE

HORDES OF TITANIANS

CHAPTER THIRTY-FOUR

Caleb Hook considered it fair enough – if only according to the Back-to-Earthers' peculiar view of fairness – that he should be executed. He had killed a man. It had been an accident, of course (and Caleb considered it typical of Jedidiah Bates and his vindictiveness that he should have died so easily), but the new authorities had only his word for that. To them, it was clear: they had sent their new ally, the Primary Preacher of the Lazarines, into Caleb's cell to recruit the Head Keeper of Jerusalem to their magnificent cause, had respected the Primary Preacher's request that the meeting not be monitored or otherwise witnessed, and had returned to the cell to find the man on the floor, dead. Although the alliance with the Lazarines had survived – in fact, Jed's number two had apparently turned out to be even more enthusiastic than Jed – murder was still murder. Of course, the Back-to-Earthers did plenty of killing themselves, but that wasn't murder. That was slaying. Of enemies. But when it happened to a friend of theirs, it was murder, and the murderer had to die. It also helped that Caleb, in refusing to join the Back-to-Earth effort, had established himself as an enemy (he was sure that if he had joined, the little murder matter would have been overlooked), and for that reason alone, he'd still have to be executed. Fair enough – according to their logic – but what saddened Caleb almost as much was that his Chief Deacon was being executed too.

The reason he knew the Deacon was being executed was that his name was there on today's schedule. What was it about the Back-to-Earthers? Ignorance, naiveté, carelessness, thoughtlessness, stupidity, cruelty …?0 Every morning with breakfast, they gave every prisoner a schedule of the day's executions, as though these were some kind of recreational activities, so that every prisoner knew who was going to die every day and, on the day that his own name appeared, precisely when his time would come. For Caleb, today was the day. It was probably about 8:30 now, and after they eradicated what appeared to be the entire national council of the Titanist Association (it had taken them days, but yesterday they'd finally finished with all the former government ministers and party leaders), they would come for him. That would be at 14:30, and he would die some time before 14:45, when they would be ready for the Deacon. But why the Deacon? He was only an administrator. There wasn't a serious theological or political opinion in him – instead of killing him, for Christ's sake, they could have hired him.

Or, to be fair, maybe the Deacon had found some point of principle within himself and, surprised by it, had stood by it. Or maybe he'd protested in some way about the treatment of Caleb. Maybe he'd done something spectacular and outwardly foolish. People can change – it was a fundamental tenet of Caleb's religion, and if he wasn't thoroughly convinced of that, he'd have wasted his life's work. On the other hand, change of that kind was supposed to help people have a better, more fulfilled life, but in the Deacon's case – if, indeed, that was what had happened – it would have brought his life to an end.

Made him a martyr. Aside from the difficulty of imagining the Deacon with a halo, martyrdom itself was a concept Caleb had always been uneasy with. This was because martyrs – true martyrs – automatically went to Heaven, and since life in Heaven was supposed to be infinitely better than mortal life, what exactly did the martyr sacrifice? The standard answer to that, of course, was that the true martyr died in the cause of pure righteousness, with no thought of his eternal reward. Otherwise, the act that led to his death would be nullified. But could there be anyone so completely in control of his thoughts that he could prevent even the quickest flash of speculation on his heavenly prospects?

The hell of prison was that it gave you too much time to think, even on the last morning of your life. And why was he worrying about the Deacon when he himself was about to be martyred? Maybe he'd been thinking about him because he didn't want to think about himself. (Or maybe he didn't want to think about Heaven. But he'd already done that – so it was too late.) He'd been lying on his back on the bed, hands folded across his stomach as he focused on the ceiling stain that, during his second or third day in here, he'd decided was shaped like a rhododendron. There were also the explosion, the open-shelled pistachio, the hat, the frowning face and the turd, and the one he chose to focus on at any given moment was the one that best reflected his mood, or the mood he wanted to induce. The rhododendron was for hopefulness, and right now he was hoping that something might happen to cancel his martyrdom.

And that was sad. In fact, it was pitiful – His Eminence, the Very Reverend Caleb MacPherson Hook, really, really, really didn't want to die. And the fact that he didn't necessarily have to die made it that much worse. The Back-to-Earthers badly wanted his support, and he was sure that some time between now and 14:30 a representative or a delegation of them would visit him and give him a last chance. He had no doubt of that, and he hated anticipating it almost as much as anticipating his execution (by particalisation, a process that, for some now obscure reason, Caleb's church opposed – even as a way of disposing of people who were already dead; actual execution by particalisation was so unheard-of it wasn't even mentioned in the canon). He didn't want to be a martyr, but he didn't want to be tempted not to be one either, especially by so idiotic a cause (the whole Back-to-Earth mission had reduced in his mind to a war in Heaven over the original Jerusalem) for while Caleb had theological trouble with the concept of martyrdom, he was simply helpless in the face of temptation. Food, drink and even occasionally sex – anything at all that made life good – he always took as it came. How, with death on today's schedule, was he going to turn down life itself?

Maybe summoning up hope wasn't such a good idea. Without thinking about it, he shifted his gaze to the frowning face. Maybe, on the day of your death, it was only right to feel depressed. Certainly the thought of an afterlife wasn't much consolation, at least not for a Christian. The ancient Egyptians and the ancient Chinese had afterlives everyone could look forward to – eternal comfort, or at least no particular discomfort, for all people – but Christians had to contemplate the possibility of Hell, which tended to take the shine off. How could Caleb know how he'd be judged or how stern the judging would be? Of course, he was a leader of the church, he gave sermons, he exhorted people to have faith, he saved souls. You'd think that would be enough get him through; but he was also a glutton, an occasional drunkard, a fornicator and, as such, a hypocrite. But how much did that really matter in God's eyes (or whoever's: as biblically unsubstantiated as it was, he couldn't help seeing himself standing before a bench of magistrates)? Maybe the view would be that, having been granted life, it was commendable he'd so enjoyed it – or that, on balance, he'd done more good in his time than bad. Who could know?

And what was the evidence that there was even an afterlife at all? Or even a God? He was sometimes amazed to realise that he hadn't really changed his view of God or Heaven or any of the other Christian trappings since he first came to terms with all that as a child. (The seminary and a subsequent lifetime of theological discussion had only ever, it seemed, confused issues.) But now, on the day of his death, he also had to admit to the possibility that there might be just nothing. Could he allow that thought even to cross his mind? Would that constitute loss of faith? If so, what a time for such a mind-crossing to occur!

But no, you couldn't simply cease to exist – to have no mind, no awareness, blankness, nothingness. You wouldn't even be experiencing death, because you wouldn't be experiencing anything. You just wouldn't be. And that would mean there was no great Father to look after you and for you to appease. Impossible, he thought, but from this side of death, he could never really know. And after death, if there was nothing, he would never know. But wasn't that what faith was – not needing to know? Uh oh. He was suddenly aware of a full-fledged belief crisis, and if he didn't solve it before 14:30 and went to die with doubt in his mind, the only alternative to nothingness would be Hell. What he needed was some more time – time to solve this uncertainty, to regenerate his faith. Time to be sure. Oh God, oh Whatever. And as far as he could see, there was only one way to get the time he needed: recanting to the Back-to-Earthers, joining them. He wouldn't have to mean it. It would just be a way to stay alive a little longer ... As he was shockingly, painfully, ruefully conscious of what he was going to have to do, his gaze, which had been wandering across the ceiling in the direction of the turd, suddenly shifted to the door, which had swung open.

Caleb quickly sat up. This would be the inevitable representative or delegation, he supposed, and though he couldn't see yet who it was exactly – from the bed, the open door blocked his view – the voice that was chatting with and thanking the jailer was a woman's. They didn't need to go to that extreme, he instantly thought – sending a woman. He was going to give in to them now, and anyway wasn't the possibility of a reprieve temptation enough? Did they imagine that if he wasn't going to forsake his principles for that, that he'd give in to some floozy? It was insulting, and typical of those morons, those humiliators, those sadists. But when the door shut he flushed with embarrassment: the woman standing there, whatever else she was supposed to be, was certainly no floozy. She had a pleasant enough face and was smiling, but otherwise she was a large woman, dressed very neatly and primly in dark blue, with her high collar and her long sleeves fastened tight. She had shortish hair, dyed black, and was probably somewhere in her fifties. In a gentle voice, she said, "Good morning, Your Eminence. I'm Ruth Goertz, your counsellor."

"My counsellor?"

"You're going to die today. Can I sit down?" She looked around the cell as though she was surprised there wasn't an easy chair or a conference table.

Caleb stood up. "Sorry. Where are my manners? Sit there." He indicated the bed. "I'll take the toilet." He stayed standing until she'd sat, smoothed her lap and crossed her ankles. Then he went over to the toilet, lowered the lid and sat on it. "Why am I supposed to need a counsellor?" he said, clasping his hands and leaning forward. Was this on the level? Was he supposed to recant to her? God, these people knew how to make life difficult.

"Well, why wouldn't you? Not every day of your life is your last."

"But counselling – and I've done a bit of that myself – is more for the, uh, long term. At least I've always thought of it that way."

"There's nothing longer term, Your Eminence, than eternity."

"You're counselling me for eternity? Listen, I've just decided I'm not ready for eternity."

"Of course you're not. It's a big step from mortal life to immortal. I'm here to help you prepare for it."

"What I meant when I said … But wait. Isn't that what priests have always done? And since I'm a sort of priest myself—"

"Yes, priests pray for you, for your soul, but they're talking to God. I'm here to talk to you. With you. I want you to tell me how you feel."

"Feel about what, Miss uh … What did you say your name was?"

"Goertz. Ruth Goertz. Mrs Ruth Goertz. What I want you to discuss is how you feel about the transition." She uncrossed her ankles and leaned forward with her elbows on her knees, clasping her hands in imitation of his. Her face was still strikingly pleasant, but the smile had been replaced by pursed lips and her forehead was just slightly furrowed. Caleb might have been the one sitting on the toilet, but there was something about Mrs

Goertz's posture and expression that suggested she was too. "What are your expectations?"

"About what?"

"Eternity, Your Eminence."

"Really, Mrs Goertz, the Church's teachings on that aren't complicated. I suspect you know them as well as I do. And you don't have to keep saying, 'Your Eminence' – I'm not feeling all that eminent right now. Just call me Reverend Hook, or Caleb even."

"Yes, of course, I know what the Church's teachings are. Like most people, I was raised in the Keepers of Jerusalem, and I guess that's why it's hard not to call you by your title. Anyway, we Pilgrims have a lot of respect for the Keepers, and there's not really that much disagreement between us."

"Well," Caleb said, leaning back and crossing his arms, "one small point might be our reluctance to overthrow democratically elected governments and kill all the politicians. But right at the moment I'm willing to overlook that."

"I'm not here to discuss politics," Mrs Goertz said. "I'm only here to help you. Now please, sir, if you would—"

"Excuse me, Mrs Goertz, but I really don't understand why you are here."

"To prepare you for —"

"... for eternity. I got that much. But I don't see how you can do that, since you don't know what it's going to be like any more than I do. Eternity – that is to say, Heaven – isn't even conceivable to the mortal mind. Or are you an angel who's come back ..."

She smiled. "You, the leader of the Church, don't know what it's going to be like? Well, that's probably true, but I can remember you yourself telling us what it was going to be like. It was in your broadcasts. You said it was a state of everlasting bliss, a oneness with God and the universe. You also said – just as you said a second ago – that it was unimaginable to mortals. Well, how could you tell us it was everlasting bliss and then tell us that it was unimaginable? We Pilgrims have been waiting for a long time, for generations in fact, for our sign from God, and while we were waiting we had plenty of time to explore the spiritual dimension, and we imagined it, Reverend Hook. We've always been persecuted, don't forget – illegal, according to the old laws. We don't have public buildings. We don't have churches. We've always met in secret, in people's homes and in groups of five or ten or twelve, never more. And that's what's made us strong. We know each other intimately. Our brains, our minds, belong to each other, and what may be unimaginable to a single mortal can be imagined by the combined brainpower of a group, and we have imagined it. We know the experience of eternal bliss. And that's why I'm here – to get you ready for it." She unclasped her hands and held them out, palms up. "Do you understand now?

"Goodness, Mrs Goertz. I don't know what to say. Um. It's very charitable of you, I'm sure, but, um … Listen, do you offer this service to all the people you're, um, about to execute?"

She clasped her hands again. "What do you mean?"

"Well, there must be a battalion of counsellors just for this prison."

"Oh, we don't bother with most of the prisoners because they're going to Hell. We pick out the ones we think might qualify for—"

"But wouldn't somebody who was going to Hell need counselling more than somebody who was lined up for everlasting bliss, however unimaginable?"

"People who go to Hell deserve what they get."

God, Caleb thought, this was one religion that did need to be persecuted. "You know, there's something that strikes me about your sect that's a little, let's say, inbred. Uh, claustrophobic. All that multi-brain pondering on everlasting bliss. But what about everlasting torment? What happened to your compassion? Myself, I feel sorry for people who are going to Hell. Which brings me to a point I've been trying to make. I'm not ready for …" No, it didn't work putting it that way. "Look, let me say this: despite what I've just said about your religion, I've seen the light."

"You, too? Now we're getting somewhere. What was the light like for you?"

"What?"

"What colour was it, for a start?"

"No, no. What I mean is, I'm ready to cooperate, to convert, to join the Back … the Pilgrims."

"Oh, Reverend Hook, I don't take conversions."

"What do you mean?"

"I'm an eternity counsellor, sir."

"Well then, could you go out and get me, uh, a whatever, a conversion-taker?"

"No sir, no. This wasn't anticipated. You're on the schedule. It can't change now. And the jailers aren't due back for an hour. Until then I'm as much a prisoner as you. And I'm not quite sure what you're getting at, anyway. Has somebody offered you a deal or something?"

"Well, not explicitly, of course, not since Jed was here, but—"

"I don't think so, no. They would have told me. They wouldn't even have sent me. An eternity counsellor's time is pretty valuable, you know, and you and I have hardly talked about eternity so far. So what I suggest is that you close your eyes now and concentrate on ..."

Caleb closed his eyes – not because he wanted anything in the way of eternity counselling or even to listen to another word from this woman – but because he had to think before he went numb. In fact, he not only closed his eyes but bent forward with his hands over his face. He'd have put them over his ears if that wouldn't have been too obvious an insult: after all, he had to stay on the right side of Mrs Goertz because she, however odds-against, was his only hope now. He didn't know who would be escorting him to be particled, but what if it was just the jailers? He couldn't recant to them. They had come with the jail and had nothing to do with the Back-to-Earthers except to follow their orders. Oh Jesus, why hadn't he taken Jed's offer instead of fighting with the old bastard? Caleb would have had endless scope for mischief if he'd been a nominal ally. But now he was going to be killed without even a chance to ... God, what was she talking about?

"... say it with me. Reverend Hook, please say it with me."

He lowered his hands and looked at her. "Say what?"

"What I said to say. Come on. And close your eyes."

"I'm sorry, but I—"

"Om. Ommm. Say it."

"Why?"

"I told you. It's how you start to create the mood, how you summon up the spirit. Close your eyes now, keep saying it and concentrate on the power of the drawn-out *mmmmm*."

"Have you ever studied ancient religions, Mrs Goertz?"

"No. Now close—"

"Buddhists used to do that – say, 'ommm'."

"Well, at least I got you to say it once. You're very difficult, Reverend Hook. If you're sincere about wanting to convert, it would be much better if you ... What are Buddhists, anyway?"

357

"I thought you didn't take conversions."

"Well, I don't as such. I can't officially enroll you in the movement. That's very complicated for us – we've always had to be so careful about spies – but you can still convert in your own heart, in time for eternal bliss. But tell me, what are Buddhists?"

Caleb despaired of getting through to the woman. But he was already as good as dead, he supposed, and so they might as well talk about Buddhists as anything. Maybe it was some kind of God-sent luck that she'd said 'omm'. Maybe he should die a Buddhist. Had that religion had a hell and a paradise, or was it reincarnation? Seminary was too long ago – he couldn't remember. "Buddhism was once one of the Earth's great religions, but all the Buddhists died in the Apocalypse, and there weren't any, apparently, at any of the stations. So that was that for Buddhism. You've always got to remember that then there were only about a thousand people altogether on Mars and the moons – pretty amazing when you think that there are almost a hundred thousand now. Anyway, none of those thousand happened to be Buddhists, or not enough to keep the religion going."

"That is interesting," Mrs Goertz said, "and they used 'omm' too. Hm. Well now, we better get back to—"

"But there's something even more interesting about Buddhists, something I found when I was reading those secret archives."

"What archives?"

"Oh yeah. I keep forgetting that that part of my talk wasn't transmitted."

"You mean your last sermon? Yes, you were only on for about half a minute. Then our committee came on to announce the new government and that we were all going to Earth. It was the happiest day of my life."

"Anyway, I got hold of some secret archives – logs, diaries and stuff – and a lot of them were about setting up these communities of immune people. You know about the immune people, I take it."

"No, I don't think so. Look, I know this is difficult for you, sir, but I've come across this before. You don't want to contemplate eternity. What you're doing is a kind of denial, but you'll find that—"

"You have to realise what it was like at the time. That handful of survivors at the stations saw the Apocalypse, the almost instant death of billions of people as, as humanity's own fault, as a sort of stupid mass suicide. They thought—"

"Reverend Hook, please." Her eyes were getting damp, and there was a catch in her voice. "I have a job to do here, and time's going to be running out. This is for your own good. Eternity. Think about what that means."

"I will, Mrs Goertz. I promise. But let me say this first. You're probably the last person I'm ever going to talk to. And nobody else – on Titan, at least – knows what I know, or only knows a warped version of it. They won't let me record anything in here, and they won't even give me writing material. Let me tell you a few things, and then I promise we'll have some time for eternity."

She narrowed her eyes. "Can I trust that promise?"

"Of course you can."

"I guess it's better than fighting the problem. Okay. But be quick."

"Thank you," Caleb said, standing up. "I talk better on my feet – because I'm a preacher, I suppose. Or is it the other way around? Anyway ..." Mrs Goertz, he noticed, had folded her arms, lowered her head and seemed to be gazing at her shoes. "... those people in the rest of the Solar System – after their initial panic and despair and whatever else ... I mean they were cut off from their terrestrial support and had to become entirely self-sufficient. Can you imagine? I think those people were heroes. Anyway, after things had been settled and organised a little and they had time to reflect on and even philosophise about what had happened – I'm talking about ten or fifteen years on – people were, a lot of them, getting bitter about the whole thing. In one communique I found, from the Martian chief scientist to the chief scientist here, the Martian was saying that the virus had been inevitable. I mean, nobody knew where it had come from – nobody knows yet. Everybody's best guess was that it was man-made, probably during some kind of biowarfare research – definitely man-made, though, and almost certainly for war, because while the virus could survive in almost any living organism, it only killed humans – well, humans and great apes, but there were only about a dozen of those left, all in cages. But where the virus came from, this scientist said, and what it was for was beside the point. The cause, he said, was humanity itself. Humanity had killed itself."

Mrs Goertz looked up from her shoes. "Reverend Hook," she said, "I know I agreed to let you have your say, but do you seriously want to waste good counselling time making a point that's made a million times a day? I know – war, pollution, overpopulation et cetera, et cetera. It might interest you to know, now that you want to convert, that we Pilgrims have never subscribed to that view."

"That doesn't surprise me, Mrs Goertz. To be honest, I've always thought it was a little simplistic myself, and I've argued before that there are elements of God, the Flood and the Ark in it. I only mention it now just to show how people were thinking then. The enormity of what had happened was only beginning to sink in, and people were feeling ashamed of themselves, ashamed of their whole species. But you have to admit that, without war, there would never have been biological weapons, and without overpopulation, the virus wouldn't have been able to spread so easily and quickly. But never mind that. What I want to tell you about is what happened next, and in the process I can mention something very interesting about Buddhists."

"Just don't forget your promise."

"Don't worry.

"I worry about the time."

"Your counselling won't take long, Mrs Goertz. I've spent my whole life preparing for eternity." Fat lot of good it's done me, was the thought that flashed by before he continued. "Then in a little while, maybe another five years – I can't remember the exact dates now – the sterility suit was perfected, and small expeditions started going to back to Earth. And it was on one of these – I'm leaving things out here because I'm trying to keep my promise – that a man was discovered, a living human man, raving mad and roaming the streets of ancient Philadelphia."

"That can't be true. Whoever wrote that was fantasising."

"It's gospel, Mrs Goertz. "There's plenty of proof today."

"What proof?"

"I'll get to that. Now, this man, this living man. They wanted to examine him to find out why he wasn't dead, but as you can guess, they had no end of trouble doing that. He couldn't speak, was scared to death of them and was alternately meek and violent, there was no way of decontaminating him so that they could take him into their ship, the time they themselves could spend outside the ship was limited, and they were only provisioned for about a week. There were all sorts of other logistical problems that mainly had to do with the impossibility of decontamination – brain-twisting riddles about how to get object X to place Y without taking the virus along—"

"I don't believe a word of this, Reverend Hook – so at least spare me the details. Time's running out."

"Okay, okay, I'll try. Another ship came from the Moon – this was before the Earth Headquarters Satellite was built – and the two crews worked in shifts in a lab they'd found in Philadelphia. Can you imagine what it was like for them, Mrs Goertz? The city was overgrown and full of wild animals, mainly rats and insects but also snakes and ferocious dogs and cats, and they had to keep kicking aside piles of human bones. You go inside anywhere and there are skeletons sprawled on the floor and sitting in chairs—"

"Reverend Hook!"

"Okay. They established that the man was about thirty years old and hadn't seen a living human being since he was about seven. In fact, he'd come to think of himself as a dog and was actually the leader of a large pack, which insisted on following him wherever he was taken – another problem. But they did manage to do a DNA analysis and found the gene that made him immune to the virus. There was one on each of the, if I remember, ninth chromosomes. I had a lot to read that night, but as I was able to understand it, that meant that the gene had to be recessive … or was it dominant … I can't remember now."

"I don't care, Reverend Hook. I don't believe it, and I don't care."

"Of course, it was a pure accident that the gene happened to confer immunity. I hadn't realised this before, but we all carry lots of junk genes that may have had survival value once but are now useless and meaningless. So the scientists had to assume that this man wasn't some new mutant, that the gene had been around here and there in the human population for a long time, maybe since humans evolved and probably long before then, something inherited from an amphibian or a fish.

"You're getting into dangerous territory for a man who's about to go to God."

"They figured that while the immune condition would be very, very rare … What do you mean, Mrs Goertz?"

"God created man and woman."

"Of course he did. And natural selection was how he did it. Pretty ingenious, I've always thought. Anyway, rare but not unique. There had to be other survivors. If they could find them and bring them together, they could save humanity on Earth. In fact, they could restart humanity on Earth."

"And now you're going to tell me that's what they did."

"Yes, Ma'am. It took years. The whole search and round-up took about twenty years. Now, Mrs Goertz, let me remind you how they were thinking then."

"If you have to."

"They figured that humanity's fatal flaw had to be something cultural, rooted deep in the past. After all, they thought, it was one culture in particular – our culture, as it happens, Mrs Goertz – that had taken over the planet and, for all practical purposes, destroyed it, and certainly destroyed itself. They thought the best thing for the new humanity was to start again from scratch. And now they had the perfect raw material. They'd scoured the Earth, concentrating, of course, on what had been the big population centres. Actually, at the time of the Apocalypse, big population centres were about all there were – when you think about it, it's phenomenal how humans had spread like syrup over the surface of the planet – and the scientists eventually found a total of about two hundred people. Two hundred, on six continents. And each one of that two hundred had been living in complete isolation for decades.

"At about this point, I looked up from the papers and realised it was already seven in the morning. I had to deliver my sermon at nine, and I hadn't even prepared it. I'd made the mistake of reading the archives from the beginning, getting lost in the morass of information and the heroics of those scientists and forgetting what time it was. So now, at seven o'clock, I had to start skimming, and I'm not sure if I perfectly understood everything from there on. But let's see ... They separated them out by age, I remember that. I couldn't find any reference to what they did with the older people, but they took the ones who'd been children when the virus hit – people in their thirties and early forties by then – and settled them on good hunting land that was well out of sight of any of the remains of civilisation. Domestic livestock, pets, escaped park animals – park animals were animals people used to bring from other places and put on display – had all gone wild and begun to take the place of the original wild animals, most of which had long been extinct. So there was plenty for the people to hunt. The scientists generally got them organised and showed them how to make and use some rudimentary tools and hunting weapons. Useful measurements of time and space, that sort of thing. And of course they already had a certain awareness of their own past culture. The idea was to stay with them – the scientists did this on a shift system – until the second generation was safely on its way up. The original people, after all, were pretty difficult – hard as hell to socialise, apparently. Most of them couldn't read, which was good, but some of them couldn't talk, either, and had to be taught all over again. But the second generation children were sort of okay, however strange their parents were, and the scientists figured it was it was safe to leave them then. I don't know whether they monitored them after that, but they did have a way of keeping them from straying off their land. Exactly how and why, I don't know. But the basic idea, I think, was to let six different cultures develop undisturbed and uninfluenced. So maybe they didn't want the descendants discovering and being corrupted by any of civilisation's remains. Then what? I didn't get any farther. That's it, Mrs Goertz."

"Well, what do you know? At last. We've got about twenty minutes. Twenty minutes to get ready for eternity."

"But Mrs Goertz, doesn't it strike you as somehow wrong … I mean, through all the centuries since then – through the various dark ages, all the Lunar coups and revolutions, the Ganymedian Caliphate, for goodness sake – the original policy, the project, has been more or less respected. Okay, I accept that the big difference now – Jed said there had been comms saying your people were outside on Earth, and I don't see why he'd risk his own entire congregation if he didn't have good evidence of that – the difference now is that the virus may be gone—"

"Oh, it's gone all right. I can testify—"

"… but do we have to plunge right back to Earth with all the same old prejudices and heresies and religions and discredited values before we even investigate how those people—"

"Those people don't exist, Reverend Hook."

"What makes you say that?"

"I've never in my life heard anyone mention them. You would think that, for as long as the Pilgrims have been around, someone at some point would have brought the subject up. You're trying to tell me that all this time there have already been people on Earth. That's simply ridiculous. And why are we talking about this anyway? We need to be—"

"But they've been a state secret, by treaty among all the stations, since – I don't know – for a very long time. I was skimming at about a century a minute by then, but I gathered it was decided that the general public shouldn't know about them. Simple jealousy, not to mention misunderstanding, was in danger of fuelling, well, rebellions and more movements like yours. From what I've heard, you people are even jealous of animals for living on Earth."

"You people? Is that what you're saying now? I thought you wanted to convert."

"Not much point any more. I only wanted … Never mind. But listen – they were thinking very long term. That was back, I guess, in about the twenty-fifth century. Everyone knew about the immune people then, and there was nothing any of the governments could do about that. You can't just suddenly make everyone not know something. But what they could do was gradually stop mentioning them and then gradually introduce laws forbidding anyone else mentioning them, in public anyway – to start wiping public records and stop teaching about them in histories, so that by a couple of hundred years after that, the immune people had mutated from fact to myth. And if myths are never referred to or reinforced in any way, in time they disappear. Of course, the people who needed to know about them – the Lunar authorities, Earth Rangers, people like that – have always been told in strictest confidence. But for everyone else, there were simply no humans on Earth. There was obviously going to be some danger when the holoparks were invented and became so popular, but I suppose that whatever it was that kept the immune people on their reservations also kept Earth Rangers, who did the imaging, off them. Maybe – I don't know. But I guess the authorities didn't worry too much, and I guess they should have worried a little more, because somehow it did happen."

"What did?"

"One of them got imaged."

"When?"

"What do you mean when? That was the holopark man. The man who set you people off."

"Wait a minute. Are you saying that … that our sign is just a human, an ordinary human?"

"Well, not all that ordinary. He's an Earth-living human – the first one that's ever been seen by the general public."

"You've been telling me one of the most elaborate lies I've ever heard – and, believe me, an eternity counsellor hears a lot of well thought-out lies, lies that people have convinced themselves are true – but you've ended this lie, almost like the punchline of a joke, with a sacrilege. I know you're being executed for killing Preacher Bates, but nobody really believes you did, and anyway Bates was beginning to make a lot of demands – so nobody's very sad he's gone. That's why we believed that, on balance, you'd probably go to Heaven and deserved to have a session with me. But now you're telling me that our miracle, the one we've been faithfully waiting for all these years, is just some plain human with a couple of fish genes. He spoke to us, Reverend Hook. He spoke to us."

"He can't have spoken to you. Holoparks don't do sound, just light. I know there are some holopark managers who put on recorded—"

"That's part of the miracle. He turned and saw us and spoke."

"Who'd he speak to?"

"The Pilgrims who were there. He did it here in Jerusalem and in Jericho, in Salem and in Bethlehem, everywhere – also on Mars and on the Moon and even on the godless EHQS. Nobody knows about Ganymede, because it's—"

"I know, I know. But did he speak just to Back-to … to Pilgrims, or to everybody?"

"That's not clear yet. But we certainly are getting a lot of popular support. So maybe—"

"The way I heard it, Mrs Goertz, he just wandered around a bit, was joined by a dog, shot something out of a primitive pipe thing and walked off-sensor. What's he supposed to have said?"

"He turned, spread his arms and declared, in the clearest, gentlest voice you can imagine – like satin, the people who saw him say, like satin – 'I am the truth and the light. I am on the Earth and of the Earth. The curse is lifted. Come to me, and I will protect you for ever more.' And so we're coming, Reverend Hook. He is not an ordinary human."

Mrs Goertz – Caleb couldn't help noticing – had been getting increasingly agitated as he was telling his story and evading her counselling, but now her pupils were rapturously dilated and her face was as smooth as … as satin. She leaned back against the cell wall, her arms spread in a supposed re-enactment of the gesture of the holy holopark man. And Jesus, Caleb reflected, walked on water. If earlier he'd had doubts about what would happen after death, he had none now. There was only one possible outcome. Anything else was either paranoia or wishful thinking.

Suddenly the door opened. Mrs Goertz, who was sitting where Caleb had been before she herself had come in, leaned forward, her beatific expression instantly turning to a frown. She said, "We still have a few minutes, jailer." But what Caleb, standing in the middle of the room, could see was that it wasn't just the jailer. It was the jailer letting someone else in – a big man with large brown eyes and sleek black hair, a sort of male version of Mrs Goertz. When he came further into the room and she saw him, she stood up. "Mark," she said. "I didn't know you were—"

"It was a last-minute decision, Ruth. Good Morning, Your Eminence. I'm Mark Maynard-Fletcher. I represent the Presidency." He held out his hand, and Caleb, mentally shrugging, shook it.

"The Presidency," Mrs Goertz said, "is our ruling council. I understood, Mark, that I was going to be the last person he'd see. The eternity counsellor, you know, always has to be the last. It works better if—"

"I know, Ruth. But as I said, it was last-minute."

"To tell you the truth," she said, "it's just as well. He spent the whole time telling me about some archives or something. I didn't believe a word."

Caleb registered the fact that the door was still open and that the jailer was still there, slouching against the doorframe with his arms crossed. Were they thinking about letting him out, or was it just execution time?

"I've come with an offer," Mark said. "Some of the other leaders of the Keepers seem to need your guidance, Your Eminence. And we thought if we could persuade you to, well – to put it bluntly – to see our side of the story. Then maybe if you presented our side to them, we could see our way to a reprieve. In fact, you'd have an honoured place in our organisation. You could even help with the first Earth mission. What do you think?"

"Oh, aren't you lucky, Reverend Hook? Mark, that is exactly what His Eminence was saying he wanted. He was saying he wanted to convert."

"Really? Is that so, Your Eminence?"

To Caleb, everything seemed so clear now. It was wrong for these people, with their ignorant, evil ideas, to go to Earth and start its destruction again, and it would be extremely wrong to join them. It was wrong because it was wrong, not because somebody said God said it was wrong, or because some imposed morality said it was wrong. God, Heaven, Hell, bullshit – wrong is wrong. "I'm sorry, Mr uh …"

"Maynard-Fletcher," Mr Maynard-Fletcher said.

"… Mr Maynard-Fletcher, but you see, I'm on the schedule, and we have to go by the schedule."

With an incredulous look, the jailer stood away from the doorframe. Mr Maynard-Fletcher opened his mouth to say something and then couldn't seem to think what that something might be, and Mrs Goertz did say, "But you said you wanted to convert. He did, Mark. He did."

"Omm, Mrs Goertz," Caleb said. "Ommm. You know, there was one part of the story I never got to. The part about the Buddhists. Remember the Buddhists? Do I have time to finish telling her that?"

"Of course, Your Eminence. Listen, you can have more time to think this over or—"

"Among the many things those scientists didn't give the people on the reservations was any information about religion, any kind of religion, and when the scientists' descendants checked on those people's descendants a couple of hundred years later, all six of the reservations had religion of some kind – beliefs they'd just collectively made up, usually involving animals or stars or clouds or rocks, anything. Except one group – on the continent of Asia. They were recognisable, practising Buddhists. Through all their individual isolation and the early days of their settlements, with their initial grim craziness, and even though not all of them had been Buddhists before –Buddhism survived. How do you account for that, Mrs Goertz? I don't know how to account for it."

"I don't even know what Buddhism is. Please, Reverend Hook, please at least take Mark's offer of some extra time to think things over. I mean, you haven't even had proper counselling. Aren't you afraid you might—"

Caleb flicked a thumb at the jailer. "Let's go. The schedule says now. We'll be late. And the answer is no, Mrs Goertz, I'm not afraid. It's really hard to be afraid of nothing."

CHAPTER THIRTY-FIVE

Whatever else could be said about all the things that had been happening just lately, this was turning into one hell of a Long Walk Out. Once upon a time, Gibbous reminded himself, I kissed Paintbrush goodbye and, following a dog that didn't even have a name yet, started up the Trail towards Big Rim and beyond, headed for the notional Endless Water. I'm still not much closer to that than I was then, but somehow I've also managed to wander into another world. He could remember times, especially as he started getting older, when whole days, whole sequences of days, whole phases of the moon, whole seasons would pass without very much happening. The biggest excitement was watching the hunters come home, seeing what they'd killed and hearing them brag about it. Now you'd hardly notice a band of hunters, and you certainly wouldn't look twice at a dead cow – not with things like this going on every time you turned around.

In the late afternoon of what had already been the most eventful day of his life, he'd experienced the loudest noise (with the possible exception of some really powerful thunderclaps) he'd ever heard. It was the sound of crashing skyships. Before that, Allaby, who was sitting in the pickup pointing a gun at the man from the screaming skycouple – Jacob, he was called – had told Gibbous and Paintbrush to get back to the shelter and hold the knife to the throat of the woman, that another ship was coming with guns and that they needed to be seen to be keeping both people hostage. Gibbous had kept hostages before – you could hardly have a war without a few hostages – but there was something that didn't seem right about putting a knife to the throat of that poor woman, who'd probably proceed to lose whatever mind she still had. Anyway, Paintbrush said a flat no to the idea. So Gibbous asked Allaby if the voice in the pickup could speak to the ship that was coming, and when Allaby nodded, he asked why he didn't just tell the voice to tell the ship that the couple were hostages and to go away or they'd be killed. For the previous few minutes, Allaby had had a funny, pop-eyed look on his face and seemed to be having trouble thinking, but he said, "Of course, Gibbous," did something with his finger and started jabbering to the voice. The voice jabbered back. Then Jacob jabbered. And then all three were jabbering at once, while the ship was getting closer and closer. In fact, it had turned into two ships – a small one in front and a great big one behind it. Allaby and Jacob were still shouting at the voice and at each other, when both ships came to a stop in the air, and the smaller one started to come slowly down towards a spot about fifty paces from the other side of the pickup.

"Go grab the woman," Allaby yelled. "The bastard in the outrigger wants to be a hero. Hurry. He can move in the gravity."

It was as Paintbrush was running towards the shelter and Gibbous was following at a fast limp that it happened. From behind him came an enormous crunch and an even more enormous screeching sound, like a thousand copulating cats. When Gibbous turned around there was nothing to see but a thundercloud of dust and, across the plain, animals stampeding in all directions. His first thought – mainly because at this moment any other appropriate thought was too big to grasp – was how lucky it was that the combined noise of the skywoman, Yellow and the baby had already driven away all the animals from anywhere near here, so that there was now no danger of anybody being trampled. Then in a while, when the hoofbeats were more distant and the dust had begun to settle, he could see what had happened – the big ship had somehow fallen on the little ship, and the little ship was more or less not there any more.

Now there was a silence almost as enormous as the crash had been. Gibbous looked back at the shelter. A wide-eyed Paintbrush was standing just this side of it, holding the baby facing outwards, and he was looking too. In the shade under the shelter, all Gibbous could see of the skywoman was her eyes, but he could see them as clearly as a pair of flames. Over at the pickup, Allaby was standing just outside the door, absently pointing the gun inside as he, too, stared at the pile of ships. Gibbous couldn't see what was happening inside the pickup, but he had no doubt that Jacob was doing exactly what everyone else was.

The silence didn't last long. The first to break it, of course, was the skywoman, who let out a shriek that, while not quite as loud as the crash, went on for longer and was lot more chilling. That got the baby going again, starting with a hoarse howl of the kind that always lasted until his lungs were empty and Paintbrush worried about him suffocating. (Nothing, though, from Yellow, who Gibbous assumed was doing some stampeding of his own.) Then Allaby snapped to and began waving the gun and yelling something at Jacob before shouting to Gibbous to come help him.

It seemed to Gibbous that, the way things were going, there wasn't time to figure out what had just happened before something else started happening. It was too much. He felt a need to get away somewhere and think, and there was a real temptation to walk up to Allaby and then past him and to keep right on walking towards the horizon. But when he reached Allaby, he stopped and said, "For God's sake, what now?"

Still pointing the gun at Jacob, he said, "Whoever's in that shuttle isn't coming out."

"In that what?"

"The big ship, the one on top. I've got to try to get her out. And anybody else who's in there."

"Her?"

"Yeah. The, uh, voice said that a woman was flying it. The man in the outrigger was taking the shuttle to the liner, but they told him to come straight here. He wanted to just destroy the shuttle then, but they wouldn't let him – they had to find out where it was from. So he could only bring it with him. You know, that outrigger was their only other auxiliary ship, and he was their only Earth-adapted crewman."

Gibbous understood almost nothing of that, but he wasn't about to ask.

"Anyway, what I need you to do is take Jacob back to the shelter."

"Again?"

"I can't leave him in the pickup or he'll fly it away. I have a feeling that deserting Rachel wouldn't bother him a lot."

"Yeah, and I guess that would be the worst thing he could do to us. Okay. Get him out."

Allaby jabbered to Jacob, signalling with the gun for him to move. Jacob was obviously trying his best to be quick, shifting from one seat to another and lowering his legs, but Allaby was impatient and kept hurrying him, finally grabbing an arm, pulling him out and causing him to fall in a heap, his legs pointing in almost opposite directions.

"Calm down, Allaby. Go do what you think you have to do. I've got Jacob." Gibbous put his hands under Jacob's armpits and heaved him to his feet. "Allaby, what's the matter with you anyway?"

Allaby started towards the big ship and then stopped and turned around. He looked like he wanted to cry. "Gibbous, I don't know how to explain it. I can't explain it, not to you. So don't ask me."

Standing behind Jacob and holding him by his elbows, Gibbous said, "Okay. I won't." He pushed Jacob a step towards the shelter.

"It's all my fault, Gibbous."

"What is?"

"All this. Everything."

"How do you figure?"

"I can't explain it to you," Allaby said and started towards the big ship again. But when Gibbous had marched Jacob a few more steps, he heard Allaby shout, "And it's your fault, too."

Obviously, Allaby had gone peculiar. He'd been lying on the Far Plain with cracked ribs when the liner appeared – if that's what he meant by all this and everything. How could it be his fault? Or for that matter, his, Gibbous's? When the liner came he didn't even know what a liner was. Something had affected Allaby, though – maybe the crying skywoman. She was enough to make anybody crazy, and it was probably worse if you could understand what she was crying about. Then Gibbous realised that at the moment she was quiet, and when he got Jacob back to the shelter, he could see why – she'd fainted. The baby was quiet, too, because Paintbrush was feeding him. She was sitting on the ground beside the unconscious woman, holding the baby to her breast with one arm and using the other arm to dab water on the woman's face. Jacob indicated that he wanted to stop right there, and Gibbous let go of his elbows. The man then very laboriously crouched and sat. With a nod, he took the cloth from Paintbrush and began dabbing the woman himself. Then he said something and grinned up at Gibbous.

Gibbous sat, too, against one of the poles, and looked out at the crashed ships and at Allaby. "I think," he said to Paintbrush, "your husband's gone a little strange."

"What do you mean, Granddad? What's he doing?"

"He's gone to that big ship to see if anybody's in it. That's what he said. But as far I can tell, he's just standing there throwing rocks at it."

"That's what it looks like to me, too. That thing's already a mess. I don't think rocks will make much difference."

"No, he's not trying to … I don't know. I got the feeling that whoever is in that ship is on his side – our side – not these people's side, if there are sides. But I don't know and don't really care right now. Is there much water left?"

"A little." She handed him the skin, and he took a couple of swallows and handed it back. "God, it's nice and quiet for a change. Have you seen Yellow?"

"I think he ran from the noise."

"He'll be back. One thing I learned yesterday is that I can trust Yellow. Look, Paintbrush, I'm going to close my eyes now. I don't think I want to sleep yet, but I think I want to think. So treat me as if I'm sleeping. And keep an eye on those two. Okay?"

"Sure, Granddad."

Now that he was finally set for some thinking – the idea was to review everything that had happened from the time he entered the strange dome of light to his arrival back here in the pickup, to make some kind of sense, of story, of all of that – all he could really do, it seemed, was just picture the light, that blank, shadowless, stark, awful light that no creature could hide from. It had got into everywhere, as though the air itself had been on fire. Skypeople were ordinary humans – no doubt about that – but something had happened to some part of their humanity if they could tolerate that light, could live out their lives in it. Allaby had said once that their ancestors and Gibbous's ancestors were the same, that all people had lived here on the ground once. And then, as far as Gibbous could make out, some of them got in their ships and went to live in the sky. But what kind of life did they have up there? Was the way they lived in that liner the way they always lived? If so, the poor damned people. All right, they were having trouble with the gravity – and it must be pretty unpleasant to feel as if you've turned to stone – but what did gravity have to do with the kind of nasty food they ate and the suffocating air they breathed? And the sound? Inside the liner, the sound had been like the light – everywhere, ceaseless, a din of jabbering human voices echoing back and forth and all around. Just as there were no shadows, there was no silence and no variation in tone or loudness. When they'd first led him in, he'd been a little overawed. The liner was full of colours he'd never quite seen before and pretty impressive straight, smooth walls, floors and ceilings. There had been a fashion once at the Ledge to make the walls of your housecave as straight as possible, and Gibbous and a lot of the other men had spent much time hammering at their walls' juts and edges, but the fashion had petered out when people began to realise that straight walls were a little boring. They hadn't quite known it before, but they actually liked their familiar, comforting irregularities. Well, irregularities were absolutely absent in the skypeople's world. The light, the sound, the walls were always the same and the same everywhere. All skypeople – both men and women – even wore the same kind and colour of clothes. No wonder the woman here didn't like life on the ground – and that's what Allaby had implied that her wailing was about – the world down here was too damned interesting.

God, how long had it been since he'd slept? He couldn't remember, but he didn't want to sleep now, not at least until Allaby came to his senses. So he opened his eyes to have a look at what Allaby might, at the moment, be doing. The first thing he noticed, though, was that Jacob was cradling the still unconscious woman in his arms and that he himself had moist eyes as he looked down at her. Paintbrush was putting the baby in his little bedpit, and beyond, the sky was just beginning to get a tinge of pink. Over at the ships, Allaby appeared to have found some kind of pole (made, apparently, of that strong, hard material skypeople used, something Gibbous would have liked to salvage to build an extension to this shelter, if they were going to stay here any longer) and was using it to bang the side of the big ship. Gibbous couldn't guess what Allaby imagined he was doing, but it was pretty certain he was still off his head. If he's no better by morning, Gibbous wondered, what will we do? Does he still count as one of us now that other skypeople are around? Will Paintbrush and I have to leave him with Jacob and the woman and the pickup and go on walking towards the mountains? No, Paintbrush will never do that – she loves him. For that matter, I've got used to him myself. He definitely is with us now, and yes, he will snap out of it, as surely as Yellow will come back. Quit worrying. Learn to trust.

Gibbous closed his eyes again. The main thing he didn't understand about all these skypeople was exactly what it was they wanted. They were obviously unsuited to life on the ground, but on the other hand, they didn't seem to be just visiting. Of course, there was no question now of running back to warn the Chief, because they were too pitiful to be any kind of threat to anybody. It was sad in a way. He'd gone through a range of opinions about skypeople since, well, since he'd had any opinions about them at all. They'd started out as vaguely benign figures, known mainly from ancestral pictures on the Cavern wall and as characters in the old stories, to the one Paintbrush had dreamt about and Breeze had seen; to Allaby, first as a real skyman and then finally as … Allaby; to killers of innocent travellers; to this collection of jabbering incompetents and apparent child-abusers. Okay, they had lots of faintly mysterious things –

373

voices that came from nowhere, pictures they'd shown him that were complete in the round, not just flat on a wall, as well as smooth surfaces, dead-hard building materials and ships that could fly – but the people were essentially ignorant. That was it, ignorant. He didn't have to know what they were saying to tell that much about them. Allaby seemed to regard them as evil or something, but Gibbous couldn't see that. With him, they'd been hospitable enough, deferential even, and as for the way they were treating those kids, who could know? There might be an explanation – although it was hard to imagine what. But look at the wailing woman here: she was a pain in the ass, for sure, but she was no worse than very frightened and very sad.

Gibbous opened his eyes again, saw that Allaby was still beating the ship with his pole, and shut them again. The next time he opened them it was dark. He'd slept, damn it. Why did people think it was kind to let you sleep – especially to sleep sitting up? The first thing he noticed were pains in the small of his back and in his neck, the second was that a fire was going, and the third was that Allaby and Paintbrush were sitting by it, talking in murmurs. There was nothing particularly odd about that, except that right behind them was their bedpit, and it was occupied. But of course that would be the skycouple under the blankets, and Allaby and Paintbrush were sitting by the fire because it was the only way to keep warm. Nice of them to let the skycouple have the … Then he realised he himself was chilly as well as stiff, and wondered why they at least couldn't have thrown his own blanket over him. He looked to his bedpit to see if the blanket was still there, and it was – with, it appeared, somebody under it.

"Who the hell's that?" he said.

"Oh, you're awake, Granddad. Shh."

He lowered his voice. "But who is it?"

"It's the most wonderful thing, Granddad. Come over here."

With his hand on the back of his neck, he got up, went around to the fire and sat on the other side of Paintbrush.

"It's Allaby's sister," Paintbrush whispered.

"His sister? Allaby's sister?"

"It really is, isn't it Allaby?"

Allaby made a slight nod, but from what Gibbous could see of his expression in the firelight, he wasn't entirely happy about his sister being here, if that's who it actually was.

"She's been looking for him, Granddad. It was her in the big ship. Allaby got her out. He saved her life, and then he realised it was his sister and that she'd been looking for him. He was really surprised, weren't you, Allaby?"

Another short nod. "Very surprised," he said flatly. "Very, very surprised."

Gibbous said, "How did she know where you were?"

"Oh, she's been looking for him all over. All the time he's been with us, she's been flying around looking for him."

"Even so—"

"She thought I might be around here," Allaby said, "because she knew I was interested in your people."

"Why didn't she look here first then? A ship that big – you'd think we'd have seen it flying around."

"Before these people took over the Moon," he said, jerking his head towards the sleeping skycouple, "flying ships above here wasn't allowed. Maybe she didn't realise until now that the Moon had fallen."

The moon fallen? Gibbous looked up. No, there it was, way over there, about to set. There wasn't much left of the night, in fact, and Allaby was still in his strange mood. Was Yellow back? Oh yes, there he was, lying with the baby in the baby's bedpit. That was something, anyway.

"Otherwise, I don't know," Allaby went on. "I didn't have a chance to ask her much before she collapsed."

"She collapsed?"

"There was fire inside the ship," Paintbrush said, her eyes bright with the excitement of it all. "She was black from smoke, and she'd breathed a lot of it. She only had time to hug Allaby and say a few words to him, and then she just coughed a lot and fell. Allaby dragged her back here. He couldn't carry her because of his ribs, and I couldn't help because I had to stay here and watch the woman and the man. Anyway, she's been out since then. I hope you don't mind us putting her in your bedpit."

"Have you tried to bring her to?"

"No, Gibbous," Allaby said. "I thought she was probably exhausted. We're just letting her sleep."

Gibbous tried to bend his stiff neck sideways and couldn't. "It isn't always best to let people sleep," he said. "Besides, there's a difference between sleeping and collapsing. When someone collapses, you should usually try to wake that person up, if you can."

"Well, Gibbous, I guess you're right. You're the medicine man around here. But I'm going to have to wake her up pretty soon anyway."

"Yes, Granddad. Allaby says it's time for us all to go."

"Fine with me," Gibbous said. "Any idea where?"

Paintbrush said, "That's what we were just talking about. We can go anywhere, and that makes it hard to decide. Allaby, explain what the problem is."

"Again?"

"Granddad needs to know."

Allaby put his hand over his eyes, sighed and took the hand away. Then he said, "Of course you do, Gibbous. I'm sorry. It's just that I've had a shock, and I—"

"What? Seeing your sister?"

"Oh, that was a shock, too, but no. Before that. Something Jacob said. I can't explain it, but never mind. Our immediate problem is that that liner over there isn't the only big base ship on the ground. There are others, apparently, in other parts of the world."

"How do you know?"

"They're such morons, Gibbous. This is hard to explain, too, but you know the voice in the pickup?"

"He's been in the pickup most of the night," Paintbrush said, "listening to voices."

"I'm the enemy, right? And I'm keeping two of their people hostage, right? If you remember, Gibbous, this was your idea – for me to talk to them, to the voices, which come from the liner. I was a little stunned at the time – still am – and a good idea from somebody else was needed. So thanks. Anyway, I told them to keep the channel open so that I could talk to them whenever I wanted to. In other words, to keep the thing working, even though we might not be saying anything."

"I see what you mean. Go on."

"Good for you, Granddad. He didn't even try to explain that to me. Did you think I wouldn't understand, Allaby?"

"I was going to get around to it. But now that both of you are listening, I only have to say it once."

Paintbrush said, "I'll have you know I understood that perfectly well."

"Then both of you understand it better than they do. One of the many things they don't know about is the workings of pickups, including the comms on them. People don't use pickups on the Moon. They're only any good here and on Mars and, with modifications, on Titan – places with air, because pickups fly by air particle displacement. That liner is almost certainly a Moon–Mars Express, and normally there's a whole fleet of pickups in one of those. But those idiots left for here in such a half-cocked hurry, they didn't check to see how many pickups were aboard, and then they discovered they only had one and that outrigger." He pointed in the direction of the crashed ships. "The pickups were probably being serviced or something. That's routine when a liner's in dock. And when the people got here, they only way they could use the pickup they did have was to start reading the manual on the panel—"

"Get on with it," Gibbous said. Understanding, hell. The only thing he was understanding now was that Allaby seriously needed a lesson in storytelling, especially the part about being clear and avoiding digressions.

"Sorry, Gibbous. Sorry, Paintbrush. This whole business gets me carried away. So ... one thing they didn't know about the comms on pickups is that if you leave the channel open, the person in the pickup can broaden it – this is so he can have several conversations without having to fool with the controls – and so they didn't know I could hear what they were saying on all the other channels and to each other."

"For God's sake," Gibbous said. "Is that all you're saying – that you eavesdropped on them?"

"Uh, yeah, I guess so. More or less."

"So what did you hear?"

"Okay, listen. They don't know what happened to the outrigger. All they know is that it stopped transmitting – it stopped talking to them – as soon as it landed here. So I told them the outrigger had been destroyed, and then I never said another word. Their own imaginations took it from there. It was really interesting what they turned us into."

"Yes, Granddad, Allaby says they think we're a band of great warriors."

"Yeah, Gibbous. Here I am with a Titanian accent – in case I haven't mentioned it, Titan is the place in the sky that I come from – and they've seen you, some kind of magical incarnation of native humanity. Among other things, they think you have godly powers because you not only brought a dead man back to life but you rescued him from Hell—"

"What did I do?"

"It's got to do with the man you darted – they completely misunderstood what happened. They don't know how many more of you there are or of me there are – maybe hordes of both. Even better, they've been getting

377

messages from Titan, from people with the same religion as theirs, warning them to stay away from various places. And now we've captured two of their people and destroyed their outrigger. They can hardly move; the only ship they have is the liner itself, which can take all day to get going and is really awkward close to the ground, and they might be facing a hostile alliance between Titanians and native superhumans. I don't know how they figure the Titanians got here – the trip would take almost a year – but when they have time to think about it, maybe they'll figure that some Titanians were already here or something. Anyway, they've been frantically talking to the other ships – all pretty far away – where the people are just as disorganised and prone to fantasy as they are. But the other ships have said they'll send some armed outriggers, which is why we'll have to go somewhere pretty soon, because at the moment they know where we are. But altogether it's not bad, is it?"

"Not bad, Allaby? It sounds damned dangerous."

"But don't you think it's better for them to think all that than to know what we really are?"

"No." Gibbous said. "If they knew the truth, they'd probably just leave us alone. That's all we want, isn't it?"

Allaby leaned forward, picked up the fire-poking stick and poked the fire.

"Here," Gibbous said. He reached for a cowpat and tossed it on.

"Gibbous, that's pretty much what I thought when you and those two turned up in the pickup. Seeing you made me as happy as I've ever been, but the last thing I wanted to see were any, uh, skypeople. I had just discovered that I could walk again, and all I wanted was for them to take the pickup and leave and for you, me and my beautiful wife to go on walking to our new beginning. But things have changed. We can't do that now. For one thing we've now got Jenny with us – Jenny, my sister. For another, I've since learned exactly who these people are, and they certainly wouldn't leave us alone, and they wouldn't leave your people alone either, not after they started to get used to the gravity – and that won't take that long. And remember those kids? Jacob still hasn't told me what they were doing to them and why – or even whose kids most of them are. Then there's also the basic fact that they're a bunch of careless morons with a very nasty, very crazy form of religion. They don't mind who they kill or what kind of damage they do. And there's another really important reason, probably more important than—"

"Okay," Gibbous said, "okay. They're bad people, and somebody ought to do something, but we can't—"

"There is no somebody, Gibbous. They say they've taken over all the stations – all the places in the sky where people live. There's even one place, I heard one of them say, where they wiped out every single person. He called it Sodom, which means a place full of sinners, and said that it suffered God's vengeance. But it was a nice place. People worked and lived there, and had fun there. I used to go there myself twice a year. The bastards killed everybody. At least that's what this man seemed to be saying."

"Look," Paintbrush said, nodding in the direction of the woods, "The sky's a little lighter over there. You said we'd be going at daybreak, and we don't even know where yet. And Allaby, what is that really important reason you were talking about? You told me all the reasons you just told Granddad, but you didn't tell me any more than that."

"Oh, it's awful, Paintbrush. The reason we have to do something ourselves is because it's our responsibility. Well, my responsibility because it's my goddamned fault. I made an awful, awful mistake, but it involved you, too, Gibbous."

Gibbous said, "I thought you'd got over that. Paintbrush, he was doing it yesterday – his fault and then my fault and probably your fault, too, not to mention the baby's fault and Yellow's fault, that the skypeople are here at all."

"Allaby how can it possibly be—"

"Well, it can be and is my fault. But it'll take some explaining, and I suppose we ought to get moving now. I promise you both that when I get enough time I'll tell you how it happened." He started to get up. "But now—"

"But now," Paintbrush said, looking at him as he rose, "we still don't know where we're going to go."

When Allaby was on his feet, he said, "Here's the problem. We need to get far away from here. I can make sure the tracker in the pickup is off, but the more time we spend in the air, the more likely it is that the liner can find us or that one of the other ships' outriggers can. Maybe Jenny can help. Yeah, that's what I'll do – I'll ask her. You're right, Gibbous – it's past time to wake her up. What's also going to be a problem is getting everybody and everything into that pickup. I've been thinking maybe we

379

ought to leave Jacob and Rachel here, along with the shelter and some other stuff—"

"Allaby," Gibbous said, "your mind is flickering. First you say something smart, then you say a whole lot of things nobody can understand, and then you say something stupid."

"We couldn't leave those poor people here," Paintbrush said. "They'd die. The water's almost gone."

"Then tell me how I'm going to get everybody …"

Standing up and taking a step towards Allaby, Gibbous said, "Keeping them is part of your plan. Have you forgotten that already? They're our hostages, for God's sake. What happens if they don't die, and somebody comes to get them. There goes your big bluff. Even if they do die—"

"Okay, what?" He was almost shouting now, and various sleepers were stirring. "What do we do?"

"Allaby," Gibbous said, "think." Allaby opened his mouth, but Gibbous said sharply, "No, don't speak. Think." With his fingers in his hair, Allaby took a couple of steps away and then a couple of steps back. Paintbrush stood up and started to say something, but Gibbous put his hand on her shoulder and shook his head. The answer was obvious, but he really did want Allaby to work it out himself. If he was going to be chief of this imaginary band of warriors, he was going to have to start thinking like a chief.

Finally, Allaby said, "Help me, Gibbous."

"Okay," Gibbous said. "The first problem. The longer we're in the air, the greater the chance of being caught. So?"

"So we don't spend a long time in the air? But—"

"As long as we're not right exactly here, it doesn't matter where we are, does it? So we just go a short distance. Anyway, they'll be thinking like you, expecting us to try to go far away – but that's only if they think we are what we are. What you say, though, is that they're not thinking that. They're imagining a band of us, and so they'll be imagining lots of ships all over everywhere. And that's one more reason not to show ourselves in a single crowded pickup. If we want to keep them worried, we have to make sure we don't show them anything at all."

"Of course, Gibbous, of course. But even if we do just go a short distance, how does that solve getting everybody in?" He paused. "Oh. We make two trips."

"Or three. That thing's so fast, we can do it in no time."

"Where do we go? Back to your settlements?"

"Oh no, Allaby," Paintbrush said. "We can't—"

"No," said Gibbous. "No reason to bother the people in the settlements. If your plan works – and by the way, I don't know what your plan is, I'm sure you don't either, and I don't think it has a chance of working anyway – but if it miraculously does work, those people back there will be better off if they never know anything happened. Believe me, I know what they're like."

"So where do we go?"

"Where do you suppose?"

"Back to the woods? To the river?"

"Good thinking, Chief."

CHAPTER THIRTY-SIX

"You married her?" Jenny said. "You married an Immyo?"

"That's right," Peter said.

"How?"

"What do you mean how?"

"Where did you find a preacher, for a start?"

"We married according to their tradition."

"Which is?"

"The storyteller conducts the ceremony."

"Don't tell me – the old man's the storyteller."

"That's right."

"Oh, boy. I bet that'll stand up in court."

"What court, Jenny? From what you've just told me, there aren't any courts any more. Any genuine governments even. You can't imagine what hell it is knowing the whole damned mess is my fault."

"Don't be too hard on yourself, Peter. Gus blames you, I guess, but in a way you even saved his life. When they killed all the other execs they missed Gus because he was in jail for transmitting your illegal image. Anyway, those assholes have been planning it for years. All you did was trigger it. If it hadn't been you, it would have been … Who knows? I'm just glad you're alive. I'm glad I am. Here we both are, living and breathing – breathing Earth air, for Christ's sake – and if you happen to be, in some strange way, married, I suppose that's just part of the bargain. Now that she's getting washed, I can see she's a pretty little thing. Beautiful colouring. Where's the baby's father?"

"Dead," Peter said. "Killed in a war."

"They have wars?"

"They're people, Jenny."

"Of course, I suppose. But tell me – what were you planning to do with your new little family? You said you were out on that plain when the liner flew over. Which means you were going away from the Immyo settlements. Where were you heading?"

"To a new beginning."

"What?"

"A new beginning."

"What do you mean?"

"We were going to find a new place where we could live, far away from anyone else, and be the ancestors of a whole new human culture. And that was it. We still might do it. Okay with you?"

"Sure, Peter, sure. Sorry. But what about the Immyo barrier? How were you—"

"I disabled it at the station before I left."

"You were thinking that far ahead?"

"At the time I was just correcting an ancient cruelty."

"I see. okay, Peter, okay. And never mind." She took a deep breath, still not quite believing that breathing was possible. Then she looked at Peter, still not quite believing it was him. (If she'd had any religion in her, she'd probably be imagining she'd died in the fire and had joined Peter in some joke of an afterlife.) "And your wife there? Is she just a convenient way of getting the ancestry going, or do you actually love her?"

"I actually do. Very much."

Okay then, love her all you like, Jenny thought as she lay back and closed her eyes. Whatever else you've done, Peter, you've just brought me the most savoury afternoon I've ever known. The two of them were drying out on a big flat rock that jutted into the river, while little Mrs Allaby continued to wash herself and her baby in the shallow, relatively calm eddies that the rock itself created by blocking the current. It was the sun that made the moment – pure, unfiltered sunshine stroking her whole body and turning the backs of her eyelids red. She'd bathed in a river, and now she was lying in the sun. She'd sunbathed on the glass balcony at her station lots of times, but that was nothing like this. There hadn't been the air and the slight breeze, and the roar and watery smell of the river, and the tingle of the water evaporating off her skin. It even helped having the insect bites she'd picked up last night. Peter had fastened her flight suit tight at the neck, but just above the line of the collar was another collar, a ring of red bites, the first she'd ever had. She'd never felt that kind of itch before, but under the warm sun, it wasn't actually bad. At this moment, she even liked the thought of insects bothering to stick their proboscos into her. She was a living, breathing Earth animal, damn it, and suddenly participating in a food chain.

She'd sunbathed in the open air on Mars, too, but that had been even worse than the glass balcony. There was no question of insects there, and of course you always had to wear a breather. And instead of a single sun, you got the puny real one plus a constellation of satellite reflectors that never did anything as luscious as stroke your body. When she, Peter and his wife had come to the river, Jenny had been afraid that the experience might bring her craving back, but to her great relief it hadn't (all she had to do to quash it was conjure up the leering boy in the outrigger), even though in this little party right now there was total nakedness. "I'll say this for her, Peter – she shows an admirable absence of jealousy. Are they polygamous?"

"No, they're monogamous – pretty strictly so, as far as I can tell."

"Then how come she doesn't mind …" She opened her eyes, leaned up on an elbow and regarded Peter again, all red and white and splotchy – short, stringy, blond beard (on a darker man it would have just been a heavy shadow), bites everywhere, wounds, a great blue bruise on his side and a makeshift splint on his wrist – but somehow looking tougher than he'd ever looked before, especially with his clothes off. "How come she doesn't mind us lying around like this?"

"Well, I've got to tell you, Jenny. She, uh, thinks – she thinks you're my sister."

"Your sister?"

"Yeah."

"You told her that?"

"Yeah."

"For Christ's sake, why?"

"As you say, look at us now. I just thought it would save awkwardness all around. Anyway, people who've been lovers are a bit like siblings, aren't they? I mean, I know everything intimate about you that there is to know."

"A lot more than a brother would know, yes, but don't be too sure. There are some intimate things about me even I didn't know until—"

"Besides, you mentioned jealousy. Ever since I met Paintbrush, there hasn't been another woman around. So I don't know if she does get jealous, and I don't want to find out. What were you saying? Until what?"

"Until … never mind, Peter." She lay back again, shut her eyes again. She had sketched Peter in on most of what had happened to her since his disappearance – his death – except for the affair with Louise. She did admit that the reason for her having swerved off course was her newfound phobia of weightlessness combined with the absence of a tracker because of the absence of any comms. Anyway, when she was explaining that, he wasn't really listening – he was still being consumed with relief at the news that he hadn't, in fact, caused the extermination of the entire population of EHQS. She hoped that her motive in not mentioning Louise was simply that it was none of his business and not something else, such as a fear that he wouldn't approve, would even be scandalised. Worse, she wondered if she herself might be ashamed of what she and Louise had done. But no, on quick assessment, she wasn't. True, she couldn't believe she loved Louise. She couldn't allow herself – not because of Louise's gender but because of her job. Love, to Jenny, implied a certain degree of possession, and there could be none of that at all of someone with Louise's chosen career. But she did like her – a lot – and that emotion deserved just as much respect. No, the shame she felt was for wrecking the shuttle and failing so miserably in her mission. How could she have indulged herself that way – the chicken casserole, the wine, the music? No, that was something she'd never tell anybody, and while it was a little too bad that the disgusting boy had been crushed, at least nobody else had seen her naked at the controls and appearing to do what he'd thought she'd been …

This was something that so far she hadn't had time to contemplate. After the boy had intercepted her, she'd been frightened for her life. After that, unconscious. And after Peter had woken her up this morning, she'd been absorbing the reality of seeing him alive, of taking in his story, and of being able to breathe on Earth. Then there was the hectic business of moving to this place, helping to manage those pitiful hostages and doing her part in setting up camp. Now, relaxed and starting to take in the wholeness of her predicament, her mind wandered over to the fact that the boy, of course, had had comms. And of course he'd been describing what he thought he was seeing, which meant that by now everybody in that liner was vividly aware, and probably everybody in the other ships. How mortifying, but at least nobody would know who the dirty woman was … except one man who was monitoring all the Back-to-Earther comms – Gus. She sat bolt upright, her hand over her mouth. "Oh my God," she said. "Gus."

"Jesus, Jenny. What's the matter?"

"Oh. Oh, I just remembered something."

"What?"

"Nothing, nothing."

Peter's woman, carrying her baby, was out of the water now and, through the speckled shade of a cottonwood, was coming to join Jenny and Peter in the sun.

On the other hand, maybe it was okay – Gus, after all, thought she was in Africa, not flying over North America. He would have assumed that it was someone else they were talking about. Sure. But really? Another woman flying an unmarked shuttle with no comms?

Mrs Allaby – what had Peter said her name translated as … Brushstroke? … came up, sat down, said something and handed Peter the wet baby.

No, Gus was bound to know it was Jenny, and so, on top of everything else, he would have realised she hadn't gone where she was supposed to go. One thing was certain: she'd never be able to face Gus again. But then, she might never again get the opportunity. She was luxuriating now in the pure air and sunshine of Earth, but she was also stranded (although, in the light of what she'd just realised, stranded was something she'd be happy to stay). On the other hand, the satellite was still blacked out, she still had a mission, and it was still her moral duty to get word to Gus somehow about the breathable air. Just a message – he couldn't reply, and so it wasn't really like facing him. There were the comms in the pickup, and she could use those, but her orders were clear: don't use comms. At all. She couldn't fly back, though, and since she'd disobeyed so many orders so far …

"Peter, did you say earlier that you were having trouble with the pickup's comms?"

"Yeah, I'd better get back and try to do something about that." Then he spoke to Brushstroke, and she spoke to him.

"What's wrong with them?"

"Nothing, really. They work all right. The thing is, I can't figure out how to disconnect them from the tracker. So I can't transmit without giving our position away."

"That's right. You can't."

"No, there's something else I want to try—"

"It can't be done, Peter. Don't you know? There's an interstation treaty. All comms in all ships – down to and including pickups – have to be manufactured with integrated trackers."

"For God's sake, why?"

"To prevent piracy. You know, I've never met anybody as naïve as you about the law. I'll bet even Brushstroke could have told you that."

"Paintbrush – her name's Paintbrush. And what kind of pirates are going to go around in a goddamned pickup?"

"You know how laws work, Peter. It's much easier to say 'all' than make a bunch of niggling exceptions that might turn out to be loopholes."

"I know about laws all right. They never prevent what they're meant to prevent – any halfway competent pirates would make their own comms systems without trackers, while for everybody else it's just a pain in the arse.

"Such a pain in the arse you didn't even know the law existed. How many times in your life have you needed to transmit from a secret location?"

"Once. Now. And that's enough. I can't even contact them to get them to widen the band again. So I can't hear what they're saying to each other. What am I supposed to do, Jenny?" Brushstroke – Paintbrush – said something at length, and when she'd finished, Peter nodded, spoke and handed her the baby. She got up, smiled at Peter and then at Jenny, went to the pile of clothes on the bank near the end of the rock and began drying the baby with a cloth.

"Peter, I think I want to make a transmission, too. I need to get through to Gus. Your plan, as I understand it, is to taunt them a little and let their imaginations go wild. But then what happens? Do they get scared and leave? Do they implode? What? You know, when you were making that plan, you believed EHQS had been wiped out. But it's still there, and if I can get through to Gus—"

"But you can't because we can't fucking transmit. Come on, we're dry now. Let's get back." He didn't wait for her, just got up quickly and strode towards his little family and the pile of clothes. That is, he took a couple of strides, suddenly remembered that his bare feet hurt and then continued on his right heel and left big toe. But with his back and shoulders, he still managed to express his sheer disgust at the Interstation Convention on Control of Illegal Interception.

Jenny didn't follow. She stayed lying on the rock, head propped on hand – feeling the sun and observing Peter in his new identity. He was earnestly talking to his bemused-looking wife as he got into his very dirty underwear and then that ridiculously small and even dirtier shirt of his. (Everybody's clothes were filthy, not least her own smoke-blackened flight suit. Next time they came here to bathe, they'd have to wash their clothes, too. Who'd care if they had to put them on wet? Who'd care if they didn't put them on at all? She'd been seen naked so much lately that nakedness was beginning to seem as normal and ordinary as … it was.) He was still talking – grumbling, obviously – as he pulled on his funny knee-length trousers and fiddled furiously with what appeared to be some kind of lacing in the front. At that point, Paintbrush pushed his hand away, gave him the baby, kneeled in front of him and did the lacing for him. Then she apparently directed him to sit on the ground, because sit on the ground was what he did, and as he continued both to hold the baby and to grumble, she began to put his shoes on for him. Rather, applied them to his feet – it was a long process – and he talked continuously as she very patiently wrapped and tied. God, she was good to him. Was that what he'd wanted in a woman all along? If so, you're welcome to him, little wife. You'd never have caught me administering to his flies and his feet.

When she'd finished doing the shoes, the little wife began getting dressed herself – in what would have been, if it hadn't been so dirty, a rather pretty embroidered skirt-and-shirt combination – and Jenny got up, went over and grabbed the flight suit. As she was fastening herself into it, Peter said, "Is that the only clothes you've got? I never heard of anybody wearing nothing at all under one of those."

"It was hot in that ship."

"It ended up hot, yeah. What did you do – take off the suit, rip off your other clothes, put the suit back—"

"Forget it, Peter. Just stay mad about the piracy clause, and leave me—"

"I am mad about it, damn it. I can't figure how to get around it."

Soon they were walking upstream beside the river towards the campsite, which was beyond a little bend about a hundred metres ahead. Low-slung willow, cottonwood and live oak trees spread out over the water, and walking along here meant occasionally ducking under a bottom branch. Peter was still carrying the baby, and Paintbrush walked next to him, holding his arm. Jenny followed by a couple of steps. Just being alive and breathing and on Earth made her feel good almost to the point of giddiness, but she was also beginning to feel the germ of an irritation about Peter's improbable marriage. It wasn't jealousy, she told herself – it really wasn't. In fact, it didn't actually bother her – not yet – but it had to do with, well, the coupleness of the couple. The conversation Jenny and Peter had had while sitting on the rock was the freest and most uninterrupted so far, but they still had a hell of a lot left to say. If Paintbrush was nearby, though, it was her he talked to and her he deferred to, and to make matters worse, he

388

did it in a language Jenny couldn't understand. Of course, he and Paintbrush were not only married, or regarded themselves as married, but were newlyweds and as such were behaving perfectly normally – probably the only normal thing that was going on here. But that, in a way, made it almost perverse. It was as bad as Jenny feeling so good. She was a complete failure and had disgraced herself to boot, and Peter had triggered the Solar System's worst crisis since the Apocalypse. Now both she and he had to do whatever they could to redeem themselves, but all she could feel were pangs of joy about the air and the sun and the river and the trees and even her necklace of insect bites, while Peter was immersed in his passion for his little bride. For Christ's sake, Rangers Romero and Allaby – concentrate.

"Peter," Jenny said, "all we need to do is fly off somewhere in the pickup, make our transmissions and fly back."

He glanced over his shoulder. "I've thought of that. It won't work."

"Why not?"

He glanced back again. "Well, maybe somehow it would. I don't know. We have to rethink everything now." He looked forward just in time to duck a low branch. Little Paintbrush had been ready and able to walk right under it, almost dragging him into it. It occurred to Jenny, as she herself ducked under the branch, that that was because Paintbrush wasn't paying attention to the fact that Peter was talking – because, to her, his words in English were just funny noises. In fact, maybe moreso to her. What experience would the Immyos here ever have had of other languages? Presumably, they all spoke the same, and since they had never been allowed to contact anyone else ... For that matter, Jenny herself only knew about different languages because she'd been taught about them and had studied ancient Russian and ancient Spanish in school. But everybody in the Solar System spoke English – except for the small Persian and Mandarin communities on Ganymede, and they could speak English when they needed to. In fact, when Peter deciphered this Immyo language, it was probably the first time such a thing had been accomplished in more than a thousand years. Whatever else he may have done, he deserved some credit for that.

They turned away from the river and walked up the sloping bank towards the campsite. The trees were a little taller, straighter, skinnier and sparser than the ones along the bank, making an open woodland that felt comfortable after the thick, low foliage right along the riverside.

Something about it seemed ineffably human. It was the kind of place humans without any manufactured trappings would choose to be – a plain on one side, a river on the other and, here, some friendly, not too imposing, sheltering and eminently useful trees. It was where useful animals would be, too – she realised she could hear chickens scratching and softly clucking a short distance away. "Chicken casserole," she said.

"What?" Peter said.

"Chickens. Shh ..."

"Oh yeah," he whispered. He pointed and said something to Paintbrush, who looked at Jenny and smiled. Then Paintbrush and Peter had a short, whispered exchange before Paintbrush took several slow steps towards the clucking sounds and crouched by a tree trunk.

Peter whispered, "I said we should tell Gibbous, and she said she's been catching chickens all her life. Women are better at it, she said, because men don't like not using weapons."

Paintbrush looked perfectly still, but somehow, without Jenny noticing – even though she hadn't taken her eyes off her – she had moved a little and was about a quarter of the way around the tree. Jenny glanced at Peter, and he was glancing back and forth between Paintbrush and, in his arms, the baby, who was silently watching his mother almost as if he knew what was going on. Then she noticed for the first time that, cleaned up, he was a very nice-looking boy, with bright eyes and a little furrow in his brow that gave him an appearance of having a sense of humour or maybe even precocious intelligence. She reflected that, in fact, Peter was pretty lucky to have found such a family – that she'd never seen anything like him for landing on his feet – when there was an explosion of squawks, feathers and scattering, half-flying chickens and then Paintbrush standing on the other side of the tree holding up, in one hand, two red and black hens by their necks. As, beaming, she came back with them, Jenny noticed that the birds were already dead. When had she had time to kill them, and how?

"I'll be damned," Peter said, "I didn't know ..." and he continued in Immyo language, saying something that made Paintbrush nearly double over with laughter. And as they all started walking again, she kept giggling and bumping her hip against his leg.

This, again, was ever-so-slightly irritating, and finally, Jenny said, "What the hell is the joke, Peter?"

"Oh nothing, nothing. I didn't think it was that funny, myself."

"But what did you say to her? Come on."

"I said, 'You mean you haven't cooked them yet?'"

It wasn't worth more than a chuckle, but Paintbrush's giggling was infectious, and by the time they reached the campsite, Jenny was laughing with her, Peter had an actual grin on his face – the first time he'd smiled since becoming aware of his transmission problem – and even the baby was gurgling a little. The old man, who had been doing something – building something – on the ground, stood up, wiped his hands on his trousers, leaned on his stick and made a remark that was obviously wry, and this caused Paintbrush to laugh even harder and to do a little dance as she held the chickens in the air. Then the woman hostage, who was tied, along with her husband, to a bed (an actual, if very rough-looking, bed; Jenny had helped the old man carry it here this morning from some former campsite), shouted shrilly, "Laugh while you can, you savages."

That got rid of Peter's grin, and it stopped Paintbrush in her tracks. With a slight frown, even though she was still holding the chickens over her head, she asked Peter something – what the woman had said, no doubt – and when Peter answered, Paintbrush looked in the woman's direction and said something serious. Then, lowering the chickens, handing one to the old man and carrying the other almost as she would her baby, she walked over to the woman, squatted next to her, indicated the bird, spoke and did an eating gesture. "God, no," the woman said. "I'd never put a thing like that in my mouth."

"Don't be stupid, Rachel," the man said. "They'll clean and cook it first."

"Even so – yuck."

It occurred to Jenny that the woman might never have eaten real food before. She joined Paintbrush at the side of the bed and said to Rachel, "Don't you have chickens where you come from?"

"And I suppose, Miss Mars, you do."

Jenny found it hard to look at her because her face was so thoroughly insect-bitten. Jenny's little necklace of bumps was nothing compared to the full-frontal, almost deforming attack this otherwise chalk-white woman had suffered during the night. There were even swellings inside her nostrils, and one eye was nearly closed. And with her hands tied to the bed, she wasn't able to scratch, which may or may not have been a good thing, but it reminded Jenny lucidly of her handcuffs and the free-fall dungeon. It also reminded her that these people belonged to the cult that had done that to her. "Yes," Jenny said, "we have chickens on Mars. Pigs, too – descendants of animals that were there before the Apocalypse. And lots of vegetables. Martians don't ever have to eat generated food if they don't want to." Then to Peter she shouted, "Can we untie them now that we're back?" Hell, let her scratch herself, she thought.

"Sure," he called. "It was only so Gibbous didn't have to watch them." Then he called to Paintbrush, who immediately started taking the ropes off the woman, and Jenny went around the bed to do the same for the man.

The woman shook her hands free, clapped them to her cheeks, rubbed heavily and said, "Well, that's Mars, isn't it? You're all barbarians there."

"But I used to go to real-food restaurants in Armstrong."

"And that's Armstrong," she said, still rubbing. "You'd never catch me in that Babylon."

"You don't like anywhere very much, do you?" Jenny said as she gathered up the ropes.

"I like Conrad. It's where my home is. It's where my children were ..." Further words caught in her throat, and tears started trickling down, around and over her fingers and the scarlet bites. She quit scratching and held her hands against her face.

"Now you've done it," the man said to Jenny. "Thanks for untying us, but if you want to talk to someone, why don't you go talk to the weird Titanian? And take the girl and her dead bird with you."

The woman began a low moan.

Jenny said, "She's only being gracious, you know. She's showing your wife what we're having for dinner."

"What you're having," he said, "and what I'm having, maybe. I've been around a little, and I can eat real food ... Don't start howling again, Rachel, please ... but she's lived in Conrad all her life – small place, Far Side – and she can't—"

"Has she eaten at all – since she's been with us, them, I mean? Have you?"

"Yes, I have," he said. "I ate some of that God-knows-what-it-was last night. And kept it down, too. But she hasn't, and she won't."

"Well, there's certainly no generated food here. Unless there's something in the pickup. Is there?"

"No," the man said. "Nothing. We weren't planning on staying."

Jenny said to the woman, "Listen, real food can be delicious, especially chicken when it's ..."

At this she finally did howl. She moved her hands from her face, which was now entirely red instead of just polka-dot, and the shriek, which was more angry than distressed, actually knocked Jenny backwards a little and made Paintbrush jump up. And when, after several seconds, it finished, she shouted, "I will not eat that stinking animal!"

"Then starve!" Jenny shouted back. "Come on, Paintbrush. She doesn't deserve your sympathy."

Paintbrush gave Jenny a quizzical look, and Jenny put a hand on her shoulder and guided her away, towards Peter and the old man, who were standing together and staring at the distraught hostage. She was making loud sobs punctuated by angry squeals. Over the top of this noise, the man shouted, "Go ahead. Walk away. I'm still tied to her. I'll always be."

What Peter and the old man had been doing, as far as Jenny could tell, was conferring about the fire, which hadn't been lit yet and wouldn't be, Peter had said, until it was too dark for the smoke to be seen. They were standing on either side of a narrow, fairly deep hole – deep, to keep the flames from being spotted – with some leaves and sticks beside it, and when Jenny and Paintbrush walked up, Peter said something to Paintbrush, who shrugged and nodded towards Jenny. So he said, "I should have warned you about Rachel."

"God, what a nasty woman. But I guess you can't run personality tests on potential hostages."

"Just wait. She can go on like that for hours."

"Peter, she won't eat real food. She hasn't touched anything since you've been holding her."

"Oh, is that it?" he said, and explained this to Paintbrush and the old man. Then he had to explain some more, because they naturally hadn't heard of generated food and of people who had never eaten anything else and gagged at the idea of ingesting something that used to be alive.

While that was going on and as the woman's howls diminished into quieter but audibly snotty sobs, Jenny cast her eyes around the campsite. The old man was nothing if not organised. If it had had walls, it could have been a room in a house. There was the bed – made with twine, tree branches and soft grass, but a bed nonetheless – as well as two hammocks, a twine-and-branch table with four stools and, on it, neat piles of blankets and other things. Over here by the fire-hole was a small platform laid out with a knife, spits, various sticks, what she supposed were flints, the old man's pipe and darts, the other chicken and, incongruously, the two guns. Even more incongruous was the bright yellow pickup. That was parked right at the edge of the site – farthest from the bed – with a layer of branches on top for camouflage. According to the this morning's arrangements, the pickup was to double as Peter's family bedroom, while Jenny and the old man had the hammocks, and the hostages, of course, had the bed.

As Jenny went to lay the rope on the table, she realised it was no wonder Peter had been so annoyed by the piracy clause. Here was everything he needed to carry out his plan (except for a decent plan). Compared to where they'd been staying out there in the open (and Peter made it sound as if they'd been stuck there for months, though it couldn't have been more than a few days), this was luxury itself: plenty of food around, water to drink and bathe in and trees to hide under, and right on site, his own little comms station. He could start each day with a few teasing announcements, listen for the reaction, taunt the Back-to-Earthers some more and then wash, dally with his wife, maybe do some hunting, finish off with a big meal, a chat around the fire and retirement to the pickup – then tuning in to transmissions, getting some sex and going to sleep. And now the piracy clause had taken the core of that away from him. But in the end, Jenny thought, it was probably just as well. Otherwise, Peter could start imagining he was already at his new beginning. He could get comfortable and complacent – everybody could – and sooner or later, they'd be caught. Besides, the most urgent job was getting a message to Gus, and now that Peter's half-assed plan was ruined, maybe he'd concentrate on that. There was, of course, no reason at all why they couldn't fly off somewhere else, transmit and come back. Peter, in his frustration, was just being petulant.

Over at the fire-pit the explanation of generated food appeared to have graduated into some kind of strategy conference. Peter was gesturing as he spoke, with a lot of pointing at the pickup and then in the direction of the liner, the old man was leaning on his stick and vaguely shaking his head, and Paintbrush, having put the chicken on the platform beside the other one, was now holding the baby, patting him on the back and listening intently. Then the old man would say something, emphasising an occasional point by hitting his stick on the ground. Peter would speak and gesture again, and Paintbrush would interject and pat the baby. At the bed, the low-key hysterics continued, with the man quietly trying – what else could he do? – to talk the woman down.

Jenny sat on a stool, leaned back against the table and gazed up at the trees. A little breeze was fluttering the leaves, and a single, small cloud hung in the sky behind. A flock of silhouetted birds, too high up to identify, briefly flew across it and then were obscured again by the leaves. She wondered what time it was. Four o'clock, maybe? Her watch was gone, along with everything else, but the sky had a four o'clock look to it. One of the great things about being on Earth, she'd always thought, was that clock-time actually meant something – it marked the real, gradual phases of the day, not the artificially imposed lights-up-lights-down you got on the satellite and on the Moon. Yes, it was definitely four o'clock up there and down here, and in a couple of hours it would be dark enough to get the fire going and to start cooking the chickens. She was already hungry, and there was a kind of sensuousness in just looking forward to dinner. What a day. She wouldn't have minded living the rest of her life like this, especially if the alternative was ever having to face Gus again.

So I do get your point, Peter, about the new beginning. But, hell, isn't that what everybody wants, and isn't that what the problem is?

CHAPTER THIRTY-SEVEN

"What does your sister think?" Gibbous said.

"She thinks we should fly away somewhere," said Allaby, indicating with a sweep of his hand the pickup flying away, "talk to them, listen to them and fly back."

"And while you're doing that, they'll know where you are?"

"While we're talking, yes, and while we're flying they might spot us."

"Or they might not."

"Yeah, but there's a risk."

"This is a kind of war, isn't it, Allaby?"

"I guess it is, yes."

"Have you ever fought a war before?"

"Well … no, now that you mention it." Somehow he felt he had, but it was true – he hadn't.

"Well, let me tell you something. Wars are risky. You can't get around that."

"You think we should do it, then?"

"I just think if you're going to fight a war, you ought to fight it."

Paintbrush said, "I thought you hated wars, Granddad."

"Well, yeah. The other choice is not to fight a war. We can just keep on hiding here. It's a pretty nice spot."

"No," Allaby said. "Sooner or later they'd find us. And if it was later, they might have had time to adapt. Whatever we do, we've got to do it now."

"Okay," Gibbous said. "So you don't have a choice. Now let me tell you something else. While you were down at the river, I went up on the plain to have a look, and as far as I could tell from that distance, everything out there is just as we left it. I could see the crashed ship, but there weren't any other ships around. And that wasn't long ago. Why don't you just fly there, do what you need to do and come back? Then they'll think you haven't moved at all. They might even think they've almost got you. They might think you're stupid, too – the best thing your enemy can ever think, unless you are stupid."

"But, Granddad," Paintbrush said. "Allaby's idea is to make them think we're better than we are – stronger and more of us. And I guess smarter, too. Not that you're not smart, Allaby, but you know what I mean."

Allaby wasn't sure he did know, but he didn't want to dwell on it. And it was true that he wasn't feeling like history's greatest tactician. Whenever Gibbous suggested something, it seemed both to make sense and to be the last thing he himself would have thought of.

"In that case," Gibbous said, "maybe they'll be in two minds – arguing with each other – and that's not a bad thing either."

That's it then, Allaby thought, wondering exactly what had gone wrong with his ability to think. Ever since Jacob had identified Gibbous as the sign from God, parts of Allaby's mind seemed to have short-circuited. Gibbous had said last night that it was flickering, and that was exactly what it felt like. It would light up in one place, turn off in another and turn on again somewhere else, and he would mistake the somewhere else for the place that just went off, and his reasoning would trail away aimlessly. He wouldn't even notice, either. All he could imagine was that, somehow, some defence mechanism was trying to save him from the dreadful act of concentration – of, in the process, accidentally grasping the immensity of what he'd done. And as that thought flicked off, too, he looked over at Jenny, who would be going with him to make the transmissions. She was on one of Gibbous's stools, with her back against the table, gazing at the sky or something. God, she was a sexy woman. He'd almost forgotten about that, about the way she had of unconsciously striking and holding powerful poses. Look at her now – legs slightly apart, elbows back, breasts forward, long, shiny, just-washed black hair spread out on the table. At the river, he'd had to make a special effort to keep his eyes on Paintbrush, who was very sexy in her own way but was now his only, as it were, legitimate ogle. It did rankle a little, though, that Jenny had so easily accepted the fact of his and Paintbrush's marriage. Was their past relationship so …

"Allaby."

"Yes, love?" he said, turning back.

"You're not listening."

Gibbous said, "He was busy staring at his sister."

"Sorry," Allaby said, shaking his head. "I was thinking about what I was going to say to the liner."

"I've been meaning to ask you something," Gibbous said. "You're very light-skinned – bright pink, really – and yellow-haired and blue-eyed, and your sister has brown skin, black hair and brown eyes. How did that happen?"

At the time it had seemed a good idea, almost a flash of inspiration, to make Jenny his sister, but now he was seriously wondering. It was the only lie he'd ever told these two, and it was beginning to behave the way lies always do. They don't just hang around harmlessly – they procreate. When earlier today, Paintbrush had pressed him on the same point, he'd said Jenny was actually …

"He's already explained that to me, Granddad. She's really his half-sister. They have different fathers."

"Yes," Allaby said. "My father died, and then my mother married again and had Jenny."

"What did he die of?" Gibbous said.

Allaby tried to remember what he'd told Paintbrush when she'd asked that, but all he could do was picture his rudely healthy, red-faced, still blond father at the gates of the holopark. "He, uh, died of …"

"He had what Allaby calls a heart attack," Paintbrush said. "You know, when your heart just stops? Like your father, Granddad. Didn't you tell me he died that way?"

"Yeah, but he was helped along by the fact that some Waterfallers had popped up and started shooting arrows at him. A heart attack's a funny thing to call it, though. We call it a heart surrender. How old was he, Allaby?"

That he remembered. He'd given his own age. "Thirty-four. I think we should be getting the pickup ready, don't you? The longer we wait, the more chance—"

"How old were you?"

"How old was I?"

"Yeah, you."

"When my father died?"

"Yeah."

Allaby suddenly understood what the old son of a bitch was doing. Gibbous knew damned well that Jenny wasn't Allaby's sister, and he was forcing him to produce a plausible fiction on the spot. He was teaching him a lesson without having to expose him to Paintbrush and making her feel betrayed, or worse. He was also saying that if you're going to claim that woman's your sister, you'd better not look at her the way you were looking at her just now or do anything else to her that's in any way unbrotherly. "I was just little," Allaby said.

"How little?"

"It's a sad story, Granddad. Don't make him—"

"I just want to know how old he was. He must know that."

Okay. Jenny's twenty-eight. Keep to facts as much as possible – six years' difference. Mother has to have time to raise son to age X, and then mourn, recover, court, remarry and produce another baby. "I was three," Allaby said. "Three." Was that right? Did that work?

"So," Gibbous said, "her father – the dark man – was more like your father than your real father, the light man. The dark father brought you up – the way you're going to bring up little Skyman … for instance." His tone of rebuke was just detectable.

"Yes, Gibbous," Allaby said slowly. "Exactly like that."

"Good. I'm glad that's settled. Now you'd better do what you have to do with the pickup." With that, Gibbous took one of the chickens, sat on the ground and started pulling its feathers out.

Paintbrush walked with Allaby over to the pickup. "I think it's because Granddad's a storyteller," she said. "He likes to get all the details straight. And you have to admit that just knowing she's your sister … I can't ever remember her name."

"Jenny."

"Yeah – Jen-ny. That's a hard one. Just knowing she's your sister is one thing, but when you think about the light father and the dark father, it makes it more interesting – sad and happy at the same time. Granddad's good at bringing out things like that. It gives you a picture of the big light brother and the little dark sister growing up together. And I like having a sister-in-law and an aunt for Skyman. It makes us more like a real family," she said, adding another boulder to Allaby's rockpile of guilt. "Allaby, is that somebody in the pickup?"

"What?" With some of the camouflage branches and their leaves hanging over the window, it was hard to see inside, but he did catch a glimpse of movement. "Goddamn, who could that be?" He pushed a couple of branches back and opened the door. The dog vaulted straight out of the dark interior and hit Allaby at chest level, nearly knocking him over backwards. As it was, Allaby instinctively put his arms around the animal to keep him from falling, and received in return a sluice of face licks. "Agh, stop," He put the dog down and, wiping his face with his arm, watched him tear over to Gibbous, who stood up and held the chicken behind his back with one hand while with the other he tried to calm the dog, who was jumping up at him.

"Where's he been?" Gibbous called.

"Shut in the pickup," Paintbrush called back.

"Poor old Yellow. I thought he was out with the hares. Down, Yellow, down."

From the bed, Rachel shouted, "You left that wolf in our nice pickup? That's top of the range. You're all vandals – savages."

"How did he get in there?" Allaby said.

"I don't know," said Paintbrush. "When were you last in it?"

"This morning, I guess, when I was trying to get rid of the tracker."

"Was that when you were lying on your back under there and you had the doors open?"

"That's right."

"That must be when, then. Maybe he got in and went to sleep."

"That means he's been there all day."

Paintbrush was leaning inside the pickup. "Uh oh, Allaby. You're not going to like this."

Rachel was screaming, "You steal it, and then you can't even take care of it—"

"You stole it yourselves," Allaby shouted back, "and you're supposed to be Christians. What about the eighth commandment?" Then to Paintbrush, "Let me see."

She stepped back so he could lean in, and the first thing that hit him, even before his eyes adjusted, was the sour-sweet smell of what must have been dog shit. And when his eyes quickly did adjust, he wished they hadn't. It was clear that whoever had designed the interior of the GM3900 Mighty Mons pickup hadn't done it with trapped canids in mind. For one thing, instead of the hard, sprung-titanium jumpseats that most other ships had, the back and front seats of the luxurious Mighty Mons were sofa-like, cushioned and upholstered. Well, these particular ones weren't any more. The dog had managed to separate every shred of soft material from every stretch of metal and had rearranged it into piles and eddies of grey foam and yellow fabric. Allaby reached down and grabbed a handful of the stuff from the floor. It was soaking wet. He dropped it, pulled back, stood up and put his fingers under his nose. "God," he said, "he's peed everywhere, too." Then he had a heart-stopping thought. He quickly wiped his fingers on his trousers, leaned forward again and, with a trembling hand, felt the control panel and the comms controls. It was all dry, thank Heaven – dry everywhere he touched, beautifully, mercifully, redeemably dry. The pickup wouldn't be very comfortable from now on, but at least it would work. With a heavy sigh, he stood back again. It occurred to him that from the day he first decided to image on an Immyo reservation right up to leaving the dog in the pickup, all that had ever saved his skin was the narrowest sliver of luck. Too bad he couldn't say as much for everybody else in the Solar System.

"What are we going to do, Allaby?" Paintbrush said, holding the baby tight with both arms and looking at him a little nervously, as though he might lose his temper or something – at the very least, he imagined she imagined, with the dog.

But it was himself who pissed him off. "What can we do? Clean it up. It was stupid of me not to notice him."

"It's not your fault, Allaby. You didn't know the dog was there. Maybe he went to sleep or something. Maybe on the floor back there. You wouldn't have seen him."

"Of course it's my goddamned fault. Of course it is. What isn't? But at least the comms and the controls are—"

"Never mind. We've got work to do. Do you think Skyman's aunt would mind holding him?"

"Skyman's … Oh. Uh, I guess not, but why not just put him in a hammock or something? She could help us here."

"It's not lying-down time for him yet. It's being-held time. You know that. If I put him down, he'll either cry or go to sleep. If he goes to sleep, he'll wake up during the night. Besides, I like the idea of—"

"Then you hold him, and Jenny and I'll clean up."

"Does Jenny know how to bale grass?"

"Bale grass?"

"You know, Allaby, there really is something wrong with your thinking. The pickup isn't only a thing for going fast in. It's also our sleeping place. Anyway, if you tried to sit in there the way it is, you could hardly see out the front. That's why I've got to bale some grass. And I don't think either you or your sister would know how."

So Jenny was given the baby, Allaby scooped out and then washed the floor (God, the proximity of a river made all the difference in life), and Paintbrush left for the edge of the plain to gather grass. Rachel was

401

bawling again, and Jacob was muttering. Gibbous wandered over to Allaby and the pickup at one point to have a look inside, shook his head, said, "Those were the nicest chairs I ever sat on," and went back to plucking the chicken and rearranging the wood in the firepit, obviously impatient for nightfall so that he could light it. Carrying the baby on her hip, Jenny had looked in, too, and after being reassured that the comms and the controls were dry, went back her stool at the table to dandle her charge and quietly talk to him. Allaby looked up once from wiping down the seat frames to see an expression on Jenny's face that he didn't remember ever being there before – a contented smile, slightly crossed eyes and total absorption. Somehow, she didn't look like Jenny at all. Damn, he thought, she is a good aunt, and for a moment he almost wished that, by way of some Pinocchio-like miracle, the lie could be made to come true.

In less than half an hour, Paintbrush appeared with actual bales of grass – long blades tied with twine into neat bundles, two of them. "Here," she said. "Start with these. There are two more. I'll go get them."

"What do I do with them?"

"Put them in the pickup, of course." And she started off again.

Allaby slid the bales onto the front-seat frame, and sure enough, they were a nearly perfect fit. She hadn't measured or anything (how did Immyos measure, he wondered), but here was a serviceable seat and the back of a seat, and there was Paintbrush going for two more. And when she came back and those were installed (she did a bit more tying so the bales wouldn't slip), she walked with Allaby over to Jenny and the baby. "Ready to go?" Allaby said.

"He's a nice boy," Jenny said, "and smart. Look, he tries to copy me. Ba ba ba ba ba."

"Ba," the baby said.

"Oh, she's got him to say something," Paintbrush said. "What does 'ba' mean?"

"Nothing," said Allaby. "Just ba." To Jenny he said, "We'd better go. I don't want to have to use the lights to get back here."

"Okay, but let me show Paintbrush this. Pa pa pa pa pa." But the baby took his eyes off Jenny, looked at his mother, smiled, chuckled and drooled a little. "He can do it. He did it a minute ago."

"It's the same as 'ba'," Allaby said, "just unvoiced. Let's go."

"What do you mean the same?" Jenny said, giving the baby a joggle and then standing up and handing him over to Paintbrush. "They're completely different sounds. Bye bye, Ba Ba," she said, fluttering her fingers in front of the baby's face. "Have to go with Pa Pa."

"Same lip movement," Allaby said. "It's just that the 'pee' sound is made in the mouth instead of the throat."

"It's pretty good, then, that he can tell the difference."

They were all walking to the pickup. "I suppose it is," Allaby said, "especially at his age. But it's not the same as two completely different vocalisations. Think of Ganymedians. They can't pronounce the letter 'pee'. All their 'pees' come out as 'bees'. That's one way you know you're talking to a Ganymedian."

Paintbrush said, "Are you two still talking about Skyman and ba ba?"

"Sort of, yes."

"Don't you think you ought to talk about what you're getting ready to do?"

"Of course we should," Allaby said. The truth was, he wasn't entirely sure what they were getting ready to do, and didn't like thinking about not being entirely sure. Any diversion right now was welcome. "Paintbrush," he said to Jenny, "thinks we ought to change the subject."

"Maybe we should," Jenny said as they reached the pickup, "because what you just said has made me realise something. You say you're not thinking clearly, but how could I have missed that?" Insofar as Jenny was capable of blanching, she did.

"Missed what?" Allaby said.

"I mean, I nearly died in a crash. Then I could breathe Earth air. Then you were suddenly alive, and I had to absorb that. Then came today, this really busy day – a great day, but busy. I just wasn't … The thing is, I don't need to contact Gus. I don't need to at all."

"But if he doesn't know that the air is—"

"That's just it. He does know. Of course he knows."

"Why? How?"

"Granddad," Paintbrush called, "they're about to go." With his stick, Gibbous levered himself to his feet and, still carrying the plucked chicken, ambled towards them.

"Gus has heard you."

"You mean when I was talking to the liner? But he can't have thought that was me. I didn't say anything specific, and anyway he thinks I'm dead."

"I'd call you a stupid Titanian if I didn't feel like an even stupider Martian. Who else on this planet would have your accent? He knows your voice, too. He knows you're alive, and if you're alive, the air has to be clear."

"I think you ought to get going," Gibbous said, glancing at the sun.

"Oh, Jenny. Maybe or maybe not. How can we know what Templeton knows or doesn't know? Everything's a mess now. As far as he can tell, there might be a force of Back-to-Earth Titanians – broadcasting from space, maybe."

"No, Peter."

"Why not?"

"The piracy clause? You've heard of that?"

"Okay, okay. But what are you saying? That you're not coming with me?"

"No, no, of course I'm coming. It just doesn't seem so urgent suddenly."

"Maybe not to you."

Paintbrush said, "Are you two arguing?"

"It's not a very good way to start," Gibbous said. "You're supposed to get them arguing."

"We're not arguing," Allaby snapped. "Let's go, Jenny."

"What?"

He'd done it again: wrong language. "I said let's go."

"So yes, let's go," she said. "After you."

"No, after you, Jenny. I'm piloting."

"All right, Peter. It's so comforting to be under the protection of a big, strong—"

"Get in, Jenny, please."

She slid in across the grass seat. "Hey, this isn't bad, Peter. My compliments to Paintbrush."

"She likes your, uh, bedding."

"I'm glad," Paintbrush said. "She's a good woman, your sister, and I want you to stop arguing with her."

"We really haven't been arguing. It's just the usual thing between brother and sister. You know."

"Oh yeah?" said Gibbous. "And did you talk to each other in those tones when you were children, living with your mother and the dark father? Tell me, which father did your mother like better?"

"Okay, Gibbous, we're going."

Paintbrush was right – he'd been picking arguments with Jenny. In fact, he knew he'd been touchy with everyone, and it was the fault of nothing other than the damned piracy clause. Besides the inconvenience and risk it was causing, it just meant that something had gone wrong, and when one thing goes wrong, other things follow. There was no connection, of course, between his finding out about the piracy clause and the dog getting shut in the pickup, except there seemed to be one, and he could have gladly done without either occurrence. He felt insecure now and, he had to admit to himself, a little fearful. He lifted and then negotiated the pickup slowly among the trees, put it on hover when he reached the edge of the plain, saw that there were still no new ships there and then shot over low and at top speed, coming down beside the wreck of the shuttle and scattering a small herd of cows and a flock of crows.

"You know what?" Jenny said as they landed. "We didn't bring the guns."

"Damn, I meant to pick them up when we ... I don't suppose we'll need them, but what's wrong with me, Jenny?"

"Peter, it's not just you. I forgot them, too. Do you think we should go back and—"

"No, hell. Let's get this over with." He put his hand on the comms controls and paused as he tried to plan what he was going to say. If there was anything resembling a silver lining in the piracy clause, it could be that it gave him an excuse for communicating only from the pickup – so he could leave the liner people to imagine that it was a way of getting through without revealing the positions of his own ships. And since he was now back at the pickup's original spot, he could pretend that a bigger ship had dropped him off for this chat. He would start, he decided, with a taunt about the liner's apparent inability to muster support from the other Mooner Pilgrims on Earth. It was an honest taunt, too – why in hell hadn't the others sent any outriggers yet? Then he'd get Jenny to say something, just to give an illusion of numbers and the likely presence of a Martian contingent. "Okay," he said to Jenny, and he turned on the comms.

Nothing happened. No sound. No light on the panel. No band-width display. No tracker tangents. Nothing. "Hello," he said uselessly. "Come in, come in, come in. I'll ... be ... fucked."

"It's not working," Jenny observed.

"It had better work." He switched the comms controls on and off and on and off. Nothing. "What's the matter with the fucking thing?" It was too much. He slammed the panel with both fists, which hurt enough to make his head reel, because he'd forgotten about his broken wrist. "Christ, what have I done?" Holding his arm, he sat back in the seat with his eyes closed, almost feeling his bones scraping. The pulsations went from fingertips to armpit and managed to create a quite separate, cold, leaden pain in his stomach. He couldn't help feeling that the comms, somehow, had attacked him. It had refused to operate, and when he'd insisted, it had attacked him. "God, Jenny, let this be a nightmare. Let me wake up now in my bed in my station. If I can wake up, I promise I'll never, ever image again on an Immyo reservation."

"Why don't we just try to fix the comms?" Jenny said. "Are you hurting a lot? Let me see your arm."

The pulsations began to reduce to throbs, and the pain in his stomach sank to his large intestine. He opened his eyes, a little disappointed to find that he wasn't in his bed in his station. He was looking out of a pickup window at the same stretch of plain he'd looked out on ages ago yesterday, searching for Gibbous in the heat haze. "You wouldn't be able to see anything," Allaby said, "and it's a bit better now."

"If you say so. Listen, Peter, you said you'd been working on the comms. What part exactly? Where?"

On second thought, it wasn't that much better. "Down where I thought it connected to the tracker." Without meaning to, he groaned, and then he pointed under the panel, beyond his knees. "Under there."

"Let me see," Jenny said. She opened the door on her side, half got out and then squirmed under the panel. "Where?"

He could feel her hair brushing the front of his leg, and when he moved the leg back, Paintbrush's grass scratched it. He said, "It's right at the end. It's got a cover on it. To open it, you push it to the right."

"You sure do," she said. "It's open now. You forgot to close it."

"I did?"

"Let me feel." She squirmed a little more. "Oh Jesus, Peter. It's soaking in there." He heard a sniff. "That's not dog pee, either. You splashed water around here, didn't you?"

That was it. Nothing he could ever do would ever be right. Nothing, ever, at all. And it was all such petty stuff – not noticing the dog, leaving a cover open, slamming the controls with a broken arm, failing to have heard of the piracy clause … If he was going to fail, why didn't he just go ahead and fail big?

"Okay, Jenny. Come up and close the door. We're going."

"Going where?" she said, squirming in reverse and then standing up, getting into her seat, tossing her hair back and pulling the door shut.

"We're going to get the guns."

"And then?"

"To the nearest working comms, goddamn it."

CHAPTER THIRTY-EIGHT

At about an hour after dark, they arrived at the edge of the liner's free-photon dome. Jenny had been flying low – just above the height of the tallest imaginable cow – and now she slid into hover, lowered the pickup to the top of the grass and hover-locked it. Gibbous, who was in the rear, leaned forward and said, "Can't she get any closer? We need to see if they've brought the kids out yet."

Allaby said, "We don't have to, Gibbous." He reached over, entered distance and direction and turned on the telescope, which in the Mighty Mons (top of the range, as Rachel had pointed out) gave a full image. On the panel was what was known as 'the stage', and on that a scale-model mid-section of the liner appeared, with tiny green-suited figures very, very slowly filing down the steps of an underbelly hatch. To Jenny he said, "At least that thing still works," and to Gibbous, "Look, they're bringing them out now, just as you said they would."

Nodding towards the image, Gibbous said, "That's not really there, I take it."

Allaby swept his good hand through it and then pointed ahead. "No, it's still over there."

"Pretty good trick. You skypeople … I don't know. You've got all this magic, but – I just don't know – you don't seem any smarter than ordinary people."

"Thanks for your confidence."

"You and that arm, for instance—"

Jenny said, "Do we go yet?"

"Wait," Allaby said, "until we can see what's happening."

"… how could you do such a stupid thing?"

It was about the three-dozenth time Gibbous had asked that. The first dozen were while he was resetting the wrist, putting a new splint on it and ordering Allaby not to use his arm for anything, even flying the pickup. The second dozen were while they were bolting down the chicken, and the rest were between there and here. Through the pain, the serious talking, the ravenous eating and the discovery in a rash of red bumps up his legs that

408

Paintbrush's grass seats were infested with mites, it had been hard enough for Allaby to maintain his anger, determination and spur-of-the-moment madness without also having to keep admitting that he'd been remarkably stupid to have lost his temper (at his several other stupidities, ultimately) and forgotten that his wrist was broken. Then it had been Gibbous's idea to invite himself along, and Allaby instantly realised that, like most of Gibbous's ideas, it was a good one (and another one Allaby hadn't thought of first) because Gibbous had a mystical significance to the liner people, had two working arms (making a total of five out of a possible six – a better percentage than three out of four) and had actually been to the liner before. Allaby's main qualm now – other than about whatever it was they were getting ready to do – was about leaving Paintbrush and the baby with the hostages. But the knife was there, the hostages were crippled by gravity, and Paintbrush, if anyone, could take care of herself.

The plan they'd settled on was vague and simple. They wanted to get to and take over the liner's comms suite. Since both Allaby and Jenny had travelled on liners, they knew approximately where the comms suite should be, and so all they had to do was fly to the liner, enter through the auxiliary hatch, dock the pickup, get out and go. In the absence of any auxiliary ships, there probably wouldn't be much happening around the docks. So it might be possible to sneak to the comms suite without being seen or at least noticed, and to make not being noticed slightly more likely, Allaby and Jenny had appropriated the hostages' uniforms. (Howls, tears, protests, curses, orders, gun-waving and a degree of embarrassment when it was revealed that Jenny was wearing nothing at all under her flight suit and that Rachel, for reasons beyond Allaby's ability of imagine, was wearing scarlet lace underwear. And while Rachel's uniform fit Jenny pretty well, Allaby went from clothes that were way too small to ones a size too big, and he had to turn up the trouser cuffs.) But in truth, they probably would be seen and noticed – Allaby's beard and the whole of Gibbous would be a little hard to hide – and would face armed resistance. Jenny and Allaby had guns themselves, though, Gibbous had his pipe, and they all had the advantage of being Earth-adapted. Otherwise, there was risk. But as Gibbous had pointed out once again, risk was what made war war.

"God," Jenny said as they watched the liner, "there are a lot of them, aren't there? You know that other bunch, Simon's bunch? I told you about Simon and the people who took me from my station – they emptied the satellite's primary school. They even snatched the tourists' kids. Then the bastards left the parents to die in the gym."

"Is she talking about the children?" Gibbous said.

"Yes."

"How come you never asked the man hostage about them, why they were doing that to them?"

"I did ask him. He more or less told me to mind my own business, remember?"

"Oh yeah. Did you ever ask the woman?"

"Yeah, but she went crazy. Two of the kids are hers."

"The man then – did he refuse to tell you anything else you asked?"

That was a point. Virtually every other question Jacob had been happy, almost proud, to answer. "No, come to think about it, he didn't."

"You know what that must mean?"

"What, Gibbous?" To Jenny, he said, "There could be a thirty or forty of them. And they're still coming."

Jenny said, "It's like watching some big black egg hatch."

Gibbous said, "He doesn't know."

"Doesn't know?"

"Doesn't know. He doesn't know why they're doing it, and he doesn't want to admit he doesn't know. It's like asking a Little Rimmer why he won't eat fat. He'll tell you to mind your own business or give you some gibberish, because he doesn't know."

Allaby said to Jenny, "Gibbous has an interesting theory."

"Look," Jenny said. "I think those were the last of the kids." She pointed at a few orange figures coming down from the hatch. "These are some more grown-ups now."

"Okay, let's wait a few minutes, let them get settled. You know, Gibbous thinks they themselves might not know why they're treating the children this way."

"Why would they do it then?"

"I don't … Jenny, they are religious fanatics. Anything could be true about them – the more illogical, the more likely."

"I was always taught that their logic was okay – it was just that it was based on wildly false axioms. And that's as far as I've ever thought about them and as fair as I want to be to them. Now, you – you were brought up a religious fanatic yourself, and I guess that exactly how they think bothers you more. To me they're just wrong and dangerous."

"I was brought up a Lazarine, Jenny. Compared to these people, the Lazarines are the Armstrong Academy of Science."

"Earth is Heaven, Venus is Hell? That kind of science?"

"Yeah, but I rejected all that a long time ago."

"You can say you've rejected it, but it's stuck in your psyche like a fossil in a rock."

Gibbous said, "Are you two arguing again? You sure do know how to pick the moment."

"We're not arguing. We're discussing religion."

"Bullshit. You know that I know that she's not really your sister, but I'm beginning to think it's worse than that. The way you two argue, it's like she's your wife. So do you have two wives now?"

"No. She's definitely not my wife. And that's the truth, Gibbous – I'll never lie to you or Paintbrush again."

"Well, even if she isn't your wife, she's something," Gibbous said.

"Okay, Gibbous. She used to be something. But she's not any more, not since Paintbrush happened. And she wasn't flying around looking for me. In fact, she thought she'd never see me again because she thought I was dead, and I never expected to see her again either, especially not here. But she knows I love Paintbrush now and not her, and it doesn't bother her at all – to tell you a little more truth than you actually need."

"Are you going to tell Paintbrush all that? That is, if we survive what we're going to do now."

"How can I tell her? You got going with the light father and the dark father, and Paintbrush fell in love with the whole story – you're too good at what you do, Gibbous. She likes Jenny, and she likes the idea of having a sister-in-law and the baby having an aunt. If I told her now, she'd never—"

Jenny said, "Peter, what do you think's going on now?"

"... speak to me again."

"Hm," Gibbous said, and changed the subject. "Is that all?"

"All what?"

"All the kids. There were more than that the other night."

"I don't know, Gibbous. It looks like that's all."

"Look at them," Jenny said, tapping her finger on the stage. There, the green figures, their backs to the telescope, were seated in orderly columns and rows ... of course they were drugged – you could never otherwise get so many children to sit that still ... and it was raining on them. Showering. They were under the liner and under a shower just wide enough to soak

411

every one of them. The adults – there were maybe ten – were all standing outside the range of the shower. A couple of them were watching the children, but most were looking around, mainly gazing over the free-photon-lit plain. Allaby kept focusing in until just one of the children was sitting hunched on the stage, water pouring over him or her. The child was perceptibly shivering but was otherwise motionless. Allaby slowly moved the telescope to the right, stopping at child after child, and the picture was the same: some were shivering and all were hunched, still and dripping.

Jenny said, "Aren't there Earth diseases you can get from being wet and chilled?"

Allaby asked Gibbous that.

"Of course. They could catch colds."

Allaby had had colds before – who hadn't? The common cold was one of a few human diseases that, even in completely artificial and controlled atmospheres, had never been eradicated. On the other hand, in a controlled atmosphere, the temperature was never below comfortable. And it certainly never rained (only Martians had weather). "Are colds all they'd get?"

"Well," Gibbous said, "if the cold gets in your lungs, that's bad. You can eventually cough to death. And anybody who sat out in the rain on a chilly night like this could get that kind of cold. Where's that rain coming from, anyway?"

"It's not really rain, Gibbous. Just water from inside the liner."

"Why are they doing that to them?"

"That's what we don't know, and according to you, they don't know either. Jenny, Gibbous says they can get a fatal lung disease."

"Then why are they doing that to them? Is it just an elaborate way of killing them? And why kidnap them just to wipe them out?"

"I don't know, but I think it's time, Jenny. Gibbous, you ready?"

"I'm not sure for what. But yes."

"Okay, Jenny," Allaby said. "Stay out of the photon dome as long as you can."

"Why? They can see us anyway."

"They ought to be able to see us, but they don't seem to. Or don't care."

"Okay, Cap'n," Jenny said. The pickup rose until it was level with the top arc of the dome, and then she shot it ahead until it was about a metre above the dome and a kilometre directly above the liner. She hovered.

"Tilt the nose," Allaby said, adding, "Damn these mites." He scratched. "They're strip-mining my legs."

"Concentrate," Jenny said.

"Ow. Okay. Sorry. Jenny, do you see that little orange dot down there, almost right in the middle of the liner's back?"

"No."

"There." He pointed.

"I still can't … Turn on the telescope."

"No that distorts. You can't fly by telescope. You know that. Look." He moved his hand so that the back of his forefinger was right in front of Jenny's nose.

"That tiny thing?"

"Yeah, that. You've got to hit it with the hatch beam. Here, I'll turn the beam on now."

"At least," Jenny said, "I'm flying a pickup. There was a point when I thought I was going to have to get a shuttle in there."

"If you'd tried that and you'd docked it as well as you ended up landing it, we probably wouldn't have a liner to worry about now."

"Very funny," Jenny said. "Have you ever tried to land a shuttle?"

"Of course not. But I don't think I'd be tempted to switch off while I was still twenty metres up."

"The read-out said I was down."

"Really? And what did your rear monitor say?"

"It was hard to tell, but the read-out—"

"You two are arguing again," Gibbous observed.

"No. Gibbous," Allaby said. "We're skypeople, and we're talking about flying."

"Sure you are."

"Jenny, Gibbous thinks we argue too much."

"We do. Are you ready? I am." She threw the pickup into full forward, and they plunged towards the orange dot.

"Uh, too fast, Jenny."

"This is a pickup. I can fly a pickup."

"But you've got to get in a position to aim the hatch beam …" Then Allaby stopped. Talking was pointless. He'd insulted her piloting, and now the only thing he could do was brace himself, and he could only do that with one arm. Jenny didn't seem to be trying to aim the beam at all. She was just hurtling. He shut his eyes in the instant before he expected the pickup to be turned into a flyspot on the top of the liner, but when he opened his eyes a few seconds later, the pickup was inside a big empty

413

docking bay, zipping past shuttle ports, outrigger ports and runabout ports and towards the pickup ports at the end. Jenny swung straight into one, stopped with a centimetre to spare and clamped the clampers.

"Okay?" she said.

"God," said Gibbous, "that was exciting."

With the last molecules of breath still in his chest, Allaby said, "Was it?"

"Yeah – so fast, and the way the thing opened up just in time. Was that the kind of flying you two were arguing about?"

Allaby inhaled, exhaled and said, "You could say that."

"Well, that was some result. You know, Allaby, from what I've seen of skypeople so far, there are some things that are terrible – this light, for one, and the food and some other things – and some I could get used to. Flying around in a pickup – God, we went faster than we could fall."

Allaby tried to remember if he'd been pressed against the back of his seat or gone through a moment of weightlessness, and indeed, he could remember both. "It did, Gibbous. It did."

"Are you just going to keep sitting there?" Jenny said. She was already out of the pickup and bending to look back inside.

"Jenny, wait. Get back in."

"What's the matter?"

"I need to catch my breath, and my legs are a little, uh …"

"Itchy? Weak? What?"

"Jenny, before you get back in, look around. From here, the whole bay looks empty. Is it?"

She stood up for a few seconds and then looked back inside. "It seems to be."

"You'd think there would be somebody around – some guards or something. Jenny, get back in so we can talk."

She slid in and shut the door. "Do you think they'd be listening to us?"

"And watching, probably. But if we keep our voices down, they shouldn't be able to hear us in here. And by the way, Jenny – you might like to know that Gibbous admires your piloting."

She peered out through the front and side windows, as though she expected someone to jump out at the pickup. Her hand was on her gun. "Where are they?" she said.

"And I agree," Allaby said.

"Agree about what?"

"I think you just did a pretty spectacular job of piloting."

"Oh, come on, Peter," she said, still glancing around. "I scared you shitless. Hell, I scared myself, but you made me mad."

"Shh, Jenny. I'm sorry. I should have known the shuttle would be a touchy subject. Gibbous really was impressed, though. He said it was exciting."

"He doesn't know how close we came ... Maybe he imagines we're infallible or something."

"I promise you, Jenny, whatever else he might imagine, he doesn't imagine that. I've lost count of the number of times tonight he's called me stupid."

"What for?"

"For breaking my arm again, of course."

"That was stupid," she said. "You know, I can't believe they've left this whole bay unguarded. They have to know there's at least one pickup tuned to their hatch spectrum going around loose.

"You know what?" Gibbous said, also peering out of windows. "The last time I was here this place was full of people."

Allaby glanced over his shoulder. "When you were first getting into the pickup, you mean?"

"Yeah, of course. There were people all around, a lot of them on them on their knees. Right along that long path there." He indicated the metal ramp walkway and the distant door at the end of it. "It was hard to get past them."

"I guess they were seeing you off, you holy man you. It'll help if they keep thinking that, as long as some are still dropping to their knees."

"Not all of them were then. Some of them were doing other things. It seems strange that now there's no one here at all."

"That's what we were just saying."

"Come on," Jenny said. "It's creepy sitting here. What have we got to talk about? Let's go." She started to open the door.

Gibbous, who'd been looking at something through the rear window, turned around and said, "You know, this could be a trap."

Allaby put his hand on Jenny's arm. "Wait," he said. "Gibbous thinks we're about to walk into a trap."

Jenny pulled the door shut, but she said, "Look, there are a thousand of them and three of us. Why trap us? They could just gun us down."

Allaby put that to Gibbous, who said, "Allaby, use your head. Have you already forgotten your great plan? They think there are bands of warriors from that skyplace of yours coming to attack them. That's who the trap's for."

In truth, Allaby hadn't thought of that at all. When the pickup's comms wouldn't work and he'd slammed his broken arm on the controls, he'd squashed forever that particular plan. He'd forgotten it, abandoned it, annulled it – it had never existed. He was starting all over. But, of course … he'd neglected to send notice of this to the people in the liner.

Gibbous said, "If you look out that way" – he pointed at the rear window – "you can see part of the big hole up there where we flew in. I assume they could close that if they wanted to. But they haven't. Maybe they're waiting for your ships to arrive. Of course, the people in your ships would be stupid to fly in here, because the liner people would probably be able to destroy them all at once. But when you've got skypeople dealing with skypeople, maybe stupidity is taken for granted."

"What's he saying?" Jenny said.

"Just a second," said Allaby, turning and leaning his arm on the back of the seat. "Gibbous, it's not so stupid at all. The pickup would be the only ship with this liner's hatch spectrum in its beam. So it would lead the attack. The other ships would follow immediately and dock, and hundreds of Earth-adapted, uh, warriors would pour out and take over the unsuspecting liner."

"Peter, tell me what you're talking about."

"Except the liner isn't unsuspecting," Allaby went on. "It just wants to look unsuspecting. That's why these people went ahead with their routine with the children. Why they're pretending they haven't seen us. They're just waiting for my other ships to arrive. When they do – I mean, if they did – you're right, their plan is get them all in here and destroy them somehow, or seal off the bay and fill it with gas or something."

"I think I understand most of that," Gibbous said. "So now that your ships actually haven't arrived, they're going to start to think they've been outsmarted, that the ships are going to attack them from somewhere else. They'll be scared and won't know what to do next. You know what, Allaby? I think you've got them."

"Except for one thing, Gibbous. I don't have any ships. It's just a made-up story."

"Well, what isn't? Anyway, it's better than that – it's a story you let them make up themselves. People believe their own stories much better than they believe anybody else's. You could announce right now that there weren't any more ships, and every person in this liner would say you were lying."

"Peter," Jenny said, "if you don't tell me what you're talking about, I'm getting out of this pickup and walking down that ramp."

"Jenny, wait. How are you at a Mooner accent?"

"I don't know, Peter. I never tried. Ugh."

"Not even when you're making fun of them?"

"I guess I could make a Martian chuckle, but a Mooner wouldn't buy it. Is that what you've been talking about?"

"Um, indirectly. Look, I did a linguistics project once on the dialect of the East Armstrong trading community—"

"You did? You never mentioned—"

"... and I can do that accent pretty well. So when we go in there let me do most of the talking. We're wearing the uniforms, and those market people sometimes have beards. Well, moustaches anyway. So the story is that we're from another Back-to-Earther colony ship. Do you know where any of the others are?"

"China, Australia, South—"

"China. That'll do. We flew over to help this ship, found the hordes of Titanians—"

"Not the hordes of Titanians, not them again. You intend to go in there talking like a petty crook and telling them about hordes of Titanians? They'll never believe—"

"They already believe. They believe in them absolutely."

"How do you know?"

"Never mind. They just do. Gibbous and I worked it out. Now, here's what happened." He cleared his throat and continued in an East Armstrong accent. "We found the Titanians, who've been here long enough to be Earth-adapted, at a big base settlement with a fleet of cruisers and outriggers, tried to spy on them, got caught, fought our way out – explains the broken arm, you see – and stole the pickup, bringing Gibbous, who'd also been captured. As the Holopark Man, he means something to us Pilgrims. Too bad we weren't also able to save Rachel and Jacob, who are being tortured and truth-drugged for information about the liner and the whole Mooner – uh, Lunar – expedition."

"Hah," she said.

"What?"

"Nothing, Just hah. Hah, hah, hah."

"Jenny, I'm serious. And, oh yeah, we were chosen for this mission because we're Earth-adapted ourselves, and the reason we are is that before we converted to Jesus we used to be involved at the terrestrial end of an illegal mahogany operation. You know, East Armstrong accent and all? I think I'm beginning to catch on to this storytelling business."

"God almighty, Peter. I know they're Mooners and religious nuts, but even they won't swallow—"

"Yes they will. Well, maybe they will. We can only try, can't we? Come on. I think we're really ready to go now. And by the way, we can't have a Martian accent either. If you can't do Mooner – and you can't – you can't speak at all."

CHAPTER THIRTY-NINE

To Jenny, the eeriest part of the whole adventure – from the time she left the satellite to being 'captured' by the disgusting boy to crashing the shuttle and getting rescued by her dead ex-lover and all the way through to coming here and diving suicidally down that hatch (she was amazed, in retrospect, at how deeply Peter could still irritate her when he wanted to) – the eeriest part was, by far, this walk along this ramp. While she veered between laughing at and shuddering at Peter's preposterous idea and struggled with the fact that he was actually prepared to go through with it, the door at the end of the ramp seemed never to get any closer. Not that she wanted it to. Not now. Not now that she had to be a mute East Armstronger while Peter – Allaby the Innocent, she'd called him once – tried to pull a confidence trick on a liner full of armed nutters. Today had started out so well, too, and tomorrow could have been the same – waking up in the woods and looking forward to another long interlude at the river.

But no. Instead, they clanged along the endless metal ramp. Well, the old man's stick clanged. Otherwise, Peter was still wearing the soft hooves that his little wife had laced and tied him into, Jenny had Rachel's shoes on – which, because they were a size too small, required her to take short, gingerly steps – and the old man was not only barefoot but looked as though he'd never worn shoes in his life. So their collective feet on the metal ramp made a soft rattling and rippling sound that was punctuated by the steady clang of the stick. Normally, Jenny would never have noticed these sounds, but since they'd decided not to speak until they were through the door (and she herself wouldn't be able to speak even then) and since the enormous docking bay was empty and echoey and since the ramp was deceptively long, the noise was enough to keep her from getting her thoughts straight and to make the door and whatever was behind it even more sinister than it probably needed to be: *kaluk, kaluk, kaluka, clang, kaluk, kaluk* …

But after a whole lot more *kaluka-clanging*, the door finally reached them (to Jenny, suddenly, it wasn't as if they'd walked along the ramp at all, but as if the ramp had somehow passed under them, like some slow conveyor belt). The door was supposed to open now, but of course – of course – it didn't. And there was no handle or anything to open it with. Had any of them imagined it would oblige that easily? Jenny hadn't. Peter, though, looked a little surprised. He turned to the old man and then to her. She shrugged. "I guess you'll have to knock," she said softly.

"Jenny, they're looking at us and listening to us right this minute. What good would—"

"Just knock," she whispered through unmoving lips, "and you've already forgotten your stupid accent."

Peter turned to the whole empty bay and the presumed tracking sensors, did an open-armed "why?" gesture and turned back to the door. Then he tapped three or four times. A mere human fist on such thick metal didn't make much sound, but it seemed that just doing it was enough, as though the people inside had been waiting for him to be polite. The door slid open, and the three of them stepped through it into a long corridor. About twenty metres away in each direction were half a dozen people in uniform pointing guns.

"Hiya, Pilgrims," Peter said nasally, while making a little wave.

One of the men in the group standing behind them said, "Who are you?" causing Jenny and Peter to swing around.

"Just a fellow Pilgrim, Pilgrim, come to give you a hand."

Jenny was glad suddenly that Peter was supposed to do all the talking. She'd have struggled to lie convincingly, and it meant she could concentrate on looking the people over: two women, three men, one of them very short and fat for a Mooner; all pretty young except the man who was doing the talking.

"Where are you from?" he said. The Back-to-Earthers had a military-type ranking system, and this man was the one with the busiest-looking epaulettes and collar.

"Thirty-fourth Street East, and I'm at your service, Pilgrims."

Jenny had to admit that Peter was doing the accent pretty well. He really was a talented linguist, and he had probably nuanced it right to 34th Street East and maybe some particular corner of it.

"No, I don't mean your home street in Armstrong, if it is in Armstrong – we're all Far Siders in this ship. No, I meant, how did you get here? Where did you come from to get here?"

"Long story, Pilgrim. Rough story, too. If you lowered your guns, it would make telling it a lot more congenial. And look, we've got him with us, too." Then he said something to the old man, and the old man, who had been facing the people in the other direction (Jenny glanced back and could see that two of them were on their knees already) turned around.

"I know," said the spokesman, "but, but … did you just now speak to him?"

Jenny detected a unspoken "Shit!" from Peter and saw him just stop his eyes from rolling. "I did. Yes, I did."

"In his language?" The man was no longer pointing his gun. No one was. Guns were either back in their holsters or hanging at the ends of arms. "How do you know his language?"

"I just … I just do. It, uh, came to me in a dream, Pilgrim."

"When?"

"The other night. Uh, last night. While we were being held by the goddamned … excuse me … by the damned, uh, darned Titanians. I was asleep, and this man here came into my dream speaking his language. And I could understand it. He told me where that old pickup was and how to steal it back and how to get to him to save him. I woke up and did all that, and when I got to him, I discovered I still knew his language. Goddamned miracle, if you ask me."

"Wait a minute. You were held by the Titanians?"

He'd said the Titanians. Peter was right – they did believe in them.

"Yeah, at their big base. They broke my arm trying to get me to squeal." He held his arm up. "But I didn't." Peter then started talking to the old man, who peered at the officer, nodded and stroked his beard.

As Peter kept on in Immyo, the officer said to Jenny, "Were you held by the Titanians, too?

She nodded.

"For how long? And how? I mean, how did they capture you? And where is their base?"

She had opened her mouth, not knowing how she could keep anything from coming out of it, when Peter said, "Funny things, miracles. You don't get them for free, you know. Ever since I've been able to speak this man's language, my companion here hasn't said a word. I swear, Pilgrims, she's been struck dumb."

Jenny silently thanked Peter but didn't know which was more absurd – his stories or the fact that these people seemed to be swallowing them. When Peter claimed to have learned Immyo overnight and via a dream, while being held by the Titanians, the ranking officer here behaved as if learning a language by dream was something people actually could do. What interested him more were the Titanians, even though they didn't seem to interest him as much as they should have, given that he did seem to believe they existed.

"… never heard of that," the officer was saying. "Have any of you?" he said to the people beside him. Mutters of "no", shrugs, shaking heads. "The thing about miracles," he went on, "is that they're free. A miracle is something God gives us. That's the whole point."

"I don't know," Peter said. "All I know is both things happened at the same time. If it's not a miracle paid for by a curse, then it's one hell of a coincidence – although I have to say it's been so damn pleasant not arguing with her today that it may have been a case of a double miracle."

Jenny had to stop herself from laughing at that. She stifled a snort under an expression of hurt and kicked Peter in the back of the leg.

The officer said, "We seriously need to debrief you – and him, now that you can translate for us – and there's no point in doing it out here. We'll take you to my office."

This was where being struck dumb became a problem. Jenny couldn't be seen even to whisper to Peter, and now that she was landed in the spirit of the whole concoction, it occurred to her that the two of them should pretend not to be Earth-adapted, saving that information for an emergency. The whole group was, in its shambling way, moving now – towards the officer's office, she presumed – and it would take more than a dream to explain why she and Peter weren't hobbling along as painfully as everyone else. Of course, it had been Peter's idea to have them Earth-adapted as a byproduct of illegal mahogany trading, but added to the overnight language-learning, the hordes of Titanians and miracles paid for with curses, it was all getting beyond the gullibility potential of even these Far Side bumpkins. They'd probably never even heard of the illegal mahogany trade, and so that would have to be explained, too. Hell, they'd probably never heard of mahogany.

Then Jenny remembered that they'd been watched as they walked along the ramp. How had they walked? There'd been no striding – that was for sure – because Jenny's shoes were too small and also because she and Peter were keeping pace with the old man. So these people wouldn't have noticed that they were Earth-adapted, and if they didn't expect … She gently elbowed Peter in the side, intending to show him how she was walking, imitating the man right in front of her. But Peter only made an involuntary yip, looked at her with surprise and held his side. She'd nudged him in his cracked ribs, of course.

"What the fuck," he said in an undertone. "What are you trying ..."

At least she'd got his attention. She did an exaggerated version of the unadapted walk – the shaky knees, the heavy breathing, the stumbling, plodding gait, as if the walker had woken up this morning with a pair of elephant's feet. But just as Peter seemed on the verge of understanding what she was getting at, the officer stopped, turned around and raised his arms. "Look," he said, "all of you don't have to come with us. These people are obviously here to help. So just Sam and Sarah are all I need. The rest of you get back to your stations or wherever."

There was a ripple of protest, and one of the women said, "But we want to—"

"I know you do. But you and everybody on the ship will hear everything later. Now go back." You'd think that, in the struggle against the demon gravity, something as subtle as disappointed slumping wouldn't show, but two or three of the people did visibly slump as they began to trudge off one way or the other along the corridor. The officer, along with the two who must have been Sarah and Sam (he was the unusually short, fat one), waited for them to get a certain distance away before he said to Peter (he didn't even look at Jenny, as if assuming that since she couldn't talk, she couldn't hear either), "I wonder how long it's really going to take. It's painful, and it's painful to watch the others."

Peter said, "What's pai—" just before Jenny kicked his ankle. She felt it was urgent now that they not be Earth-adapted. She wasn't sure exactly why, but she knew it was important, was going to be important. Peter gave her a puzzled look, and she stared back as meaningfully as she knew how.

"I'm talking about the adaptation process," the officer said as they began to move again. "How are you finding it so far?"

"Oh, we're already—" Peter said, receiving another kick from Jenny. But when he looked at her this time, light slowly appeared in his eyes. "... already able to walk up straight," he said deliberately and more to Jenny than to the officer. "We've got over the stoop."

She'd done it. She'd reached the inside of Peter's head without using any spoken language – just jabs, kicks and intense looks. It was part of the way animals communicated, and it was too hard. Words were a pretty good invention, she thought.

"Well, that's progress," the officer said. "I'm sorry to say most of the people here haven't reached that stage yet. My office is up this way." He turned everyone left at a crossroads of corridors, and they all struggled on – all except the old man, of course, who was looking like some kind of midget sprinter in comparison to the five people around him. Just after they'd turned the corner, he looked over at Peter, watched him hobble along, tapped Peter's leg with his stick and said something. With a glance at Jenny, Peter apparently explained, and the old man smiled and nodded in her direction. Jenny couldn't help feeling a flush of pride then – having the old man indicate that she'd done something smart was one of the best compliments she'd ever had. Right at the moment she couldn't have said why, but she must have been soaking up the impression, through Peter, that the old man (she was going to have to start thinking of him by his name) was really the one in charge here.

All six of them finally stopped at a door with a raised sign on it saying 'Chief Purser' still visible under one slap of white paint. Below that was a newly printed nameplate: 'Reverend Colonel Ezekiel B. Baldwin, Commander of Security'. As they went in, Peter said loudly, "Ah, you're the Colonel Baldwin they told me to report to. That was lucky – meeting you right off like that."

"Who told you?" the colonel said, easing into the swivel chair at his desk and indicating various other seats for everyone else. Sarah and Sam sat in a couple of straight-backed chairs, and Jenny sank into a sofa with Peter on her right and the old man (damn it, start thinking of him as Gibbous) on her left. He wasn't sitting, exactly, but was propped on the sofa's arm and leaning forward on his stick. Sam, as he had been all along, seemed unable to take his eyes off Gibbous. Sarah, on the other hand – she was a high-cheekboned, sleek, blonde woman, elegant for a Mooner, much less a Far Sider – couldn't seem to get her eyes off Peter.

"The officers," Peter said, "who sent us. More are coming, too – a lot more after I tell them the inside stuff on the Titanians. Pretty smart of those guys to jump the gun like that, don't you think? Pretty underhanded, too. But if I can use your comms, I can—"

"Well, you can try," the colonel said. "Obviously something's getting through, or you wouldn't have been able to respond. It's encouraging, even though it's too bad you got captured."

Peter said nothing, just gave Jenny a sharp look. The question was clear: "Aren't *their* comms working either?"

"It's so hit-and-miss," the colonel said, "with the satellites out the way they are."

The Earth comms satellites were out? I'll be damned, Jenny thought. There was only one way for those things to be out – to be jammed by a functioning EHQS. Gus had jammed the satellites, and now none of the invading ships could be in direct touch with each other. What they could do, though, was …

"I mean, all we can do – and I'm sure you've been having the same problems – is get the Moon to relay messages, but there's such chaos there now …"

Chaos on the Moon? There hadn't been chaos on the Moon the day before yesterday, when all the ships were still reporting to their leaders.

"… but somebody somewhere got our message and got it to your ship. Which one is yours, by the way?"

"Oh, it's over there, that way," Peter said, pointing in one direction and then in another, obviously having lost his bearings inside the liner. "In China. It's in China."

"Chi— Ah yes, that was a famous ancient nation. But where was it? Where is your ship, actually?"

"I think it's called Asia."

"Oh yes, of course. I know. All Armstrongers in that one. I should have figured that was the one you were from."

Jenny could hardly believe the luck they were having. The China ship just happened to be the one full of Armstrongers, a lot of them probably talking the way Peter was talking.

Then Sarah spoke – it was the first time Jenny had heard her speak, and her voice was strikingly deep and flat. "Four of the seven ships are from Armstrong. Have we asked him his name yet or why he's so dishevelled or what in creation those things are on his feet?"

"Those?" Peter pointed down. He shrugged. "I had to make those this morning. The Titanians took my shoes away. They took his away, too," he said, pointing at Gibbous's feet, "but he doesn't seem to mind as much I did."

"He doesn't look to me," Sarah said, "as if he's ever worn shoes. And he was barefoot the first time he was here. Colonel Baldwin, really. I mean, aren't you in the least bit suspicious of these people?"

"Why should I – or you or anybody – be suspicious of them? There would be no reason—"

Sarah said, "This one claims to have learned a language in a dream. Have you ever heard of anyone learning a language in a dream? Have you ever tried to learn another language? Do you know how hard that is? I studied Ancient French once, and it took years."

Jesus, Jenny thought, how did anyone with any basic sense find her way into this ship, into this movement in the first place? But maybe a touch of basic sense was why the colonel seemed to value her, and maybe her scepticism would persuade Peter to be a little less outrageous – or at least not to invent any more impossibilities.

But Sarah's task was obviously an uphill one, because the next thing the colonel said was, "Do you accept, Sarah, that this person here is the Holopark Man?"

"Yes, maybe he is. People seem to think he is. I never actually saw the Holopark Man myself, but everyone who did says, yes, that he is."

"Do you also accept, then, that he's a miracle?"

"Well, I've always thought of a miracle as not so much a person as an action, but—"

"A miracle can be anything," Colonel Baldwin said. "Don't you believe that Jesus himself was a miracle?"

"Well," Sarah said, "you could say that Jesus raising the dead and walking on water were miracles, but Jesus himself—"

"Splitting hairs," Peter said suddenly, and if he'd said it any louder or more abruptly, it would have been a shout of distress. Even Gibbous, who couldn't understand what anybody was saying, jumped a little and gave him a look. "He's the Holopark Man all right, and my companion and I are only here to help both him and all of you. It's the Titanians we've got to do something about. Never mind the miracles right now."

"See, Sarah?" Colonel Baldwin said, more or less contradicting what he'd said a few seconds ago. "Practicalities. It's the practicalities that count."

Then, for the first time, Sam spoke: "But the Titanians – aren't they Pilgrims, too? Shouldn't they and we be—"

"Pilgrims maybe," the colonel said, "but who knows what goes on on Titan? We can't even see the damned place. It's spinning away out there in the stars, spinning around Jupiter – Saturn, I mean, Saturn – about hundred thousand times the distance, maybe a million, between here and the Earth – I mean here and the Moon – and they could be doing anything. Okay, we keep in touch, but they go away and get sunblocked sometimes for months on end, and who knows what's happening out there then? Who even knows what's happening when they're not sunblocked? It takes them damned near a year at best just to get where we are already. Don't you think they'd jump the gun – as our friend here put it – if they could? They know about the forty-year rule and waiting for the sign, but they have a year's disadvantage. Anyway, why would they care about the discrimination we're suffering on the Moon or on Mars or anywhere else? They're Titanians, Sam, ordinary pig-headed Titanians. Pilgrims has nothing to do with it."

"I couldn't," Peter said loudly, "have said it better myself." Then he said something to Gibbous, who gave a little smile and said something back. Peter blinked and nodded, almost as if in obedience.

At the same time, Sam was saying, "But shouldn't we, at least check with Moon command to see if we—"

"Moon command is in Armstrong. We're Far Siders, in case you've forgotten – no offence, friend," Colonel Baldwin said, nodding at Peter, "but we can't even see the Earth from where we live, much less directly communicate with it – and with even the Moon comms satellites out we've got no idea what our own, our native, command is thinking or doing. Anyway, Sam, it's hard enough right now to get through even to Armstrong. If you want to try it, be my guest, and if you do get through …"

Gus, Jenny thought. All this is Gus's doing. He's running his own counter-revolution, using what these people think is a dead EHQS to completely fuck up their comms. It serves them right in more ways than one – mainly for being so obsessed with EHQS as a kind of Gomorrah, all of whose inhabitants deserved to go to Hell by way of a free-fall Purgatory. There had been practical reasons, too, she supposed, but practicalities, whatever the colonel might say – whatever anybody might say – were only ever props for some particular world view.

"… in fact, what we need to do – and I think I'm going to put this to the general – is what these people have had the enterprise to do and simply physically move to …"

In fact, Jenny thought, Gus has it all in hand. He knows Earth air is breathable, because he's heard Peter's voice. So what in hell are we doing in this liner? We didn't need to come, and we don't need to do anything now. Anyway, there was never an actual plan – we've been making it up as we've gone along. What we really ought to do is get back in our little grassy pickup and fly to our woods-and-river idyll. If we can. And of course we can't.

"… main trouble is that we don't have any small ships – except for that pickup you were able to rescue, my friend – but I don't know how far …"

What had made them do it? Curiosity? Heroics? Frustration? Fear? A common sense of failure? She didn't know. It was a question all three of them ought to ponder, but Jenny – being struck dumb and thus free from having to take much part in the present proceedings (Peter was busy pretending and talking, and Gibbous didn't have an inkling of what was going on) – Jenny was the only one with the mental latitude to ponder it.

Nevertheless, when the colonel finally paused in his ramblings (Sarah had been sighing and raising her eyes to the ceiling), it was Peter who thought of at least one question that really needed to be put: "By the way, Colonel Baldwin, how are you getting on with the children? We've been doing pretty well ourselves."

"The children? What chi—? Oh, you mean the Garden of Eden eliminations. We were ordered not to think of them as children, not to even mention the idea. Weren't you ordered—"

"I don't think he's ever had any orders," said Sarah. "I don't think he's—"

"Oh yeah," Peter said, "But ours are such lippy little rascals, it's hard not to—"

"Lippy?" Sarah said. "What does that mean?"

"Well, you know. Impudent, I guess."

"How can they be impudent?"

Goddamn, Peter, Jenny thought, gritting her teeth and glaring at him – they're drugged. You know that. They're probably kept drugged, all the time. What you've got to find out, Peter, is why, and being stupid isn't the way to do it.

"I think what he means," Sam said to Sarah, "is right at the beginning, when they were still children. Ours were a bit – what did he say? – lippy, too. In fact, a lot of them were little terrors."

"It didn't sound to me," Sarah said, "as if that was what he meant."

Peter said, "Oh, but it is, it is. And there's nobody lippier than an East Armstrong kid having to do something it doesn't want to do. Anyway, Colonel, what kind of success are you having now?"

"Don't tell him anything,' Sarah said. "I think he's, well, I think he's …"

She hesitated, and the colonel said firmly, "Sarah, that's enough. Let us talk. They've been through a lot to get to us: held prisoner, that one struck dumb, this one wounded. And he can speak to the Holopark Man. Can you imagine how useful that's going to be? The least I can do is answer some of his questions first. So, yes, thank God, we're down to eighty-three per cent, and we've been outdoing the other ships.

Sarah's natural elegance was suddenly marred by a scarlet blush, probably from suppressed fury, and Jenny thanked God again for the colonel's combination of middle-management dimness and superstitious credulity. But what the hell did they mean by the children not being children any more?

Then a fiftyish man with even more decoration on his shoulders materialised beside the colonel's desk. There was a knock to her left, and Jenny turned her head to see that Gibbous had just used his stick to keep from falling off the sofa. In fact, Jenny herself hadn't realised there were holocomms in this office, and this sudden appearance had also given her a start.

"Colonel Baldwin?" the officer said.

"Yes sir?"

The colonel, Sarah and Sam were all standing and holding salutes.

The officer returned the salutes and said, "At ease. Sit down. Are you okay? I see our visitors are still with you. Would you introduce them to me?"

"Certainly, General. They're from the Asia ship – Armstrongers, you know. You've met the Holopark Man already, and – would you believe? – these two have just rescued him from the Titanians. They were captured themselves and escaped."

"Well done," the general said, as though he somehow doubted that it really was well done. "And tell me their names, Colonel."

Sarah said, "He hasn't asked."

But the last word was lost under the loud voice of Peter saying. "Pete Labbaly. And this is my companion Jennifer Morero. We're at your service."

"And your ranks? Your epaulettes are a bit dirty and hard to see."

These Back-to-Earthers had their own peculiar insignia system, and Jenny had no idea what rank Rachel was and she, Jenny, was now supposed to be. She didn't think Peter knew either. How could they ever have scoffed at the Back-to-Earthers for being half-cocked?

But once again, Baldwin came to their rescue: "They're both second lieutenants, sir."

Rachel was a lieutenant? An officer? Rachel?

"I don't know," the general said, "what the discipline in your ship is like, but here when we refer to ourselves or anybody else, we always include rank. Now, I'm the Reverend Major General Michael Mitchell, this ship's commander."

"Really glad to meet you, sir," Peter said, doing a circular waving motion followed by a pointed finger, a gesture that Jenny could actually remember having seen in East Armstrong. He was so far into his character now that she wondered if he could ever be Peter again.

"And we salute here, too."

"Where's my manners?" Peter said, and he made a quick salute that, a little lower and a little quicker, would have put an eye out.

"And we stand at attention when we salute."

"Oh, sorry," Peter said, and he stood up and put his feet together and his hand to his forehead.

"Hold it there," said the general. "What about you, Lieutenant?"

Jenny actually started to look around to see who he might mean when she realised it was her. She'd become so unused to being directly addressed that she'd almost forgotten she had a physical presence. So she stood up and saluted, too.

The general sharply returned the salutes and said, "Okay. Finally. At ease. Sit down."

Jesus, Jenny reminded herself as she sat, this isn't even a real army. These people – a bunch of religious fanatics, thieves and murderers (and child murderers at that, if eighty-three per cent meant what she suspected it meant) – are just playing soldiers. On the other hand, they had managed to pull off simultaneous coups at every non-sunblocked station in the Solar System. That would take a bit of discipline – real military discipline.

"Now," said the general, "I'll get to the point. It's about these Titanians. It's already been reported to me – though, strangely, not by you, Colonel Baldwin – that our guests have actually been in the Titanian camp."

"Sir," Baldwin said, "I was just getting ready to bring them up to your office. First, I just wanted to—"

"Of course, Colonel, and never mind for now. Anyway, I'm not in my office. I'm in the comms suite, as you could tell if you bothered to look behind me."

Sam said, "Sir, there isn't anything behind you."

"Precisely. Only from the comms suite can you project yourself in isolation. There are reasons for that, as you well know, but they're not important now. What is important is that it's only from the comms suite that you can forward a holocomms image."

Yeah, yeah, Jenny thought. You're supposed to be getting to the point. Beginning to feel like an actual underling having to listen to the general's speech, she slouched down a little on the sofa and crossed her arms.

"It is typical of this man that, with the satellites out and our intercolony links broken, he should take it on himself to remedy the problem. He and his crew have relaunched their ship – a cruiser – and are now in equatorial orbit, ready to converse with the various colonies as they pass and to relay messages between them. He will restore our links. He could have asked somebody else to do this but, like the good shepherd he is, has taken the responsibility himself. But Colonel, before he does anything else, before the next stage of his mission, when he addresses everyone in this ship, he wants to privately interview your guests about the Titanians. So Colonel Baldwin, advisory officers and our guests – I give you our Prophet, the President."

Then, pop, instantly standing right where the general had been – wearing a resplendent uniform that wasn't just red-orange or yellow, but gold, and included a small-visored, high-fronted cap with a garish cross on it – was who else but the bastard Simon. Jenny sat bolt upright but was too shocked to move any farther. After staring for a few seconds, she finally thought to bring her right hand, shaking, to cover her nose and mouth. Then she saw that everybody but Gibbous – and that included Peter – was standing at attention and saluting. So she stood and saluted, too, face exposed. The only hope was that because he wouldn't expect her to be there, or anywhere else – hell, he thought that, along with the rest of EHQS, she was good and dead – he wouldn't recognise her.

Wavering in free-fall but obviously wearing ankle anchors, Simon returned the salutes. "At ease," he said, "but please keep standing." He swayed from one side to the other.

Jenny thought of bringing her hand to her face again but decided it would only make her more conspicuous. She did lower her head a little, though.

Simon raised his arms in a Christ-like, all-embracing gesture, swinging a little forward as he did. "Thank you," he said, "for welcoming me here. And God bless you. Now you two say you're from the Asia colony. I'm going east only a little faster than the Earth's spin – so that I can spend time with each colony as I pass – and it will be a while before I reach that ship's range. As soon as I do, though, I'll report that you're all right. Alive anyway, although I understand one of you is having a voice problem."

Colonel Baldwin said, "She's been struck dumb, Mister President."

Simon lowered his arms and put a thoughtful hand under his chin. This time he swung a bit backwards. "God willing, it's not that serious. Have her checked over by your doctors when we've finished, and I'll pray for her." The other hand joined the one already under his chin, as if in prayer now. "What I want to talk about – and it looks as though that means talking to you," he said, pointing both hands at Peter, "is the Titanians. I'm told that they've been threatening this ship and that you and she have actually been in their camp. Is that right?"

"You betcha, Mister President. I'll tell you, we almost didn't get out alive."

"So where is this camp and how big is it? We haven't been able to detect anything so far. And did they indicate how they knew to come here a full year before this man appeared – the sign from God? He is the one, isn't he?" He narrowed his eyes a little and stared at Gibbous, who stared back.

"He's the McCoy," Peter said.

"Thanks be to our great Creator."

Jenny had to hand it to Simon. She knew he didn't believe a jot of this religious gumph, but he put on a magnificent show of piety. Maybe, in the end, the best qualification for running a religion was unquestioning atheism.

Simon scrutinised Gibbous ("disgusting aborigine," Jenny remembered) and then shifted his scrutiny to Peter, raising his upper lip a little as he did, before moving on to Jenny. Looking her over seemed to please him – looking her over generally did please men – and his mouth grew into a little smile, but then suddenly that froze and vanished. "You know, I think I know you."

Jenny shot a glance at Peter. She could feel the blood draining out of her face.

"I do know you." Simon said in a voice that began as a whisper and then rose steeply. "You're you! You! You! God damn fucking hell – how the shit did you …"

Jenny was on her feet now. She'd drawn her gun and was swooping it around. Simon was yelling his profanities, but Jenny yelled louder,

"Nobody move!" Nobody did. Nobody looked capable of moving, not even Peter. "Peter, get up and help me here. Cover the colonel. I'll cover these two. Get Gibbous standing up. Tell him to get his pipe ready. Tell him what's happening."

"What is happening?"

"… fucking Martian bitch." Simon's cap, somehow, had come off, he was leaning left at about fifty degrees, and strands of hair were stringing out around his head. "How in hell are you even alive? Is everybody in that goddamn satellite still alive? Otherwise how did …"

"What's happening is that we're leaving this room."

"Then what?" Peter said.

"It's my turn now. I'll tell you as we go along."

CHAPTER FORTY

"Has the war started then?" Gibbous asked.

"I don't know," Allaby said. "And don't ask me what just happened in there. I don't know that either. Suddenly I don't know anything." He was holding his own gun as well as, cradled against the splint on his left arm, three others taken from the three people still inside that office and now tied up with belts and bits of clothes, while Jenny, for good measure, had put her gun on low heat and was welding the door to the wall. Allaby didn't know what to make of this. If she thought she was entombing them, it was a bit extreme, and it probably would have been kinder just to shoot them. On the other hand, she wasn't really entombing them – to reverse the welding, all anybody would have to do was to go over the melted metal with a gun set on high heat, which would cut right through. So probably the cruellest thing she'd done was to fire a shot into the holocomms mechanism, with exactly the same result Allaby had had when he'd poured whiskey in his own holocomms that time – except that instead of a tableau of Templeton pointing his finger, those poor three tied-up people had their president at an extreme angle and with an angry, open-mouthed expression and his hair all over the place.

A few more seconds of welding, and Jenny said, "Okay, this way."

"Why this way?"

"If I remember the liner I travelled on, the comms suite is up there. Don't you remember that? The bridge is up there, too."

"The bridge?"

"Come on." She started to run and then apparently realised that neither Allaby nor Gibbous wouldn't be able to and so settled for a brisk walk. Allaby felt that his only choice was to follow Jenny's lead, and Gibbous was just managing to keep up, hard-banging his stick as he went.

"Jenny," Allaby said, "what if somebody sees us? They'll know we're Earth-adapted. You went to all that trouble to—"

"Peter, there's no point now. The general will be comming everybody on the ship, telling them what's happened. We just have to get to him before too many other people do. And we have to get through to Gus now, to tell him that Simon knows."

"What did you ever do to that poor president, anyway?"

"I hit him. Knocked him out. When he came to, I tried to hit him again but ended up hitting most of his bastard henchmen. Earth strength, you know, in Moon gravity. I think we turn left here. And I think we can make better use of that strength right now. Hold this." She handed him her gun. Then she slipped her shoes off, handed him those and took her gun back and another gun with it. "If I'm right, it's the last door from the end of this corridor, on the right. I'm going ahead. You two follow as fast as you two can go. See you in a minute." With a gun in each hand, she started running. Allaby put the two surplus guns under his belt and, after a moment's thought, dropped the shoes.

"Where's she going?" Gibbous said. "Running away?"

"No," Allaby said as they clunked and strode on. "She's running straight into the middle. So are we, just slower. I don't know how to explain this, but we've got to save the satellite – that nice place in the sky I told you about – and to do that we've got to get to that door all the way at the end on the right."

It must have been a hundred metres to that door, and Jenny already seemed to be a good way down the corridor, the narrow perspective telescoping her like a ball off a bat. What a woman, Allaby thought, and for a moment he found himself remembering what she was like in bed – but only in connection with her oomph and authority and tendency to wear him out. But what would it be like to live in Moon gravity and get an Earth-weight knock-out punch from her? If you were the dictatorial president of a bunch of dumbbells and you thrived on imparting fear and projecting manliness, your image would shatter like a mirror.

This thought of Allaby's was followed by a brief consideration of their luck at not having run into anybody so far in the corridors, and that of course was followed by the emergence of two men from a door that Jenny had just run past. Allaby, from behind the two, couldn't see their faces, but their shoulders were easy enough to read. One man's arms dropped, hands dangling, in a way that would accompany a stunned open mouth, and the other's shoulders rose into an alert position as his hand fumbled for his gun. Allaby shot that hand and, having done so, wondered how and when he'd managed to raise his own gun and aim. He didn't remember, but while it was raised, he shot the other man (both of them had been staring down at the wounded hand) in the leg. Then he shot the first one in the leg. As one after the other fell, writhing, Gibbous said, "Do you want me to dart them?"

"Yeah, quick," said Allaby. "We don't need to kill them, but we can't have them yelling, either."

When Allaby and Gibbous reached the inert figures, Gibbous, leaning down to pick his darts out of their arms, said, "Oh look at this. You didn't tell me this about guns."

"Tell you what?"

"They make holes that don't bleed. With arrow holes that big we'd be wading in blood now." He put his little finger through the man's hand and wiggled the tip. "Look at that. Just a clean hole."

Up ahead, a woman came out of another door, gun already raised, and aimed at Jenny's increasingly distant back, but before she could fire, Allaby shot her in the upper arm. As she dropped the gun and grasped her shoulder, Allaby said, "Quick. Dart that one." She turned to see who'd shot her, a dart hit her in the other shoulder, and she collapsed.

Allaby and Gibbous moved on towards her, Gibbous saying, "How does it happen then?"

"What happen? Jenny's almost there. I hope to hell they're not expecting her."

"That gun holes don't bleed?"

"But of course they would be expecting her. But then why would we go to the comms suite? Do they think we're invading or trying to get out?"

"But why?"

"Why what?"

"Don't gun holes bleed?"

"God, Gibbous. The hot photons cauterise the wound. You know – instant scar tissue."

"That's clever."

"Well, what did you think? That we're still in the age of bows and arrows? Or guns that shoot lead? Look, she's made it. She's into the comms suite. The door wasn't locked. Hurry. God knows what's—"

"And maybe when you're really advanced, you'll discover darts. No bleeding, no killing, just … Look out, Allaby." Allaby felt himself being elbowed aside and then became aware of an open door just to his right and a figure crumpling out of it. There were two figures behind, and they suddenly crumpled, too. "See?" Gibbous said. "We didn't even need your gun then. But let me get those darts." He got them, and as they continued towards the corridor's end, he added, "That's the trouble with darts, though. If you don't get them back, they run out. We hardly ever use them in war because you have to keep stopping and trying to retrieve them, which can be dangerous, and then you have to redip them. I've only got about four dipped ones left. So it had better be you who shoots that person up there." He pointed his stick.

A man, gun raised, had emerged from a doorway diagonally across from the comms suite. Allaby shot once and missed, and when the man slowly turned and aimed at him, he shot again, putting a hole in the middle of the man's forehead. "Damn," Allaby said as the body fell forward. "Damn, damn, damn."

"Bad aim," Gibbous said. "but you know, in war, killings do happen. I guess I should have used one of those darts after all."

It was an accident, but just the same, Allaby had never killed a person before. People had tried to kill him – whoever had been flying that cruiser when his pickup was particled had tried to kill him. The man who was lying dead there had tried to kill him, too, and the people littering the corridor behind would have killed him if they could. But being on the receiving end and avoiding being killed was different. Innocence – righteousness – went with that. Anyway, none of the people who'd tried to kill him knew him. There was nothing personal in it – they were the same as any other dangerous force of nature. But being on the killing end, especially of someone you don't know either, made you a dangerous force of nature yourself. And of course, that man there would never again experience any forces of nature, dangerous or otherwise. What right did he, Allaby, have to … to obliterate that man's life? And from the man's point of view, he'd only been defending his own territory, the liner. On the other hand, Allaby reasoned, we're defending our own – the satellite, the Immyo reservation and, for that matter, the Earth itself.

Gibbous knocked Allaby's leg with his stick. "For God's sake we're almost at that door. Come on. It's too bad you killed him, but think about it later."

True, the comms door was about five metres away. After a last glance at the man he'd killed – almost as if saying goodbye to him (he'd been about the same age as Allaby; what had ever happened in his life, for God's sake, to lead him to join this moronic organisation and then to die defending it?) – Allaby shook his head, looked up and broke into a short, painful run so that he could open the door before Gibbous got there, to make sure that Gibbous didn't accidentally get shot. When he did open it and tried to come in, he had to use his foot to push something heavy aside. Then he realised that it was a dead woman and looked up to see an assortment of half a dozen other uniformed corpses lying at various uncomfortable angles on the floor, in chairs or over comms equipment. The general was there, too – but not dead. In full uniform, hat and all, he was standing still, almost at attention. Jenny, a couple of metres away, was pointing a gun at him with one hand while she used the other to punch at what looked like holocomms controls.

"Jesus, Jenny," Allaby said. "All these ... Did you have to, uh ... Did you ..."

Gibbous came in. "Good God," he said, shutting the door.

"You'd better lock it," Allaby said.

"What it?'

"Lock it. So nobody else can come in. I think that's a special door. If it is, its locks are photon-proof."

"How do ..."

"Just turn that thing there, where your hand is."

Gibbous turned it. "Look at all these dead people. Did she need to kill them all?"

To Jenny, Allaby said, "Did you have to kill them"

"I didn't, Peter. The general killed them. They were all dead when I got here. Except for that woman. She had just opened the door, trying to get away, and I was already inside when he shot her. None of them had guns."

"Why ... For fuck sake, why?" Allaby said to the general.

The general started to speak, but Jenny, thrusting her gun at him, said, "He's not allowed to talk at the moment. He shot them because they knew all sorts of secrets – codes and things – and if the ship was being invaded by Earth-adapted Titanians, he thought he'd send the comms crew to Heaven, where they'd be a little harder to interrogate."

"She says she didn't kill them," Allaby said to Gibbous. "Their own general did. I think he thought he was doing them a favour."

"Nice of him," Gibbous muttered.

"Jenny, while he was at it, why didn't he shoot himself and go with them?"

"I shot his gun away as soon as I could, but he could make a wrong move now, and I'd shoot him for him. He doesn't seem to want to die, though.

You should have seen how fast he gave me the holocomms code. Some people are just a puzzle."

"What are you doing with the holocomms?"

"Trying to get Gus. The satellite ought to be in direct line right now. I'm going to hate this, but I've really got to report to him."

"Go ahead. I'll take care of the general. Come on, General, you might as well sit down." Allaby pushed the nearest body the rest of the way off its chair and, with his gun, directed the general to sit there. "Gibbous, get something to tie him with."

Gibbous looked around the room for a couple of seconds and then reached down to a body and, after some study of the mechanics of a buckle, took its belt. He came over, pulled the general's arms and tied them behind the back of the chair.

Templeton materialised. There was a large cleared area at one side of the comms suite for the presentation of holocomms subjects in all their trappings, and Templeton's trappings had improved vastly since the last time Allaby had seen him. He was at the Head of Station's desk now, a grand semicircular thing with globes, monitors, pinpoint lamps, various controls and a stage for miniatures. On the wall behind, instead of holopictures (just as well, since with the comms satellites out, the pictures would have been blank) were three well known paintings – certain to be originals – and a drinks cabinet with a one-stool bar. Templeton slowly tapped his fingers on the desk, shook his head a little and said, "It seems I'm looking at the comms suite of that liner parked in the North America Southwest Sector, and what's more, I'm looking at the two most insubordinate Rangers in history. Wearing enemy uniforms, too. Is that how you got in?"

"Well, yes, and we sort of had to talk our way in, too," Allaby said.

"And finally shoot our way in," Jenny added.

"So I see."

"No," Jenny said. "I didn't … We didn't—"

"And I see he's there too, that Immyo. And who's that?"

"He's the general," Allaby said.

"The liner's commander," Jenny added.

Templeton said, "That would be a General Mitchell, I think – except he shouldn't be called a general. He's as much of a general as I'm Neil Armstrong."

The general started to say something, but refrained when Allaby prodded him with a gun.

"On the other hand, his troops probably obey him. If they're ordered to go to Africa, they probably don't end up in North America. If they're told to stay away from Immyos, they probably stay away from Immyos."

"Who is that?" Gibbous said.

"He's Templeton," Allaby said. "He's our, uh, chief."

"And he's not really there, of course."

"That's right, Gibbous. He's on the satellite, circling the Earth. The orbit right around the middle. It's called—"

"I don't want to know what it's called. Don't tell me. I'm tired of hearing about these things.

"… didn't you go where I told you to?"

"It's just as well I didn't," Jenny said. "The cruiser you sent me to look at is now circling the planet, because you shut down the comms satellites."

"I shut them down after it became clear that you weren't doing what you were supposed to do – intercepting their transmissions had actually been pretty useful. The only question was whether or not they were lying about being able to breathe, which is what you were supposed to find out. But of course I knew they weren't lying as soon as I heard that damned Titanian drawl. It was too late then – you were gone. I couldn't call you back because you didn't have any comms, and you didn't have any comms so that you couldn't give away the fact that we were still alive up here."

"Gus," Jenny said. "That's what I need to tell you. Simon, the Back-to-Earther president, knows the satellite's not dead. He popped up in a holocomms and recognised me."

"I know that, Jenny. I got that transmission. You've blown it now, and we need to… By the way, isn't there somewhere else you can put General Mitchell? It's hard to talk about things with him sitting there."

The general's eyes widened, and he started to speak, but Allaby poked him again and said to Templeton, "I don't know where we'd put him. This is just one big room. We can't open the corridor door, obviously, but there's a big double-door up there. I don't know where it goes."

"To the bridge," Templeton said. "In that kind of liner those are the doors to the bridge, the only doors."

"That's what I remembered," Jenny said.

Templeton said, "Well, you don't want to put him there. That's where you need to be. It was smart of you not to kill him, because you might need him, but can't you knock him out or something?"

The general shook his head hard, jowls shuddering. To Gibbous, Allaby said, "You say you've got four dipped darts left?" Gibbous nodded, and Allaby pointed at the general and said, "Make it three. And come around in front of him. Let him see you do it." As Gibbous was raising his pipe, there was a clang on the outside of the corridor door, and then another. There was a third while Gibbous was retrieving the dart from the general's shoulder.

Templeton said, "I said not to kill him. He had all sorts of informa—"

"Oh, he's not dead," Allaby said, "though right at the moment he probably wishes he was." Indeed, the general had that look of horror in his eyes as, with his hat on the floor and his head thrown against the back of the chair, he stared at the ceiling. "He'll come to in a little while."

Gibbous said, "I think people are trying to get in."

"Don't worry," Allaby said. "If they can't shoot through that door – and I'm pretty sure they can't – they're not going to be able to knock it down. They're too weak to do anything anyway."

"God, Allaby, you're really at home with these Immyos, aren't you? You speak their language, you know how their weapons work – everything. How in hell did you learn their language anyway? You seem to have broken every Immyo taboo there is."

"More than you know." Jenny said. Her seat at the holocomms controls was between Allaby and Templeton, and now she looked back at Allaby with a hint of a smirk.

She meant Paintbrush, of course. "Don't," Allaby said under his breath.

"Yes, don't," Templeton said. "You haven't been the best girl in the world yourself. Do you want me to tell him what you were doing in that ship?"

Jenny blushed purple, the first time Allaby had seen her blush, ever. She turned back around. "Gus, no ... Please, I ... and I wasn't, you know. The whole thing was a mistake, a kind of accident and a mistake."

Allaby said. "Oh yeah, Templeton, she told me. Something happened to her bearings reading, and she was too far—"

"That's not what I'm talking about, but never mind. Before that, she was a pretty good girl. She saved my life. She helped save the whole satellite – maybe, in the long run, the whole Solar System. What have you done,

Allaby, except start all the trouble in the first place? Start a war? Do you have any idea what it was like in that gym? Floating around with that excrement and those corpses and people trying to grab you all the time? She and that other woman, that heroic woman, rescued me. No, you wouldn't know about that. You were too busy – I don't know – outside getting dirty. Where have you been, anyway? Why aren't you dead? How did you make such a mess of yourself? I almost didn't recognise you and probably wouldn't have if I hadn't already known you were around because of having heard your ugly voice. I hate having to look at you. And in the condition you're in, I hate it even more. As for looking at him—"

"But doesn't it mean anything to you," Jenny said, "that the virus is gone, that Earth is habitable again? It was Peter who discovered—"

"It means so much that the thought is bigger than my brain. I haven't got time right now to grasp a thought like that, because now that you've blown our secret, we've got to do something, and I don't have time to think about it, about how you Rangers were always doing air tests ... Wait, I'm getting transmissions from your – their – president. Right at the moment he's ... wait ... yeah, telling the cruiser in North America Northeast to ... this is what I thought ... drop everything and join him in orbit. I reckon he's going to rally all the ships and try to kill us again."

Jenny said, "But you've got defences."

"Not many. They stole all three of our cruisers, and you took one of half a dozen shuttles. It's possible to arm shuttles, but they don't have the maneuverability—"

"You can arm shuttles?" Jenny said. "Damn, Gus, if you'd armed mine—"

"Yes, you've done something to your shuttle, haven't you? And whatever happened to that outrigger that captured you? It suddenly quit transmitting."

"I wouldn't ask if I were you," Allaby said.

Jenny said, "There was an accident. But if it had been armed—"

"Another accident? God, Jenny—"

"Well, I'd never flown a shuttle before."

"You did all right for a while, though. You were having a pretty spectacular time, I'd say."

Allaby said, "What's he talking about, Jenny?"

"Never mind," Templeton said. "We've got five shuttles and a few light-arms runabouts, and that's it. There's no chance of help from the Moon,

442

either. The Back-to-Earthers seem to be out of power at the moment, but nobody else seems to be in. They killed most of the politicians and civil servants and then started fighting each other."

"But the satellite itself?" Allaby said. "Doesn't it have artillery?"

"It does, but God knows how to … I mean it hasn't been used in centuries. Nobody's attacked this place since – since probably the time of the Ganymedian Caliphate. We'll have to see – I already have someone searching the archives, and I know there are some emergency instructions somewhere for the Head of Station. In the meantime, considering that you are where you are, a liner would make a big difference."

"A liner? This liner? This entire liner?" Jenny said. "You don't mean …"

Allaby said, "It's just us stuck in the comms suite. There's a whole shipload of people trying to break the door down. Anyway, are liners even armed?"

"They certainly are," Templeton said, "ever since the interception convention. And heavily armed, too. One liner by itself wiped out the biggest gang of pirates in the—"

"Gang of pirates?" Allaby said. "Not the fucking piracy clause."

"All the piracy clauses," said Templeton, "the whole treaty. By itself, it's made the Solar System safe for travellers. Until now, anyway."

"Gus, on that subject, ignore Peter. It's personal with him."

"Why?" Templeton said. "Have you become a pirate on top of everything else?"

"Yeah," Jenny said. "He's the notorious pickup pirate."

"The what?"

"Nothing," Allaby said. "It's just that … oh, nothing. She's having a joke." A joke. A tease. Another poke in the ribs, a kick in the ass. Gibbous was right – Allaby and Jenny could turn the most serious, most challenging, most dangerous occasion into a bantering match. But whether either of them wanted to face it or not, Templeton had just asked them to fly a liner – which was not only beyond impossibility but which involved the largest of all ships and one already full of hundreds of the same enemy that Templeton wanted them to fight. And if the liner ever managed to leave the planet, the only advantage he and Jenny had – Earth-adaptation – would be gone. Everybody in the liner would be equally weightless.

"… can be sure they can't get in," Templeton was saying. "Allaby, really."

"Sorry, Templeton. Who can't?"

"The people outside your door. Who do you think?"

"Nice of you to join us," Jenny said.

Then, as if he could understand what Templeton was saying, Gibbous – who had been sitting in a swivel chair and looking at the floor as he studiously swung the chair right and left – now stopped, raised his head and said, "It's getting louder out there."

"No, don't worry. Templeton's sure they can't."

"Can't what?"

"Get in."

"Allaby," Jenny and Templeton said at more or less the same time.

Once again, he'd been speaking to the wrong person and in the wrong language. "Sorry," Allaby said. "The idea of trying to fly a liner has caused a bit of a fizzle." He pointed at his forehead. "An alternative to screaming panic, I think. It obviously is a fortified door, but how do we know they don't have a way? A combination, a key of some sort?"

"They don't," Templeton said. "Even the ordinary ship's crew wouldn't have such a thing, and these people damn sure don't. And it's the only fortified door on the ship, mainly because the things are so expensive – sheet diamond sandwiched between titanium. Allaby, I don't know what your problem with the piracy treaty is, but you can thank it for that door. Every liner has to have at least one, to protect the comms and the bridge. So relax. They can't get in."

"Relax?"

"Think about it." Templeton said. "You two are in control of the comms suite, the transmission bottleneck. Nothing can get in or out without your permission. And when you open those double doors, you'll have control of the bridge, control of the whole ship. Unless somebody's in there now. Do you think somebody is?"

"Well," said Allaby, "if somebody is, that somebody has a very low level of curiosity. Those doors have stayed shut, and no sound has come from there. It's kind of hard to tell, though, with all the banging on the other door."

Jenny said. "But there could be somebody just waiting for us."

"There's only one thing to do," Templeton said. "Go see." He got up and walked around to the front of his desk, which because of the size of this semicircular piece of dominance furniture was a rather long stroll, during which Allaby was able to nervously wonder how, exactly, they were going to go see. When Templeton reached the front of the desk, he did what he'd

444

always done with his more modest desk and half-sat on the edge of it, arms folded. "Those doors," he said, "are outside the radius of the holocomms, but I can hear what's happening, and when you have something to say to me, just speak up. Which one of you is going to go first?"

Jenny said, "Let's make a deal, Peter. I'll go first now on the condition that if ever it actually comes to flying this thing, you do it."

"I think right now we ought to …" The end of the sentence was supposed to be "… go together", but by the time he got that far, she was already around some consoles and over some bodies and heading towards the double doors. She had her two guns. Then she had her back against the wall to the left of the left-hand door and was reaching across and nudging the handle with the gun in her left hand.

"They're locked," she said, "but these aren't fortified." She stepped out in front of the two doors and fired at them with both guns, falling to the floor as both doors sprang open into the bridge bay.

From where he stood – frozen in admiration as he watched Jenny make her attack – Allaby couldn't see any movement in there. It was a huge room with big, intimidating pieces of equipment and a screen covering the entire far wall. Jenny was still prone, moving her guns back and forth like antennae, and Allaby, with a gun in his good hand, now crouched low and moved along the right-hand wall of the comms suite, which initially meant crossing the stage and passing through Templeton's drinks cabinet. When he reached the right side of the doorway, he pressed against the wall and took a quick look into the bay. He hadn't seen anybody, but there could have been a couple of dozen people in there if they were hiding behind large objects.

Jenny said, "I'm going in. Cover me." She was the one who assumed a crouch now as she moved along the wall of the bridge bay to the left of the door. Allaby moved to the right, found a row of high stools behind a higher console, went to the far end, stayed low and peered around the console's corner, watching for movement, anything that might threaten Jenny. But nothing. He couldn't see a large part of the bay, though, and he had to listen for footsteps or rustling in the minuscule silences between the clangs coming from the comms suite. Then as he adjusted his position to give himself a better view, in the corner of his eye he did catch something. He looked to his left.

Standing upright and apparently unworried just this side of the double doors was Gibbous, pointing his stick at what looked like a large black table across the bay. "There's somebody there," he said. "Is that who you're looking for?"

"Get down, Gibbous" Allaby said.

Gibbous didn't get down. He kept pointing.

"Okay," Allaby said in a loud whisper. "What the hell do you see?'

"It's under that thing way over there. Looks to me like it's somebody in trouble."

Gibbous had eyes like binoculars. He'd mentioned once the vision exercises that Immyos did from the time they were children, and some day Allaby would have to … Yes, under that distant table was something indistinct and definitely moving a little. "What is it, Gibbous?"

"Can't make it out from here," Gibbous said, and he started walking across the bay.

"Tell him to get down," Jenny stage-whispered from her position against the left-hand wall.

"No point," said Allaby in a normal voice. "If anybody in here wanted to shoot us, we'd already be shot." Jenny didn't say anything, but she did stand up and step away from the wall. Allaby said, "Gibbous has spotted something over there, under that table thing." As the three of them, from different directions, approached the table – a large, tall, sturdy, black object with various instruments on it – Allaby could see that the figure under it was a person who was tied up in some way. A little closer, and he could see that it was someone in a uniform, though not a Back-to-Earther uniform, and, closer still, that it was a man, a bald man, not so much tied up as shackled, hands and feet, to two of the table's legs. He was gagged with a wide piece of tape and was grunting. The first to reach him was Gibbous, who squatted next to him and ran a finger over the tape, probably wondering what it was. The man stared at Gibbous with eyes so wide he might have turned his lids inside out. Allaby was there next. He squatted, too, and ripped off the tape.

The man caught his breath and then inhaled deeply. "Thank you, thank you. It stings – my whiskers had grown through it a bit – but thank you. God, I'm thirsty. Who are you anyway?" He nodded towards Gibbous.

"He's Gibbous Moon," Allaby said, "a native of this planet." He tapped Gibbous's water skin. "Give him a drink." Unstrapping the skin, untying it and holding it carefully, Gibbous dribbled some water past the man's lips. After several seconds, the man nodded, and Gibbous took the skin away. "The question," Allaby said, "is who are you?"

"Thanks. Thanks for the water. But what do you mean who am I? All you people know who I am."

Jenny, who was now kneeling on the other side of Gibbous, said, "We may not be the people you think we are."

Allaby wondered if it had been wise for Jenny to say that, but then he suddenly recognised the man's uniform – a merchant spacefarer's. He was an officer, a real one and a high-ranking one. The man said, narrowing his eyes, "You're not whatsits – Pilgrims?"

"No," Jenny said, "we stole these uniforms."

"You're really not nutters?"

"No," Allaby said. "No we're not. But who are you?"

"Oh, I'm Captain Frederick Delius Smith, and I'm very, very happy to meet you. I'm this liner's pilot."

CHAPTER FORTY-ONE

They had control of the ship, and little else mattered. That, at least, seemed to be Templeton's view, and Templeton was still with them. There was a holocomms stage in the bridge bay as well as in the comms suite – so he'd been forwarded there. Now the new Head of Station watched with delight (the discovery of the pilot had affected Templeton like a Second Coming) as Captain Smith tried to organise Allaby and Jenny into a flying and fighting team. But while Smith was perfectly willing to do his part in defence of EHQS, he was having trouble working out how.

"To fly," he'd said, "I need crew of at least four. To fly and fight I need seven, or maybe six, minimum."

And Templeton had said, "Then how did you get your ship to where it is now?"

"I had a crew of five nutters. They'd all flown smaller ships before, and so they were assigned to me. They also guarded me. I was giving orders to people who also had orders to shoot me if they didn't like the orders I was giving."

"Could they have flown it with you dead?"

"Maybe, just. But they couldn't have landed it. No other ship lands like a liner. I had three months at flying school on nothing but landing. I told them that, of course, but they seemed to believe that, without me, God would guide them."

At which point Allaby had reflected that God had surely guided him to Captain Smith. Allaby might have lifted the liner off the Earth and miraculously reached a position in defence of the satellite. Who knew? He and Jenny might even have miraculously saved the satellite. And as long he was letting his imagination loose, they might have miraculously wiped out the whole Back-to-Earth movement. But then Allaby would have had to take three months of flying lessons before they could get the ship down again. Or maybe not. Maybe he'd have simply discovered it was hard to land a liner while he was landing it. Jenny, just before she and everybody else died, would certainly have had the last laugh then.

But that wouldn't be a problem now – they had a pilot, freshly rescued from his shackles. (Jenny, cutting them off by gun, had remarked to Allaby that her time in the free-fall dungeon had been made "doubly fucking hellish" because of handcuffs, a sentiment she emphasised by a sweep of the gun that came close to shearing off some of the captain's fingers.) What they didn't have was enough crew to fly, much less fight, or any way of ever getting past the fortified door. They were imprisoned. Whatever they managed to accomplish while in these two big rooms, the two rooms were the limit of their world, a fact Templeton seemed reluctant to face. "We'll solve that – don't worry," he'd said. "You can't be in charge of the ship and captive at the same time."

But they were. At one point Captain Smith had turned on the internal viewing system, and they saw that in the corridor outside the comms-suite door were at least a hundred Back-to-Earthers. Any discipline their cold military system had conferred on them appeared to have evaporated, and though they looked as rickety as ever, they also looked panicky, angry, demented and dangerous. They were hitting the door with any objects they were capable of lifting, and every so often someone would shoot at it. Sometimes, apparently, the shooting was wild, and underfoot there seemed to be a few wounded or dead people. When Allaby saw this scene, it dawned on him that one of the fallen people would be the man he himself had killed, but somehow, appraising this mob, he felt a little less bad about that. There would also be the ones Gibbous had darted. They'd have come to by now and would be feeling like shit. The last thing they'd be able to tolerate was a rampaging, if strangely slow-motion, riot.

In the comms suite, the general had also come to. Allaby had turned him over to Gibbous, and all Gibbous had to do to maintain control was sit across from him and keep the pipe in sight. The general behaved impeccably, staying motionless, speechless and patently terrified, groaning occasionally and drawing hurricane-like breaths that reverberated all the way into the bridge bay. This vigil had been going on for about twenty minutes when Captain Smith – after a lengthy and, to Allaby, a frustrating discussion with Templeton – said, "Look, if we can get the liner up near the satellite, it won't matter that there aren't any docking facilities for this big a ship. Just load a platoon or two into runabouts and send them out to us. They can fight their way into the ship and to the bridge. Then we'll be ready to face the other ships."

"Good idea, I suppose, if I actually had a platoon or two."

449

"Volunteers then."

"I could appeal for some," Templeton said, "but they wouldn't be trained, and of course the weight advantage would be gone."

"It would be gone for everybody," Smith said, "but don't worry – we'd still have the sanity advantage. Are you receiving our internal? Can you see them out there?"

"No – your internal doesn't transmit."

Jenny said, "They've gone berserk, Gus."

"Yeah," said Allaby. "I don't think they know much about the piracy clauses either. They certainly can't come to terms with a fortified door."

"Never mind them, then," Templeton said. "What you've got to do now is start trying to get that thing off the ground."

Yes, Allaby thought, we won't exactly be rushing to the rescue. It would take an awfully long time – many hours, at least – to get the liner moving, if it was possible at all. And even if it was possible, there was still the problem of not having enough crew to fly it. And then in order to fight, to man the cannons or whatever, reinforcements from the runabouts would definitely be needed. Liners were probably the largest examples of almost everything invented and designed since, well, since humans had to make do with the sudden loss of a lot of technological knowhow and the simultaneous disappearance of the population of the Earth. If Allaby remembered his history, before the Apocalypse and the Dark Age, a ship this big (and people then hadn't actually needed any ships this big; after all, the early Solar System stations were just workplaces and dormitories, not population centres) could probably have been run by robots or computers. But now there were no computers or robots competent to do that (God, they'd had quantum computers then, machines which, however hard scientists had tried, had never been reinvented), and a modern liner, especially an armed one, would be like some ancient ocean-going battleship, with different people operating different systems while somebody shouted orders at them.

Alone at his station, Allaby had spent a lot of time reading history and thinking about it, and if it was possible to harbour nostalgia about ways of life that had come to an end centuries or millennia ago, then Allaby harboured just that. Or as Jenny usually put it – he was uselessly romantic. But whatever she called him, sometimes Allaby actually missed, as though he'd been there at the time, certain stages of, what? – the human condition, he supposed – all the different things humans could do and be and regard as normal life. He missed the pre-agricultural hunting-and-gathering societies (one reason for his initial interest in the Immyos and his reason now for wanting to get back to Paintbrush and their new beginning) and the early agricultural ones – Egypt, Sumeria, Persia, China, Greece. Imagine using scratches on stone to count the corn into the granaries and eventually turning the scratches into written languages. He missed the Assyrian Empire, the Roman Empire and the Arabian Empire and was sorry they fell. He'd love to have been around for the philosophies and sciences of the Renaissance or taken part in the Age of Exploration of the Earth, with its great bird-like sailing ships, or of the Space Age, the early explorations of the Solar System, with unmanned ships sending back close views of worlds that had only ever been seen fuzzily by telescopes or were just pinpoints of light to the naked eye. Then there were – in small, agile, intelligent, self-piloting ships – the first manned visits to those pinpoints. What would it have felt like to set foot on a moon of Neptune or on Mercury or Venus? For that matter, what would it feel like now? No one had been near any of those places since the Apocalypse.

It was such failures that made this a dark age still. People usually spoke of most of the immediate post-Apocalypse period as the Dark Age. And they spoke of it in the past tense, as though a few technological advances later on – in holography and photon engineering mainly – had brought humanity to a new enlightenment. But that wasn't really enough. Dark ages were times when truly important advances were simply forgotten and had to be learned again from scratch. The Greeks had a dark age that involved everyone forgetting how to read and write, and a couple of centuries of total illiteracy passed before they rediscovered that particular knack. The medieval Europeans had one when they forgot all notions of reason and for hundreds of years thrived on pure superstition. Humanity just before the Apocalypse was pretty dark, too, having burgeoned to the extent that it was overloading the planet. While some countries were showing off to each other by zipping around the Solar System, exploring exotic worlds and manning faraway stations, the people still on Earth were surviving in wreckage: thirst, starvation, tyrannies, atmospheric calamities, continuous murderous wars, and a population so large that when a virus appeared that could bring instantaneous death to any individual, it killed every individual. That's because people were absolutely everywhere. It was a fire in a land bereft of firebreaks, and humans succumbed to their own reproductive success.

Humanity was still in a dark age, and this liner was proof of that. Sure, there was nothing this big then, but when the time came that supersized ships were needed, the designers used the model of smaller ships and enlarged them as far as physics allowed. Now the standard propulsion systems could just barely lift a liner against any reasonable gravity – let alone Earth's. In fact, Allaby couldn't remember right now what had happened the last time a liner landed on Earth, if one ever had, and the first test of the liner's ability to help the satellite would be whether it could move at all. And just as it was as huge and heavy as possible, it was also as unwieldy and as complicated. It couldn't be flown without a pilot and a crew of four, the absolute minimum, according to Smith.

Valuable portions of an hour went by as Templeton and Smith exchanged ideas on ways a crew of two might just manage – mostly by putting Jenny and Allaby in a perpetual and impossible race between one set of instruments and another – until Allaby ventured, actually raising his hand as he said it: "You know, there are in fact two other people on this side of the fortified door – living ones, that is."

The captain gave Allaby a puzzled look, Jenny laughed, and Templeton said, "Who?"

Allaby said, hardly believing he was saying it, "They're still in the comms suite."

"Who?" Templeton said again.

"Well, there's the general – he's conscious now – and Gibbous."

"That's who I thought you meant," Jenny said, still laughing.

"Don't waste time," Templeton said, "trying to be funny."

Jenny said, "One wouldn't, and the other couldn't."

"How do you know?" Allaby said, even though he wondered if, just for the hell of it, he really was wasting time. On the other hand, it wasn't any worse a waste of time than figuring out how two completely inexperienced people could do the work of four professionally trained ones.

"Allaby," said Templeton, "just stop it. You're talking about the enemy commander and an … an Immyo."

"A what?" Smith said. "Is that what … What is that?"

"That's what he's called," Allaby said. "I mean, his name is Gibbous Moon, but he's one of the people we call Immyos. As I told you before, he comes from this planet. He's never been anywhere else, and he doesn't speak English, at least not the English you speak. But I can speak his

452

language, and he does have a scientific mind. It was a matter of seconds before he grasped the principle of the wheel."

"A regular techno," Templeton said.

And Smith said, "He's from the Earth? How can he be? What about the virus? I know it's gone now, but didn't that just happen?"

From that point, both Templeton and Jenny – she was standing more or less beside Templeton, as though she were being projected by the holocomms, too – seemed relieved for a moment to stop talking about the difficulties of flying, and they took turns telling Smith their versions of what Immyos were and how they came to be and what a mystery it was about the disappearance of the virus, given that all the Rangers always ran weekly air tests. Allaby quietly slipped down from the high stool he'd been sitting on and went to the comms suite.

At the other end of the room, Gibbous and the general were sitting in bolted-down swivel chairs facing each other – the general still horror-struck and staring at the pipe while Gibbous held it up like a wand, slowly passing it from one hand to the other.

"You know," he said as Allaby approached, "some people are more sensitive to darts than others."

"Are they?"

"Yeah. Take you for instance. Not long after you came to, you were up and sort of dancing around and yelling things. Jabbering, but yelling."

"But I'd just discovered that I could breathe, that I wasn't going to die."

"Well, maybe. But look at him. I think his headache is worse than usual. He's very, very scared, too. Maybe it's worse to get darted when you already feel as heavy as rocks. Maybe he had a vision of the people he killed. You do have visions sometimes, you know."

"Tell me – do you think he'd do anything you told him to?"

"I guess, yeah. But I can't tell him anything, can I? I don't jabber."

"What if I talked to him, and you and your pipe made sure he did what I told him?"

"How would I know what you were telling him?"

"I'd tell you what I was telling him, if I had time."

"Why wouldn't you have time?"

"Well, if we were in the middle of some manoeuvre or …" Allaby's let his voice tail off . He was jumping the gun, wasn't he? He didn't really – did he? – expect this to happen.

"Manoeuvre? You mean like sneaking up from the side instead of attacking from the front? That kind of manoeuvre?"

"Uh, yeah. Kind of that kind. On the other hand, no, not really." Templeton and Jenny were right. This was impossible.

Jenny was standing in the double-doorway. "Peter, what are you doing? We need you in here."

"All right. Coming." After a moment more of doubt, he sighed and finally said to Gibbous, "She's saying they need us in there. Can the general move?"

"I don't see why not." Gibbous got up and signalled with the pipe for the general to get up, too. The man was shaking so much he couldn't make it all the way, but Allaby took one arm and Gibbous the other, and they pulled him to his feet. Then, as Gibbous shifted his pipe and stick to his right hand, they led him past chairs and consoles and dead bodies – the shaking made it feel like walking along with a floor-polisher – towards Jenny and the bridge bay.

Jenny said, "That man's a wreck, Peter. He couldn't possibly—"

"The fact that he's a wreck probably means he could."

"Could what?" The general stammered, staring wide-eyed at Allaby.

"You'll find out," Allaby said, noting as he stared back that the general had aged about twenty years since appearing on the holocomms a couple of hours ago. In fact, his face was so drained of blood that he looked almost as much of a corpse as the people on the floor – only his wide eyes and his quivering jowls indicated any difference.

"Gus says that he doesn't want the general knowing what we're doing." As if to block them, Jenny stretched out her arms, not quite reaching with either hand the sides of the double-doorway.

"I think he's beyond caring what we're doing, but maybe not beyond helping us do it, if we're lucky."

Jenny lowered her arms. "Okay, go talk to Gus about it." She stood aside. "Your idea is at least absurd. You know me, Peter – sometimes I don't mind absurd. It's Gus who has trouble with it."

Allaby and Gibbous walked the general into the bridge bay, and Jenny followed. Gibbous said, "Oh, your chief and his table are in here now. What does he want us for?"

"I don't think that, right at the moment, he knows if he wants you. I've got to convince him, which won't be easy. I have to show him there's no choice."

"Choice about what?"

They slowed and dawdled at what Allaby reckoned was a safe distance from Templeton. He may have been only an ultrahologram, but just the same ... "About you and the general here helping us fly this thing."

"This whole big thing?"

"That's the idea."

"Why do we want to fly it?"

"To defend our chief – who's not really here, who's in the—"

"I know, I know. Up there somewhere. Who will we be defending him from?"

"Other skymen. Enemy skymen, like the people in this ship."

"By shooting guns at them?"

"Yep. Big guns, enormous guns."

"And they'll be shooting back?"

"I'm sure they will."

"But what about the children?"

The children. Jesus, what about the children? Breaking out of the colonel's office and into the corridors – all that striding and shooting and darting – reaching the comms suite, the dead people, Jenny, Templeton, the horrible prospect of flying a liner, the bridge bay, the discovery of the captain ... At what point had he forgotten about the children? And had Jenny forgotten, too? Now they were getting ready to fly a ship with a cargo of children up to, to ... "Do you know what Gibbous just asked?" Allaby said to the room at large. "He asked, 'What about the children?'"

"What children?" Smith said.

Jenny said, "They were outside before. I've been sort of assuming they were still outside."

And Templeton said, "Do you mean those children they snatched from here? They're there, on that ship? How did they—"

"No, no," Allaby said. "These children were snatched from the Far Side. But the satellite children will be on some other ship, probably the president's. I don't think it matters much where they came from. There must be some on every ship."

Smith said, "I never heard anybody mention children."

"They don't call them that," Jenny said. "They think of them as something else. They called them something else, Peter. What was it?"

In a very low and trembling voice, just above a whisper, the general said, "The Eden Adaptations."

"What did he say?" Templeton said.

"The Eden Adaptations," said Allaby.

"Oh," said Smith, "I heard them talk about those. My nutter crew talked about them a lot. You mean they meant children?"

"They're the beginning," the general said in a slightly louder voice.

"The beginning of what?" Templeton said.

In a full voice this time, the general said, "The new beginning of life on Earth. What do you idiots think?"

Still gripping the general's arm, Allaby jerked him away from Gibbous and pulled him face to face. "It may have escaped your notice that there already is life on Earth, lots of it. Gibbous, show him the pipe." Gibbous came around beside Allaby and waved the pipe slowly in front of the general's face. Allaby said, "Now tell me this. If they're your new beginning, why do you send them out to die in the wind and rain?"

"They do that to them?" Templeton said. "They're killing them?"

"They do and they are." said Jenny, "They're already down to eighty-three per cent, they say. What that means I hate to think."

The general's voice had gone quiet again and was shaking again. "New life needs ... New life needs to be started by the strongest ones."

"What?"

"What did he say?" Templeton said. "Come closer, for God's sake."

Allaby edged Gibbous and the general towards the holocomms stage, saying "I'm not sure I heard it right myself." When they stopped, he said. "Say that again, General."

"We need to get," the general muttered, still hypnotised by the pipe, "down to the ten per cent, uh, best able to survive, uh ..."

"Survive what?" Allaby said.

"Conditions."

"What conditions?"

"Conditions here. Earth conditions. The new life on Earth has to start with strength so it can continue with strength."

"Did you hear that?" Allaby said to Templeton.

"Yes, I ... Well, I think I did."

"I did too," Jenny said, "but I still don't know what he means. I think I don't want to know."

"I'm pretty sure I get what he means," said Allaby. "He means that however stupid, ignorant and nasty we thought these people were, we had no idea. They had a hundred and some children on this ship – all ages except for babies, toddlers and teenagers – most of them kidnapped and some of them donated by their own parents, these God-fearing so-called Planet Pilgrims. Right, General?" Allaby grabbed the pipe from Gibbous and prodded the general hard at the base of his throat. "Right? Am I right?"

The general nodded, his chin now juddering so much it looked as though his teeth might crumble.

"And when they got to Earth, they doped the kids senseless and took them out to be exposed for hours on end to the cold night wind and the rain – except that because it's the dry season here the ship itself had to make the rain – and let them die one by one of a kind of supercold you can get on this planet – Gibbous told me about it – and I remember the colonel saying they were outdoing the other ships. General, have your people been feeding them? Giving them anything to drink? Have they?"

It was hard to tell whether the general was shaking his head or just shuddering, but the answer was clear.

"No, I guess not, because they're too drugged to eat or drink. Anyway, if the kids weren't starved and dehydrated, it would slow the exercise down, and this ship would lose ground to the other ships. It's a kind of race, isn't it, General?"

He didn't nod, but again the answer was clear.

"It's a race to see which ship can knock off ninety per cent of its kids first. But that's just the fun part, isn't it, General? The serious bit, if I understand you, is to create a breed of humans that don't easily starve, die of thirst or catch cold – a real master race, by God." To Gibbous he said, "Here, take your pipe back before I do something really unpleasant with it."

"I wish I knew jabber," Gibbous said, accepting the pipe and immediately turning it back into a wand. "Whatever you were just saying, you really sounded like you meant it. What was it? You said you'd tell me things if you had time."

As Allaby was explaining the Eden Adaptations to Gibbous (including a long and superfluous footnote on the meaning of Eden itself), he missed most of what Jenny, Templeton and Smith were talking about, and by the time Gibbous finally understood – "... Not even Little Rimmers would have thought of that" – Jenny and Smith were sitting at the controls of the small internal monitor, and Jenny was saying over her shoulder to Templeton, "It's no good. It only works for the corridor outside."

"We've got to find out," Templeton said, "or we can't use this liner. Allaby. Allaby …"

"What?"

"Will you rejoin us in this century please? We need to know—"

"He needs to know, too. He's the one who discovered the children. He's the one who's kept reminding us about them. He's got as much right—"

"Okay, Allaby, Okay, okay. But we have to find out where the children are, and what we need to know now is why the internal doesn't work to other parts of the ship."

"How would I—"

"They've changed the codes," Smith said. "You don't need a code for the corridor. It's the default. But for the others … See if Mitchell knows. You're the one he responds to."

"It's not me. It's Gibbous and his pipe."

"Just ask him. Ask him what the code to open the internal is."

"Okay," Allaby said, "but keep in mind that he killed the whole comms crew just to keep codes like that secret."

"He didn't kill them," Jenny said without looking up from the internal monitor. "He sent them to Heaven. When will you get that straight?"

"That's me," Allaby said, "always forgetting the niceties. But I'll try. What's the code for the internal, General?"

The general shook his head relatively vigorously, his eyes for once not set on Gibbous's pipe. He was looking at Allaby straight on.

"The code, please," Allaby said.

"I won't tell you. This is my command and my ship, and you, whoever you are, have no business knowing any of my codes."

"This," yelled Smith, "is the Selena Line's ship and my command, and you'll tell us every code you've changed, you goddamned thieving, murdering nutter."

Blood returned to the general's face. He rose to his full height and, turning his back on Allaby, took a step towards Smith, fists clenched.

"Oh shit!" Allaby said to Gibbous. "Dart him."

"Again? He had such a bad reaction—"

"Do it."

Templeton seemed to have regarded that as a very bad idea, especially after Allaby told him there would be a fifteen-or-twenty-minute wait before the general surfaced again. As soon as the dart had hit him in the back of his neck, he had fallen to his knees, and now he was still on his knees but with his head and arms on the floor and his posterior in the air, looking a bit like a Ganymedian who might have fallen asleep during prayers. Gibbous had gone over to retrieve his dart, but nobody did anything to, as it were, smooth the general out. What they were busy doing was wondering why Allaby had decided to cause even more delay. Allaby, aware that the general could actually hear everything that was being said, refrained from explaining that the dart was necessary because the man had been showing signs of losing his abject terror and would have been no use to them otherwise. But he hoped they'd all get that point when he stood over the body and intoned, "Tell us, General – how does it feel to be in Hell again?"

Templeton was seething now. He was standing up in front of his desk and jabbing a finger in Allaby's direction. "The Earth is turning, you know. I don't dare switch the comms satellites back on, and so I'm going to be out your line of transmission in, in … I don't know, but pretty soon. And I've got to organise the rest of the defences, too."

"Well, go organise them. When we get high enough, we'll be back in touch."

"No, Allaby. The liner has got to be central to those defences, and if it doesn't get off the ground, if you don't turn up, we're lost here. We're destroyed. And as long as I possibly can, I'm going to keep an eye on you. I can never trust you, ever. Everything we're involved in now is some aspect of your fault, and I know that as soon as you're out of my sight – and you probably will be before you take off, because you can't do that now until Mitchell comes around and gives us the codes. As soon as time is absolutely short, you think of another way to waste it, to throw it away. Now what little time we've got we've got to kill."

Well, the general had had no intention of giving away the codes – that was the whole point. But Allaby didn't want words to that effect to reach the general's ears. He'd done the right thing but was helpless to explain why. And he really wished Templeton would stop talking about it. Somebody needed to change the subject.

"Thank God," Templeton said, "for Captain Smith here and for Jenny. They might be able to keep you from fucking up again, from doing something else that's stupid and careless and destructive, you and that trained Immyo of yours. How did you ever get hold of him anyway?"

"He got hold of me, I'd say."

"What do you mean?"

459

"Templeton, for God's sake – this is his territory, his world. I just wandered into it. Everybody did. Hell, he was on his Long Walk Out and thought he'd be alone for the rest of his life. Now look."

"What was he on? His long what?"

"It's what they used to do."

"Used to do what? When?"

"Back when they—"

Jenny said, "He's told me about this, Gus. Back in the days before even the virus disappeared, the old people used to—"

"Before the virus disappeared? When exactly were the days before the virus disappeared?"

"Fifty years ago," Allaby said. "As she was explaining, they had this custom where the old people, rather than be a burden but more to have a bit of a late-life quest and adventure—"

"Fifty years ago?"

"Yeah," Jenny and Allaby said together.

"What's the matter with your chief," Gibbous asked.

And Smith said, "Fifty years ago? Fifty years ago?"

"What is he worried about? What does that thing you people keep jabbering mean?" Gibbous said.

Allaby said, "Fifty years ago, when the virus disappeared."

"The what?"

Templeton said, "You did air tests. All you Rangers did air tests all the time. The virus was —"

"I know," Allaby said, shrugging. "I can only guess …" And in truth he hadn't had the time or inclination to give much thought at all to this. "… that it's still there and detectable but has stopped being active. Maybe it's stopped needing to be. Viruses do mutate, you know. In our stations in our sterile worlds we don't have a lot of sickness, viral illness – hell, any kind of illness. That's probably why these dumbos here think that the worst thing the Abunga-free Earth offers is a bad cold. Maybe the virus has decided to attack something else. Maybe it doesn't attack anything – there's no law that says it has to. I don't know, Templeton. Ask the virus."

"But fifty years ago. How do you figure that?"

"Are you sure you want to talk about this now. I thought time was short."

"Well, it is. It was, but now that we've got to wait for Mitchell—"

"All right. Fifty years ago was when the bleeding babies stopped."

"What stopped?"

460

"Bleeding babies. Babies that, as soon as they took their first breath, used to bleed to death. Because of the Abunga."

"But they're Immyos," Templeton said. "They're immune." To Jenny, he said, "Do you know what he's talking about?"

"Well, he started to explain that, but—"

"Okay, Templeton, pay attention. It's genetics one-o-one. The Immyos are pretty healthy people. They know all about the diseases they tend to get and how to cure or prevent most of them with stuff they have to hand. The gene that gave them immunity, though – and I'm just surmising from what I learned at the lovely campus of your renowned University of Armstrong – is a dominant gene. But there's a recessive among the people, too, that has nothing to do with immunity. So if a baby inherited two dominants or a dominant and a recessive, it was immune. But if it had two recessives, it spewed blood from all over its body as soon as it breathed in the Abunga. So about a quarter of all babies regularly died this way. Of course babies can die at birth for plenty of other reasons, but a cause of death like this – so common and so sickening and instant – put people off having very many babies at all. If they had a couple of healthy ones, they stuck with that. I don't know if they had some kind of birth control or just quit tempting fate, but fifty years ago the bleeding stopped, and they didn't have to worry any more. Gibbous, who was twenty at the time, says there are almost twice as many people now as there were then. There'd probably be more if they didn't have wars."

"Wars? They have wars?"

"Of course, they have ... You don't know the first thing about these people, do you?"

"We're not supposed to know anything about them. That's the whole point. They're supposed to develop without our knowledge or interference. Our ancestors wanted to see ... I'm not sure exactly what they wanted to see ... but it's a long-term scientific and social experiment ... maybe to see if, left alone, humanity could begin again and get it right this time. I don't know, but whatever the experiment's for, it's lasted a thousand years and will probably last a few thousand more. But it's a delicate experiment, and you can ruin it instantly if you make contact with them, if you interfere with them."

"Interfere with them?" Allaby said. "What about killing them if they wander too far?"

"That's not interfering. That's just keeping them, uh, pristine. Why do I have explain this to you? They have to think they're the only people on Earth and the only ones that have ever been on Earth. If they were allowed to migrate they'd find ruins. They'd see ships. They might see someone in a sterility suit. In time, they could even run into other Immyos, and then they'd infect each other – culturally, I mean. There are six Immyo colonies on different parts of the planet – six separate chances for humanity on Earth. On the other hand, Allaby, you've managed to spoil one, but there are still five left."

"I haven't even been to the colony. Only Gibbous and—"

"Uh, Gus," Jenny said. "It looks to me like the experiment is over."

"Why?"

"Obviously, it depends on the virus being the virus. Now that everybody can come back to Earth—"

"Why should they?"

"They just would," Jenny said. "How could you stop them?"

"We wouldn't have to."

"Why not?"

"Nobody would know. That's one of the things this battle we're going to have is about. We do what we can to wipe out the Back-to-Earthers and then say they stayed in their ships and pretended to be outside and finally did open their portals and all died. I mean, if a damned virus can keep a secret, we can."

"No," Jenny said. "Somebody would be bound to find out. What about the Martian Back-to-Earthers and the Titanian ones? They're on their way, convinced that governments have been lying to them. And this time they'd be right."

"If we can handle this bunch, we'll be ready enough for those two."

"What about the children? Are we going to wipe them out, too?"

"No. We'll find a way of rescuing them, using the runabouts maybe. But if, as you say, they've been drugged all the time, they won't know where they've been."

"Okay. Then what about the Immyo population boom Peter was talking about? They'd die like lemmings trying to migrate."

"That," said Templeton, "would be a control in itself."

"What!"

"No, Jenny – I didn't really mean that. We'd find a way to expand their boundaries or something. Don't worry."

462

The trouble is, Allaby thought, he really did mean it. He'd never doubted that Templeton was a born bureaucrat whose principal interest in life was to keep things running smoothly and to fend off change. But sometimes you can know something perfectly well and then in some unexpected future moment still be shocked by it. Templeton, a Mooner and an administrator, had never imagined travelling to Earth and couldn't understand why anyone else would. Anyway, virus or no virus, the Earth was off limits, and that was that. Also, whatever the purpose of the ancients' experiment – and Templeton had only been guessing before – it had to carry on. Why in the world – in the world of Templeton – would anyone want to discard the work of a thousand years? Allaby was ready to help fight the odious Back-to-Earthers, but in the process, what in hell was he defending?

But in a strange and maybe shameful way – though certainly not in the same way as Templeton – Allaby had a certain liking for the secrecy idea. He didn't really want anybody from just anywhere being able to come to what he thought of as his hard-edged but glorious planet and live and breathe and engineer and alter and proliferate and kill and pollute. He wanted to go to the San Juans with Paintbrush, make a new start, a new tribe, and be confident that he'd never have to see a stranger again or worry about what strangers somewhere else were doing. But he did realise that that was just a little selfish. What real harm could the relatively few people who now lived in the Solar System do? It would take tens of thousands of years for humans to reach their destructive, pre-Apocalyptic bulk, and maybe they would have learned the lesson of that by then. No, wanting the planet to himself was, at best, ignoble, but it was the soul of charity compared to what Templeton wanted.

"... really think he can?" Allaby heard Templeton say. He'd been gazing around the bridge bay, not listening to Templeton's and Jenny's continuing exchange, but watching Smith busily trying out random codes on the internal monitor and Gibbous ambling around peering at things and poking them with his stick. "Allaby, answer me."

"What did you ask?"

"Why don't you pay attention?"

"You know, Templeton, I think you think there's still such a thing as the National Park Service and that I still work for it and you still command it."

"Oh yes, Ranger Allaby, the Service exists all right, and I still run it, among the other things I run now. Whether you still work for it is a question that might need answering, but right at moment there's no choice for either of us. Now tell me if you think—"

"Come on, Gus," Jenny said. "What's left of the Service? Have you been able to contact any of the other Ranger stations?"

Smith suddenly looked up and said, "The National Park Service? You mean you're the people who do the holoparks? Damn. I go every day when we're in dock. Never miss—"

"No I haven't," Templeton said. "That was one of the things you were on a mission to do, remember?"

"Just Ben Haymark. No one else."

"... especially the North American ones. I've always loved the lions and the way they stalk so dead slow. It's excruciating sometimes." Smith made a dead-slow stalking-lion motion with his arms.

"I used to image them right around here, you know."

"You did? You did yourself? This really is an honour."

"Allaby."

"What?"

"I asked you if you actually, genuinely believe your Immyo can handle instruments?"

"I don't see why not."

Smith said, "Is his eyesight all right?"

"He's the one who spotted you from way over there. She and I didn't see you at all."

"I know what he might be able to do, Mister Templeton. I can try him out."

"Can you? Thank you, Captain."

Allaby called Gibbous. From the far side of the bay, he started towards them, his stick echoing. "Where do you want him?"

"At those controls back there," Smith said. "We'll try him as stabiliser."

"Thank goodness," Allaby said. "That was one of the things you were going to have me do, while shooting back and forth to that other one. One-handed at that." He and the gravity-crippled Smith slowly started over to the high control panel on the left of the double doors. Allaby shouted, "This way, Gibbous."

As they walked, Smith, puffing a little, said, "What I like best, though, are the horses. They have such a magnificent presence. It's great to imagine riding one, the way the ancients used to. Do he and his people ride them now?"

"No they don't. We talked about it, but it was a bit hard to get the concept across. I hope stabilising an interplanetary liner turns out to be easier to grasp."

Smith laughed. "It probably is. Myself, I wouldn't know where to start with a horse. I hope we get this battle over with pretty quick, because I can't wait to tell people I met some real Earth Rangers." As they reached the stabiliser console, Smith said, "I suppose the code on this has been changed, too." With Allaby helping, he made it onto the high stool. Then he pressed in a code and said, "It has. The default is the test, though, and that's all we need right now." As he spoke, the wall-sized screen all the way at the other side of the bay turned into a three-dimensional array of huge cubes, spheres, pyramids and cylinders, along with a small, slowly moving black dot. "I know you probably haven't seen a stabiliser before. A smaller ship doesn't need one, but on a liner it's, well, a supplement to steering. The steering can't be accurate unless the ship's got a stable axis."

Gibbous came up, leaned on his stick and said, "It's big in here, isn't it?"

"It just got bigger. Look behind you."

Gibbous turned, saw the far wall and jumped backwards a bit, nearly hitting his head on the console. "What's next in this place? What is all that?"

"Something for you, Gibbous." To Smith, Allaby said, "Should he get up there now?"

"Might as well," Smith said. "Help me down. I'm so afraid of falling here."

Allaby helped Smith down and Gibbous up, leaning the stick against the stool. Smith then explained to Allaby that the jump stick on the console moved the ball through every dimension. The stabiliser's job was to hold the ball as close as possible to the centre of one of the moving geometric shapes. The test involved several moving shapes, but when the ship was actually flying there would be only one shape, depending on the manouevre required, moving against the background of the ship's forward view. "Got that?" Smith said. If any more evidence was needed that humanity was in a technological dark age, here it was. A quantum computer could have done a job like this with the electricity off.

Just the same, Allaby nodded tentatively and did his best to translate to Gibbous. "See that ball there?" Allaby said, pointing. "Now move that thing there – yes, that – and watch what the ball does." The ball zipped around the wall – forward, backwards, up and down.

465

"Why is it doing that?"

"You're doing that."

"No, the ball is."

"You're making it do that. With that thing there."

"I am?"

"Yeah. Hold it still."

"Okay."

"Now, see. The ball is still."

"It is, yes."

"Now move it, and the ball moves."

"Yes, I see. Okay. But so what?"

"The ball helps fly the ship."

"It does? A ball?"

"Yes."

"We're not flying now, are we?"

"No. We're just testing now. We'll fly after the general wakes up."

"We have to wait for him? Maybe I shouldn't have darted him."

"No, you did right. Now see that other shape up there – like a much bigger ball?"

"That?"

"Yes."

"Move the little ball so that it goes right into the centre of the big ball."

"Okzay … Uh oh."

"Slower. You have to do it slower."

"Okay … There."

"Perfect. But the big ball is moving, too. So you have to move the little ball with it, keeping it in the centre."

"Like that?"

"Yes. Just like that."

"Well, it isn't so hard. What's hard is guessing what it's got to do with making a ship fly."

"You can say that again."

Smith said, "He mastered it really quickly. Great. Did you see that, Mister Temp— Oh."

The Earth was still turning and Templeton was gone. And just as Allaby was registering this, the general stirred. He flattened out of the prayer position, lay prone for a second or two, and then turned on to his back and released a mighty sigh. Allaby helped Gibbous down from the stool, and

466

the two of them followed Smith to the general. Jenny was standing over him. "He's saying something," she said as the others approached, "but I can't quite hear what it is."

"Get your pipe out," Allaby said to Gibbous. "Make sure he sees it."

The general, indeed, was muttering something. Jenny knelt down beside him, ear cocked, saying, "What … What?"

When he saw Gibbous, he shut his eyes and said shakily but clearly enough, "No. He's not Him. I know that now."

"That's right," Allaby said, "He's only a man who just happened to—"

"It's another lie." The general's eyes opened wide.

"What is?" Jenny said.

"That he's Him. He's not Him. He's not a sign. They lied." His voice now was weak but moderate. He tried hard to lever himself up, and then Jenny pulled him to a sitting position. "He doesn't need to shoot me again. I'll do whatever you want."

"That's fine," Allaby said. "But if you try anything—"

"I won't. You see, I want to do what you want."

"You do?" said Smith. "Why?"

"Because it's all lies. They said the virus had been gone for a thousand years and that He was the sign that God was finally ready for our pilgrimage. I heard you say that the virus was still there until fifty years ago. If the Pilgrims had tried to return before then, they'd have been killed. Our leaders lied."

Allaby said, "We could have told you that."

"It was only an accident that the virus was gone. Only an accident."

"That's right," Jenny said. "It surprised us, too."

"Have any of you ever been shot by one of those darts?'

"I have," Allaby said.

"How many times?" His voice was rising to normal and maybe above it. And it wasn't shaking so much as quavering.

"Once. That was enough."

"It wasn't. Now ask him. Has he ever been shot?'

"I'm sure he has. Gibbous, he wants to know if you've ever been darted."

Gibbous snorted. "Kind of excited, isn't he? But tell him I've had it happen a lot, and not just darted by somebody else. I don't know how many times I've pricked my finger or dropped one on my leg or foot. I shot at a bird once, bounced the dart off an overhanging rock and got myself in the ear."

Allaby translated the gist of that to the general, who, with Jenny's help, was working towards standing up.

When finally on his feet, he said, "Okay. Now ask him if he's ever been shot a second time, as I was, while still suffering from the first one."

Allaby asked.

"Well," Gibbous said, leaning on his stick and putting a hand to his beard, "When you're out you can't move, and when you come around you're useless. Nobody's going to waste poison shooting you again. Do you know how hard it is to get that stuff? The frog pools are right next to the waterfall, down a cliff and in this thick mist, and you have to—"

"Then did you ever, for instance," Allaby said, "prick your finger twice?"

He snorted again. "What, get up after pricking your finger once and do it again? Nobody's that stupid. It takes a day or two to even look at a dart."

To the general, Allaby said, "I think the answer's no."

"Then that makes me the only one, the only person ever to go to that place. I'll tell you, the first time, as you know, is pure Hell. It's even hot. Your head's about the size of a grapefruit, and your brain is trying to squeeze out of your ears and nostrils …"

To Allaby, the feeling came right back … lying beside that fire … the dog … Gibbous's unintelligible voice … Paintbrush's … Funny. In the midst of that agony, could that be when he started to fall in love with her … Nah, he didn't even know her.

"… but the second is, well, another place." He closed his eyes, ran his hand over his head and made something between a grimace and a smile. Then he sighed hard. His eyes, when he opened them again, sparkled. "You pass through the misery and pain of the first place, and then you emerge somewhere else. It's like stepping into a bright light."

Smith whispered to Allaby, "He looks loonier now than when he was an ordinary nutter."

Holding his arms out and opening them wide, the general went on: "It's not the opposite of the first place. It's not Heaven, not at all. But it's almost pleasant … it's clear." He put his hands against his chest. "It's not confusing, not confused. There's no static – that's it. You can see that all your experience has always come to you mixed with static. But now the static is filtered out. The lies are. The lies about the Moon. About the governments. About the Earth. About the Eden Adaptations. Even about God." The hands were now in a prayer position, as for a moment he gazed silently at the ceiling. And then he winked. Allaby wondered if that was meant for God or his new not-God. Was this some kind rapture of atheism? Was a double-dose of Gibbous's frog poison a truth serum in reverse – instead of bringing the truth out of a person, bringing it in? Was it actually a cure for religion?

Gibbous said, "I really shouldn't have darted him again."

"No," Allaby said, "it was good you did. If you could understand what he's been saying ... I mean, he's lost his mind, but it needed losing."

Jenny, looking puzzled and even a little frightened of what the general might do, cleared her throat and said, "About the children ..."

"The children, yes. We mustn't go flying into battle with children on board. But I'm sure they're still outside – we can check on the internal. If they're not, through the internal I can order them to be put out. They're sedated, but without their boosters, they'll come around in a couple of hours. Then, after we've lifted anchor, maybe ..."

"Wait," Allaby said. "Just leave them there?"

"Of course. When we get back in touch with your commander, he can send a ship ..."

"He needs every ship he's got right now. They'll die out there by themselves. Have they eaten anything, had anything to drink?"

"I'll order somebody to stay with them and feed them and water them – one of the Eden attendants."

"But the attendant," Allaby said, "would die, too, maybe not as quickly, but—"

"No, the attendant would lead them to safety."

"An attendant who's just been helping kill them?"

"What I say on this ship is what's done. He or she – or one of each, I think – will be ordered to let them live. To save them, in fact." The general seemed to have calmed down a little and spoke with a semblance of thoughtful sensibility, even if he didn't make much more actual sense.

So when Allaby replied he did his best to sound reasonable, too. "I don't know if you know this, General, but your people have been rioting out there. They've been quiet for a while, probably because they're exhausted. I wouldn't bet, though, that they were in any mood to follow orders."

"When the Eden attendants are outside, as I'm sure they are, they stay out of touch with the rest of the ship. Their work is considered too important to tolerate distractions, and their only contact is me."

Allaby was trying to phrase his next very reasonable objection when Gibbous said, "You're talking about the children, aren't you?"

"Yeah," said Allaby. "How did you know?"

"I guess if you're around this jabber long enough, some of it seeps through. What does he want to do with them?"

"He wants somebody from the ship to take them and lead them to safety. But somebody from this ship wouldn't know how or where—"

"No, it's a good idea finally," Gibbous said. "All we have to do is tell them exactly where to find safety."

"Oh yeah? Where is that?"

"Tell them how to get to the woods. I know they'll have to go slow, but once they're there, Paintbrush will take care of them – Paintbrush and those hostages. Some of the children are theirs, aren't they? And tell him to tell them to hurry and start, so whatever we have to do now, we can do it and get it over with. It's hard to figure how you skypeople ever win any battles if you spend all your time jabbering about them."

PART FOUR

THE SHORT WALK IN

CHAPTER FORTY-TWO

It was the first time Jenny had been back to Armstrong since she'd left university, and despite the fact that the Lunar government had just undergone a coup, a short and scary war and a counter-coup, this – the largest city in the Solar System – had of course not changed at all. She felt as if she'd never left. But what could she expect? Down the centuries there had been plenty of political upheavals here, almost all of them much more profound and long-lasting, and Armstrong had always remained Armstrong. She couldn't imagine what kind of revolution it would take to install authorities who might consider landscaping the place or putting up structures that were more than absolutely functional. Would Armstrongers ever stop painting everything in lurid colours and then never repainting until the original coat had almost entirely peeled away? Was it possible or even thinkable for them to change their transport system from the dense, clattering, tangled, ancient network of overhead trolleys to vehicles that could fly or roll quietly and independently? Would they ever switch to the modern (ie, only three hundred years old) smooth-dome architecture, replacing this array of girders and thick, towering vertical ceiling supports? Armstrong had to be the ugliest place in existence, and Jenny wished all this would be over pretty soon and that they could have dinner, which she was longing for, and a night's sleep, which she wanted even more, and then, best of all, a return to Earth.

In fact, she could have happily been on her way to Earth right after the liner had landed this morning at Port Aldrin. She could have been in the same cruiser Gus had ordered Gibbous to be put in, but he'd also ordered her and Peter to draw some money at the port and then to clean up and get some new clothes and some food and rest before going tomorrow. (Gibbous had to go right away, Gus had said, because no one who didn't absolutely need to could be allowed to see the Holopark Man. He was going to be explained away as a lifelike robot planted by Back-to Earthers wearing sterility suits.) Captain Smith had left to report to the Selena Line office, and the general, still in a state of wide-eyed righteous lunacy and proclaiming himself to be guilty of piracy and murder, had turned himself over to the soldiers who were herding the other Back-to-Earthers to a PoW stockade.

"The others will kill him." Jenny had said.

"Yeah," said Peter. "I think he thinks that's part of his redemption. It must be great not to have any static any more." He'd added that it was just as well he and Jenny weren't going back yet, because it meant they could attend the inauguration. And then he'd further added, in an undertone, that they had tactics to talk over. And it was true – ever since lifting off in the liner, they hadn't had a chance to talk at all, not in general terms. Every word, every effort, was concentrated on the job of flying and then of fighting, and anyway, as soon as the liner finally broke gravity and rose into a restored comms link with the satellite, they had Gus back with them, and they couldn't say what they had to say in front of him. They couldn't say anything now either. They were in a noisy, crushing crowd that covered the vast Presidential Plaza and, as far as Jenny could tell, branched into tributaries down adjoining lanes and alleys.

The ceremony, on a platform on the portico of the capitol, had been proceeding for more than two hours so far, and people were getting tired – shifting, it seemed, from one mass of legs to another – but no one was leaving. These, after all, were Mooners. They hadn't actually been ordered to attend, but the people here usually knew what was good to be seen to be doing. They were in many ways an independent bunch, especially in Armstrong, and even Martians would admit that there was a certain character to them – ranging from the petty chancers whose accent Peter had studied to a whole subculture of born bureaucrats and policemen to a few sometimes pompous or zany intellectuals at the university and on and on, up to a collection of self-appointed aristocrats who seemed to spend their whole lives in Armstrong's adjoining Alan Shepard Golf Dome. No, the Moon had had a succession of different kinds of governments – some fairly free and democratic, some definitely not– and while this had made most people more or less immune to a government of any kind, when the regime changed, no one ever knew exactly what to expect. The smart bet was to stay on the right side of it from the start, and if the people were invited to turn out for an inauguration, they turned out. And here they all were – all different styles and colours of clothes, a steady rumble of either inattention or feigned approval and, at appropriate moments, yips and shouts and raised arms among breaking waves of applause.

And they were applauding and whooping now. Jenny had been busy looking up at the girders and the trolleys and around at the people and the peeling paintwork and hadn't been paying attention. This was the fourth speaker so far, some kind of military man. She shouted at Peter, "What did he just say?"

"He told how he won a battle. They killed the Back-to-Earthers in their dozens. Mooners love that stuff."

Sure enough, Jenny thought, we killed them in their dozens, too – in a lot more than dozens. Because the comms satellites were out, Simon was only able to rally the other ships one at a time, and one at a time they charged EHQS, expecting to dock and invade. The liner was stationed next to the satellite by then – the general had Simon believing the ship was still on his side – and, one at a time, picked off the other ships. Gus didn't even need to send volunteers in runabouts. Since Captain Smith and his crew of four didn't have to fly while they fought, only sit in orbit, they did it by themselves. Rather, the general did. He was manning the big gun. While Gus – pointing out that the 'enemy' ships actually belonged to either the satellite or the Moon – was encouraging Jenny and Peter to use their smaller guns just to wound the attacker, the general would pull his lever and hit it head-on. Every single ship ended in a spectacular fireball. And every time one did, the general would turn around and grin at the rest of crew, while the rest of the crew shook their heads, groaned or covered their eyes. Only Gibbous, who was still stabilising, watched impassively, but then he had a delicate job to do and, Jenny supposed, probably didn't realise what was happening.

And according the official version – Gus's version – that really wasn't what was happening. What happened officially was that the Planet Pilgrims had all been staying in their ships and lying to their leaders until the leaders discovered the lies somehow and ordered them out under pain of excommunication. Since that would have been worse than death itself, they all took the plunge and did die. The ships were contaminated then and useless – sitting forever empty on the surface of the still contaminated

Earth (all except the liner – which, in the story's closest semblance to truth, had been captured by a band of Earth Rangers who came in through the airlocks, barricaded themselves in the bridge bay and flew the ship back to the Moon). As for the children, they'd never been to Earth. They'd been dropped off at the satellite, drugged and kept as hostages in the free-fall gym, which the Back-to-Earthers had captured and held until brave volunteers from the rest of the satellite retook the gym and saved all but a few of the children. The survivors were now recuperating in hospital and would be sent home as soon as they were well.

As Jenny reflected on it now, Gus's desperation to maintain the millennium-long status quo seemed forlorn, punctuated with holes and, in its way, ludicrously funny, and she let out a snort of a laugh. But just as she did, she realised that the crowd around her had gone very still and quiet.

"Jenny," Peter said in a whisper, "shh. There are probably plainclothes people in this crowd."

"But I was just—"

"Look around. We're supposed to be praying."

"Oh, sorry." She lowered her head and said, "I thought they got rid of the prayer people – that's what the goddamned ceremony is supposed to be about."

"These are Establishment prayers. Be careful."

She glanced up. It was the fifth speaker standing there now, wearing luxuriant red and gold robes and a tall, pointy blue hat. What, she wondered, made this kind of religion any less nutty than any other? Maybe you could say, she supposed, that its followers didn't kill people. But when the military man was exterminating Back-to-Earthers by the dozen, wouldn't this church have been praying for him? There would even have been chaplains among the troops. Forget it, she told herself – that's the kind of question that will never be answered – and she lowered her eyes again, her thoughts straying this time from the official children to the real ones.

They were, in fact, still at six different spots on Earth. On the general's advice, Simon had told all the other ships to carry on with the outdoor Eden Adaptations, that the ships were only going to be invading the satellite, shooting everybody or throwing them in the gym again, and coming right back – no need to interrupt the most important part of the project. Well, those ships didn't come back, and the cruisers that left Port

Aldrin this morning were on their way to pick up the kids. The one carrying Gibbous was going for the liner children, who were now having the experience of real sunshine, real woods and a real river. And unlike the other kids, they weren't drugged any more – they knew they were on Earth, and when they got back here, they'd know where they'd been and would tell people about it. What was Gus's line on that going to be? For that matter, what about the cruisers' crews? Was he going to swear everyone, even the children and the PoWs, to secrecy? Or was he just planning to cut their tongues out? And as for the kids being held in the gym, what about what the people on the satellite knew and would never be in danger of forgetting? It was only a matter of time, and not much time at that, before everybody in the Solar System knew the truth and then absolutely everybody would be a Back-to-Earther. How would Gus look then? He'd be in disgrace, that's how – certainly not Head of Station any more. But up until now the official line had only been given to Jenny, Peter and Smith, so that, once they were on the Moon, they wouldn't compromise it. In all the turmoil, the official line hadn't yet been officially issued.

"Peter," Jenny said.

From the corner of his mouth, he said, "Still praying here."

"Peter, we've got to shut Gus up."

At that point, an "amen" echoed around the plaza, the man wearing the robes and hat bowed slightly and sat down, and a judge and the new President – a minor government official, but the highest-ranking one not to have been lined up and shot by the Back-to-Earthers – rose and faced each other. The crowd applauded again.

"What did you say, Jenny?"

"We've got to ..." Then she remembered Peter's paranoia about plainclothes people. Were there really any? If so, could they be randomly eavesdropping? With phonoscopes? Surely not, but just the same ... "It's important. But let's see this through, and we can talk at the hotel."

After the swearing-in and after the President made his speech ("The price of liberty is eternal vigilance," he'd said, quoting some ancient), a band appeared on the platform, food-and-drink vendors appeared in the crowd, and the party began. Nobody, it seemed, was going home. Jenny had somehow imagined that most people would be and that she and Peter could just stroll to the hotel, which was down one of the lanes off the plaza. Instead, they had to push past dancers and general revellers, some of whom seemed to be already drunk. It wasn't that they weren't capable of pushing

475

through, but that, with their Earth strength, they were too capable. What sometimes seemed to be a gentle nudge could send a person reeling. It was beginning to make her feel a little nauseous, and when a burly man grabbed her and tried to kiss her, she realised why. It was the goddamned gym again. She pushed him so hard he went off his feet and backwards about three metres, knocking down and landing on a pile of other people.

"Jesus, Jenny," Peter said. "They're only celebrating." He stepped over, hand out, with the apparent intention of helping people up, but by then the burly man was back on his feet. He charged at Peter, who then had no choice but to give him another shove, resulting in another three metres and another pile. People were screaming at them.

"Damn," Peter said. "So much for looking inconspicuous. Let's just go." After that they didn't worry much about their pushing power, managed to leave a wake of surprised and sometimes angry people and reached the hotel pretty quickly.

But the inside was as crowded as the outside. In the hotel, though, there was a noticeable difference in class. Out there it was beer, gin and generated burgers; in here it was champagne, whiskey and a long table with platters of real food, including sides of ham and beef and trussed chickens. The people were dressed in more formal clothes, and instead of dancing, shouting and trying to hug and kiss everyone, they just stood there holding their glasses and talking – albeit loudly. And at one end of the room was a platform and podium, which could only mean one thing.

"Oh God," Peter said. "Here's where all the plainclothes people are."

"Why do you worry so much about them?"

"I don't know. I just don't like being here when the Government changes."

"That podium," Jenny said, "worries me more. I couldn't stand another speech. Look at all the food, though. I'm starving." They'd had a sort of breakfast earlier, but the fast it was breaking had been much too long for two eggs and toast to make any difference.

"Let's go to my room," Peter said, "and I'll order a meal."

My room, he'd said. She'd almost forgotten they had separate rooms. She thought of all the times they'd slept together in hotels … "With this going on? They won't have room service. The staff are all down here. Look – even the chef." She pointed to a man in a chef's hat, carving a leg of lamb.

"Well," Peter said, "if we're going to eat, we're going to have to put up with speeches."

"Maybe not. Come on." She took his hand and led him towards the long table, pushing past people as gently as she could. When they finally reached the food queue, she said, "When we get to those champagne bottles, grab one."

"I couldn't …"

"Yes you could." Quit worrying about cops or spies or whatever. There aren't any. There. One of those. Grab one." But he didn't. The problem, she realised, was that, to get to a bottle, he'd have to lean across filled champagne glasses, and the only arm he could reach with would be his broken one. "Okay. I'll do it." She reached, got her hand around a bottle's neck and, in retrieving it, knocked over only two glasses. She quickly looked around. No one seemed to notice. "Here, Peter, hold this." She gave it to his good hand. At this point they were coming to the first food, assorted vegetables.

Peter said, "We're the only ones in this queue without plates."

"We don't need them." Past the vegetables and then the bread came the first meat, a ham. Next to that, though, was a whole chicken, yet untouched. People who wanted chicken were getting it three chickens down, from a waitress with a carving knife. So Jenny lifted this chicken off its platter and tucked it under her arm.

"Jenny!"

"Let's go to your room."

With Peter either looking around wildly or just looking away, pretending he didn't know her, they managed to cross the packed lobby and to reach a lift whose doors were about to close. Jenny stopped them with her foot, letting Peter go in, and then she followed. The lift, too, was stuffed with a loud-talking crowd, but no one seemed to notice the man with the champagne bottle or, moreover, the woman with the chicken under her arm (a chicken that, by the way, was copiously leaking grease onto her brand new shirt). When their floor arrived, they got off and walked past more people to Peter's room. Once inside and as the door closed, Jenny raised the chicken over her head and did a tapdance with it.

Peter started laughing, put the champagne on the lampstand and sat on the bed, his arms around himself. "How in hell did you get away with that?"

She stopped the dance but still held the chicken high. "Just a bit of hunting, Peter dear. I reckon I can do anything Paintbrush can do, and look – mine is cooked."

He stopped laughing. "Oh, Jenny. Jenny, no."

****

Dinner, which they ate at a little table on the room's balcony (although it was beyond her why anyone would want a balcony overlooking Armstrong), was altogether more serious. As they picked at the chicken with their fingers and drank champagne from bathroom tumblers, Peter made clear what his priorities were. First, he was going to disable all the particalisation fences around all the Immyo reservations, and after that he and Paintbrush and the baby – and Gibbous, too, if he was still interested – were going to walk (yes, walk) to the San Juan Mountains, where they were going to start a new tribe.

"Is that what you and Gibbous were talking about this morning?" Jenny said, prying off a leg.

"This morning?"

She chewed a bit, swallowed and said, "Before his ship left. You two disappeared somewhere."

"No, we'd already talked about that."

"Then what did you … Where did you go?"

"Oh yeah. I meant to tell you. He had an hour or so before he had to be aboard. Remember? So I hired one of those glass-topped rovers and took him for a ride outside the dome. We drove a little way, stopped and looked at the Earth. It wasn't full, just a quarter, but the whole outline was clear. At first he didn't believe it was the Earth, 'the ground' as he calls it – which, when you think about it, is pretty much what we call it – but I'd been telling him about planets and orbits and stuff, and he understood quickly enough, just as he understood he was on the moon. There were some clouds, but you could see most of the west coast of the Americas and some of the Pacific, and he wanted to know if that was the endless water he'd been heading for, and I said that it probably was …" Peter bit off some breast and drank some champagne. "… except that it really wasn't endless, because there was land on the other side. Then I said that the Southern Ocean, which you could see a bit of just at the tip of South America, was kind of endless in that it went all the way around. And that's about all the talking we did. Oh, I asked him to ask Paintbrush to wait for me in the woods – she'll be by herself with the baby for about a day, I guess. And I told him to get his people ready for the inevitable, but we spent most of the time just sitting there looking."

They both picked and ate in silence for a little while, dropping bones in a bin beside the table. Storeys below, the celebrations were still in full swing, and shouting, singing and band music rose around them. Of course Gibbous would want to go with Peter and Paintbrush. They'd walk to the San Juans, and she'd never see Peter again. This was worse, somehow, than when she thought he was dead. "Freeing the Immyos. Walking to the mountains. These are crazy ideas, Peter." He was calmer and more premeditating than when he got drunk and took off in his pickup, but he was still just as berserk.

"Why are they crazy?"

"For a start, how are you going to disable the fences?"

"That's not crazy. That's easy. I've already disabled my own Immyo fence. I know how to do it. First I'll pick up Paintbrush, and then I'll just go to the other Ranger stations and do the same thing. I mean, why is Templeton sending us back tomorrow? To check out the Ranger stations."

That was true enough. They were being sent in separate cruisers, Peter to the western hemisphere, Jenny to the eastern. According to Gus's orders, once the ships had landed, they each were to go through the charade of putting on sterility suits – this for the benefit of the cruiser crews (it was symptom of Gus's scattered thinking that he hadn't worked out a similar precaution for the crews picking up the children) – and then fly off in the outrigger that each cruiser would be carrying. They were to visit every station and try to discover what had happened to the Ranger there.

"I mean, Jenny, we know the answer to that already. The Back-to-Earthers killed all the Rangers, or captured them, in which case they would have been in those ships that the general blew up. They tried to capture you, didn't they? And then they tried to kill you."

"Yeah, but it was my sector where their headquarters were going to be."

"So what? They just maybe tried a little harder to get your help."

"I don't know, Peter. You're probably right, but I hate giving those shits that much credit for cunning. But listen – I take it you're asking me to disable the fences at the stations I visit."

"Yeah, if you don't mind."

"I do mind a bit, yes. Anyway, I don't know how."

"I'll draw you some diagrams and give them to you tomorrow."

"One reason I mind is that I don't like doing that to Gus, deceiving him like that. He's going to be in enough trouble if we don't stop him from issuing that idiotic official story of what happened. It's too loose, too full of holes. Too many people will know better. He'll disgrace himself."

"Oh, let him."

"No I don't want to let him, Peter. Despite everything, I like Gus. I think you do, too."

"But what can we do about it?"

"Talk him out of it. Help me talk him out of it."

"I can't imagine anybody talking Templeton out of anything."

"Help me talk him out of it, and I'll help you disable the fences. All right?"

"All right, if that's what you want, I'll do what I can. When is he planning to tell that stupid story?"

"Pretty soon, I guess. The Moon's war is over. The inauguration's over. When things settle down a little more—"

"You know, Jenny, we don't need to talk him out of it. All we need to do is delay him a while. Then other people would start telling about the Earth and being able to breathe, and he couldn't say otherwise. We just have to figure out how."

They were silent again. Jenny reflected on how much cleaner bones became when you ate with your hands, and then completely out of sequence realised with a little pang how much she wanted to sleep with Peter tonight. If he didn't want to revive their relationship and instead spend his life with Paintbrush, there was nothing she could do or particularly wanted to do about it. But tonight, just tonight, just for comfort, just for familiarity. She knew he wouldn't allow it, though – the goddamned married prig. But his little wife was on another planet, for Christ's sake. Jenny wasn't about to suggest anything, though – it would be too much like begging. "I've got an idea how to delay him," she said. "Pour me the last of that champagne, and I think I'll go to my room."

"Jenny, I don't … I don't want—"

"Just pour it, will you?"

Each of the rooms in this hotel had a comms console, and if she remembered, so did the apartments in the Bachelor Technicians' Quarters. Back in her own room, Jenny tried BTQ 724, and – almost too quickly, she thought – conjured up Louise, in her pajamas and with hair unkempt even by Louise's standards. Behind her, the living room was covered with what looked like packaging litter. Louise stared for a few seconds before finally saying, "Jenny, it's you. Where are you?"

"I'm on the Moon, and you're still there. Good."

"Well, nobody's told me to leave, and I wanted to stay where you could find me. What are you doing on the Moon? Are you still on your secret mission?"

"Yes, for a little while longer. Listen, Louise – I want you to do a few things."

"Sure, Jenny. Does this mean I'll be helping with your mission?"

"You could say that, yes."

"Wow. What do you want doing?"

"First I want you to remember something. If anybody wants to know anything about your love life, say that you are very sad because you and your fiancé have split up. He's fallen in love with someone else."

"Fiancé? Me?"

"Yes. Just remember that."

"Why?"

"Don't ask. And don't mention that I've spoken to you. It's all part of the secret mission."

"Whatever you say, Jenny. Uh, who did he fall in love with? "

"That doesn't matter. But let's make up a name for your fiancé. Call him Alf. Okay?"

"Alf."

"Now take a shower—"

"Showering and sleeping – that's all I've been doing."

"Have another shower. There's perfume in the bathroom, but don't use too much. Try to do something with your hair, and put on the nicest clothes you can find in that closet."

"There are some nice clothes in there."

"And clean the place up. You're about to be visited by a very important man. Remember to act sad."

"A very important man. This is some secret mission. I'm getting nervous

"Don't be. Just be ready. I've got to sign off now. Duty, you know."

"Sure, Jenny. I'll see you when you get back."

About ten minutes later, she was saying to Gus, "... and she's inconsolable. Somebody she knows ought to go over there, because I'm afraid of what she might do. Please, Gus, will you?"

"I guess I can. If you think it'll help."

"It's about all that will help. But don't try to contact her first. Don't do anything else at all first, unless you want to pick up some flowers or wine or chocolates. But just go. Now, please."

"You've no idea how much I've got to do here. But sure, okay. I'm going."

And ten minutes after that, Jenny found herself standing on the balcony looking down at the revellers. She remembered Gus saying once that, as a Ranger, "alone is what you do." Well, she surely was a Ranger now.

CHAPTER FORTY-THREE

Gibbous and Yellow crossed the river again. Because the sun was low and directly behind them, the spray from the water hitting the stepping rocks was filled with flashes of blue and green, just like … Oh quit it, Gibbous told himself – concentrate. Hell, everything he'd seen lately, he seemed to want to connect with something he already knew. But this he did know. Nothing here had changed. The rocks were just as mossy and slippery as they'd ever been; the water and wind still smelled fresh, just like water and wind; those light green cottonwoods still spread and sagged and supported the occasional osprey's nest in their upper branches, the occasional big brown white-breasted bird sitting there and watching and wondering what was the matter with animals that didn't know how to fly.

Yellow had jumped in early on, and then Gibbous, slipping from about the second-to-last stone, ended up in the river, too. By the time he managed to pull himself upright and to shake some water out of his hair and beard, Yellow had made it to the bank and was also shaking dry, spraying his own rainbow of droplets. Luckily, it was shallow enough here for Gibbous to wade on, up to his armpits and using his stick to brace against the current. Fly – hell, I've flown – but I still can't keep my balance on these damned stones. As he pushed through the water, he curled his toes through the cold pebbles, trying to remind himself what a foothold was. I'm getting old; it feels strange somehow, as it certainly does for Yellow, to be going in this direction; and when I get there, what will I say exactly? What will they say? How will they greet me?

As Gibbous pulled, climbed and levered himself onto the bank, Yellow watched the struggle for a moment and then, apparently satisfied that the man had no intention of staying in the water – where humans were concerned, Yellow never seemed sure about what to take for granted – the dog trotted past the strand of cottonwoods and sat, waiting, at the edge of the Near Plain. Gibbous wondered if he should call him back. They hadn't been travelling for very long – they'd had a late start – and Gibbous was dripping wet and a little chilled. Anyway, he wasn't sure it was right, tactically, to make his entrance to Big Rim in the middle of the night. Now that the river was behind him, he could stop here. He'd build a fire, dry out his clothes, think some things over and sleep soundly for the first time in what seemed to be days. There was a chicken in his satchel, too – one of a couple of flocks Paintbrush had amassed, ready to pluck for the children's farewell supper. She'd told him not to take one, to catch something along the way or eat when he got to Big Rim, but when she'd turned around to see to a crying girl, he'd slipped one under his shirt. After all, he had no dipped darts left, was in no mood to go hungry all the way to Big Rim, couldn't be bothered to visit the poison pools, and … never mind, he had the pilched chicken, and that would do fine. On a low-slung branch, he hung up his wet satchel, poncho and blanket, started gathering kindling, and called Yellow.

By the time the sun had set, he had plucked the chicken and was, with a tongue-dangling Yellow beside him, watching it roast as he squatted naked by the fire. He was chilly in back and warm in front, and in a minute he'd have to stand up and turn around – but in a minute. The thing was, he didn't have to be naked. On the Moon, Allaby had offered to get him some skyman clothes, which were very light and would probably have been dry soon after he climbed out of the water. But if he'd accepted those clothes and, as Allaby had also suggested, thrown these clothes away, he wouldn't have been able to go back to settlements at all. He remembered the hysterical reaction of the Chief that time to Allaby's mask and could imagine what kind of welcome he'd have had if he'd strolled into Big Rim in a shiny skyman's suit. He'd have spent more effort explaining what he was wearing than telling people about their world's new beginning. So he was naked now because his heavy old clothes were taking an age to dry. That was okay, though. That was exactly right, in fact – a good old old-clothes-drying, chicken-cooking fire was just what he needed to get back into himself. He would get up and turn around in a minute. Meanwhile and not for any particular reason, he observed that no warmth is quite as warm as the warmth on one side of your body when other side is cold.

Well, had that been anything worth thinking about, he asked himself as he finally did get up and turn around. He was facing in the direction of the river and its roar now, and warmth crept up his back as it slid from his front. In the sky across the river was the last hint of a purple glow, silhouetting both the trees on the other side and the bats streaming up from them. He also thought he could see – because of some movement of black against black – a couple of horses drinking. No moon, though – not yet.

When it finally did rise, it would only be a three-quarter one, with not much useful light. When the ship was actually landing on the moon, Gibbous, watching the grey surface come closer in the big window, had asked Allaby what the people there did when the moon shrank – did they all migrate to the edges? – and when Allaby had finished laughing, he used his hands to give another demonstration of the way light flowed from the sun and balls moved around the sky. That was easy enough to understand, but what wasn't was why Allaby had laughed. He'd always treated Gibbous's questions seriously, even earnestly. So what had been so hilarious about that one? Was it just a funny idea, or could it have been that, as they approached the moon – after all, the most obvious of the skyplaces – Allaby was feeling back in his element, and Gibbous had just become some ignorant outsider?

But for a long time Allaby had been living down here. He had a house here – it was where, at first, they'd been heading. No, there must have been another reason, but he couldn't imagine what it was, and it didn't matter anyway. Allaby, he'd decided by now, was worth trusting. He was on the side of Gibbous and the people of the Seven Settlements – rather, six – and of the other settlements on other parts of what he now knew to call the Earth. That, in fact, was the most exciting new information of all. Going to the moon, going to that place floating around in just nowhere, feeling what it was like to weigh nothing (there was, altogether, a massive amount of nowhere and nothing in the skypeople's world) or to weigh just a little bit, helping fly that monstrous thing, watching other monstrous things through that monstrous window and then seeing them vanish in a blaze, seeing the moon approach and, best of all, seeing and contemplating the real Earth in the sky of the moon and the real endless water … and then winding up right back in the same old woods with Paintbrush and the baby and the hostages and all the children … all of that and much more … but nothing had moved him, had impressed him more deeply than the knowledge that there were other settlements, groups of settlements, like his own, and always had been. Those people had been doing the same things he and his people had always done, wondering what they were and why they were and making up stories so that they wouldn't have to wonder any more. And he'd never known about them, and they'd never known about him and his people. And they, too, had been killed for trying to travel too far. Now Allaby was going to stop that happening – saying to hell with Allaby's chief, defying him, reopening the Earth for all people, both on the ground and in the sky.

It was a noble purpose, Allaby had said, and Gibbous had agreed – even though it saddened him.

Gibbous's job now was to tell his own people about the world as it really was, and to tell them as factually and correctly as he knew how. Then when they had the facts they would go ahead and do what they needed to do. After all, they were only ignorant because they'd been kept that way. They had never been stupid.

The heat and cold had done their full exchange, and again he faced the fire and the chicken. As he squatted beside Yellow and turned the spit, it occurred to him that he wouldn't have this problem if he simply built two fires and squatted between them. How come, in his whole long life, he'd never thought of that before – had never known anybody who'd thought of it? Was it something to do with being infected by a skyman way of thinking? As he gazed into the flames, he wondered about that for a little while, considering in the process the obvious simplicity of, for instance, putting a stick between two cowpats, and he ended up deciding that – no – skypeople themselves were just ordinary people, even dimmer in their way than the ordinary, living as they did off the fat of the ideas of an eternity of individual ancestors. Allaby had said that the axle was one of the most basic of all inventions, and so the first person who put a stick between cowpats, or something similar, was probably not very different from Gibbous himself, sitting by a fire at night and being visited from nowhere by a simple notion. That, or there'd been a lucky accident. He chucked some more wood on the fire, while Yellow, without withdrawing his tongue, made a short, low whine. The dog knew by now when a piece of meat ought to be done, even if he couldn't have known why it had to be cooked in the first place.

A little later, as he chewed on his half of the chicken, Gibbous heard trees snapping. He'd been hearing this for some time but hadn't, he guessed, separated it from the general noise of the river. Still gnawing on his chicken, he stood up and walked over to the bank. There was nothing to see, of course, just a general blackness that was broken by stars above a blackness that wasn't, but he could tell that the sound was coming from a distance down-current, probably not far from the campsite. He remembered elephants passing by one night when he was camping there – yes, that was the night Allaby had first appeared – but he hadn't seen them there since.

So he supposed that they must vary their routes to the river and that it was that one's turn again, and he wondered, now that the camp had spread into something the size of a settlement itself, what kind of disruption the animals might be causing. Those kids ... first thing in the morning they were going back to the moon ... those kids would be terrified. They would never have seen or even imagined elephants, but – of course, of course – Allaby had told him about places where people could see things – animals and other things – that weren't really there, the way he'd seen Allaby's chief. But that wouldn't be the same as actually being among them, would it? Elephants were dangerous. Did the children know that? What if they imagined they were in one of those harmless places and didn't ...

But what was the point in worrying? There was nothing he could do. Anyway, they'd been out in the real world for three days already. What had they made of lions when they saw them – fierce wildcats, packs of dogs, protective bulls, snakes, bees, scorpions, rearing horses? And after what those kids had already been through, what were elephants? He turned and went back to Yellow and the fire.

When he finished his chicken, he did build a second fire. By the time it was going well enough, his blanket was dry, and he and the dog curled up in it. His last thoughts of the day had nothing to do with tomorrow's mission. He realised now that when he'd heard the snapping trees, his worries hadn't really been about the children at all. They were about the elephants. Somehow – and he couldn't say why – he felt the great creatures were doomed in this new, circular world, as well as everything he'd ever associated with them – dread, respect, admiration, awe, wonder and even worship. On these enormous balls that whirled and spun around in the sky through light and dark, Mother Elephant had already gone for good – redundant, along with Hero and all the air animals and all the wall paintings and all the blood-soaked stories, honed and changed and elaborated on through the years by storyteller after storyteller after storyteller. Anything he'd ever believed or half-believed or kidded himself that he believed or told other people to believe or never really in his heart believed ...

When the Earth had turned enough so that the spot where Gibbous was lying began to receive light from the sun again – in the form of the faintest purple fringe along the horizon of the Near Plain – he slowly opened his eyes and wished he and Yellow had left a little of the chicken for breakfast. Rising to one elbow, he checked to make sure. The combined glow of the coals and the sky was just enough to show him nothing but bones, head and feet in a little pile. It brought to mind the time, after Yellow had shared a turkey with him, Paintbrush and Allaby, when Gibbous had been woken by a gagging dog during the night. He'd had to pull a piece of wing from deep in Yellow's throat. How could that have happened? Dogs ate birds all the time, and he'd never seen one choke before. Was Yellow some kind of inadequate dog, or had he been made that way by his association with people? Somehow, he suspected the latter, though he couldn't have said why.

Never mind. No breakfast meant nothing for either of them to eat until they got to Big Rim at about lunchtime. Well, Gibbous could pick some nuts or fruit or do some dartless hunting, but what would be the point? He'd just be wasting time, and he wasn't going to starve between now and then. Still, the sooner he started, the sooner he'd eat. He extracted himself from the blanket, took his clothes from the branch where he'd hung them, put them on (they were dry all right, but pretty stiff), picked up his stick and satchel, gave Yellow a nudge with his foot, and started walking. He decided he'd follow the tree-line and thus the river until he was nearly at Waterfall and then skirt east of there until he reached the Gorge. He didn't want to be seen by anyone until he actually made his entrance to Big Rim. Whatever happened, it had to happen all at once.

But at about mid-morning he might have been seen. Just after turning east – before he'd reached the Gorge but when he was a good distance from the shelter of the trees – he spotted a hunting party. Even though they were practically on the horizon, he was able to make out enough of their dress, or lack of it, to see that they were Deep Gorgers. Whenever they got tired of snakes, frogs and fish, they would sometimes make the climb to the Near Plain so that they could shoot their arrows at big warm animals with hair. There was even a place along the rim – not too far away, actually – that they called the Chute. Whenever the Deep Gorgers killed a cow or something, they would drag it to the Chute, give it a shove and watch it hurtle, tumble and bounce, getting smaller to the point of invisibility, all the way down to what usually turned out to be the edge of their settlement. In fact, Gibbous remembered, a couple of times the animal had bounced right into the settlement, making a huge mess and knocking down one or two of those stilted houses. There were other times when it would get hung up on a crag or a branch, and the hunter who was most subordinate that day would have to climb either up from the bottom or down from the top,

488

depending on which was closer, to kick it loose. But whatever happened, by the time it reached Deep Gorge it was just a bag of bones. They had a way of cooking it, though (Gibbous and other Ledgers had been invited to their big festival a few times and had seen this) that didn't involve skinning it. They'd simply hang the whole animal high over a big fire and let it stew for a couple of days. Then they'd bring it down, slice it open from throat to groin, form a line and, one by one, reach in and pull out whatever their hands could find. The meat was full of bits of bone and smears of unidentifiable organs but otherwise was remarkably tender.

Remembering all that as he watched the faraway figures, he wondered what was going to happen to the Deep Gorgers now. Was Allaby going to have him recruit them, too? But yes, of course he was. Their lives were going to change as much as everybody else's. If Gibbous started getting sentimental about every settlement's customs, traditions and quirky ways, trying to shield people from the new, round-world realities, much worse would eventually happen to them. But how would Deep Gorgers, in particular, react? They were otherworldly even by Ledge and Big Rim standards. Gibbous had always imagined that it was their view of the world, or lack of one, that did it. All of the other settlements, except Salt, of course (and God only knew how Salters viewed the world, if they ever did), were situated in spots with some kind of aspect – a lofty, airy ledge or ridge, a misty waterfall, a languid, leafy riverside. But what did Deep Gorgers have? Almost everywhere they looked they saw rock piled on rock, along with a distant strip of sky, a sun that only directly shone on them very briefly during the day, and a muddy river prone to flooding.

So they invented their own interesting views. Their fantasies were busier, more elaborate and more preposterous than anyone else's, and on almost every rock in sight they'd painted mysterious, colourful and complicated figures. Deep Gorgers seemed to have no strong sexual morality, and hardly any one of them could say with certainty who his or her father was. They wore clothes when it was chilly, but when it was warm or when clothes might get in the way a little, they took them off. They sang a lot and danced a lot, talked and laughed and exclusively cultivated a cactus that, when eaten, made them even more cheerful. What were people like that going to make of Allaby's new world?

Oh hell, thought Gibbous, they'll probably adjust better than any of us – or probably won't even notice, just as they were obviously not noticing him now. When they hunted, they hunted. When they warred they warred.

When they celebrated … God, when they celebrated … Whenever they did anything, they were totally involved in it and immune to distraction. As he walked on and kept glancing towards them, he became certain that they would never be moved to curiosity about a distant old man with a walking stick and, of all things, a dog.

He reached the Gorge's edge and turned towards Big Rim, feeling apprehensive suddenly. The sun was just leaving the first quarter of the sky, which meant that he'd been walking faster, or had started sooner, than he thought. He'd get there even before lunch. That didn't matter, of course – it was just that he was still so uncertain about so many things. He hadn't been gone long at all, but a lot had happened and not only happened to him. There was no more Ledge, just Big Rim with a few Ledge refugees, if indeed they were still there. And he had left the Chief to stop the attack on Little Rim. On general principles – moral principles, traditional principles, historical principles, principles that in the new wide world might not even mean a damn – he hoped the Chief had done it, but if he was actually going to unite the settlements, as Allaby had said he should, Little Rim would be bound to be the most awkward. For one thing, a lot of their lies would be exposed – the ones about going up the mountains, for instance. He knew now that anybody who got to the foot of even the closest mountains would have been turned by the skypeople into thin air. Among the many things he hadn't resolved, as he kept trudging closer to Big Rim and his reckoning, was how to let the Little Rimmers save face.

Yellow had gone back to his old routine, trotting ahead and then sitting and waiting, as if making sure, every ten or so paces, that the way was clear. Gibbous hadn't actually meant to bring the dog along – supposing that at the very least he wouldn't want to travel in what he'd always considered the wrong direction. But this time Yellow was more than willing. He wanted to go anywhere. He'd just spent a couple of days trying to keep out of the way of children who were either fascinated by him or in screaming, squealing dread of him, and when Gibbous finally appeared and was recognised, Yellow ran and flew to him the same way he had that first, windy night at the liner. In fact, Gibbous's initial surprise about Yellow was that he was still there at all. This dog was an independent animal, or was supposed to be. He could hunt his own food, find his own water or find other dogs if that's what he felt like. He didn't need humans in his life, and yet he'd stayed around that teeming, raucous campsite where his only real human acquaintance was Paintbrush, and waited … that's it, waited …

for what? Of course, for Gibbous to come back. What else? What have I done to the poor creature, Gibbous wondered, as Yellow even now was waiting for him to cover the ten paces so he could trot ahead ten more. Somehow, he'd stopped being a real dog. Or had become another kind of dog altogether – another kind of animal – a loyal companion maybe, yes, but also a dependant, even a slave.

So with his enslaved animal, he was heading back to the settlements on a mission to show his own people that they could go anywhere they wanted to go and that they should. The idea was that, once they were at large, they were beyond control and could live the way everybody's ancestors had lived. They would be told the truth, and when they knew that, it would be a genuinely new beginning. They would never be the same. It had all sounded very plausible to Gibbous at the time – in fact it wasn't just Allaby's plan but, to be honest, Gibbous's as well, still incensed as he was by the generations whose explorings and Long Walks Out had been cut so cruelly short.

But as he got closer to Big Rim he was beginning to wonder. Last night's spectre of the elephants had disturbed him, and today he couldn't quite remember why. Seeing the Deep Gorgers was having the same effect. So, in a way, was the realisation that Yellow – a dog – had, in very unpleasant circumstances, waited for him. The closer he got to Big Rim, the less certain he was about what he was meant to say and do – exactly what was he was meant to mean.

CHAPTER FORTY-FOUR

It looked as though a few of the Big Rimmers were having a knockrock. If so, this was surprising because, as far as Gibbous knew, it was strictly a Ledge game – made possible by the south wall of the Gorge, which rose behind the settlement. The Ledger who was designated the chucker would climb about twenty paces up to certain little outcrop, known as the chucking platform, and underhanded (it had to be underhanded) would chuck a fist-sized rock as high as he could over the village flat. Then the person whose turn it was to throw would try to hit it with another fist-sized rock before it came down. More than that – the thrower would have to hit it in such a way that the chucked rock would be knocked beyond the Ledge's edge, to fall down into the Gorge. Scores were kept on a lifetime basis and conferred a status of sorts, and a particularly high score would often get a mention at the thrower's funeral.

Grateful for a few moments' respite from having to decide what he and Yellow were going to do next, Gibbous stood on the little rise above the settlement and observed the Big Rim adaptation of the game. In the absence of the Gorge's south wall and the chucking platform, the chucker was using the roof of the Chief's house, which was the tallest in the settlement and the nearest to the rim of the Gorge. From his distance, a good three hundred paces, Gibbous couldn't tell who was doing the chucking, but he could see by the thrower's peculiar action – pulling his arm way back and then whipping it forward without bending the elbow – that it was almost certainly his grandson Flickering Star (named, he now knew, after that nowhere skyplace belonging to Allaby's chief). Flicker was a prodigy at this game and already had a score total you'd expect of someone several years older. And sure enough, Gibbous now watched as the boy hit two out of three chucks, making a Gorge score on one. Then another thrower took his turn and missed all three of the chucks by a margin as wide as the Chief's house itself. The second chuck had even hit the ground before the thrower had managed to throw. At that, Flicker and couple of onlookers, of which there were ten or eleven altogether, had doubled over with laughter, while the rest just seemed to be standing by sullenly.

What was happening, clearly, was that some of the Big Rimmers were being taught a new game. It had never occurred to Gibbous that it could be particularly difficult to score, say, two or three out of nine, but then Gibbous had been playing knockrock since he was big enough to swing his arm. So had Flicker. But if you were already grown and were new to the game, it might be hard, maybe even impossible. Here was a skill that, however impractical (except for felling the occasional low-flying bird), was in its last generation. The Big Rimmers were never going to persist with something that they couldn't do and that caused them to be laughed at, and the Ledge refugees would lose interest when they realised that a respected competitive skill had turned into a useless curiosity. Knockrock was now just another spasm of the dying Ledge.

If the Ledge had still existed, Gibbous wondered, would he be so enthusiastic about Allaby's plan? Would he be willing to tell a living, thriving community of Ledgers, with their – with his – customs and stories and histories and friends and routines and problems and even games, that the best thing they could do now would be to drop all that and fan out into the rest of the world? He wasn't sure now if he even had the heart to tell such a thing to the Big Rimmers, not to mention the people in the other settlements.

From where he stood now he could see just about all of Big Rim. At one end was the Chief's house and the knockrock game, at the other their big meeting hall, this settlement's equivalent of the Cavern. In between, along wide and winding paths among the houses, people were doing what people do. They built fires. It was a hot day, but it was almost lunchtime, and every house seemed to have smoke curling out of its roof and wafting and settling in wisps over the paths. Along those paths, a few people walked, alone or in twos and threes. Everywhere children ran and laughed and squealed. Babies cried. A man lounged in his doorway feathering arrows. Another man walked along with a dead goat over his shoulder. Two women sat outside their houses, across from each other, and talked, one behind a loom, the other tanning a skin. Someone somewhere was banging a rock on something. A small group of people had gathered near the meeting hall to listen to an old woman speak. She gestured emphatically and pointed towards the Gorge, and the others looked in that direction. A pack of dogs roamed past the group, unremarked. Gibbous looked down at

Yellow, who was sitting in front of him. His ears were up – he was remarking them all right.

"Oh hell," Gibbous said. "Let's go, Yellow." The feeling he had was of a hand inside his body clutching at him just below the throat. Why is this so hard, he asked himself. I've helped fight a battle out in the nothingness. I know what it's like to weigh nothing. I know what it means to fly a thing bigger than all the settlements put together. I've been to the moon, for God's sake.

He skirted around the settlement so that he could enter at the end where the Chief's house was, since he'd established that his grandson was there – somebody he wouldn't have to introduce himself to. Of course, he knew almost everyone in Big Rim – even his sister was a Big Rimmer – but Flicker, when he saw him, wouldn't have to think twice.

And he didn't. He only thought once, but he thought for a while. As Gibbous and Yellow had turned the corner from behind the Chief's house, Flicker's rock was hitting the ground after knocking another rock into the air over the Gorge.

"You know what I wish, Flicker?" Gibbous said loudly.

Flicker said, "What?" and turned his head.

"I wish you were as good with an arrow as you are with a rock."

Flicker didn't move, didn't speak, even though his mouth was open.

"Who's that?" one of the Big Rimmers said.

"Good God," said – yes – Two Tornadoes, who Gibbous had failed to notice as another of the onlookers.

"You back from the dead again?" This time it was Chief Always Standing Up, who Gibbous also hadn't noticed. He was sitting in his dark doorway, and only his hands and lower legs were apparent.

"Again?" One of the Big Rimmers said.

"Yeah," said the Chief. "I neglected to tell you boys about his last visit and about the skyman's head."

"But who is he?" said another Big Rimmer. This annoyed Gibbous a little, because he himself remembered that particular man. His name was Struts Like a Crow, and he was the worst hunter anybody had ever known. That had probably been him making those spectacular misses.

"He's my brother-in-law," the Chief said, "or used to be before he died. You'll be glad to know Raincloud's feeling better now, Gibbous. She's out of the house at the moment. She hates it when the boys start throwing rocks off the roof." That could have been her, Gibbous realised, talking to that group.

Struts Like a Crow said with a slight catch in his voice, "Uh, Chief, did you say 'back from the dead'?"

After Flicker finally shut his mouth, he instantly opened it to say, "He's my Granddad. What he's back from, Strut, is his Long Walk Out. We had the fake funeral and everything. That, you know, is when the atrocity hap—

"Why are you back, Granddad? You're not supposed to … nobody's ever … The Ledge has been completely … Did you know that … Did Paintbrush— "

"Yes she did, and yes I know."

Two Tornadoes, who himself was emerging from dumbfoundedness, said, "Nobody's ever done that, Gibbous. Nobody's ever come back from—"

"From the dead," the Chief boomed out of the dark doorway. "He's come back from the dead."

Two Tornadoes said, "That is a way of looking at it, of course, Chief, and the Long Walk Out does mean death in the sense that we never see the person again, or shouldn't, but—"

"It means certain death. My father always said it, and I didn't believe him. I didn't believe him until Gibbous here came back. Then I believed him. But don't worry, Gibbous. I've got used to the idea now. Tell them. Tell them that the Long Walk Out is really the short walk to death."

"You know, Chief," Gibbous said. "Your father actually was right at the time. But now it's possible to—"

"See," said the Chief. "He's dead."

"He doesn't look dead to me," Flicker said.

"Well, when you come back from the dead, you don't look dead. Otherwise, what would be the point?"

Among the group of Big Rimmers, there was a murmur of agreement to this. Gibbous took stock. There was the Chief, or there his legs and hands were, anyway. There were Flicker, Two Tornadoes and Flicker's best friend – Bending Bow his name was. Paintbrush had said that Flicker and some other kids his age were in a housecave when the burning fat fell, and so the one of the kids had obviously been Bending Bow. All the others standing there were Big Rimmers, some of whose names he knew and some he couldn't be bothered to remember. They were staring at him, and he was staring at them.

He had to start telling them or, as Allaby had put it, rallying them. Maybe if he could get them and the rest of Big Rim to the Meeting House …

One of the Big Rimmers said, "That dog there is all by itself. It's lost its pack. I just saw a pack go by, I think."

Oh God, Gibbous thought, I shouldn't have brought Yellow. Now there's going to be another distraction. Nevertheless … "He doesn't have a pack," Gibbous said. "He's with me."

This was also greeted by a murmur, this time a little louder and a little deeper. Then Flicker said, "I remember that dog, Granddad. He's one of the ones that used to hang around our housecave. I do remember. You used to give him our salt meat."

Yellow, who was sitting at Gibbous's feet, made a swipe of his tail, craned his neck and looked up at him, almost as if he understood.

"Is the dog back from the dead, too?" Strut said.

"Just once," Gibbous said. "I gave him some meat once. Look, I've got something I need to talk to you about. All of you. The whole settlement, Chief. Could you call a meeting or something."

"I don't know, Gibbous," the Chief said. "A lot of the boys are out goating, and some others are over at Salt. When do you want a meeting?"

"Whenever you can manage it, but I can't waste a lot of time. I've got something important to—"

"I'd have thought that to a dead man time wouldn't matter very much."

"Look, Chief, I'm not dead. Really. I never made it farther than the Far Plain." Well, he'd made it as far as the moon, but as things stood right now that was beside the point.

"You've been all this time on the Far Plain, you and that dog?"

"And Paintbrush. And Skyman."

"That's what I thought. A skyman."

"No, Skyman is Paintbrush's baby's name, Chief. Two Tornadoes here named him that. Didn't you?"

"I think so," Two Tornadoes said. "So much goes on when you drink the naming brew, it's hard to separate out the specifics. I hadn't been doing it as long as you, either."

"You named him Skyman all right," Flicker said. "He's my nephew, you know."

"Do you mean to say," Strut said, "that you name people when they're still babies? How do you know what they're going to—"

"You know they do," the Chief barked and then, as if remembering his own name, finally stood up and stepped away from the doorway. His face had become much redder than Gibbous remembered. He was also a little balder and a little fatter in the belly, and his beard, though as neatly trimmed as ever, was now almost solid white. But it hadn't been that long since Gibbous had last seen him. What had happened? The Chief was squinting in the sun and raised both hands to shield his eyes. "You were with an actual skyman, too. You brought me his head, his empty head, in case you've forgotten. And you can't have been associating with a skyman, much less killing one, unless you were already dead. Now admit it."

"Why did you kill a skyman, Granddad? Skymen are good things, aren't they?"

"It wasn't his head," Gibbous said. "It was his mask. I told you ... What did you do with it anyway? You were supposed to use it to help persuade the warriors not to—"

"I don't see how that would have worked," the Chief said. "I threw it down the Gorge. It was disgusting. Listen, Gibbous, do dead men eat? Raincloud's got a pot of stew on the fire – tortoise, I think. Come in and have some lunch."

In the distractingly haphazard course of the conversation so far, Gibbous had almost forgotten how hungry he was. "Okay. Thanks, Chief."

"You boys, too, if you want. It was supposed to last a few days, but we've got two more tortoises on their backs in there. She can do another one tomorrow. Come on in. It's not every day you get to have lunch with a dead man."

Strut said, "You mean that, Chief? You're asking us to lunch?"

"We're honoured," Two Tornadoes said.

"Well, come on," said the Chief. "Come on, Gibbous."

As Gibbous stepped towards the door, Yellow got to his feet, and the Chief quickly said, "Not the dog, Gibbous."

Without thinking, Gibbous said, "He's hungry, too."

"I have no doubt you're dead, Gibbous, but if you're not, you're at least a little crazy. Dogs don't go into houses, not in this settlement. And they don't eat people food. Do you think I want it following me around for the rest of its life?"

Gibbous didn't want to argue, supposing he could find a way of smuggling something to Yellow. "Stay here," he told the dog, and a little to his surprise, Yellow actually sat down beside the doorway, his tongue hanging out as he watched all the humans approaching and filing in.

Inside, the Chief showed everyone to a stool or a spot on the floor of his big room and told the boy who looked to be the youngest to start filling bowls from the stone pot in the room's centre. Gibbous was given what he supposed was a place of honour on the Chief's sitting, lounging and sleeping platform and was second to be served, after the Chief himself, who was seated at the platform's other end. It was almost unheard-of for the Chief to invite ordinary people into his house, and the murmur this time contained breathy whistles and whispers of wonderment. The men and boys gazed at his animal-bone collection along one wall and his tattooed skins on the adjoining one. On the platform were his piles of luxurious cushions, and the ceiling was hung with coils of various thicknesses of ropes along with nets of different mesh sizes. The smoke from the fire curled and blossomed among the ropes and nets and against the ceiling before finding the hole in the centre and exiting. Coming in the other way was a tree-trunk-sized shaft of smoky sunlight. This was intersected by other shafts from the eight high windows, creating angles and crosses in the air and reminding Gibbous vaguely of the stabilising shapes on the liner's enormous wall. As soon as he was handed his spoon and bowl, Gibbous dug into his lunch and was then reminded of something else – his mother. It was, of course, her way of making tortoise stew, as taught to Raincloud. There was a certain garlicky bitterness to it that brought back lunchtimes after sunny mornings on the Ledge – playing, among other games, knockrock.

Everybody was eating in a kind of awestruck quietness, speaking, if at all, only in low tones to people nearby. Spoons clanked, tongues slurped, throats cleared. Gibbous could feel the atmosphere getting a little uncomfortable, but he was too hungry to care very much, and he was near the bottom of his bowl when the Chief finally spoke: "Well, Gibbous, this is something they'll be telling stories about for years, long after we're all dead, not just you." As he said this, he wasn't looking at Gibbous but at the room in general, and he raised his arms a little, palms outward. "You're the first person ever known to return, dead or alive, from a Long Walk Out. And the first thing you want to do is hold a meeting in the Meeting House.

I have to ask why. And I have to say to myself that you want to tell us what happens on a Long Walk Out, something no one's ever known before."

Gibbous had a few quick thoughts at once, and they were in collision with each other. For one thing, he didn't want to blow his entire message on a handful of knockrock players. He wanted the whole settlement to hear it. He'd even considered trying to call an assembly of all the settlements, but had finally rejected that as too complicated. Another thing was that he was irritated by the Chief's public-address persona. He'd seen it before, and he knew that in this mood he wouldn't be susceptible to reason – if Gibbous protested, the Chief would just be embarrassed and contrary and less inclined to call a meeting. And then Yellow was sitting outside feeling very hungry and left out. Gibbous had expected a quick lunch, an agreement on a meeting and a chance to grab a surreptitious piece of tortoise as everybody filed out. If the Chief had his way, though, they'd be in here all afternoon. As Gibbous was trying to untangle these objections, he said to the Chief, "Wouldn't it be better if I told everybody all at once? Then I wouldn't have to repeat—"

"Naw," the Chief said, still looking at the room. "I can't wait that long, and neither can these people. Think of it as practice."

"Practice?"

"Yeah. Try it out on us, and then we'll help you get your story straight. You're a storyteller, aren't you? Don't storytellers like to practise? The one around here does. He's always coming over and boring me with new tales of his."

"Well, I wouldn't want to bore you, Chief."

"You're Gibbous Moon. You won't bore anybody. Start telling."

Gibbous sighed. Maybe the Chief had something. Maybe Gibbous did need to, well, test the reaction. Anyway, there was nothing else he could think to do. "Okay, Chief. I'll do it if somebody will do something for me."

"What's that?"

"Take some meat to the dog."

"Take meat to the dog?"

"Yes."

The Chief pondered this for a few moments. "Oh hell. Strut?"

"Yes, Chief?"

"Take some damn meat to the damn dog. Why should I care as long as you're the one it ends up following around? Maybe the thing will teach you how to hunt."

499

By the time Strut had come back into the room, Gibbous was ready to start. On his way here, he'd decided that this was a story that needed to begin with the main thing these people didn't know: that the population of the Seven Settlements was not the full extent of humanity. He might not be believed at first, but at least he would be commanding their attention. He'd pictured himself delivering this revelation while standing in front of a hall full of Big Rimmers, but now that all he had were the knockrockers, he supposed he didn't need to stand up at all. He would stay seated on the Chief's platform and speak in an even voice. This wouldn't be a performance, after all. This wouldn't be some legend they'd heard a thousand times in a hundred variations. This was new, and true. This was information that would irrevocably change their lives. He cleared his throat.

After what seemed a long time later, when the fire had almost stopped burning and the shafts of sunlight were tinged with pink, Gibbous cleared his throat again, this time because he was feeling hoarse. He had told them everything he could. He hadn't meant to go into quite so much detail, but almost nothing he had to say could have gone without explanation, and then the explanations needed explaining. He'd done the gestures Allaby would do with his fists to show how enormous things spent eternity going around and around each other. He'd told them what nothingness was like, and explosions in the nothingness, and what it was like to have no weight or, sometimes, just a little weight. He'd described guns and ships and light without shadows, horrible colours, horrible noise and even more horrible food. He'd mentioned people who jabbered at each other and could understand each other's jabbering, because the jabber was just another kind of talking. He'd told them what the world looked like from the moon, in the process mentioning a fly on a boulder. He posed the riddle of the Endless Water and how it both wasn't endless, because it usually had land far away on the other side, and was, because it was on the surface of a ball. He'd picked up two of the Chief's prize flopover cowpats (the Chief had a way of curing and preserving the roundest ones), stuck a stick between them and showed how you could fix it so they would never, ever flop over. Then he told them about people who could be somewhere and not there at the same time, and you could walk right through them if you wanted to. But the most urgent thing he had to tell was about the skypeople and how they were not always good. In fact, even the good ones weren't always good – he mentioned Allaby's chief here – or were sometimes too stupid to be good. He told them about the other people in the world who weren't skypeople but were just like the people of the Seven Settlements. And now Allaby, who was a very good skyperson, was going to set everyone free. The Chief's father had been right about people dying if they tried to go up the mountains or across the desert – the skypeople had been turning them into thin air – but now anybody could go anywhere, and ought to, because a lot of skypeople could turn up at any time. Some were all right and some weren't, and some particularly bad ones were coming from so deep in the sky that it would take them more than year to get here. But whoever came and whenever, the people on the ground had to know about them and be ready for them, either to teach them how to live here peaceably – because they certainly had a lot to learn about that – or to fight them if necessary.

The boys and men and the Chief had all listened attentively enough, especially considering that Gibbous had been talking, if not somberly, at least quietly and straightforwardly. They weren't used to that, and of course the boys, especially, fidgeted a lot. They flicked pebbles and bits of dirt at each other and sometimes whispered and snickered, and after Gibbous had put the axle between the cowpats, they had a new toy, which was lazily kicked and shoved back and forth across the room. But they did seem to be listening to almost everything. The only one who'd interrupted Gibbous at any point was Flicker, after Gibbous had mentioned, again without thinking, that he'd married Paintbrush to the skyman Allaby: "God, Granddad," he'd said. "She didn't waste any time."

"Sorry, Flicker. I shouldn't have—"

"How long had Eclipse been dead by then? Three days? Four days?"

"You've got to understand. As far as we were concerned at that point, the three of us and the baby were just about all the people in the world. We were heading for a new beginning. We were all going to go live in the mountains."

"Yeah, well," he'd said sulkily, and then he brightened a little. "Does that mean ... Are you telling me I've got a skyman for a brother-in-law?"

Gibbous had answered by saying he didn't think there was a name for a man who marries your brother's widow but that 'brother-in-law-in-law' might do.

A little later, Raincloud had come in, looked around the room, peered into the almost empty pot, glared at the Chief and said, "Oh that's just wonderful. First you give them our roof, now our food." Then she took a long second look at Gibbous, who had been in the middle of explaining what a gun was. "You're supposed to be dead," she said, before walking out again.

"I told you," the Chief said, "that you should have visited her when she was sick."

"I didn't want anyone else to know I was here."

"Do you think there was any way I could not tell her you were here? After you left me with that skyman's head ... mask, whatever?"

Gibbous had figured then that his explanations must have been having some effect, for the Chief even to admit the possibility that the mask was a mask, and so he'd gone back to trying to explain to the room what guns were. And when, in advance of the twilight, he finished all his explanations, he said to the Chief that it probably had been a good idea to have a practice run-through. "I think when we have the full meeting, I'll make it a little shorter. There's a lot they won't need to know."

"Yeah," said the Chief, "most of it. The fly on the rock, for sure. I couldn't make any sense out of that. And all the roundness everywhere. God. Going west by going east or whatever." He threw his hands up. "Whew."

"In fact, Chief. Now that I've explained all this here and you've heard it and they've heard it, it doesn't seem so urgent just to have a Big Rim meeting. Maybe it would be an idea to take some time and get all the settlements together. And meanwhile all of you can tell me what you didn't understand, and I can either leave it out or explain it better. What do you think?"

"All of the settlements?" the Chief said.

"Yeah."

"All of them?"

"All of them. Even Salt. Even Little Rim – they've got to know, too."

At this, Gibbous got the first laugh of the afternoon. "Little Rim," one of the Big Rimmers shouted out. "Oh yes, let's invite Little Rim." And everyone laughed again – everyone but the Chief, who had his head in his hands.

"I know what you think of Little Rim," said Gibbous, trying to raise his voice above both the laughter and his own hoarseness. "It's what I think, too, but things in the world have changed so much now that—"

"Granddad!" Flicker shouted, getting to his feet. "Quiet, everybody. Granddad, there's no Little Rim to invite. We wiped those skinny bastards out. Except for some of the girls, of course."

"Chief, I thought you were going to—"

"I tried, Gibbous. I did try."

"You didn't use the mask. You threw it down the Gorge, you said. That's what you said, didn't you?"

"That's what I did, yes. But I did try to stop them."

"Was that what you were trying to do?" Flicker said, to more laughter.

"I remember." This was Bending Bow speaking now, also on his feet. "The Riversiders were teaching us their victory song, weren't they? And the Chief came in."

"Yeah," said Flicker. "And the Chief came in and tried to get us to stop singing. We thought we'd woken him up or something."

"I was trying to dampen your enthusiasm." The Chief looked over at Gibbous. "Really. I was."

Flicker said, "You'd have needed the waterfall to do that. What a night! I still dream about it. Granddad, can you imagine – all the warriors from five settlements, Salt too …" Rumblings and yeahs and yays surged through the room. Everyone was standing up now. "… and we all came together to do the same thing, not fighting each other for a change. Unity, we called it, didn't we, Bow? Unity! And when we marched out together – there must have been a hundred of us. Just before dawn, wasn't it? And when we got to the outside of Little Rim, the sun was just coming up. No smoke rising out of the houses or anything. They were mostly still asleep, the skinny bastards …"

"He led us, you know," Bending Bow said. "He led all the warriors from all the settlements. You'd have been really proud of your grandson."

"That was nothing, Bow. I just felt I had to, Granddad, because, well, because it was sort of my fault, the Atrocity, because I accidentally killed that Jones. I made up for it, though. We all did."

"How does that Riversider song go?" Bending Bow said. "Do you remember it?"

"Of course. Everybody remembers it. Come on, let's sing it for Granddad."

After some humming and a couple of false starts, the men and boys more or less faced the Chief and Gibbous and began to stamp their feet and sway at their shoulders, singing something about blood being warm and blood being red and enemies being dead and so on. It had three or four verses, and when they were finished, they ululated and yodelled and slapped each other on the backs and arms. "What a night!" Flicker shouted again, raising his hands above his head.

In a low tone, the Chief said to Gibbous, "You can kind of see what I was up against."

As far as Gibbous was concerned, that was an excuse. But as excuses went, he'd heard worse. And it didn't matter that the Chief had thrown the mask in the Gorge. Showing it to the fervent warriors of bloody unity wouldn't have made any difference at all.

"I know what," Flicker said, still shouting. "We've just sung a Riverside song. How about a Ledge story? The blood made me think of it. Two Tornadoes, tell us a story. The rivers of blood one. He's really good. Granddad was a good storyteller, too, but that one he's just told was very long and hard. Anyway, it's Two Tornadoes' job now. Come on, Two Tornadoes."

Two Tornadoes raised his arms. "Okay," he said. "Okay. But everybody's got to sit down. And it's getting dark in here. Somebody light the torches."

The youngest boy automatically got up and dipped the first torch into the cooking fire. As he did, Gibbous rose, grabbed his stick and started towards the door.

"Where are you going, Granddad?"

"Yeah," said the Chief. "Don't you want to—"

"No, I already know that story."

"But where are you going?"

"Outside. To talk to the dog."

504

27901506R00298

Printed in Poland
by Amazon Fulfillment
Poland Sp. z o.o., Wrocław